Carry Me Home

Other novels by John M. Del Vecchio

The 13th Valley
For the Sake of All Living Things

CARRY
ME HOME

John M. Del Vecchio

BANTAM BOOKS
NEW YORK · TORONTO · LONDON · SYDNEY · AUCKLAND

CARRY ME HOME

A Bantam Book / February 1995

Book design by Richard Oriolo

Library of Congress Cataloging-in-Publication Data

Del Vecchio, John M., 1948–
  Carry me home / John M. Del Vecchio.
    p.   cm.
  ISBN 0-553-07224-2
  1. Vietnamese Conflict, 1961–1975—Veterans—United
States—Fiction. 2. Men—United States—Fiction.   I. Title.
PS3554.E4327C37   1994
813'.54—dc20   93-31585
                                                          CIP

Published simultaneously in the United States and Canada

PRINTED IN THE UNITED STATES OF AMERICA

BVG   0 9 8 7 6 5 4 3 2 1

IN MEMORY OF

Frank Delaney
David Coughlin
Sheldon Silverman
Felix Antignani

Grateful acknowledgment is made to the following people who shared with me their memories, stories, and ideas:

Ralph Antignani; Carl Augusto; Douglas Bachman; Lee and Janice Bartels; Tom Barton; Mike Benge; Ray "Blackie" Blackman of The Ripcord Report; Harry W. Brooks, Jr., Major General U.S.A. (Retired); F. C. Brown; Jim Catlin of The Strike Force Association; Joe and Jeanne Cochran; Joe Cordova; Kathy Cordova; Frank and Carol Delaney; Bob Del Vecchio; Frank A. Del Vecchio, Jr.; Jane Diedzic of VVAOI; Larry Elliot; Mary Jo Good, Ph.D., and Byron Good, Ph.D.; Joe Griggs; Jane Hamilton-Merritt, Ph.D.; Edwin Hunter of The Undesirables; Dr. Herbert Kaye; Theanvy Kuoch of Khmer Health Advocates; Ben Cai Lam; Bob Leddlelaytner; Marcus Leddy; Bill Laurie of Cyclo Dap Archives; Ned Leavitt; Don Lombardi; Hugh Long of The Strike Force Association; Paul Lukienchuk; Gunny Doug Lyvere; V. David and Donna Manahan; Roderick MacKenzie; Gary Miller; Frank McCarthy of the Brandie Scheib Children's Fund; Conley Monk of The Undesirables; Brian Muldoon; Ron Mullins; Ron Norris; Bruce and Janice Ratcliffe; Heather Ratcliffe; Ed Ruminski; Joseph and Elena Rusnak; P. Cary Shelton; Ted Shpak of the Viet Nam Veterans Service Center; Pierre Smith; Jimmy Sparrow of VVAOVI; Tim Stewart; Thomas Taylor; Saren Thach; Dave and Karen Throm; Paul Trudeau; Karen, Robert, and Paul Trudeau; Al Santoli; Carol Verozzi; and Alan Young, Ph.D.

I would also like to thank the veterans of the Vet Centers in Greenville, North Carolina, White River Junction, Vermont, and Shelton, Meriden, and Hartford, Connecticut.

And a very special thanks to Frank and Filomena Del Vecchio.

With malice toward none, with charity for all, with firmness in the right as God gives us to see the right, let us strive on to finish the work we are in, to bind up the nation's wounds, to care for him who shall have borne the battle and for his widow and his orphan—to do all which may achieve and cherish a just and lasting peace among ourselves and with all nations.

—*Abraham Lincoln*

Author's Note

There is no Heckley County in Pennsylvania. The name was taken from a gravestone: Heckley—50th Regiment, Pennsylvania Volunteers, Infantry, 1848–1910. There is no township of Mill Creek Falls, nor, to the best of my knowledge, has anyone in north central Pennsylvania called their farm High Meadow. The communities of Ridgewater, Rock Ridge, and Coal Hill are imaginary, as are the Mill Creek Falls subdivisions—Old Town, Old New Town, New New Town, Creek's Bend, etc. There is no Veterans Administration and no State of Pennsylvania Veterans Medical Center in Rock Ridge. In California, no land exists between Sonoma and Marin counties. The city of San Martin, like Heckley County, is a figment of my imagination.

Carry Me Home is the last installment of a trilogy about America's Southeast Asia era. *The 13th Valley* (Bantam, 1982) is the story of American infantry combat in Viet Nam and an inquiry into the causes of war. *For the Sake of All Living Things* (Bantam, 1990) is the story of a Cambodian family from 1968 to 1979. The story explores the making of a genocide with emphasis on Communist factions, their actions, interactions, and ideologies, and their effects upon a people. *Carry Me Home* is the story of a medium-size aging mill town and the generation that grew up there during the Viet Nam War era. The title has been borrowed, with permission, from Marcus Leddy's *Carry Me Home* album, a collection of songs for and about Viet Nam veterans (Blue Roan Records).

I have attempted to keep major historical events and general background history accurate. Times and dates of some specific events, particularly non-news television programming, which occurred in the United States may have been altered. Certain films, TV shows, reviews, and critiques that are cited in the late 1970s and early 1980s did not appear until later.

Personal and minor events are composites, built or extrapolated from interviews, conversations, and/or official records. The characters who peopled these areas in the sixties, seventies, and eighties are fictitious.

Characters depicted from specific military units (i.e., Tony Pisano of the 2d Battalion, 4th Marine Regiment, 3d Marine Division) have not been based upon anyone who served in these units, though where unit actions are described I have attempted to be true to the history of that combat. Any resemblance to any person, living or deceased, is purely a matter of many people having shared similar experiences, held similar beliefs, exhibited similar behavior.

However, some people do live by The Code.

Part I

HOMECOMING

July 1984

I'm going to make it. I'm going to make it, Man. I'm going to make it.

Wapinski used to say it. Say it like this. He'd be standing there, like this, leaning back on the sheet-metal break. . . . Or maybe we'd be fishing the far end of the pond where the cliff comes right to the water and he'd be sitting on the edge or he'd have climbed halfway down and gotten onto that crag and he'd fish with one hand, hang on with the other. . . . Or he'd say it up here by the graves. . . .

Damn. This is hard to talk about.

He'd say, "I don't think I'd like the person I'd be if I hadn't gone." Then he'd say, "And if living with this pain, and damn it that's what it is, is the price, then I'll take it. I've seen the best. And the worst. But seeing the best, seeing it just once, that makes it worth it. That inspiration. That awareness. You become so damn aware it hurts, but you know what's possible . . . and you know the price. You know it applies here, in the World, not just in Viet Nam. You know honesty and honor and vigilance . . . the costs, and what it costs when they're forgotten . . . and that, that equates with hope.

"The best. The best here. The best in Nam. Decent. Honorable. Guts and balls and courage. Audacity. See it! That's what High Meadow's about."

Wap would go on like that, casual sometimes, ranting ferocious sometimes, go on for hours while we worked in the barn or while I'd be trying to tell him the advantages of Spredor 2° alfalfa over the old standards that don't creep out. There's a sugarbush over the west ridge there. His grandpa planted it back in the twenties. Can you imagine that spirit? It takes fifty years before a stand of sugar maples can rightly be called a sugarbush but his grandpa had that kind of optimism. Wap had it too. He had this idea that he could take the dregs, if they'd come to him, and turn em into philosophers or philanthropists, financiers or physicians. His words. That's how strongly he believed in the basic strength and value of Everyman.

Where's that spirit now? People think it's crazy. Imagine planting something today that won't pay off for fifty years? Build today for a world fifty years from now? For the year 2034? Crazy? Optimistic? I don't know. It must have been in their blood because that's what they founded here. That's what they set in motion.

I imagine High Meadow was quiet like this when Wap came back. He told me about comin to this spot with Noah on his shoulders, comin up here to talk to his grandfather and tell him his plans. To see if he'd approve. He'd come up here a lot. From up here you can see most of the place. In the morning, with the sun at your back, the pond looks so peaceful. What hell it unleashed.

The barn down there is still intact. To me the big barn was the heart of the place. Machinery's idle now, but it's usable. The farmhouse is fine. Wap never finished remodeling but the place is livable, and except maybe for the roof over Noah and Paul's room, all is tight. The path from the house to the barn is thick with grass and weeds.

I didn't stop. Couldn't. Came up the back trail, around the pond. Wap and I built that gate on the crest halfway up the drive from the road where the stream goes under in those culverts and where the school bus used to stop. We used hinges I forged in the shop that first winter when I didn't feel like talkin to anybody and there wasn't so much goin on. Used five-eighth-inch-thick carriage bolts for the pins and bolted the gate to the posts instead of using screws. That gate won't need maintenance for another decade. That's the way he wanted us to build.

There's gullies in the wheel paths on that last uphill section before the house and yard. Must have been heavy thunderstorms this spring . . . or last fall. You can't build everything maintenance free.

The high meadows are fallow. The orchard, the vineyards, and the strawberry fields are untended. We were going to have our first real grape harvest this year. Wouldn't have been much. The vines aren't old enough yet. They're nothing compared to a sugarbush for measuring optimism, but in a few years we'd have had the best vineyard in Pennsylvania. I say "we" but I should say "I." Wap set the direction, but generally he stayed in the barn running the other businesses or studying in his grandpa's office in the loft. He let me manage the farm.

It's so clear this afternoon. I can see out over the house, out over the hills, way down the valley to the edge of town where the square steeple of St. Ignatius sticks up through the trees. Back this way, where the break in the treeline is, that's the Old Mill, which closed about a hundred years ago. The next break down is the New Mill, which closed right after World War II. Then way down there, just before the creek, that's the warehouse or Small Mill area. To the left is Old Town, and over a bit, that's Lutzburgh where Bobby grew up.

Upriver, way to the left, across the new bridge, that's New Town—all subdivisions. And down there, below South Hill, is the new mall. Way east, east of Creek's Bend, is where Kinnard/ Chassion opened the new toilet paper and disposable diaper plant and where now most everyone works, just like in the old days when everyone worked at the old mills.

He carried me home. He never said that but it's true. You know, not carried, but attracted . . . all of us. And we came and we took. Seems to have happened like that, like snapping your fingers. It's nine years since we met. We were in separate isolations. I mean, that time in San Jose . . . when Da Nang was goin down the tubes. I mean I knew him from way back, from Mill Creek High, but he was a year before me. And then in Sonoma, and at St. Luke's. But we didn't really connect.

Seems like a million years ago, his coming home. I'd been back a year. I was still active duty and they sent me to Philly on burial detail, which is where I met Linda, and when I was discharged . . . I forget if Wap was back yet. I got out in April. Wapinski got out in June. Ty was still in. Yeah, I musta been in Boston.

Anyway, it's been eight years since we began this venture. Seven years ago he sent out his letters. High Meadow became our base camp, our sanctuary. We left windows open and unshaded at night because High Meadow was secure. Secure? What thoughts! Why do the voices still cry?

1

Wapinski

Robert Janos Wapinski would never remember the details of his own homecoming. In a week they would be foggy, in a year they would be out of his mind, out of the recallable memory banks as completely as if the circuits to those banks had been cut and atrophy had caused the storage area to disintegrate.

What he would remember was a few sentences a man he'd come to believe never existed spoke to him on his second-to-last flight in the uniform of his country. And he would remember his mother, cold and hard, his mother who had given him away at age two when his father left, then taken him back, reluctantly, at eight when his paternal grandmother died and his grandfather had been in such grief that he'd let the boy go. He would remember Stacy—could never forget Stacy—and what she had done. And he would remember fleeing back to Grandpa Wapinski.

But the details. They were lost, forever, for when a man returns from war his mind and soul lag behind his physical being and do not catch up for weeks or months or years.

*   *   *

Mill Creek Falls, Pennsylvania, Saturday, 14 June 1969—In the soft gray predawn Robert Wapinski quietly walked into his hometown. He stopped. He looked back at the old steel truss bridge, looked down into Loyalsock Creek, looked across to Route 154. He had walked the thirteen miles from Eagles Mere. His feet were sore, his legs tired, yet he was restless, anxious. He had two miles to go, across town, before he was home.

Wapinski reached into the pocket of his jacket, pulled out a pack of cigarettes and a lighter. He'd shipped his heavy belongings and carried only a small AWOL bag that contained his orders and records, toiletries and clean socks. Before him the warehouses and machine shops were dark. In the graying sky, silhouettes of workers' houses could be seen emerging on the hills above Small Mill. As he walked Wapinski caressed the lighter. With one hand he snapped the top back, flicked the wheel in the lee of the upheld AWOL bag, lit a smoke, closed the lid, ran his thumb nail over the engraving.

The smoke tasted good. *"Captain, I think we're making a mistake,"* a voice ran in his mind. *"Lighten up, Thompson,"* he answered back. *"We've done our job."* *"I think we should go back, Sir. We belong to that world. It's all going to be bullshit. Just like R and R."* *"Things are going to be great!"* Wapinski had said. *"Captain,"* he heard Thompson answer him, *"it's gotten into my blood. Into yours, too."*

Wapinski walked east, up River Front Road, past the aging brick warehouses and machine shops. Lights from a new rooftop billboard cast overlapping shadows on to the pavement and into the dingy alleys. He hesitated, looked up, moved toward the Loyalsock to view the sign. Four powerful mercury vapor bulbs blazed over it:

Invest in MILL CREEK INDUSTRIAL PARK
a Downtown Redevelopment Project
—Ernest Hartley, Mayor

Wapinski slowed, tensed, peered deeply into the last alley. Shadows were ebbing in the growing dawn but the alley was black, dense, impenetrable. His eyes snapped forward, he spun, looked back, searched the deserted building, the empty road, the gorge of the creek. No one. He walked on, crossed the lane-and-one-half wood bridge over Mill Creek that divided Small Mill from River Front Park and downtown. He walked quietly, caressing the lighter like an amulet, fingering the engraving. Things are going to be great, he thought. I'm not going to let it be otherwise.

The trees in the park were heavy with foliage, the gravel paths clean, raked smooth, the grass thick, lush, high. Wapinski crossed a path, headed north toward the Episcopal church. On an earthen mound in a circular clearing at the center of the park stood a granite obelisk. As a youth he had played on it, walked around it hundreds, maybe thousands, of times, but he had never read it. He walked to the monument's base, read, in the gray light, the first plaque: "ERECTED BY THE PEOPLE OF MILL CREEK FALLS AND HECKLEY COUNTY—1883—IN HONOR OF ALL WHO FOUGHT IN SERVICE OF THEIR COUNTRY." Eighteen eighty-three, he thought. Eighteen years after the end of the war. Took em long enough. "Eternal Vigilance Is The Price Of Liberty. BULL RUNN WILDERNESS."

ROLL OF HONOR
Killed
Crowley, James 1 Cav June 14, '64
Hartley, Elijah . . . .

Wapinski stopped. He counted but did not read beyond the first few names—twenty-eight. The first date struck him. One hundred and five years ago to the day. He swallowed, ran his hand through his hair, looked about. Patches of mist lay between the gravestones in the cemetery beside the church. A slight breeze brought the smell of clover and onion grass to his nose. Below the *Killed* list was a second, DIED OF WOUNDS. There were fourteen names. Wapinski moved to the north plaque.

On fame's eternal camping ground,
their silent tents are spread,
And Glory guards with sacred round,
The bivouac of the dead.*

IN MEMORY OF THE MEN WHO FELL IN THE WAR OF THE
REBELLION 1861–1865 AS DEFENDERS OF
LIBERTY AND NATIONALITY

The fourth plaque was yet another ROLL OF HONOR—TO THOSE WHO DIED IN POW CAMPS. Wapinski counted forty-one names. Forty-one?! he thought. Forty-one, twenty-nine, fourteen. Eighty-four. God! Eighty-four dead from just Heckley County! I wouldn't have thought there were enough people in Heckley then . . .

There was one additional plaque, a small one placed at the base of the obelisk. DURING WW II THE CANNONBALLS AND CANNON WERE REMOVED AND SCRAPPED FOR THE STEEL. A shiver ran up Wapinski's arms, up his neck. He did not know why.

He left the park, crossed Mill Creek Road north of the church, walked east a block on Second Street, then north on Ann Drive to Third Street. This was downtown Mill Creek Falls. Wapinski looked into the store windows. It was lighter now. Nothing stirred. No one was about. As he walked he ran the fingers of one hand along a large store window. The

---

*This poem, along with the form of the monument described, is from the 1883 obelisk at Shelton, Connecticut.

glass felt smooth, clean, not washed clean but unmolested, unworried clean. He could not explain that either. Again he stopped. It was light enough to see his own reflection in the pane.

At five eleven he felt neither big nor small. He felt thin. He'd lost thirty pounds in Viet Nam. His blond hair was military short and sun bleached. He thought it made him look younger than he felt. He smiled. "Hey, fucker," he whispered to his reflection, "you made it. You made it back."

It had been a long night, a long day and night, long two weeks, long year. Now the confusion of emotions and images, the tiredness and adrenaline rush, overwhelmed him, made him retreat into himself, numbed him, yet simultaneously he was alert, anxious. Among all the confusing emotions there was a drive, a motivation that had superceded all conflicting thoughts, that overrode all turmoil. It was a simple drive, not intellectual, not physical. It was the drive to get home.

Home. Not to Stacy, not to family, though they were very much a part of it, but simply home. Simply to stand on the porch, in the kitchen, in the bedroom of the house that he called home. He arched his back, flexed his neck and shoulders. Offers of regular commissions, reenlistment bonuses, the wonderful look and lure of a stewardess who he fantasized might be interested if he pursued, nothing overrode the force that had propelled him toward Mill Creek Falls. There was joy in the drive, pride in what he was, what he was bringing home. And there was paranoia and sadness. Home. He would go home and figure it all out from there. Perhaps establish a new home, perhaps with Stacy, from the base, the foundation, of what had been his home ever since he was eight.

Wapinski twisted his neck, stretched it left then right. Again he checked his reflection. The image was too faint to see details. "Good job, Wap," he whispered to the glass. The tiredness seemed to vanish, to be replaced by a momentary flash of energy exploding in his chest, from his heart. He wanted to run. His plodding changed to a quick, light step. In Viet Nam he felt he had had a responsibility to his grandfather, his mother and Stacy, owed them his return. He had seriously considered re-upping, staying in Viet Nam. Now he was certain he'd made the right choice.

On Third Street he passed Old Pete's Barbershop. The sign was down, the window hazed over with glass cleaner on the inside. Through scratches in the haze he could see the place was empty. No mirrors, no barber's chairs. Even the old linoleum had been removed. The only thing that remained was a cardboard poster that said BARBER SHOP: ASK FOR WILDROOT. He did not stop, did not wonder what had happened to old Pete who had cut his hair ever since he could remember.

Half a block up, across Boyd Drive, there was a new 7-Eleven. Lights were burning in the parking lot and inside. He approached cautiously. Two doors before the store a tabby cat, crouched on the sidewalk, startled and leapt away. Wapinski startled in response, immediately brought his attention back to the store. He stopped. The store was not yet open.

There were no cars in the lot, no one to be seen through the storefront. Wapinski turned, looked over his shoulder. No one. He lightly slapped his hand to his right hip. Nothing there. He stood very still. Two blocks from his mother's house, from home, he backed up. Quickly he walked south on Boyd Drive to Second Street where Morris' Mill Creek Grocery was still dark, then east to Callars Drive and north back to Third. He glanced west toward the 7-Eleven, half a block away. Jessie Taynor, a big, heavy, mentally impaired girl who Mill Creekers thought of as their village idiot, was shaking the glass doors, banging on the jambs.

Wapinski shook his head. He turned east, looked up Third Street to where it T'd into Crooked Road. Across the intersection, behind a low hedge and two small Japanese maples, was his mother's house. It wasn't yet six o'clock.

At six, the morning of 31 May 1969, Captain Robert J. Wapinski slid down against a wall on the floor of an out-processing building at Cam Ranh Bay. He sat amongst six enlisted men. His year was over. He had arrived the night before and filled out the standard forms. Now he sat and waited for the processing to be completed. Replacement Station clerks smiled awkwardly, cynically. Another grunt officer in the wrong place, he suspected them of thinking. Wapinski couldn't give a shit. He did not care about medals, either. They had given him two Silver Stars, one for a minor operation outside of Cu Chi early in his tour and one for Dong Ap Bia, plus a Bronze Star for Go Dau Ha, an Air Medal, a CIB—that he cared about, the Combat Infantryman's Badge—and an assortment of what sailors call geedunks, candy.

He was tired. He had begun his out-processing on the 26th, six days after the final assault on Dong Ap Bia. Much has been said about American soldiers being pulled from jungle battles, flown to America, discharged, and returned home within thirty-six hours. There probably exist a few for whom these events happened so quickly; for most the process of clearing company, battalion, division, and finally country lasted days. Moreover, few—except the battle-wounded who were evacuated from country and the KIAs—were in battle their last moments in the field.

Wapinski cleared company and battalion. He visited the casualties in the field hospital from his last battle. He dragged out clearing division until the 30th, wanting to avoid waiting at Cam Ranh, wanting to spend his last energy in Viet Nam consoling and supporting the wounded men he'd fought beside. Dragging out out-processing increased the weariness still on him from the A Shau Valley operation.

Captains weren't supposed to have to wait with enlisted men but he had been with two of these six men during the past month. They were not his men. He had not commanded them, although at times he had commanded other boonie rats, grunts, but he knew two of the men and he did not want to sit alone, nor did he want to drink with the desk officers with whom he had come to the replacement center.

Wapinski had no war souvenirs that needed clearing. He had already gotten his hair cut. He did not want to talk but he wanted to listen to grunts talk. The big PX, the city atmosphere, the people milling around chattering so loudly—it was almost frightening. Why? He could not get the question out of his mind nor could he bring it into focus. Out of all the men leaving or coming or working here, he thought, these six know what it's been about. There were two or three other small groups, squads, sitting against walls, amongst two hundred or three hundred men. But, he thought, then that makes sense in a war in which eight of ten are support troops.

The more the clerks laughed, the more people milled around, the more speeches he heard from "commanders" telling them how important their job had been, how well they had served, how proud he was and they should be; the more he sat against that wall with those six, an informal patrol, perimeter, keeping others away, always one awake. For two days they sat, he would think later, without communicating. If one rose to defecate, two rose to walk his slack. If they talked, he did not remember, would never remember. They may have chatted the hours away, but he did not think so.

And then onto the buses, to the plane, segregated by rank. What happened to those six he would never know. He did not see them in Japan during the short stopover. Nor did he see them at Seattle/Tacoma or Ft. Lewis.

As the Freedom Bird touched down on 3 June small cheers sounded about the cabin. Some thought they had landed at Anchorage, expected a refueling delay before the last leg to Ft. Lewis. When the pilot announced his "Welcome home. The temperature here in Tacoma . . . " the cabin erupted with applause. But the celebration was short. Everyone was tired from the flight and Seattle/Tacoma was anticlimactic. It wasn't leaving the war zone; it wasn't yet home. Further dampening spirits were two cold-turkey soldiers who had tried to make the flight without their fix. Men around them had attempted to take care of them, hold them, keep the authorities from detecting them. At first the two were restless, then buzzing, agitated, irritable, finally convulsive. A medic and doctor shot them up with sedatives. They were the first off the plane, strapped down to stretchers, carried out under MP escort.

Officers deplaned next. It was midmorning. Several small groups had gathered to greet a few of the returnees, though most men had not known exactly when they would return, had not sent word to relatives. Much of the terminal was restricted. Wapinski and a small group of officers followed a guide through the terminal toward customs and the never ending in/out processing procedures. He was dressed in a summer khaki uniform that he'd received at Cam Ranh Bay. His pant legs were bloused over jump boots, on his cap there was an airborne patch, a Screaming Eagle patch on his shoulder, a substantial patchwork of ribbons on his chest. As the returnees walked through the terminal they passed enlisted men with bare uniforms—soldiers possibly just having finished basic training. The EM stared at the returning officers singling out Wapinski. Wapinski smiled inwardly as one of them said, "Geez, look at that. And he's a captain, too." And another said, "That's a Silver Star isn't it?" And a third, "Look at his eyes, Man! I wouldn't mess with him fer nothin."

Seattle/Tacoma, buses, Ft. Lewis. For ten days Captain Robert Janos Wapinski struggled with military bureaucrats. They offered him a regular commission, they paid him, they processed form after form, and they examined him.

"Captain," an apathetic technician told him, "your ear tests indicate a loss of hearing in both ears to very low frequency sound and in your right ear a diminished capacity to hear midfrequency tones at relatively high volume."

"So what's that mean?" Wapinski asked.

"Sir"—the enlisted man stared him in the eyes, shook his head, shrugged—"it means if you sign these papers sayin it's okay, you're outa here. You're outa the Green Machine tonight. If you don't sign, we keep you here for a few weeks. Run some tests. Shit like that."

"A few weeks, Specialist?" Wapinski asked. He did not like the boy's attitude.

"Yes Sir. Then they put you before a review panel and offer you a disability. For this, maybe ten percent."

"And what does that mean?"

"Well, Sir," the technician groaned, irritated, "it means they send you maybe thirty bucks in the mail every month for the rest of your life. It means you gotta keep havin yer ears rechecked to make sure they're still bad. Look, what it comes down to is cigarette money. You can stay here for the next couple of weeks to guarantee you're in cigarette money for the rest of yer life, or you can sign these papers waiving any claims about yer ears and you're home free."

"Um." Snot-nosed Spec. 4, Wapinski thought.

"Sir, this is the only thing keepin you from bein discharged, isn't it?" Wapinski didn't answer. The technician repeated the question, a bit louder, aiming his voice toward Wapinski's left ear. Still Wapinski didn't answer. "Come on, Sir," the technician pleaded.

"Sign em for me," Wapinski said.

"What?" The technician was astounded.

"Is *your* hearing bad, Specialist?"

"No Sir."

"Then sign the papers for me and tell me where I get a ticket to Philadelphia."

*   *   *

At eight o'clock in the morning, Pacific Daylight Saving Time, Friday 13 June, Robert Wapinski called home. He had called the day he arrived, had spoken briefly with his mother. "Hi. I'm in Seattle," he had said. "Oh," his mother answered. "That's good." He had sighed. Talking to his mother was never satisfying. "I'm going to be here a few days," he told her. "I'll call when I know my discharge date. When I'm coming back." "You do that," she had said. "Mom, ah, don't call Stacy, okay? I want to surprise her." "I won't," she had answered.

Their conversation on the 13th was no more rewarding, and after having spent nearly an hour waiting for a phone that wasn't so jammed with coins that it could operate, he was angry.

"Three one five four," his mother answered with the ending digits of her phone number.

"Hi," he said. "It's me. I've got a ten-fifteen flight out of here that gets me into Philly at 7:05, your time."

"Rob," his mother said, "see if you can get a flight to Williamsport, okay?"

"I thought maybe Brian could pick me up in Philly. Have you talked to Stacy?"

"You know I never see that girl," she said. Then she added, "My stomach's been acting up."

At the gate to the flight to Philadelphia Robert Wapinski did a curious thing. He was dressed in summer-weight class-A greens, bedecked with ribbons, pants bloused, jump boots spitshined. He believed it would be the last time he would ever wear a military uniform and he wanted to wear it properly, proudly, this one last time. And yet, perhaps because he was alone amongst civilians preparing to board the flight and he wished to hide, perhaps because he had just been discharged from an institution that had owned him for the past thirty-four months and the freedom was producing an identity crisis, or perhaps because he just wished to be left alone with his own thoughts, shortly before boarding he went to the airport shop and purchased a pair of mirrored sunglasses. He had never owned sunglasses, had resisted buying a pair of aviator glasses while in-country partly because so many rear-eschelon officers wore them and he despised their clique. He put the glasses on, adjusted them at the nose and behind the ears, boarded.

He took a window seat. The plane was nearly full yet both seats beside him remained vacant. The plane taxied, waited, taxied, thundered down and was airborne.

In the aisle seat one row up from him a man, perhaps in his early fifties, turned and looked back. Wapinski tensed. He turned his head as if looking out the window but cocked his eyes toward the stranger. The man was skimming through a news magazine. Every few pages he stopped, turned around, looked at Wapinski.

What's your story, Jack? Wapinski thought. Still he pretended not to notice the man. What's he lookin at me for? The man put his magazine down, stared at Wapinski. What the hell's goin on? Wapinski tried to take in every detail. He was a large man, over six feet, at least two hundred pounds. His suit was well made, looked expensive. His tie was conservatively striped, his shoes were heavy wingtips, good for walking. Wapinski decided he must be a salesman. But his unshaven face was not a salesman's face. I bet he's queer, Wapinski thought.

The man stood, crossed the aisle, came back toward Wapinski. Wapinski searched the clouds below looking for a break to the ground.

"Mind if I sit down?" the man asked.

"Go ahead." Wapinski choked on the words. He cleared his throat, continued to search the clouds. If this guy puts his hand on my leg I'll kill him.

The man motioned for the stewardess. When she came he ordered two small bottles of scotch. "Bring two glasses," he said to the stewardess. "With ice, please."

From behind his sunglasses, out of the corner of his eye, Wapinski watched the man. The flight attendant set the bottles and glasses on the man's fold-down table. He opened both bottles, poured one into each glass. "You just got back from Vet Naam, huh?"

Vet Naam, Wapinski said to himself. Christ, we've been there a decade and Americans still can't pronounce the name of the country. "Yeah," he answered. "Why?"

"Naw, naw, naw. Here. How bout a drink?"

"I never drink scotch."

"Never? An army captain who doesn't drink scotch!"

"Nope," Wapinski said. "Beer. A little vodka. I don't drink much hard stuff. Never scotch straight."

"Well, you know, you're a man now, right?"

"I guess I am."

"Aw, you can drink it. Don't worry about it. It won't do nothin to ya. Besides, you look like you need a stiff drink."

"Okay," Wapinski said. He took the glass, tasted it, tilted his head back, gulped. The man did the same. Then he ordered two more. They each downed another drink without talking and the man ordered two more. Wapinski downed that one and removed his sunglasses.

The man smiled. He downed his drink, loosened his tie, ordered two more, finally said, "Well, what was it like over there?"

"It was all right," Wapinski answered. "It was okay."

"You see a lot of action?"

"I'm infantry," Wapinski answered.

"So was I," the man said.

"Hm?"

"World War Two. Europe. Marched north from Anzio all the way to Germany. We were in some nasty places."

"Yeah, I guess so."

For the next hour he recounted battles all over Europe in which he had participated twenty-five years earlier.

"Wow! That sounds like it was hell!" Wapinski said. He was impressed with the details of the man's stories, the comparisons he drew to Viet Nam. "Our battles were a lot smaller," Wapinski said. "At Dong Ap Bia we had fifty percent casualties in one battalion but the overall numbers don't compare with what you're talking about."

"Son," the man said very respectfully, "every man's got his own hell. You just finished with yours."

"Yeah," Wapinski answered. They were into their fifth or sixth drink.

"Never let em get to your mind," the man said.

"Um."

"You know what that means?"

"I guess."

"It means when everyone else is saying this is the way things were, and you know that is not the way things were, don't let em convince you that you don't know your own mind. That happens. Happens all the time. They make you doubt yourself, doubt what you been through, what you know and what you accomplished. They'll try to make you believe you're crazy.

"I know what you guys have gone through," the salesman continued. "Or I think I know. You guys have been terrific. Don't ever let em make you believe different. And don't ever let em paint it up like roses either. Never let em get to your mind cause they just don't understand. How bout one more?"

The plane landed twenty minutes early. Wapinski snapped awake. His sunglasses were on the seat beside him. Most of the passengers had deplaned, the line in the aisle at the door was only five or six people.

"Hey," Wapinski shouted. He stood up, grabbed his small bag and started for the exit. "Hey, what happened to that guy?" he blurted at a stewardess. She looked at him blankly. "The guy that bought me all those drinks," he said.

"I'm sorry, Sir," the stewardess answered. "I've been in the forward cabin."

"Damn." Wapinski gritted his teeth. "I didn't even get his name."

"Sir," a flight attendant addressed him from behind, "you left your glasses on your seat."

During the hour and a half layover before his departure for Williamsport, Robert Wapinski shuffled about restlessly. He called home. His mother had not asked his brother to pick him up in Philadelphia. "Call when you get to Williamsport," she said. He bought a coffee. He watched people staring at him in his gung-ho, airborne-all-the-way, ribbon-bedecked class-A uniform, and he felt self-conscious.

He sat in a lime-green fiberglass seat, stared out the terminal windows at the activity, the seeming random motion of planes, trucks, people scurrying. He winced, grabbed a magazine from the table beside him. Casually he flipped pages, then flipped back to the cover: *Newsweek*, June 9, 1969. In the "Periscope" section he found a short paragraph about the North Viet Namese using Russian-made helicopters to airlift troops and supplies within Cambodia and Laos and "occasionally across the border into Vietnam." He did not doubt that was true. He looked up. The turmoil irritated him, made him tense. He glanced at the "War in Vietnam" section.

There was *his* last battle! Chills ran up his back, neck. "The Battle of Ap Bia Mountain." He bit his lip. Couldn't, he thought, they refer to it as Dong Ap Bia like we did? Under the accompanying photo he read, "Hamburger Hill: Was the slaughter really necessary?"

The Nixon Administration, rattled by Congressional criticism over the battle, sought last week to disclaim responsibility for stepping up the pace of the war. . . . *To disclaim responsibility! What the—?* White House aides insisted to reporters that there had been no escalation of military operations by U.S. forces since President Nixon took office on Jan. 20. . . .

NEW TACTICS: As with many arguments about the Vietnamese war, the truth in this case seemed to be more elusive than was indicated by Washington's statistics. Undoubtedly, Hanoi's policy is to maximize U.S. casualties in South Vietnam in hopes of making an impact on American public opinion and improving its bargaining position at the Paris peace talks. . . . *Which is exactly our policy also. To inflict enough hurt on them to make them stop invading the south.* Cautioned by North Vietnamese President Ho Chi Minh that they must "economize human and material resources," the Communists this time are avoiding human-wave assaults. Instead it appears they have opted for radically different tactics that combine mortar and rocket attacks with hit-and-run raids by small, elite sapper squads. . . . *What's radically different about that? That's been going on for years. What the hell are these guys . . .*

When he halted the U.S. bombing of North Vietnam last November, President Johnson also approved a policy of exerting "maximum pressure" on the enemy in South Vietnam. The Nixon Administration has never thought fit to alter that policy. . . . *Why the hell should it? What are we supposed to do, exert minimum pressure? They'd simply fill in the voids. They'd be in the population centers. These people don't understand.*

U.S. military men defend this "maximum pressure" strategy as the only one that can prevent large-scale Communist ground attacks on South Vietnam's major cities. "The idea of pulling back and letting the enemy have the jungles because it would cut down on American casualties is a military fallacy," said a high-ranking U.S. officer. . . . "If we let them back in, it would increase casualties, not lower them." That may be so. *May be?* But in the meantime, as the latest weekly casualty list showed (265 American dead, 1,863 wounded), both sides seem intent on using military force to crystalize their political position.

Wapinski stopped reading. The cacophony of sounds, the buzz of fluorescent lights, the click of high heels on tile floors, the broken and static announcements, the roar of takeoffs, a baby crying, and the asinine perspective of the article tore at him. He closed his eyes, tight, opened them, took a deep breath. If we didn't, he said to himself, do they think the NVA'd stop? Do you think they'd just go away? It is a war over there. These people don't understand. They just don't fuckin understand.

He flipped further into the magazine. There was a lengthy article about the military-industrial complex, a reiteration of President Eisenhower's 1961 warning that the nation "must guard against the acquisition of unwarranted influence" by the MIC, and an assessment of congressional moves to exert control over the Pentagon.

Wapinski flipped back to the Viet Nam section. "Disclaim responsibility," he read again. He almost threw the magazine across the waiting room. He ground his teeth, lit a cigarette, flipped back to the photo of the 101st Airborne troops on Dong Ap Bia. He searched the faces to see if he knew the men. Sure, he thought, he recognized one. Again the chill. He looked about, checked his watch. Why wasn't the Williamsport plane at the gate? He flipped to the back of the magazine, to the Stewart Alsop column entitled "No Disguised Defeat?" He could not read it.

"It means—" he heard a voice, glanced left, right, "when everyone is saying this is the way it was—" another takeoff roar, another static announcement, another flyover vibrating his damaged eardrums, no one near him, yet the voice, "don't let em convince you . . . "

Wapinski stared at the column. He shook his head imperceptibly. The articles gave a different dimension to the Southeast Asia he had been dealing with for the past year. He knew the North Viet Namese had suffered seriously during his tour, that intrinsic South Viet Namese resistance had been tremendously reduced, the result of massive losses during Tet of '68 and the abandonment of their cause by so many due to the barbarity displayed by the northern Communist leadership while they held Hue . . .

Wapinski inhaled, slowly exhaled attempting to release his tiredness, his tension. He looked up. The baby had stopped crying, the flyovers and takeoffs didn't seem so loud. He unzipped his AWOL bag, stuffed in the *Newsweek*. He decided he would follow the story, the developments, closely. He would find out what was happening politically. He would speak out about what he had seen, what he knew, what he believed. But not now, not yet. Then he told himself, they won't ever get to my mind.

*   *   *

Wapinski arrived in Williamsport at ten o'clock. Again he called home.

"Rob, I'm not feeling too good," his mother said. "And your brother's not home. I forgot to call him when he came in from work. Maybe you could get a bus to Laporte and Doug could pick you up there?"

Jesus, he thought. Nothing like putting yourself out a little. "Okay," he answered. "I'll get in however."

"Oh, that's good," she said. "I don't want to have to worry about you."

"No, don't worry. I'm a big boy."

At ten P.M. there were no buses going north, although there was one that ran to Montoursville, Hughesville, Red Rock, and Wilkes-Barre. He took it to the Hughesville depot, then walked the half mile to the junction of 220, 405 and 118 and began to hitchhike. Almost immediately he was picked up by a farmer in a battered, red Chevy pickup who brought him to Muncy Valley. There he waited for an hour, finally caught a four-mile ride that took him toward Eagles Mere. A third ride brought him past the small lake, over the mountain, down and halfway up to World's End State Park. From there he walked.

The cool night air felt clean. He felt happy. Confused, numb, tired, too tired to think anymore, but happy. The sun blisters and jungle rot on his arms and legs had mostly scabbed over and cleaned up. His grunt tan— arms and neck only—had faded. Most of the pimples on his face had cleared and even though he still didn't feel completely clean, he felt strong. He was happy to be on the familiar road, at night, without a person about, without a light to be seen except for the stars, without a sound except the peepers and crickets, the lovely voices of the creeks, the squeak of bats and the silent flyby of an owl. Tomorrow, he thought, no, today he would see his mother and her boyfriend, his brother and sister, and he would surprise Stacy.

Quietly Robert Wapinski tried the screen door to the front porch. It was latched. He walked around to the back door. It too was locked. He hesitated, tried to hear if anyone was up. He looked through the kitchen window. The room was mostly dark, the door to the dining room closed. Gray light fell across the table. Miriam Wapinski hated mornings. For as many years as he could recall she had set the table for breakfast immediately after removing the dinner dishes. No one sat around her table after meals. The table was set for two.

Wapinski returned to the front of the house, picked a twig from the Japanese maple and used it to unlatch the screen door. He put his AWOL bag down on the small table and tried the front door. It was latched and bolted. Flash image in his mind—he calling out cheerfully, "Hey, I'm home," as in a normal family and then, doors swinging open, parents and siblings cascading down the steep Victorian stairs, flowing out onto the porch, surrounding him, hugging him, falling over themselves to treasure him returned to them. He looked through the beveled glass into the hall, halfway up the stairs, through the arch into the parlor. Dark grayness, stillness, polished dark oak flooring, a new large-screen TV, knickknacks in perfect order. He moved to the nylon-webbed chaise longue, slowly sat, not making a sound, not creaking a floorboard. He lifted his feet, sat back, closed his eyes. A hazy shroud of blackness seemed to envelop him, closing down his ears to sound, dulling his skin to feeling, descending over his forehead to seal his eyes and slacken his taut skin. Someplace in the distance a car, rubber tires whining on concrete, the sound soothing like that of ocean waves to beach dwellers, smooth, relaxing, home, really home.

The shroud receded. Wapinski opened his eyes. It was light. He looked at his watch. Seven ten. Without moving he took in the street, the sounds of new-day activities, cars starting nearby, old Mrs. Franklin down Third Street sweeping her sidewalk. He swung his legs to the floor. They were stiff, sore from walking and resting and sitting in airplanes. He lit a cigarette, inhaled deeply, exhaled, stood up. Doug unlatched and unbolted the front door. "Rob! When did you get here?"

"Hi Doug. About an hour ago."

"Let me get Miriam. She's upstairs." He went back in. Wapinski shook his head again. Not even a handshake. He grabbed his AWOL bag, stepped into the house. The moment he entered peaceful reentry ended. The whirlwinds began.

"Oh, Robbie," his mother said from the stairs. "I'm glad you're home. Leave that bag on the porch, please." She descended to the foyer. "Have you lost weight?" She didn't wait for an answer. "Brian's home. I don't know what time that brother of yours came in last night, but I heard the car when I was in bed. You can go over and see him and Cheryl while I clean up, okay?"

"Okay," Wapinski said.

"Your sister decided to stay at school for the summer. She wanted you to call her when you got in."

"I'll do that."

"Keep it short. This phone's going to put me in the poorhouse."

While she rattled on nervously he made small gestures, opened his arms, waiting for her to at least hug him. She seemed awkward, like a child with a secret. He stepped toward her to give her a kiss. She was short, half a foot shorter than he, and stocky and strong. "How've you been?" he asked as he stepped to her. She stepped back, grabbed out for his hands, gave them a small squeeze, let go, stepped back farther.

"Not so good," she said. "My condition's not getting any better."

"Oh!" he said. He took out his cigarettes and lighter. "How about you, Doug?" he asked. Doug had been standing in the archway, watching quietly.

"He's fine," she answered for him. "I'm the one with a condition. Don't smoke in here. It just makes ashes on the floor that I've got to clean up."

"Same old mom." He laughed. He put the cigarettes away but kept the lighter in his hand. "It's good to be back. I've missed you, and this place."

"Well that's nice," she said. "We're glad you're home safe and sound. There's so much that needs doing around here and I can't do it anymore. And Doug's no help."

"That's quite a row of ribbons there, Rob," Doug said.

"Oh, don't go into that," Miriam snapped.

There was another awkward pause, then Doug said, "Miriam, why don't we all have some breakfast?" To Wapinski, "We got a new store on Third Street. I was just going to get some eggs."

"I saw—"

"Go get the eggs, then. And Robbie, why don't you go over to Brian's while I clean up. This house is a mess."

Doug slid past him and went out.

"Did Stacy call?" Wapinski blurted.

"You and that girl. I told her not to call until you got back."

"You might be civil to her," Wapinski snapped. "Someday she's going to be your daughter-in-law." Immediately he felt ashamed, felt he should not have said it, should not have given her one more lever to use, one more weapon with which to threaten him. A thickness congealed in his gut.

Wapinski's mother's house was a nine-room Victorian built at the turn of the century when Mill Creek Falls was in its lumbering and tanning heyday. Brian's house, behind Miriam's, was a four-room cottage built in 1921 for a war-widowed daughter by the original owner of the Victorian. The two structures were still on a single gas line, single water and sewer lines, single electric meter. Miriam owned both houses. She charged Brian what she called "a reasonable rent."

When he saw Rob approaching, Brian exploded through the door. "God Damn! Good to see ya! Look at you!" He wrapped his brother in his arms, squeezed the breath out of him. "Why the hell didn't you call? When'd you get in? Oh, this calls for a celebration. Come in. Come in. Cheryl, Robbie's home!"

"I'm not dressed," Cheryl shrieked, giggled, vanished down the hallway.

"He's my brother," Brian shouted jovially. He winked at Rob. "Nice ass, huh? I'd share her but I don't think she'd put up with it."

"I got some of my own coming." Rob laughed back.

"Jim Beam?" Brian asked. He pulled the bottle and three glasses from the cupboard. Cheryl walked back in wearing a loose robe.

"Robbie." Her eyes smiled; her face lit up. "Oh, poor Robbie." She kissed his cheek and hugged him hard. He could feel her breasts against his chest. Lightly she shimmied against him.

"Oooo-oooo!" He laughed and she laughed, too.

"Here's to the soldier from Vet Naam," Brian said. He handed Cheryl and Rob double shots of the bourbon. "Welcome home." He downed his shots. "Aaaaaahh! We saw you on TV."

Cheryl sipped at the drink. "I was so scared for you."

"On TV?" Rob asked.

"Brian thinks he saw you," Cheryl said.

"Well, not exactly you, I guess. They did a little reenactment of an assault that your unit, ah . . . they killed all them Cong. I think it was your unit, wasn't it? That's what Grandpa said. All year long he cut the articles about the 101st from the paper. He saved em for you."

"Huh? Yeah?! Nice. Ah, we had a lot of units. Eighteen thousand men in the division."

"And you were with them guys in that valley near Laos. Up on that hill, right?"

"Yeah."

"So . . . ?" Brian said.

"So what?" Rob asked.

"So how many?"

"How many what, Brian?"

"How many slopes did you kill?"

"What?" Rob hadn't expected the question.

"You know, what was it like to kill a couple a hundred gooks. I want to know all the gory details."

Cheryl interrupted with disdain. "Brian just wants to be able to tell everybody at the shop."

"I don't know," Rob said flatly.

"I told everybody you were a real gung-ho killer," Brian boasted. "Each time they'd have an article about you in the paper, I'd tell em you were trying to win the war by yourself. Boy, is Joanne pissed at you."

Rob pushed himself against the back of his chair. "What articles? Joanne?"

"Didn't Mom send em to you?"

"Send what? No!"

"About all them medals you won! Silver Stars. That was all in the papers."

Cheryl put her hand on top of Rob's. "They were nice articles," she said.

Brian leaned forward, cupped his hand as if to tell Rob a secret. "There's a girl down the shop who'd like to meet you," he stage-whispered. "They say she gives great head."

"Brian!" Cheryl gasped.

"I don't know." Brian laughed. "I didn't try it. Aw," he swiped his hand in the air, "drink up, Boy. You ain't gonna be able to buy a drink in this town for a long time."

Rob sighed. "Hooo, actually I'd prefer coffee. I walked in from Eagles Mere last night and I'm kinda beat."

"Robbie," Cheryl said, "why didn't you call? We could have picked you up."

"I, ah"—he thought of saying, I called Mom, but decided to let it pass—"ah, got a ride with some guy that far and it was late and ah ... you know, it was a nice night."

"Coffee's coming up. It's all ready." Brian smiled, served his brother. He grabbed Rob's bourbon, dumped it into the coffee. "Milk?"

They talked for two and a half hours about new cars, music, baseball, Brian's work at the mill, Cheryl's new job with The Hartley Insurance Agency, people they all knew, the 7-Eleven and old Pete's retirement. Rob asked about Joanne, how she was doing in school, what she'd be doing during the summer; and he asked about Grandpa. He smoked half a pack of cigarettes, until he was out. He and Brian killed half the bottle and another pot of coffee. He was becoming wired-drunk. After each cigarette Rob returned his lighter to his pants pocket and kept his hand on it long enough to work his thumb over the engraving.

Out of cigarettes, half intoxicated, he went back to his mother's house. The back door was latched. He walked to the front. On the porch he saw that his AWOL bag had been opened. He looked in. His records were gone. He went inside. No one was in the parlor though the TV was on. He opened the door to the kitchen. The old painted wood cabinets had been replaced by new light blue formica ones with oak trim. His orders and medical records were spread on the table. He stood for a long minute, heard movement in the parlor.

"Mom," he called opening the door. She and Doug had seated themselves before the TV. "What's this?"

She looked up at him, held up a finger indicating for him to wait until a commercial.

"What is this?" he shouted. He went back into the kitchen, grabbed his records, stormed in with them. He took up a position between the TV and the viewers. "What's this?" he demanded.

"You know, Robbie," she said passively. "I thought you were dirty. You just come back from an awful bad place. We didn't know if you were sick or not."

"I'm not sick. What the—Geez!" He marched back to the porch, crammed the papers into his bag, went back to Brian's.

"That's what really happened last night," Rob said. "I called. I've been fuckin callin fer days. Then this shit."

"Look," Brian said. "Why don't you stay here? When Cheryl gets back from the store we'll figure out an arrangement. You can stay with us. Use our old car. Then you can go up to Grandpa's and stay up there. He's got lots of room. You stay here for as long as you want. I'll tell Cheryl it's only going to be for a few nights. That way she won't mind."

In thirty hours he had catnapped for less than two, had been near intoxication twice, had eaten little, traveled twenty-five hundred miles, walked the last fifteen. Now, at noon, with no wind, the temperature having risen to the upper seventies, the air thick with humidity as if August had shed a day into June, Wapinski set off to see Stacy. He had showered and shaved. He'd turned down Brian's offer for clothes, not wanting to go back to his mother's. Anyway, he wanted Stacy to see him just once in uniform.

Brian lent him his car. Rob drove slowly, circuitously through downtown and Small Mill, across the old steel truss bridge, up 154 to the edge of New New Town. His stomach fluttered. The road whipped by more quickly than he imagined it could. He headed east on the county road past the subdivision, then south into rolling country and scattered farms, then east again, the old road twisting to follow the level, finally climbing over a ridge and falling into a narrow valley. He lit cigarette after cigarette, at times realizing he still had one going in the ashtray as he lit the next. The breeze coming off the road through the floor vents was hot. His feet sweated in the jumpboots. Beneath the dress green's blouse his shirt was saturated. What to say? he thought. What to say? Ask her to marry you, he thought. Ask her. No. Not yet. Don't be stupid. Beads of perspiration formed high on his forehead. It seemed hotter than Nam. What to say? He smiled thinking about her smile, her eyes. He put his left hand out the window, tried to deflect more wind into the car. Great way to see yer gal, he thought. Stinking sticky with sweat.

This is too much, he thought, expecting her to be ready if I'm totally unexpected. I should call. He drove farther south and east then pulled into the shade at the side of the road. His thoughts were jumbled, dull. Was he going to see her response to his uniform, to him strong if skinny, hard, the conquering hero returned ready to storm the world for his lady? He rejected that notion, thought of her, of her eyes, face, smell, her poise and grace.

He was going to see Stacy whom he loved, whom he had loved for four years, lived with for one wonderful month on leave before going overseas, written to innumerable times.

He drove to her house, walked into the yard, went to the door. His feet barely touched the ground, his body felt weightless, numb, on autopilot, dumb, happy. Stacy would be—

Before he could imagine how she would look, what she would say, Stacy's mother opened the door. "Robert!" she cried. "Robert!" She threw her arms around him. Hugged him, kissed him the way he had hoped his own mother would have hugged and kissed him. He liked Stacy's mom; she had always liked him.

"Hi Ma." He smiled casually, relaxed, the nervousness dissipating at finding her there, finding the house unchanged. "How ya doin, Sweetheart?"

She looked at him smiling, about to answer, then her face contorted. She coughed.

"Ma? What is it? I'm okay," he jested, trying to lighten things up, back things up to when she was smiling. "Look, no holes."

"Robert, you're not going to like this," she said looking up at him, pitying him, pleading with her eyes as if to say, Please let him not mind, not care, not hate.

"What's the matter?" He was floating again. Jittery. "Where's Stacy?"

"She's on the sun porch."

Wapinski did not hesitate. He walked through the house to the back. Through the window he could see Stacy on the porch. He couldn't believe how beautiful she was, how sexy she looked in a bathing suit, her legs glistening with tanning oil. He stared for half a second before he saw the guy. Wapinski opened the door, stepped onto the porch, his chest puffed up, lats flared, shoulders tense under his uniform, teeth clenched. He stood legs apart, like a statue, solid, planted before them. He couldn't move, couldn't talk, then if he did move or speak he wasn't aware of it. Perhaps they talked for several minutes. Perhaps he shook the guy's hand. Perhaps he wished him well. Then he backed out, retreated, retreated to the car, withdrew, capitulated. Then all he could hear was Stacy saying, "I want you to meet my fiancé. . . . I want you to meet my fiancé. . . . I want you to meet my fiancé. . . ." over and over and over. He loosened his blouse, removed his tie, unbuttoned his shirt. He looked at the slip of paper she had handed him as she'd shuffled him out. There was a name, address and phone number. *Bea Hollands (Red).* "You remember her," Stacy had said, but he hadn't really heard, had heard with his ears but not his brain. "She said when you got back she wanted you to stop by and say hello."

July 1984

I remember when the town wasn't so big, when it was just growing. We'd moved into the New Town subdivision into one of the first houses so it faced 154 and the old houses of Creeks Bend, which Pa said were built right after the war to house all the veterans who'd just come back, built of "tin cans and cardboard and held together with bubble gum" is what my Pa would say. I remember one time my Ma, Josephine, she took us to Morris', the grocery downtown on Second Street 'cause the only market in our section was in Creeks Bend and it was owned by the Holland family and they overcharged for everything. Or so Pa said. That must of been nineteen fifty . . . four, no, five, nineteen fifty-five cause I remember Mark was just over a year and Ma carried him on her shoulder the whole time she was shopping and Joe and I kind of tagged along behind bein a bit scared cause Morris' was in Lutzburgh and most of the people who shopped there were like the Hartleys or the Merediths or the Cadwalders, which was Miriam Wapinski's maiden name and which she used sometimes and would probably always of used but the kids were Wapinski on the school register and she'd be ever explaining . . .

That's not what I was thinking though. I mean I was thinking maybe about the first time I saw Bobby but maybe it wasn't the first time and maybe it wasn't him. I never like asked him about it cause if it'd been me, I'd av been embarrassed.

I remember there weren't a lot of people in the store, but there were some, two or three in every aisle. And there were a bunch waiting to check out cause Mr. Morris' daughter was at the register and she still had to look at the keys—not like him or even most of the high school kids he'd trained who could shoot their fingers over the numbers without looking and without making mistakes either.

But what I remember, it was a real hot day, maybe August, summer, cause we weren't in school, and Ma was carrying Mark, and Joe and I were putting things in the carriage when she told us, or foolin' around if she wasn't lookin. And up there by the check out was this lady with two kids—if it was Wapinski, Brian wasn't with em cause he's about as old as my oldest brother, John, who wasn't with us either. But I think it was Miriam and Bobby and his kid sister, Joanne, and Miriam is fixing a curl on Joanne's head and we're coming up the aisle behind them. I can see this even though it's really sunny out front and the people are mostly silhouettes against the big windows. I can more than see it. I can hear it. We're at the end of the aisle near the big, three-sided Campbell's soup display and I'm getting the chicken noodle and Joe's getting the tomato because Ma said to do it that way.

"You listen to me young man . . . " That's the way it started. I turned around and she had Bobby by the arm, like right in the armpit and she's got him cranked up so one foot's just touchin the floor and his shoulder is almost in his ear. Her face was really pretty except she was red around the eyes like somethin from Halloween. "You listen to me . . . " she says harsh but quiet like nobody is suppose to hear except that there wasn't any other noise and everybody kind of put their heads down but everybody heard. " . . . if you touch one more thing, you're going to get it. Do you hear me?!"

He didn't say anything and she let go his shoulder and he sagged like his body was a sack of potatoes and he put his head down. They moved up in line so they only had one lady before them. We began the turn down the next aisle—oh yeah, I remember—we were getting paper plates too for a picnic we were going to have with Aunt Isabella and Uncle James' family, my cousin Jimmy and I were real close, and Aunt Helen was going to come, too. Joe and I were already in the next aisle and Ma was carrying Mark and maneuvering the cart behind the line and Miriam gave her a look like how-dare-you-dago-scum-come-in-here when there's this big crash and I turn and soup cans are rolling all over the place and Miriam explodes—"ROBERT!"

I mean, she like comes unglued. "You little bastard!" She grabs him again, right by the armpit again, and she lifts him and she smacks him on the ass hard enough to knock his feet from under him but he doesn't fall cause she's got him by the armpit. "You little bastard! How many times . . . "

"I didn't." His voice was high. I remember it was like high and thin.

"Don't give me that." She's shaking him with every word. "Don't give me that. Do you think I'm stupid?!" And she's dragging him to the front of the store, screaming really angry but controlling the volume and Joanne's smirking like, "Ha! Ha! Robbie did it again." And Joe and I are kind of hiding behind the carriage and Ma—only my Ma would do this—she's holding Mark and she's already picked up half the cans and is rebuilding the display like it was her job.

Miriam's still berating him. She just left their cart right in the register lane and she smacked him again good as they went through the door and I swear his pants were wet. Ma's got me and Joe pickin up the last cans and there are people comin' to the front of the store and I think they're thinkin we knocked it down. And I look out the window and the Wapinskis had a big sedan, you know, maybe a Packard, and I see her shove him in the back door and he's about to sit on the seat and she shoves him onto the floor and slams the door and I think I saw him cryin.

Then Ma says to Joe and me, she says, "Get a jar of the Heinz India Relish that Daddy likes, okay? I'm going to get in line. You don't want to be late with your paper route."

Yeah, I was almost eight, Joe was a month short of nine, and we delivered the newspapers to the houses that were already built and occupied in New Town, and Jimmy used to help sometime, too. Bobby Wapinski must of been nine, too. Nine and a half.

2

For the next seven days the heat and humidity increased. Thunderstorms erupted over Mill Creek Falls then vanished without having cooled the air or lowered the humidity. The waters of the Loyalsock raged with runoff, crashed against the high rock mounds in the creek's center, swirled in the natural stone kettles. For seven days Robert Wapinski stayed drunk. He had not yet hit bottom, wasn't even close. The homecoming whirlpool had not yet sucked him down to its greatest depths, would not until he was sickened, horrified, not by the behavior of others but by his own.

The two days after seeing Stacy, Wapinski was stupid sloppy exhausted falling-down drunk. Brian and Cheryl bickered about it, Brian telling her to give him time, yet after only two days he told Rob that his presence was wearing thin. Wapinski hit his stride with the bottle on Tuesday and for the next five days he was standing up controlled drunk, the kind of self-medicated drunken state where one no longer is aware of his feelings or thoughts yet can still function. Sunday morning would find him looking up to see the top of the curb.

* * *

"What's this?" he asked his mother.

"Your bankbook," she answered passively, as if the obvious should not need asking.

"I sent you four hundred dollars a month," he said.

"And that's what I deposited."

"What happened to the rest of the money?"

"Well, you owed us some money, you know."

"God damn it! No! No, I don't know. There should be five grand in here."

"You did maintain a room here."

"What?!" This was too incredible.

"We kept your room for you. All your clothes and other possessions are there."

"There's only three thousand dollars here."

"I talked it over with Doug and he said that we could get a hundred and fifty dollars a month for a room in this part of town. That's what some of the men at the mill pay, and their rooms aren't even in the Lutzburgh section. It's only fair. Besides," she said flatly, "the money went right back into the house. Those cabinets are all wood and—"

"And you bought a fuckin TV too."

"Don't talk that way in my house."

"You can keep your fuckin house and your fuckin room."

"You're just going to throw it away on some stupid car, aren't you?"

"That's my business." He'd picked out a car at Lloyd's Autoland. He wanted to pay cash.

"You're just like your father."

"Wha—? That again! God damn. I'll come back for my shit."

"I'm not going to say it again," she screamed. "Don't you ever talk to me that way!"

Wednesday morning. The car brought back his smile. It made him feel like High School Harry but it was a good feeling and it was his first car and it was dazzling. He had never owned a vehicle before: in high school because he was saving his money for college; in college because there simply wasn't enough money after tuition, room, board and books. Carefully he guided the used black-and-red two-door convertible from the lot at Lloyd's. His legs slid on the red Naugahyde of the front bucket seat as he blipped the throttle and the hopped-up Mustang 289 torqued over, the posi-traction rear end dropped and grabbed, the radials grabbed the pavement.

His smile spread. The waxed and polished finish gleamed in the early day sun. He unleashed the Mustang's power on Mill Creek Road, roared past the New Mill, climbed the hill past the junkyard and the town dump turnoff, slid into the ninety-degree left below the Old Mill and the cascade at the falls before throttling back for the esses. Then feeling elated, he again punched it, zooming northwest through pasturelands toward Grandpa Wapinski's. He cooled down a mile before the family farm, stopped, turned around, headed back toward town. One surprise appearance was enough. He drove his new car to the dog pound behind the town dump, parked, went to the door, looked back and felt good. He went in, checked out the animals, left, drove to the unemployment office, registered, gazed at the girls. Then he drove to the state store and bought two bottles of scotch. He bought beer and cigarettes, groceries for Brian and Cheryl and a sleeping bag.

On Thursday Bobby went back to the dog pound. He cuddled two Newfoundland-mix pups, an Old Yeller dog, a large black lab-terrier mix. In one cage, by himself, was a four- or five-month-old German shepherd–husky mutt. "Hey boy," Wapinski called. The dog growled. "Well, fuc—What's the matter?" Wapinski stepped forward. The dog leaped at the cage door, barked viciously, snarled. "Come on, boy. What's yer name? Come on."

Wapinski laughed. The pup was ferocious, yet he looked so soft and cuddly to Bobby the incongruity was hilarious. "Come on," Wap said, going to the door and raising the latch. The dog backed up to the middle of the eight-foot run. Wapinski went in, closed the door behind himself without taking his eyes from the pup. The pup backed to the rear of the cage, still growling, twitching his head quickly, not taking his eyes off the man but searching for an escape route. Wapinski squatted, spoke softly. "What's yer name, pup? What's your name? Is it Sally or Sue? Come on. How come you're so defensive? Sally or Sue or Stacy? You a bitch? Who needs em, huh? You're a boy, aren't ya? Oh yeah, I can see. Have you been beaten?"

Wapinski talked to the dog for ten minutes without trying to move closer. A warden's assistant came into the kennel room, saw Wap, said, "Are you nuts? That little bastard bit me the first day—"

"Sssshh." Wap had risen when the boy came, though he had not removed his eyes from the dog. Now he backed out of the stall and relatched the door. The pup flew at him, snapping his teeth just as Bobby pulled his hands out. "What's his story?"

"I don't know," the assistant said. "They found him and two others downtown in a box. You know them hick farmers all a time bringin dogs to town, dumpin em in front of the stores and figuring town people'll just give em homes."

"That right?"

"Yeah. We end up destroying three-quarters of em. That one's goin next. If I'd had my way, they woulda injected im the first day we got im."

"When are you going to kill him?" Wapinski asked.

"Friday. Maybe."

"He got a name?"

"Yeah. Jerk."

"Hmm . . . Jer . . . Joe . . . Josh."

"What?"

"I'll take him. His name is Josh."

"Hey, RJ," Joe Akins said over the phone. He was a college friend of Wapinski's who had stayed in school, had graduated in June '67 as Wapinski would have had he remained. "Half dozen of us from our class are going back to the house for a party," Akins told him.

Wapinski looked at Cheryl's back as she washed the dinner dishes. Brian was reading the paper. They had barely spoken to him since he'd brought Josh home. "Geez, Joe," Wapinski said. He massaged Josh's ears. The pup almost purred. "I haven't been there since . . . shit, it's three and a half years!" Josh nuzzled his head against Bobby's leg.

"That's okay, RJ," Akins said. "The guys who are going back are all guys we graduated wit—ah, I mean, you know, guys we pledged with."

Lights shown from the open door of the fraternity house and from the basement windows. The rest of the house was dark. Wapinski slowed his car. Music blasted from the cellar barroom, up through the house, out into the sticky evening air. Wapinski parked the Mustang half a block away, left Josh curled up in the passenger bucket on the sleeping bag, walked in the shadows from tree to tree up the side of the street opposite from the house. Cars were parked in all directions, both sides of the street, up the side roads. Big party, he thought. He stood against the trunk of a large maple across from the house. The music was so loud he could feel vibrations in the ground. I should have met Akins somewhere, come with him, he thought. He lit a cigarette, took a deep drag, caressed his lighter. There was someone upstairs in the house. He knew it, felt it. Two barefoot coeds in cutoff shorts and T-shirts came down the inner stairs. Through the open door he watched them emerge from the darkness, walk across the large hall, disappear into the depth of the house. A man emerged from the dark stairs to the upper floor. Wapinski felt a pang of bitterness. He walked back to his car, grabbed a pint bottle from the back seat, patted Josh, returned to his observation post.

Nittany Mountain College was a small school with a reputation for excellence in engineering fundamentals and architectural design. Bright high-school students with average scholastic transcripts often used Nittany as a stepping stone. Get accepted, buckle down, maintain a 3.0 average for two years, then transfer to Penn State. In 1963 that had been Wapinski's plan too, but he never made a 3.0, only once in five semesters broke above 2.5, and twice had dropped below 2.0. He had enjoyed a lot of parties.

Wapinski nipped from his bottle, smoked more cigarettes, crossed the street. He felt fire in his arms and in his eyes. He did not know where it came from, did not know why he felt anger, contempt for the freeness, the easiness with which the students moved. He felt something awful lurked inside, something he would have to confront. Alcohol numbed his skin, his thoughts, yet he felt wary, aware of every breathing thing, every inanimate object near him.

"Hey, hey, RJ. Well, shit it's been a long time." Joe Akins had been sitting in the darkened TV room waiting for him, nodding from the early effects of too much beer.

"Joe." Wapinski smiled. Joe rose. They embraced, slapped each other's back. "You ol' rattlesnake, how are ya?" They gripped each other's shoulders.

"I'm great," Akins said. "Good job, good wife, nice house. I started at seventeen thou a year and got a company car to boot. I'm doin great. Gahhddammmm! You're the only one to show. They all punked out. How are ya, RJ? I mean, really. Yer arms are hard as steel."

"I'm hangin in there. You know."

"Yeah. Where you been, anyway? You look terrible. You been on a diet? And where's yer hair?"

"I'm hangin in there," Wapinski repeated.

"You been in the army, huh? Yeah, I remember them guys tellin me you got drafted. You gotta excuse me. I'm looped. Me and Tayborn were tryin to drain the keg. You still in?"

"Naw, Joe. Discharged a couple a weeks ago, ah . . . I guess about ten days."

"Let's go down en get some beer. Tayborn's down there with about ten loose dollies. Gahhd, you oughta see the tits on the one in the yellow T-shirt."

The basement was divided into a poolroom and a barroom. The pool table had been pushed against one wall and covered with a plastic sheet. Both rooms were packed. Half a dozen people were dancing on the pool table. The music was loud, the floor was wet, sticky with beer. People were dancing barefoot in puddles, gyrating their bodies without lifting their feet. Akins squeezed through; Wapinski followed. He didn't recognize the song, the dance, or any of the people. People kept banging his shoulders and arms. To him the students looked young. "Let's get in there," Akins shouted and pointed to the doorway to the barroom.

"What?"

Akins squeezed between two girls standing in the doorway. They squeezed back against him brushing their breasts on him. The three laughed. He grabbed one by the ass and squeezed and one pinched his ass hard and he jumped into the next room. Wapinski slid between the girls. They were both braless. He hesitated, smiled. The girls slipped past him into the poolroom. He looked over his shoulder, down at them, at their butts. One had her mouth at the other's ear. He sensed they were talking about him. Fuck it, he thought. Drive on.

"What?" Wapinski shouted back at Akins. Akins had pulled him to the far end of the bar where the music wasn't so overwhelming.

"I said, 'Are you deaf?' Ha. This is Rick Tayborn. He's house president. Mickey's little brother."

"Pleased to meetcha." Wapinski nodded. The bar was less crowded than the poolroom, and the speakers were smaller but it was still tight and noisy. Against the far wall a group of students were passing a joint. Through the ceiling lights, the haze glowed. Wapinski was taken by the long straight hair of several of the girls, put off by the length of Tayborn's.

"You met him before," Akins shouted. Tayborn handed them each an overflowing red plastic cup of foamy beer.

"You're the guy who's a green beret, aren't ya?" Tayborn asked.

Several people at the bar turned, caught by the words. One very drunk, very large boy, maybe a defensive tackle, put his arm around Wapinski and kissed him on the forehead and laughed good naturedly, almost elfish except for his size. "Welcome to my house," the big boy said. "Ricky, gimme more beer."

"He just got outa the army," Akins shouted to Tayborn.

"Not green beret," Wapinski said, "101st."

"What's that?" Tayborn asked.

"Hundred and First Airborne Division." Wap could see that that didn't register either. "Screaming Eagles," he tried. No recognition. "I commanded an infantry platoon and then a company," Wapinski said. A few more people pushed in close. Someone turned the music volume down. It was still loud but not so loud that they had to shout.

"Is that right?" Akins asked. "I didn't know that."

"Where was that?" An older man to Wapinski's right asked.

"Huh? Ah, Three Corps and I Corps."

"Viet Nam?!" Akins said.

Wapinski's head snapped to Akins, back to the man at his right, back to Akins. Again he was caught off guard. "Yeah." He was shocked that Akins didn't know.

"Holy shit, no wonder you look so messed up," Akins said. "That musta been horrible."

"What did you do over there, Mr. ah . . . "

"Wapinski."

"Mr. Wapinski. I'm Professor Tilden. Arnold Tilden."

"Bob Wapinski." He extended his right hand. The professor either didn't see it or ignored it. "Commanded an infantry platoon down along the Cambodian border until they moved us up north. I worked in operations and as a liaison to the ARVN and to the Marines. Then I commanded a company out along the Laotian border."

"Weren't you afraid," Professor Tilden began, "of being shot by your own men?"

"Ah . . . " Wapinski floundered. He found the question very odd. He knew there were circumstances of officers being shot by their own men, but he knew also that it was rare. "No," he said. He did his best to sound professional, sincere, to hide his drunkenness. "We were a pretty tight unit."

"Did you see much action?" the professor prodded.

"I saw some," Wapinski answered warily.

"An awful lot of American boys are being maimed and killed over there for some rather vague reasons. Is it true that battle casualties are five times higher than what's being reported?"

"I don't think so. You know what—"

"I've seen the figures of the number of men hospitalized and matched them against the reported wounded and killed. It's five times higher, Mr. Wapinski."

"Of course it is, Professor Tilden," Wapinski said. He drew himself up to his full height. The condescending tone of the professor grated like an awl being dragged down his spine, but he knew he was on solid ground here. He knew the figures inside and out. "Our battle casualties account for a little less than one-fifth of our hospitalizations," he said simply. "What really drains manpower from operations are infections, like those caused by insect or leech bites, or just grass cuts. Those, malaria, diarrhea, funguses—"

"Fungi," Tilden corrected.

"Fungi," Wapinski repeated, not knowing that either was correct.

"You know a lot about the war?" Tilden asked rhetorically. Wapinski didn't answer. He sipped his beer, tried to hide his anger, his disgust at what seemed to be a setup. "It's something we can't win, you know," Tilden said.

"Why, Professor, can't we win?"

"That nation is historically predestined to be reunited. We can't win. The people will rise up and kill every American."

"What people?" The statement was so distant from Wapinski's experiences that he felt bewildered. "The South Viet Namese?! If they wanted to rise up they would have during the Tet offensive last year."

"Maybe our bombers were too much for them."

"No. No. You don't understand. Two years ago the fighting was in and around the cities and the villages but the invading army and the guerillas were pushed back. Last year they staged one major coordinated assault at Tet and they were trounced. Now most of the fighting's in the border regions."

"And you can take responsibility for that?"

"Mr. Tilden, I took responsibility for myself and my men. And I'm proud of what we accomplished. I'm proud—"

"Tell me about that responsibility. Pushing conscripted men up foreign hills to their deaths while you stay behind the lines—"

"Wait. Wait. It's . . . I can't tell you how tremendous the responsibility of being an officer is. That's almost impossible to describe." Wapinski lowered his shoulders and head, paused for a moment, calmly said,

"When you command a platoon or a company in combat, you're responsible for every man's life. Very few of my men were drafted. Very few. Most were volunteers. Almost a third were on their second tours. When you're in charge of a man in combat, it's not like in business or something. We're not talking about his job or his grade. I'm talking about his life. Do you know what that means? If you hiccough wrong you might get that guy killed. When I got there I was twenty-two years old. I thought I'd get a platoon of old-timers and I'd be the kid. Half of my platoon was nineteen. Sir, after one fight, I knew what responsibility was. Do you have any idea what it's like to have one of your men killed? Not flunked, Professor. Killed. Not even killed from somebody making a mistake. Not from bad tactics. From combat. It eats at you."

"Exactly," Tilden said condescendingly. Several of the students laughed. Wapinski felt humiliated, angry. "It should eat at you because you caused it. What it is really all about, Mr. Wapinski, and I'm sure you must agree, is the institutional rot and corruption of the Army's officer corps that allowed men like yourself to win promotions using conventional tactics to claim imaginary victories when the *enemy*, in reality, simply withdraws without you knowing it. It should eat at you even more when innocent villagers are napalmed. You see your one tiny segment and you think you know what's happening."

"Do you want to know what I did over there or do you want to hear yourself speak?" Wapinski charged back.

"You're being provincial," the professor retorted.

"And yer a fucking jerk," Wapinski snapped. "If you don't understand what's going on over there, keep your mouth shut. You're getting good people hurt."

"I believe, in this country, we have a right to speak our opinions," Tilden said smugly. "You've heard of the First Amendment?"

"You've got the right to your opinion," Wapinski said, "but you don't have the right to be wrong in your facts."

Tilden switched tactics. "Would you like to attend an antiwar rally with us next weekend?"

Wapinski stared at him. There were about a dozen people listening. "I'm not against our efforts ov—"

"Hey," a student called from behind Wapinski, "how was the dope over there?"

"I talked to one guy," another student called in, "who says everybody's stoned all the time. He wants to go back just for the grass."

"What about them Viet Namese women?" A third student said.

Wapinski turned. The students were not looking at him. "We didn't see very many—" he began but was cut off.

"This guy got the clap four times," the second student called across the top of the crowd.

"What about them Viet Namese women?" The first student pressed.

"How many babies did you burn?" A coed shouted from the other end of the bar. "How many women did you leave pregnant? How many children don't have parents because of you?"

Wapinski stammered. He knew at this point he should simply withdraw. He could not get a word in edgewise. He'd come for beer, not for debate. He turned toward Akins and was about to say, "Let's go," when an older coed yelled, "Hey, that's my brother." Wapinski turned. A smile hit his face, both because he had not yet seen Joanne and because she was relief, his tie, his legitimate ticket to the present. He was about to call to her when she said, "My brother the army captain." She did not disguise her hostility. Her breasts held out a T-shirt epigram—I SAY YES TO MEN WHO SAY NO. Again he began to speak, was about to say, "Hello Kid. I tried to call but your phone's disconnected."

"He kills people for a living," Joanne announced. "Mother didn't tell me you were back. When did you return?"

His teeth clenched. "Do you give a shit?"

More students were now snickering at him. The big elf staggered up in front of him, smiled, asked Tayborn for three beers.

Joanne snorted, pronounced, "We spend billions of dollars on big bombs to drop on little people while you turn every decent girl in the country into a whore. Then we spend billions more for their politicians to stuff their pockets. Pigs!"

The big elfish student drew up tall and stepped up to Wapinski. He towered above him and everyone else in the room. "Pig." Spit sprayed from his mouth.

"Tell em, Montgomery," someone shouted. The room reached low-level hysteria. "Pig," three or four students shouted. "Pig," a dozen joined in. Wapinski looked from face to face. He saw they despised him, that he'd entered a foreign den, an alien camp, that he was the alien and he had not known it when he'd entered. He reared back. Akins was behind him.

"Pig." Montgomery glared at him. The big boy put his beers down on the bar. He clenched his left hand. He balled his right, squared off to Wapinski.

"Throw im out," someone screamed. Students closed in. Someone screamed, "Get him, Monty." Montgomery shot his left hand hard at Wapinski. Wapinski blocked the arm, hit the big boy without thought. He hit him with such force the boy toppled. Wapinski hit him twice more as he crumpled. Skin above the boy's left eye split open. On the ground his face erupted in blood. Instinctively Montgomery raised a leg to protect himself. Wapinski, intent on the kicking foot, stomped the leg with his heel then smashed three lightning kicks to the bloody face before Joe Akins, screaming, "RJ! RJ! STOP! RJ!" and Rick Tayborn and two others could grab him. Wapinski flicked their gripping hands off like gnats. Punched, counter-punched, two of them to the floor. A girl in cutoffs screamed. Another girl shrieked. "Montgomery!" She knelt bravely, horrified, behind the boy. Everyone else backed off. Tilden had already left. The room imploded in silence. Wapinski glared at them all, looked at the bloody boy, walked through the crowd in disgust, disgust at their unthinking self-righteousness, their youthful naïveté, their rejection of him. And disgust at himself for not knowing, for once again entering uninvited, unexpected, unannounced.

"Sit down, Josh. Sit down." Wapinski turned the ignition key. The Mustang roared to life. He drank straight from the bottle as he drove, sped back toward Mill Creek Falls. "Fuckin home," he shouted out the open top. "Fuckin home. What the fuck for? Home? Eat shit. Eat shit and die." He banged the shift through the gears, holding the bottle between his legs. "Home sweet home, Josh. Buddy, me and you make a good team. They all eat shit. That's what you already knew, huh? We haven't gotten up to Grandpa's yet, Josh. If he shits on us. . . . "

Wapinski sped east on 220 to Williamsport at speeds to ninety miles per hour. He exited in Williamsport, raced through the city streets, drinking, sideswiping a parked car, finishing the bottle and tossing it, allyoop, out the car, not seeing it crash into another parked car.

He raced up the new section of 15 trying to see how fast the Mustang would go. Then he took the back road to Loyalsock skidding and sliding, then up 87 to Forksville where he went off the road but saved it only to launch the car a few minutes later over a dirt embankment on the side of 154, tossing Josh like a rag doll first to the floor then up against the dashboard base, then almost out the open roof, landing in a small clearing, narrowly missing a previously battered oak but not missing several large rocks that seemingly in slow motion tore off the oil pan, ripped away the left rear axle, the car finally coming to rest by bludgeoning a thick tree, crinkling the grill and hood like aluminum foil, springing the doors, breaking the windshield.

Noise and motion ceased.

Wapinski startled, woke to Josh whimpering and licking his temples. He stared forward. He reached down, checked the ignition. He'd already turned it off. He didn't remember. His vision was blurry. He couldn't tell if the blurriness was from focusing on the shattered windshield or if he'd damaged his eyes. He felt his face. His nose hurt, was swollen, maybe broken. Slowly he moved his toes, ankles, knees, then fingers, wrists and elbows. His left hand was stiff, the thumb sprained. Cautiously he moved his head a little to the right, a little to the left, then farther, then looking up, then down. His eyes cleared somewhat. He checked his watch. It was two thirty in the morning.

Josh licked him again. "You okay, little brother? Oh God, we done somethin bad." Wapinski tried his door. It was jammed in a position about two inches open. He climbed over the door, reached down, lifted

Josh out. "We can walk this," he said to the dog. "No sweat. I do it all the time. Walked five times this far last week. Geez! One week. Aw, Josh, look at our Mustang! Aw shit! I'm an asshole. I'm a drunk fuckin asshole. Look what I done. Shit! Better en bein put in the corner to cool! Ha. Aw . . . . there's gotta be an unbroken bottle here somewhere."

He was very drunk now. It was dawn. He'd vomited on his shirt, his pants, his shoes. He sat in the gutter. Josh sat on the curb. "What the fuck av ah done?" He looked up at the grimy brick of warehouse walls. It was Sunday, Father's Day. The machine shops and offices were closed. "What'd I do to that kid las night?"

He thought about Joanne. He was hurt, deeply hurt, shocked by his sister, by the professor and the students. And he was disappointed, bitter with himself for having lost control. He'd beaten up the big jerk, he thought, and he'd thrown Akins and two others into the walls before he'd realized what he'd done. "I didn't mean to hurt em," he mumbled to the gutter. "I didn't want ta hurt em. Why'd they attack me? I just wanted to be left alone, maybe talk to Akins. And our car, Josh." Tears welled up in Wapinski's eyes. He tried to sniff them back but his nose was clogged with blood. "Why? Fuckin why?"

He pulled the cigarette lighter from his pocket. He was out of cigarettes. His stomach retched, bile burned his throat. "All this shit, Josh. It's melting on me." Again drunken tears rushed out. "This was a mistake. There's somethin wrong. Somethin wrong. I gotta get back where I belong. We left three guys on a hill. Four guys. I gotta go back. They were blown up and charred and bloody fuckin messes. Blood, Josh. More blood than ever. Right on that kid's face. I gotta go back where I was good. Where I did good. I gotta find Doc."

Wapinski fondled the lighter, belched. The belch caused him to lose his balance. He fell back on the storm drain, rolled, looked into the drain, retched a thick mixture of bile, saliva, postnasal blood and mucus. He coughed, spit between the bars of the sewer grate, watched for the splat in the black water below. Then he brought his hands before his face. He still held the lighter. He stared at it. On one side there was a list and an inscription:

> DAU TIENG
>
> CU CHI
>
> GO DAU HA
>
> TRUNG LAP
>
> VEGHEL
>
> A SHAU
>
> DONG AP BIA
>
> I SERVED MY TIME IN HELL.

On the other side there was an outline map of Viet Nam and the inscription: THANK YOU, SIR. YOU SAVED LIVES. MEN OF 1/506.

Wapinski stared at the lighter. He held it with both hands. The sewer grate cut into his elbows. He rolled onto his side, toward the street, held the lighter in his right hand, then between his right thumb and index finger. He couldn't feel the engravings. He lowered his hand to the grate, held the lighter between two bars, then purposefully, slowly, opened his fingers. Then he passed out.

Wapinski woke at midmorning. He was still in the gutter before an alley separating machine shops and warehouses. He was broke: without his wallet, cigarettes or lighter. An old man was cleaning the blood from his nose. Before them was a familiar 1953 Chevrolet sedan. Wapinski's head hurt. His hands were bloody. He felt guilty but his head wasn't clear enough to understand why.

"This your dog?" the old man asked. "And what's this paper . . . Bea Hollands? This pup here, he's been watchin over you since I came. Nice looking animal." Concentration slowly seeped back to Wapinski. "How come you haven't been up to see me?" the old man asked sternly. His hands were gentle on Wapinski's face. "When I finally heard you'd made it back, I came down to your mother's place. Imagine that. I haven't been inside there since she chased your father away."

Wapinski focused in on the old man's face. It was a beautiful face, he thought. Wrinkled like a happy bulldog's. He could not hold the thought, nor keep his eyes focused.

"Come on up," the old man said. "I'm not strong enough anymore to lift you." He remained kneeling by Wapinski. "Well, how do they say it," he said slipping a hand under Wap's head. "If Mohammed won't come to the mountain, the mountain'll have to come to Mohammed."

"Gran—" Tears flooded Wapinski's face.

"Don't do one any good to cry and say you're sorry, now." Tears were in the old man's eyes too. "Come on home, Bob. There's fresh garden greens and corn fritters with syrup waiting."

"Granpa."

July 1984

We never related stories to each other. You know, not like we're doin now. We're all doin it now. Tellin our war stories. But then, when we were still in the Corps, or whatever branch, we never did. The extent was, "Hey, what outfit you in. . . . Yeah, I think I worked with you guys out in the A Shau. . . . " Or, "Yeah, I was too. Were you there when the typhoon hit?" That was it. But now . . . now it's time.

I know homecomings were really different. I mean, nearly 2.6 million Americans—men and women, 99.54 percent men but women too—served in Nam between 5 August '64 and 7 May '75. Official dates. Eight hundred thousand more served in the Southeast Asia theater. Three point four million Americans . . . or as Bobby'd say it, "representing fifteen percent of all American families." And each family dealt with it differently. Returning varied more than being there. No two guys came home at the same time, to the same house, same family, friends, neighbors, with the same baggage of experience.

This has taken me years to figure out, to fill in details or be willing to jump over stuff or guess about the gaps. It was difficult getting to this point. For years it was like I had this voice inside me that couldn't get to my vocal cords—like it wanted to speak but couldn't get out and then somehow it came out of him and I felt as if it had come out of me. But now, partly because of him, I'm no more that person than I am the little boy in the store watching Bobby get smacked.

What we, each and every one of us, brought to the war was a basic core identity established in early childhood. Other layers encased the core—schooling, adolescence, and military training. Then Southeast Asia. When we returned we reentered families barely changed from when we'd left. But like a ball of wax dipped and redipped, we returned with new layers, and not uniform ones either, but varying layers as if we had entered a hundred or a thousand different dipping pots. So varied was the Nam experience—from year to year, north to central to south, mountains to paddies to rivers to villages—it might just as well have been a hundred or a thousand different wars.

My homecoming couldn't have been more different than Bobby Wapinski's, yet despite the differences, the same feelings developed—alienation, estrangement from my core identity, from my layered American identity . . . as if my new wax coatings were impossible to hide or shed or deny.

3

Pisano

Okinawa, Friday, 19 June 1968—The day was clear, hot. He had been standing in line for nearly an hour. "NEXT," the clerk called.

"Pisano. Anthony F. P-I-S-A-N-O." He waited. The clerk checked the register, gave his crew the last few numbers, again rang out with a loud "NEXT." Tony stepped to the side. The crew disappeared into the shadows of the giant Quonset hut, then reappeared with four footlockers on a roller cart.

"Okay Pisano, here it is."

Tony looked at the footlocker. His name was stenciled in black on the top, front and sides. There was a combination lock at the hasp. He attempted several sets of numbers unsuccessfully. "Hey, ah, ya know," he stammered at the clerk. "How am I supposed to get this open?"

"Ferget the combination?" The clerk's tone was sarcastic.

"Listen." Pisano almost said, Listen asshole, but he just wanted to be gone. "Yeah, I forgot it." He smiled cheerfully. "I been in the bush for thirteen months"—he chuckled a self-degrading chuckle—"who's goina remember a combination after thirteen months?"

"Hey, Tony," Al Cornwall said from behind him. "I remembered mine."

"Ha!" Jim Bellows chided. "He's a dago. You know, you got to retrain em every few weeks or they forget everything."

"Bite this, Bellows." Tony grabbed his crotch, laughed good-naturedly.

"Re-mem—mem, re-mem-mem-member, re-mem-mem, re-mem-mem..." Bellows began singing, jumping side to side.

Al cut in. "You guys hear what those guys said is happenin in Frisco?"

"Wait a minute, Man." Tony threw his arms straight up. "I got to get this thing open."

"They say there's a war goin on back there," Al said.

The clerk brought a well-used pry bar. "Ah, hot-damn. Thanks." Tony jammed the bar behind the hasp. "I knew ya had ta have somethin like this."

"What guys?" Bellows asked.

"These guys here are all talkin about it," Al said. "They're sayin there's a thing called a hippie that's slaughterin Marines if they catch em alone."

"Ooof!" Tony crashed forward as the hasp snapped from the plywood. "What a hassle, Man."

"There was a guy over at chow... just back from the World. He's sayin he couldn't stand it. Sayin things like, what happens when you get to Frisco is... you know, he had a little time so he goes to a bar nearby the airport and like ten long-haired, bearded guys surround him. He said they were goina kick his ass but the bartender pulled a pistol and escorted him out. He says it was like he was slime."

"What's a hippie?" A Marine farther back in line asked.

"I heard about them," another answered. "They're supposed to be real strange. Wear necklaces. The guys! Smoke pot. Stuff like that."

"Shud up, Bellows!" Tony threw him the pry bar. He didn't care about "hippies." As he opened the locker to inspect the contents, he said, "Don't listen to those idiots, Man. You know, they all the time.... Hey, what the fuck—this ain't my shit."

The clerk came over. "Says 'Pisano, Anthony.' That's you."

"Yeah, that's me but this ain't my stuff."

"Those your records in there?"

"Ahhh... no. Look! This guy was court-martialed. I've never been court-martialed. Honest. Ya know, maybe I deserved to be court-martialed. But I never was. Look at this guy's shit. He wasn't squared away, Man. Naw, that aint my service number."

The clerk grabbed a crewman, and both disappeared with the foot-locker into the bowels of the dark hut while Jim and Al and others continued repeating rumors they'd heard about the hippies of San Francisco and Tony kicked the dry dirt showing a disgust and boredom he didn't really feel. "This is weird, Man," he said to his two friends.

"Yeah," Al said. "Imagine finally gettin out a Nam only to have to fight yer way through Frisco."

"No," Tony said. "I mean that footlocker. It's like there's somebody else, you know, somebody livin my life."

"Hey, Pisano," the clerk called. "This one yours?"

Tony inspected the footlocker. It appeared identical to the other. He tried the combination and the lock opened. "Yeah," he beamed. "See, dagos don't forget."

Anthony Pisano danced and limped through the next three days of processing on Okinawa. His leg was still hurting where he had been wounded six weeks earlier, a wound he had re-injured on his second-to-last helicopter flight in Viet Nam when the bird crash-landed at Phu Bai. He had been en route to Da Nang when the bird was hit by ground fire and the padding inside had begun to burn. The pilot had set it down fast and hard. Pisano's right thigh muscle ripped from the jounce and the leap from the aircraft.

"Hey," he had yelled at the pilots as ground crew immediately surrounded the bird and extinguished the flame. "You guys goina take me to Da Nang, or what?"

"Not in that," the copilot yelled back. They both laughed. Pisano had crashed twice before, the copilot seven times. Controlled crashes. Nam craziness—hard-nosed, twenty-year-old macho. One more adventure. One more jarring to add to the body, one more nonfatal injury to laugh at.

At Treasure Island Pisano said to Jim Bellows, "Ya know, I was standing right here day I left to go overseas. We were just gettin ready to go. And I looked up there." Bellows turned, looked. "There was some fine California woman kissin her man good-bye right up there. She had a skirt on and she had her foot up behind her like this, kind a wrapped over the lower railin, and Man, you could see all the way to Camp Pendelton."

"Ooooo." Bellows squeezed his arms in tight to his torso. "Oooo. OooooOoooo! Let's go find one."

"Yeah," Pisano said. "If they ever let us outa here." Tony smacked the back of his right hand into his left palm. He had received travel and leave orders that morning, but along with a hundred other Marines, they'd hit a bureaucratic snafu. Again he slammed his fist. "Man, I'm not staying here. They're just fuckin with us."

Bellows eyed him. "I don't know, Man. Paperwork aint right."

Tony opened his hands like a preacher. His eyes twinkled in the sun. "What can *they* do?" he asked innocently. "We got orders. They can't keep us. That's cuttin into our leave time. I'm beatin feet."

"Oh Man . . . "

"Hey! What can they do, huh?" Tony shrugged. "I'm just a dumb dago. Come on."

"Okay. Let's get Cornwall. We don't wanta be in the airport with just two guys against all them hippies."

"Aw, fuck em."

"Okay," Al Cornwall said, "this is the way it is." The Marines had broken down into destination groups—those going to New York, to Chicago, Dallas, Philly, St. Louis, moved to their respective gates en masse. "Don't anybody break up," Cornwall said. "As long as we're in a group, there's no way anybody's goina fuck with us."

"Nobody's goina fuck with us." Pisano was eyeing an older woman sitting at a dimly lit bar off the bright corridor.

"Hey! Look! We all heard them stories on Okie, right? Maybe nobody's goina fuck with us, but if the shit starts to fly . . . "

Tony turned, leered at Cornwall, pulled his head back, smirked. "Man, there ain't nobody here in the fuckin airport."

"Tony." Cornwall pulled him aside. "Look, Man, there's an honest-to-God fear factor workin here. If somebody spits at one of these guys, they might tear em to pieces."

"Geez! Look around. There isn't hardly anybody in here but us. Only long-haired thing I seen so far is that old dollie with the big ba-zooms."

"What about that creep over there?"

Pisano turned. A young man was walking down the wide corridor in their direction. He had neatly combed shoulder-length blond hair. He was wearing a three-piece business suit without a shirt. A turquoise-and-silver necklace hung against his skin. His sneakers were untied. "Hey! You!" Pisano yelled in his best DI voice, his right hand jabbing outward.

"Oh Christ." Cornwall dropped his eyes toward the floor. Several of the Marines fell in behind Pisano. The young man paid no attention.

"Hey!" Pisano yelled again.

The man furtively glanced over.

"Yeah," Pisano shouted. He gave the man his most-infectious smile, walked out to intercept him in the center of the corridor. "Yeah, you," he said more quietly. "Ken I ask you a question?"

"Me?!" the young man said.

"I was wonderin," Pisano said, "ah, see, all of us just got back from Nam and we were wonderin what a hippie is and if you're one."

"You're stoned!" The young man stepped back, then sideways, turning, continuing to face Pisano as he moved down the corridor, finally backing away still in the direction he wanted to go.

"AAaaARRR!" Pisano roared.

The young man spun, ran away.

"I can't believe you guys," Pisano blurted between laughs. "Here you been through a year a shit and you're worried about somethin like that."

*   *   *

"Passengers holding boarding passes for rows twelve through twenty-seven may now board," the ground attendant announced.

Pisano got up, shuffled to where other Marines and other passengers were forming a line. He shuffled slowly toward the door, feeling a bit disappointed because the attendant taking the tickets was a guy and not one of the pretty girls he'd seen at the other gates. He handed the worker his ticket and pass and then it struck him that he had forgotten something. "Ah . . . wait a minute," he said to the worker. "I'll be right back. Don't leave without me."

"I can't hold—"

Tony shouted, "I forgot to call"—he sprinted up the corridor to the phones—"my Mom."

As Tony deplaned in Philadelphia he smiled and winked at the stewardess, leaned forward and placed an innocent peck on her cheek, then tried to ever so lightly brush the back of his hand across her thigh, barely succeeding to brush her skirt as she stepped back. He did a little jig in the lighted bulbous pod where the ramp sealed against the plane's body. He checked his reflection in the small window, now black with night outside, then started walking up the enclosed ramp. He felt he looked sharp in his Marine Corps uniform with its three rows of ribbons, carrying his short-timer cane and attaché case, standing tall at five feet eight inches, feeling like a mountain at one hundred and forty-six pounds.

I'm a proud motherfucker, he thought. A Magnificent Bastard. I got my shit to-geth-er, rolled in a tight little ball, and the folks are goina be proud. Two-thirds of the way up the ramp he paused, switched the cane to his left hand, bent and rubbed his right thigh with the heel of his right palm, then straightened back up, threw out his chest, and marched into the terminal.

"Holy shit," he whispered. He stopped. They grabbed him. "Uncle Joe! Mom! Pop! Who's this? Maxene?" Thirteen friends and family surrounded him, twenty-six arms tried to hug him at once. He beamed, he hugged back, kissed. He broke loose, did a little jig, then let them hug him again.

Family was important to Tony. Indeed, it was the stories of his Uncle Joe—Tony's childhood hero who had been a Marine in the Pacific during World War II—that had led Tony to enlist in the United States Marine Corps in August of 1965, two months after his high school graduation, three months before his eighteenth birthday. Tony's enlistment convinced his cousin Jimmy, son of his father's sister, Isabella, and her husband, James Pellegrino, to follow suit one month later.

His family and friends had driven down in three cars, one car with four friends from high school, guys who hadn't gone into the military—Roy, Jack, Donny and Ken—all slapping him on the back, congratulating him, shuffling him toward the baggage claim area, two of them dropping off to try to pick up his cousin Annalisa, Jimmy's sister, who had just

graduated from high school and who was pretty without being intimi-
datingly beautiful. Tony stopped to let his mother and father catch up,
and his eldest brother John and Uncles Joe and James and Aunt Helen,
and his cousins Vinny and Maxene. Maxene, at sixteen, was a knockout.

He hugged his mother again, said to his father and uncles as he eyed Maxene, "We can't talk here. Let's get outa here and talk in the car. You musta
rented a bus. I thought maybe just John, or John and Pa . . ."

"We came in two cars." His mother wiped tears away as she looked
at him, grabbed him again, pulled him to her. She was short, coming up
only to his shoulders. He winked at his friends over her head. "Your
friends came in their own." Josephine Pisano sniffed. Some strangers
were glancing at them. She humbly offered an explanation. "My son.
He's just back from Viet Nam." She hugged him again, then said, "I
think Uncle James wants to ask you about Jimmy."

"Oh yeah," Tony said to Jimmy's father. "I saw him last month up by
Gio Linh. He's doin great. He loves it there."

"I know," Uncle James said, concerned, sad. "He sent a letter saying
he's going to sign up for another tour. Isabel's worried he'll bring home
a Viet Namese woman."

"Aw, that wouldn't be so bad," Uncle Joe said from behind Tony. Joe
grabbed Tony by the shoulders, clenched his hands affectionately hard.
"If I hadn't been married when I hit Japan, I might've brought home a
little geisha girl myself. You feel pretty solid. How's the leg?"

"I'm not worried about the girl," Uncle James said. "He's got that
Hollands girl here to come back to. What I'm worried about—"

"Please! Please, let's just go," Tony's mother said. "John, you and Joe
get the cars," she directed her brother and husband. "And Johnny, you
and Vinny get Tony's bags. I want to look at my boy." She stopped Tony,
burst into tears again, hugged him again. "If you only knew what a
mother goes through. If you only knew what I've been through this
year."

In a few minutes John and Vinny returned with Tony's bag. The cars
were waiting. "Where do I go?" Tony asked light-heartedly. He was
hoping to sit with Maxene. Annalisa had already left with his friends.

"You ride with me," his mother said. "In Uncle Joe's car. You can sit
in back with Vinny and John. Your father and Helen like to ride together
and Maxene can talk to Uncle James."

The Pisano family house in Mill Creek Falls was on the first street to
be finished in the 'old' New Town subdivision, which had been built
between 1951 and 1957 and backed up to the much older Creek's Bend
neighborhood. Over the years Josephine Pisano repeatedly had begged
John to sell the house and buy a larger one, but John opted to expand
the house and to add a landscaped swimming pool as the central feature
of the backyard.

It was nearly midnight. Uncle Joe turned the car onto their street. Tony's father had arrived a few minutes earlier and Annalisa and Tony's friends were directly behind. Tony was exhausted from the flights, the travel, the airports. His body was sore from fatigue and sleeping in seats and the jouncing from the last helicopter crash. He had finally relaxed and fallen asleep against his brother somewhere north of Allentown.

Suddenly twenty car horns were blasting him awake. "What the fuck—" He shot up, banged his head on the roof, crumpled to the floor. Lights exploded, flashed. All around people cheered, banged pots and pans, blew whistles. A banner, fifteen feet long, car lights blinking high-beam low-beam high-beam—WELCOME HOME. In the middle of the street Tony's father stood waving an American flag.

"Hey, what the—aw, no."

"Welcome home, Tony," his brother John said. He opened the door, got out, turned to help. Tony froze. Vinny got out the other side, shut the door. He felt self-conscious, ducked into the crowd.

"Tony! Tony! Tony!" They began to chant.

Josephine Pisano turned and looked at her son cowering like an animal on the floor behind her seat. "Tony. What—"

"Get outa the car," he demanded.

"Come on, Tony," she urged.

"No," he barked. "Get outa the car."

"Tony!" Josephine was beside herself.

"I'm stayin here," he snapped. He reached out, pulled the car door shut, locked it. Then, staying low, he turned, locked the other rear door.

"What's the matter?" Josephine began. "All these people." Her door was open. She swung her legs out but remained seated. "Nonna's here. Uncle Frank came from Scranton. They came to see you." The chanting waned. Popping started. Champagne. A neoprene cork thudded on the hood. Tony flinched. "Are you crazy? What are you, a . . ."

"Get out," Tony screamed. His entire body was cramping down, shaking. People began to surround the car.

"Josephine," his uncle Joe snapped. "Get the hell out and shut that door."

"Wha-aht?"

Tony's arms quaked. His right thigh burned as the wounded muscle tightened. "Just get out of the car," Joe ordered, and Josephine backed out, shocked, embarrassed, in disbelief. Joe started the engine. He backed up quickly making people scatter, then he jammed the lever into drive and sped up the street.

Tony sighed in back. He collapsed against the seat. Uncle Joe made a few quick turns and they were out of the development. "Where do you want to go?" he asked Tony.

"Just around," Tony said. He sat up on the rear seat, then stuck his feet over the front seat and slithered into shotgun position. Joe didn't ask anything and Tony didn't volunteer. They descended, crossed the bridge, drove through a dark downtown, up side streets, across main roads, around the old hangouts. Tony kept his face turned to his window, seeing, remembering, reacquainting. Joe drove back toward New Town. It was after one. He turned down the street that backed to the Pisano house. The party was still going strong.

"You want to go there now?" Uncle Joe asked.

"No," Tony said.

"You know it was your parents' twenty-eighth wedding anniversary last week. The party's for them too."

"Not yet," Tony said.

"We'll drive around again."

For three more hours, two tours about town and one trip to the highway for gas, Joe drove Tony. At the end of each hour they reconned the party. At four in the morning, the street quiet, only a few lights still burning in the house, they parked and went in.

The next day, before the party restarted, Tony and his father ate breakfast, alone, in silence, in the dining room. Not until they finished their rolls and juice and eggs and only lukewarm coffee remained in their cups did Tony look at his father's face. Hundreds of images and thoughts and snatches of conversations from all his years flooded Tony's mind. What's it like, Pa, to kill a man? When had he asked that? Uncle Joe talked about it, why not his father? What's this ribbon for, Pa? John Pisano had never volunteered war stories, had never displayed souvenirs. To young Tony, it was his father's past, an era in his father's life that Tony could not bring up even if his father did not actually hide it. The first time you're there, Pa . . . but he'd never asked, had never been told . . . how do you react?

Tony did not know what he would see in his father's face when he put his cup down, placed both palms over the table edge and looked up, but he knew what he wanted to see, what he hoped to see. I didn't panic, Pa, he thought. Never once. Not even when I was in the tunnels extracting bodies and the guys above pulled so hard on the rope the body broke in two and they dragged it over me. Not at Loon. Not at Dai Do. Not when Manny got it while I was holdin him trying to tell him he had a million-dollar wound when the sniper blew his chest apart. Not when I got hit, even. I did my job, Pa, Tony thought. Like you did yours.

John Pisano looked at his son. For one instant his face relaxed, tension left the room. Then he bowed his head, cleared his throat. Now he kept his head down, spoke softly. "Tony," he said, "you've seen things that no man can imagine unless he's seen them too. Or done them. Not Mark, not Joey. Not even John with all his education. They'll never understand. You're different, Tony." John Pisano raised his eyes, looked sadly at his son. "You've been to the mountain. You've seen . . . God, I hope you handle it better than I did. Jesus God, I hope you do."

*　　*　　*

A very much subdued family gathering ensued that evening. Tony apologized individually to each adult and twice to the entire clan. John Pisano said it had been stupid of them to surprise him like that, not even to wake him up and tell him a few blocks before they arrived. Josephine, with the help of her sister Helen and John's three sisters and Uncle Frank's wife, Jessie, again prepared an enormous array of food.

"All right," Josephine called into the yard and throughout the house. "Everybody, at the table."

"Dear Jesus," Tony's father began the grace. He paused as conversation stopped.

Nonna—Grandma Maria Annabella—was holding one of Tony's hands, squeezing it, repeating over and over, "Always happy. Always dignity. Always a gentleman."

"Help us," John Pisano intoned, "to remember that we share life and worship with all men. Help us to defeat hatred within us and let us and all men open our hearts to love, to forgiveness, and to self-forgiveness. Let goodness and kindness come to us and let us bring these gifts to others.

"Deliver us, Dear Jesus, from every evil and teach our hearts to rejoice in Your life." John Pisano's voice began to break but it went unnoticed. "We are happy to be Thy children, we are grateful for Your thoughts and gifts.

"And Dear Jesus." John Pisano stopped, he choked on the welling in his throat, his eyes watered ever so slightly. "Thank You, thank You for returning my son to us. Amen."

Uncle Joe broke the silence. "AAAaaaaayy! Let's eat!"

The feast was nonstop. At midnight, Aunt Ann, Uncle Ernie, and their daughters, Maxene, Patty and Julie—named after the Andrews Sisters—packed up to leave. Uncle Joe and Tony were tipsy. Tony walked his cousins to the door, hugged his aunt, shook Ernie's hands, smiled politely. He followed them onto the small porch, then gave each girl a squeeze. As they walked to their car he stared at Maxene's legs.

Uncle Joe followed Tony's gaze, put his arm around his nephew's shoulder, said, "When I got back from the Pacific. . . . " He started to chuckle, then to laugh. He didn't finish. They returned to the house. "I've got to sit," Joe said, and Tony deposited him in an overstuffed chair in the living room and meandered back to the dining room for another pastry. Why's she got to be my cousin? he thought. He could not shake the desire she'd stirred. Annalisa, at seventeen was pretty; Uncle Joe's daughter, Roseanne, at nineteen, was sexy as hell; but Maxene, at only sixteen, was so delightful Tony simply ached.

Maxene, he thought. Sweet sixteen Maxene. He opened the screen door, stepped into the side yard. The night had become cool and everyone, he thought, was inside. He stood in the darkness eating the pastry, thinking about Uncle Joe's stories about Guadalcanal and occupation duty in Japan. His eyes adjusted to the darkness. Slowly, out of habit, quietly, he walked to the backyard. The yard was dark except for lights in the pool making the water glisten and the entire pool area glow. Tony paused in the dark by the side of the house. Again he thought of Maxene. Then of a Maxene look-alike—a non-cousin Maxene without the charged taboo of cousin incest. In his mind she was a year older, a year bustier, two-thirds naked. He stopped. He heard someone. There was someone in the shadows of the lilacs at the other side of the pool. Two people. Neat, Tony thought. Neat. Vaguely he wished it were he and Maxene but he stopped the fantasy. After all, he told himself, she *is* my cousin.

He remained in the dark by the side of the house. The couple at the far side of the pool kissed. Tony imagined the passion in that kiss, began imagining. . . . He stopped his thoughts. Who the hell is it? he asked himself. He bore his eyes into the darkness. He could make out Aunt Helen's silhouette. She stepped back, adjusted her dress. His jaw clamped down tight. The rock, the foundation upon which he was built, suddenly turned to sand. His hand edged to the house for support, stabilization. Aunt Helen stepped briskly into the glow from the pool, then to the back door and inside.

Tony's stomach began to turn. He focused in on the man. Quietly he circled the edge of the yard. John Pisano lit a cigarette, faced the pool. Tony emerged from the shadows, noiselessly approached his father's back, coiled, uncoiled—POP. "Aaah!" Splash. Tony, like a cat, backed to the shadows, down the yard's edge, through the screen door and to a seat at the table. He shoved another pastry in his mouth.

For the next three weeks, until his cousin Jimmy returned, Tony's days were a mixture of culture shock, disgust, elation at being back, overindulgence in Josephine's cooking, idleness and boredom. His nights were restless.

The first nights he could not sleep at all. He was nervous, anxious, so tense his body ached. His heart beat hard, not fast, but with such pounding that his bed pulsed. It scared him. He felt his heart was about to explode, do to itself what the North Viet Namese could never do. John and Joe, his older brothers, had their own apartment, Mark had his own room. Tony could not recall the last time he'd slept alone. In the Corps he had slept either in barracks or tents or hardbacks, or he had slept in the field in bunkers or foxholes or on the ground, but always he slept near other guys, with their noises, their smells. On R & R he had slept with his Chinese "wife" the entire week. In high school and earlier he and Joe had shared this room.

Tony shut his eyes in the aloneness. He tried to relax by masturbating. He fantasized about getting it on with Maxene. He masturbated a second time fantasizing a ménage à trois with Maxene and Roseanne. He got up, smoked a cigarette. If his father knew that it had been Tony who had given the shove, he had not let on. He had come in, his clothes dripping, had laughed foolishly. "You're not goina believe what I just did," he'd announced. "I was looking for Orion and I backed into the pool." The incident passed, but the kiss, the shove, repeated again and again in Tony's mind.

He sat on the edge of the bed, looked through the window. The pool lights were off. Beyond the back fence the old homes of Creek's Bend lay in darkness. Tony sat, tried to think of his preservice life, but the past withdrew. He tried to think of the future, of his next duty station. He would go early, report in early, he thought. He thought again about his father and aunt and he felt, feared, his family, his foundation was collapsing. He thought about the guys he'd left in Nam and he said a prayer for them. He rose again, smoked again. Then he clenched his fist and snapped it in the air and smiled and told himself they'd be all right. In isolation from everything past he watched the sky gray, then turn pink through the trees to the northeast.

The Pisano family returned to their routines. John Sr. went back to his long hours as shift supervisor. John Jr. went back to his accounting office where he handled the books for Uncle Frank's store along with a hundred other accounts. Brother Joe had graduated college in May and had been accepted into medical school. He was re-taking an organic chemistry course and studying. Mark, at fourteen, was a counselor with the town's Park Department and was working, or chasing adolescent girls, seven days a week. Only Josephine stayed home and Tony struggled to be the decent, returning son, eating until he was ready to burst, struggling to repress blurting, "Is Pa having an affair? Do you give a shit?"

Then Tony also fell into a routine. He lay awake each night until dawn, then slept, restless, into the afternoon, then showered, shaved, went out with his friends, sometimes with their girlfriends, sometimes with Annalisa. Then he and they got stoned.

If his familial culture had changed little during the time he was away, the culture of his friends, or at least that segment of friends who remained in Mill Creek Falls, had changed drastically.

In high school Tony had been a rock, a hood. He had seen himself as the tough Italian kid from the good neighborhood that backed up to the bad neighborhood. His brothers had all been rah-rahs, preppies, white socks and white boat sneakers. Tony had been a slick. After he left for school in the morning, he would slick his hair back with Vaseline. He was always clean, always sharply dressed. He wore the right shirts, the right shoes with pointed toes, the right pegged pants. To Friday-night dances he wore the skinniest ties and Nehru jackets. He moved with both cliques in school, but after school he socialized with the crowd from Creek's Bend. By the summer of 1968 every boy Tony knew from his class of '65 who'd lived in Old New Town, every single one except him and Jimmy, had obtained a 2-S deferment. And every friend from Creek's Bend was in the service.

* * *

"Tonight we go to Shep's," Roy said to Tony and Annalisa.

"Oh," Annalisa said. "I've heard about Shep's."

"Yeah, it's super cool," Roy said. "Shep finally cleared Tony."

"Thanks to you," Annalisa said. Her eyes glistened. Tony opened the door of Roy's new Camaro, watched his cousin as she coyly slid in. Then he slid in beside her, put his arm on the seat back behind her, felt her warmth against him.

"Roll the window up," Roy said. He pulled a joint from above the visor. Annalisa took it, lit it, passed it to Tony.

To Tony the grass was weak. It had none of the power of the little Nam weed he'd smoked. Still he was surprised how giddy one joint made them. Annalisa began swaying, her eyes became hazy, her demeanor changed from coyly shy to giggly.

"Shep's got some great stuff, Man," Roy said. "You're goina groove on this place. It's really far out."

"Cool," Tony said. "I'm groovin on your vehicle, Man, but I need somethin more."

"Yeah. You're really uptight."

"Yeah."

Lenny Shepmann's apartment was on the second floor of a Creek's Bend four-plex. Tony led Roy and his cousin across the street, then let Roy lead them around to a side entrance. Roy knocked out a familiar series of raps: ta, ta-ta TA ta, ta-ta. A buzzer sounded, the door unlatched.

"Security." Roy grinned proudly. Tony smiled back. He could see Roy was impressed but he thought the rap was too simple, the charade dumb.

The room was dim, lit by two small candles, airless. Paisley cloth was stapled over the windows. The room reeked of smoke, cats and garbage. The Fifth Dimension's *Aquarius* album came at moderate volume from stereo speakers. Tony's eyes adjusted. Shepmann and two of Tony's old friends, Jack Roedain and Don Eisner, were sitting cross-legged on pillows on the floor. In the center of the room there was a large elaborate water pipe with a swivel tube and mouthpiece. Jack and Don sat with their backs to the stairs, motionless, apparently well on their way.

Shepmann was across the circle. He was older than the others, bigger, fat, shirtless. He glared at the intruders as if they were his prey. He sucked on the tube. His eyes bulged. Thick rolls of flab spilled over his belt. He held the smoke for a long while, exhaled, smiled a thin-lipped challenge. Tony felt repulsed. Let's get on with it, he thought.

He was about to speak when without words Shepmann opened his arms and bade his guests to be seated on the remaining pillows, indicating that Annalisa should sit beside him. Tony sat across from his cousin to Shepmann's left. He watched as his cousin snuggled her rump down into the pillows and crossed her feet under her thighs into a lotus position. Tony tried to cross his ankles with his knees bent but his right thigh would have none of it. He sat with his left leg drawn up, his right sticking out straight, aiming through the water pipe at Shepmann. The mouthpiece passed to Annalisa. She took a deep hit. Then to Roy, Jack, Don, Tony, and back to Shep.

Counter-clockwise, Tony thought. Opposite of Nam. He had smoked marijuana in Nam but it was nothing like this, nothing this intricate. The mouthpiece circled again. The weed was better than that in the joint on the way over. The record changed to the Bee Gees' *Ideas* album. Tony closed his eyes. There was little conversation. What was said seemed to be directed at the host, and Shepmann seemed intent on absorbing the praises for his hospitality and the quality of his dope. Roy arranged to purchase some from him, told him about a block of Colombian Red he had heard had reached Scranton.

Shepmann refilled the pipe three times. Each time he asked the angels of the underworld to bless his dope. Each time he bowed to the smoking water bowl and requested his guests to do the same. The mood was quiet, subdued, not quite mellow. Roy turned the stack of albums over and the stereo slowly worked its way through the reverse sides of *Ideas*, *Aquarius*, and several more. As the high came on Tony's face relaxed, his cheeks slackened, his eyes concentrated on the darkness of their closed lids. Tony's body relaxed, his right thigh felt comfortably warm as if his body had sent a surge of healing into the wounded region. Although his physical tension eased, his feelings of isolation increased. He felt homesick, homesick for *his* people. He thought about his platoon, about the good times. He did not think about firefights, shellings, tunnels or bodies. Then he heard Annalisa laugh her sweet stoned laugh and his thoughts dissipated. He felt calm. His eyes remained closed. He felt as if he were being engulfed by soft clear light blue, as if blue were a soothing substance.

"Love," Shepmann breathed.

"Love," Annalisa giggled.

"Love," Tony thought. It was a pleasant thought. He thought of Maxene. He heard a kiss. His body tensed. He opened his eyes.

Annalisa was lying back against Roy, her head turned back and up, their mouths meeting. Roy had pulled her tank top up exposing her flat stomach. The candlelight glistened off tiny, fine, almost transparent hairs on her body. Roy moved a hand under her tank top and massaged her breast. Jack had passed out. Don was totally wasted. "Love," Shep repeated in that low thick voice. He leaned over. The fat bulk of his gut shifted to his side. He kissed Annalisa's navel.

Annalisa broke from Roy, looked foggily at Shep's form. She straightened her legs, then rubbed the back of Shep's head. Again she relaxed against Roy who had raised her top above her breasts and was gently rolling her nipples between his thumbs and forefingers. Shep's mouth moved to her hips as he unsnapped her jeans.

Tony watched. He was confused. Something in him told him he had to stop this, had to protect his cousin. Something else told him he didn't have the right to interfere. He watched as Shep unzipped Annalisa's jeans, as his thick fingers curled over the waistband of jeans and panties, as he wrestled her pants down to her thighs. Annalisa leaned forward, removed her tank top, rubbed her hands over Shep's head and ears, then lay back again kissing Roy more and more passionately.

Shep massaged her, kissed her, pulled her clothes down to her ankles. He fell on her forcing her knees apart. Tony was shocked, excited. Annalisa was more sensual here than in his fantasies. Shep's face rooted into her. Roy reached his left arm over hers then slid his hand behind her back. With his right hand he grasped her right elbow and pushed it into his left hand locking her arms behind her. He continued to kiss her, to massage her breasts with one hand. She kissed him more tentatively. Her shoulders were drawn back too far to be comfortable but not so far as to hurt.

Tony did not know what to do. He watched. He wanted to kiss her. He wanted to leave. He felt it obscene to watch his cousin. He wanted a woman of his own. He wasn't sure how far to let this go, how much to watch. Shepmann disgusted him. The obese body lying on his cousin's legs, the semipublic display, the dope hitting his brain—it bewildered him.

Shep reached out, grasped the mouthpiece of the water pipe, sucked in a huge breath. Then he rooted his mouth back deep between Annalisa's legs and sealed his lips to her vagina and blew. At first Annalisa seemed to sense pleasure but very quickly that turned to displeasure, to pain. She stopped kissing Roy. Shep retreated. Her genitals released a loud fartlike noise and a cloud of smoke. She gasped.

Shepmann laughed. He rolled over on his back laughing uproariously. Roy tightened his grip on her arms. He too laughed. Tony smirked.

"Great pipe," Shep coughed out between gushes of laughter. "Pussy pipe."

"Let go." Annalisa tried to free herself. She was too stoned to make it sound convincing.

Shep rolled back onto her legs forcing her knees to the floor, grabbed the mouthpiece and sucked. "No," Annalisa began to plead but Roy had grabbed her hair above her forehead, pulled her head back and jammed his mouth over hers. Shep blew her up, rocked back again, again the noise and smoke.

"A smoking cunt." Shep laughed uncontrollably. Don came to and clapped his hands. "Smoke it, Donny Boy," Shep bellowed. "You too, Tony. Smoke it."

Don began to crawl to Annalisa. Tony put his hand out. Don stopped. Annalisa had closed her legs, pulled her knees up, but she couldn't break free from Roy.

Then Tony moved. He grabbed Roy's hair and ripped his head back. Annalisa gasped for air. Tony grabbed her arm, squeezed. "You wanta fuck around like this"—he snapped; His voice came high, dope high, then lower—"that's your business." His brain was muddled yet he was pissed. "But if I ever hear that you've led Maxene into this shit, I'll—"

"Aw, cool it, Man." Shep rolled to his knees.

"Fuck you. You're a disgrace. You're a fuckin pimp junkie."

"You smoked my dope," Shep said defensively. "You smoked my dope."

Annalisa stood, pulled up her pants, snapped them closed. "Where's my top?" She was angry, hurt.

"Not like you people," Tony said. "I've been so fuckin high I've needed navigation equipment, but I never made a cult of it."

Tony continued to smoke dope in the evenings but he smoked alone. The old friend-family network—Donny, Jack, his Pop and Aunt Helen, all of them—had changed, unraveled. He retreated within, retreated into a world that was still sane, that was still the same world he'd left. His nights remained sleepless, his morning sleep was wired, restless. He was physically, emotionally spent. And he wanted to get laid.

How he wanted to get laid. He was a returning warrior. A hero. He felt virile, at the peak, at the prime. He felt pressure—physically, hormonally, to have a girl; culturally, amongst his peers even if they weren't present, to be successful with women, a woman. He needed to make love to someone, but there did not seem to be a single unattached woman in Mill Creek Falls except his cousins.

A week before his cousin Jimmy returned, Tony received a letter from his father, a letter his father had written and mailed at the end of March, sent to him halfway around the world, only to arrive at his unit station after his unit had moved north in country, and then forwarded again and again never catching him before his DEROS, finally completing its earth orbit in ninety days. It took him back to Nam, to his perceptions of the World from Nam. He read it while he sat, alone, in his room.

Dear Tony,

It is Palm Sunday. We went to the monastery for Mass this morning and it was real nice. They celebrate Mass a little differently there. Instead of palms they gave us pussy willows. After Mass we lit some candles and said some prayers for you and Jimmy. I'm looking at your last letter. You sound pretty good. I'm sure, as you say, you'll "look back on this time with a shit-eating grin." I pray to God that you do. Maybe I wasn't in the right units. I never felt that I was "in the best fighting force in the world." I'm glad you're having an experience like Uncle Joe's and not like mine.

The weather has been real cold and we've had a lot of snow. Mark's been home two days this week with no school. Your friend Steve is finally going overseas. He came by and we gave him your address. The war news has been all about Khe Sanh but it sounds like it's tapering down. It doesn't look like the president is going to do much to them bastards. He should just keep bombing their cities until they smarten up.

I'll write again soon. Until then know that even if I don't write I do pray for you every day. Don't take any chances and be careful who you trust.

Keep down,
Your Pop

P.S. We're going to have a big bash when you come back.

Tony shook his head. "How the . . ." he muttered. "What experiences, Pa? What did you do? Geez, this . . . it's before Dai Do, before Loon. Before I got hit." He bit his lip, bit his inner cheek. "How could this have come from here?" He did not, could not, verbalize how he felt. The letter represented something, something that seemed far more real than what he had found.

Twenty-two days after Tony's homecoming, Jimmy Pellegrino returned to nearly the identical scene, the same WELCOME HOME banner, the champagne, pots and pans and whistles. Tony's father had suggested they wait one day but his aunt Isabella, Jimmy's mother, had said, "If you do for one, you do for all," and Jimmy returned to the same tremendous, overwhelming enthusiasm. Like Tony he froze, withdrew to his room locking the door, letting only Tony enter, not talking to Don Eisner or Jack Roedain, who had come ostensibly to see him but actually to see Annalisa, not even talking to Annalisa.

"What the fucks goin on here?" Jimmy asked Tony.

"I don't know, Jimmy. Same thing happened to me when I got home."

"They're so fuckin noisy."

"I didn't even come in the house," Tony said. "My Uncle Joe drove me around till everybody left."

"I don't like this." Jimmy kicked his bed. He shot his hand quickly, unconsciously through his hair. "I don't like this," he repeated.

"Hey Jimmy," someone yelled through the door. "Come on downstairs. Hey, did you kill some gooks for me?"

"Hey," Tony shouted back through the door, "we'll be down when we're down. Go downstairs."

"I'm goin," Jimmy said quietly. "Cover me."

Tony shrugged, gave him a power-fist salute. "Go for it." Jimmy opened the window, jumped out. Tony watched him hit, roll, rise and run. Then Tony opened the door and went down.

"Where's Jimmy? Where's Jimmy?" It seemed as though everyone asked it at once.

"He went for a walk," Tony said.

It rained the next afternoon. Tony and Jimmy got stoned on grass

Tony had purchased in Creek's Bend. They sat on the roof of the tool shed in Tony's backyard and looked down the back street into old Creek's Bend. The cousins talked, let the warm July rain soak into them. They watched people and cars come and go. They laughed with each other wondering what people thought about them, sitting in the rain atop the tool shed.

"All my Mom could say," Jimmy said, "was, 'Jimmy, was it bad there?' "

"I got the same thing," Tony said.

"I thought she'd shit a brick when I told her I was definitely goin back. 'Was it bad over there? Please don't go back.' "

"Aw, that's what they're supposed to say," Tony said. "Jo went crazy when I showed her my Heart. Pop hadn't even told her. He knew I was still in the bush after I got hit so it couldn't a been too bad. Man, what a scene."

They smoked another joint, split a warm beer. Tony told his cousin about Shep's, leaving out the part about Annalisa. He told him he thought his father and his Aunt Helen were having an affair. "If I had to live with that fuckin hysteria, I'd find somebody else, too." Then he told Jimmy he thought, maybe, if things didn't work out at his new duty station in Philly, he'd try and get back to Nam and into whatever unit Jimmy was assigned to.

Then Tony said, "Shit." And he laughed loudly. The rain had put the joint out. He tried to relight it and they both laughed. "Ya know, while I was over there, I forgot that it rains back here."

"This isn't rain. You remember the typhoon. . . . " They broke up.

"I wonder what the guys are doin?" Tony coughed out the words. "I wonder about Doc So—"

"He's the guy stitched your leg. . . . Ha." Jimmy rolled to his side laughing. "He's probably at Mama-san's Steam-n-Cream."

"Ooh, Man." Tony moaned. "There was this one honey I saw at the airport—right when I get off the plane, you know, up the ramp—Man, she looked so good she coulda sat on my face and farted up my nose."

"Fart up—" Jimmy squealed. "I love it." Then he said seriously, seriously stoned, "I gotta show you somethin. Don't tell my Ma. She'll fuckin go nuts."

"What?" Tony rolled to face him. "When you're done, I gotta ask ya . . . " Jimmy rolled up his left sleeve, up past his bicep and over his shoulder. "Oh wow!" Tony exclaimed. "That's really . . . neat."

"Yeah?"

"Yeah. You show it to her?—Naw, you haven't been there yet. Where'd you have it done?"

"A guy up in Dong Ha did the 'Bea.' But I had to go to Da Nang before I found a guy who could do the honey bee in red like that . . . and with all the other colors."

"Man." Tony dropped his head, dejected. "I gotta get laid."

"You comin with me to Red's?" Jimmy asked.

"You sure you don't wanta see her alone?"

"Naw. She said she's got a friend for ya. If we're goina get it on, we'll beat feet someplace while you and her friend do whatever you want."

"Geesh, Man," Tony said. "I've seen half a dozen woman with these guys, ya know, Jack and Don and all. Man, they're a hassle. It's weird, Jimmy. It's like they're all spoiled brats. I wish I'd meet somebody who was halfway fuckin, ya know . . ."

"Yeah. Maybe Red's friend . . ."

"Shee-it. I'll tell ya though, I know what I'd like to meet. She'd be about five three, five four," Tony said. In his mind he saw Maxene. "She'd have eyes that were, you know, different. They'd be brown and blue at the same time. Maybe brown or gold around the pupil and switchin to blue as you move out. Maybe turnin almost black. And she'd have auburn hair down to her shoulders. And she'd have a nice smile. A real one. Not some flaky pasted-on grin."

"Most of the jobs have been for my legs." Stacy's laugh was small, pleasant.

"Oh," Tony said. "I didn't know models specialized like that."

"Sometimes," Stacy said. "Would you like to see my portfolio?"

"Is that okay?" Tony asked. He felt out of place, intimidated, afraid her portfolio might contain naked photos, afraid he wouldn't know how to react. Bea Hollands and Jimmy had disappeared and left Tony with a woman he did not believe could possibly be interested in him. She was, he was certain, the most beautiful woman he'd ever set eyes upon—lovelier even than Maxene.

"Yes," Stacy said simply. Her voice and confidence were reassuring. She left and returned with a large zippered leather case. As long as he didn't look at her he was okay. Stacy directed him to the sofa, laid the case on the coffee table. He wasn't sure if he was allowed to touch it. "Go ahead," she said.

Tony unzipped the case, laid it flat. The first page was a typed résumé giving her age, measurements, dress and shoe sizes, and data Tony was too nervous to read. He flipped the page. There was a portrait photo of Stacy looking sideways, over the corner of a high, light blue collar that framed her face. Her blue eyes looked directly into his.

"That's your color," Tony said.

"I think so too," Stacy agreed.

Tony turned the pages slowly. Half the pictures were of just her legs, the kind of photo that might be used for a hair remover or stocking ad. He studied the photos, could not look at Stacy. "You've got beautiful legs," he said.

"Would you like me to put on a dress?" Stacy asked.

Tony could hardly speak. He gurgled. Before he could say anything she was up, out of the room. He turned to catch a glimpse of her but she had vanished. He turned back to the first photo. Her face captivated him. It was too beautiful to look at for long.

He turned away, looked about the room. It was just an average room, he thought. Why Jimmy had arranged to come here instead of going to Red's, Tony didn't know. Average house, he thought. Not really any better than mine. Maybe bigger. Tony stood, turned, looked into the kitchen. The lights were off but sunlight from the rear deck showed it to be just an average kitchen. Somehow, he felt, for a girl to grow up that beautiful she must have grown up in a very special place. Not here. Not in just an average home. Not in just an average place like Mill Creek Falls. His thoughts shifted to Jimmy and Red. Where had they gone?

Stacy returned in a simple robin's-egg blue cotton dress, stockings and heels. She stood at the edge of the hall, smiled. Then she spun. The dress rose slightly showing her legs. Tony wanted to fall to his knees, to hug her legs. Her smile was enchanting but as she walked to him his spirit drooped. In heels she was at least three inches taller than he.

They sat on the sofa again, again talked about modeling. "I close my eyes," Stacy told him, "and I think what I want to look like, and when I open my eyes, I look that way. It's a visualization technique I learned when I was in school."

"You sure learned it well," Tony said. He felt stupid, tongue-tied.

"What's wrong, Tony?"

"Nothing."

"Tell me about yourself. Bea said you're a Marine."

"Hm-hmm."

"And you've been to Viet Nam? I have a friend over there. Maybe you know him."

"Is he a Marine?" Tony perked up.

"No. He's in the army. In the parachute division."

"I wouldn't know him, then," Tony said dejectedly. "The Marines and the army don't mix much."

"Oh."

"I don't have anything against paratroopers, myself. Just Marines and Airborne don't mix. It's like throwing water on an oil fire."

"Oooo! That bad, huh?"

"Naw. Everybody just makes it out like that. This guy, he your main man?"

"Just a friend. Are you always so quiet?"

"I got some, ah . . . bad revelations since I came home."

"Like what?"

"Aw, like my father. I think he's having an affair."

"Oh, that's terrible."

"Yeah. You know what I think . . . I think it's cause I was in old Nam Bo. I think my mom was such a wreck this last year that she musta drove my father to it." Stacy didn't comment. "Hey," Tony's tone changed completely, "are you wearing contacts?"

"Hmm?" Stacy smiled, surprised at the question, the change of tone.

"Contact lenses? Colored ones?"

"No."

"I've never seen anyone with eyes as blue as yours. Really."

Stacy smiled, lowered her gaze.

"Hey, would you like to dance?"

"Where?" Stacy asked.

"Here. Look, I know I'm a short guy but . . . ah, if you'll take your shoes off . . . we could put on a few records and dance. I haven't danced in a long time."

When Jimmy and Red returned they found Tony and Stacy slow dancing to soft music in the dark.

"Damn it. No." Jimmy was raging. The argument must have been going on long before they walked in.

"Well what am I supposed to say?"

"Nothin. You're supposed to listen."

"I was listening."

"No you weren't. You got no idea what I was sayin."

"I think I understood how you felt."

"You're still not listening. Listen with your mouth shut. You can't hear if you're talking and telling me what I'm sayin and what I mean."

"Jimmeee!"

"Come on, Tony. Let's get outa here."

On the drive back into town Tony was flying. Stacy had kissed him. "Man, what's happenin with you and Red?" he asked, but he did not want to talk about it. He wanted his cousin to ask him about Stacy.

"Augh, nothin," Jimmy said. He was seething. "I fucked her eyes out and we're layin there and I began tellin her about like, like goin into a ville. I told her about the steam-n-cream and I was tryin to tell her that I didn't really like goin there. She heard nothin, Man. Nothin."

"Hey. I'm sorry."

"Naw. It's fine. It'll work out fine. We'll be back sailin in no time. How'd you make out with her friend?"

"Oh Man, I've never seen eyes like this girl's got."

"Yeah, she's pretty. She's fucked up though. A fuckin tramp, Man."

"I wouldn't mind doin some trampin around with her," Tony guffawed, but he did it against what he was feeling.

"Red said her steady guy left for Nam like a month ago. She's been fuckin round on him like a bunny. You oughta—"

"What? What guy?"

"Army guy. From down in Lutzburgh."

Tony Pisano did not have to report for duty until July 22d. On the 20th, the second morning after he'd doubled with his cousin, he packed his seabag, said good-bye to his folks and caught a bus for Philadelphia. That night Jimmy Pellegrino and Bea Hollands announced their engagement.

July 1984

I walked here. Did I mention that? I walked the last ten miles or so. Kind of a penance. Or a tribute. I left my scooter at Ma's, packed a ruck and walked here. Mostly in the dark. Guess I felt self-conscious walkin through town with a ruck and these old jungle boots so I left about, I don't know, when the moon was comin up. Got to the culverts down there about dawn then came around the back way. Real slow. Real quiet. Thinkin some about the old man but mostly not thinkin.

Sun's low now. It's too early to hear the evening sounds from the fields or woods. Too early for the deer to show along the edge. All the creatures rest at this hour—except maybe a few nonunion squirrels.

When the sun hits the ridge it'll disappear quick, like in any mountainous region. I'm going to stay. Stay here. Maybe gather some wood, make a small fire. Talk to the old man the way Bobby used to. He was really somethin. Talk to the deer and the fox and the bats, too. See if they've got any answers. Watch the garbage cans. See if the raccoons check em out. They'd stop checkin if there wasn't any trash for a while. Watch the house, too. See if a light comes on.

I've cleared a small spot for sleeping but I don't expect to sleep. Cleared a spot for a fire, too, but I'll hold off a few days. No need to announce to the whole world I'm back, back here thinkin about it. Meditating on it. That was one of Bobby's solutions . . . to clear up dreams. He'd call it "controlled dreaming," say it allows "the subconscious/conscious mind split to reconcile differences."

Dreams. I still have em. Old ones. Almost like friends now. And new ones. I don't even think of em as havin begun at Dai Do, but that's where the shrinks tried to put it. I think they're wrong. I subscribe to Wapinski's theory, kind of a Grunt's Theory of Psychoanalysis. Yeah, for me, Dai Do was there. Yeah, it was traumatic. But it's like blaming a blown engine on the thing being made instead of on overrevving the sucker. Or maybe more like blaming a crop failure on lack of rainfall in August—but when irrigation is available. Get it? There's a cause there but it's not The Cause. Not for me. Like a chemical reaction where the potential for disaster exists in the test tube—but so does the potential for something really good. And it depends on the next ingredient that's dumped in—not only on what's there. Shrink said Dai Do was it. Bobby said it was what came later. "The initial traumas may have been traumatic," he said, "but fact is you handled it then and you could have handled it forever if circumstances had been different. If somebody or something didn't mess it all up." One of the guys, this was later but I liked the way he put it, he said, "Your dreams, you know, many times they're true. They're right on target. Even when your life is a bucket of shit."

Dreams! I shake my head. Dreams unfurl slowly, begin like pinpoints then open up . . . massive . . . a pin prick into a balloon of the unconscious. Not *only* the unconscious but the subconscious and the semiconscious right up the damned ladder rung by rung till you're dreamin with your eyes about to blow out of your head like a cartoon drawing . . . dreaming awake-asleep in another consciousness that prevents sleep, that prevents rest, that prevents rejuvenation.

These problems, their origins, their complications, their multiplications—from not being able to sleep—from being so tired and still not bein able to sleep. Bobby'd say, "But think where we were, where we came from." And he'd say, "Where is that? Where?! Time, Man. Twelve-hours-out time! It can take up to three months to adjust." His words. "Blaming sleep disturbances on memories of traumatic events can *cause* additional, more prolonged sleep-disturbance problems."

Yet they all experienced it. Every one of em! To some extent or another, at one time or another. I'm not just talkin Nam returnees— Viet Vets. I'm talkin all combat veterans. I'm talkin about World War I German soldiers who had no time-zone dislocation yet who suffered the exact same time dislocation. I'm talkin American Rebs and American Union troops 125 years ago. I'm talkin Odysseus. I'm talkin a psychocauldron of wants and emotions boiling out through numbed physical exhaustion. Later, much later, Wapinski had this plaque hanging in the big barn:

> *If we go back we will be weary, broken, burnt out,*
> *rootless, and without hope. We will not be able to find our way*
> *anymore. . . . And men will not understand us.*

All Quiet on the Western Front
Erich Maria Remarque—1928

After you'd slept forever, Wapinski'd say, "Fuck it, Man! Fuck that shit! Drive on! Take your nitric-acid blood, your swirling brain waves, your numbed-out, drugged-out, burnt-out body—take all that shit, ball it, wrap it, throw it away. And DRIVE ON! If I knew, or if you knew, when we got back life was going to be like it was, we'd all have returned, gone back to Nam, without hesitation. But we didn't know. And you can't, and I can't, go back in some zomboid state."

But he didn't say that for years. He had to have his dreams first, like all of us.

It's almost dark. Lights in town are comin on. The mall lights— parking-lot cool, mercury-vapor pink at this hour—are beginning to glow. Up over the ridge, above the sugarbush, faint stars blur together. The house is dark. Behind me they're resting, comfortable. No technicolor, full touch, taste, smell, stereo dreams for them tonight.

High Meadow Farm, 24 June 1969—He rolled onto his back. Josh adjusted, snuggled against his leg. Bobby moved again. Again Josh adjusted. In his whiskey-induced fog-sleep, Bobby shuddered. His right arm fell over the edge of the mattress. Immediately he jerked it back up, laid his hand across his stomach. Dim light from the bathroom—Grandpa let a seven-watt night-light burn continuously—seeped in through the doorway. At Bobby's motion, Josh raised his head and shook it, causing his ears to flap, then lay back down, sighed, went to sleep.

Wapinski's face contorted. He did not move. For hours his mind had been snatching at images, yet the scotch had deadened it, made it lethargic, closed down each sprouting thought before it could take hold. Now the alcohol was mostly metabolized, the toxic remnants washed to the liver and kidneys for sorting, filtering, and evacuation.

He grimaced. Josh sensed his restlessness, snuggled in tighter, snorted. Wapinski's mind filled with the image of a tree-lined dirt road surrounded by lush green vegetation. He stares up the road. On the right there is a stone wall, very clear, the stones covered with blue-green lichens. He can see the wall diminishing in the short distance to the forested hill at the end of the road.

He is behind the wall. They are in numerous positions along the wall and the road, dug in, expecting an attack. He has an incredible number of weapons—pistols, M-16s, captured AK-47s, all heaped and loaded— ready. There are boxes of ammunition beside him. Somehow he has moved across the road into a gully on the left side. He is facing up the road, uphill, expecting the attack to begin any moment. He lies in the gully, in fresh orange-brown dirt, focusing on the road. Others are in positions behind the stone wall. At the end of the road, perhaps a quarter mile, there is a crossing road and beyond there is a hill that rises sharply. The hill is alive with movement but he cannot detect anything specific, for the movement is under a thick canopy of oak, ash and maple. Local land. He does not know why he is there but has been told an attack will come from the hill, a human wave determined to sweep over the land.

Wapinski checks his rifles, aims one in on the road. Stacy is behind the stone wall. He can see her crouching silhouette. Slowly the attack begins, the wave rumbles forward, hidden beneath the vegetation. The earth trembles. Still there are no soldiers. The dirt is mud. The vegetation thins. One soldier breaks from beneath the trees, begins his sprint down the road toward Wapinski's ambush. Wapinski recognizes him. The ambushers are withdrawing. He glances across. Stacy is gone. The sprinting soldier, the attacker, is running down the left edge of the road, a rifle in his hands. His legs churn. The road surface is thick mud. It slows him. He is trying hard but he is slowing. Wapinski is confused. It is Akins. Joe Akins. He aims in on Akins. Why is Akins attacking? Why must he be ambushed? Wapinski centers his bead at Akins' stomach. If the rounds are high, low, left, or right, he will still have a decent chance of killing him. Wapinski breathes in deeply, begins a long, slow exhale, begins his smooth squeezing of the trigger, begins—BAM! A round slams into Wapinski's hip. Before the pain explodes upward into him, he knows it will come. He knows his pelvis is shattered, hears the bones crunch, feels the shards scraping against each other, waits for the pain. BAMTHUD! A round hits his ribs, his chest, rips deeply into him. BAM! Another round. Another impaction. Bam! God! Help! Medic! Stacy! His company, Stacy, completely gone. Medic!

He is cool. The vegetation is gone. He is in a small room, cramped, a hundred masked people pushing, shoving. "Next," one shouts. "Next," another answers. "Not him," Akins says to the corpsman. "Put him—"

Wapinski opened his eyes, bolted up. "Don't leave me," he mumbled. He was in his own room, his old room at Grandpa's. His own voice surprised him. He knew exactly where he was, when it was. "Why the fuck?" he muttered into the dark. Josh lifted his head from where he lay by Wapinski's legs. "Akins," Wapinski said. "Of all people, Akins." Josh wrinkled his forehead, rose further, then again fell back onto the bed.

Wapinski swung his feet to the floor, stood, fumbled for cigarettes, lit one, went to the bathroom. Outside it was dark. His head hurt. His hands were sore. The knuckles of his right hand had scabbed over, on his left forearm there was a long abrasion. He returned to bed, pushed Josh over, smoked another cigarette. He did not want to think about the party, the people, the fight. He didn't understand how the flow of events led to the fight, or even to the debate that had preceded the fight. His head felt dull; his eyes itched. He got up again, put his pants on. He thought about going out for a walk but was afraid the squeaking door hinges and the creaky floor would disturb his grandfather.

It was impossible to sleep. The night was humid. More humid than Nam, he thought. Besides, he thought, Josh keeps hogging the bed. He stared into the darkness. Stacy's image was there, everywhere, in every corner, on the dark windowpanes. He looked out the window, cupped his hands about his eyes, leaned against the glass. He could see her in the night sky. Behind her image was the bloody face of a foolish boy. Wapinski felt sick. He felt for the bottle in the dimness, drank. The whiskey burned in his throat.

For the second time in his life Robert Wapinski had moved into the farmhouse at High Meadow. And for the second time he fell under the spell of the land and of his grandfather.

He knew—not consciously, not yet, that would take more time—that High Meadow would be a place of healing, a place of new perspectives, new energies, new idealism. But first Robert Janos Wapinski, ex-Army infantry captain and combat company commander, age 23 that summer of 1969, would need to be held in the grip of the land, would need to feel he belonged to that once-scarred and once-rejuvenated land.

The farm at High Meadow wasn't much of a farm anymore . . . no cows, no pigs, only a few chickens, the lower pasture rented out and planted by the Lutz boys in feed corn, the sugarbush and orchard ignored. Perhaps it never had been much of a farm. The soils were thin and the humus scant. A million years earlier the land had been seabed. Sediment had built up year after year, compressing to become the underlying bedrock formation of Pocono sandstone. Then the land had elevated in the geological Appalachian Revolution, then folded and weathered, the impervious Pocono strata fracturing into immense mile-square blocks. When the land receded, successive glaciations scarred and gouged the surface.

For 13,000 years, first microscopic vegetation, then mosses and larger green plants grew, died, deposited their organic materials. Animal life migrated to the area. Then came man. Delaware Indian oral history dates back at least a millennium. Linguistically Algonquin, the Delaware called themselves Lenape, "true, original" people, and the Monsee tribe (Mountain People) called themselves Wolf. They were the fiercest of all the Delaware, though even they did not live on the land. The mountain ridge between Loyalsock and Little Loyalsock creeks, including the land of the future farm at High Meadow, was considered unsuitable.

Europeans first viewed this land in 1681, the year William Penn the Younger acquired all of Pennsylvania from King Charles II. At that time north central Pennsylvania was covered by a forest of eastern hemlocks that rose to 160 feet and stood four to six feet in diameter at the base. In 1743 mapmakers referred to the area as the Endless Mountains and noted the gloom of the forest, the three-inch thickness of the tree bark, the thick carpet of needles on the forest floor, and the wide alleys between the massive trunks.

Prior to the beginning of the American Revolution a band of survivors of the Pennamite War between Connecticut and Pennsylvania took refuge in the area along the Indian trail north of the gap at High Meadow. They lived there for three years until the Wyoming Massacre of 1778 when British troops and Iroquois warriors wiped out the settlement at Wilkes-Barre. Fearing reprisal, the Pennamite survivors moved on.

European settlers moved west and north from Philadelphia but circled the mountain regions. Only after most of America had been settled did farmers come to the Mill Creek delta. Mill Creek Falls was established in 1849 by Raymond Hartley, an Englishman who had fallen out of favor with his wealthy family. He designed the town center, laid out the roads, built the courthouse, hotel and first school. He also established the first industry, a tannery and leatherworks. By 1860 Mill Creek Falls had grown to 800, Heckley County to more than 4,000.

In the 1870s, Williamsport, to the south, became the world's hardwood center. The demand for wood exploded the region's population. Capital poured in. Land barons grabbed up huge tracts. Eagles Mere became a fashionable resort, and much of the lumber used for the mansions there was cut from the groves about Mill Creek Falls. After the lower tracts were cut the lumber men moved uphill. Railroads were constructed to transport logs and mill products—lath, barrel staves, wheel spokes, bulk lumber—to Williamsport. In 1888 a branch line reached to Mill Creek where the tannery processed nearly three million pelts each month.

The Endless Mountains region was just moving out of log cabins when in the rest of the country electricity was coming into common use, but business depended upon trees and once the hemlocks were cut they never returned. In the late years of the nineteenth century, with the easy land stripped bare, companies moved to new tracts and pulled most of the people with them.

Then, as the century turned, paved roads and the automobile replaced the railroad. New companies built timber slides to get the highest, the farthest, the last logs. By 1910 more than 95 percent of Heckley County had been deforested. Only on the ridge beyond the gap—a natural steep-sided trough that kept the lumbermen from being able to transport logs across the chasm, the gap that would become the north border of the High Meadow farm—were any virgin eastern hemlocks left standing.

Finally the companies left for good. The people vanished. Clustered shacks rotted, caved in upon themselves during mosquito-infested summers, disappeared beneath the cover of early cycle foliage, plants that would help the earth regenerate in a process that could take 10,000 years.

To this land came Pewel Wapinski. In 1909, at twenty years old, he left his mountain village south of the city of Lwów in Polish Austria, and migrated to the United States. For seven years he wandered the eastern third of America; for seven years he worked at menial tasks, educated himself, dreamed. In 1917 he enlisted in the Army of the United States; was sent to France; fought at Château-Thierry, the first major U.S. combat role of the Great War, where he was wounded. In 1919, after convalescence, he was discharged, still alone, still to wander. On his way from Wilkes-Barre to Williamsport he took a wrong road and found the Loyalsock and Mill Creek Falls. North of the falls he discovered barren, worthless land that could be purchased for next to nothing. In 1922 Pewel Wapinski became a U.S. citizen, met and married Brigita Clewlow. In December of that year, only months after he purchased 143 muddy acres—the top soil washed away in heavy rains, blown away by dry winds, cracked and heaved in freezing temperatures—in that horrible month of that horrible year of mud slides and frozen ruptured scars, Brigita Clewlow Wapinski gave birth to their only child. They named him Pewel for his father but used the English spelling, Paul, for the new country.

For Paul and for Brigita, Pewel first built a small cabin a hundred yards beyond the northeast shore of a muddy swamp. He then tended to the highest pasture spreading clover and alfalfa seed to stop the erosion, then cut drainage ditches across the hills. He dammed the basin's outlet, built a spillway, planted an apple orchard, set to work on a windbreak along the ridge that in a few years led him to plant seven acres of sugar maple seedlings.

When Paul Wapinski returned from World War II, High Meadow was supporting a small herd of dairy cattle and enough pigs to keep a quarter of Mill Creek in pork chops and bacon. In 1946 Robert Wapinski was born to Paul and Miriam (nee) Cadwalder.

The house Bobby Wapinski moved back into in 1969 was run-down. Perhaps any home in which a man lives alone for fifteen years, alone after his wife's death, would be run-down. But Pewel Wapinski lost not only his wife in 1954, he lost his grandson whom he and his wife had raised for more than six years as though he were their own son, as though they, late in life, had been given the chance to raise their only son again, a son whose vanishing they did not understand, whose abandonment of his family horrified them. A year later Pewel caught Miriam making the nine-year-old boy eat, without utensils, from an animal bowl on the floor, calling him dog and pig, telling him he would eat there forever until he learned to eat without making noise, eat like his brother and sister who sat respectfully afraid at the table not seeing Rob on his knees, his hands behind his back, licking at his food, trying so hard to be soundless. What else she had done, Pewel did not know, refused to imagine.

Pewel Wapinski had attempted to gain custody but Miriam fought him and the court sided without question with the mother who owned a Victorian in the Lutzburgh section over the old man from the hills, sided with her without even hearing the old man's story much less what the boy might say. In Pewel's loss there was despondency. When that passed he could no longer live in the house except to eat and sleep. He rose early each day, spent the day in the barn, in a loft office he built with such intricate precision the woodwork rivaled that in the best homes along River Front Drive or indeed even those in the mansions at Eagles Mere.

The exterior of the house had been neglected. Where the grass around the barn was neatly cut, that around the house grew to its self-limiting height. Where the tree limbs at the barn were meticulously trimmed so that in the strongest storm winds the branches barely reached the roof with the tickle of a leaf, the trees around the house had grown first to brush the sides, then to jam against the roof and windows. And where the barn trim was repainted yearly, even in his eightieth year though he only did the lower sections now and hired various boys from other hill farms to do the second story and gable peaks, the house had not been painted since 1953.

The man Bobby Wapinski returned to was small, wiry, shrunken to five foot seven, only 135 pounds. Yet Grandpa Pewel was still strong, and except for when the arthritis in his shoulders, hips and especially his hands flared, he was spry. And he was happy. Perhaps that was the foundation of his spell.

For ten days Robert Wapinski and his grandfather spoke little, mostly just vague stammerings in the kitchen at the table where Robert had learned to talk.

"Bob," his grandfather said. He did not call him Rob or Robbie. It was the first evening of July. The house was hot, humid, smelled of mildew even though the old man had cleaned harder than he had in fifteen years. "I imagine, if I'd just returned from a war, if I'd just come back here, I imagine I'd feel a bit of a stranger here. And I imagine I'd be mighty restless, too."

Robert Wapinski leaned forward on his elbows, wrapped both hands around his coffee. He hadn't verbalized those thoughts to himself but as Grandpa talked he realized that he did feel like a stranger, not at High Meadow, but in town and at Nittany Mountain. And he was restless. He wasn't sure what he was waiting for.

"Well," Grandpa continued, "don't expect to feel all right overnight. It takes time. Nothing grows overnight. It takes time to grow new skin."

Robert said nothing. Conversations between grandfather and grandson were slow, unrushed. Earlier he had told his grandfather about Stacy, about the fight at the frat house, what he could remember about the ride and the crash. He had relayed these things as if he had been a briefing officer delivering an afteraction report. He had said little about Viet Nam except on the third night at High Meadow, half intoxicated, he had raged, "With all their talk, with all the words, it's like nobody here has the vaguest idea what's happening over there. They don't know. They don't want to know. They don't want to know about our soldiers. They don't give a shit about the people. I was going to go back to school. I can't go back to that place."

Grandpa had answered, "Your father felt like that some when he came back from World War Two. Your grandma and me, we pushed him back to your ma's cause we thought that was right. He sure as hell couldn't live with your ma. Well, you know, you can stay up here. Do whatever you want. Alone or bring whoever you want. Door's always open. The place is yours."

Again the fourth night Robert had drunk too much. He'd talked, raged, spewed forth indignation, but he refused to hear. And Grandpa had not repeated Bobby's comments, had not tried to reason with his grandson. He had simply sat there, listened, let the young man discharge his anger.

Grandpa finished his coffee. He rose and carried his plate to the sink. "I don't know if you know this," he said running hot water into the dishpan, "but I felt like a stranger, too, after the Great War. But, ha, I was a stranger. It was okay for me. Do you want to give Josh the bones?"

"Just one." Robert brought his plate to the sink. He picked out a bone with some meat left on it. "I don't think his digestive tract is mature enough for much more but it'll be good for his teeth." He made a chicking sound. "Come on, Boy." He opened the back door, tossed the bone into the yard. Josh scampered out.

"Granpa."

"Um-hmm."

"What makes her so cold?"

"Who?"

"My mother. Why's she like that?"

"She's a hard woman to . . . Her ma, she was a lot like that too. Them Cadwalders is like that."

"God! I wish I knew what made her that way."

"Well, she is cold," Pewel Wapinski said. "I haven't hardly talked to her since the day she—she chased . . . "

"I know," Robert said. "It's okay with me."

"It's not with me," the old man said simply. "That's not the way families are supposed to be. She broke up more'n just her own family. She broke up my family, too."

"What was my Pa like?" Robert asked. He had been told stories about his father when he was young, and he had read the letters, but he had a need to hear again, maybe to read again, in light of his own past few years.

"He was a good boy. A fine boy. When he came back from the Pacific, though, he needed time. I don't know what he saw there. He was in a field artillery unit. Okinawa late in the war. He went late. Not with the first force. He was a replacement soldier pretty late in '42. But then he went on to the Solomons and the Marianas. And he was with the first guns on Okinawa in '45. I cut articles for him, just like I did for you. When he got back your brother was three years old and your dad couldn't touch im. We didn't give him time. And she sure as hell didn't. She got pregnant. That's when you were born."

"She's always saying I'm just like him."

"You are like him. You are. You're Wapinski through and through. That's what she couldn't stand. She wanted to turn him into a Cadwalder, like she done to the fella she's got with her now."

"Doug?"

"Sorriest excuse for a man I ever seen."

"He's okay, I guess."

"He's nothin compared to your Pa."

"You know, every time she'd get worked up and start smacking me around she'd always yell, 'Yer just like him. Just like yer f-ah-ther.' I mean, I think I knew way back, even at nine or ten, she was a bitch. I think I knew that's why he left."

"That's why he left. If she hadn't been like that I'd of had a son and a daughter-in-law and three grandchildren. Your grandma and I gave your father five thousand dollars when they got married so he could buy her a house in town. That was a lot of money back then. But she turned everything she could against the Wapinski name. Only one she wasn't able to get to is you. And that's because you've got that Wapinski stubborn streak. Your father had it but she got to him at his low point. And we didn't help because we didn't know."

"Do you think he's still alive?"

"Nope. I think he died because if he was still alive he would have come back for you after he'd sorted hisself out. He loved you. He didn't know Brian. She'd already turned him into a Cadwalder by the time he come back. And, of course, he left before Joanne was born."

"Is she my full sister?"

"Maybe."

"Like Ma might have been a whore, huh?"

"She was goin with a man when your father was away."

"And me? Am I maybe a bastard too?"

"No. Your Ma wasn't playing around just when your Pa came home. You were conceived probably that week he come back. And there was a good year there. Least that's what we always believed. But then she started playin around. As I heard it."

"So my mother was a whore."

"No. Not a whore. Just she weren't your father's exclusively. She liked a few other men and that drove him crazy. But—but I think he would of put up with even that if she weren't like she was to him. And he couldn't tell me or his ma because we didn't want to know. You didn't talk about those things then."

"Great family."

"Bob, Wapinski is a great family. It's a shame you don't know more. A shame I don't remember more. But Wapinskis have always been strong. Back in our village, my father was looked up to by everyone. And my brothers were strong. And Wapinskis have always been brave and truthful. When I first come to this country I worked in every kind of job. I am always the best. But I never found in a city what I found here and that's why I stayed. Wapinskis are better than most. We serve others. But we know, you can lead others by your service. When you have children, Bob, that's something you teach. You always teach your children that Wapinski is special. That it's a thing to be honored. That way, they carry that with them and they'll always be good."

Bobby squinted. The Wapinski stuff was hard to take. "What about Pa?"

"Your pa, he . . . between your ma and what he saw on Okinawa . . . "

"What'd he see on Okinawa? I thought he never talked about it."

"He told me . . . well . . . there was terrible mayhem there. People, farmers, gettin between the armies and bein slaughtered. Maybe somewhere near 60,000 natives. Seems I read that. Fifty, sixty, seventy thousand noncombatants in just a few months. Then after . . . after the fighting was finished, he was there, then too, part of the occupation force but just a short time. He couldn't stand it. They carried so much anger, American soldiers, anger from having seen so many of their friends die. When they'd be on guard, at night, if they saw a native, they'd shoot im."

"Shoot . . . "

"Shoot em. After the war ended there."

"Um. I'm not surprised."

"Well, your father was! He didn't like it. He wanted to have some men tried. It affected him a long time."

"Yeah. I guess it could. We were very strict about that kind of thing."

"I'm glad to know that."

"Some stuff like that happened. I know some units where guys went crazy and maybe killed people they didn't have to during a fight. It never happened with my unit."

"Good. Then you don't need that."

"What? The scotch?"

"Yep."

"It . . . ah, it just helps me sleep."

"Bob, I'm only going to say this once. You don't need me harpin at you. But you're not goina find the answer in that bottle. Be careful of that. It won't do you much good and you haven't finished what you begun."

"Finished what?"

"You're here for a reason, Bob. Here, on earth. I don't know the reason but there's not a soul born without reason. You ask yourself this like you were somebody else, like He was askin you. You say, 'What have you done that you want to show me? What have you done you're proud of?' Maybe your reason is to right them folks you think are wrong."

"Folks?"

"Them newspeople you cuss at."

"About Viet Nam! Uhn-uh, Granpa, I did my part. And those people . . . they don't want to hear."

"Then you might just as well give it up."

"Give it up? Give what up?"

"Your anger. If you're not going to set them straight, you just might as well agree with them. Let them have your mind."

"My mind. My—" Bobby put his head into his hands, closed his eyes, mumbled, "Never let em get to your . . . "

"Eh?" Grandpa said.

"Oh. Nothin." Bobby looked up. "I was just thinking of something else."

"Your part, eh? Well Bob, to me, I think your part's not finished until you're finished. Unfinished business, Bob, unfinished business has a way of haunting you. Take care of business, first. You've got to plant before you play."

"Yeah. You're right Granpa. But not—"

"I know. Not yet. It's okay. You'll work it out. I know you will. I know you'll do it right. You're Wapinski."

"Yeah. Thanks Granpa."

Robert Wapinski began his third week at High Meadow by drawing up a plan for refurbishing the house, and by taking Josh on his first hike into the deep woods. His perspective changed dramatically. He gave up his morning shots of whiskey. He rose at five, made coffee, watched the sunrise. Then he skimmed the newspaper or the newsweekly for Viet Nam–related articles, which he cut and saved but barely read more than the headlines, telling himself he'd study them later. And he made a phone call.

"Bea Hollands, please."

"This is Bea."

"Oh." She had a pleasant telephone voice. He tried to picture her. "I'm Bob Wapinski. I'm a friend of Stacy—"

"Oh yes, Bob. Hi."

"Hi. I was—"

"You don't remember me, do you?"

"Uh . . . " Blew this one, he thought.

"Bob, we met about three years ago. At a party. I'm the short girl with the red hair. You and Stacy were going pretty hot and heavy then. I guess you didn't notice much else."

"Oh, I'm . . . yeah. I think I do remember you," he lied. "Bright red hair?"

"That's right. That's why most of my friends call me Red. You can call me Red."

"Okay. Red." The phone conversation was easier than he'd expected and he knew it was not because of himself. He already enjoyed talking to her. "Hey, can we get together?"

"Why don't you come over tomorrow night and we can talk."

"Stay close, Josh," he said. They headed out the back door of the house toward the pond. Josh jumped, leaped, nearly did flips in the air. Bob caught him on one of the jumps and hugged him. "Yer a good dog, Josh." He nuzzled his face behind the dog's ear. "You really are." They made a short detour to look at the car they had crashed. Pewel Wapinski had had it towed to High Meadow and pushed into the garage bay on the barn's downhill side below the main floor. "You know, little brother," Bob said to Josh, "I coulda gotten you killed. Damn. What a mess. We'll work on the yard this afternoon and tonight we'll start strippin her so we can find just how bad she is. Maybe we can pull the engine and seats and stuff and find one that's been junked with a blown engine and combine the two."

They walked down the path to the pond's edge. The morning was already becoming warm. There was a high thin cloud cover. Josh walked into the low water, lapped up some, came out shaking himself next to Bob. "Geez," Bob laughed. "You dummy. Come on. I'll take you around."

The path climbed south, away from the pond, through the edge of the orchards. Bobby was stiff. He hadn't walked much since the accident. Now climbing the small hill to the orchard his knees ached. He walked slowly. He was not in a hurry. He did not want to think about anything in particular. He felt happy. For the first time since the day he returned, he actually felt happy. They walked into the orchard. It had not been tended in years. In one tree he found the remnant of an old treehouse he and his grandfather had built. Along with feeling happy, he felt melancholy. He didn't explore the feelings.

He grabbed a branch with his left hand to help himself up a short, steep section. His thumb was still weak. The mild pressure of his grip caused some pain. He paused, examined his knuckles. They had healed from where they'd connected with the boy's jawbone. His stomach felt better after having eaten with his grandfather for two weeks and having reduced his whiskey consumption. And he was gaining back some weight.

The trail meandered over the wooded knoll at the south end of the pond. They paused. Bob led Josh to the edge of the cliff and sat and looked at the pond. The pond lay at the base of a large, hundred-acre, natural bowl with the highest rim of the ridge at the north, the bowl opening south, the east and west ridges very gradually descending, extending like two arms holding and protecting the pond and the inner farm and even the knoll upon which Wap and Josh sat. Halfway down each arm from the north crest was a sheer six-foot step, a major fracture in the underlying bedrock that ran from one ridge, under the pond, to the other. There were two springs in the floor of the pond that seeped from the fracture, oozing water that created cold spots to swim through in the summer and warm spots where the ice was always thin in winter. The pond was shaped like a Christmas stocking, or fat, squat boot. At the bottom of the toe to his left was the spillway. The dam ran up the entire toe.

The hill in front of the boot was covered with woods. Above the top of the boot there was a steep grassy area before the slope evened out into the forty-acre upper meadow. On the right side, at the back of the boot was the house, the barn, several outbuildings, the stone ruins of the old barn, and three fenced enclosures. The fences had long since deteriorated. Along the east ridge was a cluster of pines, and beneath was the family cemetery. He'd visited his grandmother's grave numerous times with his grandfather. His great aunt Krystyna, who had come to America after her brother established the farm, also lay there, and two workers had been buried up there in the 1930s, men without families, who'd died one winter in the old barn when the structure had caught fire.

"Pretty, isn't it, Boy," Bob said to his dog. "You want to keep moving, don't you? Okay." They walked back to the trail and followed it down the west side of the knoll, over the spillway and across the dam. Several trees with arm-thick trunks were growing from the earth of the dam. He made a mental note to bring the chainsaw down and remove them before their roots caused leaks.

The trail followed the edge of the pond for several hundred feet, crossed a small stream, then headed uphill. Josh scampered back and forth, racing wildly, glancing back at Bob every few seconds for approval. Wapinski laughed at his antics. A red-winged blackbird flitted across their path, then glided toward the tall reeds at the pond's edge. In the trees above, two crows screamed their intruder alarm to the forest.

Wap and Josh continued the climb, up over a set of crags, cresting then descending through a rock crevass. "Come on, Josh," Wapinski said. "You can do it." He stepped carefully from foothold to foothold, dropping quickly into the narrow chasm. Josh barked and whined. He crouched, his paws at the edge of the gorge, hesitated, peered down, shirked back, unsure. Then he stood straight up. "Come on, Josh," Wapinski called again. But Josh was now still, staring over the chasm, not listening, sniffing. Then Wapinski smelled it. A slight whiff. Entrails and fresh blood. Then full force, repulsive. It threw him back, pushed him to the other side of the world. He snapped his head around. Searched. The small hairs on the back of his neck stood. He knew where he was, but his body reacted over his knowledge. He stepped down. The scent closed upon him in the warm humid air. He looked for the dead. He mumbled to Josh, "There's got to be a cat or a raccoon here. Maybe a dog. Maybe a dog got a deer. Come on," he ordered. "Get down here. This is the path we're takin." Josh barked, whined. He came to the edge of the steep descent. Wapinski stretched up, grabbed him by the collar. The dog reared back. Wap pulled him down, caught him as he fell, tucked him under his left arm. Josh squirmed, his strong body objecting to being held. Bob descended. The odor closed in on him. The back of his throat tightened. He swallowed. He cleared his throat, spit. He descended to the bottom, put the dog down, looked into the crevices and holes but saw nothing. He searched the area beyond the path, first to one side, then the other. He climbed over a fallen tree and foraged beneath several bushes. With his head up he could smell the death but the moment he tried to home in on the origin, the smell decreased.

There was a slight breeze, so slight Wapinski could not ascertain its direction. He looked uphill at the trees. The wind should lift the leaves, he thought. If I can see the bottoms, the wind will be coming from that direction. The leaves hung listless. He moved farther down toward the pond. Again the smell came strong. He searched and the smell dissipated. He backed up and the smell was gone. He descended and the rancid, piercing smell nearly knocked him down. He felt his stomach tighten. Then he knew he would not stay, would not find the source.

He continued on the path. It rose over a small hummock then fell again toward the pond. He paused and covered his face. "Josh," he yelled. Wap knelt. The dog came over and pushed his face between Wap's arm and chest. "Josh," Wap said softly, almost pleadingly, "you smelled it too, didn't you?"

When Bob Wapinski and Josh returned to the farmhouse Grandpa was waiting for them with news. Joanne had called. Montgomery McShane was pressing charges.

Bea Hollands was dissatisfied with her life. Her boyfriend, Jimmy Pellegrino, was in Viet Nam, had been there for most of the past two years. Her last close friend, Stacy Carter, was planning a September wedding and a move to New York City with her new husband. And in nine days she would be twenty-one years old and no one seemed to know or care. Bea was stuck in Mill Creek Falls, Pennsylvania, without adventure, without future, stuck, she felt, in a backwater, back-hills town where even yesterday's Fourth of July celebration, which supposedly brought out the best of small-town America, had been a total drag.

Bea was small, barely five one and not ninety pounds dripping wet, smaller than petite, so small she purchased her clothing in the girls'

departments of the local clothing stores. As if to make up for this diminutive size, she had a wild mane of bright red-orange curls that covered both shoulders and fell to below her waist. Her hair added two
inches to her height and framed not just her face but her neck, shoulders
and her slight upper body. In the center of that frame, two hazy green
eyes tried to look languid, despite their natural vim.

"Hi," Wapinski said. "You've got to be . . ."

"Red." She gave him a big smile. She was dressed in matching pistachio-colored short shorts and T-shirt. "You're taller than I remembered."

"Yeah. Ah . . ." Two sentences, he thought. Already I'm awkward.
Does she mean I'm too tall for her? "I can slouch," he said. Red laughed.
She had an easy laugh.

"It's probably because I've only seen you with Stacy and she's tall
too," Red said. "Why don't we go for a drive. I don't want to stay here."

"Sure," he said. "Any place you want to go."

"There's a new ice-cream shop downtown that has the creamiest, yum-
miest ice cream you've ever tasted."

Wapinski didn't know what to say. She'd moved into high energy. He
felt overwhelmed.

"Stacy told me that you just came back from Viet Nam," Red said as
they got into Grandpa's '53 Chevy. "This is really a neat car. You could
put wood trim on the sides and it'd be a real woody."

"Ah, it's my grandfather's. I, ah, crashed mine a few weeks ago and
haven't been able to fix it yet."

"Why don't you just have the insurance company fix it? Look how
wide the seats are. I feel like I'm on my living room couch. This is so
much better than my car." Wapinski was about to ask her which car was
hers, but she rattled out before he had a chance. "That's mine. The Vee
Doub. It's cute, don't you think? My father helped me put the racing
stripes on it."

"Very nice," he said. He started the Chevy, backed out, and in silence
followed her directions toward the ice cream parlor. She continued chatting. Bob Wapinski liked her voice, but the chatter drove him to lean
against the door. Very gradually she slowed down as he stopped even
his occasional *um-hmms*. He liked the way she looked, too. She wasn't
Stacy, but in a very different way she was pretty. Even her legs were
nice, not model legs like Stacy's, he thought, but she had smooth skin
and firm-looking thighs and calves. He decided that he didn't like her
but that he'd like to fuck her. Then her entire countenance changed. She
shut up, became serious.

"You probably'd like to get a word in here, huh?" Red dropped her
head. "Jimmy told me I talk too much, and I know he's right. Sometimes
it just bubbles out of me." She looked up at Bob, tilted her head just so,
smiled sheepishly, said, "I'm sorry."

"No," he said. "I was enjoying listening to you."

"Yeah, but I think you wanted to talk, didn't you?"

"Who's Jimmy?"

"He's my boyfriend. Stacy said she told you."

"Oh. I must of forgot. Who is he?"

"He's in Viet Nam, too. He's a Marine."

"Man." Bob sighed. "He's got no idea what he's comin back to."

"He's been back. He's on his second tour."

"And he's still your boyfriend!?"

"Uh-huh. We're engaged. I wrote him and told him I was going to see you and just talk. He knows what Stacy did to you."

"What?"

"Well, Stacy and I doubled once with Jimmy and his cousin and once with Jimmy and Jerry."

"She was playing around the whole time I was over there, wasn't she?" Bob didn't ask it with bitterness. Somehow, he could not blame Stacy. It wasn't that he thought the fault or reason for their splitting up lay with him or with his service: it was simply a matter that he could not think badly about Stacy. To him she was perfect.

"She dated," Red said. "She wrote to you and told you."

"No she didn't."

"She told me . . . that's what she told me. She said she wrote and told you."

"She wrote and told me she loved me," he said. "What happened to her? You know we'd been going for almost four years? I sent her a long-stem red rose on the first of every month, FTD. A dozen roses, one for each month I was away."

"I know. I remember when she first went to Nittany Mountain and she met you. She was crazy about you. Really. She was always crazy about you."

"Damn! See. I don't know what happened. Did she just get tired of waiting? Did this guy Jerry sweep her off her feet? Who is this Jerry sucker?" Again Red just looked up at Bobby with her great big green eyes and shrugged. There was a short silence. Then he said, "Can I ask you . . . about your boyfriend?"

"You mean . . ."

"Yeah. Do you cheat on him?"

"No."

"Never?"

"Never. I wouldn't do that. He's, he's like—like the love of my life. He's been my only love. We've been going ever since we were sophomores in high school. I've never even dated anybody else."

They talked about Stacy and Tony and Jerry and Jimmy for an hour. They sat in the car in the small parking lot of the ice-cream parlor, ate their cones, talked more. Red sat sideways on the seat, her knees folded, her feet by her butt. Bob lay against the driver's door. Talking about Stacy, finding out that she'd been dating, dating more he was sure than what Red let on, and from almost the time he left for overseas, bummed him out, dropped him into gloom. If Red looked lovely in the amber light that came through the windshield, he didn't notice. He drove her home, in silence, until they reached her curb.

"All women aren't rotten, Bob," Red said. "I know you're feeling that way, but it's not true."

"Yeah," he said. "I know you're right. It's just depressing talking about this."

"Bob . . ."

"Um."

"If you'd like to talk again, I'd like to talk too."

"Okay."

"Call me."

Their first dates, if they could be so called, set up the next four years of their lives. Later, much later, Robert Wapinski would look back on this time with Red and think, I must have needed someone terribly then. That's why I fell in love. But at the time he did not realize it, simply went with the flow. He had had good friends in the army, friends that knew his intimate fears and hopes, that had shared his joy and his sorrow. Close friends. Better friends, he felt, than any man had a right to. Now, except for Grandpa and Josh, he was alone. Cut off. Cut off from his family by an invisible wall and from friends by seemingly infinite distance. He wondered if they were still in the A Shau, or back in the A Shau on another operation, on new hills, new or reopened firebases. Was Thompson the company commander? Had Colonel Cordman rotated? Great battalion commander. Was Quay still interpreting with S-2? And Doc Edwards and Billy Smith, his medic and RTO on Dong Ap Bia, were they okay? He hoped they'd DEROSed, unscathed. He had Faulks' address, and a few others who'd left country before him. Faulks was in Nebraska—too far, it seemed, even to call. He didn't know why. And Eton, and Bowers. Missing. Left behind when they withdrew—when the rain turned the mountain to mud and they less withdrew than slid away, involuntarily, slid down the side of Hamburger leaving Eton and Bowers wounded, getting Carino killed trying to go back and recover them. And Ty Blackwell too. Not KIA, WIA and pissed. Moaning, bitching, vengeful at the evac hospital at Camp Evans. Son of a bitch, Wapinski had thought. Son of a bitch, still a better man than anyone has a right to know: better men than anyone has the right to be befriended by, much less the privilege to serve with, under or command.

So Bobby transferred his need for intimacy to Red. Through July they just talked. Their "dates" alternated, it seemed, between fun talk and serious talk, between times when Red couldn't control her chattering and Bob was in no mind to listen, to times when Red drew the most painful thoughts out of him and if not understood, at least listened without judging.

"Sometimes it's like I don't know what I think anymore," he told Red. "I read these god damned papers. We're fighting honorably there. Damn it, I know this. I was on Dong Ap Bia. I know who was up there. I know where they came from and what they had. Then I read this shit about Nixon thinking about throwing in the towel. Or these senators. I can't believe Kennedy! I can understand the protestors. I just can't understand our own government. And I can't understand the press. Those people are way off base. They see one side of things. They've got no idea what war is and yet they think they've got the right to report it. Well, damn it, they do, but they've got a responsibility, too, to report all the different sides. God, sometimes, inside, I get so worked up.

"Red, sometimes I feel like I've been shaved all over my body. Especially inside my ears. Like I've been shaved by a razor that was set too high. You understand? It's like it's taken off my outer skin. It's like my nerves are exposed. Like everything rubs the raw ends." Bob held out his left arm, exposed the underside, and drew his right thumb up from wrist to elbow three times as he said, "Imagine it like this. Like somebody's slicing away my skin. As they lift the razor it looks clean and pink but in a second you can see tiny droplets of blood oozing from each pore and in ten seconds my whole arm's dripping blood. Real watery blood cause it drips off and doesn't scab over and the skin stays so sensitive even breathing on it hurts."

Bob continued rising at five each morning, making coffee, skimming the papers, often walking around the pond with Josh. As the mornings lightened he worked around the house at High Meadow, clearing the yard, patching the roof, replacing boards in the porches, painting. In the afternoons he worked on his car, ran errands, or set about the business of exploring options. In the evenings he read or wrote or went to talk to Red and shared with her what had happened during the day.

"Happy birthday," Bob said. "Here, they're for you." He held out a cluster of Queen Anne's lace surrounded by maidenhair fern all wrapped in white freezer paper.

"Where'd you get these?" Red giggled. "They're really pretty."

"Up at High Meadow. You should come up with me sometime. It's my favorite place. I like to walk around the pond. There's a lot of wildflowers at this time of year and the woods are full of birds and animals. I saw a fox this morning."

"A fox! I've never seen a fox in the woods."

"You've got to be quiet. You just sit still and all sorts of things appear."

"How can you be quiet with that crazy dog of yours?"

"He'll lay still if I sit with him and scratch his ears."

"Well then, so will I."

"Oooh! Scratch your ears!" He laughed.

"Come and walk with you," she giggled.

"Would you let me take you to that inn up in Towanda tonight? For a real ah, you know, birthday dinner."

"I'd like that. Did you get a job or something?"

"No. If I want one I can. My sister-in-law can get me one with Mr. Hartley if I want to get my real estate license, and Mr. Lloyd offered me a spot selling cars at his Autoland. I can also get on at the old slat factory but . . . I wouldn't work for any of em. I keep thinking I should go back, get my degree but I . . . well, you know, with this thing with McShane."

"Are they going to arrest you?"

"I don't think so. A few people told the police he threw the first punch. But I think he might try to have me pay the medical bills. I shouldn't have hit him. I don't know why I did. He was pathetic. What about you? What'd your father say?"

"He called his friend in California to see if he could get me a job with him."

"What'd he say?"

"Just, 'Maybe.' "

"That'd be neat. You'd get out of here."

"I wrote to Jimmy and told him and asked him if he'd like to live in California when he came home. I also told him that we were seeing each other. That it was strictly platonic." Again she giggled. "I said you were my buddy."

That night he again dreamed of a ground attack on his position, of lying in ambush across the mud road from Stacy, of sensing movement under the canopy, of soldiers breaking out from the vegetation, of Joe Akins and now Montgomery McShane and Wap's sister, Joanne, charging, sprinting, he aiming in, now on his own sister, squeezing the trigger and BAM! ROUNDS SLAMMING INTO HIS LEG, HIP, CHEST. His force withdrawing, leaving him. "DON'T . . . " Then triage.

He tossed, bolted upright. The skin of his head felt tight, his nostrils pulled shut by the tension. He got up, pissed, smoked, drank half a pint of whiskey, watched the moon, the night, angrily, sadly, till dawn.

In early August Wapinski thought of telling Red his dream. He'd had it in one form or another half a dozen times in the past two weeks. And he and Red were becoming, he thought, more than just buddies. But he couldn't tell her. So he related other stories.

"There was one incident, up on Highway One," he said. "Up at Quang Tri."

"I know where that is," Red said. "Jimmy was in Quang Tri."

"Yeah. Same place. I was up there for a short time as kind of a liaison to a Marine unit. It was incredible. Damn NVA kept blowing up the bridges over the Cua Viet River. The Marines had opened up a base up there. Small base. I don't even think it had a name.

"I was there waiting for a bird back to Evans. I think I was going back to Evans. Maybe Eagle. I don't remember now. At that time I was up there a lot. Sometimes Quay, my interpreter, would be with me but this time I was alone. There was a platoon of Marines on the section of the perimeter where the gate was and where the pad was. Helicopter pad. Red! Do you understand?"

"I think so. When you just said pad I didn't."

"Okay, anyway. There was the gate, and a guardhouse." Wapinski leaned back and shut his eyes. He could see the base. "There's the bunkers. I'm sitting by the pad by the gate. Comin up the road there's a sixby. A big truck. And it's full in back with ARVN troops. All wounded. All wounded, Red. All bad wounds. God, I can see em. I can see these two ARVN soldiers. One's cradling the other in his arms. The one being held is a mess. A MESS! All blown to pieces. They're all wounded. There's got to be forty of em in the truck. I found out later that they were on a bridge that got blown up while they were on it. I think they were in another truck and it rolled over on some of em cause these guys weren't just hit, you know, not just shrapnel. That would of been bad enough. But half of em were crushed. There was a Marine sergeant at the gate and he saw em and he brought em in. And this fucking colonel, I'm sorry but that's the only word. . . . "

"It's okay."

"This son of a bitch comes out and tells this sergeant to get that gook truck off his base. Tells this kid to send these guys back out. And the sergeant, he just stood there. I think he was in shock. But his men made the truck turn around and go back out the gate. These guys are dying. I remember now. There were two colonels on the base. One with a Marine Air Wing Group and one was battalion commander of Second of the Fourth Marines. Two-Four was the outfit on the perimeter.

"I think it was the Air Wing colonel who made them turn the ARVNs away. But he left on a bird for someplace. This sergeant, God bless him, as soon as that SOB left he brought the ARVNs back in and he must have got the other colonel's permission, or somehow, anyway, he got two medevac birds. And they took the ARVNs out to Quang Tri hospital.

"That took guts, Red. That kid had guts. I'd of had im in my unit any day. But those ARVNs. After they got them off the truck, the truck pulled out of there. And I watched it. I was looking at it. The tailgate was down. I don't know why I was looking at it. It lurched forward and a wave of blood just came out the back and splatted in the dirt."

By mid-August both Red's and Bob's attitudes changed. Bob lightened up again. Red was hurt. She had gotten a letter from Jimmy Pellegrino answering hers where she had told him that she'd been talking to Bob. That they'd become buddies.

"He doesn't believe me," she said indignantly.

"I don't blame him," Bob said.

"Why?"

"Look what happened to me. A lot of guys over there get Dear Johns. I think if Stacy had sent me one, maybe the first month, or, I don't know.

But I think it would have been easier than walking into what I walked into."

"But we're not doing anything."

"No, we're not," Bob agreed. He felt a tinge of guilt that he was causing this man that he didn't know anguish over his fiancée. But he also felt, felt for the first time since the very first time Red had gotten into the car with him, that he really did want to do something. He liked Red. They got along well. He was not in love with her. He was still in love with Stacy and he knew that. But he also felt that he needed a woman and Red, engaged or not, was available. "But he doesn't know that."

"Would you write to him and tell him? He'd believe you."

"I . . . I'd like . . . Hmm. Yeah, if you want me to. Of course. . . . " He backed up and gave her a silly, leering grin, then arched and lowered his eyebrows.

"Bob!" She punched him in the arm, feigning offense.

They drove to Mill Creek Falls, through town and up to High Meadow. It was Red's first time to the farm and it was Grandpa Wapinski's birthday. The early evening was overcast, humid, the wind was sporadic as if either a thunderhead was building or a front was approaching. Josh met the car as they drove in, tail wagging most of his body.

"Hi ya, Josh," Bob said. He hugged the dog. Josh tried to escape, pulled back, the loose skin of his neck rippling in thick folds behind his head. "Go ahead. Go get Granpa."

"So you're the little lady," Pewel Wapinski began, "that's got Bob's eye. Well, I can see why."

Red laughed coyly, flashed her green eyes at the old man. "Happy Birthday, Mr. Wapinski," she said. "It's an honor to be invited to have dinner with you."

"You call me Pa. That mister stuff makes me feel old. I'm only eighty."

"I told her," Bob said, "that she could only stay for dinner if she agreed to wash the dishes."

"I don't know," Pewel said. "Maybe she and I could talk some after dinner and you'll do the dishes. Anyway, dinner will be ready in a bit. You two can stay out here till I'm finished if you'd like."

"I think I should come in and help," Red said. "A man shouldn't have to cook his own meals."

"Red is it. You sure do have some hair there, Red. I've cooked for myself for fifteen years. I'm pretty good at it."

When Grandpa left, Red said to Bob, "Oh, he's just the sweetest old man."

"He is," Bob said. "He really is. But he's really not what you think of when you think of eighty. He's more like sixty. He's so damn strong. I think if my grandmother were still alive he'd be even younger-looking. She was a great lady. I think of them more as my mother and father than I do my mom. I didn't know my dad."

They meandered to the back porch, sat on the step. The wind was a little stronger. Josh jumped up, began chasing a tiny whirlwind full of leaves. He barked at it, then jumped on it but it disappeared. Bob and Red started to laugh, and Josh rolled over, yipped, sprang up and began stalking a second dust devil. He approached it more slowly this time, then snapped his teeth into it but it just kept whirling. He stood on three legs, tried to pat it with a paw but it vanished. A third whirlwind swished up in the yard. Josh sat down, cocked his head, whined. His whole nose wrinkled in puzzlement.

Red and Bob laughed, then Bob excused himself and went in to check on dinner.

"There's a card for you there," his grandfather said. "Looks a little official."

Bob picked the envelope from the desk in the living room. He sighed. He had a fair idea what it contained. Carefully he peeled the flap back, found the invitation to Stacy's wedding and a short note in her meticulous hand.

Dear Rob,

The enclosed invitation is for you, for your information, not to invite you to the wedding. I'm sorry if I hurt you. I didn't mean to. Jerry is a nice man. I know you'd like him if circumstances were different. You didn't fight very hard.

Love Always,
Stacy

That night, after they made love on the back seat of Grandpa's Chevy, Red cried. She couldn't stop. All she would say was, "I love you" and "Please hold me." Again and again. She could not tell him that she was crying for Jimmy. But Bob knew.

5

P hiladelphia, Wednesday, 14 August 1968—Tony reviewed it, re-
heard it, relived it. The hallway, the ward, painted two-tone drab,
gray above putrid green, government SOP. "I want em to cut em
off the rest of the way." Rick's voice. An inversion layer had settled over
the city, had clamped down the humidity, locked in the exhausts and
odors, echoed back the cacophony of sirens and horns and trucks, trains,
cars, construction, kids screeching, irate women, men, workers, mothers,
and rock 'n 'roll. Inversion layer condensing it all into the gully of the
hospital grounds, ramming it through the barred windows of the basement ward, barred as if a prison.

The first whiff had knocked the zeal from him, knocked the jive from
his step even before he entered. His thought of singing, "I'm - A - Mag -
Ni - fi - cent - Bastard: You're - a Bas - tard - Too!" was dashed, crushed,
enveloped in the humid reek before he even saw a single dressing.

How do these guys stand it? he'd thought.

The guy in the bed next to Rick's had groaned, pain-killer-doped
groan. Pisano had wanted to look, couldn't. He'd gone to see Rick be-

cause Rick had been in 2–4, had been wounded at Dai Do. He didn't know Rick, hadn't known him in Nam. They'd been in different companies. Still, Rick was his combat brother. Tony felt he owed Rick the visit but he had not expected the scene, the heat, the smell, the bitterness. These wounded were different than battlefield wounded. Somehow, with just-wounded, he'd always had an image of repair, recovery. Like his own thigh. Or quick death. But these broken bodies, he'd thought, they're dead but death forgot to take em.

Tony Pisano lay on his rack in the room he shared with Christopher Crocco at his new duty station. Assignment in Philly should have been ideal, could have been had he been given the duty to which he was assigned—section leader of the guards for the Marine Detachment at a substation near the Philadelphia Naval Shipyard. But they'd made him a driver and he'd spent his first weeks in modified dress blues, dress pants with the red stripes, tropical khaki shirt and white hat, looking sharp, driving Lieutenant Kevin Mulhaney and a priest or a minister or a rabbi—the local notification team—to the homes of area Marines killed in Viet Nam. If the family chose military burial, Tony Pisano, USMC sergeant, three months shy of twenty-one, would be the NCOIC, the noncommissioned officer in charge—color guard, family assistance, peon, jerk. He'd rather have spent his last year in the Corps on KP cleaning grease traps on the giant kitchen stoves at Parris Island. He'd rather have been shot himself than have to visit Rick from 2–4.

"Rat!"

Tony's head had snapped away from Rick to the end of the ward where the commotion was. "Shit," Rick had grumbled. Bullshit, Tony had thought. He viewed it again as he lay on his rack. "Rat!" the man had screamed. The ward was depressing, not dirty. "Rat!" Tony's eyes focused on the sheet covering the man, on the white dressings, on the barred windows and the view of grass and a single tree outside and two men in light blue pajamas thumping along on crutches. He reviewed it but he could not see anything of the ward except the end of Rick's bed and the white shrouded commotion, and he again thought, "Bullshit," but he wasn't sure and the last thing he had was the fortitude or desire to challenge what a legless body claimed. Lying on his rack he realized there were alternatives to challenging, like exploring, but in the ward he'd been dumbfounded.

"Up to here," Rick said. Tony looked back at him. Rick drew his hand across the crease between his abdomen and upper thigh. "That way I won't have to carry it or feed it." Rick turned his head away. Then he looked back. "They don't fuckin understand, Man. They either ignore us or shut us up."

"Maybe—" Tony tried, "maybe they can't handle it."

"Can't handle what?!" Rick snapped. "Can't handle Dai Do? Can't handle me tellin em I shot a dozen of them fuckers and they kept fuckin comin? I killed a dozen, Man, but those motherfuckers kept comin at me and I keep killin em every night and they keep comin and my ammo runs out!"

"I know." Tony said it quietly.

"How the fuck do you know?!" Rick's breaths were coming hard, fast.

"I was there, Man. Remember? I was there when we ran out."

"Well, fuck! So tell these assholes."

Tony had hung his head. He hated this, hated being there, feared it as if it were contagious. Hated the situation because he didn't have any more words to say. Hated himself for hating it. Hated that he couldn't come in and cheer Rick up, cheer up the entire ward, give them back their limbs. He was not a member of *this* club. Not even close. A few pieces of shrapnel, a ripped quadricep, all nice and clean and mostly healed, doesn't put one in the club with a guy with a shattered spine, no feet, begging to have his legs cut off.

"It's dead meat." Rick had looked back at him. "Dead fuckin meat, Pisano."

"Fuck," Tony had said. "What am I supposed to say? Hope it don't rain?"

"Yer not suppose to say nothin," Rick had said bitterly. "Just tell my fuckin Doc to cut my legs off."

"You don't want that, Man—" Pisano had begun.

"Tell im to cut em off here," Rick screamed. He drew his hand across his throat.

Tony lay in uniform, eyes closed, flat on his back, his pillow on the floor, his hands side-by-side, right on his abdomen, left at the base of his sternum. His pulse beat hard, again, not fast, just hard enough to jolt his rack—DUB DUB DUB—banging steadily, hard, not hard enough to jolt his awareness away from each thought that flitted into his head. Rick, Stacy, Maxene, Annalisa, Lieutenant Mulhaney and his Welcome Back to the World Mickey Mouse horseshit, amputees, burials.

DUB DUB DUB. He tried to clear his head but had little control over thoughts bounding in, jouncing out. She kissed me, he said to himself. He tried to force an image of Stacy into his imagination. He'd thought about her often during the past three weeks, about the kiss. She was beautiful, seemed to like him. He could not explain to himself why he'd fled, why he'd felt so angry at Pellegrino. Perhaps she's just too much for me, he thought. Too classy for a bastard like me. DUB DUB. There was a village . . . south of Dong Ha. Lots of children. A lovely young woman. DUB DUB. I wish I had a woman, he thought to himself. He squeezed his eyes hard, tensed his neck, shoulders, abdominals, let the muscles slowly relax. What's happenin, Pisano, he thought. You can't even talk to a guy from 2–4 cause he's got no legs. Can't even relate to him. And this burial shit and Mulhaney. I should grease that fucker. I should go back.

Crocco came in from the showers. Tony did not move, did not open his eyes. He knew it was Crocco from his breathing. "Hey, *paesan*, get your ass up." Crocco banged his wall locker. "Come on. Let me buy ya a beer."

Pisano remained still.

"Tony," Crocco put his foot on Tony's cot, shook it, making the steel legs vibrate on the highly polished tile floor, "what's going on with you? You're a good time guy. How come you're bein so angry? Where's this all comin from, Man? If it's Mulhaney, fuck im. He's an asshole. Don't let him get to ya."

Pisano opened his eyes without moving, without allowing any expression to reach his face.

"Hey, it's your anniversary," Crocco said. "Come on. I'll buy. What'd he do now?"

Pisano sat up. "That motherfucker, Chris. He's been riding my ass since the day I got here. I'm goina waste him."

"FUCK Mulhaney! Man!" Chris' arms snapped forward accenting his words. "Ya only go over three once. Don't let him get to ya. Do I gotta tell ya that ever day?"

"That son of a bitch. You see that candyass's uniform? One fuckin ribbon. One fuckin firewatch ribbon. He's never been anywhere, and he aint ever goina make it anywhere. Where's he get off given me CQ tonight?!"

"Geez Louise! Lambert said he'd take it for ya. Why give a fuck?"

"That's not the point, Chris. Don't ya see? He knows it's my anniversary. He's just fuckin me over."

"Here." Crocco brought his hands to his mouth like a megaphone. "Say this: 'Mulhaney Is an Asshole. He Is Not Worth My *scoraggiato.*' "

"*Scoraggiato!*" Tony laughed. "Why the hell can't you say *agita* like every other wop?"

"Come on, Man. We'll meet some townies."

"Last thing I need is to chase some chick who's playin cocktease. This duty . . . God damn thankless, gutless . . ." Pisano stood. He walked to the window, rested his ass against the black marble sill. "It's a lousy deal, Chris. Notification's the easy part. Know what happened today with that asshole?"

"What? What'd he do? He do another one of his famous Mulhaneyisms? I'm glad I don't do that shit. I think it'd be harder than anything we ever went through across the pond. God! Havin to drive a priest up to somebody's door! You got picked, *paesan*, cause you look so good in that uniform."

"I don't know if I can take another funeral, Chris."

"Yeah. What happened with that lady, anyway?"

"Shit Man, the bugle was starting, you know, and Mulhaney says to me to help her. I was trying to help her. I thought she was going to collapse. So I grabbed her hand. You know, not grab it, more like cup my hand under her wrist, give her somethin to lean on. And she turns to me and she's crying and she says, 'How is it—' Man, she says it in this eerie voice that's comin from outer space, she says it real loud, 'How is it, young man, that you are alive and my son is dead?' And Mulhaney, he laughs right out loud. Right there. Then that candyass fucker laughed about it all the way back. He repeated it a hundred times."

"Good," Crocco said. "Now you got it out. Let's go celebrate."

"Dammit, Chris. I'm an action Marine, Man, or I'm no Marine at all. They either transfer me from this Mickey Mouse unit or I'm getting out. And fuck it, I aint goin back to Nam Bo. I'm not goina let im push me into volunteering to go back."

"That's what happens to all you good Catholic boys," Crocco said. "You take this shit seriously and you end up volunteering to go back. Don't let it get to ya."

"You know what I could do?" Pisano said. He began to remove his uniform. "I could teach. That's what I'd like. I used ta think about it in Nam. I'm a good teacher. I am. I'd like to get down to Parris Island and train boots."

"Now you're fuckin with yer own head." Crocco was mostly dressed. "Eat the apple." He chuckled. "Fuck the Corps. Shit, *paesan*, some beers tonight, then tomorrow or on the weekend—"

Pisano cut in. "I'm serious, Chris. I'm a hell of a teacher. I'd train em so they don't step on their dicks first day they hit Nam."

"Screw it," Crocco said. "This weekend we'll get a stereo and get some tunes in here. Goddamn it, Man. We're alive! We made it back. It's time to start livin."

"Please come," Judy Reardon begged.

"I really don't know why you want me to go along," Linda Balliett answered. "You're practically engaged to the guy."

"I am not."

"Judy."

"Well, maybe. But we haven't been there before and it makes me nervous."

"I don't want to go. I can't imagine what it's like."

"I know. I have this image of a men's locker room."

"Yeah." Linda laughed. "Dirty sweat socks and jocks strewn all over the place. How come he wants to take you there?"

"I think it's because it's the end of the month and he's out of money. You know, sailors only get paid once a month? Paid and laid," she giggled. "That's what some of them call it."

"I could handle that." Linda ignored the joke. "What I can't handle is the sweat socks. And Judy, good grief, August isn't even half over. It's only the fourteenth."

"I've been spending all his money." Judy shrugged innocently. "Thank God Tom isn't planning a career of it. In two months they discharge him and he's free. Then he can get a real job."

"That sounds awful. Discharge. Like pus or something. I think I'm

going to pass on it. Besides, I've got the blood gases test tomorrow and
I'm on call tomorrow night."

"Please, Linda. I already told Tom you were coming. I really want you
to meet him. You said you'd come."

"I said I'd think about it. Why can't I meet him when you go out to
some place normal? Nobody goes to those—what do they call them—
clubs."

"EM Clubs. Or maybe it's NCO. It means enlisted men's club or non-
committed officer."

"I don't know about this. I don't like the idea of going over there. I
can't imagine.... I think of them as seaweed-covered cretins with
wooden legs or as scoundrels with VD and a prostitute in every port."

"Please. Just come for a little while. Follow me over in your car. Then
you can go when you want."

"Oh brother. Okay. If you can't get anyone else, I'll go. But Judy, try
to get someone else."

The club at the naval substation was small, twenty flimsy tables each
with four folding chairs, a pool table, a small circular bar, and a dance
floor. The music system and dance floor were adequate, as good as many
of the night spots in town; the band was fair; the food salty; the drinks
cheap.

"I don't believe I'm doing this," Linda said as they approached the
brick building. In the parking lot, in the light of the early evening, the
music seemed somehow incongruous. "I don't date servicemen. Number
one, we couldn't possibly have any common ground. Number two, it's
like, 'What's wrong with you? Weren't you popular in school?' "

"Linda! I'm going with a serviceman."

"That's different, Judy. You knew him before he was in the service."

"Be nice," Judy said. "Tom said he'd meet us right inside the door."

"Then the kid says to his dad," Chris said, " 'you mean, birds and
bees do it just like people?' "

"Ha." Tony laughed. "That's a good one! Just like people."

"I gotta piss. I'll be back in a minute."

"Take your time," Tony called as Chris left. "Hope it comes out all
right." He signaled the bartender. "Two more."

"You really go over three today, Sarge?" The bartender brought the
beers.

"Three down, one to go," Tony answered.

"These are on the house, Sarge. Happy Anniversary."

"Thanks," Tony said. After the heat of the day the coolness of the club
felt refreshing. The first cold beer had seemed to be absorbed by his
palate even before it reached his throat. The second just began to quench
his thirst. This one he could sip. Tony turned, rested his back against the
bar. The club was less than half full and half of those were older petty

officers eating dinner. The band finished their warmup and went on break. Chris returned from the head. Tony glanced at him; he began chuckling as he thought of what he was about to do. He poured the rest of his beer from bottle to glass, grabbed the bottle like a microphone, turned back toward Chris and began singing.

> Kicked mah ah-ahss in Phu Bai,
> Beat mah ahsss in Do-ong Ha Bay
> I'll be there fo'evah,
> Aint no one goina get in my way—
> Ba-boom—BOOM!

"Hey." Chris laughed. "That's all right! Hey, maybe we oughta go into town."

"Nah," Tony put the bottle back on the bar. "I feel good right here. I don't wanta mess with my mood."

"This is Linda," Judy said to Tom. "And this is my man," she said to Linda. She put her arm around Tom's waist and squeezed herself onto him.

"Nice to meet you," Tom said. "This is Bill Curney. Why don't we grab a table and have a drink."

Oh no, Linda thought. She looked up at the second sailor. He appeared dour beneath a flaccid smile and he towered over her by more than a foot. She followed Judy and Tom to a table by the dance floor. Bill walked behind her. Damn, Linda thought. Judy didn't mention this. What am I going to do with this creep. Bill pulled the chair out for her. She glanced quickly before she sat, making sure there weren't any food scraps or maybe a beer puddle on the seat. She gripped the seat as she sat, half expecting Bill to pull it out from her and guffaw as she fell. This is going to be worse than I ever anticipated, she thought. The last thing I need is to ruin my pants. Judy sat. Tom and Bill went to the bar for drinks.

"Judy," Linda whispered angrily. "Who's the big jerk? I thought it was going to be just the three of us."

"I don't know. Honest. I didn't . . . Well, but isn't Tom something. Have you ever seen such a hunk?"

"Beer for me, gin 'n tonic for the dollie," Bill said serving Linda. Tom moved his chair closer to Judy.

I'm going as soon as I can, Linda thought. The band began playing again. Linda glanced at Bill. He was holding his beer glass with both hands, looking down at the table. Slouched in his chair Bill looked like a child, an enormous, timid child. Creep, she snickered at him in her mind. He did not look at her. She sipped her drink. "Dollie!" she thought. "Dollie and the Creep." She finished the drink by the start of the second song. She looked over at Judy and Tom, glared at Judy who had made no attempt to include her. Bill still said nothing. Tom and Judy cuddled closer. Linda turned her seat toward the band.

"I'm goina get another beer," Bill said. "You ready for another gin?"

Linda sighed. "Sure," she said. The band launched into a rendition of The Kingsmen's "Louie Louie." "They're actually quite good," Linda began to say as she turned back toward her friend.

"Dance?" Tony Pisano was two steps from her. He had come from the bar without her noticing.

"Excuse m—"

"Dance?" he repeated. He wore his most disarming smile.

"Sure," Linda rose. Anything, she thought, to split from the creep. "I didn't see you come over."

"That's because I have magic feet." Tony's eyes were twinkling. Something about him made her smile.

Linda Balliett was wearing a pair of tan cotton bell-bottoms and a three-quarter sleeve boat-neck blouse. Her hair was bunned at the back of her head with two curled strands falling before her ears. The first thing Tony noticed was that she was three or four inches shorter than he; the second, her neck and ears were lovely, and then, her eyes were different. He could tell they were different but he could not really see them clearly in the low light.

What Linda saw was a clean, handsome young man, slight, wiry, a good dancer if a little stiff in the legs, and a smile that engaged not just his mouth but his entire face.

Tony and Linda danced two songs back-to-back. The music was loud and they weren't able to talk other than a laconic phrase or two. When the second song was over, Tony escorted Linda to her seat and returned to the bar.

"What's her name?" Crocco asked.

"I don't know," Tony answered.

"She's a real cutie," Chris said. "Here, have another beer."

"Thanks."

The band played another song. Tony drank half the beer, resisting the urge to turn and look at Linda. At the table Linda finished her second drink. Bill remained somber, still, clutching his beer, seemingly concentrating all his attention on the tabletop. When the next song started Tony asked Linda to dance again, and when the song was over he again escorted her back to her table.

Tom was at the bar. "Tom's friend had to go," Judy announced as Linda and Tony reached the table. "He's on call, or something."

"Oh," Linda said suppressing a sigh of relief. The band slowed the tempo, began The Shirelles' "Tonight's the Night." Linda turned to Tony. She had no idea what to say, what would come out as she began to speak, but she began anyway. "Why don't you—" she laughed a little girlish laugh, "sit."

"I'd like that," Tony said.

Tom returned before either could sit. "Hey, where'd Bill go?"

"Can we dance this one?" Linda asked softly. She touched Tony's hand lightly. Low voltage current seemed to come from her fingertips.

On the dance floor Tony held her gently, gentlemanly.

"So," Linda said as they slow danced, "what are you?"

"Me?!" Tony extended his arms, held her at arm's length. He was aware that this girl was pretty, not high-fashion pretty, but excitingly pretty. "I'm a dago. What are you?"

"That's not what I mean." Linda stifled a laugh. "I mean, are you a sailor? My girlfriend's fiancé is a petty officer. Something like that."

"Oh, I thought you meant, you know, like what's my sign. That's why I said I'm a dago."

"Come on," Linda smiled.

"I'm a Marine. I'm a sergeant in the Marine Corps. And I like to dance. You're a good dancer."

"So are you. I thought all the men here were sailors."

"We've a detachment of Marines to stand guard. Do you come here often?"

"Oh God, No! I mean . . . I've never been here before."

"Sure."

"Sure what? I've never been here before. I only came because my friend wanted me to meet her fiancé."

"Yeah."

"Really." Linda stopped dancing and stepped back.

"Yeah." Tony said mock sheepishly. "I believe you."

"I really never have been here before," Linda blurted defensively.

"I believe you." Tony couldn't suppress his laughter.

"I'm not the kind of girl that would come to a men's club," Linda said. "This is out of character for—"

"No. No. Look. I'm not saying that you are. I'm just saying, 'Sure.' "

"Hhmmm." Linda pursed her lips.

"What are you?" Tony asked. They resumed dancing.

"I'm studying to be an LPN," Linda said. Tony looked quizzically at her. "A nurse," she said.

"Oh," Tony said. The song ended. They walked back toward the table. "That's great. I'd like to do that someday. We had a corpsman once who cross-trained all our squad leaders and platoon sergeants in emergency medical aid. I've started IVs, given shots of morphine."

"You have! Look at this. Where'd they go?"

"Who?"

"Judy and Tom. Great! She gets me over here to meet her guy then she just about sits on him from the moment we come in and now they leave. . . . "

"Is that her? Over by the door."

"You must have really good eyes," Linda said.

Judy came back to the table. "I'll see ya later," she whispered to Linda. "We're going to a hotel downtown."

"Do you believe that?" Linda looked at Tony, shook her head. "Some friend. Oh well, tell me, how is it that you got to start IVs if you're not a medic? Who would let you do that?"

"Ah, when it's necessary, whoever can do it does it."

"Sure." Linda laughed.

"Sure." Tony chuckled back.

"Come on. Where did you get to do that?"

"Around Dong Ha."

"Where?"

"In Viet Nam."

"Oh. I see. Oh!"

The tempo changed—Isley Brothers, "Twist and Shout," then "Twistin with Linda." For an hour Tony and Linda danced. They paused for a drink, exchanged names, a few comments. And they smiled. Linda was surprised. She was enjoying both the dancing and the presence of Tony Pisano. For Tony, the more he looked at Linda, the more beautiful and exciting she was to him.

"Ah, can you drive me back to my barracks?" They had exited the club, were standing at the edge of the parking lot.

"Sure." Linda laughed. "If you can guess which car is mine."

Tony scanned the lot. There were about thirty cars. "That Plymouth." He pointed to a close-by late-model sedan.

"No."

"Uh. The Tempest?" He indicated a car halfway across the lot.

"Noooo."

"Oh no. Not that one?"

"Um-hmm." At the center of the lot there was a battered, cream-colored two-door coup of indeterminable age or make. And it was covered with large daisies. In the petals of the largest daisy, painted on the hood, were three lines making each petal a peace symbol.

Tony took a deep breath. He looked around to see if anyone was about. Then he looked at Linda. "Well, Ma'am," he said in John Wayne imitation, "let's go."

"Where's your barracks?" Linda asked after she'd started the engine.

"There." Tony pointed across the lot.

"There?" Linda burst out laughing.

"Well, Ma'am, you wouldn't want to make a Marine walk real far in the night air, would ya now?"

Linda drove across the lot and parked. Alone with Linda for the first time Tony felt awkward. And he felt very awkward before his barracks in the daisied car. But there was something about her that he liked, something different, he thought, something he wanted to understand. Her eyes were different, but it was more. For one thing she didn't seem to feel the least bit awkward or shy, defensive or aggressive. It's like we could be friends, he thought. Good friends.

Their talk alternated between serious and playful. Tony spoke quietly, sincerely, passionately about the Marine Corps in Viet Nam. Linda listened attentively, asking a few questions about the Corps but gracefully avoiding anything to do with politics and the war.

"Then a lance corporal is like a seaman or a PFC?" Linda asked.

"Oh no," Tony said. "They're the same pay grade but it's altogether different. Lance corporal in the Marine Corps is a very prestigious rank. It comes from the Latin *lancia spezzata* which is what the Romans labled their best fighters, the ones who had the most broken lances. PFC in the army's nothin. They all make PFC. Really, a lance corporal in the Corps is more like a sergeant in the army."

"But you're a sergeant in the Marine Corps. Then that must truly be a prestigious rank."

"Well," Tony said modestly, "I've been in for three years. Today's my anniversary date. I've been to Cuba and Norway, plus Viet Nam. So I've been around."

"I guess so."

"Hey," he brightened up. "What color are your eyes? They're different."

"They're hazel," Linda said.

"Let me look."

"Boy, if that isn't a line!"

"Naw. Naw. I'm serious. I was tellin my cousin . . . Geez Louise . . . you got em."

"What?"

"Naw. I'm not goina say anything cause you think I'm feeding you a line." Suddenly Tony was feeling eerie, intimidated. He almost asked her about her hair but he decided to wait.

"Tony," Linda said, "I've really got to go now. I have that exam tomorrow."

"Yeah," Tony said pensively. "You told me that before." He wanted to stay with her a little while longer but he wasn't sure how to keep her. So he said, "I think it's really neat that you're going to be a nurse. When you were telling me about that, about wanting to save people or lessen their suffering, you know, I think if I—I mean—when I get out—I think I'd like to go to school and do something like that. I think I'd be good at it. I'm good with people. Maybe be a teacher. I could teach high school or something."

"Then you should do it," Linda answered him.

"I probably will. I could go on the GI Bill and I think if I needed it, my father would help me. He put my brother through school and he's paying most of my other brother's tuition. My brother Joe is starting medical school in September. We could be, you know, like the Mayo brothers. Open our own clinic. The Dago Brothers' clinic."

Linda didn't answer. She missed the joke and was doubtful that a combat marine from Viet Nam could ever be a nurse, much less a doctor. She was skeptical but not to the point where she dared question him. After all, at twenty years old he had reached the rank of sergeant in the Marine Corps and she was now convinced that was a real accomplishment. Perhaps she was going easy on him because she kind of liked him.

Tony took her quietness as pure skepticism, as a put down. "You know," he began. He stuttered but he decided to speak his thought. "I . . . this may sound weird, but I, I feel the same way about being a Marine as you do about being a nurse. I wanted to save people. I wanted to lessen their suffering. And if I saved one other human being's life in my lifetime, never mind just if I ever reproduce myself with kids, but if I save another human's life, I've more than justified my existence. And—and—and I have. I was with the greatest fighting force in the world and what we fought for was to save lives. You know, 'The Battle Hymn of the Republic,' third verse? There's a line there. 'As He died to make men holy; Let us live to make men free.' That's what we were doing. I'm sorry. I'm sorry. I'll get out."

"No." Linda reached over and touched his hand. "No. Not . . . I mean . . ." She withdrew her hand. "Tony, that's a very beautiful thought. You, you're really a very special person. I can see why they made you sergeant. You seem really to care about people."

"I do. I think I do. Part of me always wanted to be a medic. That's why I thought I'd be a good nurse or technician. I don't think I could stand to spend so much time in school to become a doctor." He changed tone suddenly. "Hey, how long is your hair?"

"What?" She laughed.

"You've got it all knotted up in back. I was wonderin how long it was."

Linda smiled. She reached back to pull the pins out. "I'd expect that line from a sailor," she joked.

"See, you have been here before, huh?"

"No, I haven't!"

"Okay. Here let me." Tony reached over and pulled out the last hairpin.

Linda shook her head. "I had it up because I haven't washed it since this morning." Auburn hair fell to her shoulders.

Tony sat back, stared. Eyes, hair, right height, he thought. He tilted his head, closed his eyes, thought a second, then looked at Linda. "Somebody someplace took that order."

"What?"

"Oh, nothin. Nothin."

"Tony, I really do have to go."

"I know," he said. He wanted to end the night right. Wanted it to end with the assurance it was only the start. "I know," he said, "that you'd like me to kiss you good night. But, ah, I never kiss a girl on the first date." With that he opened the door and got out.

Linda Balliett did not hear from Tony Pisano for three days. It was not a matter that he was not thinking of her. Indeed, even during the two notifications and one burial at which he'd assisted he could not stop thinking about her. Christopher Crocco had noticed it the moment he'd walked into their cubicle. He noticed it as Tony sang and even danced his little jig while he dressed in the morning. He noticed it the following evening, in the weight room, as Tony went through his routine twice, pumping more weight, doing more reps.

On the second morning Crocco said, "Well, are you goina tell me about it?"

"No," Tony answered.

"Damn, *paesan*. You're floating like an airhead and you're not going to talk!"

"Nope."

"At least tell me her name. You did get her name, didn't you?"

At Linda's dormitory the scene was quite different. Though at times she found herself thinking of Tony, she spent the first two hours back reviewing blood gas theory and equations. In school the next day she concentrated hard during quiz and classes. And not until she had lunch with Judy Reardon and two other student nurses did she think about Tony.

"Who was the cute guy who picked you up?" Judy asked.

"Listen," Linda said. "He was the biggest jerk. I mean, he was a good dancer but do you know what he did?"

"What?" All three girls leaned closer.

"You're not going to believe it. This guy was so presumptuous . . ." And she repeated for them Tony's last few sentences.

"I can't even believe you went over there," one of the friends said.

"Neither can I," said the second.

"I didn't expect you to stay," Judy said. "I thought the band was terrible."

"No it wasn't," Linda said. "It was good. And he *was* a good dancer."

"But when you found out he was a Marine," Judy said, "why didn't you ditch him. Ucck! A Marine."

" 'I want a good luck charm, hangin on my arm . . . ' "

Chris Crocco looked up as Tony came bopping into their cubicle, bopping, singing, snapping his fingers, knees bent and torso swinging in Elvis imitation. "Hey, *paesan* . . ."

" ' . . . to have, to hold, tonight.' " Tony drew out the last note.

"You keep singing and the dudes in the next room are goina buy *us* that stereo. Man, there's one I saw with a built-in eight-track that'd—"

"Fuck!" Tony snarled, irate.

"Now what the hell is it?"

"Burials, motherfucker."

"I swear, you're like Jekyll and Hyde except worse. You're like Jekyll and Hyde in one breath. Simultaneous schitzo-fuck. Mulhaney?"

"No." Pisano plopped down on his cot. Two letters at the foot bounced on the tightly tucked blanket.

"What then?" Crocco was angry. Tony's mood shifts made the continuum of conversation impossible.

"Promiscuous bitch."

"Who? That chick?"

"Old bitch, Man. Death, Man. Takin another Philly boy, Man. Fuck it! But we keep linin up . . . a billion of us . . . a billion boys carrying on their generation's wars, generation after generation after *ad inf*-fuckin-*nitum* generation. I don't wanta bury em anymore."

Pisano grabbed the letters from his bed, glanced at the return addresses. One, a thin one, was from Jimmy Pellegrino. The other, a fat letter, was from his brother Joe. Tony fell over onto his rack, collapsed on his left side, his letters cradled against his stomach.

"Hey, *paesan*." Crocco shook his head imperceptibly. "I figure we each kick in a hundred and twenty—Can you swing that?"

"Yeah, Chris." Tony's voice was faint, flat, as if he'd burnt out.

"You all right?"

"Yeah."

"Didja eat?"

"Nah."

"That's what's happenin, Man. Your bod runs outa gas. You go manic until you crumble. You gotta smooth it out, *paesan*. Gotta be cool, Man."

"Yeah."

Crocco got up, left. Tony lay on his side until the mid-August sun came horizontally through the window. He thought about calling Linda, about it being Friday, about Friday night, about her telling him she doesn't date servicemen, that Wednesday night had been a mistake. He thought about the morning funeral in Germantown at National Cemetery, about the drive back past La Salle College, about going to school when he got out, about Philly General, Mercy Douglas, and Methodist Episcopal hospitals—he hadn't even asked her where she was doing her student nursing—about Philadelphia Naval Hospital, about Rick. His thoughts became vague: concepts of city-people stupidity, of slimy civilians standing in doorways, hanging out windows, bopping along streets without seeing, without looking where they stepped, where they went, stupid, so easy to shoot, to be shot by anybody, to be mortared with no hole to jump in. And he felt afraid for them. And afraid of them—afraid their stupidity might get him killed. Then he let it go, unstored, unrecallable. He rolled to his back and opened his brother's letter.

Dear Tony,

Josephine sent me a large box of oatmeal cookies, like the ones she used to send to you overseas. I'm sure it's her response to our being away. But there's too many, they'll go bad here. So I'm sending half, separately from this letter, to you. I wanted to tell you that so if they get waylaid you'll know I was thinking of you. Don't tell her, okay?

I've enclosed a few articles here for you. One's a speech by Humphrey. He's certainly the best man running this time. Look, I need your opinion on something. Do you remember my friend Todd? He's been teaching Science at Rock Ridge Junior High, but he's being *drafted*. He was scheduled to go for induction August 1 but he didn't show. He has a letter from his principal stating that there's a shortage of science teachers (which is bullshit), but the Army didn't accept it and they rescheduled his induction for September 9. He's staying with me for a few days and we've been analyzing all the alternatives—Army life, jail, splitting for Sweden. We've talked at great length but time is running out. He's filed for C.O. status but sincerely doubts he'll even get a hearing. We need your opinion.

I've thought about applying for C.O., also. I thought about it all during my senior year but I knew when I was accepted to med. school I didn't have to worry. Still I hate the draft for confining me into school as it has. That must sound trivial to you, a banality from the *unscathed*. But it does trouble me! These years are going to be of such historical significance and I've hidden behind my books. I might stop hiding and become active with the local Students for a Democratic Society. What do you think?

Back to Todd. The essence of his plight is he believes he would be double-crossing his conscience if he allowed himself to be drafted yet he is not morally opposed to *just* wars or to the military. (Mostly he's opposed to them screwing with his routine—new house, new car, and new girlfriend.) But if he goes to jail or splits for Sweden, that would upset his routine even more than the Army—and maybe forever! We really need your opinion, Tony. We need the opinion of someone who's been in the middle and who knows.

Joe

P.S. I put a tab of acid in one of the cookies!

A smirk formed on Tony's face. Before he reviewed Joe's letter he opened the one from Jimmy Pellegrino. It was short.

Tony—

Bea and I'll be in your A.O. about 2000 hours, Friday 16 August. I got till Sunday because I've gotta leave for Treasure Island on Monday. Grab a chick and LET'S PARTY!

J

P.S. Annalisa says Hi.

*   *   *

"Linda."

"Yes."

"It's Tony Pisano. The dago you danced with the other night."

"Tony?"

"Yeah. Remember? SURE!" He laughed, wanted her to hear his laugh. Inside he felt like a pincushion, tingling, tight. His breath was short.

"Yeah . . ." Linda repeated his word. To him he felt she was smiling. "SURE."

They both laughed. "Ah . . . my ah cousin, Jimmy, he's comin into town for the weekend . . ."

"And you want me to find him a date." She completed his sentence.

"No. Nothin like that. His fiancée comin with him. But I just found out like five minutes ago and he'll be here any minute . . . and I ah . . . can we go dancing tonight?"

"Oh. I wish I could, Tony. But on such short notice, I won't be able to get someone to stand call for me."

"Tomorrow night? They're goina be here until Sunday morning. Then he's goin back overseas. I'd like . . . you know . . ."

"I don't think I can."

"Um." There was a short silence. "Cause I'm a Marine?"

"No. No. Really. It's . . . I'm on this whole weekend."

"Well . . . Okay. Thanks anyway."

"Maybe tomorrow . . . if I can get someone to cover. Call me?"

"Sure."

They hung up. What a jerk, he thought. Tony Jerk. She's probably got a dozen guys callin her. Probably waitin for Mr. Right ta call.

What a jerk, she thought. "Call me!" Why did I say that?

It was warm, drizzling. The VW's windows were fogged. The radio wailed with Country Joe and The Fish, "Fixin' to Die." Jimmy drove. He was oblivious to the jarring. Tony rode shotgun. Red was in back, sitting sideways, her feet together on the seat, her shoulders against the driver's side interior, her left arm extended between the car side and the back of the driver's seat, her hand under Jimmy's T-shirt, massaging, kneading, her fingers scooping through thick chest hair. On the floor three empty quart bottles of Schmidt's beer tinked and clanged. The city street was rough, potholed, patched, neglected. Tony had suggested they leave Red's car, take the speed-line train for town, but Jimmy had wanted the car, wanted the freedom, wanted to go in, score, leave quickly.

There were few people on the narrow street. In the night drizzle the brick row houses looked grimy. Heaps of uncollected garbage crowded the sidewalks. Jimmy searched every parked car, every doorway. Tony raised up his bottle, gulped, brought it down, stifled the fizz forcing its way to the back of his nose. He coughed. Cleared his throat.

Jimmy slowed, turned down the radio, rolled down the window. Three men were sitting on a stone stoop to his left. He stopped the car in the middle of the street, let the motor idle, opened his door. "Be right back," he said. "Cover me."

Red shifted, slid down. Tony took another gulp, lit a cigarette. He wasn't worried about Jimmy. Jimmy could take care of himself. After the shit they'd been through, they were confident, poised, comfortable in situations others might deem dangerous.

Red and Jimmy had shown up just as Tony had finished showering. They were already giggling. They found Crocco hilarious. They wanted Tony to get high with them but they'd smoked up all their weed, so they'd bought a case of Schmidt's quarts, half a dozen cheese-steak sandwiches, and set off for an address Jimmy had gotten from the CQ.

Jimmy opened the door. The interior domelight came on. "What's happenin, Man?" Tony asked. In his peripheral vision he could sense Red's legs all the way to her panties.

"Man—" Jimmy slid in, dropped a lunch bag on Tony's lap, slammed the door and drove off, "do them dudes have a rap."

"Whoa! Whatcha got? Look at this!"

"One big one, my main man. Twenty-five super Js. Packed and rolled. One U.S. Grant per dozen and one for the bag cause the dude was at Khe Sanh. He's cool. They were already all fucked up. Torch one, Tone, torch one. There isn't this much dope in all I Corps."

Now Jimmy was driving fast. Tony lit a joint, sucked in a lung-full, turned to pass the J to Red. She was in the middle of the back seat, staring forward, sitting in a lotus position, her skirt above her thighs. Tony's jaw dropped. Red giggled. She reached out, grasped Tony's wrist, did not take the joint. Instead she leaned forward, continuing to hold his arm, brushed her lips on his hand, then took a hit and pushed him away. She winked, sassy, brazen. Tony passed the J to Jimmy.

"Par-Tee Time, mothafucka. Par-Tee Time!" Jimmy shouted. He turned the radio volume back up to blare. "Where to?"

"I don't know," Tony yelled back. "I don't really know Philly. There's clubs—"

"Naw. Naw, Man." Jimmy cut him short. James Brown's "Night Train," came loud from the tinny speakers. "We're clubbed out. Just get us to the docks where we can, you know, watch the submarine races and get wasted."

"Okay. Shit! This stuff's got a kick."

"No." Bea leaned forward between the seats. "I want to listen to some music." Her voice was high, the words quick, her green eyes glistening. She put her left hand on Jimmy's shoulder and Tony noticed for the first time the diamond engagement ring. "Pleeee-se." With her right hand she gripped Tony's tricep, squeezed, then released but continued to cup her fingers about his arm, ever so lightly tickling, tantalizing him.

They smoked another joint, drank another quart of beer, drove aimlessly, drank, smoked, finally parked in a closed lot somewhere between the bus terminal and Chinatown, smoked, watched cars driving by, splashing and spraying street muck and rain, chatted, especially Red, all about being a Cancer, about her desire to be consumed by romance this month of August 1968. They got the munchies, found an all-night dough-nut shop, bought four dozen, sat in the car and ate, trying to outdo the others by sensually tonguing the jelly from the pastries, and Red grasp-ing and licking the sugar off the crullers.

Then Tony lay back in the crotch of the seat and the door and closed his eyes. The world faded. His muscles relaxed, his skin went slack. If Jimmy and Red passed out, or if they made love, Tony didn't know. He felt, for the first time since Okinawa, completely and totally peaceful. Then he saw Stacy. Stacy, her incredible face and eyes. He saw her sitting up in bed, a white sheet pulled to her waist, a pure white long-sleeved nightgown primly buttoned to her throat. Her eyes and teeth glistened, her smile was inviting. Tony felt so secure, so content. There were other beds. Maxene was in the bed next to Stacy's, covered with a pure white sheet just like Stacy. Indeed the entire room was white, pure white, ex-cept for Stacy's face and Maxene's, and further Annalisa's and Patty's and Julie's and Roseanne's and Bea's. Like a garden, like blooms in a snow garden. Then Linda came, walked right through him to Stacy and Stacy said very politely, sweetly, "Cut them off, please. Up to here." She drew her long index finger gracefully across her throat. "Like everyone else."

Tony woke in his rack. He did not know how he'd gotten there. It was Saturday, early afternoon, a nonduty day, cloudy, warm, humid but not raining. Christopher Crocco was sitting on his own bed watching a port-able TV he'd bought and set up on the desk. "Eh, *paesan*, you're alive!"

"Aw, geez. Is that me?"

"It aint a dead cat under yer bed."

"Phhew! Oh Man!"

"Hey, when Jimmy dumped you off he said he'd be back about six."

"What time did I get in?"

"I don't know. I got up to take a leak about five and you weren't in. Maybe six. Mulhaney wanted you for notification about seven but Wil-liams covered for ya."

"I'm not on today."

"Yeah, but they had like six come in all at once. Gooks launched a series of attacks or somethin."

"Shit."

"Hey, ball game's comin on. Wanta watch it?"

"Naw. Shit Man, what weird dreams. I'm goina go work out. Jimmy say where they stayed or what they were goina—"

"That hot little chick with him wanted to ball his brains out right in yer rack. I swear ta God. What a sweet little ass she's got. Oh, yeah, that other girl called too. What's her name?"

"Who!"

"The one you won't tell me about."

"Linda! Linda called!" Tony bolted up, excited.

"Ha!" Crocco slapped his hands together. "Linda, is it? Linda, Linda, Linda."

"You shithead!" Tony rose, stamped. "Shithead. Leave her out of this."

At first the weights seemed heavy, heavier than their poundage. Tony began with leg flex exercises, then extensions, working his quadriceps, low weights, high reps, being careful not to re-rip the muscle. He stayed on the bench for flies, reverse flies, pull-overs and sit-ups. Beer sweat poured from his skin, its smell mixing with cheese-steak flatus, embarrassing him. He did a full set, used the bathroom, drank a quart of water, began a second set. Now he felt better, stronger.

He thought about calling Linda but his thoughts were vague. Call, maybe be rejected again. Or worse, to have her say yes and then have her be horrified by Jimmy's weed, by Red's flirting, by Mill Creek Falls–style evening entertainment. His body rocked forward as he curled the bar, snapping it to his chest, then rocked back as he slowly lowered it. He watched his biceps in the mirror, thought they looked good, thought his pecs beneath his curly chest hair looked especially sexy. What if Jimmy mouthed off? He'd talk in that dopey, macho way they always talked when together, all naws and nopes and yeahs, instead of how he'd talked when he was with her, how he spoke during notifications, professionally, politely. Does she smoke dope? God, he thought, with that car, she probably runs the stuff. Naw. He began a set of quarter squats with 250 pounds on his shoulders. What if she's weird? And I just didn't notice because I'd had a few beers? Jimmy'd see right through her. Probably knows a dozen guys who've screwed her. "Maintain," he grumbled to himself. "Main-fuckin-tain."

That night Tony, Jimmy and Red partied again, drank again, got stoned again. Again Jimmy and Red dumped Tony into his cot.

Again the effect of beer and marijuana wore thin. Again dreams came. Vivid. Confused. More intense than before. More real. It was hot, humid, sticky, filthy. He was in the tunnel. The body was jammed in, sideways, decaying, stinking in the tight enclosure. His heart pounded. In only the light from his flashlight he tried to slip the rope, the chocker, around the corpse, under one arm, around the back, under the other. He had already shot the corpse, shot it three times with his .45, shot it and seen it splat rotting meat onto the tunnel walls. He was in deep, very deep, at an angle with his feet above his head, without air, breathing in the decaying gases of the corpse, trying to tie the rope around it, him, the corpse's shirt crumbling as Tony tied the rope at the base of the sternum. To tie it he had had to rest his head on the corpse's shoulder, on the wound in the dead meat that he'd shot, blasted at first glimpse, terrified the man was alive, armed, about to blast him and stop his penetration into the inner sanctum of NVA deception, into the secret nether world the communists had designed to defeat the Marines. Tony's heart pounded. He tried to turn in the tunnel but couldn't. He wriggled back using the toes of his boots like the teeth of a ratchet, push, wriggle back, dig in, lock toes, trying to keep from sliding headfirst, diving headfirst into the stench and rot of the corpse. Back, back, only inches at a time. His breath came hard yet was muffled in his ears, dampened by the earth, by the thick air. Dirt broke from the walls, worked under his belt, beneath his shirt. Breathing hard, slipping, grabbing the rope to stop himself. Then feeling the rope go taut, the relief, thinking he'd hold on and they'd pull him out. But the corpse . . . the rope tightened, more, more. His heart pounded, the pulsing in his ears, in his eyes, in his upside-down face, pulsing—tighter tighter, dirt in his nose—the rope zipped through his fingers, the head, upper torso smashed, splatted into, onto him, drooling onto him, up top the men still pulling, below the corpse squishing the . . .

Tony jolted. Leaped from the bed. He was wet, sweat drenched, tense. His body pulsed. He stared into the blackness, ready, ready to pounce.

"Just piss, Man," Crocco moaned sleepily. "You don't gotta wake everybody."

It was overcast, drizzling again. Red looked terrible. She hugged Tony and said good-bye. Jimmy looked drained. "Cover yer ass, Man." Tony clutched his cousin's shoulders. "Stay low."

"Hey, it's cool," Jimmy said. "I'm really lookin forward ta gettin back. It's like home." He laughed, got into the car, shut the door.

Tony leaned into the open window. The car reeked of beer and smoke and was dusty with cigarette and joint ash. He hugged Jimmy again. "Write," Tony said. "Let me know who yer with. Maybe I'll be there." Tony stood back.

"Naw," Jimmy said. "I'll write, but you're under a year. They won't send ya unless you re-up."

"Hey! Maybe we'll be lifers."

Jimmy pointed a finger out the window. "Be cool, Cuz. Be cool."

6

French Creek, Pennsylvania, early October 1968: "I want you to go," Henry Balliett said. He was a large man with a large nose and a full though short-cropped beard. "It's important," he said, "that you set this example for the others." He did not look at her as he spoke but looked at the edge of the picture window as if it held his grand design for the family. "Now this program, I want to know more about it."

Henry and Norma Balliett of French Creek had six children. Linda, born January 1st, 1949, was the eldest. She was followed by Ruth, now 18; Joanie, 16; Cindy, 13; Lea, 11; and Henry Jr., 6. Henry Sr. was executive vice-president in charge of underwriting for the diminutive Penn-York Mutual Life Assurance Company of Pottstown. Norma, after a twenty-year hiatus, had returned to work as a yellow-pages artist.

"It's a nontraditional program," Linda explained. She was sitting in one of two cream-colored, glazed-chintz, overstuffed chairs. Her father remained standing, staring at the edge of the window. "Not only will I get my RN but I'll get a master's degree when I graduate. It'll take me another two years, full-time."

"In Boston?"

"Um-hmm. Two years in Boston after I get my LPN here."

"And you've been accepted?"

"Well . . . no." Linda felt the pressure of his question as she had ever since fifth grade when suddenly she was no longer his buddy, no longer his softball player but a young human sprouting breasts. "But I've filed the application and the school's sent my transcript, and . . . "

"And you think they'll take you?"

"Daddy, I'm number two in my class! Why wouldn't they?! Besides Dr. Tagesaubruch is an alumna and she's very influential—"

"Do I know him?"

"Dr. Tag—Anne. *She*. She just about started the program up there and she's my adviser. She's setting it up. Oh, Daddy, I've told you . . . "

"Okay. Okay. But how are you going to pay for all this? Boston! Philadelphia's bad enough. What's wrong with working in Reading. Or Pottstown?"

"That's not what I want!"

"That's what we can afford! Your sister just got married. Do you know what that cost?! Over three thousand dollars! We could have got a new car. And you and Joanie pretty soon—"

"I can get the financial aid. I'll tell Anne—"

"Look, Linda Lee . . . it's not that . . . it was—with the cake and flowers, really almost four thou—"

"I said I'd get it!"

"Pottstown's hiring now."

"I'm not going to work in a hospital. I'm going for a degree in family-nurse practice."

"Is this that midwife thing again?"

"That's part of it."

Henry Balliett shook his head woefully. "I may not know medicine, Linda, but I know insurance. I know who gets sued. I know what happens when a midwife loses a baby in one of those home birth attempts. I know . . . " He did not go on but stood still, his teeth clamped, his arms locked over his chest. Linda said nothing. She didn't want to rile him. He'd slapped her too many times—slapped her once they were no longer buddies and she'd discovered boys—slapped her in front of her sisters so they'd all learn the lesson.

He turned to her, she still sitting in the cream-colored chintz. "What about your car? You're not going to take that thing to Boston, are you?"

"I'll take the daisies off," she conceded. "I won't need a car up there, anyway."

He sighed. "Maybe we can swing—"

At that moment Norma Balliett walked into the living room, followed by Joanie, Cindy and Lea. "Well." Norma paused, looked at her husband and eldest daughter, smiled brightly. "Joanie tells me you've some news." She kissed the top of Linda's head. "When are we going to meet this Tony fellow?"

They drove out late on a cold Friday night in October, north from Philly, through Allentown, up to I-80 then west, then winding north up through Mill Creek Falls, not stopping, not even slowing down, Tony barely acknowledging his hometown, driving in the darkness of a deserted 154, aiming toward Forksville, searching the coal black roadside for the entrance to World's End State Park.

"You're certain . . . ?" Linda asked, repeated for the nth time.

"Very." Tony's answer was terse, his only terse answer to her the entire trip.

"I don't want to freeze. . . . "

"I'll keep you warm."

"This is really way the hell out."

"Um-hmm."

"I mean, this is like much farther out than French Creek and French Creek's pretty rural."

"Far out, Babe." Tony turned to her, flashed his smile, turned back quickly.

Linda snuggled in closer, pretending to want warmth but actually looking at the gas gauge. The road essed, rose, dipped. Inside the car she could see the silhouette of Tony's face in the faint glow from the dash and the minuscule light reflected back in from the headlights, and she tried to feel at ease, tried to feel in love with his handsome profile, but instead she felt terrified. "What if it snows. . . . "

"It'll be beautiful," Tony answered. "It's cold out but we'll be warm. I promise. I've done this in Norway in temperatures below zero."

"It *is* snowing!"

"Just a flurry. There—" He lifted his foot from the throttle, let the car decelerate, "we're here." He braked, maneuvered the car between two iron posts. "John and Joe and me and my Pop came here a couple of times and I came in scouts. . . . It's really beautiful and there's a natural pool below the falls where we can swim."

"Swim!"

Tony laughed. "Yeah. There won't be anybody here. We can skinny-dip before breakfast."

"No way!" Linda moved back from him. He worked the car through the first lot and onto a small dirt lane that led to the upper campground.

"You'll see," he said.

The tent was a two-man mountain shelter and with the small catalytic heater the temperature inside rose quickly. The air mattresses lay side by side, held in place by the narrow walls and by the wool blanket Tony had covered them with and had tucked in at the sides, head and feet, and finally by the soft cotton winter sheet. To cover them he'd layered first a regular cotton sheet, then two soft blankets and finally a thick down comforter he'd borrowed from Lieutenant Kevin Mulhaney. A warm glow came from the battery-powered lantern.

For eight weeks they had dated, for six weeks they had been lovers. Now they lay side by side, naked, uncovered, the heat of their loving having driven the temperature up until Linda's feet were sweating (perspiring she'd always correct him—girls don't sweat) and she'd kicked the covers to the bottom of the tent and unzipped both the inner and outer flaps a few inches. He lay on his back, happy, happier, he thought, than he'd ever been, and she, on her side, her hip compressing the mattress to the ground but ignoring that one cool spot and focusing on Tony's body, running her left hand—her right, propped on an elbow, held her head—running her left hand slowly, lightly, up his left thigh, up his left side, brushing his nipples which made him squiggle with delight, down his right, to his right thigh, her fingers gently entering the cleft left by an NVA bayonet seven months earlier.

"Roll over and I'll give you a back rub." Linda pushed herself up, still sitting sideways, her legs slightly askew.

Tony stared at her breasts. No matter how many times he'd seen them in the past six weeks, they always amazed him—the large aureolas, the protruding nipples, the curve, the fullness. He rolled toward her, put his right hand on her hip, pressed his face into her right tit. She laughed. He raised up on his left elbow to get better situated, moved his right hand to her left breast, moved the left breast to his ear and began speaking in a silly British accent into the right aureola. "Rangoon! Rangoon. This is Bangkok. Ah, Rangoon, you're coming in a bit heavy. Wait one." He backed away, pushed her gently to her back, then with a hand on each breast pretended he was adjusting the knobs of a radio. Then back with his mouth on the transmitter, she laughing, squirming, cocking her head to see his silliness. "Ah Rangoon, you are now clear. Do you read me? No! I've got you lumpy chicken. Eh? . . ."

"Lumpy chicken?!" She pushed lightly on his shoulders.

He lifted his head. "Loud and clear."

"Oh. Carry on."

"Now, ah yes, Rangoon, yes . . . that's affirmative. The two milk jugs are mine to keep—"

"Hey." She protested. "What's in it for me?"

"Ah Rangoon, yes, for you, yes, you get the Thunder Rod . . . No. . . Yes . . . trade two jugs plus one cracked—"

"Tony!" She pushed him off, pretending insult, pretending seriousness. "Now, roll over."

Now he did roll over and she straddled him, leaned forward, cupped her hands on the sides of his shoulders and kneaded the thick sinew. She worked toward his neck. "What's all this stuff?" she asked.

"What?" he said, embarrassed.

"These sores."

"Just zits," he said. "They come en go. Kind of disgusting. I'm sorry."

"It's not that. They don't look like pimples."

"Yeah. We use ta call em gook sores. I never had pimples, you know, as a teenager. Well, I mean a few, but not like those. But ever since Nam Bo. . . . Lots of guys got em over there."

"That doesn't look like acne to me."

"Augh, we were so dirty all the time . . . "

"Tony, it looks more like dermatophyte or a skin infection of some kind."

"What? Yeah. Maybe. I've got it on my knees, too. Never goes away all the way. Weird, huh?"

"You should see a dermatologist."

"Um." He rolled under her. She still straddled him. "Hey." He chuckled. His penis was erect. "Know what's long and hard on an Italian?"

She reached down, grabbed him. "I know what's long and hard on this one." She cooed. "God! You've got such a fat cock." She squeezed it.

"Naw," he blurted. "Not that." He laughed, coughed, choked on his words. "It's . . . sec . . . ond grade."

She laughed too but only for a few seconds before she lowered herself onto him and held him and whispered, "I love the way you feel in me."

Tony moved his hips very slowly, rocking gently, lifting her, holding her, kissing her, then holding her face, studying every lash, every pore, feeling more love for her than he ever thought possible. "You've got the most incredible eyes," he said. "I love looking at your eyes." She lowered her face to his chest. "They're really different. Like they change colors— gold, then blue, then almost black at the edge. They're really exquisite."

She lifted her head. "They're just hazel," she said.

"They're exquisite." He moved again, lifted again, but mostly they lay still, holding each other, feeling the press of the other's body.

"If my father knew we were doing this"—Linda shimmied with a small laugh—"he'd come after you with a shotgun."

"I'd risk his shotgun anytime . . . to do this." Tony kissed her. Again they just held each other. Linda could hear Tony's heart thumping. "What's your father like?" Tony asked.

"He used to be a nice guy," Linda answered. "When I was small we'd play ball all the time in the backyard. Or I'd sit on his lap to watch TV. But I think he finds women threatening. When I reached puberty . . . You don't want to hear this."

"Yes, I do. Family's really important to me."

"To me, too."

"When I get married I want to have a better marriage than my folks."

"But they had a lot of good years, you said."

"Yeah. I think they did. They hardly ever talk to each other now. And my Pop and Aunt Helen . . . my mother's sister!"

"I know. You told me. I'd like to meet your grandmother someday. She sounds like such a neat lady."

"Yeah. 'Dignity. Always dignity.' " Tony chuckled but it was now a pained laugh. "Like my father."

"But he was always good to you?"

"Oh yeah. When he was around. I mean it was usually like he was always working."

"Well, that's better than my dad. It was . . . I mean, one day we were really close, then somehow it all changed. He became the strict disciplinarian. It was nothing for him to use his hand. If he got really angry he'd use his belt. I used to hate him for that."

"Geez."

"I mean I've just distanced myself from him. But anytime we're together now there's a wall. There's a debate. If I don't watch it, sparks fly."

"That'd really bother me," Tony said. "I mean, like if I had kids. I remember one time . . . I shouldn't tell you this."

"Yes you should."

"It was at Dai Do."

"Where you got stabbed."

"Um-hmm. But it was a lot earlier in the battle. I saw this guy grease a lady and three kids. Three beautiful little kids."

"You mean kill them?!"

"Yeah."

"What did they do to him? Did they charge him . . . ?"

"No. Linda . . . "

"I think those are war crimes and men like that should be—"

"Whoa! He wasn't one of ours."

"Who?"

"Look, I'll tell you the story, then you'll understand."

"But . . . "

"This happened to me so just listen." Linda slid to Tony's side. As he spoke he stared at the tent roof. "We came on to this village, you know, a small cluster of hootches. Shacks really. And we were catching some fire from the surrounding area so we went through the normal steps—yelling for the civilians to come out, to get out in the open, to get out of the area. I mean we knew there was like a battalion of NVA—"

"Viet Namese?"

"North Viet Namese Army. Communist soldiers. They were in the area, but you know, it all went down okay. The people came out, we dumped in a shitload of firepower, and we went into the ville. And while we were in there, I mean there's this hootch in front of me, across a walkway . . . kind a path, like an aisle between the hootches. There's a double row running this way and a perpendicular row like this and I'm across the intersection of the two paths from this one hootch. And I'm trying to look down both paths and my platoon's just coming in behind me. There isn't any fire in the village but there's fire all over the god damned place. And this is my sector of responsibility, you know, and I'm really nervous. People are counting on me."

"Where were the children?"

"I'll get to that. I'm looking down one way and out of the corner of my eye I see something move and I spin an snap in—"

"Snap . . ."

"I've dropped to one knee and snapped my rifle up to my shoulder ready to fire—locked, loaded, safety's off, my finger's on the trigger. This is a combat situation. There's shit flyin. And coming out of this hootch is a Viet Namese man, like twenty yards away. He doesn't have a uniform on or anything like that, but he's got on this really heavy leather belt. I remember seeing the belt because I never saw a Viet with one like it. And this dude's running. I mean he's running like hell and you know your natural instinct is to grease the fu—you know, to shoot the bastard. But I didn't. I hesitated because this guy didn't have a weapon. Or I didn't see one on him. I didn't know, you know, was he NVA, VC, or was he just a peasant who freaked out. See, if he was uniformed, I'd of busted caps at him. Or if he had a weapon. But I didn't know, and when I decided to shoot he was already down the path and out behind a hootch and gone."

"Well, thank goodness."

"Yeah, that's what I said too. I thought maybe he had a weapon under his shirt or something, but maybe not. And I thought if he had a weapon he'd probably have shot me first while I was looking up the other path and he'd probably been watchin me, waiting until I was looking the other way. Maybe he was a trail watcher, you know, counting us. Still, I thought I did the right thing. You know, you're supposed to identify your target before you shoot. We weren't trigger happy like some of the stories I hear now, back here. You identify your target and you see beyond the target too so you don't hit somethin you don't want to hit. And I reported it and the gunny says, 'Okay.' And I say, 'I think I shoulda shot im.' And the gunny says, 'Naw. You maintained your presence of mind by not firing because you couldn't fully identify the target.' I felt okay about it until later that day and we're like at the next ville up the line and the shit's really hitting the fan. We've got platoons to each side and we're going in and the NVA—this is an old move—they'd like taken all the civilians and had them huddled in an irrigation canal and all of a sudden they make the civilians run out toward us because that makes a human screen for them to maneuver behind. But we knew it cause they've done it to us before so we're yelling at the people to split and come like in two columns forward and we're going to go up the middle with one squad while one squad watches each of the columns to make sure they're really all unarmed civilians. And there's one family just back by the canal—just this lady and three little kids—and they froze and I can see this guy on the other side, like a direct line from me through them to him and he's armed, he's got an AK and I'm running forward, me and Manny, and we're yelling for them to get down but all four of em are frozen like statues and then this motherfucker cuts loose with his AK and he's not even aiming at us but only at them and he cuts them to pieces, and we don't even get off a shot because we're diving for cover and just . . . just so horrified. But I got a glimpse of him and I'm sure he had on this big leather belt. And I fuckin sat there and cried. I'm sorry . . . "

"Oh Tony. Tony." Linda had tears in her eyes. "I'm so sorry too. You shouldn't of ever had to see that. Oh God."

In the morning they made love again, laughed again, slept till noon, got up, dressed, built a big fire and made brunch. As he watched Linda turning flapjacks and frying hamsteaks and perking coffee, as he saw her settle into the job, mastering the art of keeping all three pans cool enough so the food didn't burn, as he looked at her auburn hair just reaching her shoulders, as he caught the opalescence from her eyes, Tony thought with every ounce of his being a thought he'd had for eight weeks, a thought that had become stronger with every moment he was with her: *I'm going to marry you Linda Balliett. I'm going to marry you someday.*

Pisano stood barefoot, crouched, in only his skivvies, in the dark. The tile floor felt cold. He did not remember getting up. The momentary release from the confines of the city and the Corps that he had experienced during the camping trip had evaporated. His dreams had returned. Again and again he awoke sitting up, snapping in, or on his feet, poised. His heart would be racing, his body coated in sweat, his breath exhausting like bellows. But unlike his earlier dreams, though these were in full color, taste, sound and smell, though these still terrified him because he could not control them, these vanished the moment he woke and he could not recall details.

Chris Crocco was snoring. The night before had been a late night, a one-day-early celebration of Tony's twenty-first birthday, and the 193d birthday of the United States Marine Corps. There had been no notifications on Saturday and only one burial that Gene Lambert had handled. Linda had gone to French Creek to prepare for Tony's Thanksgiving visit with her family. So Tony, Chris, Lambert, and Reggie Williams, decked out in dress blues, had all escorted Lieutenant Kevin Mulhaney and his fiancée to a Marine Corps ball at a downtown hotel where Chris and Reggie had gotten drunk and obnoxious and nearly ripped Mulhaney's fiancée's dress off her shoulders and Lambert and Tony, drunk as they too were, had had to escort Crocco and Williams out, then return and apologize and listen to Mulhaney first quietly threatened them with "serious consequences," then in the foyer lambast them until Lambert let loose with a projectile vomit that splattered over most of the carpet and soaked Mulhaney's spit-shined shoes and half his pant legs. Before Mulhaney could come completely unglued, Tony had whisked Gene out of the hotel, into a cab, and back to their barracks.

Tony straightened, arched his back. His head ached a vodka-and-whiskey-sours headache. He glanced toward the noise of Crocco's snoring in the dark and the thought popped into his mind that it was not Crocco there in the dark but Rick, without legs. Pisano shook, brought his hands up, dragged his fingers down his face. He shook again, inhaled deeply. Then he went to the stereo, picked up the unopened cards and letters that had arrived late Saturday, and went to the head.

Tony sat on the toilet. The glare of the fluorescent lights felt like it was ricocheting inside his eyeballs. He squinted. There was a card from his mother and father, nothing elaborate but actually signed by both instead of by Josephine for both; a card from Uncle James and Aunt Isabella, one from Annalisa, and one from Aunt Helen. There were letters from his brother John and from Jimmy Pellegrino. He decided to save Pellegrino's. As he opened his brother's he thought about not having told any of them about Linda. The thought angered him, the thought that he needed to justify Linda to these people. His next thought, of this lovely girl who actually liked him, maybe loved him, this woman in whose presence he was in a perpetual state of both pride and sexual excitement—this thought eased all the pain. He fantasized about her and put the letters and cards down and masturbated. Then he returned to the letters.

Tony—

Happy birthday and congratulations. You've made it to 21. Now you're truly a man.

Tony, you forgot Jo's birthday. That was really a bad move. You were the only one who forgot. She was 52 on the 17th. You should call her and wish her a belated birthday. You know that she worries about you all the time. I think even more now than when you were overseas. You don't see it because you're never here, but her worrying is giving her an ulcer and I think it's driving Pop insane. Maybe she's got a reason to worry. When you were home on leave this last time you were pretty weird and I think that scared Jo.

Uncle James heard from Jimmy and it sounds like he's got an easy job. I think he said a "getting over" job where he doesn't have to work too hard and where he's not where they're shooting all the time.

I want to back up a minute. You should know that Jo and Pop know that you and Jimmy were smoking marijuana out back on the toolshed. Good Grief, Tony, couldn't you be more discreet! I mean the stuff is illegal. That was really a stupid move. You'd better set it straight with the folks or you're going to kill Jo with worry.

Well, I just wanted to wish you a happy 21st. Hope it's GREAT!

John

Sin Loi, motherfucker, Tony thought. He's worse than an old woman. Shit. I'd better call her. Tony opened Jimmy P.'s letter. It was neatly written and clean, unlike most letters written in the field, and decorated with three beautiful fine-line drawings: one of a water buffalo pulling a plow, one an old man's portrait, and finally a sketch of Jimmy holding a small Viet Namese child on his lap.

Hey Breeze—

Shitload of news here. I'm in a hootch in my own ville. How do you like that! We're part of Operation Le Loi—Accelerated Pacification. Really it's not new but only CAP (Combined Action Program) expanded and under a new name. It's working as well as the old CAP program and living and working with these people is really terrific. This, to me, is what the whole thing is about. While I was on leave the NVA sprang another offensive but it failed miserably. The villagers here don't want to have anything to do with them because of last Tet and then the May offensive. It makes my job so easy. We're part of 4th CAG (Combined Action Group). I think 4th CAG's plan calls for two dozen Marine rifle squads to be paired with a like number of Viet Popular Force platoons—each pair assigned to its own village. 4th is responsible for Quang Tri–Dong Ha–Cam Lo area.

Anyway, I really love working with these people and the villagers are great. The sketches are by Li, my hootch maid and best friend. She's eleven, very pretty, and as you can see very talented. She's blind in her left eye and a bit of a gimp from having stepped on a mine two years ago—a mine some jackass forgot he'd put out one night on ambush. She and her brother both took pellets from a claymore. The jackass, probably some army stooge, didn't aim it right otherwise Li would have been history. Li's really a neat kid and if I could I'd adopt her. Can you imagine the cow Isabel would have over that! Ha!

Other things going on. You know LBJ ordered a halt to all air, naval, and artillery bombardments of the North. What a dumb shit. Intel already is showing a major NVA build up in and just above the Z, and major new supply shipments coming in through Laos. Hq of 3d Marine Div is really pissed. These guys know it's only a matter of time before we begin getting hit again. Already, in one week, the number of incidents around here, all along the Ben Hai River, and—you're goina love this—around Dai Do, have increased. Same time, our CAPs are getting better and we, along with a few army units and some regular ARVN, are providing security for about 70% of all of I Corps' three million civilians. If Nixon undoes Johnson's fuck-ups we've got a good chance of ending this stupidity—forever.

Hey, by the way, I got a letter from Red and she said to say hi to you. She also wrote saying Stacy was asking for you, that if you call her she might say yes to going out!

Okay, signing off from this beautiful place—it really is a beautiful country.

J

Four hours later Tony called Linda at her parents' home in French Creek. After a brief exchange of pleasantries Linda would only say, "We'll talk when I get back to Philly."

For an entire week before they drove out to French Creek for Thanksgiving, Linda would not let Tony touch her. Nor had he been able to for the week after their trip to World's End. "Honeymoon cystitis," she'd said. "It's an inflammation of the bladder." He hadn't said anything then even though he didn't fully understand. Their loving returned in mid-November and his concentration was on pleasing her and thereby himself, and their mutual attraction became even more powerful. But just before Thanksgiving she again shut him off, physically and emotionally withdrew in a way he did not understand at all.

On Thanksgiving morning she picked him up early and they stopped at two Italian bakeries before leaving town so Tony could bring the Balletts a large assortment of pastries: cannoli, neopolitans, amaretti, strufoli and frittelle, croccanti di noce, and sfogliatelli, the latter so stuffed with ricotta filling that the insides of the box were totally smeared even before they put them on the back seat.

They drove, mostly in silence, sipping coffee from Styrofoam cups, eating a few of the pastries, Linda manically smoking cigarette after cigarette, like a Marine after a firefight, and Tony had never even seen her smoke before. They looked for gas in Coventryville but didn't find an open station, pushed on to Krauertown, filled up with an off-brand. Tony had been sullen, frowning for much of the ride.

As they got back in he looked at her, at her stockinged legs as he held her door, at her face and those exquisite eyes now so focused and determined, at her wonderful breasts so demurely covered by who knew how many layers—bra, slip, dress, jacket, and coat—at her total countenance, cigarette and all, and even rejected and sullen he could feel nothing but overwhelming attraction.

"I don't understand," Tony broke the silence, "why you couldn't tell him."

"I just couldn't," she answered.

"What's wrong with my being a Marine?"

"Nothing. It's not you. It's him. You'll see."

"We'll, I'm thinking of re-upping. You know, I might be a Marine for a long time."

"Under Mulhaney!" The conversation died then erupted again. "I just couldn't, that's all. He was . . . Look, I just couldn't. Accept it!"

"Then I shouldn't be going."

"No! You've got to. I mean, we're almost there."

"I can hitch back. It's no big deal."

"Tony, please! Don't make this harder on me. It'll be so much easier if you're there. I'll tell them immediately. Ruthie knows."

"Ruthie. She's—"

"She's the pretty one. The one that just got married."

Again they fell silent as Linda drove the last few miles to French Creek, then meandered through downtown, a short, charming main street of brick row houses and old cast-iron street lamps already decorated for Christmas. Tony sighed, simmered. He thought how Linda was the *only* good thing in his life and how even this had its ups and downs and why had she had her hair cut and maybe he should call Stacy because maybe he wasn't making decisions but was simply going with the flow as he'd been since Okinawa when he'd realized, maybe, someone else was living his life.

"You know," Linda said abruptly, "my father always says I'm either too naive or I'm too stupid . . . like I never learned, you know, to mask my feelings. He says that's a fault. That I shouldn't be . . . that I should control them. Hold them in check. That—"

"HEY!" Tony cracked.

Linda startled. "Wha—"

"Fuck it!"

"Tony!"

"Just say fuck it! You're a big girl."

"I know I'm a big girl." Now they were both yelling.

"Then act like it!"

"I am!"

"No, you're not. You're acting like a spoiled brat who's afraid Daddy won't pat her on the head."

"God! You know my friend Judy said it was a bad idea to do this on a holiday . . . because it's an emotionally charged time anyway!"

"Is that what's got you so fuckin up tight?"

"Geez!" She squeezed the wheel hard, stared straight ahead. He clamped up. Finally she said, "Mom's going to have been up all night cleaning. And cooking. She'll be a wreck. Dad will probably have slapped everybody for making too much noise and disturbing Mom. You know, that's just the way it is. And you want me to say, 'Hi. Meet Tony. He's a Marine.' That'll really blow their minds."

"You're really worried about this." Tony was calmer now. Linda, angry, still looked to him so beautiful—playfully lovely. He burst out laughing.

She looked at him, slapped his shoulder, laughed too, and as they pulled into the driveway they were laughing and poking each other and Linda nearly crashed into her father's new '69 Cadillac. They were still laughing as they got out into the crisp November air and Tony wiped pastry crumbs off Linda's chest, she catching his hands, holding them decently on her shoulders, looking to see that no one saw him touch her and seeing her sister Ruth and Ruth's new husband Jay McKinney, and her father only feet from them. Her face went pale.

"Well," Henry said. He was a full four inches taller than Tony, eight inches taller than Linda. "You must be Tony."

"Yes Sir," Tony said snappily. He extended his hand.

"So," Henry said, "you're Linda Lee's sexy Italian who's a sergeant in the Marine Corps." He grasped Tony's fingers but Tony rammed his hand in for a proper handshake.

"Yes Sir," Tony said proudly. "And you must be Hank. And this,"— he turned to Ruth, then glanced back at Linda, stage-whispering "the pretty one,"—"must be Ruthie. And Jay, right?" He shook hands with both.

"Ah, not—" Henry Balliett cleared his throat. "No one calls me Hank. Henry. Call me Henry."

"Well, thank you, Sir," Tony said. "I'd like that."

Henry Balliett smiled. "It's good to see Linda Lee with a boy who's hair is shorter than hers."

"Yes Sir," Tony answered, matching Henry smile for smile.

An hour later, in the living room with Jay McKinney, Norma, Henry and all the younger Balliett children, Tony explained somberly, "Notification just isn't good duty." There was a commercial break from a televised, pregame, Thanksgiving parade and Norma and the children were allowed to speak. "I mean," Tony continued, "it's not physically bad but it is very wearing."

"I don't know how you children do it," Norma said. "Really, I don't. I could never keep up with you. Or Linda. She looks so drawn. I worry about her."

"Me too," Tony said.

"Have you and Linda been seeing each other a lot?" Norma asked.

"Yes," Tony said. "Well except for the past few weeks. Linda's had this honeymoon cystitis thing."

Norma's mouth dropped. Henry's face snapped from the screen to Tony. "Honeym—" Norma could barely get the words out.

"Oh, I don't think it's anything serious," Tony said quickly. "I'm not even sure I have the name right. I think she said—"

"Oh, it must be something else," Norma injected.

"Yes'm," Tony agreed. "It was some kind of influenza, I think. Influenza of—"

"Certainly," Norma said firmly. Henry turned back to the screen.

"Mrs. Balliett," Tony said respectfully, "Linda said you've gone back to work."

"Oh, she told you." Norma's face beamed. "I used to do it before Linda was born."

"Did she tell you," Henry interrupted, "she was born five hours too late?"

"Five hours . . . "

"January first at five A.M. Five hours too late to deduct her on my income taxes."

"Oh, Henry." Norma laughed as if on cue. "In those years we didn't make enough to even think about deductions."

Tony also laughed obligingly but immediately turned back to Linda's mother. "What do . . . " he began.

"I draw art work for the phone company. Yellow pages. You know, when your fingers do the walking, they walk all over my drawings."

In the kitchen Ruthie whispered to Linda, "Did you see the look on Dad's face when he said, 'You must be Hank'? Nobody's ever said that to him. I thought I'd die."

"I know." Linda giggled quietly.

"Did you tell him to say—"

"No. He just came out with it. He's like that. And I forgot to warn him about Dad's handshake but I could see—"

"Linda, where did you find him? He really is sexy." Ruthie pretended to swoon. Giggled. "Oh, 'My Hero!' " she swayed. "Except he's a little short."

Linda winked. "Not where it counts," she blurted lowly.

"Linda! Have you two been—"

"Ssshhh! Get the yams." Linda looked at Ruthie, repressed a burst of laughter. She stood a little straighter, shimmied as if to shake the conspiratorial thoughts away and repeated, "Yams. To the table. I'll get the salad."

The setting could have been a Norman Rockwell painting; the beautifully glazed turkey surrounded by stuffing and cranberry sauce, mashed potatoes, yams, green and jello salads, green beens, carrot and celery sticks, a fruit basket, rolls, wine, and milk—beautiful place settings, beautifully dressed family, mother and five girls with heads bowed, Tony and Jay sprinkled in as table anchors, Henry Sr. saying grace, Henry Jr. looking out behind his father at the TV, the game about to begin.

There was light chatter through the early courses, a bit heavier as Jay and Tony began the second bottle of wine.

"You called yourselves . . . ?" Ruth began to repeat her question.

"Magnificent Bastards." Tony said proudly. "That's two-four . . . ah, Second Battalion, Fourth Marine Regiment. We were really a good unit."

"And that's where you learned to be a medic?"

"Oh! No." Tony turned to Linda, said, "IV?" She tapped her lips indicating she had a mouthful, nodded. "Kind of," Tony said. "I wasn't a medic but Doc So taught me how to start IVs and inject morphine. Stuff like that."

"Dr. So?" Henry Sr. asked. "Was he Chinese?"

Tony smiled, swallowed another gulp of wine. "No Sir. I don't know what his name was. We called him So because he was *so* neat and *so* fat."

Joanie giggled. Cindy got the giggles and couldn't stop, and it infected Lea and the two youngest girls received The Look from their father.

The conversation rocked back and forth and Cindy, Lea and Henry Jr. were dismissed from the table. Jay talked about the astronauts in orbit, about the upcoming moon shot; Linda told her parents about her financial aid package and its imminent approval. Tony smiled, glanced at Linda who began reexplaining her schedule to her mother.

"I graduate in December with my LPN. Then I move to Boston. That part's all set. . . . "

Tony felt wine confident, felt in-love confident. He turned to Jay who very seriously said to him, "Mr. Balliett—Dad—he helped me get a deferment, being that I'm married and I've got a critical job."

"Oh. What do you do?"

"I'm . . . Dad got me a job with Penn-York. I'm really just a clerk but he had them say I was handling their entire new computer system. I am learning it."

"Hm." Tony said. He heard Linda saying her classes would begin on January 6th and rotations two weeks later. To Jay Tony said, "I thought about going back to school too, but my cousin Jimmy's been sending me info on this new pacification program that's doing a lot of good. I might re-up to go back to Viet Nam and . . . "

Suddenly the table was quiet. Then Linda said softly, "Don't you dare."

And Tony smiled and said, "But then again . . . " and Ruth and Jay laughed. "Really," Tony continued, "there's word in the pipeline about drops coming down."

"Drops?" Norma asked.

"Early outs. I'm signed up until next August but there's talk, if you've been overseas, of four-to six-month drops. I could be discharged as early as February."

"And then," Henry asked, "what will you do?"

"I could go to school," Tony said. "On the GI Bill. I haven't really decided yet."

"I've got an idea," Ruth said. "Why don't you and Linda come and stay with Jay and me tonight. Then we can talk about your options and—"

"They can't stay at your apartment!" Henry Balliett interrupted. "You've only got the one bedroom."

Jay glanced up. Tentatively he said, "They can use the living room."

"They're not even engaged," Henry said.

Immediately Tony turned to Linda. "Would you marry me?" he asked.
"Sure." She answered.

"Sure!" he repeated and they both laughed.

"Humph!" Henry snorted. He rose, went to the TV, changed the channel and sat.

7

Mill Creek Falls, 4 September 1969: They had been up since five. Bobby had made coffee, Josh had eaten his first-of-the-day Milk-Bones. Grandpa was already out to his office in the big barn. Bobby and Josh strolled down the long drive to where a dented mailbox hung askew from a rusting steel post. Wapinski looked in. It was empty. He looked up at the sky. It was mostly clear. "C'mon, boy," Bobby called Josh. "We'll head on down toward Lutz's."

They meandered far down the road, Josh dashing into various fields, chasing birds or butterflies, Wapinski watching his dog, enjoying Josh's boundless enthusiasm but not concentrating on him, thinking alternately about options or not about anything but making up silly verses to tunes he'd known since childhood. He'd been offered a job selling cars at Lloyd's Autoland; Mr. Hartley had told him if he'd obtain a real estate license, he would take Bobby "under his wing"; and Grandpa had hinted that the farm was his if he'd farm it. Grandpa hadn't actually said that. What he'd said was, "Bobby, soil is a living tissue. It's the skin of the earth and as such it's very complex. It takes a special person to understand it. And still that person needs to work at it." "Um-hmm," Bobby had replied. "Well," Grandpa had said, "as long as you know."

They had reached the point on Mill Creek Road where the barren mounds and ridges had been rejuvenated by the big dollars of Adolph Lutz's horse-boarding ranch, where tons upon tons of fertilizers, natural and chemical, had turned hillside pastures vibrant green. In the field before him were two spotted grays. They looked up. Josh came scampering in from a foray to a distant field. Josh stopped at the three-board fence. He crouched, looked under at the horses. Selling cars, Bobby thought. Josh began barking. Bobby looked absently at him. After commanding an infantry company! Real estate? After planning a brigade-sized assault! He drew in a deep breath. Or farm, he thought. Then he whispered, "Josh, I gotta get outa here. What do you think?"

Josh glanced over, quickly looked back at the grays who had trotted closer. "I—" Bobby drew out the sound, "know what you're thinkin. But if I don't know what I want to be when I grow up, how can you think that?" He paused. Josh cocked his head. Pensively Bobby continued. "I do have faith. And patience. Faith and patience," he repeated to himself. Faith and patience in the pursuit of answers, in the pursuit of design excellence, he thought. It was a throw-back thought to his college days, to an engineering fundamentals class. I could go back to school, he thought. But not here. I could work in the trades. But not here. Build some decent houses instead of those wham-bam-thank-you-ma'am, don't-call-me-if-it-settles boxes they put up in Old New Town, or the slap-em-up-overnight boxes they're still putting up in New New Town. I could go back, become a designer. Maybe a city planner. But not here.

As they walked back to High Meadow, Wapinski thought of one more option—of reenlisting, of escaping by reenlisting—but it did not seem viable. He'd served his time. It was time to get on with his life.

Back at the drive Bobby pulled the morning's paper from the box. "Son of a bitch," he said. "Son of a bitch!" he shouted. "Ah . . . no offense Josh. Hot damn, look at this! Ho Chi Minh croaked!"

Bob Wapinski was now dating Red full-time. They talked, walked, made love. Seldom did he take her to anything fancier than the cinema in downtown Mill Creek Falls, though on Labor Day weekend they did go to an inn in Towanda. He had little money, no job, except that he labored around the farm and continued to refurbish the house. He had collected two unemployment checks but stopped going, saying, "I'd rather eat dirt than take their filthy handouts." Mostly he and Red spent weekend days hiking with Josh at High Meadow, and week nights, after Red got off work, lying in the back seat of the old Chevy, parked in the remotest corners of town.

Joanne had called several times in mid and late August and again in early September with the same message as before, that Montgomery McShane was going to press charges. "I'll take my chances," he'd told her. He knew there were no charges, no medical bills he'd be asked to pay. He had talked with the boy and Montgomery had apologized to Bob as much as Bob did to him, and he assured Bob that he was okay, no permanent damage. Joanne, however, continued pressing. "You might just as well shoot yourself," she'd told him. "You should have died in Viet Nam."

The weekend after Labor Day, two weeks before Jimmy Pellegrino returned, Wap, Red and Josh hiked the long path around High Meadow. The day was hot, without wind. They started at the house, followed the trail through the orchard, over the knoll, across the dam, over the rock crags. Bob never smelled fresh blood and entrails at the crags when Red was along, though he'd smelled it twice again when only Josh was with him. He never mentioned it to her. They followed the path to the fork where they usually continued to the right, around the pond, but this time they went left up into the woods, past the cabin Grandpa had built the first year he owned the farm. " 'Before he built a proper house,' is what Granma used to say," Bob said. They followed the trail up the side of the now dry streambed, listened to the birds, kissed. Red followed Bob over an old stone wall in the woods. "Granpa did this. At one time he'd cleared and cultivated this side. With these fields he had ninety acres planted. It's not a lot but it was a hell of a feat being that he did an awful lot of it by himself. A lot of it by hand." Bob led Red up the steep embankment and into the sugarbush where they made love in the cool shade of the maples.

It was pleasant sex but not passionate sex. To him it seemed as if she could not let go. He wasn't sure if it was *his* insecurities and *his* lack of direction that were affecting her. It seemed to him she had made love to him today solely to please him, even though she had no desire. It worried him.

For a while they didn't talk, didn't move. He thought of Red's aroma, then didn't want to think of her at all but of other concerns he wanted to share but couldn't. He rolled to his side. He looked at her tiny pink breasts, thought of Stacy, about to be married. And he imagined, wished, that somehow the entire time since he'd returned had been a test, a conspiracy designed to stretch to the extreme his true love for Stacy, that at any moment Red was going to say, "Ha. You blew it. We were just testing you to see if you would pass. You flunked." Except he wished he hadn't flunked. Had gone after Stacy.

Red was lying on her back, her hands on her stomach. She too was thinking divergent thoughts. In less than two weeks her fiancé would be home. In another she'd be the maid of honor at Stacy's wedding. She bit her lip, then said, "I got another letter from Jimmy."

"You told me."

"What am I going to tell him?"

"I don't know."

"I . . . I feel sad. Like I want to run away."

"Me too."

"I really love you." He rolled, kissed her. She continued. "I think I'm going to take the job in California."

"Oh. Hey, that's great. In January?"

"They want me there November first."

"November first? That's—that's only . . . "

"I know. But I've got to get away. I don't want to spend my life in Mill Creek Falls. I'm twenty-one. I want to live a little before I settle down."

"Umm." He didn't want to brood, didn't want her to brood, didn't want their fragile moods to plummet. At once he felt relieved, as if she were letting him go, and hurt, afraid to lose her.

"Will you write to me?" Red asked.

"Um-hmm. Will you write back?"

"Um-hmm. Could you, maybe, come out and visit?"

"Yeah. I could."

"Could you move out there?"

"Aw, Red." He sighed. "I don't know. I . . . maybe. You hit me with it pretty sudden. I didn't even know they'd made you a real offer."

"I start at ten thousand. That's nearly double what I make working for Daddy."

"That's great. That's really nice. Ten thousand!?"

"Isn't it exciting?"

She'd hugged him, kissed him, kissed him passionately as his hands explored her petite body, kissed him a dozen hello, welcome home, I-love-you-so-much kisses. Then she pushed away and announced, "I'm going to move to California." Jimmy Pellegrino stared at her but didn't respond. "I'm going to move in about five weeks," Red said as if she were challenging him, said as if she wanted a conflict to ease the message, wanted *him* to object, wanted *him* to be the cause.

"Cool," Jimmy said. "That'll be after my leave. You're comin with me this weekend. To Boston. Tony's getting married."

"Tony!"

"Yeah. He met some nurse chick who's in school in Boston. The whole family's going up."

"I can't," Red said. She was glad. A clean break. "Stacy's getting married. In New York. I'm her maid of honor."

"Stac—She marryin that . . . "

"Um-hmm. I'm going up on Wednesday. I thought you'd come. . . . "

"Naw. I gotta go up and see Tony. I'm goina be his best man. Ha! But California, huh?"

"Um-hmm."

"Where?"

"San Martin. My father has a friend out there. He offered me a job."

"Hey, okay!" Jimmy said. He put his hands on her shoulders again, pulled her close. She dropped her head. He kissed her hair.

She held him, not with passion, with control. "Jimmy, we need to talk." He rocked back a few inches. She took her hands from his side, with her right she removed the engagement ring he'd given her. "Jimmy, I can't do this if you're going back there again."

"Why?" He was calm.

"I just can't," she said. Her eyes began to tear.

"What if I don't go back?" Jimmy said.

That stunned her. For a moment she said nothing. Then she whispered, "Your letters said you were going back for a third tour."

"Yeah, but what if I don't?"

"I . . . " Again she couldn't answer.

"Come on. What is it?" Now Jimmy stood back. "What if I stay?" His voice was hard.

"I . . . you . . . you don't fill my needs anymore." Red said. "And . . . I've met someone." She did not look at Jimmy. "I've met someone else who fills my needs."

"Needs? What needs?" His words were fast, his tone had gone from calm to hard to angry.

"Well, to start with, I need someone who's here."

"Damn it! I just asked you what if I didn't go back?" Now he turned, stepped away. Then he stepped back. "What someone?!"

"I wrote you . . . "

"You mean this guy that you're just buddies with?!"

"Yes."

"I knew it. I knew it the first time you wrote that!"

"That's what you said in your letter, but it wasn't like that."

"Yeah."

"Really." She was crying now, looking at him, beseeching him with her tears, angry at him for not believing her. "Really," She said again. "Maybe if you'd trusted me I would have felt. . . . "

"Oh, my fault, right?!"

"If you'd trusted me I would have stayed true. But you immediately thought I was cheating . . . "

"You're being just like Stacy!"

"You know it hurts to be accused of—like Stacy?!"

"Yeah. Like when she was foolin around on that Airborne guy."

"Oh damn! It is that Airborne guy."

"What is?"

"Bobby is. That's who I'm seeing. Stacy's old boyfriend."

Bobby climbed the loft ladder, crossed the darkened wood floor with its remnant scattering of straw left from a time when the farm was active. His eyes adjusted as he approached the door, and the heavy beams and braces of the simple structure emerged as if he'd walked into a hollow body supported by an old but still strong skeleton. Grandpa had told him to go there, to spend the day, because he didn't want Bobby moping around underfoot like he'd moped all day Wednesday, and Thursday, and Friday. "Go on up," he'd said. "I left some things out. Some things a yours. And I cleared out a drawer too. That'll be yours. When you're done, file your things in the drawer and turn the lights out. You need anything at Morris'?"

"No."

"Good. I'll take Josh with me. He can't climb the ladder yet."

Dutifully Bobby had crossed the yard, opened the big door, walked by the vacant stalls, the long feeding trough, the center gutter for washing the place down, to the far end where the ladder was. He'd brought his AWOL bag, his records, a dozen magazines he'd kept, a hundred articles he'd cut from the newspaper but hadn't read beyond the first paragraphs.

He put his hand on the latch to Grandpa's barn-loft office, hesitated. It had been years since he'd been inside, years since he'd helped his grandfather raise the seven-sectioned bay window to the framed opening, pulling so eagerly on the line that ran through the pulley blocks, one on the superstructure Grandpa had built on the roof, one through the bindings that Grandpa had insisted Bobby tie about the window without Pewel watching or checking but just saying, "You're fifteen. You know how to do it." And he had raised the window alone, afraid his knots would fail or that the rope would slip through his hands, raised it easily until Grandpa had reached out and as simply as pulling in a child's balloon, pulled the window into the opening, put precut dowels through each side into the predrilled holes in the side posts, opened the center window, and untied the line.

Bobby opened the door, felt for the switch, turned on the overheads. The room glowed warm without shadow, the soft luster of oiled pine absorbing any hint of glare. He stood. A thermal drape had been pulled across the bay window beneath which a large pine desk had been built. Bobby closed the door, stepped to the desk, dropped his AWOL bag on the floor, his armload of papers on the desk. He lifted the hem of the curtain. The morning sun was rising behind the barn. Before him was the pond. He raised the hem further. Across the pond he could see the crags and the woods. To the left were the knoll, the cliff, and the orchard. To the right was the high meadow, fallow now. Above, surrounding the woods, the meadow, and the barn were the ridges, which seemed to hold and to protect everything within their expanding, descending V. Bobby dropped the drape. He sat. He squeezed his eyes shut, shuddered, opened them.

Before him was an old manila envelope that he had stolen when he was thirteen, taken from his mother's attic unknown to her then and probably to this day, had taken and run to his grandfather leaving Miriam to think he had run away. Grandpa had kept his secret, had kept the letters safe for ten years. The letters were the old man's tie to his son as much as the boy's tie to his father. Yet they'd sat, deteriorating, unread for ten years by either grandfather or grandson. They were love letters written by a man they both loved, to a woman neither loved but both accepted exactly as they accepted the physical presence of the letters, as a tie, a bind to a man who had deserted them, a man to whom neither held an iota of hate nor an ounce of grudge.

Grandpa had taken the envelope from the file drawer, had laid it on the big, oiled pine desk. With it he'd laid two file folders, one from Paul Wapinski's soldiering time in the Pacific, one from Bobby Wapinski's time in Viet Nam. Pewel had laid them side by side, his obsession with his family, driven, even back in the early '40s before Paul returned to abandon them, by Pewel's fear that he would never see his son again, driven, heightened for his grandson, because after Paul returned he disappeared and the same might be happening with Bob—disappearing, abandoning the man who had toiled for half a century to establish a home to which his son and grandson might return, might have a base upon which to build their lives.

Bobby did not immediately turn his attention to the manila envelope or to the files. He'd brought his own material and he'd brought Tyrone Blackwell's letter, which he'd begun reading in the house but which had overwhelmed him in the first few sentences. He had stopped abruptly, refolded the pages, returned them to the envelope addressed by hand, marked in the corner FREE meaning it had been mailed from Viet Nam.

He pushed the folders and the manila envelope to one corner, Blackwell's letter and his recent news clippings to the other, plopped the material from the AWOL bag in the center. That, he decided, would be the easiest way to begin.

He looked down at the desk, thought down through the floor to two stories below where his wrecked Mustang sat on blocks. He sorted pages and magazines, placing them in stacks, chronologically, the oldest on top. "What the hell am I goina do with that car?" he muttered. He turned to look for Josh but Josh had gone with Grandpa. He opened the top magazine, the *Newsweek* he'd begun reading on his journey home. "The Battle of Ap Bia Mountain," the headline said. And the photo and cutline, "Hamburger Hill: Was the Slaughter Really Necessary?" Immediately his eyes found the line about the Nixon administration, which "sought . . . to disclaim responsibility" and immediately Bobby Wapinski tensed. "Fuck em," he muttered. "They just don't fuckin—" He sat back. Never let em get to your mind, Wap. Never let em get to your mind, cause they just don't fuckin understand.

He leafed through the articles he'd read months earlier, turned to an article on South Viet Nam's president, Nguyen Van Thieu. On a trip to South Korea, the magazine reported, Thieu "was hailed as a great anti-Communist Asian leader." The article went on about the flap between Nixon and Thieu over diplomatic policies and negotiation strategies.

> ... Mr. Nixon might just agree to Communist demands for a provisional coalition government. . . . But in his statement in Seoul, Thieu made it plain that he would have nothing to do with such a proposal"

Agree! Wapinski shook his head. Agree to a coalition government with the communists! It'd be suicide. At the back of the magazine there was a column by Stewart Alsop titled "No 'Disguised Defeat'?"

> ... Nixon . . . , "A great nation that fails to meet a great challenge ceases to be a great nation." . . . the United States could not and would not accept a "disguised defeat" in Vietnam. . . .
> ... skeptic was President Thieu . . . warning . . . against a "false peace"—precisely because he was deathly afraid that President Nixon might elect to settle the war in Vietnam at the expense of the Saigon government. . . .
> ... The military and political situation in South Vietnam really is much better—the Communist wolf is really further from the door. . . . The Saigon government now controls more people than since the Diem days; the Communist "infrastructure" shows real signs of unraveling in some areas; the Viet Cong is having severe recruiting and disciplinary problems. But because there had been so much false optimism in the past, officials and reporters are chary of emphasizing these facts, for fear of being laughed at. . . .

They'll make you doubt your own mind. Hmm, Wapinski thought. Not this guy. He was enjoying this guy Alsop, thought Alsop's got his shit together, got it rolled in a tight little ball.

> ... North Vietnamese have hinted, and the Russians have more than hinted, that there should be no great problem about a mutual military withdrawal from South Vietnam, if only the political problem can be sensibly settled, on the basis of point five of the Viet Cong's ten-point program.

What ten-point program? Was I that immersed in what I was doing there not even to know about the proposal?

> Point Five proposes that "the political forces . . . that stand for peace . . . enter into talks to set up a provisional coalition government . . . [then] hold free and democratic general elections. . . .
> What the Communist side is proposing, of course, is a Popular Front government, precisely patterned on the popular fronts established under Soviet sponsorship after World War II, as a prelude to total Communist control.

Wapinski skimmed down, thought back to "administration . . . sought . . . to disclaim responsibility." "Shit," he whispered under his breath. "Never let em . . . "

> . . . This three stage process, from seemingly genuine coalition to the final . . . monolithic Communist control, is unquestionably what Moscow and Hanoi intend for South Vietnam. . . . But if the Communists are smart enough—which they shows signs of being—to offer a sufficiently thick disguise, President Nixon . . . under enormously heavy pressure may accept the defeat, as President Thieu is very well aware. . . .
>
> Senate . . . murmurs are being heard to the effect that only the "corrupt and unsavory" Saigon government stands in the way of a settlement and an end to the killing.

Wapinski's mind buzzed. He was calm and tense simultaneously, precombat relaxed. This was a completely different dimension to Southeast Asia than he had dealt with during his year.

He opened the next magazine. There was a Canadian whiskey ad that had, in the backdrop, a beautiful woman with short brunette hair, standing, looking out over a mountain lake. She wore a two-piece bathing suit and a lustrous light blue, three-quarter-length jacket. Her legs were perfect. He tried to flip by but he couldn't turn the page. Married, he thought. He checked his watch. In a few hours she'll be married. And Red'll be there too . . . to help cement it.

His mouth was dry. His head felt as if it were filling with concrete. Again he looked at the picture. The girl was looking out, across the water, her body turned half to the camera, her profile showing just the tip of her nose and the contour of her cheek. He analyzed the photo attempting to determine if indeed the image was Stacy's. One moment he was certain it was, the next he felt sure the ass was not round enough, then again with the pose, the taut muscles, the shoulders pulled back . . . the entire image not two inches high behind an eight-inch bottle of Canadian whiskey . . . "Geez, man!" He sat back. "What the hell are you doin?" Again he checked his watch. "What the hell are you doin with Red?"

He pushed on through the magazine, reading article after article— Nixon's troop withdrawals, reduction in force, Viet Namization, ARVNs taking over in the Delta, defoliants reduce land to moonscape—yet not retaining even a semblance of their content. He rose, walked to Grandpa's drawing table, looked at the old man's sketch of a school bus fitted with Grandpa's design for nylon-plastic "kid-catchers"—two-piece shields that mounted on the frame and body at the rear wheels, enclosing the wheels and curving in under the bus, designed like an old-time train's cow-catcher, to deflect an animal or a child. Yeah, Bobby thought, why not.

Bobby returned to the magazines. The September 15th *Newsweek* had five pages called "The War in Vietnam," including a column by Kenneth Crawford entitled "Kindly Uncle Ho." Crawford concluded:

> What effects Ho's death will have on the tactics and strategy of his successors is unpredictable. . . . There will be a vacuum. For Uncle Ho, like Uncle Joe (Stalin), was a genius—an evil genius by democratic lights. Both Marxians in their ideology but throwbacks to Genghis Khan in their methodology.

Wapinski placed the magazines in the empty file drawer Grandpa had left him. Faith and patience, he told himself. Faith, patient inquiry and hard work. Keep on, keepin on. For an hour he read, sorted, and filed news clippings, forcing a patience that he did not feel, forcing a focus that would not come. He thought of Red, of her eyes and smile and laugh and of how, at times, she could say exactly the right thing. Still he did not focus on her. He turned to Blackwell's letter.

Dear Captain Wapinski,
    You remember me. I was wounded on Dong Ap Bia when you were in command and now they're court-martialing me. Sir, you've got to remember me and help me. You visited me at the evac hospital at Evans before you left for the World. I was wounded in the buttocks and back by friendly fire on one of the last assaults up that bad motherfuckin hill. I did whatever you ordered. I was a good troop. I was up there when the monsoon hit and we got washed off that bad fucker, and I was the first guy back up there looking for those guys we lost. I know you remember that cause you were right there, too, like you was a regular grunt and not a replacement commander from the rear. I know you remember me because we were from the same area back in the World. I come from just outside Wilkes-Barre, from Coal Hill. The rear is where I got in all my trouble and it's like nothing I did out in the A Shau means anything cause in the rear they don't put any merit on what we done in the boonies. I got two Purple Hearts. I got an ARCOM, the Air Medal and my CIB which no one can take from me. And I should have a Bronze or maybe even a Silver Star but these motherfuckers in the rear are holding up the paperwork cause I got charged with possession of dope and insubordination to an officer—Major Krausewitz, the assistant adjutant. That son of a bitch locked'n'loaded on me in the messhall in front of about a hundred guys. I was unarmed. I pulled guard three nights straight and that fucker wanted me back in the boonies that minute. I didn't even have my ruck packed or any ammo and he wasn't going to give me time. I said, No Way, Sir! I'm not going. I wasn't even armed and he stood there with that 16 on his shoulder aiming in on my face and telling me to get up and move or he'd grease me on the spot. My wounds from Hamburger weren't even fully healed. Sir, he done this because I'm Black and because I was doing some weed when I was con-vo-

less-ing but you know I never did any in the boonies or even on guard like some of these white REMFs.

Sir, I need your help. I need you to write them a letter attesting to what kind of soldier I was. Captain Billings was killed on Dong Ap Bia otherwise I know he'd do it because he and I were really close. Sir, if you don't write, they're going to send me to LBJ (Long Binh Jail), and make me do hard time. I need your letter right away, Captain Wapinski. Other brothers that served under you said you'd do it because you were "an up front boonie rat" when you were in the bush. Thank you, Sir, for helping me. Anything you send to them, send me a copy too or they'll say they never got it.

> Your Brother-in-Arms,
> Tyrone Blackwell, Pvt 1

Wapinski reread the letter. He remembered Blackwell, remembered his anger after he was wounded, but he wasn't certain if he could recall Blackwell in the field. He pinched his lower lip, attempted to force upon an image of Dong Ap Bia the image of a black soldier he'd commanded for so short a period. Blackwell, he thought. "Because I'm black," he thought. It struck Wapinski as strange, eerie, that of all the men he'd known in Viet Nam, a significant percentage, perhaps one in six, were black. Yet here in Mill Creek Falls, with its equally mixed population, he did not truly know a black man or woman except for Johnnie Johnson, who owned the auto salvage yard behind Lloyd's Autoland, had not associated with any Mill Creek blacks since high school. He seldom even saw any black men or women or children, as if they were physically or legally segregated to the one section of town in which he himself had no business.

Blackwell . . . Bro Black from the Sugar-shack. Yeah. Maybe. Maybe that was Tyrone. He looked at the desk. There was an entire file of clippings on the 101st Airborne from '68 to '69; there was the old file with clippings from '42 to '45, and there was the envelope.

He checked his watch. She's married, he thought. Again his thoughts scattered. Again he forced himself to concentrate. He jotted a few notes on his own experiences in Viet Nam that he thought he might use in the letters he intended to send about Blackwell. It felt good. He thought of L-T Thompson telling him it had gotten into his blood and he realized that Thompson was probably right.

The notes became pages. For hours Bobby Wapinski lost himself in this writing, this cryptic memoir. Finally he sat back, his pen having outraced his thoughts and drained his mind. Yet he knew, felt, that it was only the beginning.

Grandpa returned. Bobby heard the old Chevy roll slowly into the yard. Josh yipped in search of him but he did not move. The thermal curtain remained closed. Wapinski shifted. He skimmed the file Grandpa had collected on the 101st. There were several stories on him, Robert J.

Wapinski; award for heroism in ground combat, promotion to captain, award for ... Bobby did not read the stories. He turned to the file from World War II, leafing gently through the old, fragile clippings looking for pictures of his father. There was one, a clean and happy-looking young man, from the time Paul Wapinski shipped out. Another was a one-column story from the now defunct *Mill Creek Telegram* headed

WAPINSKI GETS

HEROISM AWARD

Bobby ached to read the words but his eyes filled and his mind clouded. Somehow, to read the two files, to juxtapose father and self, would be a competition. A foreboding hit him. He was afraid ... afraid of what? He shoved the file away. Mechanically he grabbed the large manila envelope. His hands operated beyond his mind's control. Robotically they dumped the contents before him. Bobby pinched his lower lip, pulled it. He glanced at the pages he'd just written as if they were foreign. The thought of Blackwell flashed like heat lightning, then died in the storm clouds that rose from the desk. Immediately he realized there were more letters than he'd seen ten years earlier.

For two weeks Bobby Wapinski dared not set foot in the big barn. And he barely talked to Red. They dated, they made love, but they had little to exchange. Red moaned constantly about paperwork, about "Daddy dumping all this typing on me so I can't get ready. I can't wait to go." At times he thought, I can't wait for you to go. Other times he felt he was being abandoned, left behind not simply by Red but by his own inability to find a direction. And he was angry, angry at Red, for not telling him about Stacy's wedding even though he did not ask—for not even mentioning it except to say once, quickly, "That guy Jerry, he's a real wimp."

The October day was clear, cool. Bobby was in the yard throwing a stick for Josh, who reluctantly retrieved it twice but on the third toss grabbed it, plopped down six steps from Bobby, and gnawed as if to say that game's for dumb dogs. Bobby was laughing at him when he heard the motorcycle. The bike was loud, coming fast up Mill Creek Road, racing, shifting, recklessly speeding. He stepped closer to the barn, felt the hairs on his neck rise, shook it off, stared down toward the road. Josh bounded up, tossed the stick into the air, caught it as it hit the ground, stared at Bobby as if to say, Hey, play with me. I'm ready again.

Wapinski ignored him. He could see the motorcyclist sliding the corners so recklessly that Bobby was thinking of emergency medical procedures he'd perform after calling in a dust-off, an ambulance. The noise changed, the cyclist downshifted as he neared the Wapinski driveway. He turned in, accelerated up the first incline actually getting the big bike airborne at the crest, touching down, downshifting into the low ess then accelerating again up the hill to the house. He braked hard, locked the rear wheel, the back end sliding and bumping, kicking up gravel. Then he revved the engine in neutral and killed it as it idled back—a clean shut-off.

Wapinski came from behind the house. Josh ran up, skidded, barked. Wap did not recognize the rider, though he saw the man was not big, was clean-cut. "Wapinski," the rider called.

"Yeah," Bobby answered.

"Bob Wapinski?"

"Yeah."

"I just wanted to meet my jody."

"What?"

"What's that up there?" Jimmy Pellegrino pointed to a rumpled black sphere tacked to the barn wall. He kicked down the stand, got off the bike.

"That's an old bladder ball."

"Say again."

"A bladder ball. A pig's bladder. When I was a kid my grandfather'd take the pigs' bladders and blow em up. We'd use em as balls."

"Neat. I'd like to learn how. We've set up two pig farms in the provinces and that'd be great to show the kids."

"What provinces?"

"Quang Tri. Thua Thien."

"You Pellegrino?"

"Roger that."

"Hey, I'm—"

"Don't say it. You don't gotta."

"Maybe I do."

"Naw. Ferget it. I was up in Boston with my cousin. Met a few ladies up there. And anyway, I'm goin back to show my kids how to make bladder balls." He chuckled. They were now only a few feet apart. Josh sniffed at Jimmy's leg. Jimmy bent, let Josh sniff the back of his hand, then slowly reached back and scratched Josh's head.

"Third time, huh?"

"Third time's a charm." Jimmy continued caressing Josh.

"I keep thinkin about goin back. Reenlisting and going back."

"Place changes, Man. Every tour. Wouldn't be the same."

"Yeah. That's . . ." Wapinski did not finish the sentence. Seeing Pellegrino made him nauseated—not because of Pellegrino but because of himself, because of what he'd done. Go back, he thought. Fuck it. End this shit. It'd be an honorable means of suicide. "Hey, really, I'm—"

"I'm serious, Man. Don't say it. You don't gotta say it. I played, I lost. I just came up to say somethin."

"Come in for a beer?"

"Naw." Jimmy shook his head. He remounted the Harley. "I just wanted to say, you know, take good care of her."

Wap nodded. "Yeah. Roger."

"Really. I mean it. I got other things that need doin."

"You stay low."

"Ha! Hey, just one more thing, Man. Never let em get to your mind." He kick-started the Harley, rocked it forward collapsing the stand, flashed Wapinski the two-fingered V peace sign, turned slowly then roared off.

Wapinski watched him go, watched the bike and rider get airborne at the crest, accelerate out onto the road, upshift crazily, probably hitting eighty-five descending Mill Creek Road, out of sight, out of earshot.

Bobby pushed his hand through his hair. He had stolen that man's girl. He, a soldier, doing it to a fellow combat brother. It was impossible to digest, to assimilate. Four months earlier he would have risked his life for Pellegrino. That was the commitment, the promise, of brothers-in-arms. Now he was fucking Pellegrino's girl. He felt sick. And he felt envious of Pellegrino still being a part of it, a part of the cause. And Red . . . it was as if she had proven to him that she was like all the women he'd ever known—every one of them except his grandmother.

8

The dream returned. He shifted. Josh lay against his legs. There was mud. Mud everywhere—slick, yet sticky. Above, in rain-sky, came two double-rotored Chinooks, huge cargo helicopters. But not normal Chinooks. The ships' bodies were vertical, not horizontal, and the overlapping rotors were one on each end making the machine look like a giant spool. One passed over. He hunkered down, hugged the mud, waiting in ambush to look up the trail, the road, across to the stone wall. The second chopper passed. The rotor wash ripped the brush, whipped up the debris of previously exploded trees. He covered his head. In the wake of the second passing was a single disk of whirling light, a nebula spinning low toward the ground, searching. It found him. Lifted him. Exposed him. Thud! Hit! It began carrying him away. His face contorted. He tried to scream but words choked in his throat. The forces on his body were tremendous, racking him, twisting him, pulling him apart. He tensed, brought his knees to his chest, grasped his arms over his legs. He brought all his energy to bear on his cry. Still it came garbled.

"Pleeeazzz..." He screamed, sounding in his own ears as if he were yelling into a huge fan. "Pleeeazzz. Help us."

Then cool. The small room. The masked people. "Next!" The voice urgent. "Next. No. Not him." *Pleeeazzz*. The smell of fresh blood, of freshly lacerated entrails. There, on the slab below him, the body, brains flowing out. *I'm ... I'm ... I'm still alive. I'm alive ... Oh, damn you ...* The body convulsed as the masked figure probed the brain. Back-arch spasm. Tears. *Pleeeazzz* "Not him! Damn you." *pleeazz* "Put him ..." *don't* "in the corner and ..." *leave* "let him ..." *me* "... cool."

They had not had sex in the eight days since Jimmy's visit. Red passed off Bobby's somber moods to her leaving, to her inattentiveness toward him as she bustled around preparing for the move. Then it occurred to her that it was over, that he'd made up his mind to remain on the farm but hadn't the courage to tell her. He hadn't told her of Jimmy's visit but she'd heard through a friend of Jimmy's sister, Annalisa, that they— her two men—had met and had agreed upon the *swap*. The SWAP! She did not mention it to him but it angered her that "her two men" felt they could trade her as if she were a baseball mitt or whatever men traded when they traded. Still she wanted him, wanted him to come to California, to help her, be with her.

They climbed the back trail, crossed the crags, meandered past the little shack, then through the woods over the ridge and into the sugar-bush. "I'm going to miss our walks," Red said. Bobby only grunted, still she felt pleased she'd said it. Under her jacket, under her wool shirt, she wore a silk camisole and below her corduroy pants were her laciest pant-ies. The lingerie felt smooth and comfortable and it made her feel con-fident—sex or no sex—just to have it on. "I'm going to miss the smell of this place as much as the beauty."

"Yeah," Bobby said. "Me too. But we'll come back to visit my grand-father."

"He'll be all right, won't he?"

"Yeah. He's lived here, you know, without anybody."

"I'll miss him, too," Red said. She turned and looked into Bobby's eyes expecting to see hardness, withdrawn-ness, but instead saw ques-tioning, hurt, warmth.

"There's a place I haven't shown you before," he said. "It's my private place where no one goes but I'd like to show it to you."

"Really?"

"Uh-huh. That's why I wanted to leave Josh in your car. He can't make the climb. But—" Bobby laughed, "maybe you can."

"I bet I can," Red said surely.

"Come on, then." Bobby led Red to the far edge of the sugarbush, through a narrow stand of mixed scrub pines, ash and beech, over thirty feet of bare rock, to the cliff edge of the gap. "Be careful."

"Oh! This is pretty! I didn't know ..."

"Ssshh." He put his finger to his lips. His eyes lit with excitement. "We don't talk at the gap." Before them was a three-story-deep chasm eighty to one hundred feet wide. The sides were vertical as if God had descended with a giant dado blade that he'd run semicircularly through the Endless Mountains for a mile, isolating one island of old forest.

"Oh, Bobby," Red whispered, "it's beautiful."

"It's only the start. Wait till we get there." He indicated the far side.

"How?"

"Follow me." He sat, dropped his feet over the cliff edge.

"Ah . . . " Red backed a few steps away. It flashed through her mind that this was a lover's leap, that Bobby would grasp her legs and jump.

"It's like a ladder. I found it when I was eight."

"Found what?" She approached cautiously.

"It's the only way down without ropes. I think the Lenape must have carved it hundreds of years ago." Bob cleaned several handhold crevices on the upper lip, then rolled and slipped his waist over the edge until his toes found the first indentation.

"I'm not going down there." The words flew from Red's mouth.

"It's easy. I just told you I did it when I was eight. It's a ladder."

"I don't like ladders."

"I'll be under you. I'll put your feet in the holes."

"Oh God!"

"C'mon. I want you to see the Indian ring."

"You mean we've got to go up . . . "

"I found the ladder there, too. Come on. It's safer than driving across country."

Slowly they descended the cliff, Bobby guiding Red's feet. The floor of the gap was rock ledge. Scattered trees were trying to survive in debris pockets of humus and till. In spots, water was trapped in stagnant puddles that supported toads, newts, and insects. They crossed quickly then climbed the vertical wall of the far side and entered the last of the virgin eastern hemlock forest. In less than one hundred yards they hit the old Lenape trail, an eighteen-inch-wide track worn a foot deep into the forest floor by generations of moccasined travelers, a small section still well preserved after 500 years, even after more than a century of abuse to the surrounding land. In his youth Bob had shown his grandfather the ladders and the two had silently walked the trail on dozens of Sunday mornings. It had always struck awe into him, the stillness, the trees towering to 150 feet. It still did. But now, Red, exhilarated by the climbs, shifted to high-chatter mode.

"Ssshh," Bobby hissed.

"But this is amazing. Amazing. I'm going to really miss this. I'm still not sure if I should drive or if I should sell my Vee-doub and fly. What do you think?"

"Red, we're in a cathedral. You've got to keep your voice down."

"But Bobby, this is important. We keep acting like I'm not going. I'm going in eight days! I love this place. Really! But we've got to talk. I . . . you've . . . we . . . " She chattered nonstop as they hiked. He tuned her out. The trail twisted, turned, stayed almost perfectly level as it meandered between hills and gorges. At one point they passed the small spur that led to the Indian fire ring. Finally they circled out toward the back of the north ridge behind the upper meadow. There the trail, the hemlocks, stopped. Again there was the gap, but here not so deep, not so steep. The virgin forest on the other side had been cut on the last logging day some fifty years earlier.

They picked up a new path just north of the ridge. Bobby led the still-gabbing Red down the east arm, across the ridge toward the small family cemetery. "If you come out," Red was saying, "maybe you could drive the Vee-doub for me and I could fly. That'd work for us both."

Bob was disgusted. He had been looking for a cleansing ritual, a near-religious experience like he'd had the first time he found the Indian trail, a communion with the past and with the land that he and Red could share. But the chattering! He was offended. He had taken her to his most sacred site and she'd treated it like McDonald's. Again he was quiet, sullen, unresponsive. Red scampered to keep up, yakked to fill the space of his silence. Quietly Bobby parted the orderly pine break and walked into the cemetery. His grandfather was there, kneeling before his grandmother's stone, planting flowers. He looked up, smiled an awkward smile, looked back down, wiped his eyes. Again he looked up, this time with a real smile.

"Well," he said to Bobby, "are you gonna make that little lady drive that little car out or not? She must a asked you a dozen times. Answer her, won't ya?"

"I'm . . . I haven't yet decided if I'm going anyplace, Granpa." He turned. Red was behind, silent. "You drive it out, okay? Or sell it. Get something better."

Late that night they made frantic love, and for the first time in weeks, as Bobby held her, as he studied her face, her eyes, he felt in love with Bea Hollands. Over the next week they made love every night, desperate, clinging love, despite all his earlier trepidations. Then on the 31st, the eve of Red's departure, Bobby did something he had not anticipated. For three years he'd worn a silver Jumping Mary medallion, a portrait of the Virgin Mary with a parachute behind her, on a string about his neck. He was not that religious but he'd gotten the medal the day he'd earned his jump wings and had seldom removed it. He'd intended giving it to Stacy. Then, after the first time with Red, he'd decided to give it to her, but he'd held out, intending the gift for a special occasion. He had intended giving it to her at dinner earlier that evening but had decided to wait until they were in bed. After loving he decided to wait until just before she left. And when she left he decided against giving it away at all.

* * *

Turmoil. Constant, unrelenting turmoil. The morning Red left, Bobby and Josh walked the trail around the pond. While holding Josh close, Bobby cried. Whether he cried for Red or for himself he did not know, or if it was because one more person had left his life. He felt miserable at the crags, nauseated at the old shack, despondent in the high meadow. By the time he'd worked his way to the big barn he was cried out. By evening he was relieved. Within a day he was happy, within two, elated to be free, to have a thousand options open.

On the evening of the third of November 1969 he sat down before the television set in the living room of the old farmhouse and he and Grandpa watched Richard Nixon deliver to the American people his first major policy speech on Viet Nam. In the speech the president ruled out a quick withdrawal; pledged eventual withdrawal of all U.S. combat troops; emphasized Viet Namization; and stated that the U.S. would respond with strong measures if Hanoi increased battlefield activity.

"What do you think of that?" Pewel Wapinski asked his grandson at the network break.

"I don't know," Bobby said.

"Well, ha! I don't know either but then I never been there."

"Sometimes I feel like I've never been there, either. Like he's talking about a different place than the place I knew. Like they all are."

"You still angry over that 'not take responsibility' thing?"

"Yeah."

"Sounded pretty responsible to me tonight."

"Sounded good. But will he follow through? Or next time the NVA attack in force and some battalion stops em, is he going to say, 'Hey, that's not my responsibility'?"

"Eh? Let's see what these commentators have to say." Again they turned their attention to the television. The lead-in to the commentary was followed by another set of commercials, then a recapitulation of a story from earlier in the day about the South Viet Namese treatment of captured enemy soldiers—including the stabbing of a POW.

"Geez!" Bobby snapped.

The comments were mixed. Senators J. William Fulbright of Arkansas and Mike Mansfield of Montana were irate. They accused Nixon of adopting the policies of the Johnson Administration and said they would sponsor Senate hearings "to educate" the American people "to the real facts of the war." Only a brief mention was made of the NVA and VC shelling of forty-five bases and towns in South Viet Nam and their launching of a series of attacks on outposts along the Cambodian border.

"I can't watch this." Bobby stood. "Let's see what the papers say tomorrow. They tend to make more sense."

"Yep. Course this is easier," Grandpa said.

"Yep," Bobby echoed him. "Course, like you taught me, the easiest way usually isn't the right way."

"Yep," Grandpa said. He rose and turned the set off. "Glad you was listening."

On the eighth, the day Red arrived in California, Bobby turned to the recent newspapers he'd stacked but hadn't read. The stories irritated him. Gallup polls showed 77 percent of those who had heard Nixon's speech approved of his planned de-escalation. Only 6 percent were opposed. President Thieu of South Viet Nam hailed the speech as important, and Nixon, clutching a stack of telegrams, claimed the support of the Great Silent Majority. But Fulbright and Mansfield, along with a growing number of senators and representatives, denounced the president's plan—Fulbright stating that Mr. Nixon has "taken full as his own the Johnson war, based on [the] fundamental error" that the war was being fought against an international communist conspiracy. A coalition of antiwar groups was planning a massive march on Washington for the fifteenth.

Wapinski could feel the divisiveness, the polarization of the anti- and pro-war elements digging in for battle, but he could not cope with the feeling. Though he read the lines he did not fully absorb the details or the implications. Nor did he project between the lines using information he possessed as an ex-infantry captain.

On the eleventh, a letter:

My dearest Bob,

There was no doubt in my mind that I would miss you but I didn't realize just how much. As soon as I find someplace to settle I'm going to start the greatest public relations campaign San Martin has ever seen in hopes of luring you away from your grandfather and High Meadow and to me.

I'm rooming with another girl from work and her boyfriend and his sister. You won't believe how much they get for rent here. Timmy jokes that I've joined his harem and that he needed a redhead. Where I work the people are nice too, even if the job isn't exciting. But I think there is great room for promotion and growth. The man I work for is a real businessman and he runs a tight ship. I'm learning a lot and actually used my shorthand for the first time since high school. I miss Mill Creek Falls sometimes. There's 50 times the construction going on here. Things are hopping all around. Why don't you come, even if it's just for a visit.

Please come. It's raining now. They say this is the rainy season, but it's not as bad as winter back there. If you'll come and help me get out of these doldrums I'll let you play with me. Oh, I don't believe I wrote it like that. I think I'm a little homesick but mostly I miss you.

If this job doesn't pick up, I might look for another one. I told Suzie that I was getting $10,000 to start and she said, "How come you started at less than everybody else?"

Did I ever tell you it excites me when a guy talks dirty?

Love you a whole bunch,
Red

For several days Bob Wapinski savored the letter. It tickled him every time he read her sexual references. He continued rising early, watching the sunrise, walking the woods with Josh. The house was in presentable shape. There were major repairs needed, new roof, new furnace, updated wiring and plumbing. The long drive needed grading. The high meadow could be turned, planted with winter wheat. But there were problems with all those projects. Roof, furnace, wiring, plumbing, all were adequate, and to upgrade them was to make a commitment. Grandpa spent most of his time in the barn office, so it mattered little to him what happened to the house. If his grandfather had asked, Bob would immediately have set to task but the only thing the old man requested was that Bob split and stack firewood for the small potbellied stove in the barn office. Bob took the tractor and wagon up the overgrown road through the high meadow to the sugarbush, pruned the trees and cleared the deadfall. In three days he had three cords worth of branches, logs and trunks stacked near the barn, all needing to be reduced to a foot long and no more than four inches in diameter. All the while he thought about Red and her letter. At night he worked on his car, finally pulling the engine, dismantling the bottom end to assess the damage, disassembling the axles and drive train.

Suddenly a place called My Lai was in the news. First in a few newspapers, then on the TV evening reports. Policy was no longer debated, no longer newsworthy, only atrocities.

Red wrote again.

Bob, you're such an idealist. I love that in you. This is a great place for an idealist. I've been exploring the hill right behind the house. I can hardly believe I'm so winded. My goal is to get my legs back in shape before you get here. I hope that leaves me only a few weeks.

The hills are beautiful. I've already found five places for picnics and two of them are so secluded we could do anything. Even in broad daylight! I can hardly wait for you to get here. I hope I can live up to your ideal. And I hope you get here before the rains *really* start.

The job market here is really good. I know you'll be able to get a job. With your background there's no telling how much money you could make. It'll be so rewarding being with you again.

Suzie and Tim are thinking of moving to LA. We could keep this house but it's a wreck. The rent's only $325 and it has a large yard and three bedrooms. Suzie wants to leave her cats. I could say I'd take the house and then we could have Josh come and frighten the cats away. If Josh comes it'll either cost more or take longer to find a nice place. I miss you so much I think about you touching me all the time.

Red

Soon, he thought. He thought about her legs, about her thighs, about her delicate feet. He thought about "Tim" who he did not know, about "Tim's Harem," about her meeting others at work. And Bobby asked himself, what if she finds someone else? If I do go . . . I can't offer her much . . . Do I have the right to ask her to wait? Could I really leave Granpa? In his room he wrote a letter.

To the Loveliest Red in the World,

I have been keeping quite busy since your departure, trying to keep from reminiscing. Keeping busy helps little. Images of pretty curls getting tangled in the car door handle are driving me crazy. Images of green eyes, images of firm thighs.

I'm a bit surprised. This ol' head feels more emptiness than it knew it could. Your leaving never really was realized until the moment you left. I've reread your letters dozens of times. Please keep writing.

I'm goina say it. I feel terrible. I can hardly believe how hard it hit me when I saw you drive off. I watched the VW all the way down the drive and out as far as it was visible. I never realized how much you have come to mean to me. I've discovered that I think you are the most delightful, prettiest and wonderful person I've ever met. That is I'm falling in love with you more and more each day.

You don't have to sell me on California. I'm sold on you. *If you truly want me to come out, say so. I'll be there.* I want you back. Not back here, just back with me. You've been gone for twenty days. That's a terrible long time. I don't know what to say. I think I should move out there and I think we should get married.

All My Love,
Bob

Robert Wapinski stared at the page before him. He meant it. He meant it as he was writing it but he wasn't so sure he meant it on rereading it. Still he sealed it, and the next morning he drove to town and mailed it at the post office.

Several days passed. Brian called, told Bobby that Cheryl had miscarried. Bobby didn't know what to think. The news about My Lai, about a guy named William Calley and a newsman named Seymour Hersh, had become an uproar. The *Cleveland Plain Dealer* published graphic photos of the April 1968 massacre. The Army announced Calley would be tried at general court-martial for the premeditated murder of 109 Viet Namese civilians. At first ex-Captain Robert Wapinski was defensive, explaining to his grandfather that a unit in the lowlands might have gone berserk in a village if they had been hitting booby traps and ambushes, and had been losing soldiers to snipers—AND if they found evidence that the villagers were participants.

"You watch a buddy get killed, you get angry," Bobby said. "You watch a lot of them get wounded or wasted, you want revenge. That's probably what happened. A good commander, though, would of reeled in his men. He'd have controlled it."

"Good men," Grandpa had agreed, "don't always exhibit good judgment."

But soon—based solely on TV news, for he was still clipping, saving but not reading the newspaper—Bobby came to think they should convict Calley and execute him, if the charges had any substantiation.

That day marked the beginning and the end, the resolution and the commencement. It marked the end of Wapinski's questioning, the end of investigation, the end of his concern over Viet Nam, for five years, years in which other concerns would be paramount.

The barn office was silent except for an occasional muffled crackle from the old potbellied stove. The quietness invaded Wapinski, oozed into his mind, seeped into his heart. For an hour he read his clippings, ordered them, made a few notes, a few underlines. If his ire rose over the story of a university professor's home being bombed because he did not teach the left's perspective on the war, it quickly diffused as he plodded on, pushed ever deeper into not only what the news said, but what it *was*. After an hour he began jotting notes about his own experiences and about himself.

> I grew up on Grandpa's farm—until I was 8—and later spent many summers and weekends there. I fished, hunted, trapped, and spent many days by myself in the woods. I would have been a great point man—I think I was a passable company commander.

He stopped to think, think back to himself at Go Dau Ha, at Cu Chi, at Trung Lap, to picture himself at Quang Tri, at Evans and Eagle and on various firebases, in various NDPs. It surprised him, in his calm, that he could actually see himself as if he were someone else, see himself talking to Quay, to Thompson, to Billings, to any of a score of his troops. He could see the vegetation, taste the water from the mountain streams, hear and fear the crinkle of dry leaves as he stepped cautiously along a trail in the defoliated regions. He could not see the firefights. He could not hear the cracking of small arms or the booming of artillery. He could imagine them, force them, but he could not, at will, recreate them as if they were happening in the here and now, as they sometimes happened in his dreams. That did not bother him.

For another hour Bob Wapinski chronologically organized his military records, wrote brief descriptions of various places he'd been, various actions he'd seen. Then he came to May 1969, Hill 937, Dong Ap Bia, Hamburger. Still he maintained his calm but it now was more difficult. He had not written to Blackwell and that unfinished task ate at him.

NVA from across the border, in Laos, registering their rocket launchers and guns—122s, 130s, and heavy mortars—in anticipation of our move into the A Shau. When our troops first air-assaulted to the valley the NVA were ready, waiting, with reinforcements, open supply lines and on-call supporting fire. How did they know, before we launched even our first helicopter, where we were headed? What would they have done if we had not stumbled across 937? Would they have attacked us in force or only have sniped at us? Mortared our NDPs but not have engaged us fully? Waited until we'd reported "The A Shau has been cleared," let us leave, and then carry the war forward into the populated lowlands—attacking our bases, Viet Namese towns and cities on their own schedule? By Day 2 our units were catching sporadic mortar fire. By 3, 300 rounds of mortar and rockets! By the time I arrived I knew we'd be hit again. It was only a question of when. We monitored radio traffic of all the allied companies—listened to some being mauled. Still, as good as the NVA were, with the advantage of being dug in, of being nearer to their supply lines and sanctuaries, of having on-call artillery and numerical advantages, AND with weather and terrain on their side—we did finally overrun them—sheer stubborn persistence called Airborne Spirit by some, stupidity by others. How else could the battle have been fought? *Generate alternatives.* Was it worth it?

Wapinski wrote on, listed the corps, division, brigade and battalion commanders, their radio call signs and even frequencies if he recalled them, summoning far more detail than he realized he'd retained. He listed every company, every commander he could recall, the name or nickname of every troop he could remember under his own brief stint as leader of Alpha Company, 1st Battalion, 506th Infantry, 3d Brigade, 101st Airborne Division (Airmobile). Then he stopped. There were images of Dong Ap Bia he was not certain he wished to explore. If Blackwell was Bro Black of the Sugar Shack, Wapinski could indeed send him a positive response. But was he? It then occurred to Wapinski that there were no slackers at Dong Ap Bia. Perhaps there were men who had been afraid. Fear was an appropriate reaction. Half the company was either wounded or killed. Images, feelings, physical sensations flooded back, deluged his mind—lost there, left on the hill when they withdrew under intense enemy kill-zone fire. Were they KIA, MIA, or POW? On the next assault they could not find even a trace—not a piece of uniform, not a traumatically amputated limb.

Wapinski wrote to Blackwell, wrote to all levels of command, to the adjutant's office. He had nothing but praise for every soldier who'd served in the A Shau. He suggested the defense lawyer obtain affidavits from Thompson, from Quay Le, from Billy Smith and Johnson and Edwards, the medic who treated Blackwell in the field. If Tyrone Blackwell refused to return to the field, Wapinski wrote, it was likely because of rational and justifiable fear based on self-preservation—which the man had earned. Before he finished the last letter he realized his eyes were clouding; he was choking. There was before him a loaded chopper, the smell stuck in his nose, a chopper full of dead Americans.

He breathed heavily, ran the back of his wrist across his cheeks. Could we have lured them into ambushes in the valley? Could we have cordoned off 937? Waited them out? Bombed them out? He did not answer the questions but instead flipped to a news story of accusations made by Senator Ted Kennedy. His concentration faltered. He skimmed the article, whispered with little conviction, "He doesn't understand. He just doesn't fuckin understand."

More hours passed. Bob Wapinski read the file his grandfather had assembled on the 101st. Then he read the stories his grandfather had collected for his father from '42 to '45. As he read, it again hit him that *news* was something more than what it reported—something much more. And that answering the question, What is today's news? with a recap of the stories was like answering the question, What is God? by saying the Our Father.

Bobby Wapinski opened the manila envelope, opened the first letter. There was no date of writing, but on the envelope, Miriam, in her efficient manner, had noted "Received: 11 Oct. '42." The penmanship—pencilmanship—was crude. Bobby had not recognized that in 1959 when he'd last read those pages. Nor had he recognized how simply the letters were written, as if his father were a young boy who'd grown up poor on a farm in the mountainous outback of the Alleghenys. Letter after letter repeated the same phrases, made the same grammatical and spelling errors. Bobby almost began correcting them. Letter after letter asked about Brian, asked for a photograph of their baby and a photo of mother and child. There were no mentions of having received one. And all the letters from the Pacific ended with "I pray for you. Pray for me. I'm a melancholly baby until we meet again."

Bob Wapinski paused. Ah Pa, he thought. Pa! Pa! Why? He closed his eyes. In his hands he still held the new letters, letters written after Paul Wapinski abandoned his family, abandoned his son Robert who so wished he'd not. Pa! he thought again. His face sagged. Pa, I wanted to come home to you. You know that? Sometimes I thought, sometimes over there I thought maybe when I came home, you know, maybe I could bring you home, too. I would have told you all about it. You could have held me. Once you did. I know you once did. With you Pa ... why do I have to think patient inquiry? Obligations? Responsibilities? I wanted you to be here ... to hold me ... to tell me it ... it was ... What drives this thing, ME? What steers it? I—I feel like a damn raft on some damn river. Pa, we could have come home together!

January 14, 1948

Dear Miriam,

Cleveland is a big city. Bigger then I like. I got a factory job. The pay isn't much but I don't need much. I'm sending you everything I can. Don't try to get to me. I got things to work out and I can't do it with you harpin on me. I guess I'm not enough man for you and you deserve more then me. Buy Brian a baseball glove and some cracker-jacks. There's extra money here for it. And something for the baby. I pray for you.

Paul

Bobby stared at the letter. Again he'd expected more. How badly he wanted his father to be more, wanted to see in those letters the man his grandfather described. The second and third letters were similar, each mentioning money sent, requesting she spend some on the boys. The fourth acknowledged Joanne's birth. The fifth was postmarked St. Louis, December 1952. It too mentioned money sent, indicating Paul Wapinski had been mailing cash to his wife every month for four years, that there was trouble at work and he'd been laid off. Finally there was only one more; the postmark was but half-printed, the date barely legible. Bobby deciphered 53 and *Texas*. Miriam had not re-ceipted it.

Dear Miriam.

I'm working again. The boys here drink a lot. They are good friends. Everyone of them went through the same stuff I did and I finally have found a place where I can talk and not be crazy. Tell Pop and Mom where I am. I'll get a letter to them too. I'm really sorry that circumstances have forced this on us. I pray it would be differ-ent. Tell Brian to help his brother and sister more. Sometimes I recall that littlest guy and I even miss him spitting up on me. I'm not a very good man for what I put you through. I know that. I'm makin a lot of money right now with the oil coming in and I'll be able to send you a lot.

The letter stopped in the middle of the second sheet. It was unsigned. In the envelope there was a simple blank card scribed by a different hand. It said: "We're sorry about Paul. He was a fine, fine friend." There were four signatures: Tom. Jack. Omeed. Jimmy.

Bobby Wapinski was stunned, stunned beyond shaking, beyond anger, beyond belief. Why had no one shown him this letter? Had they contacted this Tom, this Jack, Omeed, Jimmy? What did his ma, his grandfather, know that they hadn't told him? Had Miriam written back? "Has he," he'd written in one letter, "settled down for you?" He knew. He knew I needed him. She must have written. What else had they known for sixteen years? Since he was seven! He felt tears well to his eyes but they did not fall. He felt injustice, anger—anger, anger—but it would not focus and he felt helpless, empty. He pushed the letter out of reach, stared at the desk. He wanted to get up, run to the house, shake the letter, the card, in his grandfather's face. But he was spent, exhausted, numb. He lay his head on the desk, looked at the letter, the envelope, a foreshortened plane with illegible pencil smears. It was late afternoon. Bobby Wapinski fell to sleep; fell not asleep, but into a semiconsciousness similar to the half sleeps he'd had for nearly a year in Asia, an infantryman's sleep.

Now they are shooting. They had come from the mountain, a human wave. Behind them, unseen, there is the vibration, the trembling, the roar of tracks, tanks, self-propelled howitzers, unseen. He is low, crawling, positioning himself. The crack of small arms comes from the far side, from the lead element of his ambush, comes premature setting off a torrent of return fire that isolates the lead element from the long base. The enemy spreads out, continues advancing. The mud surface is slick. He slips as he crawls forward into the midst of his men. The mud is thick, deep, grabbing, sucking him down. He strains to move forward but is mired. Overhead a new roar, a beating mixing with the downpour, and now mortar explosions mixing with thunder and the trembling ooze of the earth. Bam. Thud. He is hit. He doesn't feel it. He crawls on. They advance. Behind him men move up, before him they fall back. All know the lead is isolated, lost, out of contact. Still the enemy advances. Now they return fire. Friend, foe, locked in face-to-face slugfest. Across the trail, behind a hummock, his unit retreats. BamThudHitAgainPain. Now they are sliding away. He is sliding away from himself left in the mud, left on the hillside. "I pray for you. Pray for me." Sliding away. BamThudBamThudBamThud. There is no pain, only the smell of blood and shit and blood and flesh and blood. There is no sight except the last view of himself in the mud as he, they, slide back, last glimpse of himself, on the mud floor eating mud, trying to hide, to eat mud so quietly. Then there is the room, the masks, the hustle bustle, "NEXT." Get up! He lies there. Get up! It is not a busy day after all. There are nurses leaving, going to the club, corpsmen chatting softly, betting on a ballgame, smoking. They've decided not to treat him because they are tired. It has become habit because of the worst days of mass casualties, the busy days, to let the goners go—but today is a slow day—s l o w d a y. He can see it. See into their minds, see how tired they are, see how they think about him, how they see his glassy eyes, how they don't think of him. "Covered with mud! Dirty. Like a pig. Sounds like a pig. When you learn to eat like a human being we'll—Jesus! I can't stand it anymore! Put him in the corner to cool . . . in the corner to cool, inthecornertocool."

Wapinski woke. His head snapped up. How much had been a dream, how much did he control, he did not know. "Fuck it!" he said aloud. "Fuck em all! Drive on!"

Winter arrived at High Meadow in mid-December. The temperature dropped thirty degrees on the night of the 10th and on the morning of the 11th it barely warmed at all. That night the temperature dropped to single digits. On the 13th a low front swept in and precipitation fell as frigid rain, then froze into a layer of ice. By noon the ice was half an inch thick.

It was transition time. At the back of Bobby's mind were Viet Nam, his father's letters, Red. Viet Nam, he thought, had become a hook to his past, a momentary identity penetrating into some deep layer of self-definition.

Grandpa had heated up a pan of chicken broth and the two of them sat, sipping the steaming broth. "Do you know what you asked me once when you were a little boy?" Grandpa asked Bob.

"Unt-uh," Bob intoned.

"You once asked me if being truthful meant not telling a lie even when Pinocchio would tell a lie?"

"How old was I when I said that?"

"I don't know. Five. Maybe six. Do you know what I told you?"

"No. I don't remember."

"I don't remember either." Grandpa laughed and Bob laughed too and Josh jumped up and slapped both his front paws on the table and seemed to want to laugh with them.

"G'down." Bob pushed him, still laughing.

"I mighta said something like this," Grandpa said. "I really can't remember. But I mighta said, being truthful means doing what your heart tells you is right. That's about the way one talks to a five-year-old, isn't it?"

"What are you trying to tell me, Granpa?"

"I'm saying, don't get hooked on values that aren't valuable to you."

"Um-hmm. You taught me that way back."

"You like the farm, don't you?"

"Of course. It's always been my favorite place."

"Mine too. But you aren't much of a farmer."

"Nope. I guess not. I, ah . . . "

"Doesn't make much difference. None of the farms around here produce enough income to keep a family anyway."

"The Lutz farm makes money."

"Adolph'd make money if his place was solid rock," Pewel Wapinski said. "What I'm saying is, I don't know if you're being truthful with yourself. You've got that gal out in California and you're over here. You could have a job in town, work up here. You could work the farm. You could run a business from up here like what's his name two places beyond Adolph's does. But Bob, I don't want you attaching your life to this place if it's not valuable to you."

Bob Wapinski leaned his forearms on the table, grasped the soup bowl with both hands. "Why didn't you tell me about my father?"

"Tell you what? Oh. Texas?"

"Uh-huh."

"Well . . . well, tell you when?"

"When you knew."

"Me an his ma went to Texas to search for him. You wouldn't remember that. Put ads in all those papers. Figured that odd name'd get us some results. But we never come up with a single thing. I thought later, maybe, being that he was kind of hiding his exact whereabouts from Miriam, that maybe he was really in Oklahoma but sent that last letter from Texas . . . or they did it for him."

"She knew where he was. She must have written him."

"We all wrote im. Always to general delivery. But he never had an address after Missoura."

"I could have been told."

"At seven or eight!"

"Yes."

"Bob . . . we still don't know. Maybe he's hiding. Sides, sometimes a man has to discover things in his own time. What could you of done at seven?"

Over the next month, through Christmas and New Year's and into the coldest days of January, Bob Wapinski fantasized about Red. He wrote her almost every day and received a letter from her as frequently. Whatever their relationship might have lacked when they were together, whatever their trepidations, the voids were filled in their letters and in their minds. Their plans took shape. Bob asked Red to find out about residence requirements for California state schools. "I'd like to take some courses in engineering, in city planning, maybe a few art classes," he wrote. "What would it cost if I were a resident? I can use the GI Bill for tuition."

Red called, told him the addresses to write to for brochures. It was their first live communication since the day she'd driven off. He hadn't expected the call. When it was over he felt odd, dissatisfied, yet he told himself it was because it had happened so suddenly and he had not been able to get his mind into the right gear. If anything, his move to California went from possible to certain, his letters became more amorous and her expressed apprehension dwindled.

"This past week," he wrote in January, "I've felt your absence the most. I cannot think of a thing better than being with someone you love—especially if that someone's like you."

In turn she answered, "When you get here, if we can afford it and I can take the time, let's go to a big hotel in San Francisco and get reacquainted. I can't wait to take you to North Bay Mall. It's such a pleasure to be there, to walk in the open air down the esplanade between the stores and to look in all the windows, or just to sit on the benches and watch the people. They are much happier than people in Mill Creek and it shows. I'm so happy to be here—even if it rains so much. One of the jewelry shoppes has the most beautiful rings. I hope that we'll be able to work out our differences and live happily ever after like in a goddamn fairytale. I say HURRAY for goddamn fairytales. At work, Pauline is getting a divorce. We went out last night and drank three bottles of wine."

If Red's January tone was relaxed, expectant, and Bobby's was peaceful, transitional, Pewel Wapinski's bordered on frantic. "Bob," Pewel addressed his grandson at breakfast, "a man lives easier when he has a set of guidelines he lives by."

"Makes sense," Bobby answered.

"A code," Grandpa said. "You know. That way you're not having to figure out everything from scratch. You plant in the spring, you reap in the fall. You know that. You don't have to waste time or energy or seed experimenting."

"Yes Sir." Bobby teased the old man, teased him politely, lovingly, thinking he knew what his grandfather was doing, thinking that his grandfather didn't need to do it for there was plenty of time and California wasn't permanent, wasn't a disease.

At lunch Grandpa gave Bobby a photograph of himself and Brigita taken on February 22, 1947, their twenty-fifth wedding anniversary. At dinner Grandpa produced a photo of himself and Bobby and Josh, which Red had taken in September. With the second photograph he gave him a simple list.

1. Lead others through your service to them.
2. You are special, your family is special, your country is special. You and they are something sacred, something to be honored.
3. You are here for a reason.
4. A man must be able to make money and be able to keep some of the money he makes. Take care of business first—plant before you play. You're not finished until you're finished. Unfinished business has a way of haunting you.
5. Don't get hooked on values that aren't valuable.

Each day from the moment it was acknowledged Bobby would move, Pewel gave him something. At one dinner Pewel handed Bobby an envelope with one hundred twenty-dollar bills. "I can't take this," Bobby said.

"Yes you can," Pewel countered.

"No Granpa. It's not right."

"It's seed money," Pewel said. "I can do it and I want to do it."

"I can't do it," Bobby said. "If I ever need it, I'll ask you for it. Okay?"

"There's a card in there. It's something I remember from my father. The words mighta changed but the meaning's the same. He said it was the oldest prayer of the Old Testament. Maybe older than Judaism itself. Keep God in your life Bob. Someplace. Not necessarily like they teach at St. Ignatius', but someplace."

"I think He's in the land," Bobby said.

Pewel Wapinski nodded. Then quietly he said, "Dear Lord, please bless us and watch over us; deliver us from evil; forgive us our trespasses; and give us the strength and guts to try hard and never give up." He paused again. "That's for your sons."

"Sons! Granpa, I don't have—"

"That's for your sons when you have sons."

Every day Pewel Wapinski gave his grandson something more, and every evening Bobby Wapinski packed the items in his footlocker. Still what grandfather wished to give to grandson was not physical or financial but spiritual—words, ideas, ideals that to the old man were poignant. "Civilized people . . . civilization, Bob, this is a gift of God or of circumstance, and of five hundred generations that have gone before us. You've got the ability to control, to some extent, today's circumstances. That's a responsibility. Try hard. Never give up!"

"Granpa, I never knew you were such a philosopher!"

Pewel chuckled. "Only on midwinter nights like this when there's not so much to do around here." The old man lay back in his overstuffed chair in the dimly lit, dingy living room. "Take these with you, Bob," he said. He did not move. Inside, dimly, he was thinking about his daughter-in-law, thinking vaguely, She drove my son away and now she's driving away my grandson.

"What?" Bobby asked.

"These words," Pewel said. His eyes were closed. "Integrity. These words are principles. Virtue. Pride. Confidence. Responsibility. A man must live not by expedience, not by quick gratification, but by principles. Liberty. Independence. Freedom. Faith. Family. Courage."

During the last week of January 1970, after having rebuilt the Mustang, Bobby sold his car to John Lutz for $900, not even the price of the parts. He finished packing his footlocker, sent it via Greyhound to the depot in San Martin where Red said she'd pick it up if it arrived before he did.

He heard from Red one more time. She was taking a real estate license course at Academy Schools and already had a test date of Saturday, February 14th, Valentine's Day.

On January 27th Grandpa drove Bobby and Josh to Williamsport. He put them both on a flight, via Philadelphia, to SFO.

August 1984

"You can control circumstances." That was the birth of the code. He didn't listen. Not at first. None of us did the first time we heard it. And I'm not sure I can interpret it now. Isn't that the way it is with codes and canons, principles and plans? They're okay until you hit an extreme, then it's a matter of figuring out how they apply, how to decode them, what's relevant.

The raccoons haven't come. For a week there's been no lights in the house. None in the barns. It is cool, cold. My body is stiff, chilled, and I can barely bend my right leg. The fire hardly warms me. Three days ago I dug the pit and chimney. Nothing much, really—a small one-man kitchen with a flat stone over the fire pit, an entrance flue downhill, a six-inch-deep exit tunnel-chimney, a covered trench, snaking back up into the pines there, maybe thirty feet away. The tunnel-chimney controls smoke. Moisture and particulants cool, condense, fall out. What comes out the far end is pretty minimal—a crude scrubber, the kind the VC used in old Nam Bo when they didn't want us to know where they were.

This morning, at first light, I got off my duff, descended to the pond, washed my stinko bod, my pits. Shaved. Dove in with my clothes on and used the soap to wash them before I took em off and washed me. Could hardly believe yesterday. Of all people! I'd slipped back into the pines to watch. Thought maybe she'd notice the firepit, start snoopin around—maybe freak out, split, notify the authorities, send somebody up here to evict me. I didn't realize it was Joanne, Wap's sister, till she parked behind the house and got out of the car. I'd already sanitized my camp as much as I could. There wasn't much I could do with the firepit except cover the opening with the dirt I'd dug out making it. Still, I'm pretty sure she didn't notice. Of all people she woulda been the last I'd of expected to come up and plant flowers. It blew my mind. Couldn't rest, couldn't meditate. Felt like shit at first light. That's why I went down below, cleaned up, filled my water blivet, changed my duds, came back up and hung the wet ones on a line I'd stretched at the back of the pine break. Controlling circumstances.

While I was in Philly there was always something in the pipeline—something from the rumor mill about drops—early-out programs tied to Nixon's reduction in force. It was really a matter of laying guys off, of firing them, because Viet Namization was going to turn the war over the ARVN. No severance pay. No bonus. Just get out. I was discharged 123 days early—discharged not with a bang, barely a whimper. Crocco, Williams and Lambert went out and got drunk for me, then they disassembled Lieutenant Mulhaney's car—doors, wheels, hood, wires, even the windshield—and left it there for him to put back together. The rumor mill said I did it but I was in Boston and Mulhaney never laid that rap on me. Still, I say, thanks guys. Mulhaney deserved it. I left without a whimper. Just collected my pay, signed the papers, caught a bus to Scranton and one to La Porte where my mom came and got me and drove me home and all I could think of was leaving for Boston and the most wonderful woman in the world. But first there had to be another family party! I hung around for a respectable bit until I figured I could go to Boston to "visit." Oh God, how I missed her.

In Mill Creek Ma'd say, "Tony, you decide yet what you're goina do?" She really liked having me home but the nicer she was the more I wanted to go. I felt like I was caught in a niceness trap and bein mushed to death like when I was seven and she'd make me sit on her lap and hug me against her big plump motherness while she'd be talking to Aunt Isabella who'd be doing the same thing to Jimmy. "I think I'm goina go to school," I'd tell her. "Maybe become a doctor like Joey." She believed me. "Ma, I'm going to be a college kid." She believed me and that meant it was okay for me to believe it too. "Where are you going to go to school?" Mark asked. "I don't know," I lied. I'd already applied and gotten the conditional answer. "Maybe BU, you know, in Boston."

Jo would never of understood if I'd said, "I'm going to Boston to be with Linda." At least that's what I thought. I mean, her boys didn't set their life's course by following girls to far-off cities. Go to Budapest or Timbuktu to go to school, or to Guantanamo Bay or Dong Ha to shoot people, that'd be respectable . . . but to Boston to get laid!!!

Jimmy came back from his second tour more gung-ho than ever but that's not surprising. He spent the entire time with 4th CAG doing combined action duty. They kept moving him, letting him help set up CAP units in five or six different villages. He was becoming a real papa-san to a lot of people. He loved it, they loved him. And he was great for Marine morale. Sixty percent of the enlisted men in CAPs extended for at least six months. That's how much they believed in the program. But he came home to

completely different circumstances than the first time. This
country was different. Our family was different.

And I was up in Boston with Linda, in an apartment she'd
found just off Commonwealth Ave., in Allston, the cheap side of
the Ave. with lots of students, versus the swank side, which is
Brookline. Linda was studying really hard and working hard too,
at Brigham and Women's Hospital. I got a job almost right
away—driving an ambulance. Anything, I reasoned, to be near
her. She was so damned focused at that time. I was anything but
focused—except on her. But she had the drive for both of us. It
was Linda who'd gotten the applications, who'd gotten me to
enroll at BU where I started classes in September '69. I was a
"conditional" student and had to take a study-habits course that
summer—but Linda was really all I could think about.

"You can control circumstances." But we didn't know, hadn't
developed the code, had left previous codes behind. The new code
would need to be tempered in the ovens of alienation,
estrangement, self-imposed exile, expatriation. Where once we
believed in everything and our beliefs were supplanted,
suppressed, or shattered, in the void we lost all beliefs or came to
believe in someone else's beliefs. When we lost our beliefs we lost
too the adjunct discipline and were without discipline. When we
gave our minds to someone else, we adopted disciplines attached
to their interests. We wallowed, unfocused, numbed out, wide-
eyed, movin 'n' groovin without thought. We floated, without
production, without achievement, without direction, without
ideals, without ends. There was no one, no thing, to follow—no
leadership of ideas, no models of service, no rituals, no codes.

9

Boston, August 1969: Tony was tense, cold, wet. He'd dreamed again but was again unable to recall the dream. Scattered flickerings of city light came in through the narrow French doors. He looked at Linda. In sleep her mouth maintained a slight smile that warmed him but which could not dispel his tension. Quietly he pulled back the sheet, rolled off the bed, fell into a crouch. He scanned the room, the French doors that led to the two-by-six-foot third-floor balcony, the transom light of the interior bedroom door. It was four o'clock in the morning. He heard squealing tires on Commonwealth, the crashing of garbage cans in the alley behind their apartment, the moan of an airliner circling, awaiting clearance to land at Logan, and the barely audible riffs of Judy Collins's "Vietnam Love Song" seeping up from the apartment below.

Slowly Tony rose. He stood perfectly still, listening, sensing. He walked around the bed staying close to the foot, away from the French doors, walked to the bedroom door, froze. Again he listened. Linda had studied all afternoon and into the early evening while Tony had watched first a Red Sox–Yankees game, then several game shows. At each break she'd encouraged him to hit the books but he'd been unable to tear himself away from the game and by the time it was over he'd gelled into position on the sofa. She'd finally gotten him up when Rachel and Larry from the studio upstairs came in with a six-pack. They drank quickly. In the heat the alcohol gave them an immediate buzz and they'd decided to catch the T up to Clarendon Street and walk to the Combat Zone— bars, dancing, music, prostitutes, booze, hippies, go-go girls, drugs, more music, more dancing. They met other friends, and all danced and drank till midnight. Then Tony and Linda left, rode the T back as far as Nickerson Field, walked the last half mile, laughing, looking into each other's eyes, running, chasing each other all the way to Long Ave., Tony catching Linda on the first landing, she escaping then trapping him on the second, laughing, kissing then darting up the last flight, Linda fumbling with the two keys in the two dead bolts Tony had insisted upon, Tony fumbling with Linda's clothing, unbuttoning her blouse as she'd opened the door and pulled him in by the belt.

Quietly Tony turned the knob. The bedroom opened onto the living room. This room too was at the front of the apartment building, and it too had French doors and a small balcony. He visually checked the balcony, then the door to the stairs, finally the hallway to the bathroom, kitchen and second bedroom which they used as a study. For a moment he looked at the sofa where earlier they'd made love.

Tony stepped into the living room. He moved along the sofa to the front wall, to the edge of the curtained French door. Slowly he slid a hand beneath the curtain, checking the lock. He knelt, checked the floor locks, moved to the stairway door, checked the locks there. The hall was dark. He didn't turn on the light but slid into the darkness. He checked the bathroom, the kitchen, the windows above the alley, finally opening the study door where Linda had a desk clock with a backlit face that Tony abhorred because of the glow it cast, backlighting anyone in the darkness of the room, freaking him out because there could be someone outside, someone who could shoot in without detection. Tony turned the clock facedown, covered it with a dark shirt.

Now he breathed more easily. He shuffled to the desk, ran his hands to his own small pile of books, felt to the side for the cigarette pack. It was easy during the day to read, to smoke, but at night it was nearly impossible. He removed a cigarette, closed the pack, replaced it. He put the unlit smoke between his lips, touched the tobacco with the tip of his tongue. Now he needed to taste smoke. He moved back to the living room, into the bedroom. Linda had rolled onto her stomach, her feet protruding from the sheet. To Tony she looked wonderful. Downstairs someone had flipped the albums. Judy Collins's voice seeped up with "All Things Are Quite Silent." Tony'd read the album, knew the song from which the royalties were being donated "to people dedicated to resisting the United States draft on the grounds that it is unconstitutional, immoral and indecent." Collins's voice was soothing. He tried to tune it out. He sat on the edge of the bed tonguing the tobacco, its taste stinging like spicy food.

Then came shouts. Nothing serious. Kids—13, 14, 15 years old. Tony's tension skyrocketed, his heart pounded, driving pulsing throbs down his chest to his thighs. He stood. The kids were shouting, cursing, banging a board on the wrought-iron railings of the stairs three stories below. Tony moved to the front wall, edged to the French doors. He shook. He peered out without moving. He wanted to open the door, yell at them, scream, "Get outa here!" but he couldn't move. He saw two run across the street, rake the board up and down a railing there, shout obscenities at the darkened facade.

Night after night, after the first awkward nights of May, Tony's night ritual evolved. After work, study, party, love, sleep, he rose, tense, watched Linda sleep, then walked quietly, vigilantly, protecting, hovering until first light. Through job search and hiring, furniture shopping, opening checking and savings accounts, through school enrollment and life planning—degrees, marriage, maybe a house, maybe a small farm— the evolution continued. Despite breaks when they borrowed a friend's motorcycle and rode to the bird refuge on Plum Island 40 miles north of Boston, despite the terror and thrill of notifying parents of wedding plans still unresolved—wait until Linda's graduation, elope now, a church, a hall, here, in Mill Creek Falls, where?—despite it all Tony's night ritual persisted, evolved through June into July and August.

A few times Linda too had gotten up. He'd feigned flashes of inspiration, or pulled out VA pamphlets listing entitlements, duration of eligibility, restrictions, or flipped open his study habits journal. But she'd seen through the scam, sensed his discomfort, knew because of the stories he'd told her that he'd been dreaming about the tunnel or Dai Do or Manny, dreaming something terrible she could not take from him because she could not study and work and love him and be his emotional self. For his part he did not want to tell her any more, did not trust Linda to hear more, afraid she, who'd been so awestruck by his being a sergeant in the Marine Corps, who was so loving, and supportive, would be horrified by his recurrent dreams, would withdraw.

Ceasing to talk locked a part of him in a cell, froze that part like a butterfly encased in a transparent plastic cube, left him to fit his new role, his new self-image—no longer the dago hick from the Endless Mountains or the Marine Corps sergeant Viet Nam returnee. He had to project a countenance required of the big city with all its blue-jeaned, long-haired male students his age, to project an identity he did not possess.

At times Tony and Linda did talk, yet he barely made sense anymore even to himself because he no longer remembered his dreams. And Linda, stretched to the very limit, found it easier to make love to him than to try to be his therapist.

The sky softened. City lights lost their gleam. Tony turned on the television but kept the volume low. For a moment he watched soundless broadcasters—the silent talking heads—but quickly he turned his attention to his study-habits workbook, practicing the concentration technique prescribed, easily answering the few general questions about the "article" he'd chosen to read—a section from his emergency medical technician's course. He smoked, rose, showered, dressed in the uniform of AmbuStar Ambulance Service, Inc. He brewed coffee, drank a quick cup, woke Linda with a kiss and left for work.

"Pisano."

"Yo."

"You work a double today?"

Tony glanced around the small AmbuStar office. He was the most junior of the drivers. "Yes Sir."

"Good. Fill in for Carlucci. You know the streets now. Lewis'll be with you first shift. And ah—" the dispatcher-owner, Ken Charnowski, checked his clipboard, "I'll put Pomeroy with you on second."

"Those are emergency routes, aren't they, Sir?"

"Yep."

"Ah, I've been doing only, you know, critical care transport, oxygen therapy . . . "

Lewis came over. He was a thin black man, about thirty, Tony's height. "Pay's better," he said quietly. "Help you pay for that engagement ring."

"You're doing the EMT course, aren't you?" Charnowski was gruff.

"Yes Sir, but—"

"Hey, no big thing. Lewis and Pomeroy are qualified. I need a driver. I've got two on vacation and Carlucci called in sick. Work his double."

"Yes Sir."

At nine they answered their first call—a young boy had fallen from a tree and broken his leg. Alvin Lewis gently applied a splint and they drove the boy and his mother across the bridge to Beth Israel Hospital. All routine. At ten thirty they answered their second, a chaotic mess in Tony's own neighborhood—where Commonwealth Ave. bends from west to south and Brighton Ave. meets the intersection. There, a visiting Taiwanese businessman had misunderstood the lights and T-boned an MTA railcar injuring himself, his two passengers and twenty T riders. Traffic immediately clogged the access. Police, fire and other ambulances had all been dispatched and all fought to get to the scene. Treatment and evacuation took over two hours.

"Hey," Alvin Lewis said to Tony after they'd treated several of the passengers, broken out of the clog and delivered two to emergency rooms, "you're pretty good. You act like you've been doing this for years."

"Naw," Tony said. "But thanks."

"Really Man. I seen you with the Chinawoman. She was hysterical and in like one second you had it all sorted out and calmed her down. You must of done this someplace—the way you take charge."

"Naw," Tony smiled. "Not this. But, you know . . . I was a sergeant in the Corps."

"What corps?"

"In the Marine Corps."

"Oh! You mean . . . " Lewis waved his hand back and forth pointing out Tony's window.

"Yeah. This is pretty tame."

"Yeah," Alvin said. "I bet so." He became quiet and Tony said nothing more.

In the high heat and humidity of midafternoon Tony and Alvin answered more calls in South End: two heat prostration cases and one old black man who'd had a heart attack climbing his tenement stairs and who died on the stretcher in the back of the ambulance as Tony drove and Alvin held an oxygen mask over the man's face.

At four Lewis left. Tony gassed up, checked the oil and medical supplies, and picked up Quentin Pomeroy, a chubby young man with beautiful shoulder-length blond hair tied back in a ponytail. Through the late afternoon and early evening they were on the road, minor accidents and minor heat-related trauma, and one puncture wound of a young man's shoulder, which bystanders swore was a stabbing by another young man, a fight over a girl, but which both young men insisted to the investigating officer was an accident. As a favor, Tony took and concealed the switchblade, dropping the evidence as he turned from Tremont Street onto Mass. Ave. heading down toward City Hospital.

Tony was sleepy. He'd grabbed four Styrofoam cups before they'd left City, filled them with coffee, and stowed them on the shelf above the dashboard. By the time Pomeroy returned with the paperwork Tony had drunk two, discarded them, was drinking one he'd gotten for Quentin. He started the engine, wiped a hand over his face. "Hey, got ya a cup of coffee."

"Oh. Thanks, guy," Pomeroy said. "That's really white of ya."

"Don't mention it." Tony chuckled.

It was near eleven. Tony'd been in and out of the vehicle for fifteen hours, up since four on less than two hours of sleep. Pomeroy too was nodding. Tony aimed northwest toward Symphony Hall, driving sleepily, thinking about nothing in particular other than getting off duty and going home to Linda, thinking fuzzily that he wouldn't be able to pull doubles when he started school full-time, thinking how he hated it when Linda had doubles. The night dispatcher radioed.

Pomeroy jolted up.

In seconds they were wailing up Mass. Ave., lights flashing, speeding to a head-on on Storrow Drive—Storrow, a four-lane limited-access disaster of a highway with nothing but a guardrail between the on-coming lanes, built at a time when cars were rare and forty-five was an average speed.

The air was still, warm, muggy—air that refracts light, holds it, forms a halo around on-coming headlights, around the harsh blipping bubble-top red, blue, white from the police cruisers. It was as if no time had passed from the moment of the call to the moment he was there, outside the ambulance, hearing the horns, the curses, the wailing of an infant—as if he, they, were slides clicked to a new frame, from sleepy to the hectic horror of the Storrow Drive accident scene.

More horns. Behind them the eastbound lanes backed up, the cumulative headlights glinted from every shard of tempered windshield, every torn fragment of sheet metal, every pavement smear wet with fluid. There were two cars, both inverted. A Volvo had come from the westbound speed lane, slid, caught the center guardrail and flipped into the eastbound lanes, smashed head-on into a second, spinning both vehicles out, the eastbound Plymouth rolling like a punted football, finally crashing against the outer guardrail and stopping. The westbound vehicle—driver drunk, sleepy, just distracted changing tapes or flipping buttons looking for a different song—had spun on its roof, crashed backward into the center rail.

Tony smelled gas. Officers closed the eastbound lanes behind them. Others whipped orange-gloved-hands at westbound cars, demanding they maintain the flow, demanding that drivers, passengers, not slow down to gawk. Tony sprinted to the Plymouth, knelt, crawled. There was wailing coming from inside. Pomeroy shouted at one of the cops. Passersby began to crowd near. Tony heard nothing but the wail. He did not search for a source. Instead: Ignition! Ignition key. On the passenger side the roof was flattened to the base of the windows. He rolled, low-crawled, scampered to the driver's window. There was blood on the door. Tony lay on his back, his legs kicked up as he forced his right arm in, feeling for the steering column, the key.

"Get back! Get back!" The cop's voice was nasty. The growing crowd shifted, milled. Tony felt dripping—warm, wet—then the chain, the key. He turned the key. Now he began to assess the situation. There was still the wailing but the interior was dark—the bright lights from the cruisers, from his own ambulance, from the fire truck that had arrived on a parallel side road, made it impossible to see into the car. A firefighter began dumping bags of Absorb-all about the car. Another firefighter, with a flashlight, bent with Tony, tried to see inside, saw wet shreds on the inverted driver's door above Tony as Tony too saw them; saw the neck, the hair, the piece of skull—realized immediately the driver's head had been caught outside during the last rollover, had been trapped between road and car and scraped away. Still there was the wailing. More firemen came, worked the car with bars.

"Back there. Point it back there." Tony glanced at the man with the flashlight. He too was young, clean-cut.

"Christ!" The man aimed the light. Both peered, searched. "What a fuckin mess. You with Dust-Off?"

"AmbuStar," Tony answered. They could see the car was full of children, saw the cocked head and glassy eyes of one who was dead, but they could not tell about the others, could not be certain, could not even determine how many.

"Let us open it up, Man," the man with the flashlight said. "Then you can do your thing."

Now Tony stood with Quentin Pomeroy, watched. A metropolitan ambulance had taken the driver of the first car; a wrecker had flipped the car and was towing it. One eastbound lane opened. People gawked, drove by very slowly, then accelerated away.

For forty minutes the firefighters worked—finally cutting holes through the floor and removing first one dead child, then a second and a third. Then they found the infant, and Tony and Quentin took over and strapped the small body to a backboard and applied tourniquets to one leg that had been severely lacerated and crushed and to one arm with an amputated hand, neither of which had bled the baby to death because both the amputation and the lacerations were beyond the crush points.

Linda heard the keys in the dead bolts. She glanced at the desk clock. Two twenty. She pursed her lips, thought to get up and release the locks but didn't move, feeling peeved, suspecting Tony had gone for a drink with his coworkers. She had been anxious every night since the accident, had been doodling instead of studying, sketching big plump flowers on her notebook's inner cover, circling her pen over and over the petals, adding weight and refining details. Now she covered the sketch, hunched down over the text, *Medical Care of the Surgical Patient*, highlighting normal hemoglobin and hematocrit value. Time had seemed to both accelerate and stand still. They were doing a thousand things, yet nothing seemed near completion. Two weeks after the fatal accident on Storrow Drive Tony had notified AmbuStar he'd be starting full-time at BU and could only work part-time. To them he'd proved himself and Charnowski wanted him full-time, but Alvin Lewis and Quentin Pomeroy had convinced Charnowski that a guy like Tony Pisano was too good to hold back—that he'd only stick around if Ken backed off. Linda too had had a major change, an unofficial graduation to the equivalent of RN, which allowed her more responsibility at work, but in her Family Nurse Practice program there would be no real graduation, no certificate, no degree, until the program was completed eighteen months hence. And Tony and Linda still had not decided on a date, a church, a hall, or even a city for their wedding.

"That you, Babe?" Linda called.

The door was shut, rebolted. "Naw, not me. It's the boogie man."

Linda stifled her anger. "Did you and Quentin go up to Mondo's?"

"Naw. I don't like that place. Too many kids. All the kids are coming back. Shee-it! I don't know how I'm goina be a freshman with these . . . teenyboppers."

"You won't see them so much when classes start. Want to quiz me?"

"Sure." Tony leaned on the door jamb, stared at Linda, flashed a lecherous grin.

"No way!" Linda snapped. "I've got to finish this."

"Finish what?"

"Thrombocytes and hemostasis. Ask me what needs to be excluded by diagnosis before a thrombocytopenic patient can be operated upon."

"Okay. What needs to be excluded before the thrombocyto . . . before a trombone can be tooted?"

"Thrombo . . . never mind. Leukemia."

"Oh yeah. I knew that!" Tony chuckled.

"You've been drinking!"

"Oh, just a wee tad."

"At that Irish pub . . . "

"Aye! Cept I don't think it's a real Irish pub. It's, ya know, a bar without . . . a working Joe's bar without a million kids."

"When are you going to finish the EMT material? Tony, classes start in less than two weeks. You've got to get the EMT—"

"I'll finish it. Geez! I gotta whiz." Tony left the doorway, entered the bathroom.

"Your mom called earlier." Linda's voice was controlled, neutral. "Did you send your grandmother a birthday card?"

Tony returned. He rebuckled his belt as he spoke. "Look, I can't deal with this now. Do you have any cigarettes? It's been one more bullshit day. Money's great but I can't wait till these doubles stop."

"More accidents?" Linda grabbed, shook the Winston pack.

"Yeah." He watched her tear the top off.

"Bad?" The pack was empty. She crushed it and tossed it into the grocery bag that was their trash basket.

"Aw . . . not really. Not like that first Storrow one. But Jesus God, don't ever let anybody tell you gettin shot is the worst thing possible."

Linda stood. She came to him, wrapped her arms around him, buried her head in his chest. "They're lucky they have you out there," she said.

"And I'm lucky to have you in here." He hugged her back. They stood still in the center of their study for a long moment. Then Linda leaned back and said, "This won't go on forever. We can deal with it."

"Yeah," Tony said. He released her. "You're losing more weight, aren't you?"

"A little."

"How much?"

"I'm down to a hundred and seven."

"I don't think you should lose any more."

"Four more pounds. I think one oh three's my ideal weight."

"That's too thin."

"Oooo," Linda blustered playfully. "You want me to be a big fat mama like one of your Italian aunts!"

"Aw, come on," Tony said. He yawned. "That's the last thing I want."

She grabbed his hands, pulled him in close, stood on her tip-toes to kiss him. "Go get us some cigarettes, okay? Winstons. Not those awful Pall Malls. Okay? I've got at least two more hours."

Tony had not been drinking at an Irish bar. He had been downstairs in the first-floor apartment of Tom McLaughlin, a returning senior at BU, smoking dope. Now as he passed by he paused, listened to see if Tom or the other guys he'd met were still up. There was no sound. He went to the foyer, stared through the door glass. He clenched his teeth. His respiration rate jumped, his muscles tightened. The street was calm. There were a few people walking on the far side, a couple sitting on the stoop of the building next door. Tony's breathing came fast, shallow. There was an all-night Purity Supreme market up on the corner of Commonwealth and Harvard avenues. Tony grabbed the door handle, froze. His jaw quivered. The door handle was warm, warm like the infant's blood, like the blood of the children at Dai Do, like the blood on the ignition key on Storrow Drive. He released the knob. His arms were shaking uncontrollably. He wobbled, pushed himself against the wall to keep from falling. A dark figure, man, head down, walked by and Tony knew it was Manny, Manny who'd been shot, whom he'd cradled and who'd been shot again while Tony cradled him. Warm like Manny's blood oozing through his fatigue pants. Tony squatted, peed in his pants, thinking without control, he'd left this all behind; thinking of severed heads, chopped off, scraped off. He opened his mouth, sucked air over his teeth, saw the floor rising up, he falling. Then—FLASH—out.

Then pain. He looked up. He felt his head. He felt dizzy. He raised his torso from the floor. He looked at his hand. It was wet. He put it back to his head, felt the cut, brought it back before his eyes. There wasn't much blood. Some had already coagulated. He was not shaking, not breathing hard. He stood, looked out the door. It was still dark. No one was on the steps next door. Tony turned, climbed the stairs back to his apartment.

"That you, Babe?" Linda called. She'd been unable to settle down, to concentrate, had again been doodling, now cute plump cats with big heads and big eyes and navels, round and round over the lines. "What took so long?"

"Ah . . . I'll be there in just a minute." He headed straight for the bathroom.

"What took so long?" she repeated.

Tony removed his pants, tossed them in the tub. He quickly wiped his legs with a damp washcloth, then grasped the exposed cold water pipe that ran from ceiling to floor and leaned in toward the mirror. The cut was in his hair two inches above his forehead. He flushed the toilet to mask the sound of his washing off the wound. He dried quickly, combed his fingers through his hair to cover the small gash.

"Tony!" Linda was in the kitchen. He could hear her open the coffee pot, hear the water running in the pipes as she filled it. He walked quickly to the bedroom, grabbed a pair of gym shorts, put them on.

"Tony?!"

"Yeah, yeah. I just had ta go. You know what beer does. God it's hot! I can't believe it's still this hot this late."

"Where are the cigarettes?"

"Cig—Oh shit. I . . . I ran into that guy we met dancing. You know, the guy with the acne."

"So?"

"Oh, we started to talk . . . I guess he's been up here for four years. The Red Sox won the pennant two years ago. Did you know that?"

"Tony, what are you talking about?"

"We were talking about baseball. I musta left the cigarettes on the counter. I'll go back and get em."

"Oh, forget it! Baseball! Let's just go to sleep." With that she turned off the unit under the coffeepot, then she glanced up at Tony's face. "Are you okay? You look really pale."

"Do you love me?"

"More than anything."

"Why don't men say, 'I love you'?"

"Because those are just words."

"But a woman likes to hear it."

"If you hear a guy say it, it's probably cause he wants to screw you and he knows that's what you want to hear. He's probably lying so he can get laid."

"Tony Pisano! That's just more of your bullshit."

"I love you."

"Oh, see! You just want to get laid."

"But I do love you."

"I'm on to this now." Linda rolled over onto Tony, pinned him against the sheet. "How much do you love me?"

"Seven inches worth."

"Oh!" She punched him on the chest. "I swear you've got a penis obsession."

"My penis is obsessed with you."

"What if I wasn't sexy?"

"Who said you are?"

"Oh!" She punched him again. A weather front had come through late in the night and finally cooled the city. Sun blazed in through the French doors. "Maybe a little, huh?"

"Maybe a little. Can you really stay home today?"

"I never have before, so I think it's . . . you know, they'll think I really am sick. And I am. What about Charnowski?"

"Let Carlucci pull a double for once. Geez! He owes me. . . . "

Linda slid down, licked Tony's nipple making him shimmy. "Do you really love me?"

"Yes." Tony mimicked her tone. "I really love you?"

"Really? I'm serious. Enough to live with me for the rest of your life? I mean . . . it's about one hundred days that we've . . . you're not sick of me?"

"Miss Balliett," Tony intoned. "I am more infatuated with you every day."

"Enough to love *me* when I'm old and gray and I've got a fat stomach."

"Why are you doing this?"

"Maybe I'm feeling, you know, insecure. You're going to start classes. There'll be a lot of pretty girls in those classes. You'll be the man of the world. You could sweep any one of them off her feet. Just like you did me."

"Linda, I love you. You are absolutely everything I ever wanted in a girl and more. You're—you're—I mean, with all the stuff you know, with the nurse practitioner stuff, it's more likely you'd meet some rich doctor."

She hushed him with a kiss. "Then let's not put it off anymore. Let's get married."

"Today!"

"No, silly. But . . . maybe in November. Let's get married here in Boston in November. I could call Ruthie. I'd want her to be my maid of honor."

"I'd want Jimmy as the best man."

"Your cousin?"

"Yep!" Tony rolled onto his side, propped his head upon his hand. Immediately he jerked his head away. "Ow!"

"What'd you do, Babe?"

"Oh . . . ah, yesterday I was getting supplies in the storeroom and I banged my head. It's nothin. But hey, Jimmy, I think, is back end of September. We could get married next month."

"Really?"

"Would you want to?"

"We couldn't get a hall or a church or anything in a month."

"We don't need a hall."

"Yes we do. When I get married I want to have a nice reception. I'm only going to do this once, Tony. I don't believe in divorce."

"Neither do I. I don't even believe in foolin around." Tony kissed Linda. His hard-on touched her leg.

"Now put that thing away. We have to talk. I'd want my folks and sisters. And Judy Reardon."

"Yeah. I'd want my family, too. But most of all I want Jimmy. I can't get married unless he's here."

***** URGENT *** SPECIAL DELIVERY *****

Sergeant James Pellegrino
United States Marine Corps
4th CAG
FPO San Francisco 94900

JIMMY: There is truth to rumor Linda & I getting married. Invitations mailed—yours to your folks. 27 SEPT. You are best man. Hank & Norma want to give us r-t tickets to Europe for X-mas h-moon. Don't know how to blow it off. Need your ass home ASAP. Understand, L is great. Double that. Is maybe pregnant, too! H & N don't know. I love her much. Need your ass here to advise, celebrate w/ me.

Tony

Through the entire month leading up to the wedding, Tony couldn't get over how, on such short notice, both families had thrown time, energy and money into the hundred details he thought he did not care about until they began happening. Henry Sr. somehow convinced the Lenox Hotel on Copley Square to free up the small ballroom for the reception; and Linda, against her own family's beliefs, and enough to make Josephine Pisano lament for years, somehow arranged with the pastor of the United Universalist Church on Arlington Street for a marriage ceremony on Saturday, September 27th, 1969, at eleven o'clock in the morning.

All month Tony had attempted to think of something he could give Linda as a wedding gift—something that would have meaning. He was still struggling with it when Jimmy arrived, met him at BU on Wednesday, and convinced him to skip his last class, to see Jimmy's new bike— a '68 Harley-Davidson FLH-tourer, 74 CID shovelhead. "The ultimate V-twin," Jimmy quoted the salesman—and to go for a ride and a drink until they were both wasted. Since Wednesday Tony had not taken the time to think further on the topic of a wedding present.

Jimmy was already wasted. He'd started drinking even before he left Mill Creek Falls. He drank all night Wednesday, the 24th, first with Tony and, after Tony crashed, with Tom McLaughlin. He drank on Thursday. On Thursday night he, McLaughlin and Quentin Pomeroy took Tony bar-hopping in the Combat Zone and they all got wasted and McLaughlin got them stoned and for hours Jimmy said over and over, "She dumped me! Man, she dumped me! She dumped me. I . . . 'I don't fill *her* needs anymore.' What kind of way is that to talk?"

Jimmy was wasted; Pomeroy was wasted; Tony was tipsy. "There's a chick I know. . . . " Pomeroy swayed with Jimmy. "Cool chick. Long legs. Big boobs." He had both arms on Jimmy's shoulders, their foreheads touching. "Lucy Green. Lucy Goosey Green. Big Boobs. Long legs. Likes to do it. We gotta get Tony laid one last time. Fore he does the dirty deed."

"Lucy Goosey." Jimmy laughed. "Let's get Lucy Goosey. She per. . . pert-ee as Tony's girl? Where's Tony? Did I tell him Linda's great? Great. I love her. She's a knock out."

"Big boobs." Pomeroy stumbled, laughed.

"Don't you say that." Jimmy shoved Quentin's arms from his shoulders. "Dohnn say that bout my cousin's girl. Take that back."

"No. No. No. Lucy Goosey's. Not Linda. She's a saint. Linda's a saint."

On Saturday morning Jimmy drank, now Bloody Marys at Tony and Linda's, until Judy Reardon and two Boston friends—Rachel and Gina—and Linda's sisters Ruth and Joanie, drove all the boys out so Linda could get dressed. Quentin Pomeroy and Alvin Lewis had used the ambulance to pick up tuxedos and deliver them to the Lenox where the Pisanos were staying, and to the Holiday Inn for Henry Balliett Senior and Junior, and finally to Tony's for Jimmy and Tony and John Jr., Tony's oldest brother, who'd attached himself to the group so there'd be at least one sober head.

The boys, in their tuxedos, took the T up to Arlington Street, walked to the church, then waited for the limo to bring the bridal party. Jimmy, Quentin and Tom McLaughlin got stoned and hawked out the arriving girls—Tony's cousins, Linda's sisters and friends—and laughed at Tony's 15-year-old brother, Mark, making an awkward attempt to talk to Linda's 14-year-old sister, Cindy.

Tony was neither nervous nor tipsy. He'd gotten up at five thirty, put on his old jungle boots and run from the apartment, up Commonwealth to BU, then across the BU bridge into Cambridge, then upriver to the Larz Anderson Bridge and back through Allston until he was sweating profusely, yet still exhilarated, adrenline rushing, knowing he was marrying the most perfect woman God had ever created.

When she came down the aisle, when everyone rose, Tony saw nothing except Linda. She wore her mother's dress from twenty-three years earlier, an ivory brushed-satin gown with sweetheart neckline, cinched waist, and chapel-length train which had been shortened considerably. She carried a bouquet of white and wine roses surrounded by ferns and ivy, and in her auburn hair she wore a tiara of ivory stephanotis and green ribbons that brought out the green in her eyes, those exquisite eyes, and Tony knew he would love her forever and the proudest moment of his life would always be the moment she said, "I do."

Now Jimmy was miffed. They were at the Lenox and it was nearly time for him to give the toast and he'd just found out that Linda's father, that Quentin Pomeroy, that Tom McLaughlin and Charnowski and Carlucci and even Tony's own brothers, none of them knew anything about Tony's Marine Corps time. Even Reggie Williams, who'd been stationed with Tony in Philadelphia and who'd come in just for the reception, didn't know. Jimmy was miffed and stoned and wasted. Linda was bubbles and smiles and laughs and shining eyes as she and Tony moved from table to table talking to the guests. "Doctor Tagesaubruch, I want you to meet my husband. . . . " "This is my uncle Joe, Roseanne's father.

You met Roseanne, Vinny and Sante over . . ." "I remember . . ." "Uncle Joe was always my hero. He was a Marine in the Pacific during the big one." "Oh! I'm impressed. You're where Tony gets his spirit from. . . ."

"Ladies and gentlemen—" the band, Stevie and the Deceptions, all black, friends of Alvin Lewis, jazzed out a fanfare and drumroll, "the best man, Sergeant James Pellegrino, will now give the toast."

"I—I—" Jimmy paused, the guests quieted. Tinkling of glasses and dishes came from the hallway. Then Jimmy blurted, "Tony, I gotta tell ya, you are marrying the prettiest girl I've ever seen in my whole life. And Linda, you're . . . this guy you're marrying . . . this guy you married, I . . . nobody up here seems to know who this guy is." There was muted, good-natured laughter. "Anthony Pisano was maybe the greatest platoon sergeant the United States Marine Corps has ever known. Anthony Pisano is a ferocious fighter. Your husband, Linda, should have gotten a Congressional Medal of Honor for his actions at Dai Do, Quang Tri Province, the Republic of Viet Nam. He saved lives. He saved hundreds of lives. After two-four—Golf, 2d of the 4th Marines—after they ran out of ammo and while they were being slaughtered by an attacking battalion of communist soldiers, Tony Pisano stood up and with a machette in hand"—John Jr., Tony's oldest brother had moved to Jimmy's side; now he put a hand on Jimmy's shoulder trying to stop him, but Jimmy violently whipped his shoulder away, doubled his volume—"an entrenching tool in the other, he charged the NVA slashing and hacking until he had a pile of heads and bodies around him and they were beatin feet back north. . . . Geez, I can't believe you don't know. . . . That doesn't include what he did out at Loon or—he's a hero. A legend. My hootch maid, Li, she draws pictures of him because the villagers still revere him—"

"So let us lift our glasses," John Jr. interrupted, lifted his glass, smiled brightly, put his free arm around Jimmy's shoulder, "and drink a toast to the future, to happiness, to long productive lives, and maybe to some nieces and nephews."

She had smiled at him, in class, English 101, smiled as if she knew, he thought, sitting there with her long straight black hair falling over the back of her chair all the way to the seat. And Tony had smiled back, sheepishly, then averted his eyes and attempted to listen to the instructor. He kept his head straight, shifted his eyes, trying to see if she might glance again at him, trying to determine her origin. He'd entered class late, just late enough to miss the role call, to miss her name. She was new.

"Pisano, Anthony?" the instructor, a part-timer, a fill-in in the department, had asked as Tony slipped into a seat.

"Yes Sir," he'd answered. Several students had snickered as they always did at his brisk "Yes Sir" to professors or instructors, but she had glanced over, smiled, then turned her attention back to the instructor.

Tony had been dazed. Not because she was pretty, which she was, or because she'd smiled at him, of which he was certain, but because she was Viet Namese.

"God, she's really talented," Linda said.

"Yeah." Tony agreed. It was late night, mid-October. They were sitting on their bed, going through wedding presents, Linda writing quick thank-you notes. "I think she's kind of the reason for him goin back."

"You should write this one," Linda said. She adjusted the drawing so the light fell on it at a more obtuse angle. It was an intricate pen-and-ink sketch of a jungle-uniformed Tony before a village home, holding a Viet Namese infant while a toddler hugged his leg. Leaning against the board-shanty in the background was an M-16 rifle and a machete.

"You write better," Tony said.

"You know"— Linda huffed —"*these* are to you too! Especially this one." Linda picked from the small stack the most masculine-looking thank-you note and handed it and a pen to Tony. "Is he going to marry her or something?"

"Marry Li?!" Tony chuckled.

"Well, you said that's the reason he was going back!"

"Naw. No. He ... " Tony didn't know how to explain it. Looking at the drawing made him nostalgic, made him feel as if he were missing something important, made him feel he too should be there—not for adventure but for meaning—made him feel as if "compare and contrast" essays were meaningless, and his present life self-indulgent and unjustifiable. "Li's about twelve," he said. "She's blind in one eye and has a short leg because she walked into a mine. She's a kid ... like she's his kid. It's not just her. It's so many of em."

"She's twelve and she drew this!"

"Yeah. Pretty good, huh?"

"I think we should put it up in the front room."

"Aw, no. I don't think ... you know, it's kind of inappropriate here."

"Inappro—"

"Well, not inappropriate. It's just really personal. You know, it's not like McLaughlin's poster of the guy with the artificial arms and legs that says—"

" 'The Army Builds Men.' "

"Yeah. You know, can you imagine the guy who's in that poster—can you imagine him putting it up his front room?"

"That's different, Babe. This is really nice."

Tony lay back, rolled to the side, put the card and pen on the floor. "I'll write him later. I can't send him a thank-you. I'll write him a letter." Tony rolled back, put his hand on Linda's shoulder and massaged gently.

"Don't do that," she said sweetly.

"I can't help myself." Tony slid his hand down her back, under her sweatshirt, back up to her bra.

Linda shifted. "Not tonight, Babe. There's too much to do and tomorrow . . ."

"I know."

"Why don't you come with me to the doctor."

"I really can't miss another class. I cut two filling in for Carlucci."

"Hm."

"And I'd feel a little out of place. . . ."

"Hm."

"You know," Tony pulled Linda down on the bed, "I'm going to love you forever. I'm going to be the best husband and the best fa—"

"It's a pact then. Because I'm going to be the best wife."

"You already are."

"Tony, not tonight. I'm . . . I'm really scared."

"Pisano."

"Yo."

"See me when we're done here."

"Yes Sir."

When only Tony and Ken Charnowski were left in the AmbuStar dispatch office, Charnowski, face averted, mumbled something Tony didn't understand.

"Ken?"

Charnowski grumbled lower, still did not look at Tony.

"Hey, Ken! You called and I came. I'm cutting another class and you obviously don't need a driver."

"You finish the EMT course?"

"Yeah. Well . . . I did all the work."

"Did you pass the test?"

"I haven't taken it yet."

"Oh Boy!"

"Somethin wrong?"

"No. No. Remember that Storrow Drive accident in August?"

"Yeah."

"You helped Pomeroy with the baby?"

"Yeah."

"Oh Boy!"

"What?"

"Look kid, I . . . you can't work here for a while."

"What?!"

"That baby's father filed suit."

"Filed . . . Why?"

"You know that kid died?"

"Aw, no. I didn't."

"The father's attorney claims we were negligent and—"

"NEGLIGENT!"

"Yeah. Negligent."

"There's nothin I could of done more than I did! Shit!"

Charnowski sighed. "I know. But you shouldn't have even touched the baby. You weren't certified. Attorney got the records."

"But Pomeroy was."

"You were only supposed to drive."

"You gotta be fuckin shittin me!"

"That's what the suit says."

"What was I supposed to fuckin do? Let the kid bleed to death?"

"Listen . . . we'll beat this. I know you're a good kid. I know you're real cool and I know you know procedure. It's not you anyway. It's me. I shouldn't have had you out there. I can't let you work until this is settled. And kid, for God sakes, take the god damned EMT test."

"I am pregnant."

"Wonderful!" Tony had not told Linda that he'd been to AmbuStar, that he'd cut class. "Whoa-whoa! Whoa! Whoa! Wonderful!" He did a jig, leaped to her, wrapped her in his arms, legs, entire body curling about her. She let him hug her for a moment then slithered out of his grasp. Tony stood in place, running, his feet beating the floorboards like jungle drums.

"Tony!" Linda backed away, turned half away from him. "Tony, you don't understand. I don't want to be pregnant. Not yet."

"Huh!" Tony's face was a mix of fading smile and confusion. "I thought. . . . We agreed on wanting a family."

"Just not yet. I mean I do. I really do, Babe. I want to have a big family with you. Just not for a few years. Damn. I'm still an LPN." Tears formed in Linda's eyes. "Tony, I've worked really hard for this. I really want to graduate. I want a real graduation. Not that phony bologna pat on the back."

"What are you saying?"

"I don't know. I don't know. God! There's . . . you know. Nobody our age is having kids. You know, not yet, not with all the overpopulation. And we've been fighting . . . you know, at the hospital, we've been trying to educate the minorities and the poor for zero population growth. It's like this . . . like this is immoral."

"You can stay in school. They won't throw you out for being pregnant, will they?"

"I don't know. It's . . . The program goes on for sixteen more months. I'm two months along."

"Don't drop out." Tony went to her, gently grasped her hands. "You can do both. Really. Fuck everybody else. Fuck what they think. I know you. You can do this. Really."

"It's going to be expensive. How can we pay—"

"You stay in school," Tony said. "Let me worry about getting the money. Really."

"But I want you to stay in school, too," Linda said. "That's really important. Maybe I should switch programs."

"No. I know you've got this mission. . . . "

"Or maybe . . . "

"Maybe what?"

"I told my friend Cathy. She said, you know, 'Like this isn't the dark ages. You don't have to go through with it.' "

"Linda! What the hell are you saying? You told Cathy?!"

"She was pregnant last spring. No one knows. . . . "

"CATHY! GEEZ!! You tell her even before you tell me! Am I even the god damned father?!" Tony spun around, angrily stomped a foot.

"Of course . . . " Linda began, but even as she said it her own ire erupted.

Her anger fed Tony's. He was near the TV. Suddenly he thrust out a hand to the set's side, pulled, shoved, violently lifting the set from its shelf, ripping antenna and power wires from the wall, shot-putting the TV halfway across the room where it crashed, then popped, the picture tube shattering. "Do whatever the hell you want! Cathy!" Tony stormed out, banged the door.

Two weeks had passed. Decisions had been made.

Linda lifted the lid of the big spaghetti pot. Steam billowed up, rolled in under the old, oft-painted kitchen cabinets. She noted the rolling boil, thought briefly that the old stove took an awful long time to heat eight quarts, then nimbly slid in one large lasagne noodle after another, stirred, thought about Tony's return. The day was bright, crisp, clear—the first truly nice fall day of the year. Earlier, walking up to the Purity Supreme, she'd caught the change in the Commonwealth Ave. wind full-face, the change, the significance, the end of summer, the end of so much but the start too—yes the start too. She stirred the noodles. Simon and Garfunkel's "Bridge over Troubled Water" was turning in the living room. Variously she thought the music was like this fall day, like the cool clear breeze in bright sunshine; then she hoped Tony would make it back before nightfall; then how proud she was—no not proud, as if that detracted from the others—how delighted she was with the results of the Medical Care of Surgical Patients exam: highest mark in her class.

Linda set the timer, left the kitchen, sat in the study, began to reread, to smile as she read, the chapter on childbirth. It was exciting—scary but thrilling. It was her program, her emphasis. She hadn't planned to be her own first patient but Tony had convinced her. How badly, how adamantly he wanted to have this baby! She did not understand it but she could not deny it. All week she'd worked doubles in the GWYN pool— the go-where-you're-needed pool—floating to ICU, to the outpatient clinic and twice to maternity. How it excited her to hold the newborns, just to look at them in their Plexiglas bassinets, to watch the fathers come in, look, maybe touch. How it frightened her—not knowing what to expect of herself or Tony, physically, emotionally. And financially. She'd seen Tony buckle down. He'd put his studies first—reading, writing essays, copying notes, actually being ahead on assignments—and not once had he gone to AmbuStar! How mature he could be. And how boyish.

"Is that you, Tony?" Her voice had been soft. She'd cried, had been so frightened by his burst of rage, his smashing of the TV, his stomping out. Yet three hours after the incident of two weeks earlier, he had come back loaded like a packhorse. "Tony?"

"Linda."

"Babe, I'm sorry I told Cath—"

"Geez," he'd said. His eyes flashed, his face beamed with his most disarming, infectious smile. "You already cleaned up!" He dropped the boxes on the sofa, danced a little jig, then sang out like only Tony Pisano could sing out in his off-key baritone, " 'I want a good luck charm, hangin' on my arm, to have, to hold, tonight.' "

Then he bent down, lifted a box and went to her. "Linda Lee," he said mock mockingly, "whatever you decide is all right with me. And this is for you."

"What is it? Not because—"

"No. Naw, not this." He indicated the spot on the floor where the TV had shattered. "I'll—I'll—I've got to square that away later. I—" again the smile, "never got you a wedding present cause I just couldn't think of anything, but when I went out it hit me. Open it."

Linda hefted the box. Shook it. "What is this?"

"Open it."

Gingerly she untaped the wrapping paper. "What is it?" Her brow furrowed as she looked at the picture.

"It's a Bell Star."

"A . . . a helmet?"

"Two. I bought one for me, too."

"A motorcycle helmet?!"

"Yeah. And look what else I got." He went back to the sofa, brought back a large flat box.

"Tony?!" Linda couldn't imagine what was in his mind.

"Open it." He drew out the words.

Again she carefully unwrapped the paper, opened the box. Then she lifted out the jacket, "Oh! Oh, it's so soft." She held it up against her chest. "But . . . "

"It's moose hide."

"Moose?! Tony, this is beautiful but where would I wear a motorcycle jack—Oh you didn't!" Her entire face changed. "You didn't buy a—"

"No. Naw . . . "

"That money's for . . . that's our wedding money."

"I know. I know. You know, Jimmy's goina let us use his scooter. You didn't see it, did you? I mean really see it. It's real cool. I can get a ride down maybe next weekend and ride it back."

"But he . . ."

"He offered it to me that first day. I just . . . you know, had too much on my mind. But he called before he went back. He left it at my folks'. In the toolshed."

Linda became excited by the idea. They had borrowed Chas and Cathy's bike for their forays to Plum Island and she'd loved the freedom and excitement. "Tony!" She held the jacket up again. "You know, in about another month I won't fit into this."

"Aw, in another month it'll be too cold anyway. Here, I got one more thing."

"Now what? I'm afraid to look."

Tony picked a sheet of paper from the sofa. He looked at her—she was donning the leather jacket—then stepped to her, put his arm about her shoulders, kissed her on the forehead. "Reservations for the first weekend in November out on Cape Cod. It'll be our honeymoon."

"Oh, Babe, you're so sweet. . . . "

"I'm sorry I—"

"No, it was my fault."

"I shouldn't have hit the—"

"I don't like to watch it, anyway."

"Yeah, still. I was being a jerk."

"You know, you're the only man in the world I can imagine having a baby with."

"You don't have to. Really. Do what's right for you."

"This is right for me," she'd said.

The buzzer sounded. Linda popped up, her thoughts returned to the present. She removed the pot from the stove, poured the noodles and water into a colander in the sink, then tried to lift the top noodle. The entire mass was stuck together. Again she tried. The noodle ripped. "Oh damn," she muttered. Tony might pull in any moment. She'd been unconsciously listening for the guttural roar of Jimmy Pellegrino's Harley-Davidson in the back alley from the time she'd begun the sauce early that morning.

During the weeks before leaving for Mill Creek Falls and Jimmy's bike, Tony had been especially diligent about his studies—especially his English 101 compositions. Completely unknown to Linda, there was a draw, a lure, a curious attraction to that class that Tony could not identify, though he now at least knew her name: Nguyen Thi An. He had not spoken to her, had but silently nodded each time she'd entered. And very properly, almost imperceptibly, she had acknowledged him with momentary eye contact, the wisp of a smile, the slightest tilt of her head. She sat in the first row, center, he two rows back, left side. And through the entire fifty minutes—Mondays, Wednesdays, and Fridays—he stared at her.

The teacher, Associate Professor Mathew Groesbeck, was thirtyish, had long unkempt brown hair, an untrimmed beard, an old OD green field jacket he wore to class every day and didn't remove until midway through the hour. On the back of the jacket was a large bright yellow peace symbol. To Tony it was a game Groesbeck played on the class as he played the class itself, played for the two-thirds of the students who were young women, played like a con man among yokels.

"What," Groesbeck's voice was mellow, almost apologetic, "is the connection, if any, between the counter culture, freedom, the youth rebellion, the war, minority repression, big money, women's rights, morality? Certainly"—the class sat rapt—"that topic is too grand for a twenty-five-hundred-word essay. Take two elements, whatever is most important to you, investigate the ... "

Tony scribbled, "War and Morality," then again looked at An. Where most of the American girls sat akimbo—a foot tucked up under their butt, arms sprawling or hooked on the back of their seats, some even with their legs up, their feet hanging over the chair in front of them—An sat primly, her feet and knees together, her back straight, her thin arms bent and resting lightly on the fold-down writing top.

"Melyssa?"

"Uh-huh."

"If women are paid at a rate equal to one-half of that of men, for the same work ... "

Tony tuned out Groesbeck's words even though he remained aware of his speaking. He looked at his scribbled topic, scratched it out, wrote, "Freedom and women's rights," immediately knew he could not write well on that and crossed it out too. Then he wrote "Envy." He thought about it for a moment, thought about Groesbeck, thought about himself, how incompetent he felt as a student, how old he felt in comparison to these children, old not so much in years but in attitude. He felt he knew more than any of them—he'd been around the world, fought in the war, buried the dead—yet he felt as if everything he knew was either insignificant to them or outright repulsive. And he'd heard that Groesbeck was boffing at least three coeds with whom Tony could barely even communicate. Tony crossed out "Envy" and wrote "Fuck it." He looked at An.

"But it's just so unfair," one girl was saying. "They define what's of value and they control how women are compensated. They make sure the compensation is low. In that way they keep us down."

Groesbeck nodded emphatically.

Tony blurted, "Who's they?" Everyone turned. Except An. "You ... " Tony began choking on his words, "keep saying 'they.' I'm just wondering who's behind this conspiracy?"

"Ah ... Pisano. Anthony, isn't it?"

"Yes Sir." Not laughs now but a cacophony of low hoots, sighs, and catcalls.

"Well," Groesbeck came to his rescue, "that is a valid question." Then he dropped him. "One, I'm afraid, we'll have to explore next class. Our time's up."

An was up first. Tony scrambled to cut her off. He did not exactly know why. He had no intentions toward her—had no thoughts of infidelity—was as crazy about Linda as ever, perhaps more so, but he felt propelled toward her. She reached the door first, exited. He brushed past two girls, stepped awkwardly in front of An, looked into her face. Immediately she lowered her eyes. Quietly Tony whispered, "*Chao Ba.*"

An looked up, laughed. "Oh, yes," she said, and she laughed a disappointing, unpleasant, childish laugh. She side-stepped Tony, disappeared deeper into the building. Tony stood still. He did not follow her, did not gaze after her. Someone bumped him. "Uh . . . you're right in the middle . . ."

"Oh." He said absently. He moved to the wall. "Sorry." He continued to stand there, to the side of the door, crushing the spines of his books, grinding his teeth, feeling rigid, hurt, put down.

Linda heard the throaty popping of the Harley's cylinders as it entered the alley, heard the blasting growl as Tony revved it just before he killed the ignition. It was just dark. She'd cooked a second pot of noodles, this time leaving them in the water, dumping out half the hot, added cold to stop the cooking. They'd come out manageable, exactly as the cookbook said. Then she'd tiered sauce, ricotta, noodles, and mozzarella— Nonna Pisano's directions from the St. Ignatius Guild's *Treasury of European Recipes*, which she'd given Linda as a wedding present along with a check for one hundred dollars.

The wine was open, the lasagne cooked, the small kitchen table set with tablecloth and candles. Linda scampered to the front room, raised the record stack on the chrome spindle, watched, listened as the Carpenters' *Close to You* album dropped and the lead song of side two, "Baby It's You" began to play. She adjusted the volume, ran to the bathroom, adjusted her hair, pouted, thinking that her face was getting puffy.

Immediately Tony wanted Linda to come out, go for a ride. She smiled. "You'd think, being on it for five hours, you'd want to stay in."

"Just around the block," he said. "Maybe up around the Combat Zone and back."

"But dinner's ready."

Tony sipped wine, washing down the first mouthful of lasagna. "God! This is just like Nonna's. Where'd you learn—"

"I'll never tell." Linda rubbed her knees against Tony's. "Is it really okay?"

"It's stupendous!"

"No. It's just okay, huh? It's the first time I ever made it."

"Well, if it's only just okay, I'll make you a fluffer-nutter and we'll save it all for me."

They laughed. Then Linda put her finger to her lips. "Sssh!"

"What?"

"Listen to the words." The album had changed. From the stereo: *They call me baby driver / And once upon a pair of wheels / Hit the road and I'm gone 'ah,' What's my number? . . .* " Tony and Linda joined in, "*I wonder how your engine feels.*" They burst out laughing and chimed in with the refrain, "*Ba ba ba ba, Scoot down the road / What's my number / I wonder how your engine feels.*"

"Oh! Babe . . ."

"Hm-hmm."

"I forgot to tell you. Mr. Charnowski called. He said you should pick up your check. Is—is anything . . . you know . . . "

"Naw. I told him I was needing to hit the books. But . . . you know, he doesn't really pay very well. I was talkin to a couple of guys who'r workin for a developer out in the Watertown-Arlington area. Puttin up condos. They make four times what I get from AmbuStar. Now with the bike I could join em. Work less hours, have more time to study *and* make more money."

"And still have time to see how my engine feels?"

"I've always got time for that!"

Late that night Linda woke. Light from signs and cars on Commonwealth and Long avenues glittered and danced on the walls. She looked at Tony, asleep, his brow creased, his eyes wrinkled at the corners. They'd had such a wonderful evening. How they loved, how much in love Linda felt, how certain she was of her decision.

Reflections danced on Tony's face. Linda propped herself up on her elbow, watched his face. With her left hand she lightly rubbed her rounding abdomen. Tony grimaced, shook his head. Linda smiled, thought he was probably riding the Harley in his dream, probably cussing out some stupid driver as he always did when they took Chas and Cathy's bike—cuss em out, drop back a bit, then let er rip, zinging by the offending vehicle, scaring her, pushing her out of herself, out of her conventionality, her security, into exhilaration, into an outrageousness she'd never have attempted on her own, into her taking over the chore of flipping the bird at automobile drivers who'd cut them off.

Again Tony grimaced, his whole face jerking, his shoulders trembling. "It's okay, Babe," Linda whispered. "It's okay. Sail on. Your silvergirl will lay me down." Linda rocked forward and ever so lightly kissed Tony's shoulder. He completely stilled. She nuzzled his chest, kissed his nipple.

"AAAA!" Tony bolted up, grabbed the head before him, grabbed it hard in both hands, threw. Then he bound to his knees, feet, crouched, grappler's position. Linda was on the floor, dazed, shocked, hurt, too soon to be frightened, to cry out—Tony's feet dug into the mattress, still low, in a fighting stance, ready to strike.

"Babe! Babe! Babe, it's me."

His head snapped robotically back forth, backforth.

"Tony! Babe." Now Linda was crying.

He was coming to—out of it—awake, aware. He saw Linda on the floor shielding herself. He could not fathom why she was there.

Tony rose at four thirty. He had not been sleeping. His night rituals had evolved to a state of perpetual vigilance. Since the incident of two weeks earlier he had not trusted himself to sleep but had instead cat-napped at various times during the day—sometimes in class, often in the early evening on the sofa, listening to records. After a week he stopped going to classes altogether. He hadn't been to his English 101 section since the day he'd been shot down by Nguyen Thi An, though he'd made the large lectures where all the sections met and he'd seen Groesbeck privately, explaining how he had a pregnant wife and was now working for Stites and Emerson Construction, and Groesbeck had been understanding and allowed Tony to turn in his essays without at-tending classes. His Spanish professor was also sympathetic. Western Civilization and Religion were lecture courses. Tony paid Tom Mc-Laughlin to sit in for him. No one cared. His Biology instructor objected, not because this one student might miss something she considered im-portant, but because the entire student body seemed to have rejected her, rejected all science as being somehow tied to old thought, past genera-tions, status quo, the war. She entrenched. Only when Tony banged his fists on the desk and snarled, "God damn, I've got a baby on the way. I'm working full-time. And I've done all the reading," did she reluctantly agree to let him make up classes by attending evening lectures.

By five A.M. he had eaten, made a thermos of coffee, rechecked apart-ment security. Mid-November, there was no natural light in the sky, would be none until nearly six thirty. He paced. He did not want to wake Linda but he needed her. He couldn't find his socks. James Stites expected him in Watertown by seven. The carpenters didn't show up until seven thirty or even eight but the laborers—gofers, buggy-luggers, and mules—needed to start early, needed to break down the lumber stacks for the sixty-four condominiums in various phases of simultane-ous construction, carry the studs, joists, headers and plywood to the designated cutting sites, then restack the material ensuring each crew could work without pause.

Tony went to the bedroom door, stared in to see if Linda was awake. She wasn't. He needed to wake her yet he knew she'd worked yesterday, had classes yesterday, made them dinner, went to the laundromat, and studied while he slept on the couch. He walked back to the kitchen, banged around making two sandwiches. Again he went back to the bed-room. Still asleep! To the bathroom. He flushed. The pipes in the old building resounded with the rush of water.

By 5:40 he couldn't stand it any longer. "Linda . . . Linda." He kissed her gently on the cheek. She smiled, still asleep. Her head rolled on the pillow. "Linda." He kissed her again, this time on the ear.

"Ummm," she moaned.

"Linda, I can't find any socks."

"Un . . ." Sleepily. "Oh. They're in the basket in the study."

Two minutes later he was back. "Linda."

"Un . . . un." The sound of a small animal crying.

"What about T-shirts. And my quilted—"

"Oh Babe . . . wait." She sat up.

"I'm sorry. But it's getting late."

"What time is it?"

"It's just about six."

"Oh God! They're all in the basket, Tony." She yawned.

"I looked."

Linda sighed. She rose, groggily slipped into her satin bathrobe. "It's freezing in here. Why don't you have your shirt on?"

"You said you'd rub that cortizone cream into my shoulders."

"Oh. Yeah. You really should see a dermatologist."

"Maybe. If this doesn't work. But I gotta do somethin cause carrying those boards is killin me."

For the next half hour Linda readied Tony for work—including remaking his sandwiches and repacking his lunch. When he went to leave, he kissed her tenderly, squeezed her ass with one hand, rubbed a breast with the other. She shook him off. "Babe, don't do that. Go. I'll see you tonight. What are you going to do about school?"

Things had changed, perhaps had changed the moment two weeks earlier when Tony had grabbed Linda's head and thrown her from the bed. There had been no sex between them. Linda dismissed it as exhaustion from work, school, taking care of the apartment and her husband, and growing the fetus. She had no desire to have Tony.

Early evening, the blasting revs of the Harley filled the alley, then died. A few moments later, "There's a card from your folks, Babe. Must of got held up in the mail. You're home early."

"Huh?" His utterance was curt.

"A card from—"

"I heard you." Tony plopped down on the couch. "Those assholes," he said. His voice was controlled but bitter. "I'm so fuckin tired of working with assholes. I've seen things they can't even imagine. And I'm a good worker."

"What happened?" Linda sat on the coffee table opposite him.

"Nothing. I'm just so damn tired. And you should see the crap they're building. None of em give a flyin leap. With my hands"—he held up his right hand, examined it as if it were a bear paw—"I could push over one of those boxes. They grease the fuckin nails so they slide in. But by the time they finish a wall the nails are already poppin out. Shit! Those condos aren't rigid until they slap up the sheetrock!"

"Did you say something?"

"I told Stites. I told a couple of guys I was working with. They look at me like I'm nuts."

"What did Mr. Stites say?"

"He gave me some bullshit about meeting code. Half the guys nip Old Grand Dad or toke up."

"You don't." Linda got up, stepped to the stereo shelf where she'd left the card.

"Maybe some." Tony leaned forward. His arms hung limp from his shoulders, his fury spent. "I'm not a goddamn head. Not by a long shot. And I'm no juicer. But, Babe, if I get fired—"

"Would they?"

"We . . . this weekend . . . down on the cape . . . maybe we should put it off."

Linda handed Tony the card, sat beside him, put a hand on his shoulder. Lethargically he opened it. "For Our Son With Love . . . "

Under the verse Josephine had added:

Lovingly, Mom and Dad. We're anxious to have you and Linda here for Thanksgiving, with John, Joe and Mark. I get to see Joey at least several times a month, but you and Linda seem so far away. Here it is your birthday and I'm talking Thanksgiving. But we want to see you. Call collect.
P.S.: Johnny's bringing home his new girlfriend.

"Tony, will you read this now?"

"Naw, Uncle James, I don't think I oughta. You know, not here at the table. Later." They were at his mother's house. Earlier Tony had been upset. He'd wanted Linda to see the Pisano family Thanksgiving tradition, contrast it with last year. "We decided to do it different this year," Josephine had said. "This year we'll be like Lutzburgh. With a turkey."

"Ma," Tony had objected. "You gotta be kidding. No pasta! No braciola! Geez. For this I coulda taken Linda to HoJo's." And he'd been upset by Aunt Helen's presence and by the beginning of Jimmy's letter, which he'd started in the kitchen.

"Please," Aunt Isabella said. Everyone had finished eating. "Really, we can't make heads or tails of it."

"Read it later, Tony," John Sr. said. "In private."

"It's not good dinner talk," Tony agreed. He cut and served himself second servings of the apple and pumpkin pies.

"Hey, Tony." Joe pointed at Tony's plate. "Who's pregnant anyway? You or Linda?"

Aunt Helen pinched his cheek. "He is getting a little heavy, isn't he?"

Linda patted his cheek on the other side, "I like it," she said. "And with all the lifting he's doing"—she socked his chest—"look how strong he is."

"Geh-yett off it!" Tony poked Linda's belly. "I know what the scale said when *you* stepped on it. . . . "

"That's enough!" Josephine stopped him. "She has to gain. It's not healthy if she doesn't. Now read!"

"Ma! Even Pop says no."

"Don't 'Ma' me. You sound like a cow. Read." John Sr. quietly excused himself, left the table.

"Geez." Tony flashed his hands straight up. "Okay. But . . . " He read aloud.

Dear Mom and Pop,

Save these notes for me. Mr. K. was up here from Saigon for four hours. I overheard him talking to our head honchos (the top brass, Pop). This is evil. I would have expected it from LBJ but I thought Nixon would be different. You know I've developed a deep compassion for the South Viet Namese people and for their military forces. I've worked and lived extensively with Popular Forces. [You can rewrite this and send it to the newspapers.] I've lived at hamlet level, I've helped set up CAFs (combined action forces)—training mostly old men and young kids to defend their villages. I love it. I love them. There's no getting around it. They are superb. They might be rice farmers but they want to learn. They want to be able to defend themselves. They treat me and all CAP and CAG personnel with a great deal of respect. I have shared food with them, slept in bunkers with them, stood watch, gone on patrol with them. Although they are peasants, they are better soldiers than us simply because they know how to walk in their own area, down their own paths, through their own groves. We don't. We learn, but they've known since childhood. And they know who belongs and who doesn't. I teach them how to tear down an M-14 or an M-1 carbine, how to shoot straight, how to build a bunker, drive a jeep, make up a watch schedule, call in artillery when they're attacked. I thought I could teach them about moving at night. Forget it. They taught me! These guys don't have uniforms. They've got old weapons—some impossible to get ammo for. Still they've developed into a force to be reckoned with. Constantly they come to us with information (to MIT—Military Intel Team). We have come to depend upon them—they depend on us.

That's why that bastard from Saigon has me so riled. What I overheard was this. "We're pulling out. Don't tell anybody," K said. "We're going to pull out and let the communists have the country." He told them, absolutely instructed them, "Don't waste your people on the indigenous population. Cut back materiel and effort."

I almost fragged the bastard. I think mainly he means the farthest out villages and hamlets—which is exactly where CAG operates and where we've had great success. How will this bode for the next circle in? Seems to me, it will make "that" circle the outer ring of our defenses.

The bottom line is this. We've been used. The PFs and RFs have been used too, but we've been used far worse. Men get used in every war, but they're especially wasting us in this one. I think, if we really are pulling out, and who's higher in country than K, I think we'll see it as the dumbest thing we've ever done in our entire history. All our efforts, wasted! This country pockmarked for nothing.

The real sad part, if we pull out, is we will have wasted the virtues of an entire generation of American boys—its will, its patriotism, its concern for those beyond our own borders. What will be left? We are the Will. We are those who have said we will defend those who cannot defend themselves from tyranny. We are the Will. We are those who have said, "We will squeeze the trigger in defense of liberty, in defense of self-determination, in defense of self-rule." We are the will and they are wasting us. That will have a profound and detrimental effect on America for a long time. And the South, with M-1s and M-14s, won't be able to withstand the North. Again—for America, if we destroy the will to go *conventional*, the alternative warfare will be much more horrifying. I am the Will. The Will is being destroyed!

Tony stopped reading, stared at the letter, worked his tongue anxiously against his teeth, did not look up.

"What do you think?" Uncle James asked.

"Who's Mr. K.?" Isabella pressed.

"What's he talking about, 'destroying the will'?"

Tony looked up. He felt grave. "I don't know," he answered. "I don't know."

"Is this about the peace protestors? Burning flags, indeed! Or the Chicago Eight? Or this My Lai place?"

All Tony would say is, "I don't know." He read the remainder of the letter, which was cheerful, newsy. Li had sold a sketch of three marines and three PF soldiers to a major British magazine. She had sketched a portrait of Jimmy with his new rank insignia. The fighting, very sporadic, was going well for the ARVN, the RF/PF, and the Americans. Viet Namization was heavily underway farther south, but in I Corps the region's security still depended upon the Americans.

"I still want to know about this Mr. K.," Uncle James said.

"I see it this way," Tony finally responded. "Jimmy's a professional Marine now. He knows what he's doing and I trust him. I've got complete faith in him."

At dusk Tony and Linda rode through Old New Town and New New Town, circled back through Creek's Bend, then down, across the river into Lutzburgh, up River Front Drive, past the great homes, the Mansions of the Five Families. Then they looped back behind the town offices, down Second Street to Mill Creek Road, through the Warehouse and Small Mill area, across the old truss bridge and back to Tony's folks' home.

All the while Tony kept feeling—I should be there. I should be helping out. I've left them. I should be there to help them win. He thought about K. but he didn't know if K. was Komer or Ky, Kissinger or a code name. And all the while Linda clung to Tony's back, trying to stay warm, trying to squeeze her husband in that special way that transmitted her love and her warmth.

"Tony," Linda said before they got off the Harley, "you don't know how lucky you are. This is a wonderful town. I could live here."

So things went through November and December and into January 1970. Tony and Linda spent a shallow, walking-on-eggshells Christmas in French Creek, spent New Year's Eve back in their own apartment. Tom McLaughlin, Chas and Cathy, Alvin Lewis and his wife Luann, and Tom and Gina, all stopped in on their way to parties but at midnight Tony and Linda celebrated alone. "It's going to be a great year." Linda kissed her husband.

"To the best year of our lives so far," Tony promised. "To the three of us."

Then came finals and Tony's last papers. For English 101 he wrote an essay titled, "The Hidden Pullout: To Will or Not To Will." Still he worked for Stites and Emerson, a mule in the coldest month of the year. On the twelfth of January Tony received his first grade, a B in Western Civilization. Then came a C in Spanish, C in Biology and B in Religion. Linda was thrilled. On the cold night of the seventeenth Tony rode in from Watertown, the wind in his face numbing his nose, his lips, his unshaven face even through two layers of scarf, freezing the skin of his exposed forehead above his goggles, below his now long thick dark hair and the brim of his watch cap. He refused to wear the Bell Star he'd purchased—except when Linda rode behind him. He stopped at BU to see if Groesbeck had posted grades. "Incomplete," was written opposite his name.

He was dumbfounded. He stumbled away, muttering, anger growing, hoping it was a mistake, thinking he'd have to come back during the day, miss half a day's work, talk to Groesbeck. Then he rethought the conversation he'd had with Groesbeck where the man had agreed that Tony could turn in his essays at Groesbeck's office. Now Tony thought Groesbeck had played him, had fucked him because he didn't like him, fucked him because of the "Hidden Pullout" essay, the "will to squeeze the trigger" paragraph. Tony went back to Groesbeck's door, rechecked his grade. He checked the entire list. All of Groesbeck's Girls, including Nguyen Thi An, had received A's; the plain-looking and the boys had all received B's; Tony's grade was the only variant.

For half an hour Tony circled the blocks about BU. He crossed the BU bridge into Cambridgeport, circled, came back, putted in and around the apartments of the thousands of students who occupied much of the area. Vaguely he searched for An, vaguely—thinking he'd ask her if she knew Mr. K. from Saigon. He'd learned she was from Saigon—that her family had a home in the resort area near Da Lat. Her father was an importer and an adviser to President Thieu.

A week later Groesbeck withdrew Tony's incomplete, changed the grade to an F for "missing more than half the classroom hours." Tony was confused. At first he did not recognize that his 2.3 grade point average without his English mark was now a 1.875 average, and that as a "conditional" freshman he was on academic probation; he did not realize that he could not work days and be a full-time day student; did not understand that he had, in effect, dropped out. When the realization hit him he bought two pints of Jack Daniel's, shared one with the carpenters, drank one himself, and late afternoon on the twenty-sixth of January, 1970, James Stites of Stites and Emerson Construction of Boston, fired Anthony F. Pisano, also of Boston, for "drinking on the job."

So things went and thus it was two days later Tony was in the apartment when the phone rang.

Tony is slumped on the couch. Linda is in the study. From the stereo, volume low, seeps the rich voices of Gary Puckett and the Union Gap, *I've tried so hard but I can't bring you around. . . .*

Outside it is cold, the wind of Commonwealth Ave. rattles the old French doors, teases its way though cracks to puff out the curtain. Tony's eyes are shut. In two days he has not slept for more than one hour straight, has not slept when not stoned or drunk in weeks. He has been thinking about school, about jobs, about Linda and the baby. . . . *To bring back the love that's crumbling down . . .* Tony has not carried a single thought to completion but as each solution begins to congeal in his mind, he allows it to be replaced with words from one of his albums. He worries because he is not union, has not yet joined, word might spread he'd been drinking on the job—actually that he was a troublemaker, greased nails indeed!—and in the dead of winter jobs were scarce; that Linda at five months pregnant would slow down, would soon need to take a leave of absence—he'd spent too much money on weed, on booze, on accessories for Jimmy's Harley—there isn't much in their accounts. He wants Linda to quit work, wants her to want to quit—some level, not conscious—she is working, he isn't; she is going to school, he isn't; she is handling the apartment, food, clothes, bills, he isn't. He lifts his legs, flops, scrunches deeper into the cushions, flips restlessly. He opens his eyes, cranes his neck, stares through the curtain at the muted dusk, looks up, about the room, back to the French doors, the billowing curtain. He sits up, his feet still on the sofa, scratches his shoulder, scratches his right thigh at the scar, crashes back onto the couch jamming his eyes into the pillow, forcing the pillow to force his eyes to stay shut. *I'll be anything you want me to be. . . .* Still he can see light. *Like clay in your hands, you can mold me. . . .* Up again, down again. He puts the pillow over his face, tries to let his mind run on its own, go its own course. *What good can I do by refusing you. . . .* He hasn't thought about it in a long time but suddenly he can see Annalisa, naked, with Shepmann, held by Roy. The image is pleasant, disgusting, exciting, like watching a porno flick, gross, she is his cousin and he knows they are about to hurt her. His mind floats. *I'm losing you. . . .* There is Dai Do. There is Jimmy at Dai Do.

Tony sits up. This thought too is unpleasant. His body is vibrating, tense, like a rung bell, but soundless. He leans forward, puts his elbows on his knees, rests his eyes on the heels of his palms, works his palms circularly, scratching his eyes. The phone rings.

"I'll get it," he calls. The record is over, the stereo shuts off.

"If it's personnel, I'm not here. I'm not going to work an extra shift tonight."

"Okay." He lifts the receiver. "Hello."

"Tony?" It is his father.

"What? What is it?" Anxious, not angry. His parents have never called on a weekday. Only weekends. "What's happened?"

"It's Jimmy . . . "

"Augh fuck. Augh Jesus Christ God no. What's happened?" He is crying. He is already crying. He knew it, knew it last night, knew it a minute ago.

"Tony," Linda calls from the study, "is everything—"

"He's been killed," Tony's father begins.

Tony screams. He screams. Blood-curdling pain yell. "NOOO!"

"We saw the car pull up . . . "

"Nooo," he wails. He jerks the phone up, rips it from the wall. "Nooo!" His body quakes, racks spasmodically. He smashes the phone against the wall. He grabs it with both hands, shatters it against the wall, beats it into the old plaster. "God, no. No. No." He falls to his knees. "No. NO, no, no." He whimpers. "Oh God!" he shouts.

Linda is on the floor with him. She touches him lightly, one hand on his shoulder, one hand on his arm. "Tony! Tony?" She's alarmed yet calm. "Tony," she repeats trying to break into his consciousness. "Tony, what is it?"

He takes a deep breath. The spasm ceases. His arms still tremble. "They killed my cousin," he says. Then the tears start again.

Linda inches forward. Tears fill her eyes. She puts her arm around him, pulls him to her breast. Tony resists. He pushes away. He sniffs hard, sucks the mucus back up his nose, swallows. "Those god damned motherfuckers. God damn fuckers. God damn fuckers." He jerks his shoulder from under her hand, rocks, stands. He does not look at her, does not help her up. "I'm goin out. I gotta go out."

I buried my cousin on 1 February 1970. I buried him in full uniform. Both of us. I was strack, Man. I mean I was ultra strack spit-shined, polished, clean. I don't even know how Linda got to Mill Creek Falls. I can't talk about this to anyone. I just can't. I buried so many Marines it ripped my soul loose—but when I buried Jimmy it ripped the soul right out of me. I remember the priest from St. Ignatius, I remember his words. And Uncle James read the Prayer of St. Francis.

Lord, make me an instrument of your peace. Where there is hatred let me sow love. . . .

I did not shed a tear. But I did not say a word either, could not trust myself to utter a single sound for fear I'd offend Aunt Isabella and Uncle James and every member of my family and all the Pellegrinos and even Shepmann and Roy and all our friends from town who came. At the grave I moved in on the color guard the Corps provided, I told—I must of told him, the sergeant in charge—told him this was my duty, this was my cousin.

> Lord God, through your mercy
> let those who have lived in faith
> find eternal peace.

I can see the dirt walls below the casket. The walls are perfectly carved.

> Forgive the sins of our brother
> whose body we bury here.
> Welcome him into your presence.

Linda is there. She is so beautiful. She is a pillar of strength for my mom, and for my pop, and for Nonna who mumbles and prays and says over and over, "Dignity." I can just barely look at them.

> Our brother has gone to his rest in the peace of
> Christ. With faith and hope in eternal life, let
> us commend him to the loving mercy . . .

There is snow on the ground but it is not cold. Or I do not feel the cold. The sky is cloudless—opening to allow Jimmy's soul easy access to the grandeurs of eternity. Isabella is wailing with unabashed grief. Annalisa holds her hand. Uncle James is stoic, arms crossed. He looks pissed.

There is singing—communal grief. I could not participate. This was too personal. His conscious was my subconscious, his laughter was my joy, his deep compassion, my heart. With him died anything in me that was worthy. With him died the Will.

I do not know how Linda returned to Boston. Maybe Pop drove her. I remember she told me later that he said something like, "Geez, he acts like Helen and I are having an affair!" Linda told him that I suspected they were—that I was worried he and Jo were going to divorce. He was shocked at that. Linda told me he said that he and Helen were a lot alike, and that they both loved Jo, that he'd kissed Helen once—when they were celebrating my homecoming. Someplace, time, in here I don't know when, I was robotic, I took a copy of the death notice, stuck it in an envelope, got the address from her mom, sent it to Bea Hollands in San Martin, California.

10

For a week, ever since returning from Jimmy's funeral, Tony has not been able to close his eyes without dreaming, without finding himself stuck in a dank fetid tunnel, without smelling the rotting flesh, without seeing himself chopping heads as they attempt to thrust bayonets into him, without holding Manny, without Manny being shot again, without Manny becoming Jimmy. No longer are they mere dreams, night-day-mares, but now full-blown night-day traumas where Tony relives every sight, every action, every odor, every corpse.

Linda was petrified. Tony would not come into the bedroom with her, would not lie beside her in bed. She had called her folks from Mill Creek Falls, had thought they should know. "Tony's cousin—you met him at our wedding . . ." she'd explained to her father. He'd been nonchalant, cold. "That happens in war." She'd told Chas and Cathy. They'd replied, "That's what happens when you go sticking your nose someplace it doesn't belong." She'd told Tom McLaughlin. "Oh Linda, you poor woman. He must be a bear to live with. I've got some stuff that'll mellow him out. If he gets too bad, come down and sleep at my place." No one, she felt, gave her the right answer, the expected response, anything the least bit helpful. She worried Tony would never smile again, would never again do his crazy little jig, never again include her in his outrageousness, never let her be close to him. She worried for herself, for their baby. Tony was glum. He went out for hours without explanation, returned angry, tense, physically rigid, silent. Still she carried on, working, going to school, studying, doing all of the apartment chores. After ten days even she could no longer take it. "Come on, Babe. Let's talk about it."

"I don't want to."

"Look, I can't do this all by myself."

He did not look at her. There was no gentleness in his voice. "Can't do what?"

"All the cooking and cleaning and your laundry and—"

"God damn it! Then don't do it. I don't give a fuck. Leave my clothes alone."

Her face pinched, her eyes tightened, moistened. "Babe . . . "

"Jesus Christ! Don't start that sobbing bullshit!"

The pain dropped from her face, replaced by her own rage. She stamped toward him. "You bastard! I didn't kill him. Don't take it out on me!"

"Fuck off!" he snapped angrily.

"Fuck off, yourself!" She slapped him. She slapped him as hard as she could across the face.

The slap jolted him. Physically. His eyes bulged, his hands closed to fists, he stepped into her. She banged his chest with the heels of her hands. "Get out of here!" she screamed. Tony raised his hands to grab her. Again she hit him in the chest. He stopped, froze for one second, then spun on his heels, grabbed his jacket, gloves, cap, keys, and left.

For hours Tony rode the Harley through the streets of Boston. On side streets with patches of ice or sand he purposely skidded the 700-pound machine, half-thinking he'd not be able to catch it, right it, that he'd slide it into a curb, highside, smash his brains against something hard, end it all. He blasted up Storrow Drive, hitting ninety, the frigid wind in his face so severe he could not see. Still he did not crash. He exited, came back the other way, half-hoping he could hop the center guardrail, meet a semi face-to-face, half-fearing he might hop the rail, hit a car with a mother and her children. He exited, rode about BU. He could have gone back. At Thanksgiving his father had taken him aside, had told him what with Linda pregnant and all, that he *wanted* to assist them. Between Tony's GI Bill benefits and John's help, Tony wouldn't need to work while in school. Tony had told him he'd think about it—a polite refusal.

He circled by the building where his English section had met. He spotted Nguyen Thi An, rode by, circled two blocks, came back slowly. He knew she'd be there. He'd spotted her a week back. He'd stalked her, honed in on her, tailed her for hours, for days. At night he'd parked the

Harley across from her apartment, sat, silent, straddling the big machine, watching, a stakeout, a compulsion, an obsession with Viet Nam, with Nam in Boston in 1970.

Nguyen Thi An was walking with two other students, all bundled up in coats. Had it not been for her long black hair he'd have missed her. Slowly, from a block away, the Harley throbbing quietly, almost at an idle, he followed her. One of her friends left at Babcock Street. The two continued on to Fordham. Tony hung back as far as he could, kept as close as he could to the line of parked cars. He felt the compulsion, the drive. He *had* to . . . he had to at least talk to her.

Her friend entered a building at midblock. Tony moved in, close but still undetected. He studied her walk. Even over the high piles of snow at the corners she walked lightly, elegantly. She stopped before a town house, took keys from her coat. He rode up, parked, dismounted. She was just closing the door when he tapped lightly on the glass. "An," he said. His eyes were bright, his smile beguiling. "Miss An. Tony." He pointed to himself. "You remember me from English."

She looked at him through the glass. He stood back respectfully. She opened the door. "Oh yes," she said. Her voice was squeaky. "Tony from Professor Groesbeck's. How are you?"

"I'm very well, thank you." In his thick jacket, his face unshaven, his hair short from the funeral yet uncombed, he was very respectful, very formal. "How are you?"

"I'm very well, too," An said. Then she giggled a nasal raspish giggle. "Are you very cold?"

"Uh-huh." Tony wrapped his arms about his chest for emphasis. "May I talk to you about Viet Nam? I was there for a year, mostly in the north. It's such a beautiful country. And I wish to talk to you, for a paper I'm working on. I can come back if this isn't a good time."

"No, please come in. I wish very much to talk of my country."

Through every word that Tony spoke, through every pore of his skin, he fought back the impulse, the show of the impulse, which was consuming him. They went upstairs to her one-bedroom apartment. The rooms were clean, bright, without clutter. They sat in the kitchenette, An dressed in blue jeans and a white sweater, Tony in grungy work clothes he'd worn for days. An made tea, wrapped the pot in a thermal cloth to keep it hot, sat back down. Tony stared into her eyes. His smile slowly shifted from sweet, jocular, to obsessive leering. He told her of life in Anh Tan west of Chu Lai. She told him about her mother and father whom she missed dearly, about vacations in Da Lat when she was young, about their family customs at Tet. Tony compared them to his own family's traditions at various holidays. After an hour Tony grabbed her wrist. He held it lightly, between two fingers, almost as if he were taking her pulse. He moved closer to her. She giggled the raspish giggle. He grasped her wrist more tightly, pulled her to him. She spoke, objected, but he did not hear. Again he was robotic. He kissed her, kissed her lips, ran his hands through her long straight hair. She struggled but did not scream. Now he pulled her to the floor. He pressed her to the floor with his body weight. He forced her wrists together, over her head, held them with one hand, smothered her mouth with his mouth, raised her sweater with his free hand. She did not fight him but resisted passively, resisted by acting dead, being a corpse. He let her wrists go, pulled her sweater up, off, unhooked her bra. He opened her jeans, lifted them, shaking her out of them, leaving them at her ankles. He kissed her shoulders, her arms. Then he sat up, pulled her up, wrapped her in his arms, hugged her to his chest as she pulled herself into a fetal tuck. He did not remove or open his own clothes but sat there on the floor in her kitchen, hugging her, rocking her, caressing her naked shoulders, pulling her naked legs more tightly together, kissing the top of her head.

She did not look at him but when she felt he was calm she whispered, "You must go now."

He continued to hold her, to rock her. "I'll protect you," he whispered back but he was no longer whispering to An, was no longer even aware of her presence.

"You must go now," An repeated.

"Yes," he said.

An hour later he was frantic. I had to, had to fuck her, he thought, fuck Nam. I had to fuck it one more time. And it's fucked me again. It's fucked me. He parked the Harley in the alley, strained to hear sirens approaching. They'd get him for this. Inside he was speeding. What the fuck have I done?! What have I done?! How, he thought, could I have done this to Linda? He climbed the first flight of stairs, paused, tried to get hold of his thoughts, thought coalescing, cascading, everywhere in his mind. What would he say? What would he tell her? What would he do if the police came? If they broke down the door? If they attacked? He climbed the second flight. He was panicky. He opened the door.

Linda came from the study. She'd been crying. "Babe ... I'm ... "

"It's me." Tony's words flew. "I can't live here anymore."

"Don't leave ... " Linda began. Tears dripped from her cheeks. "I didn't mean—"

"No, Linda, not you. Me. Us. I can't live here anymore. I can't live in a room where I heard that voice, where I heard, 'It's Jimmy.' Don't you understand. *We've* got to move. I can't stay here."

"Oh Babe." Tears still slid down her face. "We'll move." She stood still, before him, like a punished child awaiting her parent to come to her, to hug her. "Babe, I love—"

"We gotta move right away. I don't want to stay here tonight."

"We'll get another apartment."

"No. You don't understand." Now Tony did move to her. He hugged her.

Linda hugged him back, buried her head in his chest. "We'll call right now. The agency that—"

"No. No, Linda. You don't understand." He held her at arm's length. His smile returned. "I've got to move out of here. Out of Boston. I want to move back to Mill Creek Falls. You said you could live there. You're going to have to drop out of school anyway. You can finish up by mail. We've got to go."

Linda sat in the kitchen, erect, one arm resting lightly on the tabletop, the pressure from her womb bearing straight down, forcing her knees and feet apart. Before her were bills, receipts, the new lease. She edged forward until her chest just touched the table edge. For an hour she'd been organizing the records of their new lives. She could barely wait for Tony to get home, to tell him the news.

In early March they had moved into the apartment in Creek's Bend. If Linda was heartbroken because she had not completed the Family Nurse Practioners course, she did not show it, did not mention it to Tony, or to John Sr. or Jo, or to Tony's brothers who'd helped them move in. Nor did she mention it to Annalisa, who came by every noon to talk to Linda, to tell Linda little things about Jimmy, about the extended family, about Mill Creek Falls. Perhaps she let a few words slip out to Jessie Taynor, Mill Creek's hefty, mentally impaired street soul, but if so, she did not believe Jessie understood.

A sense of fate had engulfed her, not a permanent fatalistic doom but a tranquil self-satisfaction, perhaps progesterone induced. Linda was certain she would return to her studies and she was convinced that Tony was happier, calmer than he'd been not simply since Jimmy's death but probably since before their wedding. The worst part of moving, she told Annalisa, was leaving the obstetrics group at Brigham and Women's. Still, it was her new doctor, Simon Denham, who'd given her the news.

Linda opened each bill, discarded the coupons, flyers and notes, stacked the bills with return envelopes in priority of payment. Organizing their new life was important to her. She'd arranged the largest bedroom for her and Tony, the second as a nursery, the small front room overlooking the street as a library for when she and Tony returned to their studies. The afternoon was warm, clear, the sun higher each day. If she looked close she thought she could see buds beginning to swell on the trees. Quickly Linda added up what was due, compared it to what they had, projected how much Tony would earn, estimated what could be spent on additional nursery furniture.

Tony was not at work. In three weeks in Mill Creek he'd already begun and left two jobs. He sat at the corner of the bar in the White Pines Inn. The room was dingy, hazy with smoke residue from lunchtime clients from the warehouses and small mills. Most had returned to work, three older black men remained in one booth.

"Another?" The bartender wiped the counter.

"Yeah, one more."

"Ya'rn't workin today?"

"Naw. Lookin though."

"Mill's got a few openings."

"I was there. Bout a week. Couldn't stand it."

"Which place?"

"Ah, you know, they're all the same. People were fine. I just can't work inside. I gotta find an outside job."

"You try the little farms across Old Bridge?"

"One there. One in Hobo Hollow."

"Nothin?"

"Nothin."

"What about up Mill Creek Road? Up past the Old Mill. There's Adolph Lutz's dude ranch."

"Yeah. Hey, yeah. I might give that a try."

"Nice bike you got there."

"Thanks."

Tony finished his draft, ate the last of the pretzels from the free-lunch bowl, walked out into the bright afternoon sun. He straddled the bike, rubbed his right thigh with the heel of his hand. The muscle had been ticking and cramping ever since their move, had been sending sudden stabbing pains up to his hip. Linda, in her first long discussion with Dr. Simon Denham, had convinced him to give Tony a prescription for Darvon. Tony removed the vial from his jacket pocket, plucked out a capsule, examined it briefly, then popped it into his mouth. It stuck to his palette. He dislodged it with his tongue, felt the flow of saliva surround it, soften it, make it slippery. He swallowed. He sat on the bike allowing the heat of the sun to bake into his leg, allowing the Darvon to seep into his blood. Since the first Darvon capsule three weeks earlier he'd been more relaxed, happier. The Darvon took all pains away for at least a few hours. He could concentrate, work, smile, feel alive. Supplemented with a few beers or a toke of marijuana from Lenny Shepmann, Tony could feel in control. When the alcohol, marijuana and Darvon wore off, the dreams, night-day terrors, returned with a vengeance. For months he'd fought that inner fury, frenzy, attempting to erupt out of him. At best he laid on a shield, a lethargic countenance encrusting roiling magma. Darvon cooled the magma.

Tony rode slowly out of town, downriver toward Forksville, then back. His relaxation had peaked, was gently retreating, being replaced by the onslaught of his demons. He crossed the Old Truss Bridge, rumbled east, then north on 154 by Old New Town, past the backyard of his folks' home, into Creek's Bend. Flash images crashed on to his consciousness. Annalisa at Shepmann's, Jimmy and Tony on the roof of the toolshed, the dead children on Storrow Drive, the NVA stabbing him, the tunnel body, Manny, Rick, Jimmy. Shivers rolled up his sides, his back. He squeezed the throttle grip more tightly, wished, willed the images away.

He parked the bike, forced a smile. He was cognizant that he could not share his thoughts, his mental images, with Linda. Quietly he hummed to himself. The sound chased the images away but did not chase away the thought that the images were unworthy, were wrong. He felt ashamed. Before he went in he reached for another Darvon. The vial was empty.

" 'Ain't no use to sit and wonder why, Babe . . . ' " Tony sang cheerfully. Linda had finished the bills, packed up, turned to decorating. Tony continued, changed the words. "We aint got no choices, anyhow. . . . "

"Hi Babe. You're home early."

"Aw, just a bit. My leg was bothering me so I cut out a few minutes early."

"I've got something to tell you." Linda held out her hands. Tony grabbed them, playfully exaggerated leaning over her belly, trying to kiss her. "Oh, you . . . " Linda pulled him in, kissed him.

He rested one hand on her abdomen, one on the side of a swollen breast. "Whatcha been up to?"

"I've been rearranging the nursery. Wanta see?"

"Yeah. But—" Tony paused. "What's that?" He indicated the living room wall where Linda had hung three framed certificates.

"They look nice, don't they? The IGA had a sale on frames—"

"I don't want that stuff up there. And didn't I tell you, Morris' is where we shop."

"I just stopped in on the way back from the doctors. And Babe, those are your—"

"I know what they are—"

" . . . medals. Your Purple Heart and Silver star—"

" . . . and I don't want them up there!"

"You used to be so proud of being a Marine."

Now Tony was curt. "I just don't want them up. That's all." He walked over, took them from the wall.

Linda shook her head. She was still proud of his citations, of what he'd done, did not understand how he could turn his back on what he once loved so dearly. And she felt rejected. "In here," she said quietly.

They entered the nursery. "Hey," Tony attempted to be light, "why'd you cram it all to one side?"

Linda looked at him, reached out, grabbed his hand. "Doctor Denham says we need another crib."

"Another crib? What's wrong with . . . wit—wha . . . aaahhHHH!"

"Uh-huh," Linda beamed. Her eyes twinkled. She tilted her head, looking to Tony for one instant like a pixie, a bulging-bellied pixie. "Twins."

The increase in future responsibility settled Tony some. He'd met with Simon Denham privately for a few minutes after Linda's eighth-month appointment, showed the obstetrician his scarred thigh, and explained briefly how the pains came out of nowhere, shot up to his hip, racked him out of bed, or threw him when he was riding.

"You know, Mr. Pisano, you really should go over to the Rock Ridge Veterans Medical Center. What you describe, you could have a deep infection in there. It might just be the damaged nerve, but that's not something I'm willing to guess at. You've got to—"

"I will." Tony rocked back and forth, kneading the quadricep with the heel of his hand. "It's just when it gets like this, I can hardly think. One Darvon and I'm okay all through work."

"What are you doing now? Linda says you've changed jobs again." Simon Denham reached over, grabbed his prescription pad, wrote something unintelligible.

"I'm with one of the ranches up off Mill Creek Road."

"Oh. Adolph Lutz's?"

"Ah, he hired a kid day before I got there. Next one up. Wapinski's."

"I don't know that one. Does he board many horses?"

"None. It's just the old man. Right now we're tapping the maples, boiling away, making syrup."

"Syrup?" Simon Denham snickered.

"Yeah. I think we'll get a hundred gallons. It's a farm. That's his first crop of the year."

"Well, good luck. Take this. Be careful with these. Especially on that bike of yours. Darvon's nothing to fool with."

But Tony was not fooling. By mid-April he had prescriptions from four doctors. At three Darvon a day Tony felt relaxed, alert, alive, in control. With a little alcohol, a little weed, he was happy.

Then on 30 April 1970 Tony heard President Richard Nixon announce he was sending U.S. combat troops into Cambodia to destroy the sanctuaries and root out the communist command and control headquarters, COSVN. Tony felt nauseated, irritable. His jaw tightened and he withdrew for three days, opening himself up again only to hear that the Ohio National Guard had fired into a crowd of protesting students, had killed four, wounded eleven. Darvon or not, Tony could not handle that. He did not sympathize with the students but instead felt that the country's reaction was ripping him apart. He withdrew more deeply, plunged and hid in the depths of his being, hid from himself, from his thoughts. After the fourth of May he no longer stopped at the White Pines on his way home but instead purchased a six-pack at the local state store. He'd drink two on his way home, drink the rest with dinner.

He purchased a shotgun. "For protection," he told Linda. "This hippie element's gone nuts." It was not an elaborate gun, not expensive, just a single-shot, breech loader with full-choke 30-inch barrel and an ash stock. Tony bought two boxes of shells—one double-aught buck, one number 7½ upland game or fowl. On the first day with the shotgun Tony fired half of each box from the back of the sugarbush, fired the rounds at nothing particular, just shooting out over the cliff, listening to the reverberations as they rolled through the gap.

To Linda, it seemed like such a good time, a happy time, an expectant time, just before the births of the twins. Then on 12 May 1970, Gina was born first, at 7:56 P.M. Michelle followed five minutes later. That night, after kissing Linda good night, after watching his cute little girls for two hours, after stopping by to tell his folks, Tony went back to the empty apartment. It was very dark. A light rain had begun falling. Tony did not turn on any lights. Slowly he worked his way to the bedroom, kicked off his boots, lay back on the bed.

He is alone. Raindrops patter softly on the roof. The streets are quiet. He does not want to dream, does not want the demons thrashing in his mind. He closes his eyes. Lights flash. He opens his eyes, rolls quietly, slowly reaches under the bed, grasps the shotgun, lifts it, lays it on his chest. The barrel is cool against his chest, the stock smooth in his left hand, the trigger housing and hammer functional in his right. He thinks the chamber is empty, isn't certain, thinks an empty gun can be more dangerous than a loaded one if someone breaks in. Again he closes his eyes, again the flashes. He sits up. In the dark he breaks the breech, feels for a shell. The chamber is smooth, empty. Again he reaches under the bed, feels a box, removes a shell. It makes no difference if it is double-aught or number 7½. He loads, snaps the breech shut, lies back. The sound was nice, well-machined metal, precision fit. Eyes open or shut, flashes. It makes no difference. He wishes so badly that Jimmy could meet his daughters, that he could show them to Manny. The instant he thinks of Manny, of Jimmy, he sees himself with his daughters, sees himself unable to speed them up, unable to carry them both, and Linda, unable . . . A flash. One cries. A flash. The second is blown apart. Then Linda is shot and he, Tony, can't stop it, can't halt it. Flash. He fires, he fires, he fires only to hit one himself. He cannot get it out of his mind. He will kill them. Slice them. Hack off their heads. I am the Will. I am the Will. Tony is crying, rubbing his face on the barrel. I am capable of the most brutal murder—murder in defense of myself, of others. I am capable if pushed. I am the Will to fight, the Will to pull the trigger. Tony is so proud of having been the Will, but that was a different Tony. It is comforting to know he can fight to defend; it is frightening. It makes him secure when threatened, but without the threat, need he manufacture a threat, a demon?

I am the Will, he thinks, but I can no longer control the Will. He nods more deeply. His nightmare expands. There are heads, three, huge, bigger than beach balls, eyes, beautiful, exquisite eyes. . . . Tony's entire body convulses violently, jarring him back awake, alert. He is cool, wet. His nares are flared, feel permanently splayed trying to sense the wind. Now he is angry, furious at his demons, at his horrible thoughts, at his disgusting self. He should be so happy, elated. He has two beautiful daughters, each with whispy strands of red hair, with exquisite eyes, he thinks, like Linda's. And his thoughts are on seeing them die, causing their deaths, killing them!! He cannot stay down, cannot stay still. He paces, frantic, in the dark, frantic, holding the shotgun, panicky, afraid he'll quit again, afraid he'll drag them down, afraid . . .

"Go home, Babe. You look terrible. Didn't you sleep?"

"I'm okay. Really. How do you feel?"

"I'm exhausted." Then Linda laughed. "God, look at this. I'm already soaking wet."

Tony was sitting on the edge of her bed. He slipped a finger into the neck of her nightgown, pulled it out glimpsing her skin. "Mmm-mmmm." He laughed with her.

"Of course, it's just colostrum. There won't be any milk for a few days."

"Of course." Tony chuckled.

"That Gina, I think she takes after you. She's already a little barracuda. She wants to feed all the time."

"And Michelle?"

"She's a little lady."

"And what can I do for my big lady?"

"Nothing, Babe. I just want to sleep. They'll bring them back from the nursery when they wake. Babe, why don't you go home? Were you up all night?"

"Yeah, I think I will. I was like speeding all night. I'm goina go up and see Mr. Wapinski first. And my pop. We need a car."

"You're a Viet Nam soldier, eh?"

"No, not me, Mr. Wapinski." Tony and Pewel Wapinski were in the Sugar Shack, the small outbuilding where the maple sap was boiled down.

"No?"

"No Sir," Tony answered.

The old man stared at the boy. "Why do you say that?"

"Sir?" Tony was struggling with the last of the ash from the firepit under the huge evaporator tank. He'd enjoyed the work, was sorry it was over.

"I know who you are," Pewel Wapinski said. "I read the papers. I know your uncle James and your pa, too. From church. Even if I don't go much. Now why do you say that?"

Tony was stunned. The old man had never let on. Tony had felt anonymous, free.

"You served in Viet Nam," Pewel said flatly.

"Hm-hmm," Tony mumbled. He wanted to leave, grab his pay, split.

"Then why do you deny it?" To the old man, the boy was virtually the same age as his grandson.

"Because they hate us, Mr. Wapinski. Because everybody hates us for having been there."

"Humph!"

"And they try and make us hate ourselves."

"That skin a yours don't look so thin to me."

"It's not my skin. It's my ears and eyes." Tony paused. Pewel said nothing. "I'm done here," Tony said.

"Come back next week," Pewel said. "We'll plant the lower field. And turn the high meadow."

"I won't be here. I'll be in Mexico," Tony snapped.

"Mexico?"

"Or maybe Wyoming. There's so much shit comin down, if I stay here I'll kill someone."

"Yer pa know?"

"Nope."

"You goina tell im?"

"Nope."

"When—"

"Soon as you pay me."

"Want me to call yer pa? Let him know?"

"Sure. In a few days. Just tell im I'm tired of the killin."

Part II

EXPATRIATION

August 1984

Six-in teen-out. Seven-in teen-out.

Counting breaths. Trying to meditate through it.

I'm just over the west ridge at the edge of the sugarbush, out of sight of the house, the big barn, the outbuildings. A short crawl to the ridge in the light would reveal the high meadow, the vineyard, pond, all that rests in the arms of the ridges. But I will not go, will not look, in the dark.

Night descends with a vengeance. It is very dark. There is no moon, no stars. There is a wind. Cutting. Raw. Sometimes I can read the wind but I cannot read this wind. Heat lightning flashes to the west. I hunker down. At fields' and orchard's edge weeds and brush grow quickly, thick, to armpit height. Like a buck on his day bed, I've crushed a small area, left a thin trail, a single field of fire to me; me, low, hugging the earth, camouflaged beneath a poncho, beneath wild brushweed, beneath darkness. Wind swirls the weed tops. Rain begins. Droplets lash my face. I close my eyes, let the rivulets run awash on my skin. Lightning moves closer. I lie perfectly still. My heart is racing. My eyes are closed yet I see flashes—not just the lightning but thousands of overlapping flashes taking up random quarters or thirds of my eye-frame. Interspersed are a million pinpoint flashes. My brain is speeding out of control. Forty-in two-out. Forty-in three-out. Forty-in four-out. Thunder rumbles.

I cannot describe how angry I was during this period. I cannot come close. Even now when I think back to that time I am enraged, livid, pissed beyond words. Damn, shit piss damn. That doesn't even begin . . . That's surface anger. That's what splashes from the spout of a boiling teakettle, the splattering mist of mad agitation, symptomatic of what's within except what's within you can only guess at. You can't see it. You can't see the numb volcanic rage feeding itself without sensing itself; a self-consumptive fury that the VA's perverted therapists labeled guilt-ridden, depressive, schizo-psychotic; that commentators deemed deserved purgatorial flame—that is, blame the victim—until later when they recognized the victimization (without recognizing their role as assailant) and assuaged themselves by pitying us only to rob us of any vestige of pride, of humanity. And when they decided to heal the national gash, they identified it as its veterans and not themselves, decided to *heal* us, as if we'd started the entire affair and somewhere had taken an aberrant route. If only they could design a program . . . If only they could figure *us* out . . . Fuck em! They couldn't and can't figure themselves out—don't realize that they have an effect on every man who is not an island. Perhaps this is what drove us to High Meadow, but that is much later—which is perhaps what has driven me here, now, an island in the weeds, a renegade on the rural edge of civilization practicing evade, avoid, escape. *Their* sickness, *their* unwillingness to recognize it, *their* scapegoating or displacing it, was the trigger of rage, was the very heart of the out-of-controlledness that has held sway over America for fifteen years and that shows no indication now, in August 1984, of self-correction BECAUSE there is no recognition of the source problem, of the depth and breadth and scope of this 3-D mosaic problem. The rage they cause, the overwhelming fury they describe as being set off by trivial events—which is the definition of neurological impairment or psychosis—because they do not recognize their provocation of us, do not recognize the great frustration that would redefine our rage as ordinary, justifiable anger. Rage, justified or not, causes further problems, more rage—unjustifiable rage—because rage damages the brain, imbalances frontal lobe chemistry, and fosters "disinhibited" dementia. More simply: some of you motherfuckers drove us crazy.

Nearly every Viet Nam returnee I know split. Bobby called it expatriation. From east they went west; from north, south. Or some, like me, went no place and every place—the road, the open, unending, ever-shifting road. As near as I can tell, virtually every one of us at some point or another moved because of restlessness, alienation, an itch within; moved, got the fuck out, beat feet, skyed. Some hid it in corporate transfers, like Tashkor and Rasmuellen, who later became our attorneys at High Meadow; some hid it in numbed-out self-medication; some in their own planned "accidental" permanent checking out.

One problem was the seemingly amorphous shades-of-gray conflicts in everyday life. Enemies were indefinable, indistinguishable—CONTRARY to popular myth, *UNLIKE* Nam where the enemy *was* definable and distinguishable, just elusive, excellent at self-camouflage, able to leap uncrossable borders to unassailable sanctuaries. But back in the World, there seemed to be only gnawing, ungraspable problems eroding strength, integrity, resolve. Bobby called them Gumption Suckers. Spirit usurpers. Like being in thick pea soup, like Nam mountaintop fog so thick your eyes played tricks on you and when they told you there was something out there, you saw things that were not really there—and when they told you there was nothing, something unseen would emerge and grab your rickety ass. Who was the enemy? Certainly it varied man to man, woman to woman, vet to vet. Demons: the absence of full-blown Post Traumatic Stress Disorder does not mean one is not continually attempting to cope with his combat experience. More ambiguous, insidious enemies: The System, drugs, agent orange, crime, money, the Me Generation, bad marriages, the VA, prison, filmdom, and the media. But again I am far ahead of myself. I still did not know Bobby Wapinski. And he too had a row to hoe.

11

Under all is the land. Upon its wise utilization and widely allocated
ownership depend the survival and growth of free
institutions and of our civilization. . . . The interest of the
nation and its citizens requires the highest and best use
of the land. . . . the creation of adequate housing, the
building of functioning cities, the development of
productive industries and farms, and the preservation of
a healthful environment.

—The Preamble to the Code of
Ethics of the National Association of Realtors

S an Martin, California, Sunday, 14 June 1970—It was cool, wet, already the wettest June on record and June not even half over. It was
barely five A.M. Wapinski parked his Chevy sedan on Aaron Road,
just out of town. He'd driven from Bahia de Martin Mobile Home Community, under Highway 101, north on First Street, west on Miwok
Road—The Strip—driven in the rain past the darkened downtown
stores, past "his" office, Great Homes Realty, to Aaron Road where he
turned right and descended to the small gravel parking area and trailhead by San Antonio Creek.

He was vaguely aware of the overcast, of the smell of Josh's damp fur,
of this anniversary date. He got out, opened the back door. "C'mon Josh.
We don't have much time." Bobby checked his watch: grabbed his vest,
rod and reel, bait can and hat. It was less than half a mile up Cataract
Trail to the first dam and lower reservoir, maybe three-quarters of a mile
to the hole he wanted to try first before he worked his way up the north
side of The Res, as everyone called it, to the upper section of creek where
he'd been told by Coleman there was decent trout fishing. Wapinski had

in mind he would meander along the upper creek to the Upper Reservoir and fish that small lake too before he headed out at ten thirty to be back by noon to be cleaned up and to his open house—his first listing—by one P.M. "C'mon Josh! Get the lead out."

Away from the road the trailside quickly became dense with fir, pine, scrub oak and beech, a stand of redwood, more pine and oak cloaking the slopes from the river up to North Peak. In the stream the water was high. The rain came steadily, not hard. Bobby crushed his hat down on his head; Josh lagged a dozen paces back.

Before the first dam there was a picnic area and the trailhead for Gold Mine Trail which ran away from the creek and into the glades and grassland on the east slope. In February Bobby and Red had followed Gold Mine for a hundred yards, then fifteen feet to the side into a small secluded clearing where they'd made love. He paused, reflecting on that one time which now seemed long ago. When he and Red had returned home they'd found the envelope without return address and the obituary of James Pellegrino, and Red had cried and Bobby had tried to comfort her but she hadn't wanted his comforting. Instead, she'd discarded the article. That night Bobby'd picked it from the trash, reread it, filed it in the bill box, then gone out and walked to town, to Miwok Road where he'd watched kids in Camaros and Firebirds and Bonnevilles cruising The Strip, older people with older sedans pushing cartloads of groceries from the all-night Safeway, two officers in a police car, barely older than the kids they tailed. For a moment that night he'd hated it all. For a moment he'd thought he did not belong there, did not belong in a town or a city or with people, but belonged in the hills, in the woods, alone.

Bobby climbed to the base of the dam. The gates were high. Four-inch-thick water crested the concrete barrier, shot down the slides, roiled and foamed at the base.

The morning after they'd learned of Jimmy's death, Red had been up early, off to work before Bobby realized she wasn't taking the day off. That night she'd worked late. The next day was the same. And the next ten.

"Please don't be upset if I work seven days a week," she'd said. Perhaps it was early March when he'd suggested another hike. "Just right now I have to. You'll have to share me with my work."

"All work and no play . . . you know," he'd said apologetically.

"Really," Red had answered as she'd donned her new suit jacket, "when I get home." She'd come to him, kissed him. "Maybe I should have kept working for that friend of my father's but he was, you know, just creepy. And besides, it was only ten thousand. If I make only one sale a month I'll have more take home. . . . " She hadn't finished but had checked her watch and said, "I've got to go. My appointment."

Quickly he climbed the trail stairs beside the dam. He breathed deeply. Three flights and he had to rest. Their loving had returned for three days straight, then subsided again: yet because of it he believed that the hiatus had been an aberration, a temporary result of heavy work schedules, initial adjustment to their reunification, and the shock of Pellegrino's death. Now he did not analyze the long chasms at all.

Wapinski topped the dam shoulder, struck out briskly for the three-tree deadfall overhanging The Res and the hole he wished to try. The Res trail was raked gravel, in places at water's edge, elsewhere meandering into the trees. Bobby set his bait can on the trail, removed a fat night crawler, worked the hook into the soft body below the radial ring. The worm squirmed, elongated, thinned to the diameter of ten-gauge wire. "C'mon you little slimehead," Wapinski muttered. The hook tip broke through the worm's side. The rain increased in intensity. Josh nuzzled Bobby's hand. "Not now," Bobby snapped. He backed the hook tip into the worm's seeping side then manipulated the skinny body over the barb, around the curve, until the entire hook was concealed. Josh shimmied, throwing mud droplets from his coat, covering the side of Bobby's face. "Geez!" Bobby lurched, the rod slipped, fell, pulled the line, the hook tip broke through the worm and stuck in Bobby's finger. "Owooo!" He pulled it out. Shot a glance at the dog, then at his watch—twenty to six—then back at Josh. "Just sit there. I'm goina go down and get us some fish."

Day broke gray. The rain increased. Bobby stepped off the trail, slipped, caught himself, gritted his teeth. All he wanted to do was fish but his mind wasn't with it. New thoughts, half thoughts, rushed in, on. The nation's economy . . . another sharp increase in the jobless rate . . . sharpest continuing climb since 1958 . . . California jobless rate up to 5.9 percent . . . real estate market tightening . . . his first listing, a twelve-year-old four-bedroom home in the Martinwood subdivision with pool for $41,500 . . . $4,000 overpriced . . . never sell it . . . eating nothing but raw rice and the office's coffee-service sugar cubes . . . like being socked in without resupply . . . Cambodian Incursion elation, Kent/Jackson State depression . . . fuck em all I gotta eat, I gotta sell . . . anniversary of Hamburger Hill come and gone without my notice except Coleman and Bartecchi mentioned something . . . 1/506th at a place called Ripcord . . . Grandpa's letter . . . knee-deep in maple syrup?

Wapinski flicked the rod tip aiming under the deadfall. The worm arced in low, just nicked a twig, caught, then whipped around a branch wrapping the line tight. "You slimehead," Wap growled. He pulled. He yanked. The rod bent, the branch swayed, the worm remained tangled. "Shit. First damn cast!" He reeled in as much as possible, grabbed the line beyond the rod tip, pulled until it snapped. He tied on another hook, impaled another worm. The rain came harder. He cast again, timidly, the bait falling short of cover. He let the worm sink, reeled in, added a split shot eighteen inches up the line, recast and caught the same branch as on his first cast and again couldn't dislodge the hook. His ire multiplied. Again he reeled in, snapped the line, tied a new hook. One fuckin year, he thought. One fuckin year home. No dough. Lots of bills. Living off Red, who's intermittently frigid ...

San Martin considered itself to be a canyon town, a perfect all-American community, a municipality with well-kept homes, manicured lawns, excellent schools, and state-championship quality tennis, golf and baseball teams. That very little of the town actually stretched back along San Antonio Creek into the ravine—it wasn't really a canyon at that point but a pass between South and North Peaks—made no difference to anyone.

Highway 101 through San Martin was a four-lane limited-access highway. Driving time to San Francisco at midnight was thirty minutes, up to triple that during commute hours. Radicals may have been burning Carl Street in the Haight-Ashbury district of San Francisco; Native Americans may have been in their thirtieth week of occupation of Alcatraz; UC Berkeley Professor Angela Davis may have been fired by university regents because of her proviolence, pro-communist rhetoric; and two lovely blondes, tall and thin, may have been walking hand in hand with a bearded dwarf on Market Street—all three naked—to protest the war in Viet Nam; but in San Martin the main concerns were still family income, the price of groceries, the high-school baseball team's record, and the proper length of one's lawn. Indeed, the most controversial issues in town were whether eighth grade girls should be allowed to wear strapless gowns to the Moving Up dance, and whether town fathers had the right to ban municipal workers from wearing crotch-high miniskirts. The 1970 census placed the population of San Martin's perfect All-American community at 22,646, of which 98.6 percent were white.

Bobby got a hit, just a tap, yanked immediately, hard, pulled the bait out of the fish's mouth, the worm, line and sinker snapping back, overhead, tangling in a bush behind him. He did not turn but stood rigid. Jilted by Stacy one year ago ... Jody-ed Pellegrino ... He checked his watch. It was six thirty and he'd barely had his line in the water. Again he reeled in, now following the line to the bush and untangling the snarl in the leaves. On the trail a man and a woman jogged by, oblivious to him and to Josh, who had sought silent refuge under a bush.

For another half hour Bob Wapinski fished the hole under the deadfall catching but two sunnies. The rain abated. Two more joggers went by. Wapinski followed the shoreline rushing his casts, not concentrating, thinking he and Red should move south into Marin County, work Tiburon where four-bedroom condominiums with views of San Francisco were selling from $55,000, even $60,000. Or Belvedere with homes in the $80,000 range. Now *there* was a commission! And those people were buying! He bit the inside of his cheek, thought, We've got no plan, no future, just two nice people living together, trying to make some money. A third set of runners appeared on Cataract Trail. One saw Bob, waved, called out, "Fishin's better at the Upper Res."

Now Wapinski passed from the Lower Res into the ravine of the upper creek. The trail here was much farther from the water. He slowed, watched the fast water, the pools. Fishing currents was different than fishing lakes or even slow water holes in streams. One can catch fish in still water without concentration but fishing riffles and rapids requires intense focus. Wap climbed the bank, studied the stretch. Water cascaded over a series of large boulders about five hundred feet upstream, then eddied into the bank, dumped and narrowed into a deep channel. He descended toward a switchback, approached the water cautiously, squatted, added a heavier split shot, edged forward. Now he cast across and upstream. As the current propelled the bait downstream he reeled in, then let out as the worm tumbled by. He reeled in, cast again, this time closer to the opposite shore. Now he was fishing. Now there were no thoughts of women, of money, of politics. He worked the far bank dropping his worm at one-foot intervals up the creekside, missing a few casts, recasting before moving up, always working the bait downstream after the initial upstream toss. He felt a hit, a light tap through the line, the rod, into his wrist. He paused, counted . . . four, five, six . . . flicked the tip. In still water one lets the fish take the bait because the fish isn't in a rush. In rapids a trout will dart from an area of protection to the rushing bait and back to its cover in the snap of your fingers, perhaps still not taking the bait but certainly testing it, moving it, mouthing it. Wap reeled in, replaced his worm with a fresh one, recast toward the exact same spot, missed it by two feet. Again he reeled in, recast, aiming, hitting the spot, the bait dropping into the current, then Tap! Pause. Pause. Flick! The line came alive. Wap raised the rod tip, kept the line tight, not really interested in playing this fish, his first real fish of the day, wanting to have one in his creel before chancing a play. The fish tugged, leaped slapping the water surface, tail-walking, a beautiful spotted pink, gold-green rainbow flashing, then under, dashing downstream slackening the line, Wapinski reeling like mad trying to keep tension, trying to keep the trout from throwing the hook, adrenaline rushing. Ten feet away Bobby raised and reeled and lifted the trout and flicked him up on the bank where the fish flopped wildly and did throw the hook and fell back toward the water as Bobby dove into the bank grasping, fins and hands flashing until Bobby clutched the trout in both hands, laughing and smiling and estimating it was at least thirteen inches which he was certain was huge for the San Antonio and wait until he showed it to Coleman in the office on Monday.

Every fish is a thrill to catch but none as thrilling as the first trout of the year caught in rapids. He pulled two more, smaller ones, from that spot, then worked up to the eddy below the large boulders and caught a brook trout, then another rainbow which he played until the fish was exhausted, then carefully brought it in, unhooked it and let it go.

Now he again checked his watch. It was 9:50. He had not made it to the upper reservoir, had never been there, decided he'd push on then speed up his return. Near the upper dam he climbed back to the trail, clambered up the steep staircase to the top and beheld a lovely, seemingly secluded mountain tarn. He thought to check his watch but purposefully decided against it. Quickly they set out.

A quarter mile up the narrow trail, the trail several hundred meters from the small lake, he smelled smoke. Just a whiff. He glanced back, up, left and right. He stepped off the trail, glided smoothly, silently into the thick stand of fir, listened. From the lake he heard voices. Josh sensed his caution, stepped close, quiet, glancing curiously with that furrowed brow, head atilt. Bobby put his hand lightly on Josh's head, ran his fingers to the back of his ears, massaged softly, slowly. Quietly they moved through the trees toward the tarn. There was radio music playing very low, the voices of a man, a woman, the giggle of a child. He could not see them. The radio ceased. Back on the trail he heard the footfalls and heavy breathing of another jogger. The jogger passed. Wap could not get a fix on the voices. Slowly he and Josh descended through the forest. Through branches he saw a hint of fluttering cloth. He stopped, crouched. Through the lower, less dense foliage the image was clearer yet he was still uncertain. He discerned a dark plane—interpreted it as the roof of a tent. He was about to reverse his course when he saw a whitish cloth move and realized it was a woman's dress. He focused on her as intensely as he'd focused on the cascades, connecting her to the tent, the other voices, imagining her movement pattern as he'd imagined that of the unseen trout, attempting to devise a means of happening upon her. Again voices. They were quiet, nearly camouflaged. He suspected they were hiding, squatting illegally on water district property. He backed out, coaxed Josh back, then penetrated the woods fifty yards down trail and noisily worked his way to lake edge. There he saw a young man attempting to fish clear water with white string and a branch.

"You're more apt to get a hit under those branches—" Wapinski began.

"Wha!!!" The man startled. "Where'd you come from?"

"Just walked in." Bobby smiled attempting to set the man at ease. "Didn't you hear me?"

"Christ no! You a goddamn warden? I didn't catch nothin."

"Geez, no." Wap rested his pole on the ground, held his open hands out, palms down. "Just came to fish. You catch anything with that string?"

"Not trying to catch anything. Just watchin the lake. Julie wants to document who's . . . ah, I mean . . . nobody comes up here but those idiots preparing for the Dipsea or the Cataract Trail Run."

"The Dip . . . ?"

"Dipsea. The race. Like the Cataract Trail, except down in Mill Valley. Starts with like seven hundred steps."

"Mill Valley?" Wap played dumb. He flicked his worm into the lake, glanced peripherally at the young man, thought he's eighteen, maybe nineteen.

"You're not from here, are you?" The young man stood. He looked shabby.

"No. From Pennsylvania. Just out here—"

"If you're thinking of moving out here"—his voice was defensive—"don't. And don't get caught without a license."

"Eh?" Wap reeled in, cast farther out, let his worm sink.

"You want to help us?" The young man's voice changed.

"Help you do what?"

"You're not a developer, are you?"

"Me! No way. I'm just—"

"Why don't you talk to Julie and Presnell. We could use a little help. I'm sick en tired of this. I'm Baba."

"It comes down to this—" Presnell said after Baba had led Bobby into the fir thicket of the small camp, and Presnell and Julie were comfortable that Bobby was neither a politician nor a developer, "last year the federal government ordered the town to install like this really expensive filtering system on the reservoir water."

"Here?!" Wap was surprised. The lakes, especially the Upper Res, seemed pristine. He continued to assay the camp. The setup was shoddy. All four people, the three adults and a small child they called Natasha, looked gray, damp, undernourished. Presnell was particularly gaunt.

"We've been up here three months," Presnell told Wapinski. "We drink directly from the lake. I record our daily intake. Look at Natasha." Presnell gestured toward the child. "Perfectly healthy. But the town, instead of filters—"

Julie finished his sentence. "They drilled six wells into various levels of the aquifer."

"That's cheaper?" Bobby asked. He wanted to ogle Julie—dirt-coated, gray, thin, she was still attractive—but he turned back to Presnell.

"That's how they sold it," Presnell continued. "But this is what's really going down. San Martin officially abandoned the reservoirs except the other side of the Lower Res, which they designated open space."

"That's good, isn't it?"

"No. Now the state Department of Public Health can change the land classification—no more protected watershed. This happens all over. That's what we're protesting. When the state approval goes through, the zoning can be changed. Then the Water District can sell the land. And the lake! Then it's open to development."

"Wait a minute." Wapinski dropped his gaze, shook his head. "The people I'm here with, they're real estate agents. I don't think they know anything about this."

"Of course not."

"Of course not?"

"Where're you from, Man? The moon? Wake up. The politicians, Man, and the developers already have options on the land. But they don't want anyone to know. We've got people who can prove this." Presnell leaned close to Bobby, then in conspiratorial tones added, "Options like the land's worthless. Undevelopable. Cheap, Man. They're stealing it. That's the way it goes. Look out there. There'll be roads coming right up here. A bummer, Man. We're in somebody's backyard. On top of their septic system. There'll be a dock right there. And fuckin real estate agents and open houses inviting everyone—"

"Holy shit!" Bobby checked his watch. It was already noon. "Ah, I gotta go. But I want to talk more. I want to know about this. Presnell, wasn't it?"

"Right on, Brother."

"Okay. I'll be back. I'd like to help."

"Good. They sell it all off, it becomes private. No fishing."

"You want some fish?" Bobby opened his creel. "To eat?"

"Oh, yeah. Yeah! Thanks."

"Victoria, Timmy's sister," Red said. "I guess you never met her. She moved in with Gino before you came out."

"I thought, you know, we'd just go out and eat." They were in the bedroom of their trailer on Bear Flag Place in Bahia de Martin. It was warm, windy, nearly six P.M. "Just us. To celebrate. It's my first commission."

"Oh Bobby, I'm so proud of you." Red knelt coyly on the corner of the mattress where Bobby sat. The mattress lay on the floor. They used it as bed, couch and study/work/reading area. "I know you're going to be a great salesman. Peter's really impressed. They all are. But I told Victoria we'd come. Can we go to dinner tomorrow?"

"Ah, sure."

"Please-ee." Red moved closer, swayed her shoulders.

"Yeah. I said it's cool. It's—it's—you know, only . . . If we go to their place, we can't really invite them here. We don't even have a kitchen set."

"We don't have to. They'll understand."

"Well, you know. It's nice to reciprocate."

"We will. When we can. When we have a sofa and end tables and . . . I saw the grooviest lamps at the mall. They had a tarnished brass sculpture as the base . . ."

"We should buy a house first."

"Oh Bobby, that'll take . . . well, even with both of us getting commissions . . . the down payment would take . . ."

"I could use my VA entitlement."

"Really?"

"That's what it's for." Red nuzzled her face into Wapinski's neck, kissed him there, worked her lips up to his ear. He wriggled, backed away a few inches, put his arm around her, pulled her onto his lap.

She resisted, backed off. "Maybe later." She winked. "Let's go to Victoria's. She said Gino had a hot tub installed."

For two and a half months, with the exception of the one small fishing excursion, Bobby Wapinski had immersed himself in the business of real estate. And his efforts were paying off. By July 3, 1970, he had listed two homes, sold and closed on a third, had a $39,000 counteroffer out to clients of a Golden Hills Realty agent on his $41,500 Martinwood listing, and had another sale in escrow. His conversation with Julie, Presnell, and Baba was all but forgotten.

"So you're the new man who's doing all the business at Great Homes?" Bobby and Victoria were in the kitchen of Gino's home, an isolated custom-built structure way out on South Peak Road. They were there ostensibly to get more crackers and another bottle of chardonnay. Red was on the deck with Gino and Brandon. Dawn was already in the hot tub.

Bobby laughed uneasily. He felt out of his element. Gino was wealthy, his home beautifully appointed. "Not all," he said. He did not look at Victoria but pretended to read the wine label. "I've been pretty lucky. Especially for this market."

Victoria moved closer to him. She had on a white lace camisole and long denim skirt. She raised a hand to his face, pushed back a blond lock. "Let your hair grow," Victoria said. "It's too short."

They had eaten dinner, Mexican, had consumed five bottles of California chenin blanc and chardonnay, had smoked a few joints. Red was giddy, flirtatious. Dawn had withdrawn, become serious. Victoria had removed her vest letting Bobby and Brandon behold her bosom through the lace camisole while Gino shifted his attention to Red. After another joint and another bottle of wine Dawn had stepped up to the elevated deck about the redwood tank, had unabashedly stripped and dropped into the dark steaming water.

Bobby looked up, pushed a hand through his hair. "This is about the longest I've ever worn it," he said.

"Are you always so quiet?" Victoria asked.

"No," he said. She grabbed his hand, squeezed, then pulled him toward the deck.

"Far out, Man," Brandon teased.

"Well I think I could." Red's tone was intoxicated, slightly defensive yet bouyant.

"Then why don't you?" Gino laughed.

"Why don't you what?" Bobby and Victoria joined them.

"I think I could run that office better than that *dildo* who's running it!"

"Than Peter Wilcox!?" Bobby blurted. Red flashed him a hurt glance. "I mean, you just started and . . . "

"Not that office." Red turned from him. "I mean," she continued to

Gino and Brandon, "Myra had Pauline and me completely convinced we were totally inadequate."

"Oh! Before . . ." Bobby tapered off. Victoria was by his side. She leaned into him, put an arm about his waist. He responded putting his arm about hers, feeling her long straight blond hair on his arm, looking momentarily into her upturned face. Her face was lovely, her eyes deep blue, her mouth sensual, her chin and cheekbones sculptured. Only her nose, he thought, was too large. In all he felt her enticing. Then he looked away, shook his head as if to shake off the spell.

"Idealist-ti-cul-ly," Red stuttered. "That's a hard word to say." Gino and Brandon chuckled with her. Gino's hand made a small, light circle on her back. "I-deal-is-took-ca-ly."

"Ideally," Bobby said from behind her.

"Whatever!" Red giggled.

"Isn't anyone else coming in?" Dawn called. "Brandon, come in here with me."

"Are you embarrassed?" Victoria whispered in Bobby's ear.

"No," he said softly. "I just wasn't expecting . . ."

"You don't have to feel self-conscious," she said leading him toward the elevated deck. "Even if you get a hard-on. I'd feel hurt if you didn't get a little excited."

"I'm already a little excited." Bobby stifled his laugh.

Dawn turned as they approached. She was very tan except for the points of her breasts which were white and barely submerged. "Did you hear KFRC this morning? The DJ was telling jokes about that state supreme court ruling. I think he's indecent."

"Me?!" Brandon was a step behind Bobby and Victoria. He smiled broadly. "Me? Indecent? I think"—he said as he removed his shirt, dropped his pants, tossed his clothes to the side—"I'm very decent. Don't you think so, Vikki?"

Victoria patted his chest. "Yes," she said. "Kinda decent." Facing Brandon she unsnapped and dropped her skirt. Her panties were of matching lace to the camisole: her legs were smooth and muscular. Again she patted Brandon's chest but now slid her hand to his abdomen. "A bit of a gut, though." She pushed Brandon toward the hot tub. He stumbled back, caught himself, climbed in, and stood next to Dawn, smiling up at Victoria.

"Not like you, eh, Vikki?" He teased. "What legs! Whooo-wee!" He turned to Wapinski, said, "She gets those legs from running that Cataract Trail."

"I was talking about that ruling," Dawn said, "that killing an unborn fetus doesn't constitute murder."

"Come on, Hon." Brandon shook his head, sat beside her. "Let's not get into that. Nobody wants to talk about that stuff."

Victoria gracefully removed her lingerie, stepped into the tub, moved to the far side. Red and Gino stripped and slid in next to each other on the near side, and Bobby, feeling lost, removed his clothes quickly and dropped into the only space left—between Red and Victoria. For a moment everyone ooohed and aaahed as the air jets blasted the 101-degree water onto knees and backs and shoulders.

"You know," Dawn began, seriously again, "they were also talking about that crazy guy in Burlingame who the police shot."

"Give it a break," Brandon said lowly. To the others he said, "She gets a little distant on grass."

"He was a former army captain who went nuts because his wife didn't come home one night and—"

"God!" Brandon snapped. "If you're going to talk about it at least get it straight. It wasn't Burlingame. It was Burlington. Burlington, Connecticut."

"Hey, did you hear the one about the newlyweds"—Gino overpowered the tiff—"who didn't know the difference between Vaseline and putty?" Red put her hands to her face covering a shriek. In the water Bobby could feel Victoria's calf and foot caressing his. Gino finished, "All their windows fell out!"

Red laughed, coughed. Brandon handed her the bottle. She took a short swig, passed it back.

"How come no one wants to talk about real stuff?" Dawn did not look at them but kept her eyes on the bubbling water. Unseen, beneath the dark roils, Victoria's fingers lightly brushed Bobby's left thigh.

"Do you really run Cataract Trail?" Bobby asked Victoria, trying to control himself.

"We could talk—" Red began, blushed, finished, "about women's orgasms." Brandon's foot stretched across the middle of the tub, brushed by Bobby's and Victoria's knees on its way to Red's legs. Suddenly Red shot up with a loud, "Ooooo!" Then she laughed and settled back in.

"I try to do at least a race a month," Victoria said to Bobby. Her hand found his cock and began stroking it. "I'm getting ready for the Dipsea at the end of August. Do you run?"

"We could talk about Charles Manson and that new crucifixion stance of his. . . . "

"Dawn, Honey, we're naked. We're not going to talk about those things."

"A little," Bobby said. Her hand felt wonderful. Careful not to show the slightest movement of his left shoulder, he moved his left hand between Victoria's legs and slowly allowed his middle finger to nestle between her labia. "I did a lot of hiking but lately I've done nothing but sit. Either in the office or in my car."

"We need more wine," Gino said. "I'll be right back." He got up and left, and Red stood, her small breasts red from the hot water. "I've got to sit out for a minute," she said. "I'm getting light-headed." She raised one foot to the seat to step out, swayed. Brandon popped up, grabbed her shoulders. "I've got you," he said gallantly as he pressed the front of his body to her back. "Just lay down right there." He indicated the deck. "Sometimes the heat gets to me, too."

Red lay on her stomach, her legs together, her hands under her chin.

"Take a few deep breaths." Brandon continued to help her. He sat beside her, gently rubbed the small of her back.

"Oh." Red sighed. "That feels much better." She arched her head back then pushed up with her arms, raising her torso from the deck. She inhaled deeply, held it, slowly let the air escape and lowered herself to the deck—seemingly oblivious to Victoria and Bobby though cognizant of Brandon, and of Gino who now knelt by her with the chilled bottle and let her hold it to her forehead before she took a swig.

"I'm too hot, too," Dawn said. She stood exposing her large breasts. "Did you hear about the hippie protestors up by The Res?"

"Ah, no." Gino eyed her, expecting a joke.

"They busted their asses—" Dawn giggled, "for smoking grass."

After the hot tub party Bobby and Red had returned to their trailer, in silence; had made love without talk, Bobby, so stimulated, ejaculating only seconds after penetration, and Red, still intoxicated, in no mood to give him a chance to recharge before falling asleep. In the morning they had had their first full-blown argument.

"You didn't tell me Gino and Victoria were so classy."

"What'd you expect?" Red snapped. She jammed an orange juice carton back into the refrigerator, slammed the door.

"Well . . ." Bobby paused. He was not ready for her anger. "You know, I thought they'd be like Tim and Suzie."

"What's that supposed to mean?"

"C'mon, Red. You know."

"What?"

"Suzie was a slob. That house was filthy, and like, you know, half the stuff she had in the refrigerator was covered with gray fuzz." He opened the refrigerator, removed the O.J., poured himself a coffee cupful. "I couldn't wait to get out. . . ."

"Well, you could have cleaned it up." She turned her shoulder to him.

"Aw . . . that's not the point." He stood over her, sounding like a father lecturing a thirteen-year-old. "I just wasn't expecting, you know, last night. . . . Such a nice place. I thought they'd be more like . . . hippieish."

"You certainly seemed to be getting along with Victoria. She was hanging all over you."

"Me! I didn't even know we were going to take our clothes off!"

"What do you think you do in a hot tub?"

"I didn't know. I didn't think . . . For one thing I didn't think you'd let those guys rub your ass."

"Like you and Victoria weren't playing footsie in the hot tub!"

"I didn't start—Geez, you went up there to get naked with those two guys. I don't think we should go—"

"I didn't do anything but have a good time. And I don't have to justify that to you!"

His voice rose. "I'm not saying you've got to justify it. Just tell me first."

"Why?! Do you own me?"

"Oh geez!" His hands flew in the air. Orange juice splashed from the cup. "Wouldn't it be common courtesy—"

"You just want to piss on my fire. If I break out, even a little. . . . "

"Aw hell"—he flicked the back of a hand at her—"break out all you want." Wapinski stalked off toward the bedroom, grabbed a towel, stomped to the bathroom, snarled, "I've got the Pierces coming in today at one. I'm showering."

"On July Fourth?!"

"Yeah. On July Fourth! He doesn't get a lot of days off."

For the next six hours Wapinski had again concentrated on the needs and capabilities of "his" buyer, on the availability and suitability of MLS homes. By seven he'd shown John and Joan Pierce a dozen homes—four the Pierces could afford but didn't like, four that would be a stretch, three they could afford only if John's father gave them the down payment, and one in Golden Vista which was out of the question. Joan Pierce wanted the home in Golden Vista.

Bobby had returned to the trailer exasperated and drained. He'd met Red returning from North Bay Mall with a new kitchenette set tied to the roof of her pistachio-colored Pinto. The incident at Gino's was sidestepped, repressed.

He sat there, not actually surveying the conference room table but feeling the presence of each individual, feeling the positive charge of their interaction, sensing them as a team, a platoon, almost as a family. At the head of the table was Peter Wilcox, Great Homes Realty's dynamic, nearly manic, office manager. Then eleven salespeople including Bobby and petite, bubbly Bea Hollands.

Bobby listened as various conversations went on around the table, caught bits and pieces, lost most because his damaged hearing could not sort out single voices amid cacophony.

Alfred Bartecchi and Dan Coleman were evidently against it but Ernest Schnell argued, "I hope they do legalize gambling here. Why not? Why should all the money go to Nevada? Imagine how much this building'd be worth if it were a casino."

"Yeah, but imagine what would happen to the properties if every place along The Strip had one-armed bandits."

"Value is determined by the amount of income the property produces—" Ronald Colson chimed in.

Coleman cut him off. "San Martin's desirable because we don't have a bunch of ticky-tack. You bring that trash in here . . . "

On the other side of the table stocky Lisa Fonari was baiting Tom Houghton, using her impressive cleavage to befuddle him. "I'd strike too if they sprayed that poison stuff on me while I was working," she said.

"It's harmless and it controls the weeds. Those sixteen in Tulare . . . "

"They sprayed it to kill bugs, not weeds."

"I think it was that 2,4,5-T stuff. Weed killer."

"If it's bad enough for them to ban it, they shouldn't spray it. They should destroy the remaining stock . . . "

" . . . I think they got sick from food poisoning. They leave their lunch bags in the sun . . . "

"Yeah. That's what the growers want you to believe. Ya-di ya-di ya."

Beside Bobby, Red conversed with Peter Wilcox. "Really, I think it would be wonderful to live in San Francisco. In the Marina. I love it there."

He patted her hand. "Then you should go for it," he said.

"Or maybe Sausalito," Red added. "I think that would be exciting."

"There's nothing holding you back." Peter looked deeply into her face, smiled his perfect smile.

Bobby glanced over the unsigned deposit receipt he'd prepared for John and Joan Pierce, but he did not read it. "Okay, people," Peter began. The conversations spurted as the salespeople attempted to get in their last phrases. "Come on, quiet down. We've got a lot to cover." Bobby glanced past Jane Boswell to Dan Coleman. For a week he'd been meaning to ask Dan if anyone in the office was going to run the Dipsea. "Let's go over the status of our listings." Peter began with the standard agenda. Over and over again the listers lamented, "No action," or "Not even shown," or "I could use some help on this one."

"Listen people," Wilcox finally said. "I know there's a lot of talk about the recession reaching us but don't believe it. You bring in a deal and I guarantee you we'll get the financing." Wilcox eyed each salesperson. "You've got to realize we're in the demand path. People have to buy. People have to sell. When they can't buy in Marin they come up here or go to the East Bay. Great! Send them there. Set it up with Concord or Danville or Livermore. But put it through Concord. The central office has to know for you to receive your referral. You all know how it works, right?"

Red raised a shy hand, one finger extended, about two inches above the table. "I don't," she said sweetly.

"Lisa—" Peter Wilcox turned to Fonari who screwed her eyes up toward the chandelier, "will you go over that with Red?"

Lisa clicked her tongue. "Why not?" She smiled, waved an arm bedecked with bracelets at Red. "Don't get frazzled over it, honey."

"Look, people," Peter continued, "we should be in a warm-weather blitz. Into the home stretch before school starts. People *are* moving. We're better priced than Marin. We're closer in than Sonoma. First-home buyers can't buy into Marin. Nor can people who need bigger homes. Get em up here. Sell em on San Martin. Let the San Rafael office list their home. Twenty percent referral. Twelve hundred and five homes sold in our area last year. We did twenty-one percent of that. But, damn it, this year, of five hundred seventeen closings we haven't even been a part of ninety. Eighty-seven for thirteen salespeople! That's less than seven each in seven months! Jon, can you live on six thousand a year?" Jon Ross lowered his eyes. Wilcox fixed his eyes on Liza Caldicott. "What about you?"

"Henry makes enough for us to get by." Her voice was loud, miffed.

Wilcox gasped. "Some of you aren't even paying for your desk space."

"Pete—" Al Bartecchi challenged the office manager, "cool it."

"Damn it, Al. You guys have got to sell. Sell! Sell! Maybe you, Dan and Ernie are doing okay but I want you all to be rich. Money!" Wilcox rapped the table. "Money! Money! Money makes the world go round. Listen people, I'll get your buyers financing. Just bring in somethin reasonable. We'll make it fly. Okay?" No one answered. Red nodded. "Okay, that's that. Anybody have anything else?"

No one spoke up. Those with pads and pens began gathering them. A few comments wafted between the salespeople.

"Ah—" Bobby Wapinski stuttered. He wasn't certain if he, the new guy, should ask, should change the subject. "What's going on up at the reservoirs? I've heard the town's going to open them up for development."

"Who'd you hear that from?" The question shot from Ernest Schnell's mouth.

"No way!" Lisa Fonari squawked. Then she laughed. "My great grandfather would roll over in his grave."

"There's been rumors about that for years," Peter Wilcox said. "Just talk. By the way, did the Pierces sign the deposit receipt on that Golden Vista place?"

"No." Bobby picked his pad and pen from the table. "His father drew the limit at six thousand. They're asking her mother for four more."

Peter collared Bobby. The others cleared the room. "I've got an old client up there who's been thinking of selling. If I can get them to put the house up, say for forty-four—"

"Pheew! I'm stretching them at forty-two five. . . . "

"But listen. If it's our listing, there's a twenty-six hundred and forty dollar commission . . . let's see, that's about eight hundred to Concord . . . that'd let us give them back eighteen hundred as a hidden second. Particularly if the sales price is forty-two thou but we get Hinderman at S. M. S & L to appraise it at forty-four. We can make this thing fly."

"You mean . . . "

"Yeah. The extra two grand covers their closing costs, plus they get our eighteen hundred. At twelve percent."

"I don't know if they'd go for that. They're pretty straitlaced."

"See me on it tomorrow, Bob. I'll make a few calls. Tell em the other place—who's got it, Everest?—tell the Pierces Everest took a deposit on it."

He had not expected any of it: the charge card bills, the articles, the letters, the magic brownies, his own bizarre reaction. It was a bright, clear, beautiful mid-September morning. Sun rays filtered through the sheer curtains Red had bought—"but they were on sale"—and hung over the large window. Wapinski was preoccupied, serious, exhausted, attempting to work through it. He sat at the new table in the single-wide trailer in Bahia de Martin Mobile Home Park. Sunlight bathed the bill box and personal financial files Bobby had spread out. He'd ignored so much the past few months it was imperative he take the day off, re-entrench.

Since July he had sold and closed two more homes, and had listed and had sold by others three. His commissions to date totaled $6,930, a yearly rate, if he could keep it up, of nearly $17,000. And he had thus far managed to avoid—on the advice of both Coleman and Bartecchi—the pitfalls of taking commissions as hidden second mortgage notes, or helping buyers create financing beyond their means. Unfortunately he had not avoided the pitfalls of preferring the comfort of self-deception to the anguish of truth.

Wapinski sorted the stack of bills. On the back of an envelope he listed each: rent, Red's car payment, auto insurance, medical insurance. When he came to the credit cards he listed total balance and minimum due—thinking it would be best to pay the minimum due, except that the mortgage company might pick up unpaid balances—still $125 to the Emporium . . . What the—? What'd she buy? He pulled the statement from the household receipt file: Estée Lauder—$43.58; women's undergarments—$56.40; cutlery—$37.50. He pulled the BankAmericard statement: Le France Boutique—$109; Mitchell's Jeans and Tops—$86.50. Crocker Master Charge: Sausalito Food Factory—$36.80; S. L. Davis European Design Furniture—$266.67. Goddamn it! We're supposed to be saving!!! He bit his lip, fumed beneath his breath. "Necessities!" He growled. He wrote out minimum checks, filed the receipts, suppressed his anger.

Red was out shopping, again. She was no longer associated with Great Homes, no longer in the real estate business.

"That bastard," she'd seethed one August evening.

"Who?" Bobby'd asked.

"Wilcox," she'd stammered. "He told me I could make twenty thousand a year. That's like forty sales. More than three a month! Nobody can do that! I bet even Schnell doesn't make that." Bobby had been silent, empathetic. "I can't even close one every other month." Red had plopped down on their study-work-reading mattress. "And once you do sell one, it's over for five years."

"Well, you build up a clien—" he had begun.

"I'm going to sell insurance. I talked to the most wonderful man. At least in insurance the commission comes in every time people renew. *And* you get a base salary."

It was her fourth job in ten months. Red was now training across the bay in Richmond with People's Life and Casualty. By October she'd be working out of the Larkspur branch office, fifteen miles south. Today, however, she was playing hookey, out shopping—out, Bobby prayed, only window shopping—for items for their "maybe-new-home."

Bobby rose, poured himself another cup of coffee. Dishes from breakfast, from last night, the night before, were all in the sink. The trailer needed vacuuming, dusting, a general pickup. It seemed to him the more time Red spent in the trailer, the messier the place became.

In July Bobby had listed a fixer-upper at 506 Deepwoods Drive in Martinwood Estates for $29,900. For a month he'd held open houses, advertised, prodded other salespeople to show it. He'd even offered a fifty-dollar bill—on Peter Wilcox's suggestion—to any agent bringing in an offer. "The owner's old," he'd told all during an office meeting. "Eighty-two. She's not in good health. And she needs the proceeds to get into a nursing home. She really needs help."

"My heart bleeds," came Lisa Fonari's brassy retort. "Tell her to clean the place up."

"She doesn't have the money," Bobby had countered.

"Tell her I'll clean it. She can pay me in escrow."

"Sure," Liza Caldicott charged. "You'll clean her out."

"I get along well with old people," Lisa had snapped back.

"People!" Wilcox had stopped them. "Let's move on."

In August Bobby had himself offered Mrs. Angelina Tomassino full price if she was willing to sell VA—that is, to pay the points and other Veterans Administration required fees (almost $2,000), and to put up with the uncertainty and potential problems of VA appraisal and structural inspection. She reminded him of his grandmother—and of his grandfather, living alone, widowed, who would be entering his eighty-second year in one week. Bobby wanted to help, wanted to be fair. And he wanted out of the flimsy trailer. Mrs. Tomassino had accepted. To avoid potential repair costs, Bobby and Dan Coleman had done an informal termite inspection and Bobby returned, cleaned, replaced and repaired every bit of damage he suspected might be called. Now, in mid-September, with no word from the mortgage company except to verify receipt of his certificate of eligibility, it was a matter of waiting, hoping the VA approval would arrive *before* the loan points rose further.

Bobby took out the vacuum cleaner he'd purchased secondhand. Quickly he ran the machine over the gold shag of the aislelike living room, then through the bedroom. Strands of Josh's finest hair floated and glittered in the sun. He put the machine away, grabbed the broom, swept the galley kitchen. Most of the pile of dirt was mud Josh had dragged in. He pushed it into the dust pan, opened the back door, dumped it on the gravel under the trailer. Josh was out, roaming. Cars were zipping down the off-ramp. Bobby bit his inner lip. If the Deepwoods home came through, he'd be able, he thought, to let Josh run in the grass and glades of South Peak.

Bobby returned to the kitchen. He washed the dishes, the sink, the countertop. There was something wrong, he thought, living the way they did. Not just he and Red. There were things there, too, but he was thinking more about Bahia de Martin and all the eastside developments and even much of Martinwood and Golden Vista—something wrong with living *on* the land versus *with* the land as one does when one lives in the hills. All the subdivisions were on cleared and leveled land—decent farmland. Developers with big cats had come in, stripped the land bare, removed the topsoil, poured concrete slabs on the denuded clay. Houses had risen as if they were not even part of the earth. Then the developers had sold the topsoil back to the new homeowners who could afford it. Flatlanders, Bobby thought. Versus hill dwellers. But even that wasn't true because these people weren't flatlanders in the traditional sense of the flatland farmer, but simply people who never touched the earth because they went from house to paved walk to paved drive to car to roll on air-filled rubber balloons over paved streets with concrete curbs to concrete freeways to concrete offices and shopping malls and suddenly Bobby wanted to walk the path around the pond at High Meadow, to descend into the gap and rise to the old Indian trail and walk through the cathedral of virgin eastern hemlocks. He could see it, feel it. He wanted to sit with his grandfather.

The Res, the upper creek, the Upper Res, Dong Ap Bia, A Shau—hills, valleys, mountains—he'd grown up in the hills. He belonged in the hills—even in Viet Nam he'd been comfortable with the mountains of I Corps. Now he bit his lip hard enough to hurt, hard enough to chase the thought away. Gotta eat. Gotta pay the rent—soon, hopefully, the mortgage on 506 Deepwoods Drive—506, his old battalion number, near Highway 101, his old division. The numbers were special to him.

Bobby returned to the table, closed the bill box, opened the newspaper. He had established a real estate "farm" in Martinwood, a block of 336 homes to which he mailed a monthly newsletter and in which he'd managed to knock on every door twice, first leaving a plastic litter bag with his name and the Great Homes logo, then leaving refrigerator magnets. He needed to compose his next letter, bring it to Gloria Spencer, the office secretary, for typing, then to the copy center. But first he wanted to read the newspaper, something he seldom did anymore. He skimmed the headlines. He rose, emptied the last of the coffee into his cup, saw Josh bouncing happily up the street between Mrs. Lewis' and Mrs. Stewart's perfectly maintained, rock-gardened double-wides. Bobby went to the back door, whistled his specific signal. Josh came scampering around, one furry side coated in mud, the other full of foxtails. "C'mon, little brother," Bobby whispered. "C'mere." He grabbed Josh by the collar, slipped a Milk-Bone between his lips, hooked him to his chain. "Can't go in like that. I'll bring the paper out."

Now Bobby did read the paper. The 101st was in the news again, near a firebase called O'Reilly, "much like Firebase Ripcord which the 101st abandoned July 23d . . . but this time most of the ground action is between the besieging NVA and the defending ARVN. . . ." Bummer, Man. Bummer. He skipped around. In the entertainment section there was a short opinion piece on *Hair*, which was onstage at the Orpheum in San Francisco. Tonight, he thought. Boy, will she be surprised. Tonight he was going to take Red to an early dinner at The Cherry Flower, a Viet Namese restaurant in the city on Columbus Avenue, and then to the Orpheum. He'd had the tickets for two weeks—a present from Great Homes for being July's Salesman-of-the-Month. He had told her only that he was going to take her out, for her to be ready early.

He flipped back, forth, back, forth, avoiding the financial news, reading the sports section. The Giants were more than twenty games back. There was an article on 60-year-old Norman Bright who'd won the 6.8-mile Dipsea race . . . 60! oh, a handicap race, fifteen minutes at 60 years old, in 44:46. Geez, still, 59:46 at 60, up and down that mountain! Bright had held the absolute course record since 1937 when he'd run a 47:22, but the record had been broken by one minute. . . . Bobby looked at the pictures. He had not taken up running, indeed had been putting on love handles, getting heavier by perhaps two pounds each month. He peered into the backgrounds of the photos. He had not seen Gino or Dawn or Brandon or Victoria since that first time. Now he searched the pictures hoping to catch a glimpse of Victoria . . . nothing . . . flip. More on the slaying of Judge Haley and three others in the Marin County Courthouse shooting—more on the alleged linkage of Angela Davis . . . flip. What's this? "Land Classification Changes: Sacramento—The State Department of Public Health made public an order Friday afternoon downgrading the classification of San Martin Water District property from protected watershed to . . .

"Ho!" Bobby sat up. Josh lifted his head. Bobby tore the page from the paper. He decided he'd show it to Coleman and Bartecchi. He'd been becoming better and better friends with the two of them, and with brassy, off-the-wall, stressed-out Lisa Fonari. Tom Houghton, too, though eight years older than Bobby, was becoming a friend. And Roger Fernandez had gained Bobby's respect. He would ask each what they made of it.

Three hours later, Bobby was in the office giving Gloria his farm-letter copy. Pete was in his private office interviewing a potential saleswoman.

Jon Ross was pulling floor duty, on the phone, two lines waiting, one ringing. No one else was in the office.

"I can't do it today," Gloria said. "Tomorrow."

"Oh," Bobby answered. "Tomorrow's fine." He stepped out from Gloria's office to a floor desk, grabbed a phone, "Great Homes Realty. May I help you?"

"I was calling about, ah, a house you have, ah, in the paper. Advertised."

"Yes. Which one would that be?"

"The three bedroom . . . " Bobby began waving at Jon Ross, caught his attention—"Where's that located?"—repeatedly pointed to the ceiling indicating it was an up, or prospective buyer, call.

Ross, a phone receiver jammed between ear and shoulder, pen in hand, tapped the side of his head with both hands then flicked his hands out. "Ma'am," Bobby said into the receiver, "I'm not sure which home that is, but the representative for that area is Jon Ross. He's on another line at the moment. Can I have him call you right back?"

"No!" The woman was emphatic.

"Could you hold for him, then?" Bobby cupped the air trying to pull Ross off the other line.

"I can call Everest," the woman said. "I'm sure *they'll* give me the address."

"Ma'am, Mr. Ross is right here." Bobby purposefully chuckled. "He's holding up a finger indicating one minute. Would you like to hold one minute or would you rather try Everest?"

"Oh—" the woman said, "I'll hold. One minute."

"Thank you, ma'am." Bobby immediately pushed the hold button. Ross hung up on the other line. "Hey"—Bobby flashed him a thumbs up—"she's tougher than a trout, keepin her on the line."

"Thanks. There's mail here for you." He held out a small stack, raised the receiver, pushed the flashing button, "Jon Ross speaking."

Bobby took the envelopes from Jon. "Tomorrow," Gloria called out to him. "Thanks," he called back. He left the office, got into his Chevy, examined the envelopes. There was a fat one from his brother, three pieces of junk mail, a small envelope without return address. He quickly dispatched the junk, opened the letter from Brian. It contained a letter and another envelope.

Dear Mr. Wapinski,

It is with Great Pleasure that I take this Opportunity to inform you that your Lease-on-Life has been transferred to Our account, that is The First Church of Monstrous Miriam and The Two-Dollar House of Worship. Kindly remit one half of the outstanding balance on your account or we shall be forced to collect in FULL.

Your Great & Kind Benefactor,
God

Hey Rob, it's me. This letter came for you a few weeks back—just getting around to forwarding it. Rob, things really have gone downhill here since you left. I was up at Grandpa's yesterday. He seems old. He never seemed old to me before. Miriam's been in a total rage for two months. I think she's nuts. Even Doug's having a hard time putting up with her! Cheryl and I were talking about you the other night. We've both got good jobs. Lots of guys here have been laid off. The economy's really turned to shit. Even I might be out of work soon. Cheryl thinks they're holding it together until after Election Day and then the bottom's going to drop out. Anyway, we've been thinking of moving. Don't tell anyone. If Miriam heard we'd never hear the end of it. But we've got some $ saved and I'm anxious to dump this place and start new. How's the job climate out there? Do you think I could sell real estate? Cheryl really knows insurance but we're thinking of trying for a baby again and I wouldn't want her to work if we had a baby. Hey, how's Red? Are you two going to get hitched? If you are, make sure you invite Grandpa. He said he'd fly out. Can you imagine Pewel getting on a 707? Is it expensive to live out there?

> Your brother (and fellow sufferer of M-M)
> Brian

P.S. Joanne's a bit weird but she's okay. Really.

P.S.S. or is it P.P.S.—ha! who cares? A bit of local news. The cops arrested fatso Jessie Taynor again. She's a real nut case. They say she set fire to the dumpster behind the White Pine Inn because they threw her out. Grandpa's new girl—she's a nurse, I haven't met her yet but he hired her to come out occasionally to cook and clean. He says he doesn't need her but she needs him and she's got two little girls. He told her he can't see the dirt anymore—anyway she told Grandpa Jessie needs psychiatric help, not to be arrested. I think Jessie needs to be in the sideshow.

Bobby sat for a moment, thought about Jessie, about Mill Creek Falls, about his family, about Grandpa. He thought about his grandfather needing help, about him hiring someone to cook and clean. He'd seen the dirt the old man had left because he really couldn't see it—just like old Mrs. Tomassino—and Bobby felt guilty.

He fingered the second envelope. It was written in pencil. It came from Bobby's old interpreter, Quay Le.

Dear Captain Wapinski, Robert:

How are you and your family? I hope you are well. I must ask you a favor. Please write Captain Addison who is replaced Captain Thompson who you let use the refrigerator you gave me until he DE-

ROS. You gave me the refrigerator in your hootch when you leave. You remember? You said Captain Thompson use it until he DEROS then I can take it. Captain Stephen Addison says it is his refrigerator because it is in hootch that he lives in. I say you gave it to me and Captain Thompson only have it on lease until he leave which is many months ago now and then it is mine. Please write Captain Addison. You remember my wife. She is so happy when I tell her you give me refrigerator. Now she is very angry. It is not like the good old days when you are here and we go up to Camp Carroll and down to 1st Brigade and all over. I wish you very good life in America. Please write Captain Addison so I have a refrigerator. Thank you my old friend.

> Quay Le

Geez! Wapinski thought. Can't they give the poor guy the fridge? It was a dinky little box anyway. Humph! Yeah, Quay, I'll write em. Soon as I get home. Bobby opened the third envelope. It contained only a small folded card.

Dear Rob,
    Hello! How are you? I hope you are fine and doing well. Oh Rob, I made such a mistake. I'm getting a divorce. Jerry and I separated six weeks ago. I'm living back home with my mother. I wanted to call you but I didn't want to upset you. Or Bea. That's why I'm sending this note to your office. I'll understand if you don't call or write back.

> Love,
> Stacy

It was the first time she had tasted Viet Namese food, his first Southeast Asian cuisine in more than sixteen months. They sat across the small table from each other, occasionally peering down from the second-story window onto Columbus Avenue, Robert Wapinski and Bea Hollands, smiling at each other, commenting about oddities in the street scene; about the food—Red had ordered roast crab, Bobby, the imperial roll with prawns sauté and rice—about Brian's letter and Jessie Taynor—Red, "They should lock her away for her own safety"; about the Deepwoods Drive house, the VA lender, and their anxiety about the loan's approval. Bobby did not mention the bills, Red's spending, the state of the trailer, Stacy's news. Red did not mention having to share their cramped quarters with Josh, the enthusiasm of Richard Townsmark, her new boss, or Bobby's ramblings about High Meadow.

Red looked terrific. She'd had her hair done (Done? Bobby'd thought—she was now wearing it straight, and to him "done" meant washed and combed) and she'd bought a new outfit—a chambray blue knit dress that clung to her thighs and ass and tiny waist; had purchased matching purse and shoes, and a silver necklace and bracelet. She'd been ready and waiting and looking wonderful when he returned from Great Homes with the three letters. He'd cleaned up, changed quickly and not said anything about the incredible mess Red had made in the kitchen. "It's a surprise. I'll show you after dinner," was all she said.

"So, what's my surprise?" Red asked.

"You tell me mine first."

"I asked first," Red said. "But I'll give you a hint. It's magic!"

"Magic?" Bobby pondered. "Hmm, magic?"

"Now you have to give me a hint." Red's eyes were twinkling, dazzling in a way he'd not seen in a long time.

"We have to go to it," Bobby said.

"Well, of course." Red laughed.

"I could have it here." He patted the breast pocket of his jacket. "Matter of fact, I do." He smiled, slid a finger in, touched the edge of the tickets, then thought, horrified, perhaps she thinks its a ring. "It's just for tonight," he said quickly. "And ah, you watch it."

"Watch it?" Red squirmed like a charmed child. "In your pocket?"

Bobby took out the tickets, held them out, splayed them, smiled sheepishly. "Hair . . ." he began.

Red's eyes flew from the tickets to his face. She gasped excitedly. "Tonight!"

"Um-hmm."

"Ooo, this is really far out. But what time. We'll be late. We should eat up. . . . "

He raised a hand. "We still have a good hour before we need to be—"

"But I've got something special, too. Dessert."

"Dessert?" Red opened the flap of her new purse, flashed him the contents, an aluminum foil–covered block, closed the flap. "Hmm?"

She leaned across the table. He leaned in. "Magic brownies," she whispered. "I got some hash from Gino."

From the restaurant they walked north on Columbus Ave. to the small green before St. Peter's and St. Paul's. It was still light, clear, a perfect San Francisco September eve. Bobby bought two cans of Coke from a street vendor and he and Red sat on a bench, ate magic brownies, washed them down with cold soda.

"How much did you put in these?" Bobby asked quietly.

"All of it," Red answered. "They taste terrible, don't they?"

"Sweet and bitter. How much was that?"

"I don't know. I gave Gino fifty dollars."

"Fifty!!!"

"Ssshh!" Red cuddled into him. "You'll see."

"Should we catch a taxi?" His voice was sober. Fifty bucks. Everything Red did made him angry, yet still, so much of what she was, how she looked, talked, smiled, he liked. He liked her. She was a nice person.

And he wanted her to have the things she bought. He wanted her to look beautiful. She looked so good to him right then and there he wanted to consume her. But he felt betrayed. Not at this moment, but generally—betrayed by promises made in love letters a year old.

"Let's . . . Where did we park?"

Bobby stifled a giggle. Very seriously he said, "On Kearny."

"Let's walk to the lot," Red said. She too was trying to keep from laughing. "Then we'll get a taxi."

They walked hand in hand, meandering over to Broadway, chuckling at the flashing neon bust of Carol Doda, at the lewd calls from the strip-joint barkers, at the even funnier people on the sidewalks. They strolled to Kearny hugging each other's waist, skipping, suddenly breaking out into a dashing chorus from a song from *The Wizard of Oz*, flying over the concrete, laughing, singing, "Follow, follow, follow, follow . . . follow the Yellow Brick Road!!" Before either knew it, they were in the pistachio Pinto, kissing, squeezing each other, Red's skirt up to her waist, Bobby driving, laughing, crossing the Golden Gate Bridge—the tickets, the Orpheum, *Hair* completely lost to mind, flying, floating, sailing the broken lines, feeling the canyons between stripes, the lunging climbs the Pinto made over each painted dash on Highway One Hundred and First Airborne All the Fucking Way Sir . . . Red: I've got to pee . . . Bobby: I'll hold it for you . . . tears splashing like buckets of laughter, flooding the car, vaudeville clown buckets of—SPLASH—confetti, a million colored dots, dashes, coming at them . . . how'd we get here . . . Not now Josh, ha! ha! ha! Oooo! The gold shag soft as warm cooked spaghetti enwrapping her giggle, smile, help me off with the chambray blue knit, not yet, just, giggle, hold, titter, me, snore.

She was out. Down for the ten count, down for the ten thousand count, down until ten o'clock tomorrow night.

But he was not. He was up, hard as stone, large as Coit Tower. He cuddled her, slid away, removed his clothes, cuddled her, laughed as he slid back and forth, hunched over her, whispering, singing, " 'Now my girl you're so young and pretty . . . ' " it must have been on the radio on the way home, " 'but one thing I know is true . . . ' " singing silently to her in his mind, " 'you'll be dead before your time is due. We gotta get outa this place . . . ' " Sliding back and forth, back, away, removing her undergarments—$56.40—sliding his hard-on across her hand, across Victoria's palm grasping him, perfect palm—"C'mon sweet thing," muttering, "arise, arise . . . " kissing her gently, "arise, sweet angel . . . arise, Snow White . . . boy, am I fucked up . . . " snuggling, cuddling, sliding on her thigh back and forth to ejaculation collapse but not asleep, not out, somber, angry, they arrested Jessie Taynor for setting a dumpster full of trash on fire before it could be brought to the incinerator . . . my fat friend Jessie . . . Granpa had a way with her . . . "Responds to kindness," he'd said . . . why can't they be kind? Why can't you fuck me like you love me? You bitch. You bitch . . .

Only thoughts now, not even groans, not a muscle ticking, spent, flaccid, his eyes like hers shut, but his mind exploding with rage-accelerated images. Headache, pussyache, tired, too untired, antsy, any one of a hundred excuses. Fuck it. Let her fuck herself. I'm going, leaving. It poured out of him, in his mind, in his stupor. Up. Leave. I should just get up, get out. If she asks, I'll say I'm going out to find someone who's willing to love me! Boy, that'd bring down the wrath of God. But fuck her. Out. Give Stacy a call. Give Victoria a call. Fuck her. Victoria. With Gino?! What a mismatch.

For an hour he lay there, angry, unable to focus his anger except generally at Red. He settled back, listened to her breathing. Perhaps she was asleep, perhaps pretending. Slow rhythmic breathing. She doesn't breathe like that. She snores. Not loud, but snores when she's in deep sleep. She wasn't snoring now. Well, fuck it, he thought. He began slowly fondling his penis. He didn't want to wake her, didn't want to make waves. What if he did? What if she said, "What are you doing?" Or more likely, "What the hell are you doing?" "I'm jerking off," he'd answer. "I'm jerking off because I'm so low on your priority list you never have any energy left for me."

As he fondled himself he could feel the pressure build. He slipped from anger to fantasy. They were driving, speeding down a little-used blacktop highway. Two lanes. A mile between houses. From nowhere the highway patrol car pulled out, chased them, lights flashing. He was getting too hot for details. The cops, two big guys, had them up against the car, spread-eagle, frisking them, her. The guy on him bashed him between the legs. His knees crumpled. The guy on her had his arms around her torso. He pulled open her blouse. "What we got here, sister? You carrying contrabands in your bra?" He grabbed her breasts, caressed them through the bra. "What's this here? What are these hard things?" He rolled her nipples between his thumb and fingers. He ripped open her bra exposing her skin, her wonderful curves. Bobby rose, went to beat the shit out of the cop. He could see himself grab the cop, grab the cop's gun. He went to blast . . . No. He didn't get the gun. The guy laughed at him, held his gun on him, ordered him to strip, ordered him to remove his wife's remaining clothes. "Eat me," she said to him. He was behind her, on the ground, his head between her thighs, kissing her thighs, her ass. She was naked, bent, groaning, sucking the cop's cock, the cop that had ripped off her bra. The cop had a ten-inch dick. She licked and sucked and licked and sucked. "It's beautiful." She moaned between sucks. He was getting hotter, trying not to shake the trailer, his body tensed, his dick spat its juice. He sighed, deflated. He went back to the fantasy. Both cops were about to come, one in her mouth, one in her ass. He grabbed the gun, shot them. Fucked them up good.

Still his mind was not right, still his rage, his festering wound, oozed. Still she lay on his bicep. His arm ached. His hand had fallen asleep, felt

numb, bloated, ready to burst. He chuckled quietly. "Should we amputate it, Sir?" The room was dark. There was moaning from the far
side. "It's pretty badly mutilated." "Yes Sir." "How many more are
there?" "Eleven, Sir." "As bad as . . . ?" "No, Sir. Maybe one. One's a
head case. We put him in the corner . . . " "Hm. Too bad. Put her with
him. Next."

In the dark. In the cool. In the corner. He chuckled. His eyes lit. He
could amputate it for her. He rose, grabbed the scalpel, grabbed the
Ed. Wusthof Dreizackwerk butcher knife she'd bought, she had to
have, needed to buy the best, the best steel, the finest blade, the highest price, grabbed her, lifted her, ran the back of the blade over her
arm lengthwise, planning his incision, his shredding before lopping.

Now, no longer fantasy, he had the desire. He could cut her, slice
her. He could amputate her hand, arm, heart. He opened his eyes
wide. He wanted to kill her. He would cut her. He stared at the ceiling. Stared. Looking . . . focusing . . . looking in deep, through, beyond,
into a deep dark tunnel . . . deep, so deep, a tunnel into the past, into
time gone, lost, into time measured by genetic traces. He sees himself,
there, in deep but shallow deep, a child in darkness with but a glint of
light. The tunnel does not frighten him. He peers in, intrigued. There
is his father, his father's face, in the dark, vague, smiling . . . his grandfather's face, warm, smiling too, at ease. Farther back there are others,
vague, barely discernible yet radiating warmth, positive energy, a glow
from the depths. He steps in, one step. They do not beckon him, yet
they infuse him with strength, support him in his striving. Emissive
rays, waves, telling him to search, to find, to advance the genetic progression . . .

He rolled his head, glared at the back window. He focused on the
light from the freeway ramp, forced himself to lie still, to let his hand,
arm, puff and needle under the weight of Red's head, forced himself not
to move, not to get up, to stay away from the kitchen, the cutlery drawer.
He was at the absolute limit of his drugged-brain self-control, aware the
drugs had awakened repressed demons, aware that his thoughts, desires,
were crazy.

Now he forced himself to think about his grandfather, about Brian
and Cheryl, about Jessie Taynor, about Stacy. Slowly he rocked back to
Red. Gently he raised her head, slid his arm from beneath, laid her
head back down. He stumbled to the bedroom, grabbed a pillow, a
blanket, returned, covered her. Josh had been watching them. He rose,
followed Bobby to the bedroom. "Oh boy," Bobby whispered to the
dog. "Am I fucked up. Take me out of here." Josh sprang to him,
away. He raced to the kitchen, grabbed his leash, tossed it wildly an-
ticipating a walk. Then, outside, cool air, the night glowing with freeway lights. Bobby had put on his suit pants, jacket and sneakers. In his
jacket pocket he felt the card. He sat, stared at the freeway. Stacy, he
thought. Stacy. Stacy! Stacy!!

an Martin, mid-October—"It's a steal, Bob. Really." Dan Coleman was on one end of the mattress. Bobbie carried the other. It was late morning, overcast, an omen of the coming rainy season. "You and Red'll make out well."

"You think so?" With his butt, Bobby pushed the front door open, stepped up, bent the mattress so Dan could get his end in.

"I do. And what do you have to lose? You've got nothing in it. The commission covered your closing costs, didn't it?"

"Yeah," Bobby said. "If it wasn't such a dump . . . Red's already got every minute of my spare time spoken for, for the next three months."

They worked their way through the tiny foyer, into the hallway, to the first bedroom, dropped the mattress among a pile of boxes. Behind them came Al Bartecchi and Tom Houghton, wrestling the box spring of the new California King Red had put on their Master Charge the day the VA loan was approved—and had had delivered to the trailer so the bill would come after they'd used it and Bobby couldn't send it back. "But"—she had smiled so lovingly, twinkled so coyly—"we really need it. What if my parents come to visit? Or your grandfather?"

At the trailer Lisa Fonari helped Red wrap and box glassware. "This is really so nice of you ... " Red said again.

"Agh, packing kitchens is a pain in the ass." Lisa's brassy voice echoed in the mostly empty trailer. "Ever notice how the boys always zip through moving the big stuff. You watch, when they get back they'll wonder why we couldn't pack one little kitchen—"

"We're almost done," Red injected.

"They could at least of left the radio."

"Do you—I like to listen to KFRC. That guy's crazy. Richard says—that's my new boss—he says—"

"Oh." Lisa interrupted. "Talking about new! Did I tell you who Peter hired for your desk?"

"No."

"Sharon something."

"Is she nice?"

"She's gorgeous. I mean *really* gorgeous."

Bob and Dan unloaded Red's dresser from the back of Al's pickup, shifted the weight until it felt balanced, began the short walk to the door. "What's she got in here?" Dan groaned.

"We shoulda taken the drawers out."

"How can a tiny girl like Red have heavy clothes?"

"That's exactly what Al said when we loaded it. Want to put it down?"

"Shit no. Let's just get it in there." Dan walked backward, into the door, up the step, into the foyer. On the street a few neighbors gathered, waved. For nearly six months Bobby had billed himself as the Martinwood Specialist. He'd already met half the people on Deepwoods Drive.

"Take it straight back," Bobby said.

"Yeah," Dan grunted. He backed into the living room, let Bobby swing in, then Bobby backed down the narrow hall to the large bedroom at the end. "Holy cow!" Dan said, as they set the dresser down. "I can't believe it!"

"Yeah. Wanta stop for a beer?"

"Pheew! Yeah. Hey, did you hear about the zoning meeting?"

"When?"

"Last night. It was just like you said. P and Z changed the zoning of all the watershed. Just like that."

"You're kidding."

Bobby opened the refrigerator they'd moved first thing. Second thing, he'd packed in a case of Bud cans. Al and Tom joined them in the kitchen. Sometime in the past the floor had been covered with indoor/outdoor carpeting that now emitted a sour odor. Bobby church-keyed four cans, passed them out.

"You're talking about The Res, huh?" Bartecchi said.

"Yeah," Dan answered.

"I called Roger last night," Bartecchi said. "I thought he might have known about it but he didn't."

"I don't think they can do it," Dan said. "It wasn't on the agenda."

"Anybody call Peter?" Bobby asked. Dan and Al gave Bobby a silent *Really!* look. "Well, he probably knew."

"He probably didn't," Al said, "but he'd be behind it all the way."

"He'd be the first to buy," Dan said. "Or try to sell it."

"I'd like to live up there," Tom said. "It's a great spot."

"That's because nobody can live up there," Al shot back.

"Some of these guys," Dan said, "they smell blood, they go for the jugular."

"You mean money," Al said.

"Green blood." Dan laughed.

Al laughed too, but he was serious about this business. "Fernandez says there'll be a fight. Posting a few signs along Cataract doesn't constitute public notice."

They finished their beers. Dan and Al drove back to the trailer in Al's pickup; Bobby and Tom in Bobby's Chevy. "Did you see . . . ?" Tom asked shyly. "Hanoi's rejected Nixon's proposals."

"What proposals?" Bobby asked.

"In Nixon's speech last week. For a peace conference and cease-fire."

"I didn't see it," Bobby said.

"That's right. You guys don't have a TV, huh?"

"Nope."

"They, ah, one of the communist groups rejected Nixon's thing and said there was an eight-point plan . . . "

"You can't negotiate with those bastards." The subject brought instant, unexpected agitation.

"You were there, right?"

"Yeah."

"All this stuff about Calley and those guys . . . Did that really happen? Do Americans . . . I mean, you know, like toss prisoners from helicopters? Things like—"

"I guess," Bobby answered quickly. "Some must. I'll tell ya though, where I was . . . I remember one night . . . " Bobby shook his head. They were already crossing under the freeway, approaching Bahia de Martin. He slowed. "We'd moved into this position to set up for the night and it turned out to be an NVA base camp. They'd dee-deed but they'd left a rear element, which gave us some resistance and really, you know, it messed up the plans because we didn't want them to know our location."

"Dee-deed means what?"

"Skyed. Split. Left."

"They weren't there except—"

"Yeah. Just a few guys watchin over their camp. This is pretty deep in the jungle. This one NVA lieutenant comes walking right into our perimeter to surrender but we didn't know and one of the men shot him. Not bad. In the foot. Shot him before we realized he was surrendering. You know, it's jungle and it's dark and you can't see clearly."

"Then what'd they do to—"

"Our medic patched him up. We called for a medevac with a jungle penetrator—a hoist. The bird came on station but it took fire so we canceled it till morning. In the morning my men cut an LZ, ah, a landing zone—hacked down all the trees and brush with machetes—and four birds came out, the medevac and three gunships. We got that lieutenant on the chopper and it lifted off and fifteen seconds later it exploded in midair. Took a direct hit from an RPG. Rocket grenade. Three of the crew were killed. The fourth was burned all over."

"What about the lieutenant?"

"I don't remember."

"He was in the helicopter?"

"Yeah. Must of been thrown out."

"Maybe your men killed him."

"Maybe. Maybe his own troops did when they blew down the medevac."

Bobby got out. He didn't want to talk about Viet Nam. Red came out, greeted them, gave Bobby a quick excited hug. "We're almost done. Lisa's got sandwiches and chips—"

"In a minute." He brushed by her. "I gotta pee."

By midafternoon the sky had cleared, their friends had left. Josh was out exploring the new neighborhood; Red was scrubbing their bath, making their bed; Bobby was in the small back bedroom sitting on his old footlocker, setting up the bill box and file box on an old table Al had given him. In the past month Bobby had been fortunate—had closed two more sales, one an expensive, custom-built home out on South Peak Road, near Gino's, for $66,000: with bonus for earning over $8,000 year-to-date, a $1,188 commission. Still he was anxious, touchy about money and drugs. He'd refused any more brownies, had gotten angry when Red brought home a few joints. Red's base pay was $94 per week, about $82 take-home. But her spending on the house, on clothes, on her car seemed to him to outpace their best fortunes.

He was agitated too by the letters and calls. He'd called Brian, he'd called his grandfather. They wanted him and Red to fly back for Thanksgiving but Red had refused, saying they should come out and see California. "I've really got to see my grandfather," he'd said to her. "Then go see him." She'd shrugged. "We're not Siamese twins."

He had written to Quay Le and to Captain Stephen Addison, whom he did not know. There had been no response.

And he had written to Stacy. He had not told Red. Stacy had written back, again sending the letter to Great Homes Realty.

... Jerry was really a great person in so many ways. He was bril-
liant, but kind of scattered. I really don't want to say too much. It's
just not right. Besides, you know I don't express myself very well in
letters. . . . I don't know how I fit into your life anymore, or into Bea's.
But I know that you are a part of my life. As is Bea. She was a good
friend. Just thought I would tell you, you are the best lover of anyone
I've ever known. I don't tell you that for any reason other than—I'm
not sure—it's a compliment. Nothing more, nothing less. . . . Selling
real estate!! What happened to the design process? To engineering?
To your dreams? I still have the drawings you made of the gazebo/
windmill that could play its own calliope. I keep it in my underwear
drawer and when I'm feeling down I pull it out and fantasize about
it. It's so much fun—all your belts and gears and such detail. . . . I
envy you and Red your relationship. Even if you say it's mostly a
financial interdependency. (Only a design engineer would describe a
relationship like that!) I went out with a nice attorney from Williamsport a few times. I wish I could say I'm crazy over him, or even that
I like him more than I do, but I can't. . . . Why do you think Red won't
mind if I write you? If it were me, I'd flip out. You must make her
feel very secure. . . .

"Come in and see." Red was beaming. He looked up. "It's perfect,"
she said. "At least for now. Until we paint."
Bobby rose. In his hand he had a card his grandfather had given him
in January; *Dear Lord, Please bless us* . . . He looked at Red. She was all
smiles and giggles. . . . *Forgive us our trespasses* . . . "You can't see it from
here!" . . . *never give up.* He slipped the card into the bill box, swooped
Red off her feet, kissed the top of her head, carried her sideways down
the hall to their new bedroom. "Ooo-la-la!" she cooed.
"Wow!" he said, holding her. "This really is nice. Really." He kissed
her forehead. "You're such a princess. You know that?"
"Be nice."
"I mean it nice," he said.
He kissed her nose. She let him. She giggled. Then she kissed him and
hugged him and he laid her gently on the bed and she said, "Undress me."
For two hours they hugged and caressed, massaged, made love. They
showered in the sparkling clean tiled shower stall in their own bedroom
and returned to bed and slowly loved as they had never loved. They
napped, woke, ordered a pizza, ate, caressed and massaged each other,
then just lay in the new California King, Bobby snoozing lightly, his
thoughts romping, one instant certain he was in love with Red, the next
fantasizing about Stacy or Victoria and then thinking what he and Red
had was comfortable—two nice people, interdependent—was good,
could last . . .
"Could we build a wine cellar?" Red's voice nabbed his wandering
thoughts.

"Hm?"

"In the garage? I saw one in one house. They sell these special clay pipes that you stack up like . . . well, like pipes. They keep the temperature from fluctuating. And we've got to replace that awful light in the dining room. Don't you think it's awful? I know just where we can go for chandeliers. And the kitchen flooring and—"

"Josh!" Bobby bolted up. "I forgot about Josh. He might be tearing the neighborhood apart!"

"Should we meet, ah, at the . . . White Pines?"

"Sure."

"What time?"

"Eleven?"

"Okay. Friday at eleven."

"I'll be there. I . . . Rob, I'm really anxious to see you."

"Okay. I can't talk right now."

"Okay. Bye."

Mill Creek Falls, Thanksgiving Day, 1970—What stranger event could there have been? The Wapinskis, together, seven strong with Doug, at High Meadow, in the small, high-ceilinged dining room—Miriam attempting to be nonconfrontational, pleasant, matriarchal, seated at the far end of the table from Pewel as if she'd assumed the role of Brigita Clewlow Wapinski years ago, as if Pewel had accepted her in that role. Between them were Cheryl, two months along, looking plump and busty and oddly mysterious, and Brian, treating his wife like crystal. On the other side Joanne and Doug were politely disagreeing about women in the job force. "Really, Joanne, maybe you don't see it, but women do run most of the companies around here." "They do not." "No? Even Kinnard/Chassion's run by a woman." "No it's not. The CEO's a man." "But the owner's a woman." "That doesn't count." Between them Bobby, the prodigal son for whom the turkey was stuffed, cooked, basted until it was gleaming. "You could have let me do it," he'd said to his grandfather after Linda had left. "She insisted," he'd answered. "She's like that." "But she had to come out here at five thirty to put it in the oven." "Maybe I coulda stopped her. But it's good for her too." "But I was here! She had to cart those two infants out here . . . and then back to her family. . . . " "It's his family. Hers don't want nothin to do with her." "His then. He's the one who thinned the sugarbush." "Yep. Good worker. Reminds me of you."

Robert Wapinski's mind was not on turkey. He'd taken the Tuesday-night red-eye, arrived in Williamsport Wednesday morning, rented a car, drove to High Meadow, spent hours talking to his grandfather, telling him about California, about the new house, the good people he'd chanced to acquaint, about making money, and, with chuckles, about Red spending it. Then he'd walked the path to the pond, to the orchard, the knoll, across the spillway, through the woods, the sugarbush, to the edge of the gap. He had not descended into the chasm, had not climbed to the old Indian trail, but had instead checked his watch, had thought, forty-seven hours, had wondered if she would show.

During dinner, even when Miriam ground her teeth at Bobby's "utensil noise," he was not shaken. Not even Joanne got to him with her quips about Calley and when would they try *all* the baby killers. Perhaps had Josh been there it would have gone differently. Josh lived in the now, always brought him back to the now. Instead Bobby had covertly checked his watch and thought, twenty hours.

He parked the rented car. Smiled nervously. All the way down he'd thought of not showing, thought, she deserves it, thought, if she doesn't show . . . But he'd pulled in next to the '66 British racing green MG her father had given her for graduating from Mill Creek High, and his mind fell into autopilot.

"Hi."

"Hi."

"You're on time!"

"Habit I got into in the army. You were early."

"A little. Habit from modeling. Keeps the boob-gazers away. How's your grandfather?"

"Wonderful." His entire face was smiling. He couldn't control it. He could feel it all the way back to his ears. "How's my sweetheart doin?"

"Mom? She's great. I told her you were home. She sends her love."

Bobby sat on the stool beside Stacy. A waitress came. "Lunch or coffee?"

"Coffee," Bobby answered. He didn't want to eat or drink, didn't want to sit at the bar. He wanted to face her, face Stacy, have her face him.

"You look . . . " The door opened, the waitress rattled the cups, saucers and spoons, the people who'd just come in were talking. " . . . with you."

He cocked his head. "I'm sorry. That's my bad ear. Can we sit at a table?"

"Sure. I said, you look good. California must agree with you."

"Yeah. We're in a nice spot."

"What's with your ear?"

He paused. They'd seated themselves in a front booth. He looked out the window. It was such a long tedious story. He turned back, looked at her, shrugged. He did not want to spoil the mood. She'd meant so much to him. The instant he'd seen her he knew she still did.

"Tell me." She was direct, not harsh. So he began. And he talked and talked. He told her about his tour, about things he didn't know he remembered, about the sounds, the ignored ear pains, about being discharged. She told him about modeling jobs, about traveling to places she never got to see but only to be pictured in, then whisked away.

By the time they rose to leave the White Pines Inn Bobby was quaking inside. "Pick you up at seven?" His voice was soft. He'd been thinking of it tangentially for months.

"Really?" Stacy smiled.

"Yes." Soft and firm. Could he break with Red? How could he break up with Red?

"You don't think Bea would mind? Or your grandfather? You don't have a lot of time to spend with him."

"It's okay. He'll understand. And . . . and I want to."

As Bobby Wapinski sped back to High Meadow he was flying, laughing, planning what he'd wear, thinking he'd shave again, chattering to Josh who wasn't even with him. He sang old tunes he somehow connected to Stacy even though he wasn't certain of the exact words, the real melody, belting it out to the last of the late November light: " 'We laughed in the sunshine; We sang eve-ree-y day-ay-ay; We laughed in the sunshine; till I we-ent on my way-ay.' "

By nine they had eaten, touched, held hands briefly. What was happening, the chemistry, he would never understand, but he could not dispute its validity. They walked down the quiet main street of Rock Ridge. Christmas lights glowed in a few store windows. A crisp breeze buffeted their faces. Stacy clung to Bobby's arm.

"I don't know how to explain it," he continued the discussion they had been having over dinner. "When I left Mill Creek Falls it was more to move away, really, than to be with Red."

"But you do like her."

"Oh, yeah. Stace, it's—I realized, when I got to California . . . I didn't love her. Particularly not that first month. That was hard. But as time went on, I . . . it's like I loved part of her more and more."

"Then Rob, you should stay with her. I—I don't mean you weren't going to . . . I mean, if you love her, don't let anything, even indirectly, impose."

They got into the rented car. Bobby started the engine, turned on the heat, but only sat. "Stacy," he said staring at the frost on the windshield, "I'm always going to love you. I . . . I love you now. I love what you were, what we were."

"I don't know what that was," Stacy said. She was sitting sideways on the seat, facing him, her legs tucked up, red-blue-green light reflecting off her stockinged knees. "I'd . . . I'd . . . Rob, I'd die if . . . if we got together again and you found the Stacy you loved wasn't there anymore." He turned, looked into her eyes. Her gaze dropped. "I really shouldn't have said that."

"Stace, there's something really wrong with me and Red." He shifted to sit sideways. "Really. I don't know what it is. That's why I said I love part of her. She can be very loving."

"You're an easy person to love."

"I don't know." He raised his right elbow over the seat back, touched his fingertips to hers. "Sometimes she's so shallow. She spends—"

"You don't have to say it. Just like I don't want to say anything against Jerry. But . . . I think . . . I'm really angry the war broke us up. We did have something." Her tone changed. "Do you remember our plans?"

"Um."

"You could always take a pile of junk and make it something." She smiled. "That sounds terrible. I don't mean it like that."

"I know." His smile crinkled his whole face.

"Really. Like the calliope. Your designs were always so much fun. You could do it better than anyone. With patience and . . . ah . . . How did you put it?"

"Patience and discipline."

"Um. What happened to your plans, Rob? I mean, selling real estate! I just can't see you, Mr. Design Process . . . I thought you'd go back to school. We did have dreams, didn't we?"

"It's . . . real estate . . . there's things I'm learning that complement it, complement design, make it possible to see design on a much larger scale."

"Bigger than windmills?" Her eyes were wide, the pupils dilated in the faint street light. He felt he could see into her thoughts.

"Much. As big as the land." His voice was faint.

"That's pretty big." Stacy laughed softly and Bobby glowed in her approval.

"There's a principle of real estate." He said it seriously yet happy to have someone he cared about listen. "Land, privately owned or public, is still a public trust. One owns rights, the bundle of rights specified in the deed, but under the law no one 'owns' the land. See Stace, that's where design comes in. If all land is public trust, the way it's utilized, even at its highest and best use, must reflect long-term social gain—to protect the land, to ensure that no private owner does anything to the land that will keep it from rejuvenating."

"Now you sound like the Rob I remember."

"You bring it out of me. You always did."

Stacy smiled, inched slightly forward, looked into his face, turned away.

"Remember: 'Imagine me, imagine you . . .' " He laughed. He couldn't carry the tune but he sang anyway. " ' . . . me and you, and you and me; no matter how they toss the dice; it had to be; the only one for me is you, and you for me; So happy together. . . .' "

Stacy joined in with a line, her voice tender, melodic. " 'I can't see me loving nobody but you . . .' "

And together they sang, Bobby just whispering, " 'So happy together. How is the weather? So happy together.' "

Then they kissed. Then Stacy pulled away. "Rob. Bea's my friend. I—I can't do this . . . this . . . Rob." Tears came to her eyes. "I made such a mistake. I'm sorry. I'm so sorry I hurt you." He moved to hold her but she held him back. "No. I do love you. But you're going back to California. To Bea. I—I couldn't share you . . . if I loved you. And I do. But I can't." She moved back. "I care about you. And about Bea. I don't want to be responsible for putting a strain on your relationship. But even more than that, Rob, I care about me. I made a mess of what we had. And what Jerry and I had. I always compared him to you. Just in thoughts. But I made a mess of it and it really hurts and I don't want to hurt anyone again. Including me." He looked at her with sad, puppy-dog eyes, but he did not speak. "Rob, I need . . . I know I need a lot from a relationship. I need to love and to be loved, and—Rob this frightens me. You love Red. You live three thousand miles away. You've bought a house. You're into your job. I'm not sure we should even have seen each other."

"I—"

"No. Let me finish. If—if we . . . loved . . . I mean, you're leaving again. You're going back to Bea. . . . I can't share you, even though I love you."

"Then don't."

"Don't?"

"You don't have to. It's much too . . . Stacy . . . "

"Tell me."

"Stace, I'm learning so much out there but I'm . . . I don't think I'm going to stay. There's too many people out there, too many doing nothing, being paid to do nothing. And too many double-dealing. I keep thinking about coming back—but with more knowledge and more money. I'm not going to come back and mooch off anybody. I'm never doing that again."

"I don't . . . Rob, what are you saying? Are you and Bea going to move . . . ?"

"She likes it there. She knows I . . . " He paused. He was describing these emotions not simply to Stacy, but for the first time, clearly, to himself. "To me there's something wrong with . . . not the land, but the people. Don't get me wrong. I've met some really super people. I'd like them anyplace. Maybe it's that life is too easy. People aren't properly hardened. It's like they're vulnerable. Their values . . . That doesn't make any sense. It's me. I'm incompatible with that environment. I'm there to learn, to get established financially. That's what Bea likes. Money. She won't come back. We don't have a future."

"Rob!"

"She's a great kid, Stace, but she really is a kid. That's why she fits there so well."

"Then—" Stacy's voice was low "—say—" her face was turned to the windshield "—it." Christmas lights glittered in her eyes.

"Granpa."

"Yep."

"I'm sorry I'm calling so late."

"Everything okay?"

"Oh, yeah. Fine. It's just that the roads have gotten kind of icy and this rental car doesn't handle worth manure."

Pewel chuckled.

"I'm"—Bobby said, grinning—"going to stay in Rock Ridge tonight." When he hung up he handed Stacy the phone. "Your turn." He laughed.

Tuesday, 1 December 1970—It was not a good way to go to work in the morning. There were too many things on his mind. Stacy. Red. Stacy. Red. On the flight back he'd decided to tell Red. Not out and out. Softly. He didn't want to hurt her. He'd tell her he was going to return to Mill Creek Falls—not immediately, but that that was his definite plan. Grandpa needed him. And with a grubstake from working in San Martin, he'd be able to set up an office in Pennsylvania—maybe concentrate on farms and rural retreats, maybe build a few houses incorporating some of the California design features he admired. She'd say something about it being impossible to leave Richard Townsmark and People's Life and Casualty, and they'd begin their separation by him moving into the small bedroom. On the surface they'd be a couple, until later, when they'd sell the house and he'd move back and . . .

The thought had stayed with him through picking up his bag, finding the Chevy sedan in the lot, driving north on 280 past the barren hills with boxy implants that made the ticky-tack houses of Creek's Bend look like carpenter's cream, up Nineteenth Avenue with its jammed-up traffic. Through the Presidio, over the Golden Gate and into the Marin Headlands, his attitude had softened, perhaps from exhaustion, perhaps from the beauty of the area. The closer he'd come to San Martin the more dubious his ploy seemed, and when he'd pulled in before the Deepwoods Drive house—his house, his first house that he'd worked really hard for—his resolve had puddled and Red and Josh had jumped out and greeted him and Red looked wonderful, and she hugged him and kissed him and chattered about having sold her first "set" of life insurance policies to a family of seven—Dad, Mom, and all the kids—and she didn't even shoo Josh away, and there was a black guy by yesterday looking for you—I think he was a Jehovah's Witness—and Richard helped so much with the sale—People's is such a quality company—and Peter wants you to call the moment you get in, he said he's got great news for you, but first I . . . hug, kiss, hug, kiss . . . She'd brought him to the bedroom and she'd jumped his bones on the new satin sheets and satin pillowcases over new down pillows and to him her tiny breasts seemed full and . . .

He did not drive directly to the office but instead followed Bruce Road to Miwok, then took a left and motored past the high school, the Lower Res, up to South Peak Road where he drove slowly by the driveway of the second-to-last house on the left—four driveways up from Gino's—trying to see through the foliage to the $118,950 listing that Dan Coleman got the day before Bobby left for Pennsylvania. On South Peak it was drizzling. Bobby turned on the wipers, turned into the driveway. He did not wind in through the trees, could see only a single corner, the trim painted cream, the cedar shingles weathered gray-brown. He backed out, turned around, drove to town, to Great Homes. There, for a moment, in the small lot behind the office with humidity condensing on the inner surface of the sedan's windows, he tried to collect his thoughts. He'd had no intention of getting carried away with Red, but, he thought, like the first time . . . But that was not now the case and he knew it.

As he sat pretending to sort and reorder his briefcase, he pictured Stacy, saw her eyes, every detail, every sparkling fleck, saw her legs, the Christmas lights glistening on her stockings as he held the car door. He grabbed his briefcase, held it on his lap, grabbed the door handle, just sat. A sickening feeling swept over him as if what had happened in Pennsylvania was a reentry into the past, as if he'd made love to someone who had died.

"Can't sell houses sitting there." The voice was sharp, loud. Bobby turned. Lisa Fonari smiled, wiggled her fingers in a quick wave, spun and strutted toward her car. He hadn't noticed before, not really noticed, what legs she too had, great calves, smooth, meaty, sparkling.

"Ya-di ya-di," he called getting out. She smiled, drove off.

Inside, moments later, Bobby was stunned. "What about Coleman? Or Al?"

"I offered it to them." Peter Wilcox, erect, loose, as poised and natural in his expensive suit as Bobby felt only in old dungarees and a sleeveless sweatshirt. "The bottom line is they're not interested. But I'm going to need an assistant if I'm going to establish this network."

"Offices in Petaluma, Santa Rosa and Sonoma?"

"Concord wants us to expand. They want another office in Marin, too. Maybe two. North and south of San Rafael. I'll become the regional manager. We're really on the move."

"Ah, Pete. Whoa!" Bobby slapped the top of his head. "Me? Really?"

"You're good. Yes. You. Bartecchi and Coleman are too busy with their clients. Schnell's got some major development plans. Everybody else who's qualified is commercial/industrial."

"Well, there's Tom. And Jon Ross. They've been here longer than—"

"They couldn't handle it. Never learned the art of being successful."

"What about Lisa? Or—"

"Come on!"

"Jane. Jane's been here a lot longer, too. And she's very good."

"Bob, this is between me and you." Peter leaned forward. Bobby nodded. Peter whispered. "No women managers." He said each word distinctly. "It just doesn't work."

"Pete—" Bobby sat back in the chair, looked at the desktop, "I don't want to step on anybody's toes."

"You're not. You're the most qualified. Jane's never expressed any interest in it. But you're a natural. And, you know, Hal and Sal really liked Red. That helps. That's in your favor, too."

"Mr. Woodhouse and Mr. Cugino? They don't know. . . . "

"Sure they do. As you move up it's important to have a stable home. And actually, it's better she's selling insurance."

"We're not—" Bobby began.

Peter cut him off. "We'll supplement your experience with the Great Homes' Managers Training Course."

Now Bobby smiled. In the back of his mind he pictured himself as a manager, not of a Great Homes Realty office but of an RJW Real Estate: Sales-Designs-Construction office with headquarters in Mill Creek Falls.

"As assistant you get twenty-five dollars per office closing after we've closed ten per month. You're going to free me up for expansion. Okay?" Bobby nodded. "Okay."

"Fantastic!" Pete rose, virtually pulled Bobby up, shaking his hand. They stood close, grasping hands, Pete's left hand on Bobby's shoulder, Pete saying, "Hey, by the way, don't get involved in that water district flap right now, okay?" Again Bobby nodded but he meant it not as agreement but as acknowledgment. "We don't want Great Homes associated with protestors," Pete said. He turned, opened his office door. "By the way, I want to introduce you to our new salesgal."

Pete led Bobby past Gloria's desk, gave the secretary a thumbs-up while simultaneously clapping Bobby's shoulder—Gloria already knowing, smiling, offering congratulations, Pete prodding Bobby out onto the sales floor where a young woman was arranging blank prospect cards and estimates of value forms on Red's old desk. "This is Sharon McGowan," Pete said. Sharon looked up. She had long blond hair with a natural wave, brown eyes, a stunning smile. "Sharon, this is Bob Wapinski, our assistant office manager."

Bobby pulled into the driveway of the Deepwoods Drive house. It was six thirty, dark, overcast. He'd spent much of the day on the phone reestablishing links with prospective buyers and sellers, or with Sharon—who in heels was as tall as he and who was delightful to be with—taking her to new listings that had come out on MLS while he'd been away, making her pretend he was a prospective buyer.

Bobby collected his papers, MLS books, opened the car door. It weighed heavily on his mind that he should call Stacy, should call her now, tell her about the assistant managership. He put one leg to the ground and immediately Josh jammed his muzzle into Bobby's groin. "Oh geez, you're all wet." Bobby pushed him back, held his head away as Josh leaned into his hand, squirmed his head forcing Bobby to massage his ears. "C'mon," Bobby said quietly. "Let's go in."

At the door Red wrapped her arms over Bobby's shoulders, as she'd never done before except the day before, kissed his cheek, whispered, "There's a black guy in the living room."

"What?!"

"Get rid of him. I've got something important to tell you." She let Bobby go.

"Cap'n Wapinski. Sir." Bobby looked up. The foyer was dark. He heard the deep, pleasant voice, saw the dark form, couldn't see the man's face. Bobby shuffled in. Josh pushed past Red into the living room, braced his legs wide. "Goddamn, Sir, you are a sight for sore eyes. Hot damn, Niner-niner! Seein you's better'n hot grits on a firebase. Better'n a heavy pink team bustin up Charlie's butt."

"Oh shit!" Red shot by both men. "He's going to shake. Out! Go into the garage!"

"Bro Black!" Tyrone slapped his own chest. "Whoo-weee! It sure's hell took some searchin to find ya."

Bobby still searched the man's face. He didn't recognize him.

"Blackwell, Cap'n. Tyrone Blackwell. Hamburger Hill. You remember that bad mothafucka. You remember me, don't ya, Sir? You sent them letters for me."

"Oh, holy shi—Bro Black from the Sugar Shack."

"You got it, Niner-niner. Cept now I'm Ty Dorsey. Took my mother's name, cause . . . aw that's a story. Sir, if you got the time, I brought the beer."

"Yeah. Yeah, of course. Bob. Or Bobby. I'm no 'sir' anymore. Just a PFC—like you?"

"Bet chor sweet ass." Ty laughed. "Proud Fuckin Civilian, Sir."

They moved into the living room. Bobby loosened his tie, removed his jacket. Ty held up a power-fist salute. Bobby came to him, smiling, held his fist up for Ty to tap, then clumsily (white guys and officers never did get it very well) he and Ty did a dap, tapping fists, clasping hands, sliding, ending with a four-hand embrace. Then Ty opened a beer for Bobby and handed it to him. "That's one fine-lookin missus you got there, Sir. Bob." Ty laughed. They both sat. "Bob," Ty said again, laughed again. "She told me they just put you in charge of the whole shee-bang."

"Huh? I haven't even told . . . How'd you know?"

"Some dude, Peter, called. I went out and got us a bottle a champagne." Ty bowed his head. Quietly he said, "Bea said I could stay for dinner, if that's okay with you. I was showin her how to barbecue chicken like my mama used to."

"Of course! Of course. Where are you staying? When did you get here?"

Red came back in, wiped up Josh's footprints and the splatter of rain and dog hair he'd let fly as he'd begun to shake. Then she put coasters under Bobby's and Ty's beer cans. Finally she joined them as they began recapping surface details of the overlap time to their tours, and Ty told Bobby about a few of the guys who left country after Bobby DEROSed, and about a few more who'd been wounded. They drank more beers. Red played the attentive mate, finished making dinner, served the two men, listened without much comment, smiled often, finally yawned a long gape-mouthed yawn. "Oh, excuse me," she said.

"I gotta be goin," Ty said. There were a dozen empty beer cans on the table before them (a half-full one before Red) and more empties in the living room.

"Where you stayin?" Bobby demanded.

"Jus in my car." Ty belched into his hand.

"We've got the extra bed," Bobby said more to Red than to Ty. "You can't sleep in your car."

Ty chuckled. To Red he said, "That from a man who made me sleep in a foot a mud fer—" Then to Bobby, "How long were you with us, anyway?"

"I'll make up the bed," Red said. "We really want you to stay. Besides, you've got to write down the recipe . . . "

"Honey." Ty plopped a hand on the table. "Ketchup. Worcestershire sauce. Orange peel. Bay leaf." Then he laughed. "I got so much more to tell ya. We're goina be good fer each other. Bobby, we're goina be good fer each other. I could help ya. Help ya run the whole shee-bang. I'm a good troop."

"I'm going to make the bed." Red stood. To Bobby she added, "Then I'm going to bed."

"I had pride, Cap'n Wapinski, Sir," Ty said drunkenly. "I had pride when I was with you, Sir. I had pride then. Now, what I got? Goddamn, Sir. What I . . . When I got home, Sir, there a dude in my bed. My baby, year en a half, call him 'Da-dee.' Like that. 'Da-dee.' What I got now?" Ty leaned back, laughed, blurted loudly, "Mothafucka, how I s'pose ta know? I swear my own brother set me up. Said she was eighteen. Fourteen! Oh, but she was sweet. Swee-eet! Statutory rape! How was I s'pose ta know?"

In the morning Bobby woke, dropped his feet to the floor, slumped, braced his head with his hands. His head banged, his eyes felt swollen. Then from the kitchen he smelled coffee. Red came from the bathroom. "I had something important to tell you last night." Her tone was controlled anger.

"Um." He looked up. She looked pretty in her nightgown. "So tell me."

"With him"—she wagged a finger at the bedroom door, her whole body shook—"in the house?"

"Yeah. I guess. If it's important. What—"

"I think I'm pregnant."

"Huh?"

"You heard me."

He sat up straighter. His face furrowed. A smile began to form on his face. He mouthed the word *pregnant*, stood, the smile re-forming, spreading.

She did not look at him but turned her back, cold, annoyed. "I've got a doctor's appointment at ten."

"I'll take—"

"I can drive."

"How far along—"

"Six weeks, I think."

Bobby wrapped his arms around Red even as she stood facing away. He kissed the top of her head. Her hair tickled his face. Behind his smile his head was still banging. "I love you," he whispered.

She turned in his grasp, pushed away. "But I don't love you," she said. "I'm going to shower." With that she went into the bathroom and locked the door.

Again Bobby worked a full day. Red went from the doctor's office to People's Life in Larkspur and she too worked late. Ty moved a few things into the guest bedroom, grocery shopped at the Safeway, drove past Great Homes, returned, parked his Caddy in the driveway instead of across the street, cleaned the kitchen, readied dinner. The evening was a repeat of the one before—perhaps with less beer, but with more talk—current talk and continuing stories—Wap asking about various operations, about what had happened at Firebase Ripcord. What had happened to the 1st of the 506th? How did the company commander get killed? Was it on Ripcord or on an adjoining hill? To much of the Ripcord stuff Ty Dorsey just shook his head, stammered, "Ya know, what the fuck, over." "Yeah," Bobby agreed not realizing, and Ty not volunteering, that he wasn't with the 1/506th anymore when Ripcord was over-run—indeed had been released to an administrative holding company while awaiting trial for possession of a controlled substance and insubordination to an officer.

"They both was bad mothafuckas, Bobby. Ah, but life goes on! Life goes on! Time to pick up a piece a the pie. Aint no pie at home."

"Yeah. I didn't come home to pie either."

"Yeah."

Later, in the back bedroom, alone, Bobby and Red barely spoke. "What did the doctor say?"

"I've got to call them tomorrow."

"Red . . . "

"Hmm."

"I'm sorry about Ty being here right now. I'll try to get him a room. . . . "

"Don't worry about it."

"I know you like your privacy and—"

"He's okay. He's nice. And he's a good cook. It's nice having somebody else cook. I just wish he wouldn't drop cigarette ashes all over."

"I'll mention it to him."

"And put a coaster under his beer. He's leaving rings everywhere."

"Um-hmm."

"And his boots go in his room, not in the living room."

"Okay." For a long time they were silent. Bobby tried to picture Stacy but it was as if a wall had been erected in his mind preventing him from seeing to last week. Instead he saw Sharon McGowan. She was nice. Safe. She had a boyfriend. They could be friends—no overtones. Bobby rolled to Red, kissed her. She did not respond.

On Thursday Bobby called Red at work but she was out. She didn't return his call. At three, Ty walked into the Great Homes office. He was impeccably dressed in an expensive gray twill suit, black wingtip shoes, a gold watch and gold wedding band. He'd had his hair cut, shaped into a medium-length naturally rounded do. At slightly over six foot one, strong and slim, he looked like a professional athlete about to sign a major league contract.

Liza Caldicott was on floor duty. In her loud, challenging voice, "How can I help you?"

"I would like to buy a house." Ty's voice was deep, full.

"Oh!" Liza was stunned. Seldom did buyers walk in and straightforward announce such intentions. At the same time Liza wasn't sure she wanted a black buying into great-grandfather Martin Caldicott's legacy. "How much do you want to spend?"

"Not over a hundred," Ty said seriously.

Liza gulped. She'd never sold a home costing more than fifty-four five. "We've got some in that range." Ty began to snicker but controlled it. Liza continued—she still had not even asked him his name. "Can you put twenty percent down?"

"Yes ma'am," Ty answered.

"An eighty-thousand-dollar mortgage"—she pulled out her blue-book—"runs five thirty-two a month. Your monthly salary should be above two thousand."

"I don't have a monthly," Ty said.

"But you make twenty-five, thirty thousand a year?"

"Hell no, ma'am."

"Wait a minute. Ah . . . how much do you make?"

"Nothin."

"Nothing?!"

"Nothin."

"Then how are you going to buy a hundred thousand dollar home?"

"Hundred thousand?" Ty smiled wide. "I jus said hundred."

"Hundred what?" Liza was really upset.

"Dollars, ma'am. In America our currency is dollars. Unless you find somebody willin to take pesos. I could pay in pesos."

"Now wait a minute, Mr. . . . "

"Dorsey. Mr. Dorsey. Quality Control and Sales Investigation, main office, Concord. You flunked. Is Mister Wapinski in?"

Liza was totally flabbergasted. She stood quickly, her thighs banging against the desk. She stumbled back, fumbled for words. "I'm—I'm sorry Mr. Dorsey. I . . . ah . . . "

"Please, just call Mr. Wapinski for me."

Thirty minutes later in Peter Wilcox's office with Peter and Bobby, Ty said, "Mr. Wilcox, you've got people here who couldn't sell ice to soldiers in a rice paddy. I could sell it to Eskimos. I just need a chance."

"You still have to get a license. That's normal procedure. State law. Get your license, then come back and see me."

"Let me help while I'm going to school."

"We don't have any nonsales positions. . . . "

"I'm a good worker. I was a good troop. Ask Bobby. . . . "

"There's no doubt about it. But Ty—" Bobby felt Ty had put him on the spot, "why didn't you tell me you were coming? I could have arranged—"

"I did, Bob. Las night. Don't you remember?" Bobby just looked at him. "You was explainin how to establish a real estate listin farm. I told you I'd like to do that."

"You did. You're right. We just talked about so many . . . " Bobby's voice tapered off.

Ty said to Peter, "Besides, you don't have any minorities, do you?"

"There's not many that live in town."

"See? I could bring in a whole new segment of the market. But jus right now, I'm short a funds. I need your assistance."

"Okay," Peter said. "Let me think it over."

"It sure would help—" Ty said, "to have an answer now."

Peter stared at Ty. Ty gazed back but didn't speak. Bobby fidgeted slightly. Peter and Ty remained locked eye to eye. Finally Peter said, "Get your license. If you can sell me on this, you can sell anything."

That evening Ty was hyper. He had a hundred plans, a thousand things to do. All involving Bobby in one way or another, all for Bobby's benefit. Red was somber, more pleasant to Ty than to Bobby. Red and Bobby retired early. Ty knew nothing of the possible pregnancy. He remained up, watching Red's new television ("It's only a cheap portable and certainly we need to watch the news!"), drinking beer, working on his schedule, his strategy to gain a piece of the pie.

"Ten weeks," Red answered.

"Ten. I thought you said maybe six."

"That's what I thought."

"Red . . . " He did not know what to say. Part of him wanted to call Stacy, tell her of Red's pregnancy, tell her he was going to marry Red. Part just wanted out. He did not know how to approach it—getting married or getting out. He didn't want to hurt Red, didn't even want to upset her. He eyed her, sitting on the California King, her hands folded in her lap, her head down, and he thought he should stay with this woman who'd been his partner for sixteen months, thought how much he liked her, could like her, how beautiful her face was, how content he was, now, this very moment. Then he thought he'd write Stacy, explain in detail, but . . . but that he should hold off for a few days, let things settle. This thing, he thought, this thing of Red's, "But I don't love you." What does that mean? "Red . . . "

"Um."

"What are you thinking?"

"I don't know."

"Should we get married?"

"I don't know."

"I really like you. You know that, don't you?"

"You're just saying that. . . . "

"No, I'm not. Really."

"Bobby, I . . . I like you too. But I'm not in love with you and I won't love this child."

He didn't say anything, only hung his head. The light in the room was dim. For a long time they sat in silence, not looking at each other. Finally Red stood. "I'll decide tomorrow. Saturday at the latest."

Friday morning was overcast. Red and Bobby went to work as usual— perhaps a bit early. After they left Ty showered, dressed, ate. Then he gathered up a hundred small Shopping List pads printed with

Robert J. Wapinski
Great Homes Realty
926-1010

and for three hours he went door-to-door in Martinwood Estates, ringing doorbells, announcing to those who answered, "Hi. My name is Ty Dorsey. I'm an associate of Robert Wapinski's—Bobby—of Great Homes Realty. We jus wanted you to have a pad with our phone number on it."

Other than a polite thank-you, very few residents spoke with him. In 1970 large black men just didn't go door-to-door in Martinwood Estates. Even Mrs. Grassplat, mother and housewife of the only black family in the subdivision, didn't feel comfortable with Ty looming on her porch— expensive suit or not.

By three o'clock Peter Wilcox had taken two calls (and the local police three), questioning the legitimacy of Ty's association to Great Homes. At three thirty one neighbor stopped Bobby in the Great Homes parking lot where he was returning from looking at a prospective listing with Sharon McGowan.

"You're Wapinski, aren't ya?"

"Yes. Mr. Sarkov, isn't it?" Sarkov stood so close to the open door of the Chevy Bobby couldn't stand. Sharon remained silently seated beside him.

"That's right. You got a black guy living with you."

"Huh? Ah . . . Ty? Yeah, not—"

"There's no blacks in Martinwood."

"What? Wait a sec. What are—"

"We thought he was a guest. You and that redhead starting a commune?"

"A commune. Wait a second Mister Sarkov." Bobby gently pushed him back, stood. "This guy saved my life in—" Bobby began but did not finish. It was an excuse and he knew it. Still, he now partially grasped the situation and he didn't want to offend a potential client. "The guy's my friend," Bobby said. "That's all."

"Just a guest?"

"That's right."

"Well, you can have this back." Sarkov handed Bobby the small shopping list pad. "We won't be needing it."

"What . . . ? Where'd you get—" Before Bobby could finish, his neighbor stalked off.

For the next hour Peter Wilcox told him how to handle and defuse the objections, Peter actually making Bobby write out and role-play a senario.

Xxx: You're the ones who have that new tall agent. (Peter: "They won't say black but they'll mean it.")

Bobby: Oh, you mean Ty Dorsey?

Xxx: I think that was his name. It was kind of odd having him come to our door.

Bobby: I hope it didn't upset you.

Xxx: It upset my wife some. She was home alone.

Bobby: I'm sorry. But let me ask you, if you had a man who'd saved your life (Peter: "Don't say in Viet Nam") and he asked you to help him for a few days—let him pass out a few grocery list pads so he can get back on his feet—would you be able to turn him down?

Xxx: Oh, I suppose not.

Bobby: (Peter: "You've got to say this immediately. Tie them down.") Neither was I.

Bobby practiced but it so galled him to think he owed anyone an apology, before he left the office he tore the sheet into tiny pieces and flushed it down the commode. Still it ate at him—because Ty, *unlicensed*, could not legally solicit listings, and passing out the pads could be so construed; and because they were Bobby's pads that Ty had taken, had distributed where Bobby wanted to make another personal appearance; and because it meant that Ty, having spent that much time going door-to-door, had probably not, as they'd agreed, gone to Academy Schools and registered for the Real Estate Salesman Licensing course that Bobby had agreed to stake.

From the house came Red's laughing, Ty's singing. "What the World needs now, is love, sweet love, / that the only thing, there jus too lit'le of . . ."

"Man!" Bobby broke in. "What the hell were you doin today?"

Immediately Ty was apologetic, conciliatory. "I fucked up, huh?"

"That's a fine way to say hello." Red glared harshly. She and Ty had been in the kitchen making tacos, laughing, joking.

"Did you register—"

"I didn't get down there."

"Down where?" Red pushed one more meat-stuffed taco onto the cookie sheet, at the other end of the pan one taco seemed to jump out, then fell over spilling cooked, spiced hamburger crumbs onto the indoor-outdoor kitchen carpet. Red giggled.

"Aw Man, Ty . . ." Bobby stopped. Shook his head. Decided not to pursue it.

But Red snapped at him. "What did Ty do? What's your problem?!"

Ty put his hand on Red's arm. "He's right," Ty said to Red. "I done somethin I knew after I started, I shouldn'ta done. I'm sorry, Man. I was thinkin I'd be helpin you. Get your name out en all."

"You mean—" Red started the question looking at Ty, but as she spoke she turned to Bobby "—those pads? Those stupid dinky pads?"

"Hey look," Ty said, "if I'm causin—"

"No," Bobby said. "It's okay. But tomorrow, or Monday, register, huh? I'm goina change."

In the kitchen Red was in a huff. Ty tried to cool her down. "That man, Red, that man there, he can't do no wrong in my book. He kept our shit together. You know what I mean? I bet there're still brothers in the boonies remember Cap'n Wapinski. Remember he kept our shit together. Kept us from fuckin up."

Later that night all Red would say to Bobby was, "Tomorrow."

On Saturday, Red slept late. Ty remained in bed. Bobby, taking Josh with him, left early, went to the office, plodded through various papers. It was twenty days to Christmas, the slowest business time of the year. The only other person in the office was Lisa Fonari. Bobby went to her. "Can I talk to you?" he began and he told her of his dilemma, omitting everything about Stacy except that she introduced him to Red, omitting Red's pregnant condition.

"I think you'd make a great soap," Lisa answered in her brash yet sincere manner.

"C'mon. Really?"

"Hey, so you get married." Lisa slid her legs out from under her desk, crossed them, her short skirt rising to midthigh. "If it doesn't work out, you can always get a divorce."

Bobby stared at her. She leaned forward allowing her blouse to come away from her shoulders, exposing more skin, knowing her body language was adding to his confusion. "Um," Bobby muttered. "Maybe."

His confusion was tremendous. He could not make a decision. He was at once excited about having a child, yet torn by Red's reaction. And he wasn't sure what having a child would mean. He still had not called Stacy, could not think of what to say. Suddenly he found that both Sharon and Lisa were exciting him more than Red ever had—maybe more than Stacy—and maybe it would be okay to be single for a while.

All day in his mind, interspersed with thoughts like—How did Everest Realty get that listing? I talked to those people only a month ago. And,

I'm getting fat. Gotta take up jogging. Maybe run with what's-her-name—he mulled his personal situation. By evening he was exhausted. Ty was again hyper. He'd already killed a six-pack, immediately handed Bobby an open can when Bobby walked in, opened another for himself.

"It was before Bobby came"—Ty continued what he'd been telling Red—"when I first put my hands out to pick up them mothafuckin dead bastards." Ty's eyes glowed like lamps, his voice was soft, eerie. "First time. I felt somethin that I never felt before in my life. And it jumped outta him and went inta me. Right then and there as soon as I touched the mothafucka's arm ta drag him. You know what I mean? Throw im in the pile. That was the first gook I ever fuckin touched and that fucka was cold meat. There was nothin there but there was somethin that ran right through me. Second I touched that arm, it came. And the second time I touched him it was over and the more I got to fuckin touch em, different ones, knockin out gold teeth, takin a finger off to get a ring, dumb shit like that but I did it—even in Cambo started a ear necklace—but the more I did the more I backed off. Felt bad, yeah. Aint too many fuckin times I do, though. That first sucker, he never felt nothin. He died without knowin. Me too. I hope I die without knowin."

Red's eyes were watery. She couldn't speak, could hardly move. Ty's story evoked a flood of sympathy—more than anything Bobby had ever told her, more than Jimmy Pellegrino's death.

That night Red went to sleep without talking to Bobby. When he retired he found she'd made herself a small bed on the floor, was curled up atop all their extra blankets, with all their pillows. Bobby lay on his back, hurt, seething. He could hear the TV, imagined Ty staring at the small tube steadily sipping beer after beer.

On Sunday morning Bobby woke early, walked Josh, made coffee. Ty and Red were still in their bedrooms. Bobby cleaned the living room, throwing the empty beer cans and cigarette ashes and butts into a separate bag that he immediately put out in the trash can because of the smell. He took three sweating, unopened cans from the sofa, tried to dry the cushion. Then he grabbed Ty's boots, which were askew on the living room carpet, put them in the kitchen trash basket exactly as Miriam used to put Bobby's scattered clothing or toys in the trash when Bobby was a boy. Then he left, got into the Chevy, sat. At noon he was to hold an open house with Sharon McGowan. It was only eight. He sat, tried to think, tried to reason. Nothing worked.

Bobby reentered his house. Still neither Ty nor Red were up. He went into the master bedroom, sat on the floor by Red. She opened her eyes, stretched, reached out, laid her hand on his knee. "You didn't have to sleep down here," he whispered.

"I needed to think," she said.

"Hm." He looked at her face, pushed a long errant strand back over her ear. To him she looked peaceful.

Red clutched a pillow, sat up. "You want to have a family, huh?"

"Hm."

"And get married?"

"Hm."

"Then ... I think ... Not now. Not yet. I want to have an abortion. As soon as possible. Then we can get married. And in two or three years we'll start a family."

He did not move, did not smile, did not utter a sound. What she proposed had no reality for him—not positive, not negative. It just didn't penetrate at all. But her sitting there, clutching the pillow like a tiny child, looking so peaceful, moved him. He leaned to her, kissed her hair.

"It's really best," she said. "Really."

"Okay," he said. He kissed her hair again, then hugged her.

Red rocked back, rolled to her knees, smiled sweetly. "Now I'm going to bed. Geez! This floor's hard. I didn't sleep a wink."

Again Bobby left. The Great Homes office was empty until eleven thirty when Dan Coleman came to pick up open house signs. Then Sharon came and Bobby and she left for the ticky-tack Riverside house where the asking price was only $29,950. Seeing Dan and Sharon made Bobby feel the world was okay. He told none of them anything but tried deeply to exude to them all his appreciation. Not a single curious neighbor or prospective buyer came to the open house—it was, after all, only a little more than two weeks to Christmas.

As Bobby headed up Deepwoods Drive in the fading light it hit him that his relationship with Red was over. Suggesting the abortion, then marriage, was an excuse, he thought, a way for her to get through this moment—for her to get his agreement before she split. He pulled in alongside Ty's Caddy, surprised to see Ty loading his clothes into the trunk. "What's happenin, Breeze?" He tried to be light.

"What the fuck, Man." Ty did not smile.

"What the fuck?"

"Life goes on, Breeze." Ty slammed the trunk, got into the Caddy. The car was packed with all his belongings.

"What's goin on?" Bobby was befuddled. There were tears in Ty's eyes.

"Fuck it, Man. Don't mean nothin."

"Ty, what are you doin? Where's Red?"

"I don't know. She split fore I got up."

"Where're you goin?"

"Jus goin, Mothafucka. I thought you was different."

Bobby was beyond befuddled. Obviously Ty was packed, moving on, but why so suddenly? Why so hurt? Why angry? "Goin where?"

"On my own, Man. Sometimes ... sometime you whites are crazier then blacks. You know that?" Ty pulled the shift lever from park to reverse. The car rocked.

Bobby just stared. For a second he saw Ty's leaving as a burden lifted from his shoulders, saw the expedience of it, but he did not understand it.

"I had pride when I was with you—once. I had pride, Mister. No matter you left three behind. I aint goina let you dump me." Now Ty was openly crying and Bobby was completely upset and tears formed in his eyes too. "Next time jus tell me! Jus tell me!" Ty let the car roll back. "Jus tell me. You don't gotta dump my shit in the garbage."

The Caddy swung back onto Deepwoods Drive, the transmission clunked as Ty shifted, Ty muttering, "I'll show im. I'll show im all. Get my piece a the pie. This jigaboo spade gonna outdo im . . . outdo them white fuckas . . . outdo the Cap'n." And he was gone.

On Thursday, 10 December 1970 Bea Hollands entered San Martin Canyon Hospital to have an "ovarian cyst" removed. Bobby was now sure their relationship was over except for the final separation. He still had not called Stacy—indeed, with each passing day it became more difficult for him to think of calling her; became more difficult for him to exert any control over his personal life. Yet by year-end, with the market slow and the season against him, Bobby managed to list one house and sell three more.

Mid-January 1971: How? he thought. How? How? How did I let this happen? How did it happen? He sat at his desk. Lisa Fonari was across the room at her desk, head down, diligently writing something. In the front office Jane Boswell had answered the phone, buzzed him on the intercom. Others were working at their desks. The call had shattered him but he could not, did not, let it show—but continued thinking, How? How?

"Hello."

"Rob?"

"Stace!?" His heart had jumped, dropped.

"Rob? Yes. It's me." Her voice was soft, incredibly wonderful. Why hadn't he called? Why hadn't he stopped it? Red had announced it at his office Christmas party—not actually announced it but sweetly told Lisa and Liza and the two had immediately turned the party into a celebration of Bobby's and Red's impending nuptials. The good wishes and happiness had been intoxicating. And then Liza had taken charge of arrangements.

"Stace. You sound . . . where are you?"

"In Mill Creek Falls. I haven't heard from you and I thought . . ."

"Stace . . ."

"Rob, I can barely hear you."

"I'm—I—Red and I got married." There was a pause. He wanted to say, I'm sorry. I didn't mean to. Wanted to explain. But thoughts, words were agonizing. He couldn't speak. He'd betrayed her—and himself— and he wasn't even sure how.

"Oh. Oh, congratulations."

"Stace . . ."

"Rob, speak up."

His stomach churned, tightened. He and Red had exchanged vows on Cataract Trail overlooking the Lower Res. Friends from Great Homes and from People's Life and Casualty had huddled under umbrellas. Even Josh, held by Tom Houghton, had been there. And that night, not only had they not consummated their marriage but Red had gotten very drunk on champagne and by nine o'clock she was blubbering, sobbing, then shrieking to the few friends who'd remained at their house how the marriage was going to have to be annulled because she had been forced into it against her desires. Bobby had been more confused than ever. He had not even called his grandfather.

August 1984

I'm going to make it. I'm going to make it, Man. I'm going to make it.

I'm still over the west ridge, hunkerin down on my daybed, night bed, trying to meditate, trying to see into this darkness, this true dark of true dark. What is it? What is evil? In the sixties we were taught there is no such dicotomy as good-evil. Only shades of gray. In the seventies even that became irrelevant. But how? How did civilization—American culture anyway—lose control? Lose sight? Lose insight?

What right do I have saying, I'm going to make it? I should have died at Dai Do, or at Loon, or on Storrow Drive. What I did to Linda and to my daughters is almost exactly what Bobby's father did to him except where Wap's old man was chased away by Miriam and whatever demons he had, I only had the demons—and Jimmy.

My daughters were one-day-old and I un-assed their AO. If Grandpa Wapinski hadn't called my Pa, and then gone and seen Linda, told them both I was disturbed by the war, which I don't know how he knew because we didn't ever but that once talk about it, and if he hadn't "paid" Linda all those wages I never earned, I'd probably never of come back, never of been allowed back.

I did leave Linda a note. I guess I'm trying here to justify what I did. I left a last adios that said something like:

Babe,
    I've gone to get help. I'll be away a while. I have to get my head

together—not just for me but for you and those two beautiful girls you brought into the world. I'm afraid for you and them.

Maybe I didn't include the last line . . . but I wanted to. Maybe I didn't write that note at all . . . but I think I did.

13

Seven and a half miles east of town, Sunday, 13 September 1970—It was very warm, very dry, dusty. In the ditches along the road's edge Queen Anne's lace bloomed to eight inches across. There was the smell of wheat, the smell of road-kill, of exhaust from two Kenworths pulling tandem rigs, of hot motor oil from the Harley, of his own sweat. The ride in had been fast, roaring through the night and into the dawn, moths and beetles splattering against the headlight and handlebars, forks and every front-facing surface they could possibly smash against. Oil had been seeping for weeks—typical Harley—but with dawn catching him from behind, a line or gasket had let go and hot oil had blown out, then back against his legs, boots, the cylinder heads, exhaust pipes, panniers. He'd stopped, fiddled, quickly realized he needed more than the scant tools he carried. The roadway was flat. He'd begun walking, pushing the 700-pound Harley. With the sun came flies and yellowjackets.

Tony had left another place, another job, had straddled the Harley, felt the gutteral vibration, left. He had not looked back. Could not have cared less. For a week he had shoveled sand, stone and cement into the small mixer, hosed in water, mixed, dumped the heavy sludge into a

wheelbarrow, grunted, snarled, pushing the wheelbarrow along meandering two-by-six planks to boxed sections of a meandering walkway,
working like a horse, an ox, a machine. Working ten, twelve hours without breaks, "Just pay me in cash," then collapsing with a six-pack and
whatever food the woman brought to the "carriage house," garage really, watching *Leave It to Beaver*, *Ben Casey*, *The Avengers*, avoiding the
news, falling asleep to *Then Came Bronson* or *Hawaii Five-O*. Then rising
early, starting the mixer, shoveling, trudging, one more odd job in a
string of odd jobs that lasted hours or days or this one an entire week,
then off with a bit of cash in his pocket, gas money, with a little more
time behind him, a little less in front, off to the next town, standing
outside the local Manpower office, whispering, "I'll do it cheaper and
better." Working, moving. His hair grew long, curled, frizzed; his beard
came in thick, coarse. In Ohio he'd had a run-in with some punk-nosed
college jerk whose daddy had bought him a superhawk Jappo bike and
probably a deferment as well. He'd kicked ass, taken the kid's leather
jacket with a Marine Corps emblem painted on the back, painted over
with flowers, both emblem and flowers now cracking and fading from
his harsh wear. In Illinois he'd crashed at a farm commune for three
weeks, nice people, easy style, but he'd left because of lack of privacy,
intolerance, lack of beer, of grass, of Darvon. He'd ridden south, then
west, then north, then west again, stopping, working, gruff, rough, angry, trying to stay one mile ahead of his demons.

In town: "I tell you right now," Swen Evenden said to his brother, "if
she were my daughter I'd go git er."

"She ain't your daughter," Dawen Evenden answered.

"The Lord still recognizes you as responsible for her," Swen said.

Two other men moved closer, one nodded, one quietly grunted
"Amen." The men were not large, not small, not old, not young, not
rich, not poor. They had been to church services, had gathered afterward
to talk, socialize, exchange views on the wheat crop; exchange tidbits of
local concern—pros and cons about the construction of a Dogs and Suds
Drive-In, feelings about the hippie commune east of town: "Least they're
downwind en downstream."

Dawen Evenden shook his head. "She's nearly seventeen," he said.
"You really think I can tell her—"

"If she were mine, I'd tell her," Swen interrupted. "En if she didn't
listen with er ears, I'd tell it to her backside."

"Ey," agreed the other two.

"And you wouldn't have a daughter eny all, Swen. Not in this day
and age."

"Well, it wouldn't hurt to head out there for a Sund'y visit," Swen
said. "Dawen"—he pronounced the name Dah-ven—"you maybe
should have Lottie make up some chicken and bring that out."

"I'll go too," said Calvin Eckhardt. "I've never seen the place. We've been makin jokes about em for a year but we don't know, eh?"

"You sure Lauren's out there?" Roger Minnah asked.

Swen pursed his mouth. These men were his older brother, his good friends, his neighbors. To admit that his daughter had joined John H. Noyes and his following of Iowa (they pronounced it eye-oh-way) hippies was to admit that he and Lottie had failed. Still, he was worried.

Dawen spoke for him, spoke in Swen's silence. "She been out there a good part a the summer. She en the Arlen girl."

"Melissa!?" Roger shied back.

"Ya." Dawen said.

"She came home every night," Swen said, justified his family. "She didn't stay. When school started she went right back. Just went out Friday night."

"If she were my daughter," Calvin Eckhardt said, "I'd leave the chicken home en bring out my side-by-side."

Creekside: The John Noyes commune, like many other communes of the late sixties and early seventies, offered an alternative to traditional American values and family structure. Noyes and his disciples, David, Michael and Luke Nachahmennen, were ostensibly seeking "a more perfect world, an expanded consciousness." In early 1970 the commune had been inhabited by forty-one women, men, and children. In May there had been a major flap between Noyes—a free-love proponent—and Brad Thurgood, a seeker of a counterculture with more stereotypical sex and marriage roles. By June the commune had disintegrated and only the four original men, five women, two of whom were pregnant, and four young children remained. It was then that Noyes met Melissa Arlen and Lauren Evenden—classmates, both sixteen, about to turn seventeen, farm girls with long straight blond hair, freckles, excellent grades, loving families.

On the road five miles east of town: He'd stripped to his T-shirt. Sweat rolled into his eyes, stung. He squinted, braced the bike with his leg, wiped his eyes. Still they stung. He pulled his handkerchief from the pocket of his dungarees, rolled it, tied it around his head to absorb the sweat, thought about a cold Grain Belt or Hamm's, about rolling the cold sweating can on his forehead to cool down. A car sped by. He'd heard it coming from behind, heard it longer than he could see it. Out-of-state fucker, he'd thought. Fuckin scared shitless to stop. The road had been rising very slightly for the past mile, making pushing the big machine under the hot sun torturous. Now the road imperceptibly crested, not enough for him to sit and roll, just enough so that he had to hold the Harley back. Ahead in the road he saw a prairie dog that had been clipped by a vehicle. He paused. A second animal was beside the first trying to pull it from the road, glancing furtively up at Tony, then back down, short, jerky movements. The two animals tumbled into the roadside ditch beneath the Queen Anne's lace.

Tony continued pushing, wishing he had a beer, somehow feeling satisfied in the punishment, the cruelty of the sun, the weight of the bike, the vacant blacktop reflecting more and more heat, the wheat dust and road dust and his own sweat and the oil on his pants making the cloth stick and chafe his groin and that sting added to the stinging in his eyes; thinking it was proper that he walk through hell for what he'd done; thinking without words, without analyzing what he had done. His throat was caked with dust. " 'How dry I am,' " he burst out, chuckled at himself, but only in his mind, " 'no-bot-tee knows . . . ' " He didn't finish the song but changed to, " 'In heaven there is no beer / That's why we drink it here / Cause when we're gone from here / Our friends will be drinking all our beer.' "

At the commune: "Don't go," Jennifer, one of the two pregnant women, pleaded. The men did not answer. In the house Jessica was crying. Nicole and Christina were still tripping, completely out of their minds. The infants and toddlers were crying, whimpering without understanding, one on Jennifer's hip, one in a high chair on the porch, the two toddlers clutching Jennifer's legs. "Don't go," she mumbled. Then she yelled, "Beth Ann . . . " but her voice broke and died.

The engine of the van caught. Blue-black smoke belched from a hole in the tailpipe, expanded like a soft cloud attempting to float the van up, away.

"Beth Ann," Jennifer cried again.

Beth Ann poked her head from the passenger side window. Michael was behind loading boxes, bags, moving quickly. Luke and David were inside, in back, laughing, pulling in the boxes and bags Michael plopped on the doorway floor. John H. Noyes was behind the wheel. "You'll be all right, honey," Beth Ann called. "You'll be all right. Take care of the others. You oughta get rid of those two."

Four miles east of town: He hadn't noticed it, became angry that he'd been so unaware. A quarter mile down on the right there were dual rusted barbed-wire fences running perpendicular to the road. Beside one was a mailbox. He could not make out a drive but could see a shadow line between fences. Far off to the right, maybe half a mile, there was a clump of trees.

Tony saw a van emerge from the trees. He sighed. The van kicked up a cloud of dust that hung over the shadow line between fields. It did not stop at the road but swung out, accelerated toward him. He braced the Harley, felt the weight pull on the scar in his quadricep. He raised his arms, flagged the van. It continued to accelerate, reached him, didn't slow.

"Hey!" he shouted in his best sergeant's voice. "Stop!" The driver stomped on the brakes. The van skidded. "What the hell's the matter with you?!" Tony roared.

"What's happenin, Man?" The driver's face was ashen, his smile pasty.

"Hmm." Tony eyed the long-haired driver, the chick beside him. "I need some help."

"What'sa matter, Man?" The voice was irritating.

Tony slapped the Harley. "Blew an oil line." He stared at the driver, challenging him. "Doesn't anybody up here stop? Law of the road, isn't it? People need help?"

"John, give him a ride," Beth Ann said. She leaned forward, rested a hand on the driver's leg, eyed Tony up and down. "Why don't you get in?" she said directly to him.

"I need a tow." Tony eyed her back. "Tow my scooter to town." She had on a tight cotton shirt. Her hair was long, dark, her eyes dark. Silver earrings hung like windchimes almost to her shoulders. She inhaled from a cigarette, blew the smoke toward him, ran the tip of her tongue around her lips.

"Go up the driveway," the driver said. "They'll help ya up there." With that the van sped off.

Tony spat, laughed, thought, sit on my face, babe, pushed on. He read the mailbox—Noyes—pushed through the gate. The driveway was rutted. It had once been paved but never maintained. More sweat dripped into his eyes. He was hot, tired, thirsty, hungry, frustrated over the bike, pushing with all his strength to get the Harley out of a double pothole, then holding back as the drive ran downhill into the clump of trees, shade, grass, a mishmash on the lawn—washtubs and washboards, clotheslines, a single chicken, a scrawny goat. Bit by bit he took in the scene. It was the Illinois commune again but this one had no apparent order, no rhyme or reason, appeared not so much a counterculture co-op as a total breakdown of culture. A woman sat on the ground by the washtubs, legs splayed, mumbling, nursing an infant, half her dress down to her waist. Two toddlers were on the porch. One was squatting naked, peeing; the other was hiding behind a high chair holding another crying infant. The porch railings were in place but most of the balusters were missing. Tony rocked the bike onto its stand. He saw a leg, stepped forward, cautiously, automatically checking his advance route for trip wires, checking for snipers. He became tense, vigilant. The leg—legs— were naked, on their side, curled. The woman at the washtub moaned. He snapped toward her. "What the fuck?"

Now he approached the body, a girl's body. He reached out. She was cool, not cold. He checked her neck for a pulse. There was none. He put his ear to her chest, thought he heard a heartbeat. Immediately he rolled her, cleared her mouth, cocked her head back to open the airway, blew in. Then he felt for the bottom of her sternum, up, over, both hands, pump, pump . . . eleven, twelve, thirteen . . . Again he squeezed her nostrils, breathed into her mouth. His adrenaline flowing. He worked for four, five, six minutes, broke to yell at the woman by the washtub, "Call an ambulance," continued, could see peripherally that the woman by the tub had not moved. He was in rhythm now, heard cars on the drive, thought, Thank God. He looked up. In the brush there was another body, naked, young, blond, crumpled. Get here! he screamed in his mind at the cars. Get here! Still he pumped, breathed the girl.

Two cars pulled in. Men emerged. Silent. Shocked. "Get over here," Tony yelled. There was milling, confusion, then running.

"That's the Arlen girl," a man by him blurted. Tony did not look up.

"Lauren? Lauren? Are you here?"

"What is this?" Now more voices. Then one to Tony, angrily. "What are you doing?"

"Breath o' life," Tony snapped. He returned his mouth to the naked girl's.

"Get away from that girl!"

Tony was stunned. The woman at the washtub was up, being held, dressed by two men.

"What's happened here, eh?"

"White lightning," she muttered.

"White lightnin!" a man shouted.

Tony heard him, understood, said to the man who'd yelled at him, said, his hands between Melissa Arlen's naked breasts, "LSD. They musta OD'd. Jesus. Get an ambulance."

"They were jealous of me," the woman at the washtub mumbled. "Because of my babies. He's evil. He has false consciousness. They'd be on top of us all the time."

"Get away from that girl you son of a bitch." Now two men were coming at Tony.

"I'm a para—" Tony began.

"GAAAAHHHD!" The cry boomed across the commune, the fields, shook the house. "ITS LAUREN!"

"Jealous of me because of my babies," the woman wailed. "He done it." She pointed at Tony.

They set upon him, punching him, kicking him. "I'm a paramedic. . . ." Tony blocked the punches but the punches didn't stop. There was more yelling. He could see it, could see what they saw, knew instantly they would not believe him. He lowered his guard, did not swing back, did not resist, thought, imagined, before he blacked out, How deserving.

In town: "Says here that bike was last registered to a James Pell-ee-green-ee who died in Vet Naym. You steal this bike, son?"

"Pellegrino." Tony's face was swollen, his nose broken. He could barely open his mouth. His hands were cuffed behind his back, his ankles to a bar on the concrete cot. In the cell with him was a uniformed man who had not identified himself.

"You're Anthony Piss-an-no."

"Pisano. Jimmy's my cousin."

"Report said Pell-ee-green-ee died. This bike isn't registered to you. You steal it, son?"

"Yeah, I fuckin stole it from him. Fuck im."

"You're a real firebrand, aren't ya, son?" The uniformed man poked him in the chest with a billy club. "You kill that girl with that punch?"

"I was trying to give her CPR."

"You rape her first, son? Coroner says Lauren Evenden was sodomized too. Some people here in town are downright mad."

Tony didn't answer. He was angry, pissed about being caught, trapped. And he was withdrawing. He'd gone into the hole, into the tunnel again, trying to help, feeling like a Marine again, only again to have the body break, be dragged over him.

"All them other girls is really messed up, too. And those poor babies." The uniformed man sat on the cot next to Tony. "Coroner thinks you put them psychotropic mushrooms in the punch. About fifty times too much. A glassful'd be about fifty times too much. He's surprised you're not all dead. Were you tryin to kill em?"

"I'd only been there ten minutes before those fuckers arrived and beat shit outta me. I'd never seen em before. None of em."

"Hmm." The uniformed man stood. "We've got eight witnesses say they caught you red-handed trying to sodomize that girl again. You better hope she doesn't die, son. Swen and Lottie are gentle people but Morgan Arlen is ready to string you up right now."

"I pushed my bike in there. Line blew. Because the guy in the van said they'd help."

The uniformed man snickered. He turned away, looked out the bars. When he turned back he backhanded his billy club into Tony's face.

The next day an older man woke Tony, cleaned his face, cleared the blood from his eyes, nose, lips. He was still cuffed and shackled. The older man fed him chicken broth, then milk, through straws. "Feel better?"

Tony grunted.

"Well, you look a little better."

Again Tony only grunted. He did not look toward or at the man.

"Got the readout on your prints, Mister Pisano," the man said. "Got your service record. That was pretty impressive, Sergeant."

Now Tony did look up.

"I was in the Corps—well, years ago. What happened to you Sergeant Pisano? I don't understand what that war does to you boys. Don't you have someone to call?"

Tony shook his head.

"I called Boston. You haven't lived there in some time, I guess. You're license has expired."

Still Tony said nothing.

"Your home of record is in Pennsylvania. Sure you don't have someone to call?"

Tony shook his head. How could he call? How could he call Linda? Or his father? For a brief moment he thought maybe he could call Uncle James or even better Uncle Joe in Binghamton. But then he knew he couldn't.

Twice more that day the older man came in. Twice he uncuffed and unshackled Tony, let him use the can, let him feed himself. On and off there was commotion out beyond the cell, beyond the corner of the narrow corridor. The cell itself was small, six-by-seven, no window, a hard cot, a commode, a tiny basin—a typical modern, small-town holding tank designed for overnight stays. The only light came from fluorescent tubes behind white plastic diffusers in the ceiling of the corridor. On his third visit the older man said, "Sergeant Pisano." Tony did not respond. "You're going to be arraigned on Thursday. These are serious charges. We'll follow due process. You've got the right to representation. Do you understand?"

Tony nodded. He wanted to speak but he now could not speak, was afraid to open his mouth. He was afraid he might cry but . . . it was more than that. He might give information to the enemy, break his code of silence. Besides, it was payback time, penance time. They couldn't do anything to him, his thoughts convoluted, that he didn't deserve. His thoughts scattered. Cops cannot be trusted; lawyers cannot be trusted; society cannot be trusted. He did not speak. He felt numb.

Later that night they came for him, the uniformed man and three others Tony did not recognize. Again he did not defend himself, again he passively accepted their blows, cringed, involuntarily raised his hands, arms, to protect his eyes, until they grabbed him, pinned his arms behind him, forced him to his knees, his head pulled back, a knee in his back, the uniformed man flicking Tony's mouth, lips, with the billy club. "This the way you held her?" The billy club was poked into his cheek, cheekbone, rocked his head, strained his neck. "Rammed yer club into her face, huh?" One man snickered, the uniformed man scowled, the snicker stopped. One man left, disgusted, unwilling to participate yet unwilling to stop the beating. The uniformed man rammed the billy club into Tony's mouth, rammed it to the back of his throat. "Like that, Sar-gee-nt," he mocked Tony. "Like this." He ramrodded the club back and forth, Tony gagging, his lips splitting, bleeding, then Tony gagging, convulsively racking, vomiting, gagging on the vomit, vomiting more, the uniformed man angry, backing off, then forcing the side of the club against Tony's neck, pressing, swearing, Tony's air cut off, the blood flow blocked, his eyes bulging, "Should of gone out there years ago. Got rid of you scum." Tony blacked out.

When he came to he had been cleaned up, and again cuffed and shackled. The fluorescent lights were on. His neck, mouth, abdomen ached. His right leg twitched. He tried to let go but everything was taut, shivering. He tried to sit up but didn't have the strength. He thought of Linda, of the baby on the porch, the baby on Storrow Drive, the family shot by the NVA, his own babies. Jumbled, chaotic thoughts, images, horrors against the fluorescent light coming through the bars, through his eyelids without rhyme or reason or order, and Tony, in his mind, laughing, doing his little jig, going to his death dancing.

In a hospital southwest of town: She was afraid, in tears. Her father was trying to be warm, comforting but to her he was authority, harshness, righteousness, a mirror reflecting her evil, her offenses.

"I didn't do any, Daddy."

"It's okay, Melissa. It's okay."

"We never did any. Daddy, we never did. We just watched. I don't know what happened."

"He put it in the punch."

"In the punch . . ." Her voice shook, was thin. "The punch. Oh Lord! Lauren. Lauren must have had two glasses because she was so thirsty. I thought it tasted sour. And their glasses were dirty. I only sipped . . ."

"It's okay, Melissa. We know it wasn't intentional."

"That's when Lauren began acting weird. That's . . ."

"It's okay. They caught that motorcycle creep." Morgan Arlen turned, gritted his teeth. He did not want his daughter to see how irate he was. Still he could not help but say, "We're going to hang that creep."

"What motorcycle?" Melissa wanted to piece the day together. She had not been told about Lauren's death.

"The guy with the Harley," Morgan Arlen said. His stomach was tight with anger. "The guy with the frizzy hair. Anthony some Italian name."

"Daddy, there wasn't any Anthony there. There was John, and his disciples. And Jennifer and Jessie and Beth Ann and the two earth moms."

"It's okay, Melissa. They caught him red-handed. Caught him with one of the girls."

"No, Daddy. It was John's commune. He hated motorcycles. He was afraid of them."

Rock Ridge, Pennsylvania, Thursday, 24 September 1970—Anthony F. Pisano was heavily sedated. He had been admitted to the Rock Ridge Veterans Medical Center two days earlier as a transfer from a private facility in the far Midwest. He had been heavily sedated and escorted to Rock Ridge by two men he didn't know, two men who'd barely spoken. His transportation had been arranged and paid for but Tony did not know if it was by those two men or some other. It was not part of his record. His motorcycle, he had been told, was being repaired and would be shipped via ground transport.

They had brought him to Rock Ridge because it was the nearest facility to his home of record. He had no address, no forwarding address from his last known residence: Long Avenue, Boston, Massachusetts. The admissions report noted that Pisano, Anthony F., had been indigent, that he had attempted to commit suicide by jumping out a third-story hotel window. He had been saved, the report said, by landing in a small tree that had broken his fall though it had badly bruised his face. The report noted that only days before his jump he had saved the life of a young woman by administering CPR. His depression, it was speculated, must be due to previous events. The father of the young woman, wishing anonymity, had sent a one-thousand-dollar reward to be given to Sergeant Pisano upon his release from the hospital.

"Date of birth?"

"Ten November 1947."

"Service number?" To Tony the man looked old, older than his own father. He was balding from the front. He was dressed in a loose-fitting suit, a striped tie. He sat in a chair before his desk. Tony was in an identical chair, facing him. "Dates of service?" The man had Tony's admissions form, a copy of his service record, a copy of his preliminary physical. He had told Tony his name twice but Tony had forgotten it and felt uneasy asking again. The man reviewed the information slowly, lackadaisically, as if he were killing time. Tony focused on the green blocks of the half-tiled walls of the office, thought the work was well done. He looked out the window. It was sunny, windy. ". . . Panama, Viet Nam . . ." The man talked on, told Tony a little about where he was, what to expect. "Anthony," the man raised his voice as if Tony couldn't hear, "do you know why you are here?" He looked at Tony's face with professional empathy, with no real interest.

"No," Tony said. To Tony his own voice sounded strange, far off, as if speaking inside a box.

"Do you remember being in the hotel? Up on the third floor?"

Tony shook his head. He had no idea what the man was talking about.

"How do you feel right now?"

"So-so," Tony said. His voice was flat, listless. It distressed him but he had no energy to lift it, make it a real voice.

"What are you thinking?" the man asked.

"I don't know," Tony answered.

"You don't know or you don't want to share it with me?"

"I don't know," Tony repeated.

The man sat back, eyed Tony, didn't speak, seemed to Tony to be disappointed with him. Finally the man said, "You know I want to help you, don't you?"

Tony was confused.

"I want to help you. Do you remember trying to . . . trying to harm yourself?"

"You mean . . . " Tony's voice was slow, far off.

"Yes."

" . . . like on Storrow Drive?"

"Yes," the man said. He knew nothing about Storrow Drive, guessed that it was the location of the hotel.

"I was feeling like really fucked up—" Tony stopped abruptly.

"You can say 'fucked up' in here," the man said.

"That was really fucked," Tony said. His words were intense but his tone was without spunk.

"Why?" The man tried to pull it out of him.

"Because all those kids died." Tony looked at the man, knew the man had no idea what he was talking about, still wondered how the man knew anything at all about Storrow Drive. "And their mother," Tony added.

"Hm," the man said.

"Her head was just scraped clean away. Nothin left . . . blood en bone . . . could see her spine . . . "

The man fought his immediate impulse. "Yes," he said calmly.

"Musta been caught between the car and the road," Tony said. "The blood shined in the road in all the lights. When I reached in, her blood dripped on me."

"That must have been very distressful." The man maintained his professional interest.

"Well . . . I seen a lot of that shit." The words dribbled from Tony's mouth. "But that . . . without the head . . . I mean nothin to recover, ya know? At Dai Do we hacked off a lot of heads but you know they were right there."

"Dai Do? That's where Storrow Drive is?"

"No." Tony clammed up. He could not understand how this man could make such a stupid mistake.

"Excuse me." The man attempted to recover. "Of course." Tony volunteered nothing more. "Can we go back to the hotel," the man said. It was not a question. "You tried to hurt yourself. That's when you bruised your face."

Now Tony felt more alert, mentally, even if the sedative had sapped him physically. "They beat shit outta me because a bunch a people died. But I didn't have nothin to do with it. But . . . like death follows me. Ever since Nam. Philly. So many in Philly. And Boston. And then Jimmy. It's like I'm a fuckin death magnet. Death with a capital D. Touch me and you die."

"Have you killed a lot of people?" The man fidgeted in his chair, attempted to maintain his calm countenance.

"Shit yeah," Tony said. Suddenly he blurted, "SHIT! Yeah, I killed em.

What the fuck do you think?" There was anger in Tony's voice. "And I'd kill em again. If I could find that motherfucker that killed Manny I'd kill im. Some fuckin times, Man, I can be there, you know? I can be right there and I can stop it. I can be holding Manny but let go of him and see that motherfucker before he fires and fire his ass up." Tony cocked his arms, clenched his hands as if clutching a rifle; his face tightened, his eyes intense, aiming in, searching a treeline. "Blow that motherfucker right outta a tree. Or the dink who hit the lady and her kids. The one with the belt. I can be there cause I was there. I saw him like, what, an hour earlier. And I'd grease that fucker." Tony turned his eyes on the man. "I'd waste that fucker. I'd do the same to that fucker drivin the Volvo!"

The man was shaken. He tried to hide it. He did not want this sociopath to turn on him, wasn't certain how to control him, wasn't certain if he should, if for therapeutic reasons he should let Tony run on. But he knew there would be other sessions.

Tony could see that the man was afraid and it angered him. "I thought my head was fucked up"—spit came from the corners of Tony's mouth—"you know, from ol' Nam Bo. I was the Will. I was the Will to pull the fuckin trigger. But when I got back, when I started to deal with the Mickey Mouse shit, with you slimy civilians, you fucked me over worse than Nam ever did." Tony was hissing, glaring.

"Okay, Anthony. Not me. Right? That's one of the rules in here. I'm here to help, remember?"

"Yer all fuckin here to help. Bash my fuckin head in. Fuck yer help. A fuckin grunt can cope with nerves, Man. Cope with all kindsa shit. Can't cope with slime."

On Friday the 25th of September 1970, Dr. Jonathan Freiburg officially diagnosed Anthony Pisano as suffering from paranoid schizophrenia and borderline personality disorder. He recommended an initial three-month therapy, one session per week, and prescribed Elavil and Thorazine to reduce the threat of violence to self and others, and diazepam for the muscle spasms in Tony's right leg.

Mill Creek Falls, 27 September 1970—It was Sunday, her "day off," and it was her wedding anniversary. Linda was exhausted. She had started the day early as any mother with four-month-old twins does, with a predawn feeding. She no longer checked the clock, just started by tucking Gina in on the right, Michelle on the left, football holds with the infants' legs sticking out behind, their bodies resting on pillows under her arms, their heads in her hands. She gently massaged their scalps, the tickle of their fine curls delighting her as she lay back on her own built-up pillows, relaxed, let the milk come, chuckled as Gina smacked and gurgled away at Rangoon, as Michelle, now the bigger by seven ounces, worked methodically draining Bangkok of every last drop. Then

Linda had put them in the crib they shared and still in predawn show-ered and washed her hair and even shaved her legs—luxury of luxuries.

In May Linda had returned from the hospital to her apartment, as she'd insisted—brought there by John Sr. and Jo, Isabella already there preparing the house for the homecoming and Annalisa helping her mother. Jo had stayed for the first ten days, had called Norma, Linda's mother, saying, "They're so beautiful. Come up and see them. You could stay here or in the guest room in our home." Norma had answered, "I'll have to ask Henry," and Henry had said, "We don't have a daughter named Linda." In June, John Sr. showed up with a used, gray-and-white 1966 Ford Country Squire station wagon that he'd registered in Linda's name. In July Linda had gotten her Pennsylvania nursing credentials and had landed a job with 86-year-old Mrs. Victoria Meredith of River Front Drive, who allowed Linda to bring Gina and Michelle but who be-grudged the infants Linda's time.

At noon Linda had her first visitors, Grandma and Grandpa Pisano, as she now called them, and John Jr. and his girl, Molly Kleinman. "Oh. Hi!" Linda beamed. "Did you knock? I didn't hear . . . "

"We just walked up," Jo said quietly. She gave Linda a hug. "We don't want to wake the babies."

"Oh, don't worry," Linda said. "They're in there gabbing at each other. They're so funny. They actually goo-goo to each other. Hi Grandpa."

"How are you, Linda?" John Sr. said.

"Great," Linda said. "Come on in," she said to Johnny and Molly, who'd remained on the porch. Then back to her father-in-law, "Want a cup of coffee? It's fresh."

"Linda," Jo said, "I don't know how you do it. I'm just going to peek in, okay?"

John Sr. said, "I'll get it. I brought you some pastries. From the Italian bakery."

"Oh, Grandpa"—Linda scolded him—"and me still with fifteen pounds to lose."

"Can I peek in too?"

"Of course. Bring them out if . . . ah . . . unless they need to be changed. You don't want to get a leak on your nice clothes."

"We just came from church," Johnny said.

"If they need it, I'll change em," Linda called. She already had out four cups and saucers, spoons, napkins, and was untying the pastry box. Grandma returned carrying bright-eyed Gina. Molly brought in Michelle, who the instant she saw her mom squirmed, her face furling into a boo-boo face, emitting a tiny sniff.

"Ohhh!" Grandpa Pisano drew out the word. "Look at that face. Let me hold her."

They stayed an hour. Molly confided to Linda that she and Johnny were thinking about getting married. She did not mention it being Linda and Tony's anniversary, pretended, as they all did, as if the present situation was normal, wonderful, as if nothing had happened. Except for John Sr. who lingered after the others had left and said to Linda, "Any word?"

"No."

"Not even a postcard."

"No."

"I'm ... " John Pisano's voice trembled. "If he comes back ... "

"He'll come home," Linda said softly. "Really, Grandpa."

"You don't know how sick this makes me."

"I know he's going to come back," Linda said. "I just know it."

"Do you need anything? You shouldn't have to work."

"You paid the doctor," Linda said. "You gave me the car. And the furniture and toys. You've done so much. And Annalisa and Aunt Isabella are always helping. Really, we're doing okay. And I like working."

"But with the babies ... " John Pisano shook his head. "Not even a card on your first anniversary. Not even a damn postcard."

An hour later Jessie Taynor banged on the door waking up the infants. "Ssshh!" Linda flew to the door to stop her, shook her head hearing Michelle cry.

Jessie, seeing her look, cringed. "I didn't make t'em cry," she said.

"No. No, Jessie. You didn't. Come in."

"Jessie didn't make t'em cry. They make Jessie cry."

"Ssshh." Linda raised her finger to her lips. Jessie had become her "buddy." She was good to talk to unless she was in her defensive mode. Then she neither listened nor made sense but instead struck out verbally, sometimes physically—sometimes to the delight of the twelve- and thirteen-year-old boys who would see her on the street, torment her, just to listen to her ramble and rage and watch her waddle after them shaking her big fists, her fat arms.

"Do you want a pastry?" Linda asked.

"Um."

"Okay. Sit down. At the kitchen table. Let me quiet the girls."

"Jessie didn't make t'em cry."

"No. Jessie didn't make them cry. But now Linda must kiss them." Linda went into the nursery, smiled at her two babies who were lying, Gina belly-down, Michelle belly-up, next to each other, Michelle's right arm under Gina's head, Gina's right arm over Michelle's chest. "What are you two doing, huh?" Linda checked their diapers. They were both damp but, she thought, not really wet. She cranked up the musical mobile that craned over the crib. "Let me talk to Jessie," Linda said sweetly, "then maybe we'll go out in the stroller. Or maybe read a book."

Back in the kitchen Jessie had already eaten both napoleons and the only cannoli that John Jr. hadn't eaten earlier.

"So, Jessie, how are you?"

"Jessie good," said Jessie Taynor. She had cannoli cream on her face. "Linda good?"

"Yes, I'm fine. I'm tired though."

"Jessie not tired. Jessie never tired."

"Linda get tired." Linda caught herself, changed her syntax. "I get tired," she said. "And sometimes a little down."

"We go downstairs. Go downtown."

"No. I mean sometimes I feel a little down. You know, sad. That's when I'm glad I have you as my friend."

"Jessie Linda's friend."

"I know. Mrs. Meredith . . . do you know Mrs. Meredith?"

"Merra-dit." Jessie Taynor smiled. "Big house."

"Uh-huh. You know, sometimes I get tired of her."

"She bitter old bitch." Jessie laughed.

"Nooo." Linda looked compassionately at Jessie. "No. But she treats me more like a maid than a nurse. I don't really mind. That's part of the job. But you'd think her family'd help more with that stuff."

"Jessie help Linda. Jessie tell Merra-dit go fuck."

"No no, Jessie. But thank you."

Late that afternoon Pewel Wapinski knocked lightly on Linda's door. Linda, Gina and Michelle had been on the floor in the small living room, Linda marveling at how Gina had learned to roll over and push herself against her sister until she was sitting up; and marveling at Michelle who still needed help sitting up but who, occasionally, bonked her sister with a plastic Donald Duck rattle. "Mr. Wapinski!"

"Um." He stood with his hands behind his back.

"Won't you come in?"

"Jus stopped for a minute," he said. He brought his hands forward, produced a bouquet of flowers.

"Oooo!" Linda gasped, surprised.

"Happy anniversary," the old man said.

"Oh, they're beautiful. Please come in. How did you know?"

"Remembered it in the paper last year."

"In the paper?"

"Um."

"Oh. We must still have been in Boston."

"Um."

"Did you want to see the girls?"

"Yep. But I'm bothering you. Those his certificates on the wall?"

Linda turned. She had forgotten she'd put them back. "Yes. Some of them."

Pewel knelt down, bent over, gave first his index finger to Gina, then his thumb to Michelle which she immediately seized and yanked almost toppling him. "Whoa! That's some handshake, Missy." He extricated his hand. To Linda he said, "Thank you."

"For what? Can I get you a cup of coffee?"

"No. I got to be goin. Said I'd only stay a minute. I know sometimes young boys forget. Those are really from him. Jus through me."

"Did he—"

"No. But he will. And he'd a asked me to bring em if he'd a thought and he'll think of it later and he'll be angry at his self for forgetting. Maybe in a month. And then he'll ask and it'll have been done."

"Thanks so much. That's so thoughtful."

"Maybe you and the missies could come up for dinner some night."

"Oh. We'd like that."

It was eight thirty. There were no more knocks on the door. Linda was exhausted. She had nursed and changed the babies, put them in the crib, knew she'd be nursing and changing them again in four hours. Now it was quiet. The windows were dark. She did not play the stereo. She was in the living room. She knelt, got down on all fours to pick up the rattles and stuffed animals with eyes that shimmied, tossing them one by one into the old milk crate she'd cleaned and painted for toys. In the corner of her eye she could see the flowers that Pewel Wapinski had brought and her stomach tightened. She sat back on her heels, rocked forward at the waist, pulled her arms in tight, clenched her fist to her face. Tears broke and she cried, sobbed, her arms quivering. "Come home, Tony. Dear God, Tony, please come home. Please come home. Please. Please. Please . . ."

Rock Ridge Veterans Medical Center—There is no time when one is heavily under the influence of Elavil, Thorazine and diazepam. No time, no space, no freedom. The orderlies call it liquid strait jacket. Tony is confused, cannot concentrate, standard effects of Elavil. He has been warehoused a week, no, certainly longer—he does not really care, standard effect of Thorazine. To think tires him, he is tired all the time—standard effect of diazepam. Tony too has come to call his "therapy" liquid strait jacket. He had been repatriated, almost, involuntarily, and this angers him but he cannot hold anger because of the ETD drug combo: 400 milligrams of Elavil each day, 300 milligrams of Thorazine, 40 milligrams of diazepam. One brother he's met is on 800 milligrams of Elavil, 400 Thorazine. They sleep, eat, watch TV, nod off, watch TV. When they talk they talk of Thorazine, of their strait jackets. They do not talk about combat, about Viet Nam, about their service. This is 1970. If they speak of Marines or Airborne the orderlies take note, report them, their jackets are upped. They are not here because of combat stress. Posttraumatic stress disorders will not be officially recognized for nine more years. They are here because they are psychotic, sociopathic, insane, crazy, nuts. They are here because they are poor, have no jobs in the sour economy, have refused to hold jobs, are difficult, are irritants, are bitter at a society in which—if they'd only get off their goddamned asses, settle down, get on with their lives—they would be provided with everything, absolutely anything, status quo or counterculture or in between. But no, they have essentially given the finger to everyone, maybe given the ultimate insult, attempted to check out of this society permanently.

It is early morning. Tony does not know the time but the orderlies know, mumble quietly to each other about their charges sleeping and dreaming their Thorazine dreams, sip their morning coffee, read their magazines, prefer that no one wake up—not yet, the expedience of Thorazine, the warehousing of spirit and body by diazepam.

On his cot Tony is restless. His body is paralyzed, his mind is impaired, but the drugs don't mask everything, don't keep everything from the conscious or the subconscious.

He is afraid. He is afraid he is going crazy. He is afraid he is dying. His heartbeat is irregular. The orderlies have told him not to worry, they'll watch over him. They have not told him it is another common side effect. He lies there not awake, not truly asleep. Night images splash his mind, sometimes dripping entire episodes of his life—the death of Manny in particular, maybe because one of the orderlies looks like Manny, looks as much like Manny as Tony can remember Manny looking. Except in the episodes. Then he sees Manny, sees him exactly how he was. Sometimes the images are flashes, the third child shot by the NVA, just a still photo in the mind, just the expression on the child's face, then falling, Tony's body arching, grabbing his cot, falling, the helicopter at Phu Bai, the blood dripping onto his hand as he reaches to switch off the ignition.

"All right. Let's go guys. Everybody up." The orderlies move through the ward, bang on the metal lockers that stand back-to-back separating two cots here from two there, an aisle between sections, on and on, ward after ward, but Tony is restricted to his ward, Seven-upper, they joke about it. Everyone lights up. Tony smokes Pall Malls. They are his one pleasure even if they no longer taste like Pall Malls. Nothing tastes as it did. He doesn't know why. They are herded through the motions of daily hygiene and morning meds. Tony can't shit. He feels bloated. His feet and hands feel puffed, numb. They watch TV. Then they watch more TV. And more TV. And they smoke and nod and on some wards they do talk but on Seven-upper they barely talk at all.

It is his fifth or eighth or tenth, he can't concentrate, can't calculate, session with Dr. Jonathan Freiburg. "I think we've been making some progress," Freiburg says. "Don't you?"

Tony nods. He is afraid to open up to Freiburg. Everyone knows Freiburg dictates the strength of the strait jacket.

"Tony, are there still people you'd like to kill?"

What kind of fuckin question is that? Tony thinks. "I killed enough people," he says. "I don't want to kill anymore."

"And all the people you killed, you killed during combat missions, didn't you?"

"Yeah. I guess. I told you last time that that Storrow Drive thing was an accident. I was responding. I was driving the ambulance."

"Um-hmm. Go on."

"I was angry at the guy who caused it."

"Why were you so angry, Tony?"

"Because it could have been me. I could have been driving the car he hit. So I was scared."

"Yes. That's a good reason to be angry, isn't it?"

"Yeah. And I answered a lot of other accidents. Lots of em could of been me."

"That's pretty frightening, isn't it?"

"Yeah. I ... I wasn't in control."

"Go on."

"Back in Viet Nam ... " Tony pauses. This was a bad subject unless Freiburg brought it up. Tony, even drugged, knows Freiburg can't handle it, hates it, condemns him for it. His body language always conveys a don't-tell-me-about-the-atrocities-you-committed attitude. "ah ... back then I was all spunk and courage but now I'm afraid to talk to people. I'm afraid of most everything."

"What kind of things, Tony?"

Tony sighs internally. *Beat him on that one.* "Sometimes I'm afraid people can hear what I'm thinking," he says.

"Umm." Freiburg hums.

"I'm afraid the woman who dispenses the meds at noon knows I can't get a hard on no more."

"Hmm."

"But the guys say that's cause of the meds and sure she knows it."

"Do you know that you've been on a reduced dosage this past week?"

"Me?"

"You haven't felt it, have you?"

"No." Tony immediately thinks about his strength returning but he says nothing.

"Tony, let's go back to some of the things you fear. You've told me very little about your family."

Again Tony sighs inside. *Now I got this asshole on the right track.* He has never mentioned Linda or his daughters, has said little about his folks. The not-mentioning has developed an inertia that has become drug-confused into a code of silence, a way to protect them. Still he is sad, not mentioning them here, or in the ward, sad, embarrassed, ashamed about denying them, denying the blood from which he'd come, the blood that came from him. Still, it is easier, better, less complicated, this way. "They're good people," Tony says. "I don't want to burden them. With my problems."

"Are you afraid you might hurt them?"

"Who?! My folks! Hell no. I mean, I'd never hurt em. I'm not a violent person."

"But you tried to hurt yourself."

"I told you before . . . "

"Yes. But even if what you told me is true, I'm not saying it isn't, but you said you let them hit you. You wanted to be hit. You wanted to be punished."

"Maybe it's because I should be . . . I should of been . . . I could of become, like, a doctor. I drove an ambulance. I took the EMT course. I could have stayed in school. I'm pretty smart. I should be a student now but I'm not. I'm not anything."

"Good. We'll talk more next time."

That was it for a week. Gradually, meaning returned to time. The next week it was more of the same. And the next. Tony hated the place, hated Freiburg, the orderlies, the meds, the stinking TV up on its perch, the smell of the ward. But he kept that to himself. Because he also liked being taken care of, liked the rest from having to make any decisions at all, liked not having to think, not having to be responsible. And all those things he liked he found repugnant, and he found himself liking their repugnancy. When he complained about pain and tremors in his leg, Freiburg interpreted it for him as a "physiological memory of being wounded brought on by his reimmersion into a pseudomilitary environment." Still he controlled himself, outwardly. Again his dosages were reduced. "They lookin for a maintenance dose," the black orderly that looked like Manny told him.

"Maintenance?"

"Yeah, Bro. You gotta stay on that shit for the rest a your life. You crazy, Man. You know? You a crazy vet. You always gonna be a crazy vet. Except you take your three-a-days. Whatever Freiburg say. Ha! An I wouldn't even get on that Harley fucked up on Elavil. You wanta sell it?" Then the orderly laughed. "Less, a course, you wanta keep it for knockin yerself off."

Tony let the words swirl in his mind. Crazy vet. Crazy vet. I'm not a student. I'm not a doctor. I'm a crazy vet.

In mid-December they gave him a day pass. He and three other crazy vets went and got pizza at the small restaurant next to the inn on Main Street. They walked, looked at the Christmas decorations, looked in the store windows, ogled some girls all wrapped in coats and scarves and earmuffs, even went in and purchased small gifts for each other and for the lady who gave out the noon meds.

He had one more session with Freiburg. "Do you ever have nightmares?"

"Sometimes," Tony said nonchalantly.

"You know, if you get up, take a diazepam, you've got a prescription, maybe walk just a little, you'll be able to go back to sleep."

Maybe if I ripped your tongue out, Tony thought. He smiled slightly. It was okay for a crazy vet to think that. "I'll try it if I need it," he said. "You know, Doc, down deep inside, I know if I apply myself, someday it's all gonna click."

"It will, Tony. For you I'm sure it will."

At 9:23 A.M., Wednesday 23 December 1970, Anthony F. Pisano was conditionally released from Rock Ridge Veterans Medical Center on outpatient status. In his pocket he had a hundred-tablet bottle of diazepam (Valium), a thirty-tablet vial of ten-milligram Thorazines, prescriptions for more, two packs of Pall Malls, and a thousand dollars. It was bitter cold. Tony straddled his big Harley FLH V-twin. They'd repaired it before they'd shipped it to him, one more act of atonement. He cranked it a dozen times before it coughed, two dozen before it sputtered, started. Then Tony roared off. Being a crazy vet this was okay.

There was a time when I was ten when I wanted more than anything a bicycle for Christmas. It was a lean year in our household—1957—I think because Pop was changing jobs. Johnny had turned sixteen on the 22d and Pop had bought him a wristwatch with phosphorescent hands. The tree was tall that year, but skinny. I think Aunt Helen paid for it because Pop had decided it was frivolous to waste $4.99 on a tree which we'd throw away in ten days. Oh, but how I wanted a bicycle—a red Columbia like the one Joey had gotten the year before. On Christmas morning John and Joey and I rushed down—maybe John was becoming a bit aloof being sixteen and all but I didn't notice it—and even Mark, who was only three and a half that year, rushed down, probably because our ma, Jo, had said something like "Nobody opens anything until we're all there," and Joey and I probably pulled Mark out of bed, but three and a half was plenty old enough for him to be rushing and excited too. And there under the tree were stacks of presents, square and rectangular boxes, wrapped, some of them, with last years paper that Jo had of course saved, rectangular boxes with shirts and pants for school, square boxes with wool sweaters that Aunt Isabella knitted and Jimmy and I wore ours to school in January and looked like twins and Mrs. Lusanti, our teacher that year, chided us and we both refused to ever wear them again. There were small packages, too. Red bags with pencils and erasers and plastic protractors, and each had a new pack of baseball cards and we immediately stuffed the gum into our mouths—it tasted like cardboard and felt like eating a baseball card until it softened and the sugar came out. Johnny got another big present, a portable typewriter. Joey got a horn and a newspaper rack for his bike. I don't remember what Mark got but there wasn't any bike and I was really sad, really crushed and after Ma and Pop came down I slipped out and went back up to my room and I started to cry 'cause I knew they didn't love me as much as the others because I'd come so soon after Joey—he wasn't even fourteen full months older than me—and I knew I was one of them mistake kids and that's why there wasn't a bike like Joey had gotten last year. A red 24-inch Columbia. Joey could deliver his half of the paper route using his bike with his new basket. I'd have to walk. And then Pop came up and he said, "Tony, come here." I got up. He didn't try to comfort me, he just wanted me to do something. He pulled down the attic stairs which were on a spring and

folded up and most of the time you forgot it was there except just before
and just after Christmas when we'd have to go up there and get the dec-
orations out or put them away. "Come on," Pop said. "Help me with this."
I was trying real hard not to cry because I didn't want him to know but
I knew he knew and that embarrassed me. "There's something back up in
the corner that I forgot to bring down. It's under the awnings." So I went
up to get whatever it was and it was a red 24-inch Columbia and I wasn't
sure even who it was for and I was afraid to even smile because I was
afraid it wasn't for me. I didn't even hear him come up behind me until
he said, "That's your size, isn't it?" And I couldn't even say thanks be-
cause I couldn't believe it because it didn't happen like I wanted it to. It
hadn't been under the tree.

He sat on the back porch, tight against the wall, shivering, teeth chattering, chain-smoking his Pall Malls. The night was clear. A fingernail
moon hung over the porch and lumberyard, over the town and endless
mountains. He was thinking about logistics, about infiltration, snipers,
intelligence, was thinking about invisibility, how much and how long
should he remain invisible. Then he was not thinking at all, not shivering
at all because the diazepam was kicking in and accentuating the grass
he'd smoked earlier.

Inside, Linda was finishing up the decorations, the wrappings. At
seven and a half months Gina and Michelle were sleeping longer, giving
Linda more time in the evenings, more rest through the night. They were
too young to be excited about Christmas, yet Linda dutifully, carefully
wrapped packages from Santa. She wrapped one for Jessie Taynor, too,
just a cheap bracelet, but she wanted Jessie to have something feminine.
And for Jo and John Sr. to whom she signed the card, "Love Tony, Linda,
Gina and Michelle." And to Aunt Isabella, Annalisa, Uncle James, Johnny
and Molly, Joe and Mark, and Nonna. And to her own mother and father
even if her father still would not speak to her.

Linda wrapped a present too for old Mrs. Victoria Meredith who'd
fired her in October because Jessie Taynor had told Victoria's son that
Linda was not a maid and that Mrs. Merra-dit was a "fuckhead,"
wrapped the gift for Mrs. Meredith as much for having fired her as for
having once been her employer. Having been fired had made Linda
available for her new employer, Mr. Pewel Wapinski. For Mr. Wapinski
she wrapped up packages of comfrey tea and honey, new kitchen towels,
a prism to hang in the kitchen window. Finally she wrapped one more
present, just a slip of paper with three words. And she put them all
under the tree and went to bed.

The fingernail moon slid to the horizon, hesitated in the spikes of
barren treetops, disappeared into the valleys behind the ridges. Tony
rose, stepped softly to the door. It was locked. He checked the window.
It was covered with a taut, clear plastic sheet. He moved back to the
door, knelt, felt a mat, felt under it. Nothing. He ran his hand up the

door, across the top molding, down the far side. Still nothing. He checked the window frame, right, top, left, bottom—aha! Under the sill was taped a key. Very slowly, very quietly, he unlocked the door, entered, stood perfectly still. He could hear breathing, hear the creak of the floor as he shifted his weight. The nursery was lit with a seven-watt night-light. Light came through the doorway, illuminated the short hall and the edge of the living room. He stepped slowly, cautiously. When the floor creaked he froze, listened, counted to 120, stepped again. This to him was exciting, more exciting than anything he'd done in he did not know how long—a mission. He reached the living room, made out the outline of the tree, knelt, slowly unzipped his leather jacket, unwound his wool scarf, reached into his wool shirt, removed the small boxes. Two contained plastic-bead necklaces. The third a gold chain necklace with matching chain-hoop earrings. On the tiny blank card he'd written, "Peace on earth to men of goodwill."

Tony stood, moved to the nursery, looked at his daughters in their crib. So little had he seen infants that at first he could not differentiate the scrunched up lump of one, the sprawling lump of the other, from the folds and curls of blanket and lumps of stuffed animals, then seeing them, he was shocked at their size, little people already. He imagined Linda coming up behind him, putting her arms around his waist, hugging him, saying, "They're yours, too, you know. You could be here with them." For a time he watched them but they did not move and Linda did not come. He crossed the small hall to where Linda slept, to where he'd lain that last night with the shotgun, the thoughts rushing back but now, awake, erect, watching, seeing Linda, he stopped the thoughts, stopped them dead, pushed them back. Now as he watched Linda sleep, made out the silhouette of her face against the pillow, the curves of her body beneath the blankets, the beauty of her one foot sticking out, that foot he'd kissed at World's End State Park, kissed . . . He could not watch her. Quietly, quickly, he withdrew—out the hall, the living room, kitchen, onto the porch, into that bitter cold, replacing the key, then just sitting on that top step, shivering, teeth chattering, chain-smoking his Pall Malls.

Christmas morning—It was almost eleven. Linda was beside herself. She wanted to call Jo and John Sr., call Mr. Wapinski, call someone, talk to someone besides the two babies. But say what? Say he'd come in the night! Been there! She wasn't even certain. It must have been him, Linda thought. It scared her, someone coming in while they slept. " . . . to men of goodwill." It sounded like him. She was behind schedule. Jo was making braciola, ziti, and chicken. Isabella was making a roast. Uncle Ernie, Aunt Ann and their three daughters, Linda hardly knew them, were coming from Rock Ridge, to Jo's, for Christmas dinner, plus, plus, twenty-five or -six or -seven in all and Linda had only made two pies, and Oh God the necklace and earrings were beautiful but where the hell was he! She'd looked out the window, looked quickly out all the windows searching, turning back to check on Gina, Michelle crying because she couldn't get down, no Harley, who'd ride in frigid December, except of course, he'd ridden all year up in Boston, no Tony, who to call, bother on Christmas morning—except maybe Mr. Wapinski—one more look and . . .

He was on the porch, tight against the wall, his legs pulled up tight, his arms around his knees, his face buried, an old wool army blanket over him.

"Tony," she said. He looked up. His nose was running. He looked very frightened. "Tony," she said gently.

"Hi Babe," he said. Then he cringed as if she was about to kick him, boot him off the porch, down the stairs.

Linda was dumbfounded.

"I'll go," he said quickly. "I shouldn't have come. I'm sorry." He stood. He was shivering uncontrollably.

"Come in here," she said. It was not an invitation but an order. She grabbed him, afraid he was going to topple down the stairs. She ran one hand down his arm to his hand which was in his jacket pocket. His hand was cool, not frostbitten cold, still, to her, too cool to be healthy. He squeezed the tips of her fingers in his pocket, did not want to let go. Linda did not know how to feel. Tony looked awful, drawn, pale. "Come in," she repeated. "I've got something for you, too." She was still holding him, still had her hand in his jacket pocket, could feel the bottles, vials. "What's this?" She backed away, withdrew a bottle, read the label:

> Rock Ridge Veterans Medical Center
> Anthony F. Pisano
> as needed to control anxiety
> 10mg – 30
> SK-Thorazine
> (Chlorpromazine)

"Thorazine! Veterans Med . . . Are, are you . . . "

"Crazy." He did not look at her but let her pull him into the kitchen. Gina cruised to the archway, stared up. Michelle was whimpering at the couch.

"No you're not," Linda said. "Anxiety reactions are curable." She went to the living room, helped Michelle down, went to the tree.

Tony was afraid to move. "They didn't cure me, Babe."

Michelle crawled past her sister, grunted. Gina let go, took a step, fell on her bottom, crawled too, clucking at Michelle, both moving without fear to Tony's feet, then rocking back, plopping on their bottoms, looking up wide-eyed, interested.

"That's Michelle," Linda said indicating the infant at Tony's right foot. "And this is Gina. They're your daughters and they need you. Pick them up."

"I—I'm dirty."

"I'll wash them later."

"What if..."

"You won't drop them."

Tony bent, smiled, laughed a small laugh, let the laugh be stifled by self-consciousness. Still he lifted Michelle. She grabbed his collar, looked at her mother. Gina grabbed Tony's pant leg, pulled herself up to standing. Now Tony did smile.

"We're suppose to be at your mother's..." Linda began.

"NO! Ah... I can't."

"Um." Linda said. "It's Christmas, you know. The necklace and earrings are beautiful. Thank you." Tony smiled sheepishly. "I have something for you, too," Linda said. She took Michelle from him, handed him the small light box. Then she lifted Gina. "Go on. Open it."

Tony peeled the tape back as Jo would have, so as not to damage the wrapping paper. In the box there was a slip of paper and on it were the words, "All My Love."

August 1984

One result of Viet Nam homecoming experiences was poor decision making. It was Bobby marrying Red; Ty getting involved with a fourteen-year-old; me not seeking help, losing Linda, Gina and Michelle. It was the inability to make overtly difficult decisions that might disappoint others and incur their rejection or wrath. And it was Watergate, Phnom Penh, El Salvador, Teheran, Beirut, Afghanistan, Iran-Contra. . . . The result hit more than individual returnees.

There is a system of cleansing that Bobby introduced us to. It's not original; my brother John did it in Boy Scouts when he went for the Order of the Arrow. It's much older than that, though. Native American lore contains accounts, as does the New Testament. Most famous of all is the Buddha's long and extreme exercise. One eats as little as possible. Maybe sits in a sweat shed. Maybe bakes beneath the summer sun. Maybe walks across the desert. Maybe goes to a fire circle, alone, with only water.

Cleansing. I've grown to detest the word *healing*. It's been overused, abused, mutated for political advantage. Same-same catharsis. Catharsis equals defecation—i.e., purging; the discharge of pent-up, socially unacceptable emotions, thoughts, beliefs. I'm not certain that *cleansing* is a better word. By it I do not mean to wash away but to elucidate via removing extraneous adjunct. Do not purge us of our past. The experience was not so much excrement. Purge, and the results will be additional poor decision making.

The night cleansing begins, the storms break. At first this is difficult. Blood sugar drops. You become depressive. Then your body adjusts. Soon it burns itself, burns fat, that tissue dumping, along with its stored energy, *toxicants* into the blood, to be used, to be filtered out by kidneys, liver, skin pores—whatever can handle it. What isn't handled re-lodges somewhere else—kidneys, liver, brain, balls. Sometime the tissue—active tissue versus fat, which is inactive—can't handle it and then the dioxins or the methyl ethyl ketones or the alkaloid known as cocaine, or the pesticides and herbicides, the fertilizers and PCBs and new car odor and alcohol and amphetamines and Elavils, they gunk up the cellular genetic mainframe computer and you end up with soft-tissue sarcomas or a plastic anemias, or your crazied goo fertilizes an egg and the fetus develops with multiple deformities.

Cleansing needs to be monitored. Six quarts of water need to be consumed daily to keep a constant flush going. One monitors quietly, looking inside, searching, sensing, feeling for toxicants lodging so that at that precise moment the condition can be controlled—a sugar cube injested—wash, wash, wash. It is as much a mental discipline as a physical cleansing but one no Western scientist, no doctor, will recommend. But then too, they'll tell you no one can read the wind. No one can reach back, expand the frame, the scope, seek enlightenment. What cleansing can not do is allow you, me, America, to return in time, return to remake, unmake, poor decisions.

Night-4. It kicks in with a vengeance. Tires me. I do not wish to talk. Exhausted. Both from lack of sustenance and from rising so often to pee. Yet it exhilarates me. Flying, light-headed. I rise slowly, move slowly, as quietly as possible. The night is dark—no moon, faint stars behind thin clouds, faint flickers of fireflies in the sugarbush. The storms of last week have passed leaving the hill dry, the brush and weeds brittle, the grasses golden, the pond-side rush and reed spotted brown. Bullfrogs belt out their mating calls, or so I imagine. Why else would they make such a racket? It's still warm, I'd guess 80 degrees, humid, a dog-day night. I feel toxicants bursting from their holds, swishing within, coming to the surface, oozing from pores, coating my skin, attempting to reenter. Daily I wash at first light, at midlight, at last light. I creep to the pond on fingers and toes like a sapper. The exertion is tremendous and I sweat heavily. Then I slide between rushes and reeds into the water like an otter, or perhaps like an alligator. How I wish I could be the otter. All night I lie still, except to drink and to relieve myself; toxins swishing in the flood. These days are numbered. It is not evil to die.

Bobby was in a period when his lower head ruled. Our lives continued that descending sine-wave staircase, peak, valley, lower peak, lower valley, testing, tasting of the three temptations, all three now stamped with society's approval or at least condonation, poor decisions or not, up down up down accelerating high, crashing without boundaries, without guidelines, totally free to fleece or fail. "You owe it to yourself, Boy!" "You're worth it." Passwords. Key phrases. Condonation by slogan. Morality by sound byte. Knowledge, analyses, understanding by psychobabble. Otters, it is not evil to play. Bullfrogs, it is not evil to fuck.

For months I meditated upon just that. And on Jimmy's Harley, screaming to me in a wavelength one cannot hear but can feel, sense, a consciousness emanating from molecular vibrations one

sensitizes to through practice, through meditation even if at the time
I had no knowledge of meditation—sensitizes to nature, to the
natural order which includes the life of mountains and meadows,
motorcycles and mankind. It is not evil to die. Recognizing such
alleviates the pain of living, frees one to recognize natural processes.
That freedom is very different from the "freedoms" of the early
seventies that imprisoned as much as the walls of Seven-upper, as
much as that tiny cell where my face was bashed, as much as any
poor decision. Poor decisions have a way of following you, of
multiplying themselves.

14

S an Martin, California, 29 April 1971—Bobby's stomach bounced. The stairs were higher than he remembered. Josh loped lazily as if taunting him, Get the lead out, lard-butt. Five eleven, 208 pounds—thirty pounds heavier than at induction, sixty pounds more than when he'd DEROSed, sixty pounds in twenty-three months—208 on his twenty-fifth birthday and much of it heaving and dropping with each step and him thinking, vaguely, maybe I'll catch a glimpse of Victoria, and, I don't want to be seen by her looking like this, and how did I get so fat in the first place? Blump-blump-blump. Jiggly belly bounce.

Halfway up the stairs beside the lower dam he stopped, bent at the waist, panting. The morning was warm, the sun strong for not-yet-May. He could feel its rays penetrating his neck and shoulders. Josh crested the stairs, vanished. How quickly things had happened in the last six months. He'd barely taken a moment to reflect, had done little but work, eat, drink a few bottles of beer with each late dinner, then sleep, in bed, with Red facing her side of the room, he his. Nationally the economy was still slow but locally it was spurting. Locally there was money, a seemingly endless supply if one knew how to tap it, accelerating development, expansion, growth. Unemployment, foreclosures and bankruptcies were also high, yet those that had, spent. At Great Homes Realty sales were breaking records. Robert Janos Wapinski was making money.

He stared at the crest, glanced at the dry chutes, turned, looked down to the small lot, out to downtown where Bennett, Bennett and Bennett had broken ground for their new financial headquarters, a proposed eight-story edifice taking up the entire Miwok Road block between Second and Third streets, displacing Rheem's Auto Parts and Fonari's Deli and the half-dozen one- to three-bedroom flats above. Already BB&B's steel work was at four stories and higher than any other structure in town, appearing to Bobby, with the morning sun on the far side, dull brown, even black. He thought of Dorsey. Crazy Ty Dorsey was trying to get his piece of the pie, too. Bobby had not seen him, had not talked to him since the day he'd left Bobby's home on Deepwoods. But he'd heard dribs and drabs about him and had received one note without return address.

"It promises to be a colder winter than expected," Ty had written.

> I've got no plans right now as our real estate partnership proved to be but a pleasant mirage and my money is limited. I'll be checking out the city for work suited to an ex-boonie rat.
>
> I keep wondering why my insides twist up when I think of our splitting. Our attachment is shallow so there shouldn't be no twisting. I've split from people I was with a lot longer. But captain, I guess my hopes was more embedded in our friendship then in any of those others. Tell Red I'm sorry if I messed up the house. I appreciate her helping me like she did. And you, captain, my thanks to you too. You helped me set my sights on a target I wouldn't of even seen. Just being with you, captain, watching you think, watching you move, just like in the jungle— you know what I'm saying. I'm going to strive to be like you. Except for where you make people think they can't measure up.

Peter Wilcox had let it slip—through Gloria Spencer, to Bobby—that Ty had purchased a piece of income property in San Martin's old Riverside subdivision, using Peter and his creative financing, as agent both for purchasing and for finding tenants. Ty himself was living in a fleabag boarding hotel down on The Embarcadero in San Francisco.

Bobby began again. His thighs felt leaden. He paused, tried to whistle for Josh but was breathing too hard to control the sound. He pushed on to the top, crested, walked, attempting to catch his breath, barely seeing the water of The Res, barely noting the trees, seeing little except the short stretch of path directly before him. As his breathing settled he looked up, imagined again he was running with Victoria, imagined they took a side trail like Gold Mine out a dozen meters and into a glade. The thought was pleasant.

Bobby began jogging again. He did not move quickly but plodded, pounded like a ponderous stamping machine punching out cheap imprints of his heel bones. The sun seemed to intensify. Sweat, which had been seeping from his pores even before he'd hit the stairs, now cascaded from his brow, from his fat roll and love handles, streamed down his face, down his sides, soaking his old gray sweatshirt. Over his belly the cotton was black with sweat. Drive on! It had taken him an entire month to decide to begin exercising, he wasn't going to quit before he reached the Upper Res and hippie camp. Aw, fuck it! He stopped the jog, walked, tried to catch his breath, placed his right hand on his chest over his heart, felt his ticker banging, felt the surges in his neck.

For four months he had bitten the bullet, kept an even keel, walked the straight and narrow—except on the Somner transaction where the financing had been a work of Mickey Mouse art worthy of Peter Wilcox at his best. With the sweat flowed irritability, bitchiness. Every fucking fiscal step forward was wiped away by Red's habitual need to shop. Every cushion was whisked away. Not a single pleasure was permitted to ripen, to age before instant-gratification picking. Fuck it! He didn't want to think about it. Jog, he ordered himself, jog to the upper steps.

From behind him turmoil erupted; Josh chasing a rabbit, the animals hurtling past him. He tried to speed up. Where at first he had not even seen his surroundings, now elements pulsated at him. Wooden stakes with red or blue numbered tops seemed to leap out. What are they going to build? he thought. Wish I could design it. He recalled an article in the paper suggesting a municipal golf course for those who didn't belong to the country club. Green fees, the article suggested, would make it self-sustaining "as long as the cost of land acquisition and development isn't capitalized."

"Hm. And I'd be a millionaire," Coleman had quipped at an office meeting, "if I could keep all my income and somebody else paid my bills."

Bobby had wanted to add, I'd be rich if Red didn't . . . but he'd censored himself.

He passed the cascades and switchbacks of the upper San Antonio Creek, reached the base of the next staircase. On the first step he saw a bit of fur, on the second a few drops of blood, on the third more fur. He squatted, pinched a small clump between thumb and forefinger. His eyes narrowed. The fur evoked not Josh's triumph but a poster he'd seen a month after—he did not know exactly, had kept an even keel, hadn't made waves—a photograph showing the tips of an adult's fingers holding two teeny legs, the bottom of two teeny feet with ten perfect toes facing out. The cutline read: *10 WEEKS: The structure of the human body is completely formed.*

Bobby flicked the fur from his fingers, wiped his fingertips on his sweat-soaked shirt. His quadriceps quivered. He whistled for Josh, lost his breath. Josh bumped him from behind. Bobby jerked. The dog too was panting. Bobby stroked his head. He couldn't tell if Josh had caught the rabbit.

"C'mon . . . Little Bro." Bobby puffed. "Let's go . . . back. We'll . . . try again . . . later."

As they walked back thoughts leached from data banks to consciousness. Trapped. In his thoughts he spoke to Josh. Trapped, Little Brother. I wonder if she feels it too. I wonder if she's trapped . . . or screwing around. . . . Even in his mind he couldn't admit to that. She'd written their wedding vows, designed and defined their relationship. "Robert, in entering with Beatrice into this marriage, will you honor the commitment to a new reality of joint decision? Will you respect Beatrice for who she is, and nurture her growth as she becomes the woman she wishes to be? Will you be faithful to her through changing climes, and trust her faithfulness to you?"

Trust? Joint decisions? How he craved a loving wife. How badly he wanted her to grow beyond her personal problems. How had he ended up with a woman with so many hang-ups she was incapable of being loving? Trapped. As much as if he were physically restrained by wires, by slow-hardening concrete, by thick layers of fat. Nothing more than a meal ticket!

By the time they were back to the shore of the Lower Res, Bobby's heart rate had settled down and he'd caught his breath. His thoughts changed and the ones of Red, of their wedding and home life, vanished. He thought instead of Mill Creek Falls, of High Meadow, of Grandpa— thank God he's got that lady and her husband and all that maple syrup, ha!; of Brian and Cheryl, whose child was due in six weeks; of Stacy, Miriam, Joanne. He could never go home again, never, not after what he'd done.

He reached the steps beside the lower dam, plunked down the first, second, third, fourth.

"Hi." She startled him. She was powering up the stairs, looking fresh, strong. "Wondered when I'd see you here," Victoria said.

"Oh, hi."

"Can't stop." She passed him. "Maybe see you next time," she called back, crested to the trail, vanished.

"Yeah," he called. He tightened his stomach muscles, sucked in as much as possible, jogged down, his stomach heaving and dropping.

"That's bullshit."

They had been arguing for more than an hour, though most of the time they'd simply stewed in silence in separate rooms, Bobby in the den with the new desk and file cabinet Red had purchased and had had delivered for his birthday, and Red in the kitchen listening to KGO until Bobby came in to refill his coffee cup and she'd exited through the dining area, gone into the living room and plunked down on the sofa with an issue of *Glamour*.

He did not recall the exact onset. He'd been in the den, paying bills, fantasizing about Victoria. He'd only run that once, had let six days pass, had told himself on six consecutive mornings he'd go tomorrow—but he hadn't. His fantasy jumped from Victoria to Red. "You never ask me to make love anymore," she said to him within his mind. "I've given up trying," he responded. "Why?" "Do you read the comics?" he asked. He was melancholy, maybe pathetic. "The comics?" "*Peanuts*," his inner voice said. "You know, Charlie Brown. Every fall, every football season, Lucy holds the ball for Charlie Brown. Every year ol' Chuck runs to kick it and every year just as he's about to connect Lucy pulls back. Well, I feel like Charlie Brown. But not anymore. I'm not going to try anymore. If you're interested, you instigate it." Could he say that? Could he actually lead her through that exchange? Their sexual relationship wasn't just flagging. It was dead. She didn't seem to care. Could he get her, he'd thought, to ask the first question? Or would the hiatus build its own momentum, have its own life. She never initiated sex. It was not her role, not her responsibility. He felt unloved, rejected.

He opened the last of the bills, prioritized them, totaled their debt, their minimum due, reread the offers for new cards, more credit. "What crap," he blurted aloud.

"What is it?" Red had been in the hall.

"These credit companies! What a scam. Did you see this pitch from that new store at North Bay?"

"You mean Empress House?"

"Yeah. What crap."

"They carry a very high quality line of merchandise," Red said. "I applied at the store."

"Oh geez. Don't you have enough . . . Damn it! Look at this!" Bobby grabbed the stack of bills, pulled out the BankAmericard statement, the I. Magnin statement, the Emporium, Roos Atkins, Hastings of S.F., and Saks Fifth Avenue statements . . . " 'Women's bras and girdles,' " he read aloud, " 'is ninety-one twenty-six! Petite sizes: one hundred forty-two fifty! Cosmetics: forty-three fifty-eight!' Look at this one. 'Custom file cabinets—three hundred sixty-seven . . .' "

"Humph!" Red made a face. "It's my money. I earn it. Nobody's going to tell me how to spend it!"

"That's not the point." Bobby's ire rose more quickly than he could ever remember. He was on the verge of leaping at her.

"And that file cabinet was for you!" Red stood in the doorway, feet shoulder width apart, hands on hips, leaning forward at the waist, all ninety-five pounds of her ready to tackle him.

He gritted his teeth, paced his words. "The point is we can't spend more than we take in. The interest on these cards alone—"

"Well, escuuuuusssse me! I'll have them come for the desk tomorrow."

"Geez. Let me finish."

"Humph!"

"We make just so much. If you want something, let's make the money first—"

"Fuck you!"

Bobby almost fell from his chair. He wasn't sure whether to laugh or lash out.

"Fuck you," Red repeated. "I'll open my own accounts. Pay my own bills."

Bobby stared at her. Then he quietly said, "Okay."

"Good." Red straightened up.

"I'll pay the mortgage and utilities, okay?"

"And your car."

"And my car. You pay groceries, your car, your charge cards."

"Fine. But you buy your own clothes."

"Sure. You got it. What about medical . . . "

"You're covered under *my* People's Life policy. Don't you remember?"

"Right."

"See! I'm good for something." She turned away.

The freeze continued through dinner, through her watching TV, folding clothes, ironing; through his finishing with the bills, checking oil and radiator levels and tire pressures on the cars. It thawed slightly at bedtime. Neither apologized. Bobby showered, grabbed his fat rolls, felt disgusted with himself. Red was already in bed, reading.

"If we sold this place," Red said sweetly, "would we have enough for a down payment . . . "

"Did you see something?"

"You know the house on the cul-de-sac that backs to the country club?"

"Lead End?"

"No. Farther in."

"Tin Pan Alley?"

"Yes."

"The Everest Realty listing?"

"I think so. I was just thinking . . . "

"We couldn't afford it right now."

"What if I asked my father for—"

"I don't like this idea."

"It was just a thought."

"Someday."

"Good night." Red turned off the bedside lamp, lay back.

"Good night," Bobby said quietly. He lay down wishing he could love this woman but certain he'd be rejected if he tried—especially after their money talk.

"Oh," Red said. She did not turn toward him. "Did I tell you? Richard and Kathleen are getting a divorce."

"The Townsmarks?"

"Um-hum."

San Francisco, mid-May 1971—He had seen her before though she had probably not seen him, not noticed him. He stood in the aisle, as he usually did, stood hanging on to the overhead chrome bar as the bus turned from Van Ness Avenue onto Broadway. She sat in front—sat always in the same sideways seat behind the driver. He did not know where she got on but he thought it must be at the very start of the run for her always to get the same seat. Neither did he know where she got off because he got off first. But every workday for three weeks, since he'd started the route, he'd seen her, long straight hair, long straight body, bony knees, long fingers, gaunt facial features as if she'd been starving herself—a woman in her midthirties, tired, alone, white. The bus stopped. People shuffled. Ty moved forward. He wanted to be closer to her, wanted to let his eyes penetrate her, take her in, bony knees, straight body, all. He liked her hair, long, dull blond, straight, clean, falling indifferently to the green vinyl seatback, dropping in ribbons to her shoulders, down her chest to her waist. He was neat, clean, professional in appearance among the throng of denim-clad mods and working-class stiffs. Again the bus stopped. People shuffled. He moved closer. She pulled her long narrow feet back against the seat base, momentarily glanced back, then turned forward, faced forward though she sat in the sideways seat. For two weeks he'd meant to check out her face as he boarded. Every time, with people shoving, shuffling on-off, with him trying to situate amid the crowd of straphangers, he'd missed. Now he saw her eyes. They were light blue, lighter than he'd ever seen, the color of rinse water from a watercolor brush dipped but once. Again the shuffle. Again he moved up. He held his left arm cocked at the elbow, his hand by the bottom of the lapel of his suit jacket, his little finger with a fourteen-carat gold and 0.6 carat diamond pinky ring twitching, trying to catch her attention. His eyes were intense upon her, upon her hair, her thin face, her bony knees. He wanted to speak to her, determined that today he would at least nod, get her to acknowledge him. Again the shuffle. One stop to his. He stood less than three feet from her, his eyes burning, his pinky twitching. The bus lurched. He rocked back. From behind someone hit his back with a forearm. Ty turned. "Ah, excuse me." He thought he'd maybe knocked the person behind him when the bus had lurched. A white man, maybe thirty, glared at him. The man was shorter than Ty, stockier, dressed in an Oakland Raiders warm-up jacket. Ty turned forward. Gazed at the thin blonde. They came to his stop. She did not glance at him, did not acknowledge his nod as he moved past. He stepped down, grasped the handrail, stretched to take the long step to the curb. "Uuuff!" A shove from behind toppled him. The white man, before a dozen people, fell on him, whispered, "Stay away from her," stood, backed apologetically, offered Ty his hand, loudly, seemingly horrified by his fall on Ty, roared, "Oh my gosh. I'm sorry. You okay, buddy? I'm really . . ."

Ty held up his hands. With quiet dignity he said, "I'm fine."

He rose, brushed himself off, walked up Davis Street to Vallejo, then to The Embarcadero. The hotel was mold-blackened brick. He entered. The lobby was small, the front desk a counter no more than six feet long. Ty did not look at the concierge, a young lithe white man in a spotless sleeveless undershirt. Ty walked tall, stiff, to the stairs. Very properly he climbed with minimal upper-body movement. The concierge watched him until he made the twist to the second flight.

The stairs narrowed. He climbed to the fourth floor, walked past half a dozen prune-juice brown doors, unlocked his own. Most of the guests were long-term residents, the hotel more a rooming house than a wayfarer's inn. Ty entered, relocked the door, threw the deadbolts, placed four empty bottles on the floor against the stile—an alarm to scare off intruders. The room was small, perhaps eight by ten. To one side was a twin bed, to the other a wooden three-drawer dresser. Against the far wall, beside a narrow window opening to an interior light shaft, stood a two-door sheet-metal locker. The walls were beige, the floor beige, the locker beige. The room was clean—the bed made, the sheets starched—all neat and clean yet dim and dingy. Four books were propped on the dresser. One was on real estate finance; one a guide, *How to Sell Anything;* one on expanding one's vocabulary; one on speech and diction.

Ty surveyed the room. He was satisfied. Everything he needed was here. He was ready. Able. Raring to go, to advance. Very carefully he removed his suit, inspected it for damage from the bus incident. Hell with that broad, he thought. I don't need the hassle. There was a small tear at the right knee. Tomorrow he'd take it to Li Wong's in Chinatown, have Mr. Li stitch, clean and press it. He removed his tie and shirt, hung them in the locker. Removed his ring, gently laid it in the small wooden jewelry box beside his wedding band. In only his underwear and socks he sat quietly on the bed, listened, intent on absorbing the activity of the building. Dropping through the light shaft were sixteen-inch pipes—garbage chutes. From the upper floors came the accelerating Doppler of descending waste. From the central bathrooms came the clang and flush of old pipes and fixtures. Through the walls came muted conversations, the soft lilt of music played at volumes that respected other residents' right to privacy.

Ty slid from the bed to the floor, lifted the thin mattress, worked his hand into a pocket he'd cut and sewn his first night. His hand seized a folded kit bag he'd made from one of the hotel towels. Ty laid the mattress back, unfolded the kit on the neatly made bed, removed the contents. There was $4,000 in cash. He'd sold "his" hot Caddy, the fake plates and forged registration, on the black market—to increase his stake money. He'd added a few dollars from his job as a delivery-service runner (the only one to wear a suit—he'd tell surprised secretaries, attorneys, businessmen, that several of *his* runners had called in sick so he, the proprietor, had come himself). Had added a few dollars from side deals. With the cash was a letter he'd begun writing to his brother Randall, plus two vials.

Methodically Ty opened the pages. "Ran-Ran," he'd written, "times are a little tough but I'm getting my stuff together, eeking out an existence. I don't need much. Don't eat much. If I had a little more money I'd be able to live in a better neighborhood but I'm okay. Have you seen my wife or baby?"

He hadn't written further.

Ty rose, went to the locker, removed a pack of Kools. He moved back to the floor beside the bed, took two cigarettes from the pack, gently rolled first one, then the other, between thumb and forefinger, loosening and unpacking the tobacco from the thin paper tubes, letting the tobacco pile up on the letter to Randall. Then he opened a vial of skag. He'd purchased one in Hunter's Point for $42; had cut it fifty-fifty with quinine, had a dude on Haight Street lined up to buy one vial for $45. Now he sprinkled just a portion of the heroin from his vial onto the tobacco. Carefully he stirred, coating the dry shreds with the soft powder. Then he repacked the cigarettes, carefully tamping in the tobacco, carefully cleaning the paper of every remnant. Ty repacked the kit, raised the mattress, replaced the contents in the secret slit. Now he smiled, lit the first Kool, inhaled deeply, relaxed. He was *so* careful, so controlled, he knew, just knew, he could handle it. He inhaled the thin blue line of smoke rising from the tip. He felt pleased. Two years earlier he'd been sliding on the muck of Hamburger Hill, getting his ass shot. One year earlier he'd been at Prek Drang, Cambodia, being eaten by mosquitos, scared shitless, unable to eat or sleep, stepping into a punji pit. Man, Ty thought, I owe this to myself. I missed the fun but I ain't . . . No, Man. Talk right. Words are important. I am not going to miss it now. One skag-arette made him mellow, not particularly high. Just nice. Ah, but a little H. A little heroin. What a lovely word. What a strange, beautiful word. There, inside it, was *hero.* He smiled, felt warm. He'd been a hero. He'd always wanted to have the hero within.

"Mr. Dunmore," said Peter Wilcox, "this is Ty Dorsey. He's the man I was telling you about."

Ty took in all of Lloyd Dunmore's demeanor as he produced his business card, handed it to Dunmore with his left hand, his pinky flashing the gold-and-diamond ring. Ty smiled, extended his hand, which Dunmore grabbed robustly and held as he read Ty's card aloud:

> **TYROLIAN FINANCE CORPORATION**
> of
> San Francisco
> Ty E. Dorsey   Director
> The Embarcadero   415-864-5121

"Mr. Dorsey, it's my pleasure to meet you," Dunmore said. He was an older man, late fifties, heavyset but hard. "I was telling Peter—I'm going to be very frank with you—I didn't understand all this civil rights stuff when it started and I don't understand it all now. I'm a Christian, Mr. Dorsey. I don't care if you're black or white or green. But the government cares and I do understand how maybe society has been structured to keep coloreds out. But I don't care about your color. If you can do the job, if we can work together, that's all I want."

"And Mr. Dunmore," Ty said respectfully, "I don't care about your color either. If you can do the job, and Peter's told me of your track record, that's what I'm concerned with. The bottom line. Hey," Ty winked, "ya gotta eat. Ya gotta make money."

Dunmore looked up at Ty, then to Wilcox. "Peter," he said, "I think I'm going to like this boy."

For an hour they talked, hammered out the details. "Then it's set," Dunmore finally said. "You put up three thousand, take the property in your name. I'll put up twenty-seven thousand plus closing costs. In two years we'll sell it. You get your ten percent plus twenty percent of the appreciation minus my carrying costs and the costs of repairs." Ty nodded his agreement. "Stay with me, son," Lloyd Dunmore said. "You get me off the hook on this red-lining charge and I'll send some people your way. I just have the feeling Tyrolian Finance Corp. is maybe a little undercapitalized."

"Maybe a little, Mr. Dunmore." Ty leaned back, took a pack of Kools from his pocket. "Maybe a little," Ty repeated, "but it's moving in the right direction." He stood. "By the way," he said, "when do I see the property?"

"Anytime," Peter said. "Anytime."

Neither Peter Wilcox nor Lloyd Dunmore showed. Instead, as a favor to Peter, Lisa Fonari sat in her Capri convertible before the sprawling nineteenth-century Victorian so far out Miwok Road as to be through the pass between North and South peaks, beyond the fields and pastures and low woodland and back into a tight canyon where redwoods grew from the bottom and Miwok Road—here barely a lane wide—twisted and turned between the trunks. The sun was high and strong, the air still. Lisa had parked in a filtered shaft of light, her face tilted up. Birds chirped. Squirrels scurried. She lounged, glanced at her watch, squinched her mouth, huffed to herself, feeling used, laid back to soak up more sun—waiting, attempting to be patient, growing more and more antsy with each passing second, finally thinking, Screw Wilcox! Let him wait for his own clients. I don't see why Bobby couldn't know! She huffed again, gathered herself in, grasped the steering wheel, turned the ignition key, began to leave.

A late-model Chrysler sauntering up the canyon blocked her retreat. "Hello." Ty leaned from the window, waved. "Sorry if I'm late. You're Lisa, aren't you?"

She backed up, reparked. He followed her, parked grill-to-grill with her Capri. "You're Wapinski's friend, aren't you?"

"Yes." Ty smiled broadly, displayed himself before her, before this lovely woman, he in his finery, his expensive if rented car, his muscular six-one frame. They stood downhill from the Victorian. The stairs and walkway were stone, laid perhaps eighty years earlier, not once repaired in all that time. "So this is it, huh?"

"That's it." Lisa shrugged. "How come you're using Wilcox," she asked, brash, forward, "instead of Bob?"

Ty looked down at her, didn't answer. "Are you going to take me through?"

Lisa flipped a hand up the walk. Some stones had separated leaving large gaps; some had slipped one atop another; some had slid sideways out of line. The huge veranda matched the stone entry, corners sagging, boards askew, base so eaten by powder-post beetles that crossing to the door was hazardous.

"This is it, huh?" Ty repeated.

"This is it," Lisa answered again. "She's got six apartments inside, and the toolshed out back has its own bath and is rented out to a student from College of Marin. How come you're not using Wapinski?"

Again Ty eyed her. Then he said, "I don't think he wanted me to buy anything."

Lisa smirked, thought, I wouldn't sell this place to a friend either; but for once she held her comment.

"This is a dump," Ty said. They passed from one room to the next, through makeshift doorways, jerry-rigged halls. The floors tilted as much as those in a fun house, creaked as if splintering under their weight. They climbed the stairs. The banister and balusters were ornate, carved, turned, and built-up, but many of the joints had slipped and even under dozens of layers of paint the gaps were wide. The separate rooms, "apartments," were without exception messy and filthy. Every tenant was a student or ex-student. Walls had been papered with rock-concert posters or sprayed with fluorescent paint. Windows were covered with sheets or not covered at all. In one room the tenant had half a dozen photos of herself, naked, with half a dozen different partners.

"What are you going to do with it?" Lisa asked.

"With what?" Ty was nauseated. The building that he'd just sunk most of his money into was worse than anything he'd seen in Coal Hill, dirtier than most of the refugee hootches he'd seen in Viet Nam. Yet in every apartment he saw expensive items: stereos, radios, cameras, make-up mirrors, lava lamps, leather pants and jackets, musical instruments, bicycles. All the good items were covered with dirt, stained, thrown in heaps with unwashed clothes, sitting on counters with week-, month-old pots and pans and pizza boxes.

"With this place!" Lisa snapped. "You know the units are illegal. This is single-family zoning out—"

"I know."

"So?"

"So what?"

"Do you know what you've bought?"

"I can see." They moved outside, strode to the toolshed where Ty looked in, gagged, almost fell through the floor where it had rotted out and where the tenant had lifted a covering strip of plywood so as to use the hole as a garbage chute even though the ground was but two feet below and there was no place for the garbage to chute to.

"Maybe he didn't show it to you because he didn't think it was worth it." Lisa was angry. Her time was being wasted, and she felt her favor was part of an overall sham she hadn't been told about.

"Maybe he jus don't believe in me." Ty too was angry. He needed to justify himself, needed this woman to know that he knew what he was doing, to know he hadn't been taken, to know he was on the move, advancing. "Look there," Ty said indicating nothing particular but gestering toward the house. "Right now she's making $720 each month. That'll carry it. More than carry it. And I've got a silent partner. In a year we'll gut it; restore it. This place is going to be a mansion. It's going to be worth a quarter million dollars. You watch. You'll see."

Tuesday, 15 June 1971—He had been winning but now was no longer winning. He was anxious. He did not let it show. Instead he joked, continued to work methodically, drew on his every reserve of patience. His last three transactions had fallen apart in escrow. He had not closed a deal since mid-April. There had been no commissions. He had no sales in escrow, no imminent prospects. The market spurt had soured and the entire office staff was in a slump. And now these reports: one more load of shit dumped on his head, one more load to carry through the day.

Dan Coleman poked his head through the door of the conference room, saw Wapinski with the morning paper, cleared his throat. "Hi." Wap looked up. "What's happening?" Coleman said.

"Hey," Bobby answered. "Didja hear the one about the landlord with two vices?" Coleman began chuckling even before Wapinski delivered the punch line. "He became the lessor of two evils."

Again Coleman laughed. Then he said, "You get to the local yet?"

"No," Bobby answered.

"I'll wait till you read it."

"Read what? There's all this stuff . . . " He paused, turned back to the front page, read the four-line headline aloud. " 'Viet Nam Archives—I: Pentagon Study Traces Three Decades of Growing US Role in Indochina.' Did you read this?"

"I only glanced at it. Probably read it later. That's yesterday's, isn't it?"

"Yeah. Listen to this. 'A vast study of how the United States went to war in Indochina, conducted by the Pentagon three years ago, demonstrates that four administrations progressively developed a sense of commitment to non-Communist Vietnam, a readiness to fight the North to protect the South and an ultimate frustration with this effort—' "

"Yeah," Coleman interrupted him. "Talk about a sense of commitment, have you met Olivia yet?"

"Who?"

Coleman patted his hand on the air signaling Wapinski to keep it down. "Olivia," he whispered. "Twenty-seven. I don't know where Peter finds em. Goddamn, Man, another knockout. Between staring at Sharon and ogling Olivia, I'm never goina get anything done down here."

"Well"—Bobby stood—"tell me." For a minute they stood in the doorway peering into the hall, looking like two shy high-school sophomores hoping to catch a glimpse of the senior cheerleaders, Coleman sighing, offering to help Bobby train Olivia.

They realized how silly they were being, chuckled at themselves. Coleman said, "Read the part on The Res. Today's paper. We'll talk after the meeting."

"Good."

"Why's it Tuesday this week, anyway?"

"Ah, Peter's got business in Santa Rosa tomorrow."

"New office?"

"Hasn't told me." Coleman left. Slyly Bobby gazed forward, hoping to catch a glimpse of the new agent.

An hour later all of the salespeople were seated about the table in the conference room. They'd completed old business, new business, introductions to Olivia Taft, Peter's bottom-line talk. "I expect people to deliver, to produce, to keep their commitments. Maybe that's hard but I'm not doing anybody a favor here by letting you work if you're not making money. That's the bottom line. . . . "

Peter turned the meeting over to Bobby, left for an appointment.

The salespeople began chatting. Al went to the kitchenette for more coffee; Jane Boswell passed around a tray of homemade tea cakes. Bobby turned, waiting for Al, attempting to let his gaze pass nonchalantly over Olivia. He raised his eyes to Sharon, glanced to the other women, trying to hide that he knew they knew he was ogling the new saleswoman.

Olivia Taft was beautiful, another beautiful woman in an office blessed with well-dressed, good-looking women. She had all the perfect visual qualities of Sharon, the best of Jane and of Lisa—yet she looked nothing at all like any of them. Her hair was dark, yet her skin was light, almost ashen—winter colors that she accentuated with black eyeliner, crimson lipstick, a white dress with a high-contrast pattern of small navy roses. Her eyes were blue, her earrings, bracelets, sandals silver.

Bobby's heart thumped. Somehow, to him, in contrast to his personal life, it did not seem fair. "Respect," he said quietly. Al Bartecchi poured coffee. "Respect for your clients, for people in general."

Lisa clicked her tongue, her eyes flashed to the ceiling. Bobby glanced at her. "Only kidding." She smiled sheepishly. But she was not kidding and everyone knew it, tolerating her as she tolerated Bobby's pontifications.

"There are three sayings that irritate me in this business and I'm going to ask you to refrain from using them in this office."

"Is this from Hal and Sal?" Liza Caldicott interrupted.

"No." Bobby was terse. "It's from me."

"Then we don't . . . " Liza began.

"They're not orders," Bobby said.

"Then . . . " Liza began again.

"Perhaps we should listen first," Olivia said firmly. Her tone was sweet but she did not smile either with her mouth or her eyes.

"So say it." Liza fell against the back of her chair, crossed her arms.

" 'Buyers are liars; sellers are story tellers.' " Bobby delivered the real estate salesman's axiom. "Don't say it. Don't think it. It separates you from your clients. And 'Lookie-loos,' as a label for potential purchasers, 'nosy neighbors' or not . . . that's a slur. The one I dislike most—please, do not refer to a property owner who's attempting to market his own property as a 'Friz-bo.' Do you know the general public rates real estate agents next to used car salesmen? That disrespect and distrust may simply be a reaction to the disrespect the average agent shows the general public. Let's not do it."

Without further discussion, without comment, the meeting broke. Only Dan Coleman remained. With his notes he had Tuesday's paper. "You read it yet?"

"The Pentagon . . . "

"The local. Today's. Look here. Eight hundred and seventy-six units."

"Eight hundred? Whoa!"

"Up at The Res. It's already approved. Last night. Some developer from San Diego. God those fuckin idiots want to fuck up northern California just like they've done down there."

"Eight hundred!" Bobby repeated. He took the paper from Dan, laid it open on the conference table. There was a schematic of proposed streets, lots and improvements.

"Eight seventy-six," Coleman reiterated. "All single family but clustered. Eights, tens, and twelves mostly. It's a great plan. But great or not, it's going to ruin The Res. They're goina take the entire north side half a mile up the upper creek."

"Hm. Extending Aaron Road . . . Fuck up the fishin, huh?"

"Fuck up a lot more than that. You said something about this last year. I . . . geez! I really didn't think it'd happen. And I don't think they've projected out the figures."

"Who's doin . . . MacMulqueen Corp."

"Not the developer," Dan said. "The town. Figure it out. Nine hundred houses, four people per, thirty-six hundred people, eighteen hundred kids, eighteen hundred more cars. We'll need a new elementary school. They'll have to add more lights down The Strip, maybe widen it. Probably widen Aaron Road. Maybe need a new fire station. A few more cops. Cry'n out loud, Man. I grew up here! You didn't know the town . . . You know my mother's house on Third? When I was five I used to walk from there across Miwok. You take your life in your hands now. There used to be fields . . . filled, I mean filled, with jack rabbits and snakes. You name it. The creek down here used to have fish, turtles, muskrats. We used to catch the biggest snapping turtles . . . Geez! In the spring these old snappers would come out, come all the way up to lay their eggs. Even they'd cross Miwok. . . . "

"You show this to Peter?"

"He knows."

"What'd he say?"

"What's he always say? 'People've got to live someplace.' "

"And, 'And life goes on.' Right?" Bobby said. Dan clammed up, glanced at Bobby, then away. "Right?" Bobby repeated.

"I grew up here," Dan muttered. "It's becoming a goddamn city. That's the last . . . aw, fuck it." Dan walked out.

Bobby didn't go after him. Instead he reread the article, noted on his pad the names of the MacMulqueen attorneys and executives. He closed the paper, stared at the front-page headline:

No One Really Foresaw
Pentagon Papers—II

> . . . The Phase I deployment of American troops, which was now (Nov '65) nearing its 175,000-man goal, had apparently stopped deterioration in the military situation.
>
> But at the same time, the narrative relates, the enemy had unexpectedly built up . . . 48,550 Communist combat troops in South Vietnam in July 1965 . . . by . . . November . . . 63,550. . . .
>
> The Pentagon study says that the carefully calculated American strategy, with its plan for the number of American troops required to win, did not take escalatory reactions into account.

One more article to cut and store and read when work wasn't so pressing and Red wasn't so . . . He didn't finish the thought but flipped the paper over to fold it and give it back to Dan. On the back was a full-page ad for women's stockings—a fly-away skirt, one fantastic set of legs, surrounding print. Immediately Stacy Carter flashed to his mind. He folded the sections, folded the paper again, huffed, looked down at the date. Only now did he realize it was his anniversary, two years from the day he returned to Mill Creek Falls, to Miriam, to Stacy's "I want you to meet my fiancé."

Wapinski put a hand to his forehead. He did not want to think back to all that shit. He did not want even to think back to last night, back to his breaking down, his caressing Red's shoulders in bed, her immediate tensing at his touch, her silent rigidity as he rolled away.

All day people came and went. All day he was vague, preoccupied. At six thirty Olivia brought him a young couple who'd been sent to her by a friend of her mother's. "Mr. and Mrs. Klemenchich . . ." (*Olivia*, Bobby thought. He liked the way the word felt in his mouth.), "this is Mr. Wapinski, our office manager."

"Bob," Bobby said. "Please call me Bob. And I'm just the assistant manager."

"I'm Rod and this is my wife, Estelle." Rod was big, burly with a full beard and thick uncombed hair. Estelle was dressed in a nurse's uniform, white shoes, stockings, jumper. They exchanged handshakes, pleasantries. Bobby looked to Olivia for an introduction to their housing needs, but none came. Rod wasted no time. "I'll get right to the point," he said. He whipped out a five-by-eight-inch green sheet of paper. "Is this worth squat?"

Bobby glanced at the VA Certificate of Eligibility, noted the issue date—Nov. 28, 1970: the Branch of Service—Army: the Entitlement—PL 358. He nodded, thought to ask Rod about his service, tell him he too was a vet, but he let the urge pass. "With a quarter," Bobby said, "it'll get ya a cup of coffee."

"See!" Rod blurted at Estelle.

"Well, at least we tried," she shot back quietly.

Rod began to rise.

"Wait a minute," Bobby said. Rod paused halfway up. "You want to buy a house?"

Estelle was firm. "Yes."

"Down payment?" Bobby said.

"Squat." Rod collapsed back into the seat, humiliated, angry, looking away from the other three.

"That's why we thought we could buy through the veterans' program. My sister and her husband bought a veteran home in Texas last year and I had a patient who said he bought one in San Leandro. . . ."

"They're more common in the East Bay," Bobby said. "But they're pretty hard here. North Bay sellers just aren't accustomed to paying points and putting up with the delays and restrictions. But there's other ways."

"I don't want to live in a dump." Rod turned, challenging, looking as if he were about to punch out the fat blond boy in the suit across from him.

Bobby smiled. "I'm not talking a dump. What do you do?"

"Duct work."

"Heating and air conditioning," Estelle expanded. "Rod's a private contractor."

"Good," Bobby said.

"I can't stand bosses," Rod said simultaneously.

"File taxes?" Bobby asked.

"No," Rod said angrily. "I'm fuckin Al Capone."

"Oooofff!" Estelle ground her teeth, twisted in her chair. "Can't you even once control your mouth!" To Bobby she said, "Yes, he files. I file for him. He had a profit last year, on the Schedule C, of thirteen thousand four hundred something."

"Four fifty-six," Rod added. "I'm not a bum. I just sunk it all back into a pickup with a utility body. And into my shop."

"I make eighty-five hundred—" Estelle began.

"Eighty-six," Rod corrected.

Bobby took out a form entitled Buyer's Profile; pushed his pen quickly; asked a few questions about debts, loan payments; scribbled a few notes. "Any kids?"

"No."

"Expecting any?"

"Fuck you."

"Rod! Please!! No, we're not."

"Present rent?"

"Two hundred seventy-five."

Bobby mumbled loud enough for Olivia, Estelle, and Rod to hear " . . . twenty-two divided by three point five . . . this is just ballpark—" he flipped to the amortization table, "fifty-seven, fifty-eight thousand dollars . . . You could buy one hell of a house."

"But not VA, huh?"

"We could try, but—" Bobby slapped the desktop, got loud. "Before you clam up, hear me!" That got Rod's attention. Bobby continued. "The market right now, for sellers, is slow. You won't believe some of the financing owners are offering. You qualify for a decent size loan. I could put you in a house, very comfortably, let's say with an eighty percent, forty-thousand-dollar first mortgage—that's about two eighty a month— get the owner to carry a second for the rest—ten thousand at ten percent, fifteen-year schedule, ah, about one ten monthly. All due and payable in say five years."

"Three ninety," Rod stammered. "I'm comfortable with—"

"Wait a minute." Bobby worked the figures quickly, " . . . reduce your taxable income by ninety-five . . . Do you have, let's say three thousand for closing and a little cushion?" Bobby asked.

"Gotta be a catch someplace," Rod snickered.

Estelle's face fell. "Not really," she said.

"That's okay," Bobby said. "We can work around that, too. Try and put some money away. Borrow some from your folks. Put it in an account in your name. Just something to show the bank loan committee. I know the appraiser. I can get him to up his appraisal enough to cover the closing costs. But you've got to make yourselves look good on paper."

"Is that legal?" Rod asked. Though his eyes betrayed disdain, his manner had softened.

"Borderline," Bobby said. "I don't much like bosses either." Rod chuckled knowingly. "The trick here is to find a house you like with a seller willing and able to carry the second and work with us. But there's more out there than you might think."

After the Klemenchichs left, Olivia came back to Bobby, thanked him profusely, then took his hands, tenderly kissed him on the lips, twice. "You look like you needed that," she said sweetly. She did not smile but turned, walked toward the door, turned back, her eyes meeting his. "See you tomorrow."

The evening was cool, misty, typical San Francisco July weather—winds gusting in from the Pacific, thrashing Dutch and Murphy windmills, lifting the scent from the Buffalo Paddock, dipping and churning, buffeting the Portals of the Past, becoming a breeze to the lee of Strawberry Hill, aromas mixing with rose essence from the Japanese Tea Garden and music from the Golden Gate Park Band Concourse. He had come to escape The Embarcadero, the dark halls of the residence hotel, the dim lobby, the concierge's watchful, desiring eye. He had come to ponder, to assess, to plan. The big Victorian fixer-upper at the end of Miwok Road was now in his name. So too the small two-bedroom house in Riverside—that one without covert contracts. But Ty Dorsey was nearly broke. The purchases and unseen fees had taken all his capital. He had barely enough money for the seven-dollar per week rent, or for an occasional peroshki from the Russian kiosk just south of Kezar Stadium and the park. The kiosk was closing, the merchant lowering the shutters, locking them to the narrow grease-splattered counters. Ty's stomach gurgled. His tongue rolled in his mouth coaxing the heavy flow of saliva back to be swallowed, unused. He walked on, following South Drive to the Baseball Meadows, trying to walk gently so as not to wear out his shoes, trying to think of a new way to make money, big money for more property, thinking of dope, grass, hashish, heroin, thinking it was not enough money and when was Lloyd Dunmore going to send him someone with cash to invest as he had promised.

She had driven up from Palo Alto or Menlo Park or Atherton. The car belonged to her father whom she despised because he worked and earned and was serious and could afford the Oldsmobile which used precious fuels and polluted the air and was a symbol to her of their bourgeois decadence which she despised as much as she despised the car and her father and, she said the words as she searched his face for acceptance, "racial intolerance."

He was tall, strong, black. She was hefty, of medium height, white. He was impeccably groomed: his shirt, trousers, shoes meticulously worn. She bordered on slovenly, her dungarees worn at the knee, ripped at the ass; her tank top stained, loose, a shoulder strap falling, exposing the plump upper skin of a tanned, braless tit.

She was starry-eyed, yet serious. She wanted to give herself to him, had come to the city to give herself to a black man, on a blanket that she'd brought, under the exotic trees of Strybing Arboretum. Her love was free. Her body was a political statement. The act, in some small way, was repayment for what her father, and all her white forefathers, had done to the Africans, repayment for dislocation, enslavement, carpetbaggers, segregated lunch counters, George Wallace, J. Edgar Hoover, the KKK and the FBI.

He was not starry-eyed but horny. He had not been with a woman in a long time. They cost money. They'd have to wait. But she was free. He didn't have to buy her a drink, dinner. Indeed, she'd offered, during intercourse, to take him to a restaurant! She was passive, detached as he worked away. He liked her hair, long, straight, spreading like rays, like a halo on the blanket under the trees in Golden Gate Park on an evening in mid-July 1971. Afterward he wanted to wash, talk a little, maybe make a date to do it again. She just wanted to leave—like someone coming into court to pay a parking ticket, "You got my payment, now let me out of here!"

"Hey, wait a minute," Ty said. He felt bewildered.

She carried the blanket, paced steadily toward her father's Oldsmobile, barely glanced back.

"Wait a minute," Ty called louder. He jammed his shirttails into his trousers, jogged toward her. "Hey, I—" She opened the trunk, tossed in the blanket, slammed the lid. Her breasts bobbled. He caught up to her. "Hey, I don't even know your name."

"Names are meaningless," she said. She opened the driver's door.

"Come on, Lady." Ty smiled, attempted to be charming even as he rushed to intercept her fleeing. "You know, you've got a lovely shaped face. I'd like—" She got in, slammed the door. He placed his hands on top of the half-opened window, clicked his pinky ring against the glass. "Aw, don't just split."

"I have to go."

"My name's Ty. Ty Dorsey. Let me give you my card. I'm a financial—"

"No." She said the word sharp, loud. "Don't tell me. That's not what this is—"

"Oh, for God's—"

She started the car. He held the window. She began to roll it up. "Maybe another time, Mr. Black," she said, or at least he thought he heard her say.

He withdrew his right hand, she shifted into drive, rolled forward.

"Hey! Stop!" He screamed. He ran. His left hand was stuck in the window. He ran trying to extricate his fingers. "STOP!" She gunned the engine. The Oldsmobile's suspension compressed, the car leaped forward. Ty stumbled, his left arm jerked, his shoulder, elbow stretched straight. Then the car was gone and there was terrible pain in his wrist and the back of his hand and he grasped his left hand with his right. He was on his knees on South Drive in Golden Gate Park, cradling his left hand to his stomach, afraid to look, afraid, finally opening his right, seeing blood, knowing it was staining his trousers, his shirt, seeing fingers, sighing with relief, turning his hand to see the cut, seeing the bone, the last socket, the pinky and ring gone.

The pain in his hand, his entire arm, up through his shoulder to his neck, was incredible. For three days he'd suffered in his room, alone, afraid. He had no insurance, no money, none for doctors, none for emergency rooms, none for someone who might ask who he was, or had been. He smoked a skag-arette, another, another. There was money for that—not a lot, enough to let this one pleasure pay for itself. He smoked, lay on the bed, thrashed back and forth, angry at the pain, the loss of the pinky, the ring. The fat fag upstairs, that's how he always thought of him, the fat fag, he'd been there the evening Ty had returned, Ty's hand wrapped in toilet paper and paper towels from a gas station rest room, had seen the blood on Ty's shirt and trousers and shoes and had helped him upstairs to his sixth-floor apartment, a real apartment with kitchenette and its own bath, where they'd unwrapped the paper towels and toilet paper and Ty babbled uncontrollably, unstoppable, exactly what had happened, right down to the carats of the ring and he bet that the bitch wouldn't even try to return it to him, but had probably thrown ring and finger out on Nineteenth Avenue and was too dumb to stop. The fat fag had washed the wound then rolled Ty's good right arm over, tied off, slapped up a vein and shot in a speedball that almost knocked Ty to the floor as it blew the top of his head off, the IV heroin kicking in a hundred times stronger than anything Ty had ever done in his life.

The next day, before dawn, he'd been awakened by the pain, waking in only his underwear on the fat fag's sofa, as horrified by what might have transpired while he was in la-la-land as he was by the stabbing, pulsing realization that his finger had been ripped off. He'd stumbled out, nauseated, scared, stumbled to the stairs, descended the two flights, retched dry bile heaves, only then realizing he didn't have his pants, his keys, wincing, climbing back, knocking for the fat fag, begging for his clothes, the man so sweet, so concerned, begging him to come back in, to let himself be taken care of until Ty became ornery, then enraged, and the man gave him his clothes and tried to help him but Ty shrugged him off and the man followed him a cautious three or four paces back until Ty opened his own door and slammed it. For three days he suffered, alone, afraid, smoking all the dope he'd bought for resale, injesting nothing but Coca-cola from the glass bottles he'd purchased to use as additional alarm bottles at the door-stile if and when he ever drank the contents.

"He's going to China."

"Who's going to China?"

"Nixon."

"Nixon's going to China?!"

"Don't you listen to the news? It was on the news last night."

"I—I didn't watch it."

"The paper?"

"Haven't read it yet."

"Bobby!" Sharon began to laugh, not cruelly, not with the least bit of reproach, but with mirth and amusement. "You know, this is really a big story."

"Is it?"

"Yes, it is. He said he's going to seek normalized relations."

"Who?"

"Nixon." Sharon smiled, shook her head. "I think it might mean the end of the war."

"Oh." Bobby screwed up his eyes, his nose, pursed his mouth, knowing it would make Sharon laugh again. "Really?"

"Oh." Sharon jabbed him on the shoulder. "You knew it all the time. Stop pulling my leg." Bobby glanced down at Sharon's legs. She was wearing pants. Still she fidgeted playfully. "I bet I do know something you haven't heard," she said.

"What's that?" His mind had not assimilated, processed, projected anything about the China news which he had not previously heard.

Sharon moved closer. "That big turkey that Peter listed and sold . . . " Her voice was conspiratorial.

"You mean the Victorian way out on Miwok?"

Sharon moved even closer. "Um-hmm." She whispered, "The town's seeking an injunction against the new owner."

"Why?" Bobby had not heard this either.

"They were fixing it up . . . " Sharon began.

"Yeah," Bobby said. "It certainly needed it."

" . . . but they were also expanding it and keeping the apartments. I think Peter made a deal with the building inspector that it could be fixed but the inspector said okay only if they stayed within the existing foundation. Lisa says they pushed out the back about twenty feet for four more units."

"That's zoned single-family . . . "

"Hm-hmm."

"I bet they get away with it."

"I don't know."

Bobby didn't answer. He looked Sharon up and down, looked away. He wanted to compliment her, wanted to tell her how much he admired her, her smile, her pleasant approach to life. He fantasized about her on and off, but had always remained perfectly proper. In some fantasies she had left her boyfriend, Red had been killed in an auto accident—something very clean and very sad—and an appropriate amount of time had passed. They were in the office, alone, exactly as they were now.

"Anyway," Sharon caught his wandering mind, "I think if you get the listing on that old Third Street duplex, I've got an investor who'd be interested."

"What perfume are you wearing?"

"Hmm?" Her whole face lit.

"Ah . . . it . . . it's really nice."

"It's just Chanel," she said. "Nothing fancy."

"It's really nice," he repeated.

"Thank you," Sharon said. Then she laughed and smiled. "You're losing weight, aren't you?"

"A little," Bobby said. "I can't believe how fat I've gotten. I've never been fat."

"You're not fat."

"Fatter than I should be. But I've cut out drinking beer with dinner. I think it's the beer doing it."

In August the Klemenchichs got their house. The widow, Mrs. Watercross, was delighted. Bobby had listed her property for three thousand dollars more than he (and she, too, after seeing the comparable sales list Bobby had prepared) believed was top dollar. Then that lovely young woman had brought her a full-price offer with a thirty-day close. Together, Bobby and Olivia Taft showed Mrs. Watercross how she could have the best of both immediate cash plus income. Mrs. Watercross adored Estelle Klemenchich. She was happy that Estelle was thinking of raising a family in the same house that she herself had raised her own children. Bobby too was thrilled. The commission broke his dry spell. He was back on track. He had money in his pocket. And luck upon luck, he'd just "made" another ten at North Bay Mall, "the easiest ten bucks I ever made" is how Al Bartecchi quoted him when Al told Dan Coleman later that afternoon.

"Naw," Dan had said. "Wapinski wouldn't do that."

"That's what he told me." Al flipped a dispirited hand, grunted.

"He didn't say anything?!"

"Nope." Al was disappointed. His feelings infected Dan.

"You mean he knew the store undercharged him and he—"

"He was bragging about it."

"Maybe he's been around Peter too long."

"Maybe. I mean he was *really* happy."

"What'd you say to him?"

"Nothing at first."

"Nothing?"

"Well, Jane was there. She likes him, you know."

"What'd she say?"

"Nothing. But I don't think she liked that either. When she left I asked him."

"Same as you did with Peter that time?"

"Yeah. I said, 'Bob, what did you just sell for that ten dollars?' He looked at me kind of puzzled. 'Nothing,' he said. 'Yes you did,' I said. I said, 'You sold your honesty for ten bucks. Isn't it worth more than that?' "

"What'd he say?"

"You know. What could he say? I pressed him though. I said, 'Didn't you just sell your integrity for ten bucks?' He said, 'It was Sears! They were probably overcharging me anyway.' I said, 'Probably. But that's not the point. What they do to themselves doesn't concern me. What you do to yourself . . . ' He said, 'Aw, cut the crap. It was a lousy ten bucks,' I just dropped it."

"Well, let it work on his head," Coleman said.

Al chuckled. "Just like you did it to me."

Bobby hated the summer nights of 1971, hated going home, avoided the Deepwoods house like hemophiliacs avoid razors. But he did not know what to do. Occasionally he entered additional thoughts into his journal.

4 July: In the whole time we've been together, I've never asked her to do anything because whenever I have she resents it.

17 July: If I look at Red as a woman she thinks I'm lewd and disgusting. If I don't look at her as a woman she thinks I don't love her.

3 Aug: What I say I want for her, I want for everyone, and I want it badly for her and me. This world is going nuts. There's got to be a better way.

14 Aug: I want to leave her. I don't love her. I do love her but she doesn't love me. I love her but I don't need her. She doesn't want to be married. Cramps her style. She can't fuck around. She doesn't really want me. Not how I want to be wanted.

I bully her. Tell her she's not doing it right. Shoddy. Half-ass. Never finishes anything. Richard Townsmark has been transferred to L.A. Without him, she's in trouble at work for not following through. I love her but I can't live with her like this. If she gets fired . . .

Occasionally he called home. "Happy Birthday, Granpa."

"Bob. Where are you calling from?"

"My office. Did I wake you?"

"Nope. Jus watching the news. Australia and New Zealand say they're goina withdraw all their soldiers from Viet Nam by year's end. You're workin late, eh?"

"It's, ah, only eight ten. How are you?"

"I'm doin jus fine. My friend Tony's not, though."

"Tony? Who's Tony?"

"Linda's husband."

"Oh! You mean your housekeeper . . . with the two babies?"

"Yep. Cept the babies are toddlin all over the place now. How you doin?"

"Fine. Great. I'm sorry I don't call more often. I'm making good money though. I can afford to call more if you don't mind."

"I don't mind. You could write, too. Stamp's only eight cent. Eleven cent air mail."

"Well, I can afford the calls now. Really. I'm sorry I haven't called more. How are you doing?"

"Good. I get a crick in my hip. Sometime it jus gives out but mostly it's okay. When Tony's here he helps. He turned and planted the fields and was doin the barn roof but . . . Ah, well."

"Um."

"How's that little lady a yours doin?"

"She's fine. She might be changing jobs again."

"You two goina come back for that celebration I promised?"

"Not quite yet, but . . . "

"Maybe Thanksgiving? Like you did last year."

"Maybe. We'll have to talk about it."

"Hard to leave all that sunshine, eh?"

"Oh, it's not that. As a matter of fact, sometimes I think I should just pick up and leave."

"How come?"

"You know. There's a certain craziness to this place. Like up at The Res, the local lake. It was all pristine forest and watershed. Then some developer bought it and got permission to put in a subdivision. Wouldn'ta been so bad if he did it like the plans said but instead they just clear cut everything. I called them, tried to get an exclusive right to market their units but they've got their own sales division. Sometimes I wish . . . Sometimes I wish I could design a community where this stuff doesn't happen."

"You can," Pewel Wapinski said. "But you have to start with yourself. It'll come. That was a nice card you sent to Cheryl. Yer brother's been smilin like the cat who got the canary for the whole past month."

"Why'd they call him Anton? That's kind of an odd name, isn't it?"

"Brian said it was Cheryl's idea. She heard it on a soap opera she was watchin before he was born and she fell in love with it."

"Yeah, but *Anton*! Don't they think kids'll make fun of him when he starts school?"

"Maybe. Maybe less than if he were named Pewel. Then he'd really have to fight."

"Oh, ah . . ." Aside, "One second." Then back to the phone, "Granpa, I've got a client just walked in. I'll call next week. Happy Birthday, again."

Bobby hung up. Olivia rested her buttocks on his desk, her stockinged legs, feet together, slanting down beside his chair. "Granpa?" Olivia teased.

Bobby chuckled self-deprecatingly. "My grandfather. He's eighty-two today. I didn't know anyone else was in the office."

"Just me," Olivia said. She lifted one foot and crossed it over her other. Her calf muscle bulged. The ceiling fluorescents glowed ambient but the curve of the bulge still formed an accent shadow that caught his eye. "I heard from Estelle, today," Olivia said. She did not smile but looked sad, serious.

"Klemenchich?" Bobby said.

"Uh-huh. Rod had an accident last Friday."

"Oh." Bobby could barely think with Olivia next to him like that. "Is he okay?"

"It's not life threatening," Olivia said. She uncrossed her legs, put her weight on the one that had been on top, lifted and pointed the other foot, stretching the ankle, rolling it slightly.

"They still like the house . . ."

"Oh. Estelle loves it. But Rod . . . I guess he slipped with a large sheet of metal. Estelle said it split his right palm right to the bones. Almost cut his hand off."

"Ow!" Bobby squirmed in his seat, almost could feel the metal slicing his hand. He twisted toward Olivia.

"Estelle said he had to have major surgery to reattach the tendons or something and that he might not be able to use it for an entire year. She said he might not ever get the use of his fingers back because of nerve damage."

"Oh! The poor guy. He's got insurance though, right?"

"She's got major med that covers him. And there's workman's comp. But they don't think they can keep the house. Could we sell it for them for three thousand more—"

"Three—!"

"To cover the cost of selling—"

"We already boosted the cost."

"I know."

"They've only been in there, what, a month?"

"That's what I told her."

"I don't know. In this market . . . we could try, but . . ."

"It's okay, Bobby," Olivia said. She slid closer. He had one hand on his desk by her hip, the other at the back of his chair, opening himself to her. He leaned back slightly, looked to her face. Slowly she bent, put a hand to his face, kissed his lips. For a moment they remained close, still, their hands met, softly pulled, they kissed again, gently, softly. "I—" Olivia began, stuttered, "I don't want you to do anything to upset your wife."

"She—" Bobby also stuttered, but then blurted, "she doesn't care."

"She doesn't?" Olivia's tone was sad, empathetic.

"No," Bobby said. "She . . . we don't have very much of a relationship."

"I'm sorry."

"It's okay. It's—it's all kinda for show."

"My marriage was like that too."

"That's why you divorced."

"Um-hmm." They kissed again. Olivia slid further along the desk edge until she was in front of him. He stood, kissed her again, again softly, gently, their bodies barely in contact. "Maybe we shouldn't," Olivia said. "At least not until you settle things with your wife."

Confusion continued to reign. Nothing was right. The world was out of kilter and Bobby was perpendicular to the slant, knew he was tilting, knew he'd fall. Half of him didn't give a fucking flying leap. Half of him dreamed on, worried on, bemoaned his lot, his fate. He loved his job, he detested it. It was exciting—the hunt, the tactics of list and sell—but he was not interested, not committed. It was for show. Each time he thought of quitting he'd told himself he would again become engrossed in this business when the commissions became larger. But the opposite was true. He worked for his commissions, worked hard, but whenever he had enough to pay his bills he slacked off. On the drive home he thought of Olivia, of Sharon, of Jane. Even of Lisa Fonari. He thought maybe he wouldn't even go to the office if it wasn't a matter of seeing them. What in hell he was doing with Olivia he didn't know but it was exciting and pleasant and thrilling and everything he could want it to be and everything it wasn't anymore with Red. And yet he knew that he'd rather be with Sharon. Or Victoria. Or Stacy. Aloud he said, "For ten bucks I would sell my integrity if I could undo . . . "

Red's pistachio Pinto was in the driveway. Josh was lying on the small porch, alert, ears up, smiling that happy Pennsylvania Husk-perd smile, his coat glistening in the porch light. Bobby's mind flipped as if he'd not seen him in a long time, not seen him for what he was—not just a dog, not just a faithful friend who could at times be ignored, not even just a symbol of nature, but Bobby's attachment to the world beyond himself, beyond the limits of human concerns, beyond money and bills and shelter and governments and self-promotion.

Bobby opened the car door, reached to gather his books, decided to leave them on the seat. Josh nudged him. He turned, still behind the steering wheel, massaged the dog's ears. Josh groaned.

"Ya know, Little Brother," Bobby whispered, "I've got a dream. I've got this dream of a community where you and I live, where people design and build in harmony with guys like you, ol' buddy. Aw, I'm just getting stupid, Josh. C'mon. Let's go in."

Red was watching TV. She did not look up when Bobby came in, didn't budge until Josh stepped with his front paws onto the living room carpet. Then she clapped her hands twice, glared. Josh backed up, lay down on the mat in the small foyer, his back to the living room, his legs stretched and straight as if rigor mortis had set in, his back and neck arched so he was watching Bobby and Red and the TV.

"What are ya watchin?"

"Ssssh."

"Is it almost over?"

"SSssshH!"

Bobby walked to the kitchen, opened the refrigerator, grabbed a can of beer. But he put it back. Instead he grabbed a glass, ran the tap, drank water. He went to the bedroom, to the closet, pulled out the Saucony running shoes he'd bought but had never used, decided—Tomorrow, I'm really going to start. Red came in.

"Good show?" Bobby asked.

"So-so," Red answered.

"What was it?"

"Oh, it's too complicated to go into. It was pretty good though. You smell like perfume."

Bobby turned his head, sniffed his shoulder. "I do!?"

"Yes."

"Hmm! I don't know . . . Oh. Maybe it's from Olivia. She got a new listing and was so excited she hugged everybody in the office. I was on the phone with Granpa. Today was his birthday, you know. She came around hugging everybody."

"Um."

"Red."

"Um."

"I've been thinking . . . "

"Um."

"Maybe we should look for a different place."

"A new house like the one on Tin Pan Alley? I'd love that. This is such a dump."

"I was thinking . . . "

"We could put in the offer they have to leave the dining room set. It's absolutely perfect in that room."

"No. I mean, I was thinking someplace else."

"Where?"

"I don't know where. Someplace that's got more of a sense of community. Someplace that's not so damn expensive."

"What are you talking about?"

"I mean, like if we helped develop a community."

"You're not talking Pennsylvania!"

"No. Not necessarily."

"If you go back to Pennsylvania, I won't go back with you."

"You won't . . . What the hell's that suppose to mean?"

"I mean I won't go back there. I hated it there, and if you go back, I'm not going."

"What are you saying?" His voice spiked angrily. "You'd leave me?!"

Red backed up, sat on the bed. She eyed him warily. "I won't go back. If you go back, you go back on your own."

"Well, what if I do want to go back?"

"Go back then!" Her voice was hard, not loud. "Take Olivia with you. Don't you think I know?!"

"Know?"

"Cheater! Don't you think I know!" It was no longer a question.

"I haven't cheated on you. I've never cheated on you." Now his index finger, hand, arm were jabbing the air, pointing at her face, eyes, knocking her glare down. "Even though you've given me every reason to cheat," he said loud, angry, "I haven't."

"I still won't go back with you."

"So what's that mean? You want a divorce!" Bobby was livid, feeling self-righteous, abused, more attacked than attacking. Red did not utter a sound. She sat there on the bed, now more passive, eyes down, shoulders curled in. She sat there a victim, incriminating him with her victimization. "Well, fuck you," he roared. Her silence angered him more than any words. "Fuck you. You want a divorce, you can have a divorce. There. Ha!" He stomped. Slammed the door. The entire wall shook.

Still she said nothing. Still she sat there, looking to him as if she weren't a part, weren't a cause, as if she thought she were totally innocent, as if she were the one who'd been abused, who'd suffered through their togetherness. He snorted, still seething yet closer to control. She looked at him. Mumbled something.

"What!?"

"We never should have gotten married," Red said. Again she hung her head. Again he snorted.

Then he went to the phone, dialed, almost as if he were being guided by an outside force, almost without conscious will, as if in a dream:

"Hello."

"Hi, Brian."

"Huh?"

"Oh. Did I wake you?"

"Who . . ."

"It's Rob. I forgot about the time difference."

"Robbie. Geez. It's two o'clock or some . . . You okay?"

"Yeah. I'm sorry if I woke you. But I wanted you to know. Red and I are getting a divorce."

"What?"

"Yeah. I'll call ya tomorrow. Don't tell Granpa, okay?"

"Yeah. Sure."

"Or Miriam."

August 1984

A grunt can cope with monsoons, with leeches, with searing heat, suffocating humidity. The savagery of war does not strip him of his humanity. These things are external. They are not of the self. One does not say, "I am the pain of leeches." One does not say, "I am a firefight." "I am Manny's death." "I am an atrocity." It requires a return to a civilized World to complete that dehumanization.

This became Bobby's theory of the self. As you witness our destruction, you should have our criteria for evaluation. It was maybe six years ago that Bobby said, "In finding one's self one loses one's self and no longer needs to define one's self because one simply is. That is the true self. When one no longer needs to define one's self in terms of possessions, actions, or relationships, the self falls away, opening one up to actions and relationships. Losing one's self frees one to do, to observe, to be observed, to interact without the constraints of looking at one's self through others' eyes, or even one's own. Praise and criticism, real or imagined, block one from developing a value system based on criteria beyond the immediate, beyond the past, beyond projected opinions, polls, the people's will, election results, resale values, net-net-net and myriad other less-than-ultimate criteria. Our problem is searching for ultimate criteria; interpreting actions and thoughts against those criteria; establishing a guide, a code, an ethic, that reflects those criteria."

It was not new, but to him, to us, it seemed like something lost. It had been lost to "our people," lost to our country; and our people and country were floating, a rudderless ship—the rudder voluntarily destroyed or purposefully disconnected in the name of criteria driven by the three great temptations: greed, lust, and power; insidious, manipulative forces like unseen toxins coursing through the system tripping, cutting, causing us to lose our way, to lose opportunities, to feel guilty for what might have been.

The bells of St. Ignat's do not usually ring at this hour, at night, but they are ringing now, shaking me from my thoughts on self. It is day six of my fast. Owls howl. Bats scat. I've deluged my body with so much water it is running out of my pores and orifices and my ass is *so* sore. But it is nothing compared to my mind, my sense of self, at that time.

I want to be fair. Not all private or state or federal veterans medical facilities were as fucked up as Rock Ridge. And even those that were, including Rock Ridge, changed as the 1970s progressed. Change, however, did not necessarily mean improvement.

15

Mill Creek Falls, 1 February 1971—The dawn is winter gray, muted, as if everyone and everything has entered the first stage of a cryonics experiment to suspend animation until a cure is found. Uncle James, Aunt Isabella, Nonna all wear black coats over dark suits, dresses. Annalisa's coat is deep beige but in the winter light inside St. Ignatius' main hall it looks as gray to him as this new layer enwrapping his core, coating all previous layers, his new grayness.

Tony hangs on to Linda's arm, his hand and wrist through her crooked elbow while Linda sits holding Gina, looking forward, listening to the young priest, rapt, attentive to his every word. Twice she has taken Tony to Rock Ridge Veterans Medical Center, twice she has tried to find out what is the matter, what is the illness, the diagnosis, the prognosis. She has talked to clerks, orderlies, secretaries, and the "pharmacist," an orderly at GS-6. Dr. Jonathan Freiburg has not been available, has sidestepped making a firm appointment. The orderlies have told her Tony is a crazy vet.

In the pew beside Linda is Jo. She holds Michelle, is as attentive to the young priest as is Linda but while Gina is asleep in her mother's arms, Michelle is alert, twisting, wanting to crawl, wanting down, and Jo struggles in perfect dignity to subdue her without upsetting her. Next to Tony is his eldest brother, John, who does not touch him, and by whom, because he senses John's revulsion, Tony does not want to be touched. Tony presses closer to Linda, his arm tightening in the crook of her elbow, she aware, stolid, solemn, cutting him no slack. Beyond John Jr. is John Sr. Jo has accepted Tony, accepted the fact that he is ill, infected with some alien virus that will be defeated and soon her son will again be healthy; but John Sr. has not accepted the illness, cannot help but think of a time when he had said to Tony, "God, I hope you handle it better than I did," cannot help but be disappointed, ashamed at the countenance and behavior of his third son.

In the first pew is Uncle James, Aunt Isabella, Annalisa, and Maria Annabella—Nonna, 81 years old, solemn, stolid, dignified; by her presence in the first pew more in control of the mood of the entire congregation, 90 percent Pisanos, Pellegrinos and DeLeones for the first memorial mass, than the young priest at the altar. Uncle Ernie and Aunt May, Maxene, Patty, Julie have come from Rock Ridge, Aunt Mary from Wilkes-Barre, Uncle Frank and Aunt Jessie from Scranton. Even Uncle Joe from Binghamton has come, Joe who is Tony's mother's brother and thus not a "real" uncle of Annalisa and Jimmy but who is, was, will always be Jimmy's uncle in that he will always carry that layer of being a Marine. And on and on back through the church, family, friends, neighbors, even old Pewel Wapinski, whom Linda has told of the service.

Tony clings to Linda. He has dreaded this moment, this day, dreaded it because it again smashes Jimmy's death into his face; dreaded it too because it is his coming out, his first family reunion. He'd hidden in the apartment through Christmas and New Year's and though Linda had told Jo and John Sr., they had allowed him to hide, had not mentioned him to the family, agreeing he needed time to adjust. Tony would like not to be sick but sick is the only justification, in his eyes and theirs, for his behavior. His eyes are red, swollen, sunken, dark. His mouth is dry. He keeps his head bowed as if to hide between his shoulders. He thinks it is better, here, now, to be perceived as a naughty child than as husband, father, cousin of the deceased, Marine. He wishes to leave, to hide. He does not look at his brothers, cousins, does not meet their eyes. Still the double dose of diazepam he has taken has taken the edge off; and clutching Linda, being close to her, bolsters him, bolsters not his spirit but his self-righteous feeling, unverbalized—if she, whom I have so betrayed, accepts me back, so too must all of you. And Linda, like Jo, like Maria Annabella, is stolid, solemn, dignified.

The young priest is preparing the Eucharist, praying over the gifts. Tony has never understood this—this mystery of faith, this essence of the religion in which he was raised. The congregation is singing "All Saints Hymn" but Tony's mouth is too dry. He cannot even hum.

" . . . may your soldiers, faithful, true, and bold; Fight as the saints who nobly fought of old. . . . " He tunes out, thinks he cannot go to Communion, cannot consume the Eucharist, the body and blood of Christ, with diazepam in his stomach. His thoughts flow quickly. He feels the change, the brain numbing, the shutting down. He is holding Manny, who is wounded. His mouth is trembling. He is telling Manny, "It's cool, Man. It's cool. Not bad. Grab your ass and haul it off for like six weeks of R n R. There's a soul sister at the evac gonna do sweet nasties to your bod, Bro." Tony jerks Linda's arm. She jerks back, glares from the corner of her eye. He sees Manny's chest erupt, feels the impact through to his abdomen, feels Manny's splattering spittle and blood . . . Linda jerks her arm again, first forward, then back, hitting him with her elbow. John Jr. glances, glares, pretends to ignore. Tony cowers lower. He can smell the dead gook, the rotten meat, the goo drooling on him as they pull the body, the club being jammed into his face, he is panting, diazepam or not, drooling from the corners of his mouth, dry mouth or not, and then they are outside the church.

"That's incredible." The voice is behind him, soft, sad, concerned. He's not sure how, why, he heard it. Another voice. "He's like a zombie." "She said it's the drugs. They've got him all drugged up." Tony turns. It is Maxene and Annalisa. They turn away as he looks. The sky is light gray, winter overcast, yet to him, bright, making him squint. The words hurt, anger him, he who has protected Annalisa, he who has . . . He cannot think. In deep, below the deadening, he is enraged and the ire splits layers like magma squirting through mantle cracks reaching the lower strata of crust but not breaking through.

More voices. John Sr. to Aunt Helen. "It's a temporary phase. I went through it too." "Not like that you didn't." Like fuckin hell. The words are in his mind, in his throat, trapped. If they acknowledge it, if they deny it, it makes no difference—both piss him off. "We're working on it," Linda says. More anger. Standing in front of the church on a cold, threatening winter morn as if it were some kind of party and not one of them speaking Jimmy's name because that's been left inside with the priest.

More anger. He wants to go to Linda's apartment, he does not think of it as home—but he is helpless. Since the ride on Christmas Eve he has not been on the Harley, has not driven. Linda has taken over all the duties, all the driving. She is so very capable. He wants to go to the apartment, watch some TV. He has taught his daughters to laugh at cartoons though they are too young to pay attention for any length. Still, it is his only chore. Entertain the girls while Linda makes breakfast or dinner or washes the laundry or readies for work where she'll bring the girls with her and he can watch TV and smoke Pall Malls and don't forget your noon meds and I'll be back between five and six depending on how many people are in Morris'. More anger. More anger. His head is throbbing. Gina is crying. These idiots, he thinks. They think they know all the answers. They don't know shit. Jesus Christ, at least with goddamn Darvon I could function. Fuck this Thorazine-diazepam shit.

"Ma." It is John Jr. "I gotta get to work. Are you and Pa goina be at Aunt Izzy's?"

Tony does not hear the answer. Pewel Wapinski is standing before him. "Time to get the maple taps ready, eh?"

"What?"

"Syrupin time, eh?"

"I . . ." Tony looks to Linda, who is rocking back and forth trying to keep Gina from crying so that she can finish her conversation with Dr. Joe, Joey.

"I'm counting on you," Pewel Wapinski says.

It is. It is going to be okay. It's going to be a good year. Like I promised her. Tony is in the sugarbush collecting the first of the thin sap, picking old buckets and new plastic milk jugs from the taps, dumping a cup here, a few drops there, a whole quart—wow! so early—into the larger bucket that he then carries to the tractor and empties into the tank.

In the house Linda is washing dishes as a lasagna, Nonna Pisano's recipe, bakes and fills the house with its aroma. The girls are napping. Pewel is in the barn office designing a "pipeline filter system" so the sap tank on the tractor can be drained into the pipeline which will direct the sap through a series of ever finer filters and deliver a cleaner product to the evaporation tank in the sugar shack. It has been a good few weeks, she is thinking, an amazing turnabout. Together she and Tony flushed the last of the Thorazine tablets down the commode in their apartment. For days he was nauseated, afraid, from withdrawal. She held him, reassured him, read him the Thorazine withdrawal symptoms from her PDR. Then she took the diazepam, and he'd agreed, and she meted it out, one each evening, only if he asked. She is happy to be helping her man. He is gaining back his health. If he is still secretive about his absence, about his hospital stay, that's okay. Someday, she thinks, he will tell me. She smiles as she sponges the counter and drapes the dish towel over the rack so it will dry.

It is almost her fantasy come true—almost like being a family nurse practitioner—caring for the elderly, the adult, the infant. And in the setting of the High Meadow farm. She feels like a country doctor. She looks out the window wondering if Grandpa W. will be in early, if she should make him a snack. Dr. Simon Denham, along with seven other doctors, is planning to open a small medical office complex in the late spring. He's offered her a job. But, she thinks, I'll only work two days a week so I can still work here. This is paradise. Linda has even suggested to Tony that he should think about returning to school.

In the high meadow Tony is trying to get the old tractor started again. It is dusk. His hands have gone numb. His toes sting. "Come on moth-afu—" He clams up. No way, he thinks. I am not going back into that frame of mind. He opens the side cowling. His arms are quivering. He doesn't want to have to walk in, maybe have to leave the sap in the tank—it'll freeze overnight—have to thaw it in the morning before he unloads it. Not enough choke, he thinks, or flooded? "Come on! Damn!" Again he tries to start the engine. I can deal with it. I can deal with it. "Start, you motherfucker!" I can deal . . . Now he does not notice the cold but feels his arms, stomach quiver with anger. He edges out the old choke knob. The motor coughs. "Come on, Babe, you big blue snot." *Ba-da-lumb ba-da-lumb.* Then nothing. "You motherfucken scumbag whore!!!" He is trying to control the volume if not the words. The motor catches. He laughs. "In we go, Babe."

It is now three weeks, three good weeks, each week a little better than the one before. Tony is in the living room with Gina and Michelle and they are "watching" *Leave It to Beaver.* Linda is on the phone with her mother, Norma's third call since Christmas. She has called collect. Henry has been promoted, is in Dallas on business; has been away at least one week each month.

"You don't have to," Linda says. "We're really glad you call."

"I insist. I'll send you the money. It's my call. I just can't let your father . . . "

"I know. I just wish"—Tony walks into the kitchen, opens the refrigerator, takes a can of beer, returns to the TV— "he could accept . . . "

"It's his nurses thing," Norma says. "That and how rude Tony was to us . . . "

"What nurses thing?"

"Oh, you know."

"What?"

"About only sluts being nurses. Oh, I can't believe I said that word."

"Mom!"

"Well, I don't feel that way. Really, Linda, I'm glad you and Tony are back together. Ruthie told me everything. I wanted to call you every day . . . "

"It's okay. Things are going great. I know Daddy . . . "

"He's checked—how do I say this?—he's checked with his attorney for you."

"Checked what?"

"About divorce. If you divorce him you can come home. Henry agreed—"

"That's enough! How can you even say that?"

"Now Linda, you are our daughter first . . . "

They talk on, Norma sympathetic to Linda's plight, Linda not wishing to say anything the least negative that Tony might overhear, unable to detail or defend her situation.

For the twins it is late and they are cranky. Tony, before the optical tranquilizer, is oblivious, as stupified by the commercials as he is by the programs. There is a patient on *Ben Casey* who is beautiful. Tony stares, his eyes focusing on her neck, her chin, hair, face, following the camera's sweep, she is lying on a gurney, her breasts peaking the hospital gown. For Linda and Tony, February, now into March, has been good but it has been sexless. Tony is afraid to sleep with Linda, afraid he'll hurt her, afraid, if she tries, he won't be able to perform, afraid he'll be as he was in the hospital. And Linda's body is no longer taut. He spies on her when she dresses. He sees the dimples on her thighs, the stretch marks on that once perfect abdomen, the heavier breasts with their long nipples which Gina, with her first tooth, has scarred. Still, the more his health returns, the more desirous he is of her. He does not know how she feels. He does not know that she is depressed by her body, her weight, thinks she's gotten ugly. He does not know that she is tired of being touched by others, the nursing babies. He does not know if she will ever be willing, will ever forgive him.

Now he rises. Linda has nursed the girls, changed them, put them in the crib. He does not remember her coming in, taking them. *The Avengers* comes on. He gets another beer, checks the door, windows, looks down back into the lumberyard, out front across and along the street. He goes in, checks on the girls, returns to the TV. Linda sits beside him, puts her arm behind the small of his back, holds him. He has not done this in a long time, not passionately, but he now kisses her, smiles, laughs, the happy-go-lucky Tony there, at least on the surface. Linda giggles too. He kisses her neck, kisses down her blouse, nuzzles between her breasts. He is more erect than he's been in a year, still he is afraid. He pauses, looks back at the TV, is captivated by an image. Linda runs her hand through his hair. She feels his fear, doesn't understand, still she whispers, "It's okay, Babe. We'll take it slow." He does not connect her words to him, to *The Avengers*, to anything at all.

More time passes. Syruping is over. The lower fields, then the high meadow, are turned, fertilized, turned again, planted. Pewel instructs Tony in every aspect, careful at first not to inundate him, but soon finding him eager to learn, eager to do. Tony has never been a good student but now he reads every article Pewel gives him, devours issues of *Farm Digest*. He arrives on the Harley at five, paces until Pewel gives him something to do, works feverishly until Linda and the girls arrive, breaks briefly, then again attacks his chores. March passes; 17 April, the second anniversary of his discharge, goes by. He no longer takes diazepam but has found in Lenny Shepmann a source of weed, marijuana, and yellow-jackets, street amphetamines. He is sure these are good drugs. He again feels alive, positive, in control. Still he hides the grass, the yellowjackets, from Linda. When he can't get yellowjackets he substitutes Benzedrine or Dexedrine—even over-the-counter diet pills. And when he is exhausted, coming down, he drinks beer and smokes grass, sucking smoke to mellow out without the catatonia of the Veterans Medical Center drug cocktail. Most nights he paces the apartment like a caged animal.

Linda is baffled. He was easier to manage when he was helpless. Still there is no sex. Tony can sit, lie still, only when watching TV. But he is positive, playful, occasionally irritable. He talks about another baby, a son, how wonderful it would be to have a son. He caresses Linda, whispers, "How'd you like a dick up your ass? How'd you like me to lick your entire body?" He comes in from the field, fondles her in Pewel's kitchen, holds her from behind, kisses her ears as she squirms to get away. The work is good for him. His arms are hard, sinewy, his stomach flat, strong. But at night he paces or passes out.

Linda worries. She feels like a janitor in a candy shop who isn't allowed to touch the goods; working her ass off but only able to stare into the case. She gets headaches. They become more frequent and more severe and only when they are very bad will he stand still. But her worry drives him away and after work he stops at the White Pine Inn where he makes new friends, biker friends, shooter friends, acid-head friends, flipped-out friends. Gina and Michelle's first birthday party is held at his folks' house and he is so proud of his daughters and his wife and that night he is zinging on yellowjackets and mellow on grass and he makes love to Linda but immediately after ejaculation he leaps from bed so sensitive to the touch even a fold in the sheet is unbearable. He is happy, thrilled, delighted that his dick stayed hard, is still hard, would probably stay hard if he slammed it in the bedroom door. He feels cured, free of the fear of impotence. For a week they make love. He is cured, freed, free to attack.

"Babe."

"Um."

"You could do that."

"What?"

"Be like Ben Casey."

"Huh?"

Linda is smiling. She is barefoot, in shorts and a loose shirt, standing between the living room and the kitchen. "Like your brother. You could go back to school."

"Don't like bein a farmer's wife, eh?"

"Oh, it's not that."

"Rich doctor'd be better than a farmer, though, huh?"

"Tony! That's not what I mean and you know it. It's . . . you always said you wanted to go on with school. You were a really good paramedic. You liked it."

"Phaaftt. Those people wanted to sue me, remember? I'd be crazy to—"

"What people? Who wanted to—"

"Aw, nothin! Let's just drop it."

She stands in the archway to the kitchen, glares at him sitting, watching *Ben Casey*. He sits there hurt, rigid, feeling a failure, unable to earn beyond his dole from Pewel Wapinski, unable to promise Linda, his daughters, a future. Become a doctor, he thinks. What a fucking pipe dream.

Mid-June: The Pentagon Papers are heavy in the news. Jo and John Sr. have celebrated their thirty-first wedding anniversary. Linda has dressed Gina and Michelle in identical yellow-and-orange sunsuits they received from Norma for their birthday and is about to head over to the Children's Free Clinic run bimonthly by Simon Denham and his new group in their new building.

"No fuckin way."

"What?!"

"What do you think?"

"What's the matter with you?"

"Nothin's the matter with me. Free clinic! Goddamn welfare."

"We qualify."

"That's because Wapinski pays me cash. Don't you dare take them there." His voice is harsh, loud, the babies begin to cry. "What's that goina teach em?"

"That I care," Linda screams.

"Care! That's shit!" He storms out. She hears the Harley start, hears him run through the gears, blast down Route 154.

The early July sun blazes, bakes the ground, soaks into the tiers of new shingles already halfway up the barn roof. Tony is shirtless. He has a green bandana tied about his head, soaking up the sweat, holding back his long hair. He has carried up the ladder every bundle they've nailed down, all the bundles scattered to the ridge. His right thigh aches from the ladder, from kneeling, nailing. Sweat drools through the bandana, rolls to his left eye, stings. He holsters his hammer, pulls the bandana off, wipes his eyes. His third of the roof is way ahead of Jeffery Mitchell's, who Pewel has hired to help, is ahead of Mike Pritchard's third too. Son of a bitch, Tony thinks. The heel of his right hand and the side of his right thumb are beyond blistered from the hammer, the skin broken, sweat stinging there too. Tony looks over to see how Jeff and Mike are doing. They are not on the roof. He stands, looks over the edge. Linda is walking back to the house. Jeff and Mike are drinking ice water from quart jars, eating potato chips. Fuck, Tony mumbles. He turns, kneels, nails in another three-tab shingle, slides, aligns, nails, again, again, quick, rhythmically.

"Hey, Tony," Jeff calls up. Tony ignores him. "Hey, Tony, that line's getting crooked."

Tony backs up, sights his line.

"It's got to be up a little more toward the center," Mike calls.

Yeah, right, fuckhead, Tony thinks. He nails another course. The sun is beating him. His nail belt chafes his side where it is already bright red from the sun.

"Hey, Tony. You're just about a half-inch down."

What the fuck? You stupid jerk. What is this shit? Tony turns. "Hey, fuck you."

"What?" Jeff and Mike simultaneously.

"You heard me." Tony flips his nail apron dumping a pound of nails on the roof, the nails rolling, bouncing, flying off.

"What's the matter?" Jeff moves to the bottom of the ladder, looks up, climbs six, eight rungs, turns, says to Mike, "Steady it for me, okay?"

"Sure. Whoa. He's comin down." Tony looks down, flips his hammer out, lets it fall missing Mike Pritchard by six inches. "Geez, Man! What the hell are you doin?"

"Comin fuckin down," Tony snaps.

"I'll get off—" Jeff begins but Tony leaps, jumps right off the roof, jumps from twenty feet onto the grass, hits, rolls, jumps up, smacks his hand into the bag of chips.

"Geez, Man!" Pritchard sees the anger in Tony's eyes. Jeff is coming off the ladder. "You gettin sun stroke?"

"I'm not fuckin sun stroke."

"What's the matter?"

"I'm sick of you fuckin cocksuckers."

"What are you talkin about?"

"I fuckin humped all them shingles up. I fuckin nailed off half what's done. You fuckin crybabies are eatin potato chips."

"Hey, ah, have—"

"Yeah, sorry, Man."

"Sorry's right. *Sin Loi,* motherfuckers."

"Tone . . . "

"Stuff it. I'm the idiot. I'm the crazy fuckin idiot. Pull yer fuckin weight. I quit. I'm outa here." Tony grabbed his T-shirt, strode to the Harley. His left ankle felt broken but he refused to let it show. He got on, kicked it over, roared off.

It is mid-afternoon when Linda arrives at the apartment. Tony is there, in the kitchen. He is not there but is over Phu Bai, has been over Phu Bai for hours, falling, crashing, his whole body racking with each fall, each stupid, mechanical-failure fall with him so short, so ready to leave, to go back to the World, to the land of the big PX where everything will be all right, be ALL RIGHT!

Linda bolts back, almost drops Gina. Michelle is in the car, asleep, strapped into the homemade kid-seat Pewel has made for her. Tony is at the kitchen table. He has ransacked the apartment, even flipped the sofa onto its back, has found his shotgun in a closet. The stock of the gun is resting on Gina's high-chair tray, the barrel is in Tony's mouth. Linda gasps. Tony's eyes light up. He flashes his teeth, bites the steel barrel, waggles his fingers, moves his hand down the barrel to the trigger. He is laughing, sucking the barrel, feeling the billy club rip his lips. Linda screams, squeezes Gina, tries to shield the girl's eyes. Tony pushes the trigger, the hammer snaps, he snaps his head trying to feel his brains blowing out, laughing at Linda, trying to make her as fuckin nuts as he. Linda is crying, Gina is crying. Tony is laughing, his eyes are bulging. "Didn't know," he shrieks. He's laughing out of control. "You didn't know, didja? You thought I'd do it." He stands close to her, almost on her, leers into her face. She pulls Gina back, holds her with her left arm, rocks back, twists, winding up, closed right fist round housing, missing, connecting with her wrist and forearm into the side of his head, actually knocking him down, she screaming, "Don't you ever do that again!" he scrambling, jumping up, she cowering back unable to wind up for another blow, trying to protect her baby, he banging his chest against her, knocking her to the wall, pinning her, then quivering all over, running down the back stairs to the Harley, still holding the shotgun, fleeing.

"Father."

"Yes."

"You got a minute?"

"Of course." They are on the porch of the manse of St. Ignatius. Tony relates to the young priest how he has quit his job, how he worked and worked and how the others stood around and ate potato chips and how he got angry and quit. He does not tell the priest about jumping off the roof; he tells him about the fight with Linda, leaves out the shotgun.

"I've got to find something to do," Tony says. "And it's got to be outside." Tony is repentant, centered on his problems. Thomas Niederkau, the priest, asks questions, wants to know more. Tony tells him about jobs he's had, machinery he's run. He does not tell him about the Corps, about his service, about drugs or Wapinski's or Rock Ridge or a small town out west.

"Do you know Mr. Lefkowski?"

"The old guy who—"

"He's been the custodian here for forty years, but he doesn't want to do the cemetery anymore. I need someone in the cemetery," Father Tom says. "Mow the lawn, trim the trees, dig the graves. You can work a backhoe?"

"Um-hmm."

"Clean up after funerals."

"I'd like to do that."

In the apartment Tony is apologetic, self-deprecating, pleading for forgiveness, withdrawn. He is mellow on grass, on Darvon, on Dexedrine, each drug pulling his mind and body in a different direction, pulling more gently than Elavil and Thorazine but still slowly tearing his mind apart. Linda is angry, suspicious, untrusting. Covertly she blames herself, fears that she has not met Tony's needs, has not made him happy, has not been good enough to him. She is determined. She will make him sane if it drives her crazy. For two weeks things improve. She is happy, happier. She has made up an excuse for Tony, has told Pewel Wapinski that Tony has decided to go back to school, that he is studying, that he's happy Pewel has Jeff and Mike to take over.

In the cemetery Tony is meticulous. The job is good. He can be alone, be responsible only to himself. He mows, trims. Daily he visits Jimmy, takes flowers from new graves, just a few each day, brings them to him, brings too a small pipe, a little weed. "Remember on the shed roof . . . " Sometimes he cries. It's okay. There is no one there.

Some days he digs, some days he backfills. On days he digs he makes the first cut with the backhoe, first from one end, then the other, clawing, scooping, removing the dirt, dumping it, smoothing the pile with the side or bottom of the bucket. Then he cleans the hole with the bucket making sure the corners are square, the sides straight, vertical, smooth. He dismounts, tosses a shovel into the hole, jumps in. He likes backhoe work but the tractor and bucket and hydraulics are machine, not like a shovel, a wood-handled, once alive, common garden spade. He talks to his shovel as he cleans this particular hole. He wants the mourners to see perfect walls. He puts the shovel down, scrapes, smoothes the dirt walls with his fingers. He drops to his knees. He has never knelt in a hole. It feels deeper than he expected. He tosses the shovel out, sits. It feels even deeper, feels peaceful. He lies down, looks up the tall vertical walls, grins. With his hands by his sides he pats the ground. The earth sounds hollow, hollowness around him, under him. He likes this. He is with the dead.

By late August Tony is spending less time watching TV, less time in the apartment, more time partying with his new friends, biker friends who are helping him chop his Harley: acid-freak friends who like him because he is so paranoid they feel safe when they are tripping, safe because Tony, that ex-paramedic, that strong and vigilant friend, will take care of them; speed freak friends who like to supply him; downer friends who like to mellow him out. He tells Linda about the pot. She is furious. He tells her to come with him. She refuses. He spends more time away. He misses John's and Molly Kleinman's wedding and his mother and father are furious. Linda worries. Her headaches become unbearable. She worries Tony will split again, abandon them again, embarrass her by leaving her again as if she isn't capable of keeping a man. She trusts him, believes him, does not trust him at all.

Ruthie, Linda's sister, visits. She and Jay are thinking of starting a family. She wants Linda's advice, wants to stay a few days, spend time with the babies.

"Come with me," Tony says to Linda.

"I shouldn't."

"Ruthie can watch the girls."

"I won't smoke any pot."

"You don't have to."

"And if I don't like it you'll bring me right home."

"Um-hmm."

"Promise."

"I promise."

"Oh, Tony, I don't know."

It is early September 1971. The sun is low, the evening pleasant. They have ridden Route 154 to Old River Road, have followed its twists and turns down Loyalsock Creek valley to a creek-side meadow where Tony and Linda dismount and Tony is greeted by half a dozen young men, a few young women. Linda is not greeted but is ogled by every man.

"Oh Man, you got the new tank."

"Yeah." Tony is proud of the Harley. He has stripped off the panniers, replaced the stock seat with a double-tiered high back, replaced the tank with a bright yellow teardrop, the mufflers with fishtail pipes, the original handlebars with a set of easy-riders that swoop out and up then curve and fall as gracefully as the neck of a swan. In the gleaming yellow of the new tank there is a brown, gold and black Harley eagle. One talon grasps a flaming skull and crossbones, the other a Marine Corps emblem. He has a long way to go, he thinks, custom carbs, air cleaners, forks, maybe a hard-tail frame, but the bike, as it is, is okay—Jimmy's respectable dresser transforming into Tony's chopped outlaw.

"Far out, Man." The speaker is Ken Bonnell, Big Bonnie; he is at the top of the pecking order. Little Bonnie, Bonnie Conterelli, is his "syp," sweet young pussy, his princess, his property. "Far out," Big Bonnie says again. He checks out the tank painting, checks out Linda.

Sitting on a bike fifty feet away is Zookie, Gaylord Sutthoff's main meat. Zookie is an "ocie," old cunt. She is smoking, checking out Linda, too. Her neck tattoo, a small garden of flowers circling to the left like half a collar, catches Linda's eye. Linda immediately looks away. Big Bonnie, all smiles, puts an arm over Tony's shoulder, hugs Linda with his other arm, pulls her in tight, the three musketeers, turns Linda so her left breast is against his side, hugs her rhythmically, Tony too. Linda cringes, tries to protect herself. They walk toward the keg where others are chugging plastic cupfuls.

They too are happy, smiling, laughing. Gay hugs Linda about the waist while Big Bonnie still holds her about the shoulders. Slowly, gently, laughing, Gay pours beer into Linda's mouth. "Drink. Drink up. Everybody must drink." Linda swallows, laughs too, thinks these are two good-hearted men, thinks Tony is there to watch over her. Gaylord does not force her to drink any more quickly than she's willing.

Zookie watches Gay spill beer on Linda's chin, Linda so genteel dabbing her chin against her shoulder, her arms now around Big Bonnie and Gay. Music is coming from the shade under a large solitary elm where most of the bikes are lined up. It is a Hendrix song but Linda does not know which one. Gay begins pouring another beer into Linda but Zookie grabs him, breaks his hold on the new girl, takes the beer and finishes it.

"Zookie," she says. Linda stares at her, has no idea what she's said, thinks instantly this older woman must once have been very beautiful, but is now . . . "Zookie. That's my name." She glares at Big Bonnie. He drops his grip from Linda's shoulders.

Linda is baffled. "Linda Pisano," she says. "I'm Tony's wife."

Zookie laughs. Her laugh is deep and broad, full of tones, meaning. To Linda it is eerie yet pleasant. "Tony," Zookie says. "He's such a nice'a boy," she says playfully. "Whats'a nice'a girl like you doin with a nice'a boy like that?"

Linda has no words. She thinks Zookie is playing with the accent but she isn't sure. She notes Zookie's hair, long, dark, shiny; notes her earrings, long dangling silver elipses with inlaid turquoise flowers. "We met when I was in nursing school—" Linda begins.

"You've got pretty eyes," Zookie interrupts.

More couples arrive on bikes, a few in pickups. There is another keg, bottles of Boone's Farm wine. Tony and others go into the woods, return with dead branches, build a bonfire in the pleasant September darkness. Between trips they drink, then settle, toke up, suck smoke, pass joints. In small groups away from the flames others are popping pills, snorting powder. Around the fire they are passing tiny pipes.

Linda is loose, happy. She and Tony sit side by side, he instructing her in how to hold a joint, how to hold in the smoke, she turning to him, sad, exhaling a cloud, saying, "You know, this'll be the end of us," then giggling, sucking smoke again, passing the joint.

The evening cools, the fire dies to glowing embers. Tony rises, walks toward the solitary elm, pees in the field. By the scooters he hears another group. He stands still, intent, invisible. "One big fuckin bitch, Man"—Tony does not recognize the voice—"more than anything, more than coming back and findin my old lady'd been fuckin around . . ."

"Sixty-seven?"

"Yeah. Two fuckin divisions of Marines, Man. Never saw nothin like it. We had M-14s one day. Next day we had M-16s. Alien, Man. And they didn't fuckin work. And they never did a fuckin thing about it. Not like nothin was done, Man, but like nothin was done about the guys that got greased. Guys wasted in the rice paddies, Man, cleaning rods jammed in these alien plastic pieces a shit, rods jammed down the barrels tryin to poke out rounds that wouldn't eject. Can't bring those guys back, Man."

Tony is frozen in a time-space warp, angry, stoned. He had not known that some of these guys were Nam returnees. He's never told them his stories, has no desire to talk, does not wish to hear.

"I was in a fuckin hole on the perimeter with a kid from California. His name was Lassen. And he was curled up in the bottom of that fuckin hole. Petrified. Petrified, Man. He was in my squad and I grabbed him by the shirt and yanked him up top of that motherfuckin hole and by this time they're on us. They Are On Us. I had a sixteen. I jumped out the back and we pulled back. The Rome plows . . . they'd pushed up berm enough to cover the tracks, APCs, ya know. And just high enough so the turret . . . the 50-cal could stick over. And the 50s were pumpin. We were in front of the fuckin berm and we pulled up outta the hole and got back on top a the fuckin berm.

"Guy on the 50, Charlie somethin, I ferget his name, he gets fuckin blown away. They got right up on him. Lots a guys got fucked that night. One five five howitzers fired point blank inta them motherfuckers. Then Puff comes in. Artillery poundin all around. Off to my left the listenin post got hit. They were just gettin ready to set up and they got fuckin hit and they were comin back in and the dinks were hot on their fuckin asses. We went out there and fuckin got em. Guys are fuckin hollerin, they're fuckin kickin. Charlie was right on top of em. We ended up with about three hundred bodies that night. Next morning, right in front of us, there's a fuckin gook layin there and he was sittin like this, you know, with his back up against a fuckin stump and his eyes straight ahead. In shock. Still alive. But he didn't move. That fucker was stoned, Man. He was outta it. He didn't know if he was dead or alive . . . numb functional, Man. I came up on him. You know, we had to bed-down the whole motherfuckin perimeter. I come across him and he's starin out, his arms up like this. I shot that motherfucker in the head. He was . . . ya know . . . he wasn't breathin. I don't know if he was breathin or just playin possum or stoned. I just fuckin pumped im."

Tony is cold, stripped of clothes, skin, nerves, stripped of layers, coatings, time. He is raw. He can hear the chanting in the valley, knows the attack will come. He hears the bugles, hears the sounds oozing from the earth, from the core, from hell. He cannot talk, cannot move toward the speakers, the bikes under the solitary elm. He thinks to tell them of his brother, how his brother once held a wounded friend whom a sniper killed, how his brother saw women, children, human shields, murdered, how his brother . . . He cannot think, cannot talk of such things. He turns, looks at the fire, the glow of the coals, the occasional spurt of flame, the dark silhouettes sitting on logs, laughing. He hears Linda's giggle. Big Bonnie rises, comes to the field, sees him, speaks but Tony doesn't comprehend. No matter, Big Bonnie is stoned. Gaylord is laughing, pressing a joint into Linda's hand. Zookie is aloof, eyeing them. Big Bonnie stands next to Tony, faces the dark, pees. Zookie moves to Linda's side, opposite Gay, rubs Linda's back. Tony is thinking how pretty Linda is, how he'd like to make love to her right now.

Big Bonnie hugs Tony. They eye the fire, the women, voyeurs in the dark. Linda's laugh is louder than the others. Zookie hugs her, kisses her ear. Linda laughs, playfully pushes her away. "Neat old lady," Bonnie says.

"Yeah," Tony says.

"Nice chest," Bonnie says.

"Yeah," Tony says. "She's still nursin. Ever taste tit milk?"

"Naw."

"Sweet, Man. Sweeter en candy. You wanta taste it?"

"Yeah."

"I'll get her over here. You can taste it."

"Yeah."

Tony kneels behind Linda, puts his hands on her waist, her hips, puts his chin on her shoulder. Linda turns, "Oh," so happy, so light. Zookie caresses Tony's arm. "Go ahead," Tony whispers. "You can do anything you want." Linda does not understand. Tony caresses her stomach, kisses her gently. It turns him on thinking how much Gay, Big Bonnie, even Zookie, want her. "Go ahead," he whispers again, kisses her again, moves his hands up so the backs lift her breasts.

"Let's play carnival." Gay laughs.

"How do you play that?" Linda.

"You sit on my face and I try to guess your weight."

Linda tries to stifle her laugh, covers her face with her hands, squeals. "Do I"—she brings her hands down, still laughing, stoned, hesitating with her hands—"get to"—her hands up, shy, blurts—"pull the lever?"

"Darlin"—Gay says, he has a hand on her leg—"you can plunk my magic twanger."

Zookie beams, puts her hand on Gay's on Linda's jeans. "He's a frog," she says. "Long tongue."

Gay leans forward, his mouth open toward Linda's.

Suddenly Tony pulls her back. She slips off the log onto him. He stands, lifts her, Zookie and Gay left agawk. Tony bends, grabs Linda's legs, lifts, she falling over his shoulder. He carries her into the darkness, to Big Bonnie, past Big Bonnie, to their bike. Big Bonnie follows. Linda is laughing. Tony is inflamed. His eyes glow like a vicious dog's. He shoves Bonnie into one of the bikes.

"Hey. What the—"

"Fuck off!" Caustic, not loud.

"Huh?"

Tony radiates anger, hate. He seats Linda on the Harley.

"One fuckin minute . . . "

Tony turns on Bonnie, nostrils flaring, breath coming from deep within the earth expelled through nares like jet exhaust, radiating danger. His mouth, lips, are wet. He hisses, seethes, ". . . kill you . . . " Bonnie backs off, stumbles into a bike, backs farther.

The bike explodes to life, the big chrome headlight casts its beam across the field, into the hill. They are on the road, Linda hanging on for dear life, stoned but scared shitless by the speed, by Tony's blasting through corners, charging rises, down dips, she is rigid, epinephrine overpowering alcohol and cannabis, terrified sober.

Then home, in bed, confused, Tony on top of her banging his pelvis angrily against hers, thrusting deep, trying to hurt her, and she, hurt, still stoned, still terrified, refusing him her warmth, punishing him back for being such an asshole, withholding her excitement, her love, nothing more than a limp bimbo.

Ruthie leaves the next morning before Tony emerges from the bedroom. She feels the tension but Linda assures her it is nothing, hangovers, a crazy party. Do I smell like a campfire? Crazy people hanging all over each other. "It's not *me*," Linda says, "but, you know, some were actually very nice."

Tony sees red. He is in bed, lying on his stomach, a pillow over his head, the blanket pulled up closing off all light. In the blackness he sees red, a triangle warping, stretching, zinging high thin, pulled wide flat, jumping, jerking, drug-induced responses to sharp sounds, bitching.

Linda is bitching, grumbling, sniveling loudly enough for the kitchen noise to pierce the walls, the blanket, the pillow. Pots bang, spoons fall, oatmeal—three spoonfuls, how did she hide it, hold it in her mouth—spurts from Michelle's mouth. Bitch, bitch, bitch. "I could use a hand out here."

He doesn't answer. Problems, he thinks. Always fuckin problems. Always something wrong. Solve the fuckin problem, he screams at her within his head. He grits his teeth. Life is a fuckin problem. Success in life is measured by how you solve the problems that come at you. It is a Marine instructor's voice from long ago. Still he lies there.

"Dirty dishes," she moans. "How do we create so many dirty dishes? I'm so tired of doing dishes."

I'll do em, to her in his head. Just leave em. Aloud, "I'll do em when I get up."

"I'll do them," she calls. "I just don't get a chance to do anything with the girls screaming. And my head's splitting."

Tony gets up angry, residual anger from last night, from last year, from last forever. He puts on a pair of u-trau, walks into the living room. There are toys, books, gnawed teething biscuits, scattered all over the floor. Even the milk crate Linda has painted to hold the toys is overturned.

"Look at this mess," Tony snaps. "This place is a goddamn shithole." He stands amid the clutter and with a bare heel grinds a plastic boat into the carpet. The toy cracks, splinters, a spring flies out throwing small jagged plastic chips. Shrapnel, he thinks. He stomps a plastic blow-up pink panther. It pops, sighs as the air runs out. "They got too much damn stuff."

"About time you got up." Linda comes from the kitchen, stares at him.

"This place is a shithole," he snaps.

"Then clean it up." Linda is in no mood. She's been up with Gina and Michelle, and Ruthie until Ruthie left, trying to keep them all quiet, trying to let her man sleep.

"They're not so fuckin young that they can't learn to clean—"

"For Pete's sakes, they're only sixteen months."

Gina and Michelle stand together, behind their mother, under the kitchen arch. They look at Tony without expression. Already, at sixteen months, the pattern has formed, *stay away from him when he's angry*.

"What the fuck are you looking at." Tony leaps at them.

Linda shoves him with the heel of her hand. "Don't you ever—"

The twins cower. Michelle begins to cry. Her cries make him angrier. He backs from Linda, snarls at the girls.

Linda shakes her hand at him. "Stop that. Leave them alone."

"You want to cry?" Tony snaps at the girls. They are now both wailing. "I'll give you something to cry about!"

"Stop that!" Linda shrieks at him. "What's the matter with you?"

"With me? You goddamn tramp. Were you going to let em go all the way last night?"

"Huh?"

"I've got eyes."

She is furious. "What is this—this monster coming out of you?!"

He growls. He storms back to the bedroom.

"You know," she screams after him, "you don't do a goddamned thing around here. I'm sick and tired of it. Not a damn thing. You don't even work half the time. And what you do bring home, you spend on that goddamned bike. You're so goddamned selfish."

He seethes in the bedroom, she in the kitchen. She quiets the girls, hugs them, gives them the big spaghetti pot to play in, goes to the living room to pick up, thinks, I'll be damned, plunks down on the couch, leans back, closes her eyes. Her head is pounding.

Tony dresses, hunkers down on the floor beside the bed, waits for the attack. Gina and Michelle are banging on the pot. Tony grits his teeth. He can hear the metal ripping, the car impacting, ripping the station wagon to pieces, flipping it, babies flying. He hunkers lower. The door creaks. He leaps, hits it, slams it—the wail is instantaneous, high, painful. Immediately he is back to now, throws the door open. Linda rushes from the living room. Michelle screams, shakes the walls with her scream. He's slammed the door on her hand.

Linda scoops up the girl, rushes to the kitchen sink, cold water.

"I . . . I didn't mean . . . " Tony apologetic.

"You are such a . . . " Linda is livid. The words get stuck in her throat.

"I didn't know . . . "

" . . . such a time bomb. You're a walking time bomb."

"I . . . "

"Get out of here. Get out of here! You could've amputated her hand."

Tony goes down the back steps. He is shaking, confused. Gotta change, he thinks. Gotta keep changin. Go. Get the fuck out. He gets on the Harley, cranks it up. His mind is cranking, racing. He runs the front wheel straight into the side of the house, revs the 74 CID V-twin engine for all it's worth, de-clutches, the rear wheel spinning, digging, he thinking, I'm the idiot. I'm a fuckin idiot. I should never have come back. The

Harley hopping, trying to break through the wall; Tony snarling, smash you motherfucker, the rear wheel half-buried, fishtail pipes on the ground, chain eating dirt, engine revving, revving as out of control as Tony's head, then kur-kur-Chunk. The bike dies. Tony's arms quake, shivers run through his legs, his jaw twitches. He dismounts. Runs.

Through the noise Linda holds Michelle on her lap, rocks her, her little hand wrapped in a washcloth with ice cubes tucked inside. Gina is next to them on the sofa, Linda rocking and holding both girls. Then the noise stops. She sits still, the girls leaning against her too afraid to even lift their heads from their mother's body. She remains there ten, twelve minutes with her eyes closed, then rises slowly, gently lays the girls down. She grabs the box for the wood blocks, kneels, begins sorting the toys, putting them away. She works steadily, feels a small sense of satisfaction when the room is clean. She picks up every piece of the shattered plastic boat and takes it outside to the garbage. Tony is not there. Linda no longer cares.

New York City, Saturday, 6 November 1971—For two months Tony wandered, slept in doorways, begged for quarters, dimes, drank rotgut wine, ate little, smoked whatever dope he could mooch or steal. He was unshaven, unwashed, living in the clothes he'd worn on the day he left Mill Creek Falls. He'd been in a dozen fights, lost a dozen times, cut, bruised, punks without will, he'd thought, rolling a drunkard, taking his change, but unwilling to put an end to it all for him. He despised them. He withdrew further, became more confused, numbed out but not, to his mind, enough. He was in escape-and-evade mode, attempting to stay one step ahead of his own mind, attempting to kill every thought, afraid he wouldn't be able to. He was trying to work up enough courage to go into the subway, wait for an uptown express, fall from the platform in time to be crushed.

His existence had been day-to-day, sometimes hour-to-hour. He had barely spoken in five weeks, had been alone except for the brief plea, "Spare a quarter, Friend," and the occasional moment, they avoiding his eyes, "Sure," digging for change, dropping a few coins into his paper cup, careful to avoid touching him. Some nights he sang to himself, using song as a thought depressant. " 'Ain't no use to sit and wonder why, Babe . . . ' " He couldn't continue with that one, it evoked too many images and he wanted to evoke nothing. "Strafe the town and kill the people . . . " An old aviator's song to the tune of "Wake the Town and Tell the People." It evoked nothing. If he could have concentrated, he might have been able to uncover the enemies who had done this to him. Yet the deepest he dared go was, "I can't even be a good father, a decent husband." That evoked self-pity, his new pleasure.

On the night of 6 November Tony was sitting on the curb of West Fifty-fifth Street between Seventh and Eighth avenues. Across the street, before a café, there was commotion, a big fight, people swearing, shouting, screaming from the sidewalk, retorts from the door. It subsided, the people dispersed. Then it erupted again. The bouncer emerged, one man raised his arm. There was a shot. Tony jolted, nearly peed his pants. The bouncer crumbled.

Tony was out of control. He did not evade but ran in paramedic mode, knelt beside the man, rolled him gently. There was blood on the man's chest, left-center, well placed. People gathered. Tony checked for a pulse. There was nothing. He lifted the man's head, then his own head snapped up, eyes searching, checking for snipers. He released the head in his hand. It thunked to the sidewalk. People shied back horrified. Tony looked up. Words sputtered from his lips. "He's dead. He's dead. He's—"

"You better come in till the cops come. C'mon, I'll buy ya a drink."

Tony was in a fog. They were feeding him drinks. Someone congratulated him, slapped him on the back. Someone swabbed his hands with chemicals to test for nitrates—the Greiss test. If he'd been clear he would have known what was happening but he was not clear. He babbled. "Follows me. Wherever I go. Killings. K-fuckin-IAs." He drank more, more, was very drunk, was sick, fell flat on his face. The results of the Greiss were negative—no charges, released, drunk. Someone, his arm about Tony's waist, heard Tony babbling, asking for refuge, asking for Rock Ridge.

Tony did not remember how he got back to Pennsylvania, did not remember being readmitted to Rock Ridge Veterans Medical Center, did not know he'd been admitted into alcohol detox.

"I don't"—his eyes were red, watery, his voice small, weak—"mean to keep pestering you," he said to the therapist. "I don't have—" he couldn't finish aloud but in his mind said, "a human in the world I can discuss this crap with."

"Are you familiar with AA?" The therapist, Daniel Holbrook, was in the doctoral program at Penn State. He was a year younger than Tony. Dr. Jonathan Freiburg had been kicked upstairs, replaced by Nelville Chapman, MD, psychiatrist, and by this young man. Policies, programs, procedures and personnel were in flux at the hospital. There were seeds of change, of social recognition, that alcoholism and drug abuse are illnesses, not crimes, and that talk therapy for "psychotic" war veterans might be at least as effective as pharmaceutical therapy; seeds germinating because the number of Viet Nam returnees at veterans medical centers, or in prison, was skyrocketing. But at Rock Ridge these were just seeds. Elavil and Thorazine were still the treatments of choice; and Haldol and diazepam (and Inderal to control the cardial arrhythmias caused by the antidepressants) were still prescribed as quickly as trick-r-treat candy on Halloween; straitjacket cocktails to guarantee institutional efficiency—no muss, no fuss, no flare-ups, no riots—just docile sheep without hard-ons.

Holbrook pitied Tony. He cared. He truly wanted to help. This was his first job. He wanted to be good at it; he dreamed of great break-throughs. Tony did not answer him. "Do you get drunk all the time?" Holbrook asked. Tony shrugged. He was in the detoxification program, not the psycho-schizo-borderline-personality program. They had given him lithium carbonate, not the strait jacket. His past RRVMC residency record had not yet caught up with his new admission. "Why do you drink?" Holbrook asked.

"I . . . " Tony garbled his words, felt isolated, claustrophobic in the tiny office.

"Please. Speak more clearly."

"I got a case of the ass."

"Hmm?"

"I get drunk so I can go to sleep."

"Um-hmm."

"Go to sleep. I don't want to be conscious."

"Go on."

"That's all."

"When you say, 'a case of the ass,' that means angry?"

"Yeah."

"Why are you angry?"

"I don't know."

"You're angry at somebody?"

"I guess."

"Um-hmm." Holbrook paused, wanted Tony to fill in the gap but Tony remained silent. "Who makes you angry?"

"I don't know."

"Are you angry at your mother?"

"No."

"Your father?" Tony didn't answer. Holbrook remained silent. Tony shifted. "Your father?" Holbrook repeated.

"My enemies," Tony said.

"Who are your enemies?" Holbrook said. He mentally chastized himself, thought he should have simply fed back the words as the question.

"I don't know." Tony felt that Holbrook was becoming impatient. "Maybe my father." For a few minutes he told Holbrook about Aunt Helen, about the suspected affair, about how it seemed it was all a misunderstanding, nothing more than his father's joy at his return.

"Have you confronted your father with this?"

"No."

"Why not?"

"I don't care anymore. It wasn't true."

"Then why be angry about it?"

"I'm not."

Silence.

"I . . . I . . . I guess I just said that because I needed to tell you something. I was really hard on him when I thought, you know. He went through shit too but he handled it. I went through shit and I'm fuckin fallin apart. It's eatin my fuckin mind."

"Um-hmm."

"I killed eight motherfuckers with my hands. With machetes. Sometimes I want to kill eight more. Eight more motherfuckers. Ever since I did that it's been followin me."

As Tony told Holbrook about Dai Do, the young therapist could feel Tony's presence in Viet Nam, could vicariously experience the intensity even with Tony being lithium calm. He had never placed himself, mentally, in such an intense, life-death struggle. As Tony talked, Holbrook buzzed the orderly, told him to delay his next appointment. Tony continued. Holbrook tried to remain professional. He listened empathetically, interpreted the story as "an atrocity," just like the atrocities he'd been reading so much about.

"Now," Holbrook said in a pause, "you said this place ... "

"Dai Do."

" ... Dai Do, it's been following you."

"No. Not Dai Do." It angered Tony that after all his explanation Holbrook still didn't understand.

"What's been following you?"

"Death. Fuckin Death. Last week I saw a guy get greased in New York. Zapped right there on the fuckin street."

Now Holbrook was lost. "Okay," he said. "Let's back up and clarify some things. You said you're 'fallin apart and it's eating your mind.' What's eating your mind?"

"You don't fuckin get it, do ya?" Tony clamped his teeth, twisted away.

"Don't get what?" Holbrook asked.

Tony sneered at him. "If I don't drink or smoke a fuckin joint ... Jesus fuckin H. Christ ... I can be so fuckin tired I can't move but I can't sleep. If I aint movin, if I aint drinkin, or smokin dope, or poppin that diazepam shit ... that shit's nowhere near as good as yellowjackets ... I can work on yellowjackets ... if I'm not doin somethin, I can't sleep. My head's crankin, you know? Crankin all the fuckin time. I'm fuckin wide fuckin awake, thinkin. Gotta move. Gotta crack some motherfucker's head open. Or drink myself to death. Maybe jump in front of a fuckin subway."

Later that afternoon Holbrook's report was read by Jonathan Freiburg. "Expressions of suicidal and antisocial ideations. Sociopathic tendencies ... " Freiburg also received Tony's RRVMC history. In consultation with Nelville Chapman, who had never seen Tony, they merged the reports, did their administrative duty, reassigned Tony, first to be physically stripped and restrained and pumped with Thorazine, then to be moved to Seven-upper, the schizo-psycho ward. Full pharmaceutical therapy was prescribed. On the positive side, Freiburg, now with Tony's home address and phone number, directed an orderly to type a standard letter to be sent to Mrs. Anthony Pisano. The letter sat for three days.

Tuesday: Tears ran down Linda's cheeks. "Oh Babe." She bent to him. "What have you done to yourself?"

Tony was numb, twitching, unable to connect, unable to even think left-right in sequence, or one-two-three, or who the fuck are you? The Elavil-Thorazine-diazepam-Inderal cocktail had been maximum-dosed with the plan to reduce to therapeutic maintenance levels over a period of six to ten weeks.

"I've been so frightened for you. We all have. Your folks hired an investigator and Mr. Wapinski went through all the back roads and even searched over by the gap. Father Tom . . . " Linda couldn't continue. Tony showed no response. "What do they have you on, Babe?" No response. "Damn it, I'm going to talk to the orderly. Your folks are down in Admin. They wouldn't let us come up. Who's this Dr. Freiburg?"

Linda looked around. The patients in Tony's ward room, the ones whose dosages had not yet been lowered, who could not yet go to the day room to watch TV, were all zombies. She kissed Tony on the forehead. "I'm going to find somebody. Oh God! Oh God! Look at you."

"Tony!" It was his father. Tony's head felt like it was erupting. He knew Linda had been to see him but he wasn't sure if it was today, yesterday, last week. "Tony, we're going to get you out of here. It may take a little while but we're going to find a better place. This is really . . . " John Sr. didn't finish either. Thank the Lord, he thought, Jo didn't come up. Neither of them would have been allowed had his father not bribed an orderly.

Downstairs, in the administration and therapy offices, Linda was determined. She was not going to fail. She was not going to let her marriage fail. "What kind of therapy do you have him on?" she asked Dr. Chapman. Her tone was sweet, nonthreatening.

"He's on sedation right now," Chapman said. "I wish you had called first. We can't bring him down right now, and you're not allowed up there."

"Um-hmm. I understand. What sedation?"

"It's just standard—"

"Doctor! I asked you what medications my husband is being given. And why? What's the diagnosis?"

Chapman clasped his hands, looked up, away, as if trying to find words simple enough for this woman to understand. "Do you know what schizophrenia is? Sometimes there are imbalances in—"

"Has he been diagnosed as schizophrenic?" Her voice was firm.

"It's a preliminary diagnosis, but yes, we think he's suicidal, perhaps antisocial, certainly paranoid. He was admitted for alcoholism, but we immediately found these other problems. You understand, this is his second admission. It seems he can't cope outside."

"So you've drugged him up. I want to see him."

"No visitors are allowed for the first twenty-one days."

"Do I need to call my lawyer? I want to see my husband and I want to know what medications you have him on."

"You'll be able to see him," Chapman checked the file, "after December fifth. And ah, he's on Elavil. Does that mean anything to—"

"Yes, it does. I'm an RN. Going for my PA. Does that mean anything to you?!"

"Oh. Well, why didn't you say—"

"Elavil and what else?"

"Thorazine. Diazepam. Inderal. If the Thorazine—"

"He was admitted because of alcohol and you put him on Thorazine. They're additive."

"Well. Yes. We may put him on Haldol instead. It's new. Haloperidol. Do you know . . ."

In the car back to Mill Creek Falls John said, "What do you think?"

Linda answered, "Is there someplace else he could go?" Neither wanted to show their fears and trepidations before Jo.

Over the next two weeks Tony's dosages were gradually reduced until he was minimally functional. Linda, John, Jo all visited but weren't allowed to see him again until Monday 6 December. They met Daniel Holbrook and were impressed by his attitude. Later John and Linda, with Tony's brother Joe, agreed that perhaps it was best not to move him.

Tony saw himself as nuts, saw RRVMC as a viable fallback position. He came to trust Holbrook and he told him his craziest thoughts, whatever came to mind, about Nam, about himself, about Rock Ridge.

"Ya know how sometimes you hear about crazy guys locked up in an insane asylum?" Tony chuckled. "The kinda guy who's in a padded room, mattresses on the walls even. And he's always naked. Sittin in a corner. Jerkin off. Jerks off fifteen, twenty times a day. Nurses bring him food—slide it through a slot in the door. He sticks his dick out at em." Tony enjoyed telling stories, enjoyed entertaining Holbrook. "Guy doesn't have a care in the world. Crazy as a loon, jerkin off to his fantasies all the time. That's the guy I wanta be."

Holbrook smiled, said, "Last week you told me you wanted to make an honest effort to reestablish your life with Linda."

"I'm just talking, Doc. Come on, cut me a huss. Don't take everything I say so seriously."

"How do I tell which Tony to take seriously?"

"There's only one, Doc. Just me. God, Doc, when I'm jokin I'm jokin. When I'm serious, I'm serious."

"Can Linda tell?"

"Yeah. Ya know, we had a real good thing going. I know I split. Twice. But I can't stay away from her. Sometimes I just can't be there but I can't stay away, either. We love each other but she . . . Sometimes the apartment is like a battle zone. It builds up and up."

"What builds up?"

"Oh. The anger."

"You're still angry, aren't you?"

"I don't know." Weekly they broached the subject without breaking through. Individual talk therapy is ineffective when the patient is stoned or strait-jacketed, or chemically confused.

By New Year's Tony was into the routine at RRVMC. He went to art therapy and painted like a second grader; went to craft therapy and made a leather belt like his brother had made one summer at camp; went to walk therapy and hiked the grounds of RRVMC until his feet froze; went to work therapy and mopped the floor of the main kitchen. He convinced Holbrook that further customizing his Harley and rebuilding the engine would be great therapy and Dr. Joe brought him his bike and he was allowed to keep it in Building 27, a greenhouse.

In talk therapy Tony brought up Viet Nam. Sometimes Holbrook let him talk, sometimes he stopped him. Holbrook never brought up the subject himself. In mid-January Holbrook said to Tony, "Your war's over. Give it up." A week later, "Put it out of your thoughts. Once you do, those headaches and nightmares and fears will vanish." Next session, "It's time to grow up, Tony. If Viet Nam still bothers you so much, why don't you write to your congressman?" By early February Viet Nam was off-limits in their discussions and if Tony mentioned it Holbrook would say, "Why do you resist the positive direction our talks have been taking?"

Now there was group therapy, too. In the first rap session Tony was shocked. He had been moved to Seven-lower, had been weaned from Elavil-Thorazine-diazepam, was now on lithium. Tony saw the patients, really saw them for the first time, recognized in them Jimmy and Manny and Rick, Al Cornwall, Jim Bellows, recognized in them half the guys from his Nam platoon, company, regiment—The Magnificent Bastards. Why are they here? Why are we all fucked up? Before Holbrook arrived, they talked quietly in twos, threes, fours. "Lotsa fine bros went down. Never got short. No fuckin Freedom Bird for them. Fuckin waste, Man."

"Fuckin waste. I can't even remember all their names. I'm ashamed cause I can't remember their names."

"Don't let em be forgotten, Man."

"We did in a L-T who got like twenty guys greased. That asshole Freiburg says I've got an unresolved killer-self."

"What's he know? He talked to me about the sin of killing. I thought, Right! Mothafucka! That's when I got switched to Holbrook but he's just as wacked. He can't take hearin nothin."

"Sssshh. He's comin."

"Don't talk Nam, Man. You'll never get outa here."

Monday, 28 February 1972—It was a clear morning. The weather for five days had been unseasonably mild. Tony felt almost cheerful. He was as crazy as ever but now he felt more comfortable with his craziness, with being lost. Holbrook had recommended he be released on long-term outpatient status—for which Holbrook was writing a program proposal. Tony agreed. His lithium dosage was reduced to 300 mg t.i.d. He had no desire to drink, to do other drugs. He was happy to be un-assing this AO, yet he was afraid to "go home"; afraid he'd hurt Linda or his daughters. He knew he was dying. He had reached a certain, if uneasy, peace with his craziness, his life, his death. He wanted to say good-bye, maybe collect the maple sap one more time for Old Man Wapinski. He felt he owed him that.

16

She'd left, driven away, driven that pistachio Pinto loaded to the roof out the driveway, past the FOR SALE sign, down Deepwoods Drive, away, forever. He'd stood there watching, barely caressing Josh's ears as the dog pressed his head into Bobby's leg. She had returned only to file the Dissolution of Marriage petition at the county courthouse and to lay claim to every remaining decent household item they owned (or still owed on). Her last words to him were, "I can't see you as a divorcé." That lay in his ears, he standing there seeing not Red, not even himself, but Jimmy Pellegrino on that big Harley that he handled like a dirt bike, seeing Jimmy Pellegrino and thinking, for this he got greased.

Then he'd turned, gone in. It had gotten dark but he did not remember the dusk, only the dark and he not having the impetus to turn on a light but sitting in the dark listening to Josh scratch. He heard other noises, rose, turned on the porch light, just enough light coming through the windows to give the few furnishings an edge, sat restive, afraid of the dark like a child, afraid of the same boogeyman that scared him when he was eight and he'd moved back into the house on Crooked Road.

Months passed unnoticed, unrecallable, except for the repeated personal justifications, the evaporation of the weight of his once oppressive marriage, the new place, running, that honky-tonk song and Olivia Taft. He was sad but free, alive, feral.

> Got a dollar in my pocket, got your letter in my shoe,
> Fresh out of the infantry, and tryin to find you.
> Old 43 is slowin down, the road around the bend,
> I'm on my way to see you again.

He couldn't get it out of his mind. He'd heard it on the radio late on a foggy night, a distant station bouncing signals off the clouds, maybe Reno or Phoenix or Albuquerque. They'd played it twice by request. He'd stopped everything to listen to it the second time, but before it was over the clouds shifted and the signal fell elsewhere.

> I think it was in April but it might have been in May,
> I got on board my Freedom Bird, leavin Cam Ranh Bay.
> I was nearly left in Tokyo, when I couldn't find my plane,
> I was on my way to see you again.
>   —static—
> This time I need more than just a friend . . .
>   —static—
> Woman don't you know that I am not a settled man,
> And life don't seem the same to me since leavin Viet Nam,
> Somehow this time it's different like it's never ever been,
> Now I'm on my way to see you again.
> On my way . . . again . . .
> Honey please don't ask me where I been,
> From Maine . . . where between . . . see you again . . .

Who was this guy? How did he know? Bobby took solace in the song, the lively honky-tonk lilt, the references. He pressed on in a daze, sang the lines over and over to himself in his monotone, singing it as if it were a marching song. He thought about writing to Stacy, about calling, letting her know. He sent a silly "Missing you" card much like Red had sent him when he'd remained at High Meadow. No response.

His new place was on Old Russia Road, a road that predated all the subdivisions of San Martin, stood in a cluster of six cottages on the slope of North Peak mountain. He'd rented Number 101. It called to him the day he saw the data sheet in his multiple listing packet. Hillside, view, remote, the number—it was in his blood. He had taken Olivia Taft there and made love with her on the living room floor before the unlit fireplace, had made love to Olivia who was very beautiful, very sensual, who never smiled. He had sold the Deepwoods Drive house, paid himself the realty commission, split the equity fifty-fifty, the check his last note to Red.

Birds sang along Old Russia Road. Flowers grew wild. The sky was clearer, closer. He broke out his running shoes, found a way to run from his cottage to Cataract Trail, then up the dam steps, those damn steps, and back—a seven-mile loop. He ran daily with Josh, sweating like an overstuffed pig, dropping from 208 in May to 195 in September to his 178-pound target weight by late October. While he ran he composed lines in his mind. When he returned to the cottage he scribbled them down, scribbled them as the sweat from his hand and forearm soaked into the paper and the pen skipped and he'd get frustrated and scribble on the page edge until the pen wouldn't write there either.

Dear Stacy,
   By now you have probably heard from Bea and you know we are divorced. I [scratched out]. Things are going well for me, and I pray for you also. Our divorce was amiable. . . .

How could he include that? He put it aside, thought about running, planned his assault on the Cataract Trail New Year's Day Run. That would be his first. Then the Bay to Breakers, then the real Cataract Race which attracted top runners from all of northern California, and next year's Dipsea and dozens of 10-Ks between. He planned meticulously, studied training literature. He took a large desktop calendar, plotted the weeks, designed daily workouts, projected weight, times, courses, to New Year's Day, to RACE ONE.

He knew the course, as much as anyone could with the construction, the benching, blocking and stripping of the land in total contrast to the spirit of cluster-house development. Mud, silt, and gullies from the first rains of the wet season were already destroying sections of the trail, making the run more steeplechase than trail race.

Bobby's pants had begun falling off his hips, he'd had to buy new clothes because even his old clothes from when he was 178 didn't fit. He ran, composed lines, scribbled notes, worked, loved Olivia on occasion, ran, the hog transforming into the gazelle. He listened to the radio, listened for that song, heard that Medina was acquitted of the My Lai massacre. It meant little to him.

Dear Stacy,
   By now you have probably heard from Bea and you know we are divorced. Although it was mutual the transition has been more difficult than I expected. My emotions swing from elation to depression, from rapture at being alive to loneliness—though not for Bea. I'm exhausted, though I think stronger and wiser. I pray things are well with you. I'd love to be there for autumn, I miss the colors, I think of you. I'm sorry for this past year, for what happened, but I cannot tell you all because the secret is Red's as well as mine.

Bobby stopped. Reread the last line, decided to leave it.

   I once had a dream. You remember? I still have it—expanded. I dream of a community, exactly where I don't know, but a community of friends, clear thinkers, hard workers. A contrast community—set apart but not isolated—apart from the callous, chaotic and corrupt world which I see about me. A community *designed* to exact the best from the individual and the whole. Most people are either unable or unwilling to take responsibility for themselves. People are capable of thinking. The problem arises from lack of motivation, from the near universal desire to get something for nothing, from the corporate mind-set of selling nothing packaged as something. Daily my apprehensions rise as to the ability of this country to avert a major economic crisis. Talent and materials surround us, but the desire to produce seems to have died.

Is it possible for a loose community of individuals to be responsible for what they produce and what they consume? I think it is.

Please tell me what you think. Help me.

Love,
Rob

He had mailed it, gone for a run, bested his previous record on the Old Mine/Cataract Trail loop to 49:49 or 7:07 per mile. His weight dropped to 174.

San Martin, California, Friday 26 November 1971—He sat at the dining area table. Josh lay in the living room before the fireplace. Bobby glared out the sliding glass door, over the small deck, not conscious of the gold-brown fields dropping away, the clumps of tree-green in small draws. On Wednesday he'd received a note from Red. "The time we had together was for the most part enjoyable," she'd written. "We're just finished with those episodes and moving on to a new series. . . . " Bobby thinking, like we were a damn TV show. "My therapist says we shouldn't judge our time together by the last few months . . . "

That had put him in a funk but nothing like the letter that had just arrived.

Dear Robert,

I do not know you. You don't know me. It is difficult to harbor ill feelings toward you, but wake up. Stacy and I are very much in love, we're planning on marriage, we don't need or want love letters from an "old flame." You'd agree if you were in my shoes.

You have recently separated and are divorcing. I sympathize with your emotional swings, but you must direct those emotions elsewhere. Stacy assures me you are "no threat" to us. Still you are an unwanted intrusion. Maybe someday we'll all be friends but in the meantime I hope you understand our feelings and respect them.

Sincerely,
Harlan LaFacetie

He read it, reread it, erupted, gripped the table, banged the two legs on his side on the floor like a pile driver trying to smash through. "I am such a fucking fool." He sat, jerked up again, his lap crashing the table against the glass door. He punched his face, raised a lump on his cheek. One year from the weekend with Stacy, he thought. "HOW in Hell did I LET this Happen!?"

Montage: A client's home. She was divorcing. Her husband had moved out. "I'd really love to cook this for you someday," she said. He smiled. Their business over, they had turned to cookbooks, South American cuisine, photos of the ruins of the Inca empire. The conversation seemed unique. "Have another glass of sherry," she said. By the gods, he thought, *she's* trying to get *me* drunk. She leaned forward, kissed him, grabbed his hand, lead him to the living room, seduced him.

Later, on the drive back up Highway 101, one hand over one eye to keep his drunken vision single, he thought, the old Wapinski charm still works. Then his monotone bellowing, " 'I think it was in April but it mighta been in May, / Got aboard my Freedom Bird leavin Cam Ranh Bay. / I was nearly left in Mill Creek, when I couldn't find my dame, / I'm on my way to find some again . . . .' "

> The land war continues to make news. Yesterday [2 Dec '71] North Viet Namese troops overran government forces at the central Cambodian city of Baray, killing perhaps half of Lon Nol's 20,000-man force. . . .

Numerous nights, numerous bars, singles' bars, looking for Miss Goodbar, looking really for . . . He didn't know. He laughed, smirked, downed his scotch, flipped another sawbuck on the bar. Behind him ladies cruised the floor. One pinched him. "You got a nice ass." She moved on.

Work was going well. At the company Christmas party he met an agent from Concord. They compared sales, incomes. She made more than he so took him home, fucked his eyes out, told him to leave.

He lost more weight as if breaking through his target pulled the floor from beneath him. He crashed uncontrollably to 166, to 164, to 162. He was too sick on New Year's Day to run the Cataract Trail race.

> Senator Hubert Humphrey today threw his hat into the presidential ring, declaring, "Had I been elected, we would now be out of this war." Humphrey, a presidential candidate in 1968, added that it is taking President Nixon longer to withdraw American soldiers from Viet Nam than it took the allies to defeat Hitler.
>
> U.S. troop strength in Viet Nam is 159,000, down 70% from its peak three years ago. Last week Nixon announced the planned withdrawal of 25,000 to 35,000 more Americans.

"He's a Husk-perd," Wapinski said into the phone. "They're really a great breed and he's best of the breed."

"Well, I'm sure he's a lovely animal," Mrs. Closson said. It was the first he'd spoken to her. She lived at 103 Old Russia Road. "But Tabitha is scared to death of Husk-perds. Do keep him away from her, please."

"Oh! Certainly." Bobby bit his lip, stared at Olivia who'd just come into his office. "And, ah, if you could keep Tabitha out of our yard too, that'd make it easier." Bobby hung up. "Bitch." He looked at Olivia who'd come next to him, leaned back against his desk.

"The Klemenchichs listed their house with Everest Realty," she said.

"Bitch." He ground his teeth. He didn't need them. Business was good. He looked at Olivia's legs, raised his eyes to her hips, waist, breasts, face. A testosterone tingle elevated him.

"Not this week," she whispered.

Bitch, he thought.

Stresses built. Bars were out. He couldn't take it, told himself he was more selective. He bought a new car—a sexy California-poppy yellow Capri. He paid cash. He bought new clothes. He spent money on expensive restaurants, on trinkets and trash. He took one woman up to the wineries in Napa (my bed or yours?), one to dinner and films (do you like to be on top?), one to parties (your body is sooo warm), one to a jazz club. He was getting good at being single.

"Robert, we can do better than that."

"Well, Mr. Everest, I'm not exactly sure."

"Read it over," Everest said. He handed Bobby the papers: Everest Realty—Manager's Employment Agreement. "You wouldn't be working in the shadow of Peter, anymore," Dirk Everest said. "You'd take over completely. Build it how you want. Bring some of those salespeople with you. You'll have my complete backing."

Bobby scanned the top sheet. "Manager shall receive an override on each closed escrow in the amount of $80.00, which will be paid . . . " He suppressed a smile. Double his Great Homes deal. "Let me get back to you, Mr. Everest."

"Dirk," Mr. Everest said. "Call me Dirk."

President Richard Nixon arrived in Peking today [21 Feb '72] declaring this "the week that changed the world." The president met with Prime Minister Chou En-lai and the two leaders predicted an early peace in Viet Nam. North Viet Namese officials in Paris voiced exception to both Chinese and American statements. Analysts believe the North Viet Namese fear that China, which recently doubled its military aid to Communist Viet Nam, will make a deal "behind closed doors."

Other news: Efforts to halt plans for the development of North Peak Condominium World failed today when state Water Resource officials misfiled their Application to Review with the state Department of

Environmental Protection. Also spraying of Atlantic-Pacific timber-lands in Sonoma and San Martin counties with herbicides designed to kill broadleaf vegetation was declared the "only economically feasible method to promote fir seedling growth," corporate officials said today on conditions of anonymity.

"Rob."
"Yes"
"Brian."
"Hey, Brian, how—"
"You gotta come home."
"What? I can't just—"
"Granpa's in a real bad way. He must a fallen last week and broke his hip or something. They didn't find him until this morning."

He did not stop to see his mother or brother but drove the rented yellow Mercury Capri—exactly like the one he'd purchased except this yellow was more banana than poppy—directly toward Grandpa's. As he motored past the Episcopal church, the cemetery, past Third Street, up Mill Creek Road, he muttered, "Screw the bitch. I'll call from up there." Then the lyrics from the Turtles' "Happy Together" wafted into his mind: *Me and you and you and me, no matter how they toss the dice, it had to be....* He gritted his teeth, wanted to turn it off. He passed Lloyd's Autoland and Franklin GM, passed the dump road, slid the Capri through the icy esses by the falls and the Old Mill. Snow was packed in berms at roadside, salt and sand splotched the road. *I can't see me lovin...* It was dusk, 4:15 Leap Year Day 1972.

Grandpa Wapinski had fallen Saturday morning, the twenty-sixth, from the ladder leading to the second-floor barn office. He had lain on the unheated barn floor in those cold Pennsylvania mountains with a broken hip until Monday the twenty-eighth when Tony Pisano, newly released from Rock Ridge, had shown up out of the clear blue. Tony had wrapped him and carried him to the house and called Linda, who had been planning to come to High Meadow after she did Grandpa Wapinski's weekly shopping as she was now doing every Monday morning before coming with the twins to stay for the week.

Linda had called for an ambulance, beat it to the farm, found Tony whimpering, warming the old man, rubbing his feet which were blue, doing all the right things as he'd done in Boston on Storrow Drive, as he'd always done in crises. But he was now shaken to the core—Tony's last anchorline was but a thread, hanging. She had not greeted him but ordered him to get the girls from the car as she checked Pewel's vital signs—which were barely existent. Then together, as the twins watched cartoons on the old TV in the living room, they tried to warm him.

The ambulance had arrived and she asked Tony to stay with the girls while she went with the old man. When Brian reached Bobby late that day, the doctors had just told them about the old man's hip.

No one was at High Meadow. The '53 Chevy was gone. There was no answer at Brian's. He dialed 3-1-5-4, hung up before it rang. How could he call Miriam? How could he call, divorcing, without a meaningful soul in his life, defeated? How could he not?

He went to the back door, the way he'd come in. He lit a cigarette. The path to the barn had been shoveled. The sides of the snow trench were perfectly smooth, perfectly straight. He laughed, realized that the old man must have shoveled the last snow himself because no one shoveled a trench like that. Bobby reentered the house. On the old refrigerator, held by magnets, were a child's drawings. In the living room there were toddler toys. Across the stairs was a folding gate. He stopped, dialed Miriam again. As it rang he thought about Stacy. And Harlan. Thought about his grandpa's comment on "unfinished business," thought about Olivia.

"Three-one-five-four."

"Mom."

"Who's this?"

"Rob."

"Oh."

"I was calling about Grandpa."

"He fell and broke something. He's in the hospital."

"Where?"

"St. Luke's in Rock Ridge, I suppose. Or maybe Divine Providence down in Williamsport."

"Haven't you ca—Ah, is Brian there? There's no answer at his house."

"He's probably not home from work yet. Where are you, anyway?"

"I'm up at Grandpa's. I just got here."

"Humph. Why don't you call that Eye-talian girl he has clean up after him?"

"Do you have her number?"

"Am I information?"

"No. I'm sorry. What's her name? Pisanti or something, isn't it?"

"One of those names. Pisano. It's P-I-S-A-N-O."

"Thanks."

"Are you going to grace us with your presence?"

"I'll be there after I find out . . ."

"Well, call first. You know how I feel when people just burst in."

There were five Pisanos in the book. He dialed one. "Hay-lloh."

"Mr. Pisano?"

"Yes."

"This is Robert Wapinski."

"Oh. Pewel's grandson."

"Yes." Bobby was amazed at the instant recognition. "I'm trying to find out about my grandfather. Is it your wife who takes care of him?"

"Oh, no. He calls you Bob, right?"

"Um-hmm."

"Bob, that's my daughter-in-law. Let me give you the number. Do you have a pen? Ah, I've got the number at the hospital, too. But try Linda at home first. She'll probably tell you more than the people at St. Luke's. Cheryl's there too. That's a cute nephew you've got." Eerie. The man knew more about Bobby's family than his own mother did—or even he himself.

At the hospital Bobby met Linda. She hugged him. She was warm, physically warm, a bit plump, not a California-woman, comforting, sensible. "Go in and see him," she said. "He's on pain killers for his hip. And his body's still cool but ... Bob, even if he doesn't respond, he'll hear you."

Bobby looked down the hall. He was afraid to go.

"The doctors can't believe how strong he is. The fracture's a crack—" she showed him with her hands, together, flat, then she bent them slightly, "not a snap. For a man his age, they say he's got the bones of a forty-year-old."

Bobby smiled faintly. He wanted her to come with him, to lead him, but he couldn't ask.

"I'm sorry you missed Brian and Tony," Linda said. "They just left. Go in and see your grandpa. It'll mean a lot to him to know you're here. He talks about you all the time."

Pewel Wapinski's shoulders and head were propped slightly. His nose was covered with a translucent green plastic oxygen mask. Saline was dripping from a bottle into a regulator into a tube that ran into his left arm. Wires ran from his chest to a heart monitor. A tube came from beneath the blankets, fell from bedside to a collection bag near the floor. His feet, legs and hands were wrapped in electric blankets or pads. A temporary cast immobilized his pelvis, back, legs. His face was pink, almost ruddy, not ashen as Bobby had expected. Still, to Bobby, he looked dead.

"Hi Granpa." Bobby reached to grasp the old man's hand but it was wrapped. He touched his grandfather's face. "It's me," he said. "I'm sorry I didn't make it back for Thanksgiving." There was no movement, no response. "You know, I think about coming back all the time but it just isn't the right time yet." Bobby felt frustrated. He wanted his grandfather to know he was there. "This is like ... how old was I? I think I was a sophomore when Aunt Krystyna broke her hip. You told me that that happens with women because the angle of their hips are wider and therefore not as strong. Remember? I was fourteen or fifteen and I thought well why not redesign their hips." Bobby chuckled, closed his eyes, flashed on Linda.

That night Bobby slept in the waiting room. Linda woke him at eight thirty. She introduced him to Tony. The three barely spoke. Brian and Cheryl arrived, then Aunt Isabella Pellegrino.

"Are they going to amputate his legs?" Brian asked Linda. That shocked Bobby. No one had mentioned that to him.

A somber Filipino doctor with a thick accent approached them all in the waiting room. "You come down, now," he said.

Linda shuddered. She knew. She'd been there before, numerous times, working, training in ICUs and CCUs. She smiled but her eyes were wet. Bobby and Brian and Tony remained silent, not looking at each other, looking down.

Pewel had been awake since six thirty. He didn't know about the contingent of visitors hovering, waiting, expecting the worst. His hip pain was excruciating. They'd given him Demerol. More than anything he was feeling cantankerous, irritable, angry that somebody had shoved a catheter up his urethra. At eight the doctor had told him about his hip, had shown him the X-ray and pointed out the shadow where no shadow should have been, had told him he'd had a close call.

Bobby walked in first. Brian and Cheryl were directly behind. Immediately Pewel boomed, "Fine thing. I've got to break my hip to get you to visit." Bobby's, Brian's, Cheryl's mouths dropped. Linda pushed in. Tony and Isabella stood behind, peered between heads. "Hey"—Pewel's voice was hoarse—"why's everybody here? Aw! You thought . . . eh?" He shook his head. "Nothin wrong with dyin." He lifted his head, shoulders, pushed against the cast, winced. "We're all goina do it. But not jus yet."

Bobby slapped his own face, laughed, gently hugged the old geezer.

"Fine thing," Pewel repeated.

Laughs, chuckles, apologies. "And you," Pewel pointed at Tony. "Daylight's burnin. Now I can't bring wood to the evaporator but I can stoke the fire and I'm sure's hell looking forward to being warm."

"Granpa," Bobby blurted. "You gave us such a scare."

"One of these days," Pewel snarled but not angrily, "I'm going to teach you two boys how to live. Life skills. Just like runnin a farm. Doctor said my feet'll be fine. Just tender for a while."

"When I came in last night I thought . . . "

"Nothin wrong with dyin," Pewel repeated. "But I'm conservative. Don't rush into things. Now I got this worked out." He pointed at Bobby. "You gotta go back, eh?"

"Not right away."

"Soon enough. And I know Linda here, you and Tony"—Linda sniffed—"I know and I sure's hell don't blame you. So Tony you live with me. For six months. That's your penance before you can go back."

17

Mill Creek had been but a respite, a temporary remission. On the return flight, staring at incredible cloud formations—pure white fluff sparkling in the sun's brilliance, intricate nooks, crannies, crevices, dark canyons, immense cotton-ball head walls to thirty-six thousand feet—Bobby's confusion exacerbated. That guy gonna live with him for six months? Penance? He's *my* grandfather. Bummer, Man. He knows I couldn't stay. Then without inner verbiage, which he could control, but with inner images, which he could not: Stacy—should have called—couldn't—the Capri parked uphill on her street, an OP. His insides roiled, the clouds darkened. They don't understand, he thought. But he knew it was he that did not understand, did not comprehend what had happened, was happening. How badly he wanted to do right. He'd never lost his belief in doing right. But now he felt guilty for fucking up, for running away. How could he ever go back?

Jane picked him up at the airport. "No problem," she'd said. She drove him home, to 101 Old Russia Road. He thanked her. Did not invite her in. Not staid Jane. He spent the night with Josh and with whiskey.

In the morning he ran. His weight seemed to have stabilized between 157 and 160. He felt ill. His nose ran, his chest was tight, he coughed. Still he ran, feeling the alcohol and whiskey toxins surfacing. He went easy the first mile, picked up the pace on the second. Felt nauseated by the fourth. He coughed and phlegm broke loose, came to his mouth. His sweat dried. Chills skittered across his shoulders. Inside, sitting, he broke into a sweat. He called in sick, went to bed. The next day he again called in sick. And again the next and the next. He saw no one, spoke only to Josh and even to Josh he spoke sparingly. He felt his neck. The lymph nodes at the base felt like sacks of BBs, the glands under his jawbone felt like plums. I am sick, he told himself, yet lingering beneath the thought he suspected the lethargy was not the flu. He piled on more blankets, plus the sleeping bag he'd bought but never used, and his new trench coat. Still he shivered. He coaxed Josh up. Bobby ached. He rolled to his side, brought his knees up, arms crossed. He nodded, slept, dreamed but did not recall the dream, woke wet, the sheets and covers soaked. Josh's head was on the pillow. "Ghee-it down." He pushed Josh away, threw the covers back, got up. His skin felt cool as the sweat evaporated.

Bobby picked up where he left off. "I can't put my finger on it," he said to one woman, one afternoon.

"You're just feeling guilty about having a good time," she countered.

He let it go, sipped the superb zinfandel, cut her another piece of cheese, pinched off another piece of French bread. The day was warm, the sun high. In the shade of the ancient stone bastion of Buena Vista Winery, he kissed her. She was delightful. Something was not right.

"I decided to stay with Great Homes," he said.

"Oh," she said. The reference meant nothing to her and he realized that he'd told someone else, some other her, about Dirk Everest's offer.

In Viet Nam the Easter Offensive began.

North Viet Namese divisions continued their massive offensive in the South with attacks on dozens of allied positions below the DMZ. The attack, which began with a 5,000-round long-range artillery barrage across the DMZ on March 30th, has become a general offensive with the NVA opening secondary fronts in the Central Highlands and in Bing Long Province north of Saigon. Observers have reported sighting Soviet-built tanks on all fronts. Military analysts estimate the North Viet Namese strength at 150,000 troops. Observers say ARVN forces have generally elected to withdraw rather than stand and fight and some American advisors have denounced the South Viet Namese for their lack of offensive spirit. In the north, the NVA have launched assaults from the A Shau Valley which have quickly overpowered ARVN and the remaining American defensive fire support bases. . . .

Bobby paid little attention. He was disillusioned, tired. He wanted to prepare for the Bay-to-Breakers race in May but his times were worse than they'd been six months earlier.

> After a three-and-a-half-year halt, the United States today [6 Apr. '72], in response to the communist offensive in South Viet Nam, resumed its bombing of the North. .

Over the next few months Bobby spent more time with the guys from his office. He had a full-size basketball court built on the downhill side of the cottage and mounted lights on the building so they could play at night. Sometimes as many as fourteen of them played ball on Bobby's court, drank beer from his cooler. Basketball gave him courage. Self-confidence. It also gave him much greater speed in his kick when he ran the Cataract/Old Mine Trail loop. He lowered his personal best by a full minute but still skipped the Bay-to-Breakers race, decided instead to aim for the Dipsea. His weight increased to 168. He felt healthy and strong, yet he was not out of the rut, had not stopped the spiritual descent.

Spring passed to summer. The Democratic National Convention Platform Committee adopted a plank establishing the primacy of immediate withdrawal of all U.S. forces from Viet Nam. Bobby agreed. Why not? What was the use of continuing the war? He wasn't following the action but then few, it seemed, were. The greater portion of the news was given over to antiwar maneuvers. He tuned most of it out. "It's best if we just get out and get on with our lives," Bobby said to Olivia—Olivia who was back in his bed again, whom he now grasped as if she were his salvation though their occasional afternoon trysts were still completely secret. "Those people obviously don't give a damn about their own country."

On the 26th and 27th of August he was ill again, and again he decided against running the Dipsea.

Bobby thought constantly about Pennsylvania, about "home." He followed Pewel's recovery, which according to Linda Pisano was nothing short of miraculous for a man of 83, recovery moving from cast and bed to walker to canes. To Bobby his grandfather sounded old. Pewel complained about not being able to get to his barn office. Bobby researched, sketched, sent his grandfather a design for an elevator that could be built cheaply, that would operate on old electric motors that Bobby knew were stashed in a bin in the barn. Tony, he wrote, could build it in two or three days.

Olivia blew him off again, and he ranted about the promiscuous psycho-bitch from hell. Alone, in the cottage, he skimmed AP refugee and escapee reports of atrocities committed by communists in areas they'd taken during the Easter Offensive.

> As refugees tell it, 40 civilians in Quang Ngai Province were locked in a building and blown up with dynamite because they were considered unsuitable for indoctrination.

In other cases, wives and children have watched their menfolk shot in batches of a dozen following "people's trials." ... Their crime: lack of enthusiasm for Hanoi's brand of liberation.... Since the offensive began, authorities have reported confirmation of 2,558 civilian assassinations, 9,313 abductions ...

His ranting doubled but he did not know why.

"Another beer?" He and Al had played some one-on-one half-court under the lights, had worked up a good sweat.

"Yeah," Bobby said. "I'll get em."

"Nah, I'm up. You're really on a bummer, Man."

"Yeah," Bobby said. "You know, except for Josh, I'm ... I'm really fuckin lonely. I don't want to live like this."

"Um." Al uncapped the long-neck bottles, handed one to Bobby. "What are you gonna do about it?"

"Finish that case a beer," Bobby grumbled. "I'm a serious guy, Al. Ladies don't like that. You know, all the time they want you to make em laugh. I'm not good at that. You ever try talkin to a woman about work? I don't mean in the office."

"Maybe you're talking to the wrong ladies," Al said.

"They're all like that." Bobby rose, stumbled.

"Jane's not."

"Staid Jane. Aw, she'd never look twice at me."

"I think she likes you, Man."

Shortly after Richard Nixon humiliated George McGovern at the polls, Bobby Wapinski began quietly dating Jane Boswell. Jane, like all the Great Homes Realty female agents, was pretty, yet with Jane it was more subtle. And for the first time in a long time Bobby experienced, recognized, saw the person he was dating, and not a projection of himself. They attended a personal-growth workshop. "For life to be better to you, you've got to be better." "Set your goals. List the reasons why you want to reach those objectives." "Become attractive and you will attract what you want." "Attitude is ultimate. It makes the ultimate difference in the quality of life."

Bobby was enthralled. Someone was revealing a format upon which he could hang various elements of his disgust. Jane too was excited. He told her about his rebound from Stacy, his marriage to Red. She told him about moving from England when she was thirteen, about feeling an outcast all through her teens because she had so few common reference points, about a brief marriage that ended in annulment.

They attended more seminars, arrived separately, left separately, met afterward at his cottage, talked long into the night, hugged, kissed, not lovers but loving. The only drawback, for Bobby, for Jane too, was the reaction of Al Bartecchi. He was Bobby's friend, Jane's friend. He'd even been the one who'd steered Bobby to her. Yet he'd become sullen, subtly exuding a sadness whenever he saw them.

On a night in early December, Jane said, "I love to touch and I love to be touched."

"I do too," Bobby answered. They had never been so close. He certainly, and he thought she, was thinking long term. "Sometimes I like to be alone."

"Me too."

"And someday I'd like to have a family."

That drove a wedge between them, but it did not seem insurmountable. They continued to keep their relationship private. Al Bartecchi continued to suffer in silence until Bobby realized that Al must have come by to play hoops, must have seen Jane's car.

"Hey Man, you comin up tonight?" Bobby.

"You got a group comin?" Al.

"Naw. Just a little one-on-one. I don't want to go too hard. I'm going to run the Cataract New Year's race. I don't want to get hurt."

That night they played but they played hardly at all. The court was slick with mist. "Al," Bobby said when they went in, "I've got a dilemma. You know I've been dating Jane."

"Yeah." Al did all he could not to let his sadness show.

"And I like her. She's a hell of a person."

"Yeah. Seems to be."

"But you know who I'd really like to be with"— Al looked quizzically at him, uttered nothing— "is Sharon."

"Sharon!"

"Yeah. Is that stupid?"

Al suppressed a smile. "No. But she's living with some guy."

"I know, but I don't think it's very stable. I overheard her telling Olivia about some problems."

"I don't know, Bob."

"Yeah, me either. But she's so attractive. I think sometimes I go in just to see her smile."

"Well, go for it, Man."

"I'd feel better about trying if you'd—this is kind of hard to ask—if you'd maybe take Jane out. You know, we . . . I feel like this obligation to her and if you guys went out that would break it."

That night Bobby swore he saw Al float to his car. That night, with only Josh to talk to, he whimpered, alone. He made a try for Sharon. She was physically more beautiful than he'd ever realized, as if his eyes had just focused or adjusted to low light. She was more poised, too, more intelligent, more active, and her beliefs seemed more in line with his own. She wanted to have a family—not yet, but she loved kids. He developed a crush, spent hours thinking about her. He confessed to her his love. Sharon never led him on. "I'm a one-man woman," she said to him, "and my man is a one-woman man." He felt like a fool, but he couldn't control himself. He'd found her. She was, to him, perfection. But she was unavailable, uninterested.

He attended more seminars. "In life, do all that you can; be all that you can; read, design, create, feel, earn all that you can. Keep testing the outer limits of your ability. . . . How would you be if you were the person you truly wished to be? What do you need to do to be that person?"

Create. Design. Build. Strengthen yourself, he told himself. Wapinski building blocks. What would Granpa do?

Still he sank lower.

And PEACE was NOT at hand. The negotiations in Paris had failed. Everything down the tubes. America resumed the bombing of Hanoi and Haiphong. The press labeled it the Christmas Bombings. He heard but he couldn't pay attention.

Friday, 22 December 1972—"Oh, Bob, it's very good to see you here."

"Mr. Everest."

"Dirk. Come on now. Hey, I want you to meet my wife. She doesn't usually come to these Realtor parties, but I got her involved in this one by putting her in charge of the Christmas decorations." Dirk Everest turned, looked for his wife. They were in the main dining room of the San Martin Golf and Country Club clubhouse. At least 150 people were in attendance. Bobby had come alone. He had been hoping that Sharon and her one-woman man would be there, had thought all day about what she'd look like in a formal gown or a party dress. He'd come standing tall, clean, in a new lightweight wool-blend suit. "Honey," Dirk said, "this is Robert Wapinski, the man I tried to steal from Peter Wilcox. Bob, this is my wife."

"Diana," she said.

"My pleasure." He bowed slightly, gulped. She was twenty years Dirk's junior, appeared more like his daughter than his wife.

"Would you two excuse me a moment," Dirk said. "I see Ernie Schnell over there. We've got something going and I've got to ask him . . . you understand."

Diana understood. Bobby didn't but he willingly followed. She was attractive, perhaps a little heavy in the hips, perhaps too much make-up, too red lipstick, too black eyeliner but certainly lovely, and lovelier as she and Bobby danced, as they drank champagne cocktails through Santa-hat straws from white-bearded glasses, as she dragged him around to chat with others as if they, Diana and Bobby, were a couple. Later they spoke privately, sweetly, on the patio overlooking the eighteenth green. There she kissed him, lead him into the shadows where they kissed like adolescents. She pulled his head to her bosom, exposed her shoulders, her bra. He worked frantically to unfasten the front bra clip as she pushed her breasts into his face. He kissed that wonderful skin until suddenly she shuddered, stiffened, pulled back, covered herself. "Dirk's watching," she whispered indignantly. Then she strutted away.

At noon on the 23d Peter Wilcox called him, laughing, thinking the whole thing hilarious. "I heard Everest caught you in bed with his wife last night."

"What?"

"What a foxy broad, huh? You're pretty foxy yourself, you sly dog."

"In bed? I wasn't—"

"Yeah. Yeah. Dirk called himself. He was pretty upset."

"Wait a minute. I wasn't in bed with her."

"That's what Dirk said."

"No way. We got smashed on those Santa Claus drinks. We kissed some. That's all."

"Yeah, yeah." Peter cracked up. "He might be out gunnin for ya. But I'd risk that for a night shackin with Diana. Are those tits as nice as they look?"

"Damn it, I wasn't . . ."

By Christmas Eve Bobby had heard from Al and Dan, Tom, Jon Ross, Lisa Fonari and Liza Caldicott. He'd cuckolded Dirk Everest. Everest was steamed, Lisa told him, already had his attorney draw up divorce papers.

"Mr. Everest."

"Yes. Who's this?" The voice on the phone was terse.

"Robert Wapinski."

"You've got one hell of a nerve—"

"I called to apologize. But I also want to set something straight. I wasn't in bed with your wife. We didn't do anything—"

"That's bullshit. I saw what you two were doin with my own eyes."

"Look. You're right. We were out on the patio. It was way out of line. We kissed. Nothing more."

"You're amazing."

"Really, Mr. Everest. I'm sorry. I'm really very sorry. I drank too much. But really, nothing happened."

The phone was banged down.

Another guilt trip. Bobby hung his head, beat the heel of his hand into his forehead, moaned angrily, "Welcome to my comic strip." Then he fell to his knees and repeated over and over, "Never again. Never again." For five days he beat himself, physically, emotionally.

Again Bobby skipped a race that he'd prepared for. He hurt physically. He was sure he was going blind, knew he was dumb, knew his kidneys were failing, his heart valves leaking and his brain becoming mush. Night after night he sat in that isolated cottage, in the living room wrapped in a blanket, freezing in that warm house, keeping the interior lights low, the curtains drawn, staying away from the court, afraid Dirk would shoot him, perhaps shoot through the curtains at his silhouetted shadow.

An Agreement Ending the War and Restoring Peace in Viet Nam was signed today [27 Jan. '73] in Paris by representatives of the United

States, North and South Viet Nam, and the Viet Cong. The United States and South Viet Nam signed different versions of the peace agreement because of South Viet Nam's intransient position and their unwillingness to recognize the Viet Cong's Provisional Revolutionary Government.

Over. End of an Era. Last US Troops Leave Viet Nam. Bobby clipped the articles, but read only the first few paragraphs, perhaps a cutline if it caught his eye.

Under a picture of Le Duc Tho, the North Viet Namese negotiator in Paris:

> For the fifth time we have declared clearly that the DRV (Hanoi) and the PRG (Viet Cong) have never wished to force a Communist government on South Vietnam. We only want there to be in the South a National Reconciliation government supporting peace, independence, neutrality and democracy.

Over. Ended. He'd blown it. Aloneness became the anvil against which he attempted to hammer himself, to forge a new being. He began drawing at night. Small sketches on scraps of paper. He drew plans for a desk organizer, for a running-shoe rack, for closet and cabinet organizers, dish stackers, camping equipment holders. " 'This time I need more than just a friend,' " he sang quietly in his monotone honky-tonk, " 'I'm on my way to see you ah-gheen.' " He designed and began to work on an office-mobile—his old '67 Chevy sedan. He brought it down to the edge of the basketball court, ripped out the seats making one large open compartment, carefully measured the interior. He drew orthographic and isometric sketches, labeled all dimensions. Then he overlaid tracing paper and sketched in a driver's chair that could swivel to shelves along the passenger side, to a desk where the rear seat had been. He drew a collapsible desktop that, with the driver's seat folded flat, became a six-six bed.

Late, very late, after the hit-man hour (when no hit man would think to come because all the lights would be out and there would be no shadows to fire at), Bobby walked. He walked without a flashlight because there was always enough ambient light—either from moon and stars on clear nights or from the reflection off the firmament of the mercury bulbs blazing at North Bay Mall on cloud-cloaked nights. He walked with Josh, quietly, slowly, following Old Mine Trail to the remnant of Cataract, past the very first sold and occupied cluster homes, through the construction site, more than a mile of ripped-up land with varying dark monsters: backhoes and cranes looking like brontosaurs bent, eating the earth; past row-house condominium frames looking like a forest seared by wildfire; past huge piles of white plastic drain pipe looking like the last burial ground of the mastodons, their ivory tusks collected and stacked for shipping, powdering, an aphrodisiac to humanity fucking the earth. Some nights he raged inside about inflation or crime or toxic dumping. A male agent from Golden Hills Realty had answered an up-call, had met this "client" at a vacant house, been robbed, beaten, shot in the head, and abandoned. One more downer. One more reason to say fuck it all.

He walked slowly, delicately. He crossed small sand-gravel gullies, stepped into slippery clay-silt deltas, buildups that sucked his running shoes from his feet, stood upon large newly exposed boulders or smaller rocks, the size of basketballs, washed clean by the last downpour, the last torrent eroding North Peak mountain. In the dim light the creek waters looked gray, murky. He thought of the time he'd fished this stretch, of the trout that hid in the cover along the edge. Now he stood on a lip directly over the water's roil, peering down into the spindrift above the gray cascade. To the north, behind him, he heard the predawn chirp and trill of songbirds. He turned, glanced back across the dark blocks and skeletons of North Peak CondoWorld.

The lip beneath him shifted. He shifted his weight, began to step back. It happened as if in slow motion, the earth giving out, sliding slowly then avalanching, he twisting, hand reaching to the stable ground just inches behind, one leg, foot rising, the other falling with the lip, then quickly his legs out from under him, thwack, his head, the gravel, the immediate feel of blood followed immediately by inundation and the roil of the cascade.

His body lies in a shallow paddy. He is on his side. The water is five inches deep. He has sunk two inches into the mud beneath the water. Grass, rice, offer little cover. The air is thick, humid. The water is foul, oily, sticky. He lies on his side keeping half his face out of the water, just high enough to keep from drowning. The top and right side of his face are exposed, bloody from hitting the gravel. Rifle fire comes from the tree line. Undefoliated. Assholes, he thinks. The water is getting cold. Damn cold. Better cold. Better to feel cold than to feel nothing at all. In the water there are swirls of violet and blue from the oil and of red from the blood. Has he been hit? No one near. The water is stagnant. Maybe it's blood. Something moves before him. A trout, he thinks. Or a turtle. He wants to reach for his 16, for his bayonet. He wants to stab the ripples. What the hell's there? But he does not want to move. What if they see him. There isn't enough concealment to hide a swimming duck in this paddy, much less a moving man. He lies perfectly still, on his side, his legs beneath the water. His right hip protrudes. In white. White! What the fuck am I doing in white? They'll see me. He cannot move. Where are the others? Why doesn't he have on fatigues, cammies? Why is he in this foul stench of a paddy? Couldn't be a paddy. Paddies don't defoliate. Must be a manioc grove, a teak stand, something, and someone must have cut all the wood, carted it away for fuel, left this rotting barren bog. Bog, that won't be a fish. Water spider? No. No fuckin way. He does not move. They are firing at him. He cannot move. Where's his 16? Has he fallen on it? The swirling before him comes closer to his face.

His waist is completely submerged but his hip shows white in the marsh muck, against the graying sky. His torso emerges from the water just below his arm pits. It is wrapped in white. His right arm is behind him. Tied. Tied to something. Lines into it and tied to something. He can't move. His neck is below the waterline. Submerged. Half his head. His heavy head. Have to keep it up. Can't let it drop. His neck muscles cramp from keeping his head just so, his nostrils above water. They're going to shoot me. Don't let them shoot me. White! For God's sakes! Who put me in white? He coughs. Something bites him, inside. Something bites his lungs. He tries to raise his face just an eighth of an inch, just enough to get his lips out of the water. He coughs on the red swirl in the water. It is seeping into his mouth. Don't let them shoot. Under the water, something on him. A hand? A crab? A spider? Sudden jerk. A leg. On his face. He opens his mouth to scream. Red swirls gushed in. Drowning. Bit. Bit my face. Get it off my face. Get it off. Pulling, ripping, surging with all his strength. Get it off! His right arm breaks away, reaches his face, grabs the crab/spider but it is locked on his face biting his eyes.

He lets go, falls, falls into his own mind, swirling, seeing himself as Stacy, as Red, as Olivia. Seeing himself in a rushing swirl of colorful dresses, of perfect teeth, makeup, eyes, hair, Lisa, wine, women without names, Jane Sharon Diana. Seeing himself without self, seeing un-self prodded by corruption; by crime unreacted to; by toxic assaults unopposed; by political lies condoned; by ambient cultural masturbation acquiesced, assimilated, accepting the path of least resistance, the easy way, the tons of regret; by denial of self all swirling together losing what was good, losing values—take these with you . . . Integrity. Virtue. Pride. Responsibility. Freedom. Faith. Family. Courage.

Then there is the noise, the sharp cracking barks, repeated yips, whines. Like Josh chasing a jackrabbit. Josh.

Bobby is at the side, the bank. His face aches. His body is limp. Dawn has broken. The sky is overcast, rumpled, splotched bright to gray to black. Josh paws his shoulder. Bobby laughs weak, but laughs. From the ground the Lower Res looks immense, a sea edged with trees, the earth. The small gully in which he lay towers over him. The sky stretches forever.

18

San Francisco, mid-September 1971—Ty stood in the aisle. His hand throbbed; his groin ached; his head hurt. He held the chrome overhead bar with his right hand as he had each workday evening for the past month. She sat in front, as always, sideways as always, behind the driver. He kept his left hand in his jacket pocket, slouched, stared up, forward, aware of her yet not looking at her, aware of her long straight hair, gaunt face, long straight body. He wanted to watch her, catch the light blue of her eyes if she raised her face. But he dared not. The man in the Raiders jacket was not behind him. Behind him was a haggard black woman with two children. Since they'd boarded she'd been berating the boy, perhaps eight years old, for having dropped ice cream on his pants. "How'm I gon clean em tonight? En have em dry fo tomorrow fo I get you to school? Bran new pants! How come you do this? I work, en fo what?" Loud. Pained. Sharing her plight with an entire bus of strangers; the boy shy, slouched, his head down but nowhere to hide; the girl, perhaps six, assuming a posture that said, "Not me. He did it." And Tyrone Dorsey in front of them in his suit and fine shirt and polished shoes, not turning, assuming too a posture that said, "Not me. They are not with me. All blacks are not like them."

His eyes itched, were watery and red. The bus stopped. People shuffled. His eyes darted to the gaunt white woman who timidly glanced up, back, then tightened her knees against the seat and twisted her feet attempting to keep them from the aisle. In his mind he apologized to her but he knew now he would never apologize, knew he would never speak to her. Indeed he was afraid she might actually acknowledge him, might read him and know. He felt ill, ached all over. The lymph nodes at his groin were sore, swelling again. No amount of washing would take the sensation away. His hand throbbed from the abuse it took every working day—packages, papers, crates, stacks of manila envelopes, every conceivable form of mail needing whisking from point A to point B, ASAP. Tonight, he told himself, as he now often did, I'll take a little something to ease the pain.

By the tenth day after his finger had been ripped off he had felt as if adjustment and recovery were imminent. Tyrolian Finance Corp. had received its first investment capital, $7,600, via a referral from Lloyd Dunmore. Peter Wilcox had immediately provided a borrower for a short-term second mortgage of $8,000 minus ten points up front and $150 in fees. Ty, on paper, earned $950 though he retained only $450. He had yet to register with the state or the IRS.

Then the pins and needles had begun and he'd thought it was nerves over his first loan transaction. The swelling and soreness and itch had followed. Then pimplelike sores burst into blisters on the head and shaft of his penis; the inside burned. Herpes. Herpes from the woman who'd stolen his pinky ring and his finger. He'd called into work, said he had a summer flu, locked himself in his room with his few books, weathered the first bout alone, angry, withdrawn, disgusted, unable to concentrate even through a single page.

The bus swerved, rocked like a giant ark, halted, lurched, halted. He'd become aware of the feeling at ten o'clock this morning as he'd waited before a pretty receptionist, needing the signature of her boss, in an office on Montgomery Street. As he waited he'd chatted her up, chided her about working for a white guy. "Nice-looking sister like you!" Ty, cocky, proud, smiling. "Why don't you come and work for me? I've got eighteen runners." Ty kept his left hand in his pants pocket. "Couple of em out today so the boss—" he tapped his chest, "is filling in. But I need help in the office. Someone to take over. Break me loose to expand. I can't do it if I'm tied to a desk all day. Great opportunity."

"I don't think so, Mr. Dorsey." She smiled. She answered another call, put the caller on hold. "Really, I'm very happy here."

"Nice-looking sister like you," he repeated quietly. "Working for a honkey." She excited him but the feeling in his groin wasn't excitement. By noon he'd begun feeling ill, had recognized the prodromal symptoms. By three he was having chills. By five thirty, on the bus, sidling past the long, thin woman, he felt as if bugs were creeping out of his abdomen, out of his anus, creeping to his groin. He felt as if everyone could see, as if even the small boy being berated knew, and all the people with eyes darting at the haggard woman saw instead herpetic Ty Blackwell Dorsey. He felt exactly like the little boy, embarrassed, shamed, nowhere to hide.

By six fifteen Ty was sitting alone in a dark wooden booth in a small dimly lit bar a half block off The Embarcadero. Before him was his half-finished beer, the crumbs of a Reuben sandwich, a stack of thick home fries coated with ketchup that he'd aligned neatly on the plastic plate. With his fork he separated one fry from the stack, cut it in half. Eat, he told himself. "Keep yo strength up, Son," his stepfather used to say. He forced the forkful to his mouth. "Keep yo from gettin sick. En ef yo get sick, keep yo from gettin real sick."

Ty sipped his beer. Half a dozen patrons were seated on the stools chatting or watching the news on the TV. All were white. The bartender was white. Only the cook, who emerged occasionally from the small kitchen beyond the end of the bar, was black. Eat, Ty told himself again but he did not want to eat anything more. Herpetic cunt, he thought. Goddamn herpetic white pussy. My ring, my finger, my fuckin johnson, my whole fuckin body. He ground a forkful of fries into the plate. Carve a big *H* in her forehead, he thought. Goddamn. He sipped his beer, glanced to the stools, to the TV, caught a few words: ". . . new American chief delegate William J. Porter . . . Paris talks . . . " It flashed in his mind that maybe it wasn't the bitch who'd stolen his finger but perhaps the fat fag had done something to him that night after his first speedball.

Ty did not linger on the thoughts. He believed thoughts like those would keep him from advancing. He still had plans, herpes or not, nine fingers or ten, honkeys or whatever. He glanced to the TV. The white customers, even the bartender, were rapt. The story was: black GIs; soul alley; drugs; black/white incidents. It was not a new story, not a new exposé. In the fourteen months since Ty had been discharged he'd seen scores of TV reports about how black and white GIs in Viet Nam hated each other, how they warred against each other, how blacks were abused, used as infantry fodder, treated unfairly for promotions and medals. There was not a single story on interracial cooperation, harmony, friendship.

Fuck em, he thought. Fuck it all. I go god damn Airborne. Prove my manhood. Then some honkey major . . . then some honkey bitch . . .

The TV caught his eye again. The scene could have been I Corps, could have been Camp Evans. A black soldier was standing by a sandbag wall. The reporter was letting him ramble. In the background a white GI was waving a Confederate flag. One of the guys at the bar glanced at Ty then quickly turned back to the TV.

"You know why we here?" the black soldier was ranting. "Economics. Even these white dudes. Suckers, Man, suckers. The Man, he lookin for an openin, you dig? He lookin for a foothold, dig? He want them rubber plantations. He want ta drill for oil. He want these little yellow people to work like ants. You understand what I'm sayin? Have these little people make radios an tape recorders. Pay em in rice. We here because of eee-co-nomics! We here to line the pockets a The Man. No matter we dyin. No matter we killin these little people. There plenty mo."

Ty stared at the TV, at the backs of the other patrons. His thoughts were not on the validity of the assertion but, why didn't they get a brother who could speak clearly. They do it on purpose, he thought. They find a stereotype, broadcast it, reinforce it.

"Who gettin killed, huh?" The soul brother's arms were now flailing. "Bloods, Man, Bloods. You dig? Brothers. Twenty-five percent, Man. You tell me this aint no race war."

It was dark in Ty's room. Late. He needed to pee but he dared not move the bottle alarm, open the door, go down the hall to the common toilet. He was sweating, feverish, delirious, shaking, twitching like a fish too long out of water. He did not like the dark but was afraid to turn on the light. Had to, he thought. Had to. To control the pain. To control the anger. To forget those honkey motherfuckers absorbed in the TV-nigger's babble. True or not.

Even before he'd reset the bottle alarm Ty had rolled back the mattress and taken out his "works." He'd been shaking, sweating, aching all over, itchy at his groin. He'd weathered the pain of his traumatic finger amputation with the fat fag's speedball and with skag-laced cigarettes; had weathered the first herpes bout snorting a little coke, smoking a little heroin. After they'd passed he'd prepared, bought the works for recurrences. Then, tonight, returning, he'd been all jitters. He'd paced the small room, removed one shoe, placed a few bottles, unfolded the kit, removed his shirt, back to the bottle alarm, checking his stash, his cash, his dope, back to undressing—nothing in straight-line order. Carefully he'd mixed the coke powder and the heroin powder—his dealer had called it Indochina Ivory—a little water, pure, clean, distilled, kept in a sterile bottle in his sheet-metal armoire, mixed in a clean spoon—so careful not to spill it, not to use too much, a quarter of a tenth of a gram of heroin, 60 percent pure, and a third of a tenth of cocaine—I can handle it—it's too expensive to get hooked, steal my piece of the pie—then crushed a pure white sterile cotton ball into the mix in the spoon, a wadded sterile filter absorbing impurities—so careful—then inserting the needle into the cotton, drawing that beautiful mix into the syringe. He'd checked the room. His head, body, groin, had ached but the anticipation of the hit had overridden the prodromal creeps. Ty had tied off, a length of surgical rubber tubing above the left elbow, had slapped up a vein, jabbed in the needle, felt good, satisfied that he'd become proficient at self-injection. Then fifteen seconds later—Contact! Ambush! High, wide, dull, loose, BANG!

Sweating. Delirious. On his back, on his bed, in the dark, alone, needing to pee. Alone. Alone from day one, from moment one back in the land of the big PX, the pig PX. They'd snubbed him. Right down the line. Those white boys he'd sat with on the Seven-oh-Sweet Freedom Bird: moment minus one aboard, all friends and thrilled to have returned from that bad motherfucker; moment one, on the ground, "Don't even look me up. I know we been through the same shit, Bro. I know we been close. But it won't work back here. They won't even let you come down my street." Worse, honkey number two simply refusing to talk, refusing to look at him, walking away. Home. Luwan. Shut off. Keeping his daughter away from him. Randall, Phillip, all surface. Alone with them cause they couldn't understand. Alone too, with the Captain. Not a single person to confide in. Not a single friend. Has to be. I gotta be alone. Isolate myself. I-so-late me from them hos-tile mothafuckas. Nice-looking sister! Soiled brother. Marred, Man. Diseased. Just another incurable retched niggar staring at them with their flag, them shoving that Confederate flag in my face. Kill for whitey. Killed by whitey. Brother abuses brother for The Man.

Alone like blue-eyes. Maybe she's got it. Maybe that's why she all the time sits like she does, like she's holding herself in. Same as me. Cept she's brand name. I'm generic. Yeah. Same as me. Long, straight, nice arms. Same as me cept light blue eyes and dark brown eyes. Vanilla and chocolate. We'd be perfect together. Brand name aint no better than the generic. I'll show em. I'll show her. When I get my piece of the pie.

How in God's name . . . this little black boy from Coal Hill who split from his baby . . . Jessica, baby, Daddy gonna come back someday. . . . Prove your manhood. Go Airborne!

Ty rolled, grabbed an alarm bottle from before the door stile. He was high, mellow, coming down, aching, shaking, sad, afraid to go into the hall. He urinated into the bottle. His johnson burned.

OPM. OPM became his opium as much as speedballs became his addiction. OPM—other people's money.

Ty's second herpetic eruption lasted half as long as the initial attack. In its wake, partly because of his perception of his new vulnerability, he doubled his financial efforts, his assault on that piece of the American pie he so desperately wanted, needed, needed to assuage all the assaults and abuses by which he'd been victimized, stigmatized.

"Mr. Jackson," Ty said, "I'm not going to play games with you." It was the evening of Sunday, October 3, 1971. Ty was in Richmond, California, about a mile from the end of the Richmond–San Rafael Bridge. He was sitting in the comfortable living room of Elmont and Mabel Jackson, on the edge of Elmont's large overstuffed chair with his papers, pencils and charts on the hassock before him. Mr. and Mrs. Jackson sat side by side on the sofa facing him, looking first to him, then to the papers, then to Ty's business card and back to Ty. "Some people invest in real estate," Ty said. "And I don't want to discourage you from exploring that option. But allow me to point out two things. When you own a piece of property you have to maintain it, don't you?"

Elmont nodded.

"You have to clean up after the tenants if they mess the place up, huh?"

Again Elmont nodded. He was old enough to be Ty's father. Mabel was younger but not by much.

"And you have to pay the mortgage and taxes whether or not you collect the rent, right?"

"Honey," Mabel said, "I been cleanin homes so long that aint gonna stop me."

"No, Mrs. Jackson," Ty said. "And it shouldn't. But let me continue a minute. If you take the money your brother left you—"

"God bless his soul," Mabel injected.

"And you buy a house and rent it . . . You see, so many of these stories about buying low, letting appreciation push the price up, then selling high and making huge profits"—Elmont Jackson suppressed a smile; Ty was describing his fantasy—"well . . . appreciation, actually, is the increase in cost as measured by the selling price minus your purchase price and closing costs and your selling closing costs and minus the value your money loses over that time to inflation. Most people don't minus out the inflation. They also don't deduct any out-of-pocket expenses for unpaid rent. Or for their labor in fixing the place back up. That's where you get these high figures for appreciation. Look, Mr. Jackson, I'm not going to play games with you, it's your money. I just want you to understand the alternatives."

"Give you the money," Elmont said, "and you turn aroun an loan it out."

"That's right. Totally secured. You get ten percent interest on the face value of the note. Unless you want to go the unsecured route. Then I can get you sixteen percent."

"Sixteen!"

"Oh, yes. But I wouldn't advise—"

"Sixteen percent a year?"

"Uh-huh. Well, ah, it's not for everyone. Actually it works out even more. See, ah, let's say we lend out ten thousand at sixteen percent. But we don't actually give the borrower ten thousand. They pay points up front—"

"Like I did here when we bought the house."

"That's right. But on these unsecured notes I can get you three points up front, so instead of you actually giving me ten thousand, you give me ninety seven hundred. But you still collect interest on the ten. So—" Ty wrote out the figures on a piece of paper on the hassock, "it's sixteen hundred divided by ninety-seven hundred, which, ah . . . Look, I'll do those calculations later if you want but it's probably closer to eighteen percent. And of course you get some of the loan fee too. It's not much, maybe seventy-five—"

"That sounds—" Mabel sighed, slapped her hands on her ample thighs, "like highway robbery."

Ty smiled sheepishly. "It does, doesn't it?" He leaned forward. His voice was soft. "It's not for everyone," he almost whispered. "But the truth is, you know, as a black man, I like owning a piece of white people's homes. They owned our homes for so long. . . . It's our turn."

"Aint that the truth," Elmont said.

"I don't know," Mabel said.

"It's time we got our piece of the pie." Ty's voice was soft, smooth. "You know, I've been overseas. In the army. America is the best hope for blacks but we've got to take the opportunity. We've got to grasp it. Grasp the legal opportunities. Otherwise your children and mine will be right down here where we at. Forever. And it'll be our own fault."

Mabel shifted uncomfortably. "This all legal?"

"Oh, it's legal." Ty nodded his head subtly. "Absolutely."

Elmont sat up straight as if the implications of Ty's words had just reached him. "Tyrone, you mean if I give you the nine thousand seven hundred dollars my brother left me, in a year you'll give me back sixteen hundred and I'll still have a note sayin I'm owed ten thousand?"

"An unsecured note," Ty said. "I want to remind you of that. You're protected by law, by the good name of the borrower and his legal promise to pay. But it's not a mortgage on his house. Just like a credit card. Still, people pay their credit card bills, don't they?"

"Yeah. Sixteen hundred the first year," Elmont repeated, "and I don't gotta break my back cleanin or repairin or worryin about collectin the rent!"

"That's the way it's been working. I can't promise you a note for exactly that amount, you understand. It might be two notes. You don't give me the money until I've got it sold."

"Honey—" Mable fixed her eyes on Ty's face, "you evah done this befo?"

"Oh yes," Ty said sincerely. "All the time. Mostly to home buyers up in San Martin." Now Ty chuckled. "There may be hardly any black families up there, but pretty soon blacks will own ten percent of the entire town."

Elmont turned to Mabel. "What do you think, Mabe?"

"Might be nice to sit back and not worry . . . "

"We've got a little bit"—Elmont turned from Mabel to Ty—"a little bit of savings too."

"Oh, wait!" Ty held up his hand. "Now I don't want you to give me all your rainy-day money."

"Well"—Elmont was nearly bursting now to hand his money over to Ty Dorsey—"not all of it. We could go, um, maybe twelve thousand."

Ty interrupted. "Look, this sounds like this is a bit too much for you."

"When do you need it by?" Elmont shot back.

"I'll need a cashier's check on Friday," Ty said softly.

* * *

"Mr. Ellis. Mrs. Ellis. I'm not going to play games with you. . . . "
Again and again. "Mrs. Carr, I'm sure if your husband were still alive
he'd want you to invest in the future of your children. . . . " "Mr. Brown
. . . I've been overseas. America may have problems but it's our best
hope. I don't want to rip it down. I'm no Panther. I'm just like you. Only
I want our people to partake of their proper share."

In San Francisco's black neighborhoods, and in San Bruno, in Foster
City, all the way south to San Jose and back north through Milpitas,
Fremont, out to Martinez and across to Vallejo, Ty Dorsey's spiel flowed,
telling people what they themselves were thinking, good people aghast
at the radicalism of the times, hard-working people hoping, praying to
take a legal step forward. From them Ty collected funds—from generally
older black men and women whom he found by searching year-old obit-
uaries in local newspapers in municipal libraries, generally calling on the
listed survivors exactly a year and a day from the death of their loved
one, calling them as if by chance.

By the end of 1971, Ty Dorsey had collected just under $200,000 from
thirty-one sources. He had placed $160,000 in loans on which he'd
grossed nearly $12,000. For the remaining $40,000 Ty issued fake notes
to the sources—those he judged most gullible. From the principle he
made all necessary interest payments (which not only kept everyone
happy and at bay but also generated dozens more "sales" leads).

Ty Dorsey purchased two more investment properties—small, run-
down Riverside subdivision homes—in his name. He purchased another
with Lloyd Dunmore as a silent partner and three more in which he was
only owner-mortgagee in name, under aliases: Tyrone Blackwell, Ty E.
Dorsey and T. E. Wallace.

Through autumn and early winter Ty concentrated on his pyramiding
real estate "empire." His herpes infection recurred for a short bout prior
to Christmas but subsided within days. He still dared not think of sexual
contact, still believed, if the thought flashed across his consciousness, that
he'd been sexually scarred, devalued, but he barely thought of it now.
He had his stash, his kit, his work, his "works." Carefully, very carefully,
aware of the potential for robbery, for violence, for addiction, Ty pressed
forward. He spread his drug purchases thin, buying only a little from
any one junkie, always complaining about the price, always lamenting,
"Damn, Man, I work my ass off. This drainin me, Man, a ev-rah cent."
After a purchase Ty always returned to his hotel by a different and
circuitous route, never returning to his own building without entering
another by one door, leaving by a second. In his room, too, he became
more cautious. One day he quietly cut a hole in the plaster behind the
bureau, inserted a portion of his cash and stash, sealed the hole with an
old piece of wallpaper so it appeared the room had once been painted
without the furniture being moved. On another evening he pulled a section of the baseboard that ran beneath the bed away from the wall, made

a second hiding place. Then he found that at the back of the base of the sheet metal armoire there was an opening and if he kept the cabinet an inch from the wall he could easily insert and retrieve envelopes. He also took the precaution of leaving ninety dollars in cash, several costume-jewelry rings, and a single vial of skag in the box on the dresser—enough, he reasoned, to satisfy any creep who'd break in. Enough to keep them from searching for more.

Ty Dorsey was careful, too, in how he administered his speedballs, how much heroin and cocaine he used. Over and over, long after it had become a nightly, then a twice-daily habit, he admonished himself, "Don't get hooked. It'll steal our piece a the pie. Just tee-tee, Man. Just a little now and then. Take the edge off. Keeps us goin." When his left arm became swollen and sore he taught himself to shoot with the left into the right. When those veins collapsed, he found he could shoot his thigh or the top of his foot. "Just a little, Man. If we get hooked, The Man'll come. Take our piece a the pie. Take our portfolio."

There is an old adage: "You can't bullshit a bullshitter." Ty would never understand, not even years later, that perhaps the negative corollary is more valid.

"I've got a little problem," Lloyd Dunmore said. It was midafternoon, mid-January. Dunmore, Dorsey and Peter Wilcox were standing in the sun, in a small parking lot in Sausalito, following lunch at the 7 Seas. Their backs were to the bay, their eyes sweeping Sausalito's two-lane main street, taking in the tourists, hippies, street artists, shops, and colorful old homes stepping up the steep verdant hillside. From the crest above town a thick low fog was cascading down the hill.

Ty did not look at Lloyd Dunmore. "If it's only a little problem, Lloyd, you probably wouldn't even bring it up."

"Well, it's little and it isn't," Dunmore said slowly. He opened the door of his Mercedes, rested one arm on the roof. "I'm getting up there in years." Ty turned, looked Lloyd in the face. Peter pretended not to hear. "Not old, mind you. But I'm financially set. Except for my youngest, the kids are grown and out of the house. What I'm saying is I want to cut back. I'm still going to be in charge of my operations but the daily management—"

"Come off it, Lloyd," Peter interrupted. "How old are you?"

"I'm fifty-eight."

"And you want to retire?!"

"No. No. Don't get me wrong. Madeleine . . . she'd like us to do a bit of extended traveling. Believe it or not she wants to see Asia. Most of what I've got going takes care of itself. But there are a couple of properties . . . Look, I know you two. You're both good men. Peter, that strip shopping center we've got in Terra Linda, buy me out."

"Really?"

"Come up with a price. What it's worth. And Peter, I'm willing to let you clip me on this one." Lloyd laughed, patted his hand on the car roof. "Not by too much. Ha! I'll even carry the paper." Dunmore shifted. "And Ty, that big Victorian we've got way out there on Miwok . . . "

"The slum?"

"Ah, you haven't been out there to see what I've done, have you?"

"No. Just that one time."

"Go out and look at it. The construction's almost finished. We've got eight nice units in there, Son. Tore down all that crap out back and carted it away. Some of those people were absolute pigs. I don't know how anybody could have lived in that filth."

"You had a problem with the building inspector. . . . "

"Naw. I took care of him. It's tenants. Peter won't service it. . . . "

Peter cringed. "Way out there?!"

"See," Lloyd said. "I just don't have the time. But you, Son, you could live out there."

Ty's stomach knotted. He raised a fist to his mouth, stifled a belch, retasted the hot prawns curry he'd had for lunch.

"Now"—Dunmore patted his car again—"hear me out. You buy me out. Move out there. Ty, the amount you spend on rental cars and coming up all the time, you'd be better off living out there."

Ty slowly shook his head. He resented Dunmore telling him he'd be better off living in the damn woods.

"Truly, Ty. I'm just getting too old to do it. I've sunk nearly thirty-six grand into that rebuild. I'm not looking for a profit. And like with Peter, I'll carry a note, ah, unless you have the OPM to cover it. You can do a wraparound. Shouldn't cost you an out-of-pocket penny. Add to your portfolio, too. For real. Not just on paper."

"Hmm." Ty did not say more but purposely let Lloyd babble on.

"My wife bought a new car. You've seen it, right?"

"The Jag," Peter remarked.

"Yes." Dunmore glanced at Peter, back to Ty. "You might be interested in her old one. Basically she only drove it to the country club and back. I'd make you a good deal on it, too. Include it in the wraparound. We can make this thing work."

"I'll think about it, Lloyd." Ty looked across Bridgeway, stared into the sun at the shadowed street scene.

"Good," Lloyd said. Now he moved quickly into the car. As he started the engine, he said, "I'm late. Call me tomorrow."

"Hey," Wilcox said watching Lloyd's car pull away, "have you talked to Bobby Wapinski lately?"

"No. He doing okay?"

"Sure. Fantastic! You know he's got that new cottage."

"Yes. I heard."

"And, ah, maybe he told you about the house on Tin Pan Alley."

"Which one?"

"Up by the golf course. You know, in Golden Vista Estates."

"We haven't talked. Maybe he tried to leave me a message. . . . "

"Yeah. Probably. He's thinking of putting in a low-ball offer. But you know, he's stretched right now."

"Golden Vista's pretty expensive."

"Sure. But this seller's desperate. Transferred . . . to Houston, I think. Or Dallas. The place's been vacant for months. Except for the dining room set. It'd be a great rental for families transferred in, you know, for maybe just a year. People who don't want to buy but want to live in a nice house."

In April Ty drove by Bobby Wapinski's cottage on Old Russia Road, drove Madeleine Dunmore's old Audi 100-LS up the North Peak slope not once but three times. Each time he was happier, more reassured, delighted to find Bobby apparently not home, thrilled that 101 Old Russia Road was a shack when compared to his own new Tin Pan Alley residence which backed up to San Martin Golf and Country Club's fourteenth tee. Happy that he had made it, that he now owned six properties, "owned" fourteen more under various aliases, and held notes totaling $67,000. In only a year and a half he—little Tyrone Blackwell-Dorsey-Wallace-Green, the jigaboo from Coal Hill, the disenfranchised spade veteran of Hamburger Hill, the coon rejected by his mentor—had eclipsed his own symbol of exactness, of making it, of the American pie. He had surpassed The Captain.

"Do all black men have huge penises?" the woman whispered into his ear. They had been making love for an hour. He was spent. She was on top of him, holding him, tickling him, attempting to reexcite him. She nuzzled her chin into the crook of his neck making him squirm. Her skin was pale, white-white, not ashen, not sickly—ice milk. Her hair was black, blacker than his. The contrast of the chalk white of her arm against his rich deep brown chest aroused her, yet making him convulse or fidget under her was what she found truly sensual.

It was hot, a mid-July afternoon. Occasionally a burst of laughter from the fourteenth tee penetrated the sheer curtains of his room.

"Only one." He chuckled.

"Only one?" Olivia teased him.

"One each," Ty said.

"One each what?" She shifted, straddled him. "Say it," she ordered.

"Say what?" he countered.

"Penis," Olivia said.

"Why?" Ty asked.

"Why can't men say *penis* to a woman? I like your penis. I'm glad it's huge."

"Well . . . " Ty chuckled. He really couldn't say the word. Not to Olivia. "It likes you too," Ty said.

"What does?" She tickled his ribs. He squirmed. She tickled harder. "What does? Say it." She collapsed on him, pinned him.

"My johnson does," Ty blurted.

"What's a johnson?" She kissed his earlobe, blew gently into his ear.

"My wang. My dick." She was tickling him all over, poking her chin into his clavicle, gently digging her knee into his thigh just above his knee. He wriggled, gasped, "My meat. My ding-a-ling."

Afterward she backed into him, cuddled, snoozed in his arms. He held her, hot afternoon or not, kissed the back of her head. Better than the Captain, huh? he thought, but he did not say it. She'd told him that they'd had "several afternoon dates. You know, private. A girl can get a reputation in an office." Ty hadn't pressed. It was enough to know that she wanted him more than she wanted Wapinski, that she was with him now, that she thought his penis was huge even if he thought it was probably only average. He kissed her again, little pecks on the nape of the neck. Then he rolled, grabbed his Kools from the bedside table. She'd come onto him for reasons he didn't know. He hadn't pondered it, had thought instead, later, and laughed thinking it, and she had made him say it out loud—"Now this is true affirmative action." She had not laughed with him, had not smiled, but she had kissed him passionately and he'd whispered to her, "I think I'm falling in love with you." He did not tell her about his herpes infection. It was dormant; had not flared in five months.

At four they rose. A steady breeze came from the golf course, billowed the curtains. Olivia closed the glass slider, stood nonchalant, naked, facing Ty, teasing him with her matter-of-fact posture.

"Why'd you close it?" Ty asked.

She did not look at him but coyly gazed to the side. "I'm run down."

"Hmm?"

"Let's do a couple more lines. Then I've got to go."

"I never expected him to move in."

"When the hell did he decide . . . What the hell's he thinking?"

Their voices were harsh, hushed. Peter Wilcox, Lloyd Dunmore, Dirk Everest, and Howard Trimball, president of San Martin Savings and Loan, were in the country club locker room. They had played eighteen holes, had had a quick sandwich and beer, then had come down to shower and change. The room was clean, fluorescent-light bright, royal blue carpeted, mirrored between the banks of lockers.

"Damn. I never thought . . . " Peter Wilcox stepped one foot onto the bench, untied the lace on his golf shoe. "When I told him about it, I thought he'd rent it like he's done with all the others. Have you been there?"

"God damn, no." Dunmore sat on the bench.

"He's a slob. There's not a stick of furniture in that house. Except the dining room set that came with it."

"Well, where's he sleep?" Howard Trimball placed a foot on the bench.

"I suppose he's got something in the bedroom," Peter said.

"Who gives a damn where he sleeps." Dirk stammered, "Th-this is bad."

"Yes, it is bad," Dunmore said.

"There's no blacks in SMGCC," Trimball said.

"I don't want this setting a precedent," Dunmore said. "And I don't want this becoming a court case."

"You know, Lloyd"—Everest tapped a fist onto his locker—"you and Peter did this. And you, Howard. Why in hell did you give him the god damn loan?"

"Shit! He's got half a dozen loans with me. This way I can show we make loans to Negroes."

"I thought he was going to move into that eight-plex out in the canyon." Lloyd grabbed his chin, pushed his fingers up against the grain of his beard, removed his shirt.

"So did I," Peter said.

"Well, he hasn't." Dirk straightened, banged his locker with his fist, removed his pants. "Figure some way to call his loan."

Howard Trimball pursed his lips. "I can't do that."

"Why not?"

"Come on, Dirk. You know as well as I do."

"Well, what the hell are we going to do if he wants to join?!"

"I really never thought—" Peter began.

"I don't care what you never thought." Dirk cut him off.

"He hasn't submitted an application—" Howard began.

Again Dirk cut in. "But if he does . . . He owns property abutting the course. It's supposed to be automatic."

Now Lloyd Dunmore stood, broke up the group. "I'll buy him out," he said. He opened his locker. "He's money hungry. Where's he coming up with all this money for notes, anyway? Unsecured! Damn, what a salesman! But"—Lloyd turned to the other three—"he doesn't have a pot to pee in. Let him buy what he wants. He'll need capital to keep it. And, damn it Howard, he bailed your butt out. I'm just a shareholder."

"My butt?!"

"You bet your god damned ass. Now you let me know the first minute he's late with a payment. I'll tell him Madeleine and I are divorcing and I'm getting the house for her." Lloyd paused, stood naked, hands on his hips, his knees stiff, his belly bulging. He fixed the men with his stare. "I don't," he said emphatically, "want this to go to court."

"Execrable." Ty chuckled.

"I don't know," Olivia said.

Three months had passed. Their first tryst had ended not with a bang, not with a wimper, but simply without word. He'd been perplexed, bothered. She had given him back his manhood and had vanished. He had not chased her. He had a piece of the pie to get and the exact size of the slice was yet to be determined. And he was having problems with his veins. In August his left arm had swelled so horribly he'd been unable to wear any shirt, suit or jacket he owned and he'd gone nearly stark-raving mad trapped inside that Tin Pan Alley house, feverish, nauseated, self-dosing with black market antibiotics so as to avoid medical reports. He felt caged. Very late at night he escaped, drove to the Safeway on Miwok Road, shopped, returned, paced. He bought a ten-inch black-and-white portable TV, watched as Ramsey Clark visited Hanoi and averred that U.S. POWs were being treated well; as the last U.S. ground combat units in Viet Nam stood down; as the ARVN recaptured Quang Tri City or what was left of it; and as Henry Kissinger, in Paris, announced an agreement in principle accepting a cease-fire–in–place and agreeing to give the communists nearly one-quarter of South Viet Nam's land area.

During the entire time Ty Dorsey did not see or hear from Olivia Taft. He did not "raise funds," did not expand his portfolio. Being sick dropped his resistance. The blisters and burning returned and added to his misery, pain, and self-imposed incarceration in that home on the fourteenth tee. Slowly it subsided. He fought the desire, the need for speedballs. He locked his "works" away but needed it, had to have it. He wrapped his "works" in plastic, put it in the freezer so that when he needed it, it would be uncomfortable. He smoked grass, smoked skag-laced Kools, snorted coke. Anything to stay away from the wonderful feel of the needle, the conditioned pleasure now so tightly locked in his mind that the very touch of the kit bag sent waves of joy trembling throughout his body. Slowly he gained control and the infections sub-sided. He analyzed his spread sheet and saw that his cash on hand had collapsed to $19,000, that other expendable items (drugs) had been de-pleted, that his net worth had plummeted to under twenty grand. Still he was current with all payments. And with a 6 percent adjustment of property values—he was certain the market had jumped at least six per-cent—he could increase the assets side, and the bottom line, by $17,600; and $37,600 was still a pretty good bottom line for a twenty-one-year-old black man.

Then Olivia came back. He did not question her but loved her and shared his coke with her and when she told him about a triplex on Fifth Street he agreed to buy it. On this property Ty gained a $70,000 asset, yet via the Mickey Mouse of financing, a total loan liability of $75,111. He put $3,592 cash in his pocket. The monthly principal, interest and tax payment was $688.13. The rental income was projected at $460 per month, but in mid-November 1972 the big first-floor apartment was va-cant and the income was only $260.

"Execrable," Ty repeated. "Utterly detestable."

"I would never use that word," Olivia said.

"Well, it's good to know them."

"I couldn't use it. It doesn't sound right. It'd be like speaking a foreign language."

"How about *hauteur*?"

"Beats me."

"Come on."

"I don't know."

"Haughty spirited. You know, snobbish. Disdainful. Kinda the way you act."

"I'm a snob?!"

"Aw, come on." He grasped her. Pulled her onto him. Kissed her. They were on the bed, partially dressed.

"I think it's snobbish using those words," Olivia said.

"I don't use em much," Ty answered. "Just . . . I need to know em so if they get used on me . . . "

Olivia hushed him by putting a finger to his lips. Then she kissed him, then raised her torso above him by planting her elbows on his chest and said, "What's really snobbish is what they're trying to do."

"Who?"

"The board of directors. You must have heard."

"You mean Lloyd? Peter? They're my partners."

"I heard . . . you know, just a rumor . . . you know, you've caused quite a stir moving in here. . . . Some of them want to buy you out."

"What are you talking about?"

"Just a rumor, I guess."

"Yeah. Just . . . ha! I'm probably their worse nightmare. Ha! Me puttin my black johnson into a white woman."

"Penis."

"Pe—" Ty broke into a laugh and Olivia laughed with him.

"Let's do another line." She rolled off him, stood. "Then I've got a word for you." She shimmied.

"Umm?" He sat on the edge of the bed, placed his hands on her thighs, ran them up over her hips to her waist. She grabbed them, arched her back. He rocked forward to kiss her stomach.

"Hooters." She jumped back.

"Who-dares?" He laughed, rose. "What are who-dares?"

"You'll have to catch me to find out." She ran to the door, glanced back, saw him, his eyes revealing he was ready to take up the chase. "You can't catch me," she squealed, bolted down the hall toward the living room. He sprinted after her. She darted to the far end by the archway to the dining room. He stood, poised to move either through the kitchen to capture her in the dining room or lunge straight through the living room. She too tensed, ready to move opposite him. Then she quickly straightened, arched her back, shimmied, sang out, "Hooters," disappeared into the dining room.

Ty froze. She couldn't see him. He could hear her. He crouched, silently edged into the kitchen.

"Where are you?" Olivia sang sweetly.

Just then he lunged, burst through the dining room door, his arms extended to tackle her. As he lunged his foot caught the carpet. She was at the far side of the table, pulling her bra straps off her shoulders, teasing. Then, BAM! His face, his mouth, the entire mass and force of his movement, right into the table edge.

"Oooph! Shit!" Garbled. "Shit."

"Ty. Oh Ty!" Olivia came to him. He was on the floor, a hand covering his mouth. "Are you . . . " She could see blood behind his hand. "Let me look."

Ty tilted his head down, dropped his hand. Amid the splatter of blood were two ivory tiles—his upper incisors. "Shit. Lthk at thhis! Shit!" He covered his mouth, looked up at her. "So what are who-thares?" He chuckled. Then he groaned.

"Would you talk to him?" Peter asked.

"I didn't even know he was living there."

"But you do now. There's going to be incidents. I don't want it to get ugly."

"What do you want me to say to him?" Bobby was miffed. According to Peter Wilcox virtually everyone else in the office knew that Ty Dorsey was living in Golden Vista.

"Tell him it's for his own good. And Lloyd will make it worth his while."

"You're fuckin crazy!"

"You brought him out here," Peter said. "You're partly responsible, you know. If they burn a cross on his lawn or something, San Martin will suffer. The town will be in every newspaper in the country. Is that what you want?"

"Don't put that shit on me, Peter. I just came down to see Al. If Ty's living there, if he bought that place, that's his business. He's got every right to live there."

"Yeah," Peter scoffed. "Some friend he is of yours. You don't even know. . . . "

"Know what?"

"Forget it. That's his business too, I suppose."

It was rainy, cool, gray. Inside, even with the bathroom light on, it seemed gray. Ty Dorsey, wrapped in a towel, stood before the sink, leaning in, one hand on the sink back, the other holding his upper lip, leaning in close to the mirror inspecting his new gold caps, real gold, gleaming like his grandfather's one incisor had gleamed when Ty was small. There were other teeth, too, that came to mind—incidents, intrusive connections that hit him the moment a month earlier when he'd looked down and seen the white chips amid the red splatter. He'd told himself it was nothing. Don't mean nothin. Drive on! Don't mean nothin. Those fuckers were dead. Dead meat. Dead meat don't hurt.

Ty stood straight, used both hands to raise his lip. Then he let his lip go, experimented with different smiles, different facial expressions. This one got too much teeth, he thought. Not enough, he thought of the next. He practiced a demure smile he found visually pleasing, professional.

When Ty was satisfied with his appearance he retreated to the bedroom. He glanced through the glass slider at the drizzle, at the gray-green of the fourteenth tee. "Dead meat don't hurt," he muttered. "What the fuck he mean, sixty-four grand!" Ty sat on the bed, pulled on a gold-toed sock. One good thing, he thought, one good thing about smashin my face—he leaned back slightly, caressed the mattress where Olivia had spent the night—she's got a debt attitude. Ha! Like Bobby and those goddamn shopping list pads. She owes me. But I don't owe him nothin. Nothin. Nothing. Don't talk like trash. Sixty-four thousand dollars. Get yo black ass . . . your black . . . being . . . out of the country club. Fuck you, Lloyd. I can't believe . . . For Madeleine, my ass. Needs her own space! That bimbo wouldn't leave sugar daddy for all the tea in China. I can-fuckin-not believe he asked. We've been partners. We've had deals. I've put a quarter of a million dollars out through him.

As Ty dressed for his appointments in Oakland anger touched off anger—thoughts of Olivia, of his new gold caps, no match for the realization of what had happened. He had taken Lloyd Dunmore at face value, had told him he'd consider it. He'd told Olivia about the offer.

"They want to buy you out."

"No. Not Lloyd. We're tight. Really. Something to do with Madeleine needing to find herself."

"Get real. There's eight homes in Golden Vista on the market. There's a beauty on Silver Spoon that backs up to the course. And it has access to the open space slope and riding trails of North Peak. And a pool. For sixty-one nine. Why would they want yours?"

"Maybe my financing's better."

"If he asked you to secure him a second on Silver Spoon, you'd do it, wouldn't you?"

"Of cour—"

"See? I can't believe you're being so naive."

Naive! It was her word. He had never seen himself as naive. Not Ty. Not Tyrone Blackwell-Dorsey-Wallace. Not Mr. I-won't-play-games-with-you. It took time to settle. Naive. Get the nigger out of the country club. For God's sake! This wasn't the South. This was California! This was 1972! He'd been an American soldier! He'd fought for The Man. And there were laws. Laws! Laws to protect him. He steamed inside. But I—I couldn't go to . . . They'd want to know who I am. And who the fuck am I?

In January Lloyd Dunmore made Ty Dorsey a new offer. This time he attempted, after beating around the bush during another Sausalito luncheon, to be up front. "Ty, I'm getting lots of *flak*."

"About what, Lloyd?" Ty flashed his demure golden smile.

"You."

"Me?"

Dunmore tucked his chin, glanced up. "I don't want to do this. I like you. We're friends. And I'm not a racist."

"What's happening, Lloyd?"

"Ty, it's for your own protection."

"What is?" Ty acted concerned for Lloyd Dunmore, acted as if he wished to help the older man. Beneath, he laughed. Naive, my black ass. Squirm, honkey.

"Ty, I'll buy your place for . . . I'll give you seventy-four. That's twenty thousand more than you paid. People up there are really upset and I'm taking the heat."

"Is my yard maintained okay?"

"Of course."

"And the house?"

"You know that's not it."

"Am I dirty?"

"Ty! Don't make it hard on me."

"How can you offer me this and say you're not a racist?"

"Because I wouldn't offer it to you if it were only me."

"So, you're fronting for racists."

"Listen, damn it. I've been protecting you. I got you started. Tyrolian Financial'd be nothing if I didn't . . . Damn! And I know you're balling that white woman. They're going to lynch you. Or burn you out. Besides . . . I know, I know you've got cash-flow problems. This'll solve it. You can't afford—"

Ty glared. He'd heard enough, had let Lloyd talk enough. "Who?" he demanded.

"Seventy-four thousand. That's my final offer. Move into the Miwok eight-plex. No one will bother you out there."

The two sat silent except for Lloyd's heavy breathing and the ticking of Ty's right foot. Lloyd kept his eyes down. Ty stared past him, out a window to the boat slips and across the bay to Angel Island. For minutes on end neither spoke.

The waiter came. "Are you finished, Mr. Dunmore? Mr. Dorsey?" Both nodded.

Finally Ty broke the impasse. "I've got to get down to San Bruno," he said. "Tell them not to do it. Tell them Blackwell says there's more trouble in it for them than for him." Ty stood. His heart was racing, his legs felt weak. "And Wallace and Dorsey agree. You guys can't afford my house."

"Hey, you look different."

"Naw, same old me."

Bobby cocked his head. "No, there's something different."

"Just serve the ball." Ty laughed, turned away from the net, then turned back. "You any good at this?"

"No." Bobby chuckled too. It was late June. School was out for the summer. They were on one of the green-painted asphalt courts of the school complex between Sixth and Seventh streets. "This is only my fourth time. How about you?"

"You're up on me by one. Olivia needed somebody to beat!" Bobby and Ty were now next to each other, the net between them. Olivia was back at the baseline, stretching.

"I didn't know you guys knew each other," Bobby said.

"Yeah. I bought a couple of houses through her. You know, they say you're not there anymore."

"Aw, you know, a little. I'm trying to line up something with the regional planning board. I . . . I guess I'm really not much of a saleman."

"Oh Man, Bobby, I know you were good."

"Maybe. But . . . Ah, hey, you know, this with Olivia, it's awk—"

"No big deal, Man. You guys dated some, huh?"

"Yeah, a little."

Ty laughed again. "We'll just volley, Captain."

"Hey. Maybe after"—quietly—"just us"—then louder—"a few beers up at my place."

"Gotcha." Ty chuckled, flashed his smile.

Through an hour of volleying, of laughs, good-natured taunts and quips, of Bobby and Olivia carefully not looking at each other, Ty laughed. He laughed openly and happily. He'd beaten Lloyd Dunmore. He'd beaten Bobby Wapinski. He had very simply, in his own mind, won on every level. Even Ty's tennis gear, Pallucci clothes—presents from Olivia—were better than Bobby's cutoffs and sleeveless sweatshirt. By the gods, he said to himself, I am happy. And to it all Ty added, in his own mind, his own clean arms (Olivia's pressure—she found the "works" repulsive so they only snorted and smoked), his legal registration of Dorsey Financial Services, and this beating of Bobby's ass on the court. Ty's laughter rolled, his smile glistened. Bobby too, even confronted with this ex-girlfriend, looking battered and broke, seemed happy. Only that bugged Ty.

"You know what it is with those two fuckers?"

"Take it easy, Dirk."

"I've had it. I know how to come down on those sons of bitches."

"Dirk, why don't you—"

"Peter, nobody humiliates me. I was going to let that bastard run my company. And that nigger! Every time I approach that tee, I can smell him."

"I don't even know he's there."

"That's because you don't live down here." Now Dirk Everest jabbed Peter Wilcox in the chest with an index finger. "You know what it is?

That jackass and that jigaboo, they were in Viet Nam together. God-damned losers."

Throughout the first eight months of 1973 Ty Dorsey adjusted his port-folio. To his numerous unsecured notes he added mortgage liens secured by property whose value was highly inflated. To his real property assets he had added the Fifth Street triplex, and in April he included a duplex on Second Street that huddled in the shadow of Bennett, Bennett and Bennett's eight-story financial complex. In short, on the day the OPEC ministers announced their agreement that became the Arab Oil Embargo of 1973, Ty Dorsey's financial summary, had he been honest with him-self, would have looked like this—Assets: Real property (liberally) val-ued at $432,100; Cash: $16,050; Notes owned: $86,600; Drugs: $1,000; Vehicles: $1,600; and personal property (including two-dozen fine suits): $6,500. Total: $543,850. Ty's liabilities: Loans against real property: $373,000; Unsecured notes owed: $266,000; Unpaid taxes, fines, etc.: (est.) $50,000; Miscellaneous debt: $10,000. Total: $699,000.

Worse, his yearly cash flow from rents, loan fees and points, and in-terest on notes owned, minus expenses to interest, taxes, and insurance, was a net negative of nearly $20,000. Indeed, the only way Ty Dorsey was staying financially afloat was by using monies collected by Tyrolian or Dorsey Financial and purportedly loaned.

Southeast Asia was dropped from the news. All U.S. troops were out of Viet Nam. U.S. bombing of the Khmer Rouge in Cambodia had come to a legislated halt. Despite numerous omens and perhaps because of that long conflict, most Americans were caught off guard. Still, war trig-gered it. War in the Middle East.

The first Arab oil embargo hit in the late summer of 1973. In San Martin the Shell gas station on Third and Miwok was the first to run dry. Then the Mobil station a block away. Then the Stop-n-Go pumps next door to the Safeway. Lines formed. September '73 was hot, dry, nice weather for cruising with the top down but too warm to sit and bake and not know if there'd be gas when one's turn finally came. Tempers flared. Fights broke out. Dozens of out-of-gas cars lined the shoulder of Highway 101 through town; hundreds sat in garages or driveways.

The biggest problem, even though two of every three working towns-people commuted to San Francisco, was not gas but the new local cost of living. By November the initial impact of high energy costs was fol-lowed by a loss in San Martin of 17 percent of the town's appeal as an All-American bedroom community, as measured by the average sales price of a home. Those who were caught financially extended or over-extended, found their worlds quaking.

By December '73 capital had dried up. Those who had, held on. Those who had lent, demanded their due. The financial rains stopped. Ty's out-going cash depleted his reservoir. And someone, somewhere was watch-ing.

* * *

"What the fuck!" His voice was loud, booming, angry. Even cushioned by the dense vegetation and towering redwoods the sound reverberated in the canyon. He hollered it again. He stomped the broken macadam of Miwok Road. He jumped, turned, kicked a clod of dirt that had fallen from between the treads of the D-7 Cat. "No fuckin way!" He gritted his teeth, seethed at the building inspector, the three policemen, the city's wetland's officer. Only a half hour earlier he'd been home, with Olivia, doing a few lines, laughing, when the tenant called. "Impossible," he'd said.

"Mr. Dorsey, they've made us remove all our personal things. We've got it all scattered out on the lawn."

"They can't do that!"

"They have. And they're unloading the bulldozers. You'd better get out here."

Now Ty exploded again. "You goddamn son of a bitch."

"One more crack like that out of you"—the police sergeant stood, squared, one hand on his belt, one gesturing at Ty—"and I'll bring you in for disturbing the peace."

Ty threw his hands straight up, his lips pulled back, his gold caps flashing. He was speechless, overwhelmed, overpowered. Finally he blurted, "You CAN'T do this!"

"Certainly can. You should have answered all those summonses," the sergeant snapped. "You expanded this way beyond the original foot-print."

"That wasn't me. That was Lloyd."

"Your name's on the papers."

"Where my tenants goina go?"

"That's their problem."

"Come on, Mr. Bailey," Ty pleaded with the building inspector who was ten feet beyond the sergeant. "Give me one day. One day!"

"I've given you six months," Bailey called over his shoulder. The two dozers were now positioned against the northeast side of the rebuilt Victorian. On the opposite side, corralled by additional police officers, stood eight tenants amid piles of their clothing and effects. "Court says it comes down. That expansion was illegal and you knew it. This is single-family residential."

"One day," Ty shouted.

"Time's up," Bailey said. He raised his right arm.

From above came the increasing revs of the diesel motors, then the clank and squeak of the plow blades being raised by the hydraulic pistons, then the *ka-thunk* as the operators shifted. Ty closed his eyes, turned away, put his hands to his ears. Of all his real assets this was the only one with substantial equity, and within thirty-five minutes it was nothing but a crushed and broken pile of boards heaped into a foundation hole.

Even the foundation the dozers broke here and there, wherever they could get traction in the dirt, which had been a new lawn.

"You owe Elmont. You owe me. You owe anybody else?"

It was now 10 December 1973. To add insult to injury the city of San Martin had sent Ty a bill for $3,700 for destroying his Miwok Road Victorian. Now here, on the front porch of his Tin Pan Alley home, was this man, this very big man who said he represented two of Ty's clients, this very big man who said he'd bought a note himself, discounted, six months earlier and the balloon payment—of $16,000—had been due on Halloween. He hadn't received one red cent!

"Come to my office tomorrow morning," Ty said calmly.

"What office?"

Ty's eyes skittered. "Great Homes Realty," he said quickly.

"You son of a bitch," the big man said. "I want my money. Now!"

"You think I keep that kind of money here? in my house?" Now Ty acted angry. "I do business during business hours. Ten o'clock tomorrow morning. In the office. Bring the note and I'll give you a check for—"

"You pay me in cash, Mister."

"What are you, some kind of idiot?" Ty stepped from the doorway to the porch, aggressively confronting the big man. Again he felt sick, stress-induced sick. Even the bitch had dumped him, had blown him off only moments after she'd inhaled his last line. Ty shoved the big man in the chest. "Get the hell outta here!"

"Tomorrow, mothafucka. Tomorrow. You hear me!"

Inside, alone, Ty leaned back against the locked door, held his head, tried to breathe deeply but his breath came in quivering gasps like a small child crying.

Like Jessica crying, he thought. Like his own daughter crying. "Dear Uncle Phillip"— Luwan had helped her write it and Phillip had sent it on to Ty—"for Christmas I want a skip-rope and some beads. Love, Jessica." Nothing more. Not even a "Hello," from Phillip. "Aw shit, Man. Shit." His jaw quivered. His quadriceps felt like jelly. He thought of her but he could not picture her.

There was so much shit coming down. If it wasn't, Ty thought, for moving in . . . No. If it wasn't for them white racist fuckers . . . The Man's system. Set up to separate blacks from their money. They won't let us get no piece a the pie. Set me up.

He stumbled into the dim light of the living room, searched the window wall, which faced the golf course, for shadows. He did not concentrate, did not extinguish interior lights. Instead he went to the closet in the middle bedroom where he'd maintained his cache: works, skag, cash. Without the Victorian eight-plex, he knew, even without laying out the spread sheet, that his bottom line was out-of-reach negative. And notes were coming due, secured notes on which he was sure he could default with impunity, but also unsecured notes that would bring civil action, and fraudulent notes that, sooner or later, would bring criminal action.

He went through the procedure, tied off, slapped up, shot up. Heroin. No money for cocaine. No cocaine for speedballs. Better this way. Duller. No psycho-bitch . . . she'd used the term herself, about herself, said Wapinski had called her psycho-bitch. They had laughed. Laughed together . . . He was floating now—dull, without pain, hours without feeling.

"One minute." He raised his face to thumping on the door. It was midnight, perhaps two A.M. His mind was barely clear enough for him to reassemble and recache his works. "One minute." He buckled his belt, straightened his clothes. Opened the door.

Two men burst in, slammed the door.

"Whaaa . . ."

"You don't hear well do you, mothafucka?"

"Get outta—"

One man punched Ty in the face. "You dumb!" He growled, ranted as Ty fell, folded, crumpled to his knees. "Dumb. You know that?"

Ty looked up. One man was white. One black. The black man was not the same one who'd demanded money earlier. Ty's mind was too dusty to feel frightened, his body too dull to feel pain. He rocked to one side, began to kneel. The white man grasped Ty's hair, squeezed hard pulling the tight curls, banging Ty's head against the wall. He pulled Ty's head up straight so Ty was staring at the black man. "You didn't hear Mr. Dee," the man said.

Ty was dumbfounded.

"You don't hear, do you?" the black man said. In Ty's mind the words mixed with the words of the big man earlier. "If you don't hear, you don't got much need for this, huh, mothafucka?" The black man nodded to the white man. The white man hammer-locked Ty's head, squeezed hard.

Ty felt a sharp prickling at his right ear, heard the material being sliced, did not yet feel the pain. The man released him. He felt warm trickling on his jaw, down his chin. Then the man dropped Ty's ear on the floor in front of him.

"Ya don't use em, mothafucka. Ya won't miss it." The black man laughed and the white man laughed, too.

Ty escaped, fled. He left the house, left his fine suits and shirts and shoes, left the car, the secured and unsecured notes, left San Martin, left the North Bay. He took his works, his skag, $3,000 cash, the clothes he wore. Nine-fingered, one-eared, gold-toothed Ty Dorsey, under the name of Theodore Darsman, moved south; finally, after two months, he took up residence in a one-room unit in a run-down flophouse near San Jose. His hair grew long. Picking it out covered his ear space. He ate little, talked to almost no one, shot up the last of his skag. By March 1974, not yet twenty-three years old, he was broke, on the lam, hopeless, dopeless. On the eighth Ty, now Theo, broke two of the glass bottles of his door alarm. Then he picked up a bottom shard with his left hand. Crying like a baby, wimpering, "Dead meat don't hurt!" he placed the sharpest edge on the heel of his right palm, pressed hard, jerked the glass back.

September 1984

There are studies that have concluded that more Viet Nam veterans have died by their own hand since returning from Southeast Asia than were killed in combat. It is difficult for me to believe this even though many veterans I have known, including Ty, Bobby and myself, have been at one time or another "suicidal." But being suicidal and committing suicide are not the same. And coping behaviors learned in Viet Nam—learned at the edge of life—have helped many of us, on that new edge, to choose survival, to choose life.

Some people have tried to make political hay from the issue—people apparently from both sides. I kid you not on this; this was said to me by a professor at Nittany Mountain College, and I've heard others say it and lots of the guys reported it said to them too—"They all killed themselves because they were guilty of atrocities and they couldn't live with that guilt any longer." Horseshit! On the seemingly other political side there have been some veterans advocacy groups who have pointed to the figures and used them to convince Congress and charitable donors that *their* group should be highly funded. It's a two-edged sword. These groups have provided excellent and necessary crisis-intervention services. Yet they have a vested interest in these figures, and their campaigning may actually exacerbate the problem by lowering the suicide threshhold for some vets.

There is no doubt that there have been thousands of Viet Nam veterans suicides. The figure, "over 60,000," however, is very much in question. If I had died on Storrow Drive while racing Jimmy's Harley like a possessed pariah from paradise, would that have been suicide? And if it had been, was it caused by Viet Nam? And if that is answered yes, is it because of my guilt feelings from surviving mostly unscathed while Jimmy and Manny got greased and Rick lost his legs? or guilt from atrocities I committed?

Even the VA, later, when it finally recognized PTSD, blew it. They were not there, generally, to *cure* guys. They were there to warehouse—and later to establish an excusable process, a complex set of obstacles for vets to hurdle on their way to collecting a lifetime "percentage" disability. Screw curing! Screw curing and assisting and returning the vet, healthy, to a productive life. Pay him off! Let him subsist. I'm overstating this, of course, but that's because of how I personally was treated. Some guys were helped. Some VA programs were and still are beneficial. And lots of the suicide attempts, like Ty's, were calculated, escapable, pleas. Had Ty slit his wrists vertically instead of horizontally, he would have died in San Jose.

19

"How's it going, Tony?"
"Good."
It was Tuesday, 4 April 1972. Tony Pisano was at the start of his third outpatient therapy session at Rock Ridge Veterans Medical Center. Why he had come again, this third time, he wasn't certain. He was eager, hopeful. Things had changed drastically from the moment he'd moved into High Meadow. He and Linda were together again, yet not together.

Tony's new therapist, John H. Binford, Ph.D., had been brought in to implement Daniel Holbrook's experimental program—both as researcher and as therapist. Binford was six years older than Tony, the same age as Tony's brother, John Jr. That was part of the lure, the promise as Tony saw it, the reason Binford had gained a hold over him, held him through biweekly sessions that would continue for thirteen months. During the entire period Tony Pisano continued to take his three-a-day dosages of lithium carbonate—gradually reducing the amount from 300 to 25 milligrams.

"Have you been back to see Father Tom like I suggested?" Binford's face was soft, friendly.

"Ah, not yet. I ah . . . you know, was really busy these past few weeks."

"You remember what I said . . . "

"Um-hmm."

". . . about cleaning up the little loose ends first."

"I remember."

"We want to do this in order, Tony. Little by little."

"Yeah. That's what Mr. Wapinski says too."

"Good. Then you'll see Father Tom this week?"

"Yeah. I'll try."

"Not try." Binford raised an index finger as if scolding.

"Okay," Tony said.

"When?"

"Tomorrow."

"Why not today on your way back to the farm?"

"Um. Okay."

"You sought Father Tom out for that job, didn't you?"

"Yeah."

"Why?"

"I don't know. Kind of a last resort, I guess."

"You were raised in a strict Italian-American home? In the strict Catholic tradition?"

"Aw, I don't think it was so strict. You know, it wasn't rammed down our throats."

"I want to get to something here, Tony. And I think we've got to get to the root of who you are before we can go on. Tell me about growing up. Tell me about being Italian and Catholic, about what it meant to you."

"I don't see what the fuck this has to do with shit."

Binford held up both hands, gently, lackadaisically, halting Tony. "You agreed, remember? Try it my way for a few sessions. This'll help me understand where you're coming from, okay?"

"Okay."

The session lasted fifty minutes. Tony told John Binford about growing up in Mill Creek Falls, about Thanksgiving and Christmas and Easter dinners, Memorial Day and Fourth of July picnics, about Jimmy and Annalisa and playing hide 'n' go seek with them and his brothers, playing on warm summer nights under clear skies, how special it all seemed. Church was a disruption, a task, an obligation, a duty to perform, enforced by Jo and Aunt Isabella. Holy days were forced upon the children who griped and complained. "It's boring. It doesn't make any sense." Still they went. God. Duty. Honor. Country.

"And sins," Binford said quietly.

"Sins?" Tony responded.

"It would be a sin to miss mass on Sunday, wouldn't it?"

"Oh, yeah. You'd go straight to hell for that." Tony chuckled. "And for lots of other things. But I don't think that was very important to us."

"Still, lots of things could send you to hell, huh?"

"Oh yeah. I think they even told us it was a mortal sin to masturbate."

"And to steal?"

"Yeah."

"And to kill?"

"That's like numero uno."

"Tony, I've been over your combat record. I've seen your citations. I've read Dr. Holbrook's reports. You killed a lot of people in Viet Nam, didn't you?"

Tony went instantly from relaxed to tense. He felt Binford had ambushed him. "Maybe."

"Maybe?" Binford was stern.

"You got the record."

"I want you to think about this. I want you to think about *your* views of killing and *your* deeds. Do you view what you did as sinful? And isn't it that sinfulness that caused you to be guilt-ridden and depressed? Is that the key to your acting out, Tony?"

"Wait one fuckin minute." Tony slid to the edge of his chair. "That's not it. You think I shoulda been a scumbag like those bastards who went to Canada or Sweden?"

"I'm not saying that, Tony. But you didn't see yourself as a murderer before you went to Viet Nam, did you?"

"I didn't then. I don't now!"

"Right. You don't see yourself as a killer now, do you?"

"No I don't."

"But by your own accounts you've killed a dozen human beings. Maybe more."

"In combat!"

"I'm not saying it wasn't justified."

"That's right."

"But you grew up believing it was a sin. See? This is an unresolved conflict in your subconsciousness. You have to be able to come to terms with those traumatic events before those deep-seated feelings of guilt and remorse will stop manifesting themselves in self-destructive behaviors."

"That's more fucked up than I am."

"Is it?"

"You bet your sweet ass. There it is. I'll tell you what's fucked up. I'll tell you what's sinful. All this amnesty bullshit for draft dodgers."

"Does that make you angry?"

"It sure does. Did you read the testimonies before that Senate committee?"

"A little . . ."

"Kennedy and McGovern, talking like the righteous thing to do was to crawl off to Canada! I'll tell you, there was that one guy, Kelly, lost a son in the A Shau. He had it right. He said somethin like if Kennedy's definition of honor, righteousness, and high moral standards was running away, then that was labeling all of us who didn't run away as immoral and dishonorable."

"And you feel you did the moral and honorable thing?"

"I know I did. If I hadn't been there, it would of been worse on those people. I was a god damned good sergeant . . . "

"Protected your men?"

"That's right."

"But what if no Americans had ever been there? What if there had been no Marines to protect?"

"Then the gooks would have taken over and enslaved the Viet Namese."

"Really?"

During that spring of 1972 nothing could possibly have been better for Pewel Wapinski than to have a strong, trained paramedic move into Bobby's old bedroom. Pewel slept on a rented hospital bed in the dining room. His paramedic collected the maple sap, turned the fields, learned not just to plow, fertilize, and plant but how to *plan* the farm. He even built a crude elevator to lift Pewel Wapinski to his barn office.

And Pewel had a highly trained nurse come nearly every day, one who enjoyed his home and farm, who enjoyed cooking, didn't mind cleaning, who loved him as if he were her own grandfather; and he had Gina and Michelle—Rascal and Timidthia as he called them—growing, bright, babbling and cute in the way of precious and precocious two-year-olds, astounding him with their feats of physical flexibility as he himself became more mobile.

On the girls' second birthday they had a party in the kitchen at High Meadow. "You can have cake after lunch," Linda said.

"Why not now?" Tony asked.

"You're worse than the girls." Linda was happy and it showed. "You too!" She admonished Pewel as he picked a stray blob of frosting from the edge of the cake plate.

"I wanna come you," Gina said to Tony.

"Come on then," Tony said. He held out his hands.

"Wash your hands first," Linda ordered. Gina and Tony looked at her. "Yes, both of you."

Tony winked at Gina, lifted her to the sink. His relationship with her was better than ever. Michelle still would not sit with him. "What's for lunch?" he asked. He put Gina down.

"Hangerber," Gina squealed.

"Huggerber," Michelle said from her mother's side.

"Hangerber or huggerber?" Tony chuckled.

"Ham-burg-ers," Linda corrected.

Gina giggled. Then, "I wanna pick you up."

"Pick me up?" Tony looked at her. "I too big."

"I pick you up," Gina giggled again.

"She means she wants you to pick her up," Linda said to Tony. "Bring her to the table, okay?"

As they ate lunch Tony spoke to Pewel about new strawberry fields. He wanted to turn and plant one row at a time. " . . . eventually put in enough . . . We can't make any money on grain. Strawberries are a cash crop. Enough for Morris', the IGA, and the 7-Eleven. Maybe the stores in Rock Ridge, too. Even RRVMC. They've got a big mess hall there . . . "

Pewel agreed but his focus was on the little girls, and soon Tony dropped the topic though it spun and whirled in his mind as he mentally calculated planting schedules, maturity, how many years it would take to have established beds that he could trust, and could guarantee the stores and hospital a fresh in-season supply. In his head he knew exactly what was needed, knew too exactly how different this crop was from syrup—this fragile time-essential crop. He could commit the fields. Could he commit himself?

"So Tony, how's it going today?"

"Good."

"The farm survive hurricane Agnes?"

"Yeah. Pretty much so. Except remember I was putting in those new beds . . . ?"

"Strawberries?"

"Yeah. That pretty much got washed out."

"Oh." Binford sighed, rocked his head empathetically. They were now into the fourth month of therapy. Tony had come to view him as a friend, perhaps as a bit weird, ignorant about the realities of combat, but still as a friend. "And how are things between you and Linda?"

"Okay."

"Just okay?"

"You know."

"No," Binford said, "I don't."

"Not being with her . . . you know. I'm still living with Mr. Wapinski. I see her every day. And the girls. But . . . really . . . I mean it hurts like hell knowing what I did to em and knowing that I can't live with em. Linda'd let me come back. She wants to help me. You know how she is. But . . . well, she's under a lot of pressure and Mr. Wapinski, my agreement with him was for six months."

"What kind of pressure?"

"Oh, mostly from her folks. Her mother calls all the time and tells her to dump me. Her old man hates my guts."

"Some reasons there?"

"You know. I told you about the shotgun. She told her sister and she told their father."

"Um-hum."

"Mr. Wapinski says that if you hurt someone, that hurts you inside. He says it causes internal battles and that the toll on you is worse than the toll on the one you hurt because you hurting them is external. To them. Their outsides heal. But for you, it detracts from who you are and takes a lot longer to rebuild."

"Let's go back over that incident with the shotgun. Putting it in your mouth. Pulling the trigger. What were you thinking? Do you remember what you were thinking?"

"About Nam. Fuckin around. Didn't care who was around me, you know, was just goin back to it."

"Do you remember what Linda did?"

"Yeah. Started cryin and shit. Screamin. 'Don't do it.' Came over and put her arm around me. And, ah, I knew I—I couldn't do that to em no more."

"Do you ever think you maybe did that because you were looking . . . subconsciously . . . for hugs from your mother?"

"No way. Not at all. Nowhere near that. Geez. We've been here a hundred times. I told you about my cousin . . . About getting thrashed out west?" Tony paused. "You think I should have gone back, huh?"

"Do you?"

"I think of it all the time. If I hadn't met Linda I probably would of. I still could."

"Um."

"I could go back. If I could go back for just one day. One hour. Just smell the air, feel the ground, see the people again. There's like this part a me that needs to go back. Like I left part of me there. Like there's another Anthony F. Pisano fuckin still there. You understand? It's like only . . . like only his shadow came back. Like he hasn't caught up to me yet. Like it'll never fuckin happen. There's still an Anthony Pisano . . . shit! I even saw his footlocker on Okie! I just remembered that. He's still in Nam Bo somewhere. I'm just this fuckin shadow that can't see nothin. That's in this fog. Shadows can't function in a fog."

"Like you lost your soul over there? Only your physical being came back?"

"Yeah. What came back is proud, but it's only part of me. And I'm tired of livin here and there. I'm not responsible for that shit. That suffering. I can't be held responsible for that. Damn it! I was good. Everybody said so. Everybody recognized it until .·. ."

"Until?"

"Until I came back." Tony snorted, turned sideways to Binford.

"Did you ever see any atrocities over there?"

"Yeah. You know. I guess . . . Usually they talk about that being like burning a ville or raping or killing women or children. I heard of some of that. That happened . . . ah, in Delta Company. Before I got there. They had one particular guy who was notorious for ah . . . he was always on point. Big guy. He'd go forward with a fire team—very far ahead of the company. And ah, evidently he raped a village woman and held a gun to her head and said, 'When the rest of the company gets here, if you say anything, I'll blow yer brains out.' And the guys in the fire team knew he'd done it but they weren't about to say anything cause their heads would a got blown off. That's the story, anyway. That's something."

"And the time, ah, tell me again about the woman and children killed at . . . that you saw killed. The soldier with the belt that you think you should have killed first."

"Aw, Man. Again?"

"Please."

Now Tony retold the story in detail. He told the therapist about seeing the man with the belt, the firefight that ensued, the human shield tactic used by the NVA. "I cried that day, Man. I remember thinking if Pop saw me crying he'd be disappointed, but I cried that day."

"One more month, eh?"

"One more."

"You talk with Linda yet?"

"No. I . . . We're getting along pretty good, don't you think?"

"Don't matter what I think."

"But Gran . . . ah, Mr. Wapinski . . ."

"You can call me Granpa. I like it."

"Grandpa. If she lets me move back . . . "

"I'll be fine. Doin pretty good, see? I don't need to go upstairs."

"I don't wanta feel like I'm runnin out on you."

"Yep. Caused ya enough problems, runnin out, already."

"Um-hmm. Really has. As long as I've got my three-a-days, I'm pretty good. She'll let me come back, don't you—"

"Ask her."

"Yeah. I will. Tonight. At her place, tonight."

"Here, Tony. I got a little something for you." Pewel Wapinski handed Tony a piece of paper.

"What's . . ."

"It's a prayer. Nothin fancy. I say it in the mornin an at night. Keeps the crops growing."

Tony looked at the sheet. "Dear Lord," it began, "Please bless us and watch over us; Deliver us from evil . . . "

"When you understand it," Pewel said, "not just readin words, but understandin it, things fall into place."

Tony continued to read. " 'Forgive us our trespasses; And give us the strength and guts to try hard and to never give up.' "

*　　*　　*

It was difficult for the four of them to be alone in the kitchen of the Creek's Bend apartment; difficult for Tony who had frightened them here, in this apartment, difficult too for Linda, because of the hurt, the loss of trust, loss of love associated with these rooms, and because of the joys she'd shared with Gina and Michelle, alone, the hard work she'd invested in rebuilding their lives, twice.

Forgive us our trespasses, Tony thought. "Here, let me do that."

"I've got it." Linda lifted the large pot from the stove, brought it to the sink, dumped the boiling water and shells into the colander. Mist enveloped her, then vanished.

"What can I do?" Tony asked.

"See if the girls want milk or juice, okay?"

"Sure." Tony went to the back porch where Gina and Michelle were playing. The railings had been "fenced" with chicken wire so the girls couldn't slip through, and a latchable gate had been installed at the top of the stairs.

"Papa, know what?" Gina grabbed his pant leg.

"What?" Tony smiled. Gina was so open to him, Michelle so closed. Try hard, he thought.

"Deedee, deedee deedee," Gina squealed, let him go, ran to Michelle.

"Deedee, deedee deedee?" Tony laughed. Both girls, their heads together, laughed too. Tony laughed more. "Do you two want milk or juice with dinner?"

"Papa, you come inside, okay?"

Tony pointed to himself. "Go inside? First tell me, juice or milk?"

"Papa angry at Gina," Gina said to him. Then to Michelle she said, "Gina a bad girl. Papa angry." Then quickly, looking, acting sad, "I sorry, Papa."

"No. No, Gina. Papa's not angry." Tony knelt near the twins. "Gina's a good girl. And Michelle is too. Michelle's a good girl. I love you both very much. I just want to know if you want milk or juice with dinner."

"Papa angry," Gina whispered to Michelle. "Papa very angry."

"No I'm not!" Tony said emphatically. "Really." He stood. "I'm going inside. I love you."

The girls put their foreheads together, giggled again.

Inside Linda had set the table. In the middle was the large bowl of shells. Separately, so Gina and Michelle could have their pasta plain, was a gravy boat with tomato sauce and a small bowl of grated cheese. On Tony's plate was a baked breaded chicken breast. On Linda's, half a breast, the other half diced and split between the girls' plates. And there was corn on the cob, steamed zucchini and a fresh tomato salad with olive oil and oregano.

"That's beautiful, Babe," Tony said. He wanted to hug her. It had been so long! "Shoo!" He flitted his hand over the pasta chasing away a fly.

"Oh, I can't keep them out of here," Linda said. "The girls are forever going in and out."

"I could screen the porch for you."

"That'd be great."

"Who did the chicken wire?"

"One of the guys from Steve's Lumber. When I bought it and told him I lived here, he said, 'You mean right up the hill?' I said yes. I was going to buy those U-shaped nails. He said he could let me use a staple gun. I didn't know what that was and he just said he'd do it during his lunch break."

"Oh," Tony said.

"He didn't even charge me," Linda said. She had her back to Tony, was cleaning the twin's Tommy-Tippy cups.

"Damn fly," Tony said. He hunched, moved in on the table, swatted. His hand banged the tabletop. Linda jumped. "Got it," he yelped.

Linda turned. Tony was scraping the fly guts off his hand. A wet black and red splotch was on the table. "Oohhh!" Linda let out her breath. "That's gross. Did you have to?"

"What?"

Linda sighed again, put a hand to her head, "I'm going to be sick."

"Whaaatt?! It's only a damn fly. When I was in Nam Bo, geez, I was telling this to Binford just a few days ago, I remember having to eat sitting in front of a dozen dead gooks. There'd be maggots crawling out their eyeballs..."

"Ooo..." Linda slapped a hand over her mouth, ran for the bathroom.

"Let's go over it one more time, Tony."

"Doc, I've told you this—"

"Stop." Binford was being firm again, playing, as Tony thought of it, good cop/bad cop, all in one. Talk about schizophrenics! "Dr. Holbrook and I have been doing a great deal of reading on this. In our experience, in our search of the literature, the only actions we've found that could cause the degree of guilt behavior that you've been suffering from is if one committed a sinful act. That is, an act which the person who committed it perceived as sinful. Like killing a defenseless woman or her children. Or maybe one's own officer. Now let's go back over—"

"What the hell are you saying?"

"I'm saying that perhaps what happened in Viet Nam, what you say happened with that woman, is not what really happened. Sometimes our mind tries to protect us from reality...."

"No way. No fuckin way."

"Look, if you refuse to cooperate with me, I can't help you. There are no charges here. Nothing will come of this. There are no recriminations. I'm not even saying what happened was malicious. What happened there, your recognition of that reality, your taking responsibility— overtly—might keep you from covertly sabotaging yourself. I'm doing this for you, Tony. To help you stop inflicting this punishment on yourself. Now . . . can we go on? Or should we stop this therapy this instant?"

Tony stared, mouth agape. He didn't know how to respond. Binford's innuendo shocked him, rocked him to the core. Because—because, he suspected . . . it could be true. "I . . . " Tony dropped his head. He could barely make his voice heard. "I gotta take this slow."

"That's okay." Binford was back to his friendly, good-cop voice.

"If I'm guilty of something I'm guilty of not going back and seeing Rick."

"Rick?"

"In Philly. I told you about him. The guy who wanted the docs to cut his legs off. Here." Tony touched his throat.

"Tony, people don't self-destruct because they didn't visit someone they don't even know. . . . "

"But he was a Marine. A Magnificent Bastard. Like me."

"And how many others haven't you visited?" Tony looked up at Binford. "See?" the doctor said.

"What about Manny? If I'd of moved him, covered him, anything."

"But you didn't know about the sniper."

"Sometimes I still dream of him. I still feel Manny gettin greased right in my arms."

"Do you blame yourself?"

"It's—it's not a matter of blame."

"When it happened, do you remember how you felt?"

"I was ragin pissed."

"And at Dai Do, with the machetes?"

"Relieved. Scared shitless but relieved when it was over."

"And all those other times. Do you remember any time feeling like you had gotten people killed? Feeling that it was your fault? That you had screwed up? or sinned?" Tony shook his head. "Only, maybe, with that woman and the children, huh?"

"I . . . I guess."

"Let's go back over that day. . . . "

Again and again. Into September, to Tony and Linda's third anniversary when Tony moved back to the Creek's Bend apartment, through October, into November and Nixon's reelection and Tony's twenty-fifth birthday, into December and the Christmas bombings, and to the peace accords of January 1973, every other Tuesday Tony retold John H. Binford the story of the NVA soldier with the belt and the woman and children. In every way possible the therapist attempted to guide Tony to a new understanding. Tony resisted. The story evolved.

During this time, too, John H. Binford's ideas evolved. Each session he recorded Tony's responses and his own observations of Tony's behavior. With Daniel Holbrook and a third doctor, Binford hypothesized about and expounded upon his therapeutic model. By the time of the

Paris accords, the three of them were treating, or experimenting with, fifteen Viet Nam veterans—six outpatients and nine institutionalized. All the men responded positively to therapy. All reported either total or significant abstinence from self-dosing with alcohol or street drugs, a lowering in the frequency of explosive rage and violent outbursts, and fewer quasi-dissociative episodes (flashbacks). Binford's confidence grew as his hypothesis moved toward theory and as patient after patient proved, or failed to disprove, the validity of his ideas. Not only did his confidence increase, so too did his determination to affect Anthony F. Pisano.

Others who touched Tony's life changed too. Linda was ever more independent. She took another nursing course, by mail, and she wanted Tony to restart his education. Grandpa Wapinski's health gradually diminished, and for the first time Tony saw that he was indeed an old man with a limited life span.

"So you're angry about it."

"You bet your sweet ass—"

"One minute." Binford held up a hand. "Now I know we've always said anything we wish in here, but today, just today, I'm going to ask you to practice self-control over your language. No swearing. No cusses. Just as an exercise in self-control. Can you do that for me?"

"I guess." Tony scratched his nose.

"Why the anger?"

"Don't you see?"

"I see peace. I see a peace treaty."

"I see a sellout."

"I see American prisoners coming home."

"I see my cousin. I see him being killed for no godd . . . arned reason. I see the devaluation of his sacrifice. And mine."

"But you won."

"Not with the fuckin commie army in place!"

"Okay. Let's move on. Close your eyes. See Dai Do. . . . "

In early March Binford tried another tactic. "Here!" he shouted. They were in the village just before getting to the woman and children. Binford threw a seat cushion at Tony. "That's the woman. Pretend that's the woman. What do you want to do to her?"

"Doc!" Tony glared.

"Show me what you want to do to her!"

"This is stupid. If this were the woman I'd push her down and drill that motherfucker behind her."

"You'd kill again?"

"Fuck, damn right!"

"Who would you kill?"

"Not this stupid pillow."

In April 1973 Tony brought in a news article from the local paper.

"Listen to this, Doc. 'The beatings ended only when they fell to uncon-
sciousness, or when they capitulated. Or died.' These guys really went
through a worlda hurt."

"That's about the POWs?"

"Yeah. Remember how you thought it was so great of Hanoi to release
em. Listen to this. This guy was badly burned. 'About his condition he
said, "My wounds were draining badly, and were full of puss. The smell
was terrible. It attracted a horde of flies. I let them lay their eggs on the
burned flesh. When the maggots hatched they devoured the dead tissue
which served to debride the wound. Later I washed the wounds with
my urine to get the maggots off." ' Heroic stuff, huh, Doc?"

"Do you think so?"

"Yep. I do. I hurt for this guy."

"What about for the people he dropped bombs on?"

"You don't make a distinction, huh?"

"Do you?"

"You bet your sweet ass. He was a captive. A prisoner. Helpless. They
were active combatants. Engaged in battle."

"People pushing bicycles against supersonic fighter-bombers?"

"Able to attack and able to defend. Isn't that the distinction the Geneva
Accords make on treating POWs?"

"What about at Dai Do," Binford said. "Let's go back one more time.
Who was able to attack and who was able to defend?"

"All of us."

"The woman . . . "

"No. I meant the NVA. And us."

"Close your eyes."

"Hm."

"Can you see the woman?"

"Uh-huh."

"And the children?"

"Uh-huh."

"And yourself, Tony?"

"Yeah."

"Where are you?"

"I'm down. I'm in the dirt. In the prone firing position."

"You're holding your weapon?"

"Yeah. I'm trying to sight . . . trying to get a bead on the dink."

"And what do you see?"

"The woman. And her kids. And I can see this fucker behind em."

"And you want to shoot him?"

"Yeah. I want to waste im."

"But you can't?"

"Right. I can't get a clean shot. The dumb bitch—"

"You're angry with the woman?"

"Right on! Dumb! Dumb fuckin frozen! Exposing her kids to fire."

"And you fire?"

"Yeah."

"You hear your weapon, feel your weapon, see the flashes."

"Yeah."

"Your bullets hit the woman and the children, don't they." Tony's eyes are still shut. His face squinches. Binford continues. "Now you've got a clean line of fire on the man with the belt." Tony moans. "Shoot him."

"MAHAAAH!" Tony jolts up, eyes open, stares at Binford.

"Did you get him, Tony?"

"Yeah. No. No. He was already dee-dee-in. Splittin. Beatin feet."

"But the woman and children are dead, aren't they?"

"He drilled em in the back."

"No, Tony. You shot them. You shot them because you were afraid the enemy soldier was going to shoot you and you needed to lay suppressive fire even if the woman and children were in the way."

"Unt-uh."

"Yes, Tony. You could see it clearly this time, couldn't you? We've stripped away the screen memory. You were scared that day, weren't you?"

"You're always scared when you're in a firefight," Tony said quietly. "But not so scared you fire up women and children."

"And you were excited that day, too, huh?"

"Your adrenaline's pumpin."

"And you missed killing that soldier earlier and you even needed to be counseled by your superior?"

Tony sighed. "I told you that."

"And you've finally seen what really happened there. Now you know why you've been punishing yourself."

"No, Doc." Tony's voice was slow, pained.

Binford's voice remained calm, firm, bearing down like a heavy weight. "Only an act of commission causes the self-destructive behavior you've exhibited. The only way to deal with it, Tony, is to own up to it. Confront it. Then you can come to terms with it. You're not alone, Tony. Many men err under the stress of combat. You're not perfect. None of us are. You don't have to hold yourself up against some impossible John Wayne standard. It's okay, Tony. It's okay."

Tony slid slightly forward in the chair, placed his hands, fists balled, on his thighs. "You really think I shot em?"

"What do you think, Tony?"

Tony canceled his April 17th session. He excused himself by telling John Binford's secretary that his sister-in-law, Molly, was in labor and he was staying with his brother, lending support. (Adam Pisano was born 18 April at 4:54 A.M.) Tony didn't call or attend his scheduled May 1st therapy. He worked at High Meadow as he had now for fourteen straight months. He felt moody, antsy. On the 6th his supply of lithium carbonate ran out but he refused to return to RRVMC to pick up his refill. Linda noticed the change but purposefully ignored the signs. She was busy. On Tuesdays and Thursdays she worked eight to five for Dr. Simon Denham and his new group practice. Monday, Wednesday and Friday she worked for Pewel Wapinski. Saturdays and Sundays she attempted to catch up around the apartment and even cram in some study.

Saturday, 12 May 1973, Mill Creek Falls, River Front Drive, the back lawn of Ernest Hartley's mansion, the wedding reception of Annalisa Pellegrino and Edward Milne—On this joyous and beautiful day, this third birthday of his daughters Gina and Michelle, for Anthony F. Pisano everything again turned to shit.

"You look beautiful." Tony hugged his cousin.

"And you've had too much champagne." Annalisa hugged him back, turned to her maid of honor to introduce Tony.

"Wait. Just give me one minute, okay? Just a little toast between you and me."

"Sure." Her eyes were bright reflecting the sun and the white satin.

"To the unseen best man," Tony whispered.

Annalisa looked him in the eye. Smiled. "Okay. To Jimmy," she said.

Tony hugged her again. Then he slipped away, back to the patio where a few friends of Edward Milne were surrounding a keg of beer. Tony stood near them, not really with them except when he refilled his cup.

Tony watched the congregated celebrators. John and Molly were there with baby Adam, swaddled, a sun bonnet covering his face, Molly tipping up the brim, showing him off to everyone and anyone. Nonna Pisano sat on a wicker throne chair looking like the queen mother. Uncle James and Aunt Isabella discreetly directed operations. All the aunts and uncles and cousins attended, ate, drank, danced. And friends and friends of friends, after the first serving, came to celebrate, too—more lovely young women than Tony had seen, ever, in one place.

"Check out that one," one of Edward's friends said.

Tony moved to the keg to refill his cup.

"Bit old for you," a second friend laughed.

"You talking about the little one with the nice tits?" a third said.

"Yeah," said the first. Tony followed their eyes, realized they were talking about Linda. In a way it delighted him, made him proud.

"Boy," the third said, "I'd like to plow her fields."

They laughed. Tony laughed with them, involuntarily. Then the second man said, "I heard she's hot to trot."

"Man," said the first, "look at them tits. She's really stacked."

Again they laughed. Then the second young man said, "She used to fuck like a bunny for a friend of a friend of mine. He said she's a dynamite lay, but that her old man's trouble."

Tony moved off. He was wounded. He was drunk, angry, wanting to punch someone, wanting to confront Linda right there. He moved down the tree line, between shrubs, gradually closer. He heard his father's voice, saw the back of his head. "I don't understand him," John Sr. was saying. "He's not like the others. Never has been."

Tony moved on, closer, angrier yet. Annalisa was sitting in a chair surrounded by almost everyone. Edward knelt before her, was raising her skirt, teasingly pushing the garter higher instead of removing it. The band was playing little flourishes—da-dat-da-dah—with each thrust.

Linda was watching Annalisa, talking to someone Tony didn't know, perhaps one of the visiting nurses. "I thought Tony was pretty bad off with all he saw," Linda said to the woman. "But I heard from Susan about one guy out there who just realized he'd killed a woman and her children in cold blood. They say he was so overwhelmed by his behavior that he psychologically blocked it out and supplanted the memory with a total fabrication."

September 1984

It kicks in. The dream, the terror. I see a mouth. I see the mouth the same way I see the tunnel; the same way I feel the chopper going down; the same way I see, feel, hear, smell Manny, me, my arms, his face, his chest. I see teeth, a slight overlap of the incisors. I see the gums, pink, gray; the lips, gray; the tongue. I see saliva, spittle, white foam at the corners of the mouth and silvery reflections off the wet chin. I do not see the person. I do not see me. But I sense the person, the hopelessness, the lostness, the shame at being worthless, at being a burden. I sense the befuddlement, the WHY? the HOW? the exasperation yet the lack of motivation, incentive, foresight. I am the mouth. I am a vegetable.

I do not know where to go from here. Ty, Bobby and I are nearing convergence, collision. I want to tell you these stories, ideas, events, theories, simultaneously. But that is not possible.

I did not confront Linda with the fucking like a bunny for the friend of Annalisa's husband's friend, but in my state of mind, of self-esteem, I believed it. Why the hell shouldn't she? She was sensual, beautiful, and strapped to a lead weight—me. God, it hurt. I was raw inside, irate, fragile. Why? The base, the foundation that I'd worked so hard to rebuild, I let it be shattered by one sentence overheard. I was worthless, a murdering scumhead. I was not even worthy enough to pray Grandpa Wapinski's prayer. Give me the strength and guts to try hard and never give up? Try hard on what? Never give up what? Worthless scum has no reason to be strong, to persevere.

Binford's guilt therapy had me convinced I should die, rid them of me. I could not touch my daughters, could not hug them, could not play with them, could barely look at them. And if Linda was boffing somebody—probably the guy from Steve's Lumber—could I have touched her? My mania returned. I slept in the barn at High Meadow, when I did sleep, on the pretext of needing to get in the expanded crops. I skipped out and drank, alone, at the White Pines Inn. I found Big Bonnie again, scored my dope from him, fucked Zookie until I thought my balls would collapse and I'd suffocate in her neck tattoo.

In June I received a letter from Rick. I don't know how he found me. He was in school, doing pretty well amid the "influx of idiots" and the professor who wouldn't "let me in class without a haircut. Oh, by the way," he wrote it just like this, "they did cut my legs off."

On July ninth, a few days after checking on the flag on Jimmy's grave, after arranging with the Lutz boys for the crops, without telling Grandpa Wapinski or Linda or my Pop or Jo or Annalisa, I split, climbed back on the Harley, set myself free.

Free. I think of telling you of the homeless who befriended me. Some good people down on their luck. Times were tough. Some crooks. Some crazies. Some zombies. I think of telling you of the runaways—kids—some as young as thirteen. What's this country coming to?! I think of telling you of all those things I saw, things I did. But why? It is only more of the same. More of the same when I was almost arrested in Montgomery, Alabama. More of the same when I ditched a chick and took her dope and dough in Denver.

Being a two-time loser facilitates being a three-time loser. By time four it was habitual, repeating as if I were strapped to a carousel in purgatory. Intrusive thoughts, frustrations, anger, drugs, booze, splitting, danger-zone, trouble, checking into the VA, going crazy because of untreated or mistreated PTSD that was rubbed raw by current events, by cultural misperceptions, by social ostracism, by guilt therapy and strait jacket cocktails. Then deeper remorse, additional self-incrimination, self-hate.

Why was my Pop able to handle what he saw and I wasn't? Why were so many Viet vets able to handle their experiences? Why did others, like me, fold, crumble, give in, give out? There are many reasons but, to me, the most unkind booby trap, the most long-term devastation, stemmed from the liquid strait jacket "therapy" from the VMC, and that followed up by the acerbic ambush of guilt-therapy. I think I could have made it home had I not been so damaged, had I been left to my own devices.

Today I have a better grasp. I understand the booby trap of the cocktails—not just the immediate and short-term effects, but the long-term brain damage—the actual atrophying of dopamine receptors analogous to foisting Alzheimer's disease on the subject. I also understand the ambush of guilt-therapy that became prevalent after the DMS III (*Diagnostic and Statistical Manual of Mental Disorders*, 3d ed.) added *Posttraumatic Stress Disorders* as a mental illness (diagnosis), and after it became perverted by a do-gooder system that did not—a system that set up compensation for *failing* to heal, and then only if one admitted to the commission of malicious atrocities against civilians or one's fellow combatants.

* * *

A break. I get so wound up about this my thoughts short out, words are supplanted by anger, by fury—rationality is obliterated. So breathe with me. It is a technique Bobby taught. A few deep breaths, belly breaths, and a look about. The night is clear, cold, black sky and stars to the west and north; thin low clouds, and light, to the east. Morning is coming but that light is the false dawn. From up here, it's almost as though the world no longer exists. It has been destroyed in nuclear war yet without TV, radio, papers, I've yet to be informed. The mall lights to the south come on at dusk but they are automatic and maybe even if everyone is dead they would still operate for some time. My fire is not dependent on them, on any of them. Burning apple branches mostly. Cleaning the orchard earlier. Habit. Apple is a hardwood but too full of knots for anything other than small sculptures and firewood. I toss on another piece. Glowing droplets rise against the black curtain of the sugarbush like inverse rain. I follow the riselets, jar the fire for a fresh storm. First by the thousands, then hundreds, then one by one they die out and only one climbs up over the crown, into the stars.

I came back in February '74. Grandpa Wapinski was pretty angry with me but he didn't show it much. His body wasn't very healthy anymore but he had his tickets to California ready and he was like a little kid with a lollipop, those old eyes glistening. "Come with me," he said.

"I came to syrup," I said. "Then I'm outta here."

"Upset, huh?"

"Why'd she do it, Mr. Wapinski? Why'd she file . . . " I broke down that time. I cried and he let me cry. How could I have expected Linda to do anything but? She'd filed for divorce in January. I was out of my head. "Okay." I finally got the words out. "I'll accompany you." I could not have been more lost, more lame, more in need of a shepherd to carry me home.

20

San Martin, California, May 1973—Bobby was in the Safeway at Sixth and Miwok. He had just handed the cashier a twenty-dollar bill. In his bag he had two large zucchinis, one jar of spaghetti sauce, a box of mushrooms, a pound of mozzarella, a pound of ground chuck, and bread, peanut butter and cigarettes. In his mind swirled the idea to use zucchini slices instead of lasagna noodles. The entire preparation and cooking time, he reasoned, could be cut to a third, because there'd be no precooking.

"Oh, excuse me."

Bobby startled. Looked back, down. There was a woman picking up a clutter of coupons from the floor. Behind her were eight children, all about the same age. Bobby lifted a foot to give the woman room. She looked up, smiled. His thoughts crumbled. Bobby bent. He did not take his eyes from hers. Behind her the boys were pushing, pulling baseball cards from the exit displays, dashing into the path of shopping carts. The girls each had food items. Bobby fumbled, picked up a coupon, handed it to her. "Thank you," she said.

"Sure," he answered. He stood.

She too stood. She was only as tall as his nose.

Bobby turned to the counter, lifted his bag, walked out.

"Children," the woman said. "Children. Let's stay in line."

"Sir," the cashier called. "Sir, your change!"

But Bobby had already left.

He sliced, he cooked, he made notes, but he could not get that smile out of his mind. He moved to the dining room table. The sun was high and only indirect light fell on his papers, sketches, finished drawings, notes. "THIS IS A KITCHEN," read the block letters of the cutline on the drawing in his hand. Below, the text read, "This is the kitchen sink. Be prepared to spend a significant amount of time here."

Wapinski flipped back to the first sheet—the cover—his cartoon drawing of a befuddled, eight-thumbed man standing amid stacked pots, pans, and pizza boxes. A cartoon dog that looked amazingly like Josh was in the corner looking equally befuddled. Arched across the top were the words *The Feral Man's Cookbook: With Menus for 30 Days*. On the bottom, in smaller letters: "Written and illustrated by Robert J. Wapinski." Under that in much smaller letters: "Recipes tested by Josh—if he wouldn't eat it, it's not included."

Bobby chuckled. He flipped through the next few pages. Dedicated (to Grandma and Grandpa). He smiled, reread the introduction, "An elementary guide to the inner workings of a kitchen." He flipped to his menu for zucchini lasagna, penned in the word *basil*. He felt good. He sniffed. The lasagna smelled wonderful.

"You were a company commander. Earned a Silver Star with Oak Leaf cluster, Bronze Star, Air Medals. What were you doing selling real estate?"

"Well, when I first came out my wife, my girl at the time, she was selling real estate. I didn't have a job and she convinced me to get my license. Almost immediately I had a sale. Things just took off. It was a good job. I liked it. It was good to me and I think I was good to it, too."

"I'm sure you were. I can't get over this thought. I mean, it's not too often I get to interview the commander of a combat company. Honorable discharge. Silver Star. You're a little light in the education department."

"I've enrolled in a few night courses to get my degree."

"Good. It's not a problem, though. You qualify on your work record. Salesman, office manager, planning committee member of the San Martin Board of Realtors. You're . . . why do you want this job?"

"Maybe I shouldn't say it like this, but I'm tired of what the developers are doing to this town. I think I could be an effective force at helping to design a plan that they could live with and that would keep them from flattening and paving the entire area."

"You know, you're overqualified. It's an assistant plannership. You'd be more clerk than planner. And it doesn't pay nearly as much as you were making selling real estate. With your combat record, you should be seeking a better position."

Wapinski chuckled. "You're the first person that's ever placed any importance on my military service. I'm proud of it, but truth is, I almost left it off the résumé because I thought it might work against me."

"See that plaque there?" The man gestured to the wall behind him where there was a framed Bronze Star certificate.

"Oh! I didn't notice it. Viet Nam?"

"Korea. Look, I'll put your application through with my recommendation that we start you off at the top pay bracket. That's thirteen six. They don't start anyone off at the top. Chances are, if you're hired, you'll be getting more like ten five and if they start you off at the bottom, that's eighty-nine hundred. You'll have to be interviewed by a few others."

"Mr. Reed . . . "

"Tim."

"Tim. I want the job. The money's not as important as the opportunity to serve."

"To serve?"

"I mean . . . "

"I know what you mean. I've just never heard it from a man in your generation."

Where the heck could she be? It was midafternoon. He'd gone back to the Safeway a dozen times. "I'm doing a cookbook," he'd explained. "Trying different recipes."

"Ah, you're the guy . . . "

Bobby looked at the cashier. She turned away, looked at the cash register drawer, squirmed, popped her chewing gum. "Were you talking to me?"

Reluctantly she looked up. "Yeah," she said. "You're the guy that walked out without his change."

"Hmm?"

"God!" Then to the drawer. "He doesn't even remember. I shouldn't a said anything."

"My change?"

"Yeah. I can't give it to ya." Again she popped her gum. "It was ten ten. You gotta see the manager."

"Oh, when I—"

"Yeah. Sheesh!" Again, more to herself than to Bobby, "If Miss Andrassy wasn't here with her class . . . You didn't even know!"

"The . . . " Bobby pointed into the aisle behind him. "What was her name?"

"Who?"

"The woman with all the kids?"

"Teacher. Miss Andrassy. She's my sister's teacher."

"At . . ."

"Over at the elementary school."

"Hey—" Bobby beamed at the sullen cashier, "you know that ten ten?" She looked up at him. "You keep it." He smiled. "Because you were so honest."

"There's the water problem to begin with," Bobby said. "I know they're deemphasizing it but the deepest well is pumping salt water and the one south of Bahia de Martin is contaminated with chemicals from the old landfill."

"Well," Henry Alan Harrison said, "you know a good deal more about this than most. But it may not be true."

"True or not," Bobby said, "it's easily verifiable. These are the things a planner must be concerned with. How much can be pumped? What population can be sustained?"

"Yes." Harrison nodded. "We're looking for an assistant, you understand. Not a chief planner."

"I'm willing to start at the bottom."

"Um-hmm." Harrison sat behind an ornate wooden desk. He was a young man. Bobby judged him to be not more than a year or two older than himself. Maybe even younger, he thought, but he's already losing his hair. Harrison turned Wapinski's résumé over, read Tim Reed's notes scribbled on the back. "You were talking to Tim about the 'problems of homogenized communities'? What's that all about?"

"We were talking about the demise of the multigenerational, multiethnic, multioccupational neighborhood. What I said to him was that if all the people who surround you have the same problems you have, and there's no one around who had the same problem a generation or two ago, who lived and worked through it and learned, then you're apt to have to rediscover the solution. Or worse. It may seem unsolvable. It's a terrible waste not to draw on previous experience. Or from other socio-ethnic-economic groups."

"Hmm." For a moment Harrison was quiet. Then, "You were in Viet Nam?"

"Yes," Wapinski answered. "Were you?"

"No. I was lucky. I had a high draft number."

"You seem older than when the numbers . . . I mean . . . "

"I'm glad I didn't have to go," Harrison said. "I know guys who went. They're very messed up."

"I—" Bobby stuttered. He did not want to talk to Harrison about Viet Nam.

"You made it through okay?"

"Uh-huh. It was a great experience. Very interesting. Intense. Rough at times."

"You're the only person I ever heard say that." Harrison looked suspiciously at Wapinski as if Wapinski were hiding something.

"It's in the past," Bobby said.

"Hmmm." Harrison closed Wapinski's file. "We'll be in touch."

Bobby continued to work on his cookbook, continued his running regime, continued to talk to Josh, care for Josh, walk or run the mountain trails with Josh. And he tried to think of ways to meet Sara Andrassy. Finding her name now seemed the easy part. He knew nothing about her except that she taught second grade. And she had an incredible smile, a nice voice, dark eyes. Physical infatuation, he told himself. To fall . . . he thought, on sight! He chastised himself. "Frivolous!" he said to Josh. "But . . . What do ya think, Josh? Bovine scat? Good grief! In a supermarket! Dumb, Man, dumb. Not even a single word and I melted. Dumb."

At two thirty on Friday, June 8th, 1973, Bobby settled the questions. Five days before the end of the school year, he simply walked into Sara Andrassy's classroom.

"May I help you?" Her skin looked deeply tanned, or perhaps she was dark; her hair was dark brown with a few red highlights wisping in the curls; her eyes glistened like polished obsidian.

"Sara Andrassy?"

"Yes. I'm Sara Andrassy. May I help you?"

He must have looked ridiculous, standing there before her and her twenty-two second graders. Her smile was broad. The children giggled. "I'm Robert Wapinski. I'm a new clerk with the Regional Planning Board."

"Yes?"

"I . . . I wanted to catch you before you left. Maybe I should come back after class . . . "

"Certainly. If you'll excuse me . . . "

"Yes."

He began to back out of the room, not taking his eyes off her. Before he was more than a few steps she said, "Do you play tennis?"

Then three little girls giggled loudly, sang and giggled while singing, "Miss Andrassy, in a tree, K-I-S-S-I-N-G."

"I'd like . . . " Bobby held Sara close. A mile off, over the waters of the bay, skyrockets erupted in the blackness. They had been together nearly a month. He'd swept her off her feet; she'd jolted him to his core. She was exactly everything he'd always wanted though perhaps quieter, perhaps shorter too, and more fragile, though not as fragile as he'd imagined. She was exactly everything he had always imagined in his ideal except not a single facet matched the image he maintained. The night was beautiful. He released her, leaned forward, opened his shirt. "I'd like you to have this," he said.

"You never take it off, do you?"

"Would you wear it?"

"Always."

"It'll protect you. And that's more important to me than anything in the world."

"But what's to protect you?"

"You. You make me want to live a thousand years." With those words Bobby Wapinski slipped the chain with his silver Jumping Mary medallion over Sara Andrassy's head.

Sara thought they should move more slowly. Bobby had no doubts. On their second "date" (he'd taken her to a Pizza Hut) he simply told her, "I'm going to marry you someday."

In mid-July of 1973 Sara Andrassy moved into Bobby's Old Russia Road cottage. The ensuing months were the happiest time of Bobby's life. It was a time free from searching for a life partner, a time to follow his dreams, a period in which he would develop most of the concepts—though he did not fully realize it himself—of High Meadow and The Code.

Daily in July and August they walked Josh from the cottage down Old Mine Trail, circling the peak, sometimes descending Gold Mine Trail to Cataract, then climbing the old stairs by the lower dam and plodding through Reservoir Estates, into the bowels of North Peak CondoWorld. Farther on, beyond the Upper Res, they escaped into the still undeveloped west slope, then climbed Steep Hill Trail to the edge of the old Nike site, and back to the cottage. At times the sight of the development infuriated Bobby. But now, with Sara, he was often oblivious to everything but the two of them, Josh, and whatever was their current topic.

Sara was open, nondefensive. She told Bobby she was the fourth of four children, three older brothers. By heritage she was Hungarian, Chickasaw, and English. "And with gypsy and American Indian roots actually being in Asia," Sara said, "I guess I'm an Amero-Euro-Asian mutt."

"Perfect blend," Bobby said. "Look at Josh and how great he turned out."

"Oh thanks." Sara laughed.

On one walk Sara explained, "Life just sort of acted upon Mom."

"Um." Bobby wanted to know details.

"She wasn't very aggressive, but I know now she was passive-aggressive. She always got her way. She'd pout or whimper. Make us all feel guilty. Poor-me–type behavior. And everybody'd cave in."

"When you meet Miriam"—Bobby had already told Sara about his mother—"you'll see that different isn't necessarily . . . well . . . Miriam isn't passive."

"Daddy's a bit introverted. Sometimes he's nice. Now Granddad Coolwater, he was downright mean. I remember when we were little and we'd driven from Atlanta to Cleveland to visit. And George, the brother just older than me, and me . . . Granddad'd be sitting on the porch, in his chair, and he would ask us to come up and he'd say, 'Put your hand there.' He'd pat the arm of the chair. We'd put our hands there and he'd play chicken with us with his cigarette."

"What!"

"He'd see how close he could come to our skin before we'd pull away. That was Sunday afternoon entertainment at Pawpee's. I hated it."

"I guess so."

"Tamas, my oldest brother, once refused to move his hand and Pawpee refused to stop. Daddy got so angry when he found out. . . . He was my hero that day. He threw the chair from the porch and broke it. Then Lynette got angry at Daddy and they had a big fight."

"Phew!"

"I was Daddy's favorite at that time. He always said that. Lynette did too. I don't know why but when I got a little older and they would fight I'd end up being the peacemaker. 'Sara, tell your mother I won't blah-blah-blah.' 'Well, you tell him blah-blah-blah.' I used to feel like I must be this really terrible person. I mean, I felt I was the only thing holding them together."

As Bobby and Sara's relationship deepened Bobby could feel his singleness evaporating. He was as afraid of the commitment as a Dog Patch bachelor, and yet, with Sara, the evaporation pleased him. He saw in her a woman he could trust. For a son of Miriam Cadwalder Wapinski to be able to trust a woman and to recognize that, was the equivalent of popping a flare in the middle of a night-cloaked jungle.

Their relationship deepened quickly. Bobby told Sara about Viet Nam, the country, people, Americans he knew. "I must have been very fortunate to have been with the units I was because compared with some of the stuff I've read, we were outstanding."

On the 19th of August, during his birthday call to his grandfather, Bobby said, "She's pretty as Stacy, Granpa. Different though. She reminds me of Granma. She's that kind of person."

He'd driven the course—those sections that followed the road. And he'd parked and walked sections of the staircases and the mountain trails. It was 10 A.M., Sunday, 26 August 1973. Bobby was relaxed, happy, a little apprehensive as he lined up with the 1,235 other runners in Lytton Square. In the canyon the morning was cool, overcast. Bobby had not designed a prerace schedule for this Dipsea but had simply maintained his normal routine.

Numbered runners were released in order, by age, by handicap, the Dipsea being time trial, not mass release. Out of the gate, easy, not sprinting like some, loose, to the stairs, to the one hundred or five hundred cursed stairs, three cases with uphill road sections between, which better than half the field walked. He did not think of the stairs, did not count them, paid no attention to the people he passed, felt no irritation at the few who passed him. Up, up, out of the canyon, up, pines and redwoods giving way to eucalyptus, up, chuckling to himself as he burst out onto Edgewood Avenue, feeling comfortable with his steady pace, feeling strong up to Panoramic Highway. You scare me, sometimes, he said to Sara in his mind. You telling me how courageous I am when I'm such a coward. These dreams, these designs, they terrorize me. The pieces come slowly to me. The drawings take forever.

He reached the first crest at 750 feet, could see over the clouds to the Pacific, began the descent into Muir Woods. His thoughts meandered in the magnificence of the redwood forest. Suddenly he was across the gap in the cathedral of eastern hemlocks and he wanted to show Sara Muir Woods and the gap and the cathedral and he wondered how Granpa was doing. Up again, steep rutted trail to 700 feet, then down, rolling trail, then up to 900 feet, to 1,450 feet, to the edge of the woods, the sun breaking through, the protected forest giving way to open grassland and suddenly the steep descent dropping 800 feet in less than two-thirds of a mile. The trail leveled, the Stinson Beach Post Office and finish line were but a thousand feet. Bobby felt great. Sara had said to him, "There's enough gypsy in me that I could live anywhere as long as there are hills and water." He felt his long strides propelling him in harmony with an energy, a universal understanding, a power totally outside himself. A few people were clapping. He became aware of other runners and broke into a competitive sprint to the finish with a guy in green running silks and fancy shoes and he beat him by ten yards. Then slowing, turning to shake the man's hand just across the finish line, but the man collapsed into him and both fell, the man grasping his calf, panting out, "Cramp!" and Bobby gritting his teeth, a pain shooting from his left knee up through his thigh, then gone until he stood and his left leg gave out and he couldn't stand on it.

Sara hugged him. "You finished! Are you okay? What happened? You beat . . . I saw you way up there and you passed almost everyone."

"Yeah, I, ah, ha, hum. Just twisted my knee right here."

The gas and oil crisis had opened up a thousand avenues to city, regional and state planners. The possibilities excited Wapinski. By late October there was talk of constructing an experimental solar village at Hamilton Air Force Base only ten miles south of San Martin. Sara heard from friends in Davis about phase I plans for a self-sustaining community with a sewage composting plant. Bobby visited both sites, talked to everyone he could. He had laid his cookbook aside. Now he abandoned it. Energy production-consumption policy gripped him.

"Look at this." He waved an eleven-month-old *Life* magazine at Sara. "People knew this would happen. Listen, 'We can't escape shortages.' This is John G. McLean, CONOCO chairman. 'The critical "balance-wheel" will be the volume of foreign oil imports; this will be the element which will adjust for our failures or successes in other energy areas. Balance of payments . . . by the early 1980s this deficit could be twenty to thirty billion dollars per year versus today's three billion.' "

"Bobby," Sara interrupted him. She was sitting opposite him at the dining area table, correcting papers. "What did the doctor say?"

"One minute. McLean says—he's talking about the new financial centers in the oil-producing countries of Africa and the Middle East—'Most of these countries are not ready to use internally new funds of this magnitude. A large portion of the oil tax revenues will thus move into the short- and long-term money markets of the Free World in ways, and with impacts, which are difficult to predict. One clear possibility is that these countries could become large equity holders in the financial institutions and industrial companies of the United States, Western Europe and Japan.' "

"Come on now," Sara interrupted again. "I'm serious. What did the doctor say?"

"He said to live with it."

"Can you go back to running?"

Bobby shrugged. "He gave me some exercises. I could have the cartilage removed but he thought it wasn't that bad. He said something like my hematocrit was low. Thirty something. Maybe because of my cold. Geez, I wish I could get Harrison to read this stuff. Tim Reed agrees with me but he's the only one and Harrison overrules him at every turn. Listen to this. 'We need some practical trade-offs in the ecological area. The production and consumption of energy inevitably involves some ecological impairment. We can not achieve our environmental goals overnight and still give the U.S. economy all the energy it requires and the public demands.' Ha! That sounds like Harrison. Take a flying leap! It's fine to discover supplies at a faster rate, but how about using them at a slower rate?"

"I think you're absolutely right."

"You know, my position at work's a sham."

"No it's not."

"Yeah, really. We're more an arm of the business community than a planning/regulating office. Harrison's more interested in 'expanding the tax base.' " Bobby looked down, shook his head. "I feel like the office curmudgeon."

"Patient investigation and disciplined perseverance," Sara teased.

"I want to be a force, a catalyst, for changing how people think," Bobby said. "How they react and relate to the environment, to minorities, to different ideas."

"Then you will be," Sara said. They strolled between the hillside trellises with their clipped vines. Josef Andrassy I's fine home looked down upon them.

"I could be, you know, if you're with me."

"I am with you." Sara smiled.

"If you believe in me," Bobby said.

"You can't really believe in someone, and no one will believe in you, if you don't believe in yourself. That's what I tell my children. And if your self-esteem is damaged or destroyed, you won't believe in yourself even if I believe in you."

"Granma and Granpa always told me I could do anything I wanted, if I wanted to enough," Bobby said. "My mother was just the opposite. She always told me I couldn't do anything. Sometimes I have this dream of setting up a business or an institute or a community and I think I could pull it off. And then I think, What! Am I nuts? Who would listen to me?"

"I would. And I know your grandfather would. I really liked talking to him."

"Sometimes I want to get back there. Back where people are a bit more sane. Sometimes San Martin makes me sick."

"I know. All these little rich kids. And some of them are so poor. To them life already is the cost of their clothes."

"Sara?"

"Um."

"When should we get married?"

Sara smiled. "Is that a formal proposal, Mr. Wapinski?"

"No." Bobby reached into his pocket. "This is." He pulled out a small velvet box, opened it.

"In the spring," Sara said.

"You know what I like about you?" Bobby stood downhill from her, looked up into her face. "You never dish out crap."

Wedding plans moved in steps, in spurts, in rushes and rests. Bobby's new design project, blessed by Tim Reed, moved in minute steady increments—maps, charts, graphs, outlines, breakdowns.

"The most fundamental element for success," Bobby explained to Tim Reed, "is the public relations campaign. We've got to reteach the people. Change their views on energy."

"Let me see what you've got."

"Tim, before I open it up, understand it's not just San Martin. I want to affect this entire corridor from Santa Rosa to the Golden Gate."

"Good. Let's see."

"This is just the transportation end of it and it's preliminary." Bobby opened his large portfolio, laid a topographic map of the North Bay on Tim Reed's desk. Overlying the map was an acetate cover with hundreds of blue arrows representing wind currents. "First, we've got to understand our present energy consumption," Bobby began. From oil companies he'd obtained bulk gasoline sales records for the entire region. From county and state offices he'd gotten vehicle registration figures. From the Department of Transportation, daily, monthly and yearly traffic across the Golden Gate Bridge, including rush-hour surge figures. Step by step Bobby Wapinski explained his findings to Tim Reed. Tim found the details fascinating.

Again Bobby said, "This is preliminary. I've explored—"

"Skip to this one." Tim tapped the map. "This is where you're going, isn't it?"

"Uh-huh." It excited Bobby that Tim was enthusiastic. "These are prevailing wind patterns. The study's got to be expanded but for some locations, like at the Nike site on North Peak, we've got decades of year-round data. There's always the Pacific wind. It always comes through these passes here, here, here. A whole series of em. Tim, we can tap the wind. We could have a thousand windmills, some small, some large, on the ridges and in the saddles."

Tim was perplexed. "And do what?"

"Use them to generate electricity."

"For homes?"

"To electrify the third lane of Highway 101."

"Hmm?"

"Follow me. Look." Bobby opened up another folder.

"What—"

"It's an electric commuter car."

"You designed it?"

"It's preliminary. I haven't worked out all the details. But there are a lot of people working on electric cars."

"Sure, but the batteries are way too heavy. They've got no range and—Oh!"

"See?"

"Hmm. You know, I thought you'd come up with a proposal for mass transportation . . . "

"People won't give up their cars, Tim. Americans like their independence. The freedom individual autos offer is exactly what mass transit takes away. My cars become pods in a mass transit system. This is a population corridor. Here, look." Bobby quickly shuffled his notes. He was afraid of losing Tim Reed and Tim was critical to any future presentations. "Ninety-six percent of the people in Marin and San Martin—and seventy-eight percent in Sonoma County—live within fifteen miles of 101. That's the advantage to *this* mass transit system. People get all the benefits of a regular car. The privacy. The freedom. The power for the lane comes from the windmills. In spots, that wind averages thirty miles per hour for *at least* four hours per day two hundred days per year. Excess power can be sold to PG and E. Our entire region essentially becomes a clean, efficient, environmentally sound power plant. And the amount of excess electricity on windy days can offset the costs of electricity needed on calm days.

"Where are you going to get all these cars?"

"Build them."

"Come on, Bob. You mean everybody would have to go out and buy a new car?"

"Tim, this is a ten-, maybe fifteen-, year project. The average household"—again Bobby shuffled his papers—"buys four cars in that period. I don't want this to be a revolution. It should be an evolution. By 1983, or maybe even '93, we'll have transformed northern California's perspective on transportation and energy. Personal consumer habits will change. They're going to change anyway. We can impact the direction of that change."

"Hmm." Tim Reed rested back in his chair. "Let me go over this for a few days. You know, PG and E might be interested. They could own the windmills and be, ah, or have a public utility branch responsible for that third lane. Hmm. Oh, by the way, can I give you this? Save me the stamp."

"Ah . . . of course."

"Jinny and I are really happy you invited us. Jinny likes Sara."

"You can make it?"

"To dance at your wedding! You bet your sweet ass."

Saturday, 23 March 1974, Sonoma, California. They stood, he in front as tradition dictates, in the chapel of the San Francisco Solano Mission—the northernmost and last built of the Spanish missions along El Camino Real, the Royal Road. He was nervous yet tranquil. Others chatted quietly, smiled, nudged one another now and again, turned often. The guests stood, more than one hundred, because there were no pews, no chairs, no furniture except the two individual kneelers the couple would use. The room was small, dim, cool, with thick walls, tiny windows and a low ceiling, constructed at a time when the average man in the territory stood only five feet two inches tall and fossil-fuel heat was unknown.

On the right, facing forward, was Pewel Wapinski, clean shaven, spiffed up in a new suit, leaning, on one side, on his brass-head cane, on the other on Anthony Pisano's arm. Tony, too, was in a suit and tie, clean, his hair pulled back, a leather thong with a carved apple-wood motorcycle-wheel slide holding his ponytail. Beside him were Miriam and Doug. Behind were Bobby's friends; in the back Dan Coleman and Tom Houghton, officially ushers, held Josh, officially the Best Dog.

In front Bobby turned to Al Bartecchi, stammered, "The ring?"

"Right here."

"They should be here, shouldn't they?"

"It's still early. Jane's with em. They'll be okay."

On the left stood Josef and Eva Andrassy, Sara's grandparents, and her brothers Tamas and Peter and their wives, Colleen and Donna, and the youngest and unwed brother, Gyorgy (George), and Aunt Karolyi, and behind them, the principal of San Martin Elementary and twenty teachers with spouses or friends, plus friends of Sara from Sonoma and Davis and Berkeley.

Finally Dan Coleman escorted Lynette, Sara's mother, to her place at the front. Everyone turned, expectant.

The rehearsal dinner had been held the night before at La Casa, Sonoma's classy Mexican restaurant on The Square across from the mission. Before most of the participants had arrived Sara sat alone with Miriam in the upper balcony room while Bobby, Doug and Tony stood at the downstairs bar drinking margaritas and Pewel sat near them inhaling the good feelings.

"You'll regret the day you ever met this man," Miriam said to Sara.

"Excuse me?" Sara said. She did not know whether to laugh or to be angry.

"I'm telling you not to marry him," Miriam said. "You don't have to go through with it. I'm telling you, he's just like his father."

"And just who is his father?" Sarah shot back. "He told me he doesn't know his father."

"Well . . . I knew his father. He's going to be just like him. He'll drink. He'll carouse. He'll do exactly what he pleases. Eventually you'll regret the day you met him."

"I resent you even saying that." Sara's voice was firm but her hands began to quiver.

"He'll knock you around and abuse you," Miriam said. "Then he'll start messing with other women. Don't marry him."

"How dare you!" Sara began.

"Oh," Miriam huffed. "You're pregnant, aren't you? You might as well admit it so I can get ready."

Sara stood. "I'm not pregnant."

"Sit down. You don't have to show me."

Sara sat, leaned toward Miriam. "What's your problem? What kind of mother would talk about her son like that?"

"I told Cheryl, who's married to Brian, the same thing. And I'm telling you. Okay, you're not pregnant. Keep it that way. It'll make your divorce easier."

"OH!" Sara coughed out the utterance in disgust.

Miriam stood, strode from the upper level toward the stairs that Al Bartecchi and Jane Boswell were climbing and behind them Bobby and Tony and Pewel and Doug. "Didn't you bring me anything?" Miriam snapped at Doug.

"They're here." Whispered, person to person. Commotion. Then a hush falling over the chapel. Mother of the bride glancing, smiling, to the mother of the groom.

The ceremony was not simple, not short and sweet. It was built around a full Catholic mass—Bobby's marriage to Red was not recognized by the church and thus the church sanctioned this rite—though extended by their own additions, and by the importance Bobby and Sara placed upon ceremony and tradition. Eleven flower girls and four "ring bearers," Sara's students all, led the procession. Then came the maid of honor and bridesmaids carrying new candles instead of bouquets and then Josef Tamas Andrassy with his daughter in white satin and lace and Sara too had an unlit candle and every guest and family member also raised a candle as the transformation of Robert Janos Wapinski and Sara Coolwater Andrassy which had begun so long and so short ago continued. Tamas Andrassy read Genesis 2:18–24 and—at the insistence of Pewel Wapinski—Tony Pisano read a letter from Paul to the Corinthians. These were followed by the reading of a gospel according to John by Father Paul Weiss, and finally by Father Paul's homily and the lighting of the candles.

> With this light, as we pass the flame from church to grandparents to parents to children, and on to all assembled to witness this blessed sacrament of marriage between Sara and Robert, we cast new light upon this couple, upon ourselves, upon each other, and upon our world. In this new light we recognize and declare a transformation of spirit, a moving from the order of the self to a higher order—to the unity of two, and perhaps in the future to yet an even higher order above the self, above this couple following their shared dreams, to a level of family—the great circle—from which this light has been passed to you to transform you to what has always been.

In the small chapel the scores of candles flickered and the light glinted from the low ceiling, refracted from the tiny windows, reflected in hundreds of eyes. It was midday and yet the ambience of a candlelight vigil enveloped all. The priest continued—changing momentarily to the earthly.

> Many do not understand what love is, what it looks like. Today we are told that love is simply a supportive arrangement, a relationship of mutual, positive reinforcement. Yet the difference is not one of degree, not one of time spent together. When you truly love, you love the other the way the earth loves the sun on the first warm morning of spring, and you know this love holds the potential for arid and parched summers, for cold autumns and overcast winters, and you must have faith that spring will come again, and again relight the land.
> Follow your dreams, Sara. Follow your dreams, Robert. Follow your dreams in the light of this new light.

"By gawd, you're an old man," Pewel, 84, said to Josef Andrassy, 87. "And you're still just a pup," Josef said, and both men laughed.

The reception was held at Juanita's in Boyd's Hot Spring, an ancient smorgasbord resort hotel fifty years past its heyday, run by an infamous ex–San Francisco madam who had crammed and choked the pink-and-white stuccoed hotel with beads, bangles, Christmas lights, stuffed owls, old gaming tables, thousands of trinkets and treasures, now mostly chipped, broken and dusty; with live animals—monkeys, pigs, a donkey; with a huge hot table piled high with delicious (if not elegant) food; with music; and finally with her brash, outrageous, hilarious self.

"Come on." Bobby pulled Pewel's sleeve.

"You too." Sara grasped Josef.

"We want a picture of the four of us," Bobby said. Then outside by the fountain, in the bright sun, "the five of us." He pulled Josh, and Josh was thrilled to get between him and Sara.

"Six of us," Pewel said. "Tony, get in here."

"Oh, this really isn't for me."

"Yeah, come on," Bobby said. He could not have been happier, livelier. It was contagious. Tony stepped closer.

"Come here," Sara said. "Before . . . ooOOH!" Josh leaped, pulled Bobby's hand into Sara's buttocks. Then he barked and dug in, pulling against the leash like a sled dog in harness, aiming for a big sow who'd just ambled out the front door.

"I'll put him in the office-mobile," Tony volunteered.

"Naw." Bobby laughed. "He should stay here and enjoy." Then Bobby turned to Tony, smiled, said quietly, "Granpa's told me about you. Thanks for helping him when you can. And ah, lighten up, Man. We gotta lotta living to do for a lot of guys who didn't make it back."

September 1984

Convergence. Change. Yet more of the same. More of the same.

I'm not sure when I decided to stay in California—probably long before Grandpa Wapinski and I even left Mill Creek Falls. I stayed at Bobby and Sara's, at first, taking care of Josh while Bobby and Sara went to Yosemite and then on their raft trip down the Stanislaus, which after his fall into the San Antonio took giant *coglioni* on Bobby's part. I put Pewel on a 707 for Philly. Miriam and Doug had split from the reception after some snide comments. I didn't see them again for years. Pewel said he could make it back on his own but I called Annalisa—I couldn't call Linda with her having filed for divorce—and she and Edward picked him up in Philly. I didn't have the Harley; no wheels, little cash, few needs. I slept in the office-mobile for a while then split for Frisco.

More of the same. Dives. Flophouses. Panhandling. Temporary jobs, dope, booze, some loose ladies who seemed to love me beyond reason. Crash. Withdrawals. Extended drugged states. Occasionally I cleaned up, sobered up, went up to San Martin, visited Bobby, Sara and Josh. Talked about his grandfather mostly. Or about the farm.

It was more of the same through the summer of Watergate and into the Gerald Ford period, which was both the sickest and the healthiest time in American history. Sickest is easy to understand, eh? But healthiest? Watergate renewed my faith in America, in our *system* of government. The *system* worked. That the individuals, principals, involved were scuzzballs makes it, the workings of the system, all the more impressive. Had we been a benevolent dictatorship, or had ethnic, racial, economic or social divisions dominated our governmental or cultural system, America would have come unglued. Put to the acid test, it was only deeply scarred: an incredible demonstration of strength.

More of the same, too, for Ty. He didn't see the system work. He saw an old system reemerging, a system of bigotry. One of the shrinks later said he thought Ty had set himself up for all the accidents—eye-for-an-eye, tooth-for-a-tooth type thing—by participating in mutilations in Viet Nam and Cambodia. When I first heard that I thought it was an earthenware vessel of excreted by-product, but after . . . I wasn't sure.

21

After three months of healing, the slash on Theodore Darsman's wrist was a long curving yellow-purple scar. Ted Darsman—a.k.a. Tyrone Dorsey, Blackwell, Wallace, Green, and others—had bamboozled the emergency room staff. "Fell, mothafucka, fell carryin a fuckin bottle a Coke. I'm suin them fuckas. Big time, Man. Lookit mah arm. Mothafucka, that hurt. Hit them mothafuckas for a million. Think I can't, huh? You watch me, mothafucka. Million bucks aint nothin to them pigs. One Super Bowl commercial. Who make the glass? Sue them mothafuckas too." And later he bamboozled the people who ran the soup kitchen just off the Nimitz Freeway, and the people of Our Lady of Hope Men's Shelter near the Bayshore Highway. "Just been down and out, Man. Just down and out. Times er tough. I owned my home. Had my own business. Had trucks. A whole fleet. You try keepin gas in a fleet a trucks at these prices!"

For more months Ty played on the sympathy of strangers, sought help, pleaded for understanding. He had, with the bottle shard, frightened himself into "cleaning up his act." The fear waned, his hyperactivity subsided. He scrounged quietly, swindled a little here, liberated a little there, petty theft from the shelters. He withdrew more and more into the private space within his mind, escaping, obsessing on what once was, on Olivia, distancing himself from welfare workers, from other homeless men, from junkies, journalists, Jesuits—anyone who wanted to control or direct his thoughts.

He became a nowhere man. A nobody. Not Ted Darsman any longer. Not Ty Dorsey. For a while Tom Davis. Then Tom Davies. Then Tobias Denny. Into and out of shelters, into and out of breadlines, into and out of social services offices. Finally he became, with forged documents, Tyler Mohammed. That made him feel like a brother. He finally belonged, if only in his mind, if only tangentially, to something, to a people. Still he remained mostly quiet, mostly withdrawn, mostly alone.

Then in October 1974, from behind, "Hey, what time are you?"

Tyler, sullen, angry. "Nine forty-five. You?"

The guy, happy. "Nine forty-five, too."

"Join the line."

"Geez fuckin Louise, Man, I told myself when I got outta the Corps I was like nev-ah ev-ah goina stand in another fuckin line. En look at me."

"Humph." Tyler Mohammed glared at the smiling long-haired freak in the OD green field jacket. Ty turned, dropped his head, stared at the green-and-black checkerboard tiles of the floor.

"Who were you with, Man?"

Tyler turned back. "Hmm?"

"Yer hand, Man. Says you was across the pond. Who were you with?"

"Who the fuck are you?"

"Pisano. Anthony F. I actually been job huntin. Went to an interview last time I had an appointment and they disqualified me. Gave me a bag a shit. They expect you ta go to like ten places."

"Man," Ty whispered, "yer coked out, aren'tcha?"

Tony just winked. About them people wandered aimlessly. Some sat on the floor. Some told those in line before them or behind them their unemployment history or practiced their stories about their futile job quest. Most people, however, stood, passive, unwavering, looking forward like zombies, not recognizing anyone, not allowing themselves to be recognized, to be penetrated in their humiliation.

"Whip some on me, Man, or I blow the whistle."

"Men's room, Man," Tony whispered. Then beside each other, before urinals, again, "Who were you with, Man?"

"No one."

"Bullshit."

"I"— Ty broke into a laugh, his first in a short forever— "shit you not."

"Right on, Bro. Here." Tony handed Ty two joints. "Gratis, Amigo."

"Where you from, Man?" Ty asked.

"Pennsylvania," Tony said. They moved to the sinks.

"Humph. Me too! Coal Hill. Near Scranton. Sucks, Man. So's San Jose. You come out for dope or broads, Man?"

"Came out for a guy's wedding. He was a screamin yellow buzzard."

"Fuckin fool."

"Yeah. Got it made, though."

"White guy, huh?"

"Yeah."

"You Airborne?"

"Me. Naw. I'm a bastard. Magnificent Bastard. Marine, Man. Pukin buzzard guy's up in San Martin. House on the hill. Got it—"

"I know a guy up there. Wapinski."

"Hey. That's him."

"Ha! We was together in Nam. A Shau. Hamburger Hill. Bad moth-afuckas."

"Yeah. Ha. Small world. We're from the same town . . . in Pennsy. I worked for his grandpa."

"Shee-it! En life goes on."

"Yeah. Ha."

"Yeah, cept lots a returnees in these lines, Man. Lots a returnees."

Thursday, 31 October 1974, San Martin Municipal Building—"What stupid, idiotic junk is this!"

"Idiotic?"

"How dare you waste taxpayers dollars on ridiculous schemes."

Wapinski stared. His jaw dropped. He had not expected—had not the slightest inkling—that Henry Alan Harrison would finally review his work this day, week, or that Harrison had not been reviewing it all along, that Tim Reed, thinking he was protecting Bobby, had kept the designs, data, and reports from Harrison.

"Who do you think you are?!" Harrison snapped. "And how could you possibly think anyone, anyone in their right mind, would approve this—this juggernaut! This spruce goose! Windmills!"

It was not yet nine o'clock. The sky was clear, the morning calm. On the way in he'd been singing like he did now virtually every morning, " 'I guess, you'd say, what ken make me feel this way, my girl, talking bout . . . ' " Then into the office, smiling, greeting the guards, the receptionists, taking the stairs two-by-two (exercising his knee), pondering how they'd get by on his salary alone, Sara three months pregnant, due in March, could she teach until spring vacation? Knowing they'd make it.

"Windmills!" Harrison screamed again. "Wapinski, you'd better justify this. You'd better come up with substantial justification for this!" Harrison's hand lashed out, tipped the edge of Bobby's thick file that lay on Harrison's desk, the top of the ream splaying then cascading down the desk and chair—off arm, seat, a drawer handle and onto the floor—cascading down like the Stanislaus flowed down the Devil's Staircase.

*   *   *

Phone conversation:

"Sara."

"Bob."

"Come home."

"Bob, is everything okay?"

"Please come home, I . . . I need you."

Then, at the cottage, Sara entering, Bobby by the table, sitting, drooped, elbows on his knees, staring fixedly at the hardwood, his voice sheepish, shaking. "I've been fired."

"Oh." She came to him, bent to hug him. "Is that it?"

He did not look at her. He was embarrassed. Embarrassed by the fact, by the tears in his eyes. Even afraid she would abandon him. He straightened, looked at her. He couldn't hold back. "They may just as well have knifed me," he said.

"Bob." Sara touched his face.

"Harrison fired me. He wants to kill me. Kill us economically. He might just as well have ripped out my heart."

"What happened?"

"He . . . in front of the whole office . . . he ranted about me wasting taxpayers' dollars. He didn't understand anything. He didn't even look at the figures. He didn't understand. He just kept badgering me, telling everyone I was Don Quixote. He said, 'Wapinski, you either begin to play ball, get on the team, or pack your bags.' I got tongue-tied. He never even gave me a chance to explain."

"What about Tim?"

"He wasn't in. He hasn't been in since Monday. He wasn't feeling well on Monday."

"Well, Harrison can't just fire you like that. Can he?"

"I . . . "

"You could challenge it. The County Board of Commissioners . . . they review job evaluations . . . "

"You know . . . just to design one . . . even one house. One good house. And see it built. One design that wasn't destroying. And see it through. They . . . Harrison . . . he kept my file. When I asked Beth for it she said Henry had ordered her to lock it up."

"Challenge him."

"I can't. Don't you see, Sara. I can't go back there."

Sara sighed, put a hand on his hand. For a while they sat in silence, Bobby in shock—shocked by his own reaction to Harrison, by how he shook, how he was still shaking, less angry than assaulted, violated. Then the phone rang. "I'll get it," Sara said softly. "It's probably Harrison wanting to apologize. Hello."

"Hello. Is this Sara?"

"Yes it is. Who's this?"

"Linda Pisano. Is Bob there?"

"Yes."

Then Linda to Bob. "Your grandfather's back in the hospital."

"Oh God!"

"I'm not sure how serious it is," Linda said. "I drove him over to St. Luke's. He's been coughing and he's awfully short of breath. And his hands are cool. They decided to admit him. They ruled out a heart attack. He's awfully strong, Bob. But I thought you should know."

"Thanks."

"Is Tony there?"

"No. I haven't seen him in, ah, about a month."

"He was in San Jose, I think. That's what Grandpa said. Grandpa was hoping that he'd come back and help out again."

"I . . . ah . . . Linda, I . . . maybe I shouldn't say this but your divorce is . . . I mean, I know how he's been. I'm not saying you shouldn't have filed, but I don't think he'll go back."

"I didn't go through with it."

"Does he know that?"

"I haven't been able to find him."

They both paused. Then Bobby said, "Should I come back?"

"Call tomorrow," Linda answered. "It may be nothing."

"Yeah."

"Could you try and get in touch with Tony for me? I know he was in a men's shelter in San Jose . . . for a while. Tell him I didn't go through with it. And that Grandpa needs him. And I . . . the girls miss him. Really."

Drugged-out, boozed-up, unemployed, homeless, unwashed, unkempt. Twenty-three and twenty-seven years old, and already old—society's dregs, falling, falling, dropping acid because it was so much cheaper in San Jose in November of 1974 than skag or coke or even grass that Tyler Mohammed and Tony Pisano could stay fucked up and flying with minimal panhandling.

Tripping: The exterior is drab—gray paint on grooved asphalt shingles banged over clapboard in the '30s or '40s, an upgrading project in Pennsylvania mountain country. Click. Ty enters the house. It is but a single room. Then, above, without stairs, another room appears. He is rising, falling up through the floor to the other room. Click. A ramp appears, brings him to a high door in the wall in the gable end. He passes through.

Click. Click. Click. Speeding. Drugged out. Fucked up. Scenes flashing like slides, like live index cards on a Rolodex. Now a corridor. The sides are Sheetrocked like the Sheetrock he carried, lugged up board ramps, manpower jobs, nigger work, vet work, until his arms are eighteen feet long, until on the left there is an interior door, window, as to an office. The door is closed, the office dark. He cannot see through the glass but sees vaguely his own reflected image sieved through the diamonds of reinforcement wire in the glass. The diamonds cut deep. The diamond-shaped pile that is him, sieved, falls, falls piece by diamond piece until he is a clutter of diamond-shaped dowels at his own feet.

Click. Past the window down the corridor to an immense room without a ceiling. At his feet the room is a gigantic pool and the pool is filled with thick translucent green liquid, splashing, huge waves splashing as if the pool in the room is an ocean. There is dry land across the ocean, through the storm spray. Click. There are boats in the raging sea, four dark gray shapes, ancient, open-topped oar-drawn whalers, or Viet Namese sampans. No one has oars. There are people in the boats. They are grotesque. He knows they are alive, sees their pained faces, knows they fear the sea, fear more so reaching, crashing into the hardly discernible far shore. They beckon him, invite him aboard to witness their plight. In the boat, through the splash and spindrift, it is impossible to see the sides of the room. The sea makes him sick. He vomits.

Click. Hands, wrists, forearms, change, turn into green-rubber lettuce, leaf lettuce, uncured rubber, smelly, sticky. He retreats. He is not of them, has not transformed. They are people. He has known for a thousand years, they, the green and red, ghastly, gruesome, grotesque, rubberized pliables in pain and fear are people. He forces the boat back toward the first shore, but he cannot leave. His feet, ankles, have transformed, have stuck. He strains. Terror. Someone is talking calmly, softly from just behind. "Don't be afraid, Tyler Mohammed. You don't have to struggle against us." His face, he can see his face rubberizing, the eyes stretched vertically to eight, ten, sixteen inches long, his head melting. He screams. He turns toward the calm voice. "Ha," he thinks. "They don't expect this. No one has ever attacked them."

Click. From somewhere, a hemlock branch is in his hands. Not a branch with prickly needles but a staff sharpened to a spear point. He jumps to the nearest boat, thrashes through broken horrified souls toward the helmsman. The storm tosses the craft. He stumbles but surges forward, stumbles again, reaches the helm. The helmsman has vanished.

Click. Fast. Faster. He wills the craft toward the far shore. Faster. The cries of pain, the fear, the woe of the melting dripping cabbage faces straining to break from him, him the helmsman, to remain adrift in pain rather than to face the unknown shore.

"Bad trip, Man?"

Blank stare. Slack jaw.

"Hey, Man, bad trip, huh? You freaked out, Man. You're a real freak-out, Man. Ha! Freak-Out Man."

Tony looked out from their squat. Then he looked back at Ty, then back out from their box. They were in San Jose, above Santa Clara Street, downtown—not old, inner-city blight East Coast downtown, but still there were alleys, dumpsters, boxes. Their box was on the flat roof of a three-story building, over a shoe store and wallpaper outlet and respectable apartments. The rooftop was safe, defendable. To one side were the boxes of Frankie "the Kid" Denahee and David "Wildman" Coffee. Sheldon "Fuzzy" Golan and Big Bro Boyson were set up to the other. The roof was OP, NDP—observation post, night defensive position. To the third-floor tenant, if they were quiet, their presence was okay. At each first light they flatten the boxes, drop to the fire escape, split up, withdraw to the park across from the courthouse or wander the few blocks to San Jose State College where Big Bro likes to leer at the coeds. They do not hang together but disperse singly or in pairs. Tony, Fuzzy, Wildman, or the Kid take turns pairing with Big Bro Boyson because Big Bro is immense and dark black and his large round face and huge jaw attract suspicion.

It was now Tony's turn, not just to hang with Big Bro, and not just this day. But outside the law, outside the civilized fringe of society's petticoat, with these homeless brothers and cousins, it became Tony's turn to function. Big Bro had been a Marine. Frankie had served with the 25th Infantry Division; Wildman with the 4th; Fuzzy with the Big Red One. Their numbers, their names, their squats changed, shifted, yet they'd become an informal network watching out for each other. They called Tony Pisano the Catcher from *The Catcher in the Rye*—whatever happened in the field was fair play but should they come too close to the edge, the Catcher, unobtrusive, no questions asked, was there to catch, to protect.

"Bad trip, Man?" Tony repeated.

Still Ty did not respond. Tony folded back the newspaper, continued reading the story inside. In Saigon there had been violent antigovernment riots. Tony had followed the story since November first. Demonstrators and police had clashed repeatedly. President Thieu's repressive policies and government corruption had been denounced by leaders of South Viet Nam's opposition. Thieu had responded by firing three of his four corps commanders and had promised to ease restraints on the press. Simultaneously he had accused the demonstrators of trying to undermine the government. Moscow responded to the unrest by pledging increased aid to Hanoi.

Tony did not tell Ty what he was reading. Nor did he mention it to the others. He knew Wildman would freak. Wildman had been a POW for ten days. He and sixteen others had been cut off and captured. During that time he witnessed his closest friend's decapitation. He saw three guys tied, stretched, eaten by rats. Of the seventeen, thirteen attempted to escape. Wildman, or so his story went, was one of six survivors. He'd been discharged in 1968, had lived on the fringe since '71.

Tony knew that Fuzzy, if he read the news, would also freak, want to take action. "You know, Man, they always sayin, 'It can't happen here.' Or they thinkin, 'Won't happen here.' Or they aren't thinkin at all cause they don't have a fuckin clue. IT CAN HAPPEN HERE!"

Tony had said nothing the first time, perhaps nothing the second, but Fuzzy was focused. "What?" Tony had finally responded.

"Terrorism, Man. Disrupt domestic tranquillity, Man. It's goina happen here cause we're goina make it happen."

"Who you aimin at?" Tony asked.

Fuzzy ignored his question. "You know phu-gas?"

"Gas and soap gel," Tony said. "Like napalm."

"Yeah. Big cans, Man. Drums. Stick a soup can in the bottom with a small sponge soaked in gasoline. And two wires. Fill the drum one-third with phu-gas. Cap it. Cover it with gravel en shit. Cheap, Man. Set em up all over the city. Wire em together, then send the spark. Gas in the soup can evaporates and gives you a perfect explosive gas-air mix that'll fire off the whole god fuckin damn drum. Cheap. Just one here, one there. Blow away a few innocents. You watch, Man. When they can't stop me, Man, you watch this fuckin government come tumblin down."

"Yeah." Tony had said. Fuzzy was still in the field.

"Yeah." Fuzzy's eyes lit.

"Then what?" Tony had asked.

"Then what the fuck," Fuzzy had answered.

"Yeah," Tony had said.

"I could use garbage cans," Fuzzy said.

"Unlimited supply," Tony nodded.

Fuzzy bit his lip. Brooded. Tony said no more.

"Whatdaya think?" Bobby was almost giddy. He'd been banging his head against the wall for eight days attempting to jar loose a decision, and finally an answer had come late on a November afternoon as he and Sara sat in the office-mobile in the parking lot of a dilapidated shopping center in Novato, the town south of San Martin. Parked in front of the A & W Root Beer stand, they sat sipping root beer floats, eating cheeseburgers and french fried onion rings to sate Sara's craving, with soft vanilla ice cream in a cup on the floor for Josh. "A and W Energy Systems," he said.

It had been a difficult week, adjusting to having been fired, first blaming himself, then rationalizing that Henry Alan Harrison was an idiot, then finally telling Sara, "I don't distrust my ability to do the work, but I've got to learn how to present it."

"A and W Energy Systems?" Sara giggled. She too verged on giddy. "Andrassy and Wapinski. But people will think it's something powered by root beer fizz." They laughed together.

"Maybe W and A," Bobby said.

Besides the adjustment to being fired they had had to deal with the crisis of Pewel's health. Bobby had been terrified. To him it was worse than the incident thirty months earlier because then he had believed in his grandfather's strength, but now he doubted the old man's resilience.

"Hydrochlorothiazide and Digoxin," Linda had explained to him at midweek. "They did a full work-up. His left ventricle's enlarged."

"What's that mean?"

"The left ventricle's the one that pumps the blood to the lungs," Linda had answered. "When a part of the muscle is insufficient, that part enlarges to compensate for the weakness. They think they can control it with medication."

"Can he come home?" Bobby had asked.

"Probably by the end of the week."

Earlier that afternoon Bobby had spoken again with Linda who was at High Meadow. Pewel was in his barn office, she'd said, working on a design for a hospital bed that could lower to sixteen inches off the floor as well as raise to forty-eight inches. " 'So a man like me, damn it' "— Linda quoted Pewel—" 'don't feel imprisoned way up there on them islands. It's undignified having to have a nurse help you out of bed when, if the damn thing was normal height, you'd just get up by yourself.' "

Sara glowed in the light from the A & W sign. Her skin was radiant, her hair shiny. She was four and a half months pregnant. She leaned toward him. "I've got it!"

Josh nuzzled his snout between them.

"Say it again," Sara said.

"What?"

"You know, when humans overcompete for resources . . . "

"Oh. You mean the stuff I was writing about if we could build energy-efficient, self-sufficient, cost-effective shelters and transportation systems."

"Yes. To lower people's . . . How did you put it?"

"To lower the competition for resources by lessening our dependence on fossil fuels." Bobby paused. Sara curled her fingers like a charades player attempting to draw out a respondent. "Ah . . . auto fuel consumption drives up petroleum costs in the Third World and forces people to burn their forests for fuel. Environmentally efficient energy systems are beneficial, both immediately to the user, and also over time because they help alleviate international tension decreasing the need for war."

"See!" Sara was excited. She bounced in her seat, massaged her fingers deeply into Josh's thick coat. "You said it twice: 'environmentally efficient energy systems.' "

"Um!" Bobby too was excited. "Environmental Energy Systems."

"Oh, I like that. Bob, I like that. Your own business."

"Me too! Environmental Energy Systems, 101 Old Russia Road, San Martin . . . "

He let Tyler Mohammed give him a tab of acid but he did not drop it. Fuzzy whipped on him a nickle bag of dew but he did not smoke it. Instead he brooded in his squat, in emotional isolation, brooded about his old man, about the old man always being angry at him, always being disappointed, except when he was in The Corps. Then the old man had had trepidations but he'd been proud.

It was November 10th, Tony's twenty-seventh birthday, the 199th birthday of the United States Marine Corps. Tony watched Ty crash through consciousness into the wherever. "Snore softly, Bro," he mumbled. He crawled from the box, quietly sidled past Big Bro Boyson, out cold, on the roof. Tony turned, came back, covered Boyson with a piece of carpeting they'd found. Then he moved to the edge, sat on the parapet. Most city lights were out. The late news was over. From the roof Tony could see the bluish light of a TV in a room on the second floor of a building across the street. Snore softly, Bro, he thought. Dream softly, Bro. Make the tunnel go away. Let the children run. Let their mother duck. Let the car crash into an abutment instead of jumping . . .

On the street there were two people, teenagers, he thought, two girls. He watched them glance back over their shoulders, then dash across to his side of the street. They brought a smile to his face, how they were dressed in bell-bottom dungarees with bells large enough to conceal small dogs, and one in a tank top even though it was too chill for that. They scurried to the corner, turned, retreated, ran into his alley, disappeared in the darkness. Don't mean nothin, he thought. Then he saw three men across the street. "What the fuck." Something in Tony Pisano was grating. One of the men had a bat. His mind began racing. The street was safe, had been safe, but things were changing. Are they after me? he thought. Would they bring attention to the roof squats? He crouched behind the parapet, glanced to the boxes, low-crawled to the alley side, peered over the side parapet. He could not discern young girls from dumpsters. His paranoia spiked. He fell back to hands and knees, began puffing, feeling drained, feeling as if he needed to lie flat, in a prone firing position, maybe crawl into a shell. He moved to the front corner, craned his head out over the parapet. Again Tony ducked, froze. His arms trembled.

Then Tony heard, "Back this way, Man."

"Yeah. They gotta be."

"Damn whore."

"Last time she does that, Man." The three men laughed.

Tony peered over. The men moved into the alley. He could see one hanging back. The other two disappeared into the dark. Tony shivered. His teeth chattered. He thought, vaguely, he could rouse Big Bro, Wildman. He could . . . Then he thought, somehow he deserved this, deserved for things to be shitty, for atrocities to follow him. It was natural. It was supposed to be like this. Then, "Like fuckin hell." The words shook from his clamped jaw. "Like fuckin hell." The words, quiet, came from his gut. He was still trembling when he dropped over the edge, softly, to the fire escape, softly dropping to the second-floor balcony above the alley. The man with the bat was silhouetted against the opening to the street. No one else was visible. Tony hugged the wall, stood stock still. He heard movement at the dumpsters below him but it was too dark to see. Then, "Ha! Gottcha! Com'ere."

"Let me go!"

"You owe me—"

"GET THE FUCK OUTTA HERE!!!" The explosion was Tony's voice, so full of violence, the young man leaped, jolted back; the watcher at alleymouth stumbled, dropped back, back-pedaled to the far side of the street. The man with the bat crouched into a fighting stance. Tony was silent, frozen, rigid. One of the girls began crying.

Then, from the man with the bat. "Just grab her and let's go."

And from the roof. "LEAVE HER. LEAVE OR WE'LL BLOW YER FUCKEN HEADS OFF!"

"Hey"—nervous, backing out—"hey. I'm goin, Man. Hey, we're outta here."

November passed. Viet Nam was creeping back into the news. Busy men like Wapinski missed the onset, ignored the page 32, then page 12, then page 8 stories, but idle men, men of the street, of the grates and rooftops, men with time to spend, talked amongst themselves of their suspicions. By mid-December they began to stir. Phuoc Long Province: Don Luan and Bo Tuc cities came under heavy attack and were overrun. Song Be Airfield, Duc Phong, Firebase Bunard all were hit. Gerald Ford, Congress, did nothing. America prepared for Christmas. The men of the street stirred.

"I been there, Man. I fired shells from Bunard," said Frankie "The Kid" Denahee.

"Yeah?" Tony.

"Yeah. We built that sucker ... in sixty-six. Or ... Fuck! I don't remember."

"Yeah." Pisano, quiet, helpless, resigned. "Hey Ty?"

"Huh."

"Wapinski says we should go up there for Christmas. House-sit while he en his old lady go to Pennsy."

"Fuck the Captain, Man. He jus gonna throw our shit out when he come back."

"Roof's gettin old, Man. He said he'd come pick us up."

"Shee-it, Man. Then what? What if somebody take our squat, Man? Roof aint so bad. You stop playin Superman to every who-ah runnin from her pimp, you live easier."

"T-n-T, Man. I thought you was wasted."

"T-n-T, Bro." They tapped knuckles, catchers in the rye.

December 18, on the road from San Jose to San Martin—"Hey!" Bobby said. He was at a loss for words. The distance between him and Ty and Tony had grown to a chasm. "It's good to see you guys."

"Long as you know it ain't me," Ty said.

"Um." Bobby said.

"An nobody know I'm there."

"Yeah. I understand. I didn't know about the fraud charges until Tony told me."

"They fucked me, Man. They saw a black livin in their neighborhood, they set him up. I didn't fraud nobody. Not one sucka woulda lost one dime if they hadn't set me up."

"Um." Bobby pursed his lips. Then he said, "So, it's Tyler Mohammed now. No more Dorsey. No more Blackwell."

"No more whitey names," Ty answered.

They fell silent. Bobby didn't know how to deal with him, and he was concerned with what Sara would think. Ty and Tony did not look dirty, but they were shabby. And they smelled. They had showered in a men's shelter the night before but months on the roof or in the shelter had left a residue. Still, it was not the visual or the olfactory but the anger that disturbed Bobby. Tony seemed happy, almost manic. He'd had a string of questions about Grandpa Wapinski's health, was disturbed when Bobby told him that Pewel had been readmitted to St. Luke's for constipation, dehydration and alkalosis; and relieved that it had only been a five-day stay in which the doctors had changed Pewel's diuretic.

"My true name"—Ty began unsolicited—"is Tyrone Dorsey Blackwell. My true name is Tyrone Blackwell Wallace. My brothers are Phillip and Randall Dorsey Simpson, and James Dorsey Wallace, and my sister is Shreva Wallace."

"Wow!" Tony said. "You got a sister, huh?"

"I got a baby, too. Jessica."

"You shittin me, Man," Tony said.

"You stay in touch?" Bobby asked.

"No Sir. When you got no name, no address, you don't stay in touch with no one." There was a lag. Then Ty said, "They call us T-n-T in San Jose, cause Tony always blowin up and I'm always coverin his ass."

"Ha!" Tony slapped Ty's hand.

"But I . . . " Ty was hesitant. "I shouldn't be comin back here. They see Blackwell, they see Dorsey . . . "

"It'll be cool, Man," Tony said. "They're only going to see Ty Mohammed."

"Shit! They ain't gonna see nobody. I . . . I don't even know who I am."

Bobby slowed for the tollgate before the Golden Gate Bridge. "So"—he snapped out—"who the fuck do you think you are?"

"I don't *fuckin* know, Man."

"Maybe you're all of em," Bobby said. Ty did not respond. Bobby continued. "Ty, you remember when you stayed with me on Deepwoods?"

"I remember, Cap'n. I remember thinkin I was goina get me a piece a the pie. Just like you."

"Man, I've wanted to tell you this ever since then."

"What?"

"When you drove away that last time. You remember, I'd come home from an appointment or something. You'd been watching TV the night before. And drinking and you'd left your boots in the middle of the room. That morning I stuck em in the garbage and went to work. When I came back you'd packed and were clearing out. I was angry. I don't remember why. Maybe at Red. But I didn't open my mouth. What I should have said then, about the boots, was not that it meant clear out but it meant pick em up and put em away. That's what my mother used to do. Stick our stuff in the trash if she found something lying around. Damn it, Man. I didn't mean for you to split. That's been bothering me for three years."

"Yeah?!" Ty stared at Wapinski.

"Yeah."

"No shit?"

"I shit you not, my main man."

"Thanks, Captain. Thanks, Bob."

eturning was scary. For Ty to San Martin, for Bobby to Mill Creek Falls. He had not told his grandfather or anyone else back East about being fired, about going it on his own. And he had not told Sara that the County of San Martin had challenged his unemployment claim, that the checks they'd been counting on would not arrive. To save money Bobby had reverted to eating nothing but raw rice bits during the day while Sara was at school. He'd been losing weight again, worrying over every dime, hiding his worry from Sara who was frugal anyway, afraid if she knew their true financial picture she too might skimp, and pregnant, he did not want her to skimp, or to worry.

As they drove in from Williamsport, Bobby said, "I hope you like it. It's not much. The house is pretty ratty and the farm's been deteriorating for years."

"Tony made it sound like the Garden of Eden," Sara said. "And you know how I like hills. If you'd been a flatlander I don't think I would have fallen for you."

"Well, you're lucky you did, lady." Bobby chuckled, kept his eyes on the road, tried to keep it light.

"And why's that?" Sara baited him.

"Cause you're knocked up and you wouldn'ta wanted ta be seein Granpa lookin like that and not bein married."

Then their first morning together at High Meadow and Sara's introduction to the farm. It was cold, windy. The leaves were down, the trees gangly gray stalks in a gray sky. The ground was brown, dead, hard. Ice skimmed the pond except above the subterranean fracture where water from an artesian spring stirred the surface. "It was a great place to grow up," Bobby said. They had descended to the pond, were slowly climbing to the apple orchard. Bobby held Sara's arm, trying to steady her. "A great place to be a little boy."

"I can do it." Sara shook her arm free. "It'd be a great place for a little girl, too," she added. They climbed on, entered the open-roofed orchard. Sara's breath smoked before her face in small puffs. She blew a stream into a puff and watched the puff and stream dissolve into the dryness.

"Sometimes," Bobby said, "in San Martin, I get the feeling God's bored with what's happening on earth and pretty soon he's going to say, 'That's all folks,' and that's going to be it."

"Maybe He said that a long time ago," Sara said. She started walking again, climbing the south knoll toward its rounded peak. "What are those funny little birds? See them?"

"Oh. Ah, that's either a nuthatch or a tufted titmouse. Or a junco."

"Don't . . . you lived here all that time and you don't know their names?"

"Oh"—Bobby turned to the birds—"I know their names. That's Chuck. And that's Diana."

Over the next few days Bobby showed Sara the barn and Grandpa's office and several of the old farmer's designs; he brought her to the family cemetery where Grandma Wapinski and Aunt Krystyna were buried; together they explored the new fields and strawberry beds Tony had begun and the Sugar Shack with its new-fangled dumping and filter system. They climbed the back trail, pregnant as Sara was, cold as it was, past the old cabin and up the high ridge to the resplendent sugarbush and finally to the edge of the gap where Bobby told Sara about the far side, the Indian trail, the cathedral of virgin eastern hemlocks.

"Someday," she whispered.

He smiled and they held each other and watched a male and a female cardinal rise from the gap and flit into the maple crowns from where their repeated shrills shook the entire sugarbush. Bobby engaged them with his own whistle—three beats, then four, then five—and the birds answered him in kind, then went back to their tiff. "Clarence and Anita," he whispered to Sara.

On the twenty-second of December Sara met Linda Pisano. They hit it off immediately. Yet there was a distance between them Sara could not understand until Linda began to talk about Tony: "When he's here, now, it's like living with a total stranger." The next day Sara met John Pisano, Sr. and Jo, who had come to High Meadow to bring Pewel a present: wool socks and insulated deerskin mittens because his feet and hands were now always cold. They were elated to meet Sara and to see that Bobby had "settled down." And then the tension again: "Tony's house-sitting for us right now," Sara said.

"If he wasn't my son . . . " John Sr. began, the zest gone from his voice. "What he's done to Linda. You've met her. She's a beautiful girl. And our granddaughters . . . "

Bobby interrupted. "He passed through the gates of hell, Mr. Pisano," Bobby said. He did not know from where within him these words came. "He defeated death, but it—"

"Then," Jo said sadly, "he should rejoice in life."

"Him!" John Sr. scoffed. "He's a death maker. Going to make the death of me." He stood, turned away. "I don't want to talk about him."

"I'm very fond of him," Sara said simply.

That startled John Sr.; and Jo answered, "So are we."

They had Christmas Eve dinner at High Meadow. Miriam and Doug were there; and Brian and Cheryl (who was pregnant again) with their son Anton, almost three and a half. Joanne came alone. And there was Linda, Gina and Michelle, and Linda's sister Cindy, now 19, and Tony's brother Mark, 20, and with them the youngest Balliett, Henry Jr., just shy of 13. And, of course, Grandpa.

In the kitchen, before dinner was served, Linda and Sara were putting the final touches on the meal while Joanne puttered and Miriam sipped a glass of wine.

Bobby entered. "What can I do?" he asked.

"Are all the chairs in?" Linda asked.

"Yep. And the table's all set."

"Did you get the serving spoons and forks?" Sara asked.

"Yes. Everything's set."

"Then would you take the turkey out and carve it. You know how to do it where you open it up like petals?"

"Yep," Bobby said. "Okay. I'm off."

"Well," Linda laughed. "Looks like you've got him pretty well trained."

Sara laughed too, but Joanne sneered, said, "You wait. Wait until after the baby comes."

"I can hardly wait," Sara said. "With Bobby . . . I mean, there's never been a question about what we want from our marriage. We . . . ah, we're two of a kind."

"Yeah, right." Joanne stirred the soup.

Bobby reentered. He stood behind his sister, looked over her shoulder. "That's ready for the tureen, isn't it?"

Joanne nudged him back. Bobby startled. Joanne quipped something about control and he wanting to keep Sara barefoot and pregnant in the kitchen.

"Hey in there," Brian called. "Let's eat. I'm starving."

The room was dark except for a single candle that Linda held in the hall to the kitchen. "Dear Lord," Grandpa began, "please bless us and watch over us. On that first Christmas Eve the angels said, 'Peace on earth to men of goodwill.' " At that Linda entered and with her candle, lit the three candles on the table and inserted the one she held into the fourth holder. Grandpa smiled. He and Linda had planned the meal and he'd so liked Sara and Bobby's wedding rite that he asked Linda to get the candles. "Did you all hear that?" He said gruffly. "Peace to men *of* goodwill."

Joanne spoke up. "They probably said 'to people of goodwill.' "

Grandpa chuckled. "I'm certain they did. I'm certain they used a word that meant all people, and all creatures too, but the monsignors and prelates couldn't translate it exactly and they skimped here and there."

"On purpose, Grandpa," Joanne said. "They were all men. They translated it that way to preserve their power base."

"Oh, come on, Joanne," Brian said. "This is grace. Let Grandpa finish so we can eat."

"It's okay," Pewel said. "She's absolutely right. 'Peace to beings of goodwill.' I want to ask you, each of you, to say something nice, to everyone here. That peace will be your present to me."

"Now?!" Miriam said from the opposite end.

"Yes." Pewel smiled. "Even you, Miriam, who looks prettier every year." She was speechless. "But I want to start with my darling, Gina."

Gina was prepared. Her eyes glittered impishly. "You make me happy," she said.

And Michelle squeaked, "Me too. For no reason any all."

Pewel leaned forward. "Why, thank you," he said.

Around the table the "grace" was said with Doug saying to Bobby, "You oughtta come over to the new KC plant. I'll show er to ya. She's a real beaut"; and Bobby saying to everyone (and holding Michelle's small hand in his), "I feel happy for no reason any all, too. When I'm here, even in winter, I see the muskrats swimming across the pond and the moths with their intricate wing camouflage and the wildflowers of June and the bats of August nights catching insects up against the windows. I feel euphoric. I want you to feel that way too."

Some of the good cheer would last forever. Some was transient. And amid the chatter of Christmas Eve dinner, 1974, the first formal wording of The Code was begun. "And now," Pewel said, "I want to give you my gift. Before I am human," he said, "I am an element of the earth, a particle of the universe, and to this I owe integrity. I am a living being and to all life, next, goes my allegiance. I am a human before I am an American. To the brotherhood of man I owe my energy and my spirit."

"You're getting sexist again, Grandpa."

"Thank you, Joanne. If I didn't have you here to guide me, I'd err."

"How about," Sara said, "I am a human before I am a man or a woman, before I am an American. To humanity, as part of the earth and universe, I next devote my energy and spirit."

"Boys"—Pewel chuckled —"the girls are refining me. Aren't you going to help?"

Sara, leaning back, around Pewel, said happily to Bobby, "I see where you get it from."

Around and around. Pewel went on, "When your self needs minimum maintenance, you can expand beyond your self and take care of others. Expanding beyond the self is also less wearing on the self and thus requires less maintenance of the self. In this way one is opened to teach or to cure; to create, to explore, to investigate; to love, to rear children, and to defend those who cannot defend themselves."

On December 26 Pewel Wapinski, suffering pleuritic chest pain, tachycardia, tachypnea, and dyspnea, was readmitted to St. Luke's Hospital in Rock Ridge. By dark, after hours of tests and hours of waiting-room pacing, doctors told Bobby and Brian, Sara and Linda, that Pewel had a pulmonary embolism. For the time being he was confined to bed, attached to an oxygen mask, and injected (IV continuous) with an anticoagulant.

"I don't believe it." Bobby was angry. "How could it happen? Just like that? Like that!" All morning and into the afternoon Sara had paced the waiting room with him but she was now sitting with her legs up, letting Bobby pace alone. At times Brian popped up, paced too. At times Linda joined them.

"It can," Linda said softly. "It can happen just like that. He's still very strong. They'll get it under control."

"Yesterday he's great," Bobby said. "He brought Sara and me out to the barn to give us another present. Do you know what he'd done? He made a crib. He made the most beautiful crib from the maples up at the sugarbush. He's eighty-five years old and when we called and told him Sara was pregnant, he took the tractor and the saws up to the sugarbush and chose a number of branches. He said he could see the crib in the branches before he cut. He said he wanted his grandchildren to grow up in a little bit of High Meadow even if they lived three thousand miles away." Bobby fidgeted, shuffled, scuffed a heel into the floor tiles. "Damn it. Damn it!"

Then with the sky winter black, the doctor came again and said, "He's stable. He's resting. There's nothing you can do here. Go home."

"I think I should stay," Bobby said.

"Take your wife home. Come back in the morning. We'll call if anything happens."

*   *   *

Friday, 27 December 1974, nine A.M.—"Helloohh!"

"Ah, hello. Can I help you?"

"I'm looking for Robert Wapinski."

"Oh. Won't you come in? He's upstairs. Who should I say . . . "

"Ah . . . my wife and the kids are in the car. . . . I, ah . . . I'm Phil Simpson. Tyrone Blackwell's brother . . . half-brother."

"Ah . . . oh . . . ah . . . " Sara recognized, then doubted, then felt confused. "Ty Mohammed, you mean?"

"Huh?" Phillip was equally confused. His tie to his brother had been reduced from a broken thread to a feeling.

"Why don't you all come in. They'll freeze out there. I'll get Bob."

A few minutes later, after Bobby repressed the frustration of being interrupted in the paramount task of going back to St. Luke's—he'd called at five and eight and both times had been told Pewel was stable and resting—"This is Jessica?"

Phillip nodded. The little girl, almost six, sat on his lap. Phillip's wife, Carol, held their son, twenty-five months, on her lap. And pregnant Sara held Phillip and Carol's youngest, the baby Cecilia.

"And you named this guy Tyrone?" Bobby said.

"Yes." Phillip nodded sheepishly. "The little stinker . . . you know, I mean my brother. . . . Look, Mr. Wapinski . . . "

"Please. Just Bob."

"Look, it takes a man and a woman to make a baby," Phillip said. "Two parents is jus natural. Maybe not necessary, but it's a primary and a back-up system for raisin kids."

"Umm." Bobby wanted to speed Phillip's plea. "You're saying . . . "

"Look now at this." Phillip hoped his thoughts would be passed on. "See how vulnerable is a person if you remove the back-up? See? You wouldn't go out an cut off everahbody's left arm. But that just what we doin with quickie divorce and lettin men run out on their families. See? I know there are circumstances. But we approachin one-third single-parent households in this country. One third! Higher then that in the black community. We allowin . . . like we approve of it . . . we allowin the removal of the back-up system. That's dangerous, Mr. Wapin—"

"Bob."

"Bob. That makes the children and the country vulnerable. Half a all divorced women with children under five end up on welfare. Luwan been on welfare. That's why Carol and me got Jess. But he her father."

"You want him to come back, huh?"

"A course."

"All I can do is tell im."

"Give im this picture a Jess. Tell im I'll pay his bus fare."

Later that morning at St. Luke's Hospital Bobby talked with his grandfather. Pewel was still propped in bed with oxygen and IV therapy but he was awake, alert, impatient with his condition yet physically tired. "They say you're going to be okay," Bobby said.

"One, two, three, four. Potatoes on your head."

Bobby chuckled. "What?"

"That used to be one of your jokes."

"One of my jokes . . . "

"When you were little. Brigita'd be spoonin potatoes in your mouth and you'd make up those jokes."

"Oh. I don't rememb—"

Pewel cut in. "Or you'd ask, 'Does being truthful mean not telling a lie even when Pinocchio would tell a lie?' "

"Um." Bobby paused. "They did say you're going to be okay."

"I know. The doctor came in earlier. Diuretics. Digitalis. Now they're sayin somethin, cow manure."

"Coumarin," Bobby corrected. "It's an anticoagulant."

"Six months." Pewel sighed. "Take it for six months."

That evening Pewel's spirits were a little better, and that night he slept well. On Saturday he was up twice, walking. Linda brought Gina and Michelle. His spirits soared. Jo, Isabella and Helen visited, as did Brian, Cheryl and Anton. Father Tom Niederkau from St. Ignatius came, followed by three women volunteers from St. Theresa's Guild. Adolph Lutz brought a fruit cake his wife had made, and Stacy Carter, how she heard no one knew, sent a bouquet of flowers. Through it all Bobby and Sara sat, left briefly to eat, read Pewel the newspaper. There was a six-line note on fighting in the Mekong Delta, and separately, three paragraphs on the Khmer Rouge having launched an offensive in Cambodia. A page 1 story about Kinnard/Chassion closing one of its Yankee Rollers, a massive heated drum on which toilet paper is made, and laying off most of its third shift was positioned next to a large photograph showing the factory with its four-foot-high rooftop SEASON'S GREETINGS sign.

On Sunday Pewel was stronger. He held one of Sara's hands, one of Bobby's. "What do you want to do with your lives?" Pewel squeezed their hands. "Don't tell me. Tell each other. Tell yourselves."

"But I'd like to tell you," Bobby said. For an hour he explained his massive design scheme for evolutionizing transportation in the North Bay area. He told Pewel of the lightweight car design, of the windmills. And he told him of Henry Alan Harrison's reaction and of his "subsequent decision to start my own company."

Pewel was excited by Bobby's bold approach and Bobby's decision to go out on his own. Between naps they talked about energy—sources, consumption, alternatives. "Oh, just think of the possibilities!" Pewel lay back. He was very happy, very tired. "They won't let you do it out there, eh?"

"No. Not a chance."

"So. How is Environmental Energy Systems going to make enough money to stay in business? Who's going to buy your crop?"

"That's the problem right now," Bobby said. "It's either huge foundations or one-man shops. There's not much in between."

"Bob, you can grow the best crop in the world, but, if nobody buys it, it sits and rots."

On Monday, 30 December, Pewel was champing at the bit. "You stay with us until after the holiday, Mr. Wapinski," his doctor had said. "Then we'll see."

"Sara's school starts on the second," Bobby said apologetically.

"Go." Pewel waved him off.

"We'll be back after the baby's born, okay?"

"Yep." Pewel pointed to the closet. "Go in there. In my jacket pocket in there." Bobby fished into Pewel's jacket. "My knife in there?"

"Yep." Bobby pulled out a well-worn pocket knife.

"Take it with you," Pewel said.

"Granpa, this is yours."

"I know. But I want you to give it for me."

"Give it?"

"To Tony. My present to him. Tell him I hope he gets a great deal of pleasure from it. Tell him a good knife is like a good woman. And vice versa."

23

L ittle by little, shit everywhere hit the fan.

"Ohhah!" Sara entered, kicked the door shut behind her, dropped her book bag with sets of papers to be corrected.

"What's the matter, Sar?" Bobby had rarely seen her agitated.

"I can hardly believe it!" she blurted.

"What?"

"Two of my students . . . " Her arms shot out, palms up, beseeching. "Second graders! With marijuana joints! In *my* classroom!"

"You're kid—"

Bobby began to make light of what Sara had just said. She cut him off. "If you ever design a town's school layout, separate the levels. That's the problem. With the middle school next door, all their problems become ours. Joints in second grade!"

"Were they going to, you know, I mean, second graders . . . They wouldn't know how to smoke them, would they?"

"That's not the point. Oh! This entire town is out of control."

It was only their third full day back. Problems had begun immediately upon their returning to the Old Russia Road cottage.

"Where's Ty?" Sara had asked Tony.

"Ah . . . " Tony had stalled.

"We've got something very special for him," Bobby had added. "And something for you from Granpa."

"But Ty has to sit down for this," Sara had said.

"He split," Tony had said. "He freaked out. Some people from your old office, Al and Jane, dropped by and they recognized him. He freaked out and split."

"Aw . . . " Bobby had opened his suitcase, taken out the letter from Phillip, the picture of Ty's little girl. "I need to get these to him."

And the next evening, the call from Linda, after Tony had left with the photo of Jessica: "He's developed another pulmonary embolism." There was frustration and sympathy in her voice.

"I thought that couldn't happen with the heparin. And coumarin."

"Well, it shouldn't but it can," Linda said. "His doctor thinks they can control it. He said it may not even be a new one but the first one breaking apart. It's very small on the X-ray."

Bobby put his hand to his head. "I—I can't come back right now. I mean, I will if . . . "

"I don't think it's that serious, Bob. But they're going to keep him in the hospital until it clears up."

Bobby stayed within earshot of the phone on the fourth and fifth. He read, watched TV, tried to think of a way to sell his crop, tried to define to himself what was indeed his crop, dozed on and off. On the fourth CBS News told of the failure of the U.S. government's clemency program for draft resisters, and of a Khmer Rouge massacre at Ang Snoul, Cambodia. Little else was mentioned about fighting in Southeast Asia. On the fifth NBC showed aerial views of Phuoc Long Province and Phuoc Binh and warned of the impending collapse of that besieged city only sixty miles northeast of Saigon. Then on the sixth came the announcement of the fall of the entire province including the provincial capital. To Bobby this was startling. Until the day before he had seen no mention of a major offensive, or even a major build up. Phuoc Binh was a provincial capital, a regional center. Not since the Nguyen Hue Offensive in the spring of 1972 had a major city been lost—and that one, Quang Tri, was 400 miles from Saigon.

Public and media debate erupted. Bobby talked to his grandfather. The old man was again doing well. Still Bobby stayed by the phone, by the TV. From the seventh to the tenth all the major networks carried stories about President Ford's Viet Nam "concern," then his "consideration" of emergency aid to South Viet Nam, then congressional opposition to that aid and State Department doomsday scenarios if the aid wasn't forthcoming. Amid the electronic reportage there was little mention of the fate of the civilian or military human beings of Phuoc Long—province and city—who'd been pounded by tens of thousands of rounds of communist artillery, crushed by a hundred Soviet T-54 tanks. And there was little mention of the *three weeks* of intensive fighting in which the out-manned and outgunned South lost 4,550 soldiers and were finally over-run by the NVA's 4th Corps infantry.

On the eleventh Sara said, "I can't believe it. They're not going to do anything."

"Who?"

"The school. These kids have the school board completely buffaloed. We're simply abdicating all responsibility."

"Oh," Bobby said, "I thought you meant Ford. And Congress. They're not going to do anything either. They're giving Hanoi a green light."

And that evening, like buckshot coming from all angles, "Bobby"—in Linda Pisano's voice there were tears—"he had a TIA. They don't know why he's throwing clots."

"Oh geez. I don't know what that—"

"Transient ischemic attack. It's an obstruction in the blood flow to part of the brain. He's had a stroke."

"Oh no!"

"He's resting," Linda said. "His vital signs are stable but he's lost all movement on his right side. And it's . . . it's too early to tell."

"I'll try to get a flight tomorrow."

"Ah . . . unless you can stay . . . call his doctor first. I had a patient when I was in Philadelphia that went through this. She regained most of her functions but it takes time. There's nothing you can do right now except sit. And he'll need help . . . Can . . . can you get Tony to come back? He might need someone full time."

More calls. Brian. Miriam. Jo and John Sr. St. Luke's. And to and from Linda, again and again. The twelfth, thirteenth, fourteenth, fifteenth, on to the twentieth—Sara trying to prepare a nursery, working, worrying about Bobby, holding him, listening to him, talking, visiting her own grandparents and parents and brothers.

And mud! Mud everywhere. North Peak cloaked continually in cool mist or drizzle, the earth turning to mud through which Bobby walked Josh, "civilization" encroaching on "their" open space, the further expansion of North Peak CondoWorld, "Keep that animal on a leash." Restless, unsettled, sell your crop, don't leave me. Bobby slept like a turning wheel. There was Bowers left on Hamburger Hill, left wounded, the rain turning the hill into a snot-slick slope, attackers marching in unseen, he hiding behind the wall, the stone wall, the road, unseen as-sailants, mud, pigs, "You sound like a pig! When are you going to learn to eat?" Masked men probing, blood, the smell stuck in his nose, his head hurt, "This your dog? Nice looking animal. How come you haven't been up to see me? There's corn fritters and syrup waiting," probing, eyes only seen in green shrouds, "I'm cold. God, I'm so cold." "Next." "And with 289,000 North Viet Namese soldiers in South Viet Nam, any emergency aid . . . " "Next." "But he's still alive, Sir." "Just push those brains back in and put him in the corner. . . . "

Bobby was pissed. It was Friday, January 31, 1975. Tony had shown up out of the blue saying it was almost time to go syruping. "Look, damn it! I went down there three times looking for you guys. There's not going to be any goddamn syruping this year! He needs help. I need help. He keeps coming in and out. He's partially paralyzed and Linda says there's a problem with fluid in his lungs."

"Well, you tell me, Man." Tony too was angry, defensive, frightened by Bobby's account of Pewel's health. "What do you want me to do? I can go back. I owe him that."

Now Bobby was conciliatory. "I've just been wanting to get in touch with you. You don't owe him anything. You don't owe me anything. Did you get that picture to Ty?"

"Yeah."

"Did he do anything?"

"He put it in his shirt."

Bobby's anger flared. "What is it with you guys?! Don't you know what the word *responsibility* means?!"

"Fuck that! You don't have a fuckin idea what we're like. Not one motherfuckin idea!"

"No wonder"— Bobby could not have said a more hurtful thing— "Linda reinstated those divorce papers."

Tony looked at him—stunned. The last strings were being cut. "Fine." His voice was low. "Fuck you."

Bobby louder, "Fuck you too."

Four feet apart they squared off, heads lowered, teeth clenched, fists balled, breathing in long deep breaths, staring, trying to stare each other down, not wanting to throw the first shot, Marine versus Airborne, ready to counterpunch, to deliver the knock out, to rip out eyes, throats.

At that moment Sara came home. "Oh—" she was surprised yet happy to see Tony, "you two must be talking about the truncation talk." She hugged Tony first, like a visiting brother, then kissed Bobby. "I've been listening to it on the radio."

"What truncation?" Bobby asked. He turned on the TV.

"In Viet Nam," Sara said. "They're talking about giving up part of the country"—while she spoke she removed her rain jacket, put her book bag by the table; Bobby flipped channels trying to find a news program—"in order to defend the heart better. Something about a withdrawal from the north."

"That's Quang Tri," Tony said. "I saw it in the paper. There's only a pile a rubble left anyway."

" ' . . . threats and scare tactics,' the senator said." Bobby backed away from the set so Tony and Sara could see. "Senator Kennedy," the anchor continued, "demanded that the administration substantiate its five hundred and twenty million dollar request. 'Once again,' Kennedy told the

Senate, 'we are hearing the same old arguments and the same old controversies over the same old war. The lingering and bloody conflict deserves more of our diplomacy, and not more of our ammunition.' " The news topic shifted. Bobby gritted his teeth. "Nice way of saying, 'Get stuffed,' huh?"

Bobby became more antsy. He could not work, could not design. He worried over every dime, every wasted minute. He felt ill. Perhaps it was psycho-sympathetic. His weight loss accelerated and Sara became afraid for his health.

Tony stopped by in mid-February. He too was anxious. He told Bobby that Ty was cleaning up his act, getting straight, that they'd been talking about going back, together, but had decided to wait until March just in case they didn't have a place to stay.

Then on Washington's birthday, Linda called with more bad news. "The doctor told me they may have to take his right leg. There's just no blood in it. It's a truncation process," she added. "You can protect the vital organs by eliminating peripheral needs."

Bobby could barely speak. He gave the phone to Sara. "Have they told him?" Sara asked.

"Oh, Sara—" Linda, she'd been strong for Bobby, now she burst into tears, "he just wants to go home. He's been pleading with them to let him go home to die. They want to put in a pacemaker, but he just wants to go back home."

Sara too was in tears. To Bobby she said, "You've got to go back. I'll be fine."

On the eighteenth Bobby made arrangements to fly back on Sunday the twenty-third. He talked to Pewel on the nineteenth and the twentieth. Bobby could not read, could not concentrate on the news. Phnom Penh was surrounded but he did not care. He talked to Pewel again on the twenty-first and the old man reminded him that the next day was Pewel and Brigita's fifty-second wedding anniversary.

On the twenty-second, with Bobby all packed, Linda called with terrible news. "He's had another stroke," she told Sara. "He's comatose. They've got him on life support. I . . . I know your situation. If you don't have the money . . . for coming twice . . . he . . . Bobby shouldn't come. Grandpa could be like this . . . he might not make it through the night but he could hang on for months."

Tony came again, gave him "as a peace offering, Man," a copy of the 27 January issue of *Sports Illustrated*, the swimsuit issue with Cheryl Tiegs on the cover. Tony was shaken by the news. The two sat in the mist and dark of the basketball court, killed three six-packs, talked about High Meadow, about Viet Nam, about women, children, cousins, wives.

"I use ta hit her, Man," Tony said. "I couldn't control it, Man. That's why I left. I figured I'd kill her. I almost chopped my daughter's hand off, too."

"She never said . . . did . . . did you try counseling?"

"Man, I did that for a year. Fuckin shrink said I killed these kids and a mama-san. Said I repressed it and it comes outta me making me act like that."

"Did you?"

"Man, I don't fuckin know. But I know I can't go there and do it again. I should go back though. It's late but I could still bring in some sap. Time to go back, Man. Time to go back."

"We're goin back."

"We're goin back, Man."

"Man, we're goin back."

"You shittin me. Sides, I can't go back. I gotta go maple syrupin."

"Syrupin?" "Wildman" David Coffee crawled over to Tony. "Syrupin!"

"What the fuck! Okay. There ain't no fuckin syrup this year anyway."

"Count in the Twenty-Fifth," Frankie "The Kid" Denahee said.

"Big Red One," said Sheldon "Fuzzy" Golan.

"One-Oh-Worst," added Ty.

"Fourth," said Coffee.

"The Magnificent Bastards," said Tony.

"The whole goddamn Corps," said Big Bro Boyson.

"How the fuck we gettin back?" Ty asked.

"Same way as the first time," Denahee said.

"I flew over," Ty said.

"That Texas billionaire's behind it, Man," Denahee said. "We're meetin here. They're meetin every place, Man. We're all goin back. Goin back."

"We need"—Ty turned to Tony—"Wapinski. Man, we gotta get Wapinski."

"Who's that?" Big Bro.

"The Captain, Bro."

"We don't need no mothafuckin officers." Big Bro Boyson pulled back from the group on the rooftop squat. "No mothafuckas," he repeated.

"Captain's okay, Bro," Ty said. "Saved lives, Man."

Then aside, later, Tony and Ty alone. "We can get you there," Tony said. "We just have to be cool about it."

"You sure it was me they was lookin for?"

"Shit! He had all your aliases on the warrant."

"I didn't fraud no one."

They converged on the nicely maintained ranch house on the quiet subdivision street in San Jose, California—not just the six roof rats, not just homeless veterans, but fifty-nine strong—men in suits and ties, men in worn field jackets and worn-out jungle boots, men pulling up in new cars, men who'd walked miles. It was March 12, 1975, Tyler Mohammed's twenty-fourth birthday. Two days earlier the NVA had detonated their blossoming lotus in the vital Central Highland's city of Ban Me Thuot. For two entire months Congress and the Ford administration had been battling publicly about aid to Viet Nam and Cambodia. Senate Majority Leader Mike Mansfield led the antiaid fight stating that he was "sick and tired of pictures of Indochinese men, women, and children being slaughtered by American guns with American ammunition. . . . " Eric Sevareid had reinforced this point of view with his "Death Rattle of a Failed Policy" broadcast on February 26th. He was by no means— in the print or electronic media—alone. On the ninth of March there had been a sudden shift in news emphasis—away from Cambodia, away from the aid debate, to the fighting at Ban Me Thuot. On the twelfth Bobby began his true reentry and reeducation into the realities of Viet Nam.

"Man, I can't fuckin believe this." Wapinski's voice was low. He was in the corner of the living room in the San Jose ranch house. He'd shaken hands with the roof rats, was standing between Tony and Ty. Before them, some in chairs, some sitting on the floor, were forty other vets— and more were arriving, packing into that small living room—all talking quietly in twos or threes or not talking at all.

"Fuckin amazin, huh?" Tony whispered.

A vet before them turned back. "What's really fuckin amazing is how those bastards have cut and run."

"The dinks, Man?" Ty asked.

"Congress," the seated man whispered.

Another vet turned. "There it is, Bro." He raised a power fist to them. "Once you commit you can't just cut loose and say ta-ta suckers."

For a moment they were all silent. A few coughed. A few fidgeted. Into Bobby's mind popped the word *responsibility*, the accusation *cut and run*. He wondered, How can these guys be responsible when there's such a lack of leadership in Congress and the administration? Irresponsibility breeds roof rats.

"Hey," Tony whispered, "any word on Grandpa?"

"He's still in a coma. My mother and sister, my brother too—they want to disconnect him. Screw that, Man. You don't just put somebody in the corner to cool."

The meeting settled down. The host introduced himself and his Viet Namese wife, who bowed slightly, then immediately retreated to the kitchen. "There's one hundred thousand of us meeting all over America," the host said. "That's the word. A hundred thousand, just like us, ready to go back. And things have just started. Plane fare will be provided for the first ten thousand. They're still trying to put together the logistics and get a manifest of who's ready to go."

Again more asides. "What about weapons and ammo?"

"The weapons are already there. Waiting to be distributed."

The host began telling people in front about his in-laws who lived in

Tay Ninh. In the back another conversation erupted. "I don't know, Man," Bobby whispered.

"Yeah, huh." The vet directly in front of him.

"What?" Big Bro.

"I want to know it's organized, Man." Bobby.

"Yeah." A seated vet. "Give us our weapons here, and we'll go."

"How the ninety thousand goin who don't fly?"

"Boat," a vet farther in said. "I went by boat in '65."

"Give us ammo and weapons"—another voice—"and we'll land a force of a hundred thousand American ex-military . . . "

"Perot's behind it, Man. He'd follow through."

"Who told you?"

"Word on the street, Man."

"Good enough for me . . . ah . . . long as we get ammo and weapons as we step on board."

"Good enough for me, too!"

"I'm not lettin it go down the tubes, Man."

"It's hallowed ground, Man. My buddies' blood's there."

"Yeah. Mine too."

"And my cousin's, Man."

"Fuckin dinks. Worthless bastards. Don't give a shit. They fight like shit."

"Ah . . . " Loud, from the front, a vet friend of the host. "I'd like to read to you some parts from these intelligence reports. These are dated January seventeenth and twenty-first and February sixth. Ah, you can all read em in full later if you want. I know what you guys are sayin. I was saying it myself last week. ARVN ain't worth shit."

Called from the midst, "Right on." Murmurs of assent.

"Well, you were right. They weren't worth shit. Especially if you saw em in '65 or '67 or maybe even some units in '71. How it got to the point where regional forces, ruff puffs, Man, where they could go nose to nose with regular NVA units and kick butt, I don't know. But it happened. That's what I want to show you. These guys have been fighting their asses off.

"I didn't know, Man. Nobody in America seems to know. It's like from '72 . . . like the past two or three years have been a complete blackout. You know the reputation of the 1st ARVN, and their Airborne, and Marine Divisions, and their Rangers. But I'm telling you the ARVN 3d, 7th, 9th, 21st—even the 22d and 23d Divisions—despite Saigon—they've matured. Gone in and done the job. They didn't give up. They haven't given up. And conditions are much worse than anything any of us saw when we were there. They've done things like . . . like the ARVN 7th—they had to make their own division farm to feed their people because aid cutbacks have thrown South Viet Nam into an economic depression. They've been fighting without gas for their APCs, without air cover because there's no aviation fuel. Congress has been fuckin sellin em out.

And us too! I don't give a shit about Thieu or his cronies, but I do care about those people I trained. And I care about their families. Fuck the politics. If we cut and run—that's the most dirty, filthy, obscene thing we can do. Listen to this:"

CONFIDENTIAL

American Consulate General II

SUBJECT: Debriefing (1830 hrs, 21 January) of S-3 Officer, Phuoc Long, escape to Quang Duc.

INTRODUCTION: Major ████████ is, as of this date, the last GVN soldier to escape from Phuoc Long . . . evading communist forces for 18 days.

PLACE—Sector TOC, Song Be: 3 January 1975: Shelling of the city by NVA 130-mm artillery had been intensified during the last three days (this was the 24th day of shelling) to an estimated 3,000 rounds per day . . . At approximately 1130 hours on 6 January during heavy shelling, the Province Chief with four bodyguards, plus the Sector S-2 and S-3 and 2 NCOs from each section, dodged the incoming shells and made their way out of the TOC. Their timing was essential as four T-54 NVA tanks had rolled into the area and had shelled point-blank the Province Chief's house and bunker and had destroyed the Province headquarters building and had moved up the road toward the Sector TOC. The tanks commenced shelling the TOC and surrounding bunkers. Some RF soldiers had attempted to knock out the tanks with M-72 LAWs but the weapons were ineffective against the new Soviet-equipped armor. Maj ████████ attempted twice himself with no results and witnessed one 81st Ranger soldier sneak up less than two meters behind one tank and fire his LAW, also with no results. The soldier was so close that the explosion left his face a bloodied mess. Other soldiers were seen jumping on top of the NVA armor attempting to open the hatch and throw in hand grenades to no avail as the hatches were secured. . . .

The man paused, flipped through the pages, said:

The NVA shelled the city with thousands of rounds . . . with many direct hits and the delayed rounds had further devastating effects. Most civilians as well as military were living in bunkers during these days of late December and early January. . . . With no responding ARVN artillery (it had either been knocked out or they just didn't have any ammo) NVA units moved closer. . . . The S-3 estimated that as many as 40 T-54s entered the city and crippled it. . . . Maj ████████ remarked that city had been out of food and water for days and he could hear the ill and wounded at the province hospital crying for help. . . .

The Major continued by saying that he was not a political person, but it seemed that ever since the '73 Peace Agreement was signed, the South

Viet Namese have been losing. He added that even reduced US aid and support would mean the survival of South Viet Nam. He said, "Now I talk to you as a friend. So I feel very bad and believe that my country may fall, but I will die fighting for it. The problem I will have is to understand why it fell when so may Americans and Vietnamese have died for a good cause." This reporter responded that I knew he was tired and had to rest, and take heart—everything was far from being lost. . . .

In parting the Major said, "Only the Americans, the ones who have stayed and fought with us, understand the Viet Namese. Unfortunately, the rest of the free world does not understand, nor care."

The man paused again, shuffled through his stack of reports and letters. "Here's a State Department *AirGRAM* from the American Consul in Can Tho, dated February 6, 1975. 'During the heavy fighting of December and January . . . ' " Bobby Wapinski found himself shaking his head and thinking *what* heavy fighting in December?

> . . . most public attention was focused on gains made by the NVA/VC forces against GVN defenders. Can Tho 0021 related a few examples of particularly effective performance by the Republic of Viet Nam Armed Forces during this period. . . . Attached . . . account . . . of the December 6 defense of a village in Vinh Long Province by 60 Popular Forces and Rural Development (RD) Cadre against 200 Communist attackers . . .
>
> . . . We would point out the following. First the RD Cadre are not a fully trained, heavily armed military force. They are instead lightly armed, government employees whose function is to bolster civil services in rural areas of Viet Nam. Secondly, the reader should note the extremely limited but highly effective use of artillery during the attack. Finally, we would remind the reader that the battle at Hoa Tinh village is only one of dozens of such incidents that occur throughout the Delta every week. . . .

Outside. "You sign up, Man?"

"Yeah," Tony responded. "You?"

"Yeah," Bob said. "But . . . shit, Man. There's so much happenin. Granpa. Sara's due in two weeks . . . "

"Yeah. How can you go, Man?"

"Yeah. Yeah. But how can I not?"

"God Damn It!" Ten days had passed. There had been no call. Tony had spent six nights at Old Russia Road—sleeping in the office-mobile, preparing gear, unbeknownst to Sara, for Bobby and himself. The South Viet Namese city of Da Nang, one of Tony's areas of operation during his tour, had come under heavy bombardment on the twentieth of March, and by the twenty-first the handwriting was on the wall. Still there was no call. All that night, Tony had raged silently, had gotten drunk, silently, inside the car. At first light he'd taken the car and driven to the Marine Corps recruiting office in San Rafael.

"How come Da Nang's fallin?" he demanded.

"Calm down, Pal." The recruiter had just unlocked his office in the basement of the post office.

"Why the fuck didn't they leave the 3d Marine Division there?"

"Pal, they've been on Okinawa for two years."

"What about the 1st?" Tony had demanded.

"Camp Pendelton, Pal. Where you been?"

"Why aren't they still up by the Z?"

"Here, Pal. Have a sticker."

"Yeah. Give me ten a them."

"Sure."

"An ten a them. An them. An them."

"How bout a cup a coffee, too?"

"I'm goina pound somebody's fuckin face!"

"Take it easy, Pal. Milk en sugar?"

"Fuck, I shoulda stayed in. I shoulda stayed. This wouldn't be happenin. I wanta go back. We're goin back. We're a ground swell."

Now, at noon, back at the cottage, with Bobby and Sara nowhere in sight, he stood on the roof of the office-mobile screaming, "God Damn It! I'm a bastard! I'm a Magnificent Bastard. And I'm goddamned fuckin proud!"

He jumped down, peeled the back off another bumper sticker, carefully aligned it, stuck it to the center of the driver's door. He stood back. The sticker said THE FEW—THE PROUD. There were stickers on every door, on the front and rear bumpers, on the fenders, inside on the dash. He'd plastered stickers to the basketball backboard, the pole, vertically on the thin poles holding the downhill fence. Long stickers: I'M A MARINE. THE MARINES. UNITED STATES MARINE CORPS. Round stickers: the Marine Corps emblem.

"Oh Man. He's got these little pigeon legs. He's so beautiful."

"Kids are neat," Tony said. He and Bobby were on the roof of the Chevy, toasting the birth of Noah Pewel Wapinski. It was late Saturday night, the 22d of March 1975. Sara and baby Noah were in San Martin Canyon Hospital. "You got a son, Man. Do right by him."

"Oh yeah. You gotta see him. He's so tiny. Only six pounds fourteen ounces. He was born at eight fifty-one. Man, that was the neatest thing in my whole life. I saw the head. I saw his head crowning. I was right there."

Tony bit his lip but he did not let his feelings show. "It's somethin, huh? Hey, how's your grandfather?"

"Aw, no change. Linda said she'd see him tomorrow and tell him.

God, Man! I could lose my job, my house, my life. No big thing. But I can't lose my kid. I could make it or not, Man. Sara could make it without me. But Noah. He can't make it without me."

Bobby and Sara spent the 23d of March, their first anniversary, in the hospital with Noah. On the 25th, the day they brought Noah home, Pewel Wapinski, eighty-five and a half years old, stopped breathing and died. Lynette, Sara's mother, came to Old Russia Road. Bobby flew back for the funeral.

The late March winds were warm, sweeping in from the south. Bobby glanced down from the cemetery on the east ridge. More than a hundred people had come. The Pisanos and Pellegrinos, the Lutzes and the women from St. Theresa's Guild, and Father Tom Neiderkau. Bobby had not been surprised by them but he had been by Johnnie Jackson, a wiry, middle-aged black man, and his family, who owned Mill Creek Auto Salvage and Junkyard and who told Bobby, without elaboration, that had it not been for Pewel's help, he would have lost his business in 1962. And by old man Willings and Ernest Hartley, the mayor of Mill Creek Falls, and members of all the Five River Front Families; and old Pete the barber, and Jessie Taynor and Mrs. Franklin and Mr. Morris . . . "He helped me . . ." "He laid out my store . . ." "He organized . . ." "My sons went to him for . . ." "He once . . ." And by Stacy Carter.

From the cemetery Bobby looked down at the house. It was badly in need of repair. The front porch was settling, the stone piers deteriorating beneath and the posts rotting at the base. The mortar of the chimney was disintegrating and several bricks were missing from the top tier. A gable trim board, rotted around its nails, had popped loose. Everything needed paint, inside and out. Down the drive, wheel ruts and gullies were about to make the house inaccessible, fence sections were down, the old gate sagged on broken hinges. And although some of the fields had been turned in recent years, the back of the high meadow was more new woods than grass.

The night before, after the wake, Bobby had talked with Linda. "You know, we've been married over five years," Linda had said. "We solved the same problem a hundred times but it never stayed solved. It would be like it was happening for the first time all over again."

"I know what you mean. Not exactly, but . . . When I was married the first time . . ."

"It's like pouring energy into a bottomless pit," Linda had said. "It just drains you faster than you can replenish."

"Yeah. He told me how he used to hit you. About almost cutting off one of the girl's hands."

"He didn't used to hit me." Linda had looked queerly at Bobby. "Maybe he bumped me once or twice," she had added. "And that thing with Michelle's hand, he did that because he was really irritable. But it wasn't like it was on purpose. I'm sure he didn't know her hand was in the door."

"He didn't tell me anything about it. Just that he almost cut it off and that he abused you."

"I hit him a lot more and a lot harder than he ever hit me. What was bad was we never knew who he was going to be. Maybe he was going to be happy and doing those little dances he does, or maybe he was going to be the other guy. Completely impossible. Or the quiet one, withdrawn then exploding. But Bobby, when I met him, and that first year or so, that was the best year of my life."

"You're still going to go through with the divorce, though, huh?"

"You can't have a marriage when only one spouse shows up," Linda had said. "You know, his biggest mistake was not staying in medicine. He had a real aptitude and he loved it. But he never believed in himself."

Bobby glanced back at the grave. Buried, he thought, next to Brigita. The two people that loved me more than all the world. How hard it was to step away, to join those in the house. "Granpa. And Granma," he whispered. "I'm sorry I didn't come back." Again he turned, then returned, whispered. "You've got another great-grandson."

For a long while, after everyone had gone, Bobby just sat. Then he called Sara. They talked for hours. "God, Sara, I feel like I'm going to burst. I'm so full of this place and of Granpa I think if I don't talk I'll burst." Part of the time she talked while Noah nursed and she put the phone to her breast so Bobby could hear the baby swallow. She told him all the local news except the part about Tyler Mohammed being arrested. They talked again the next day, the day Da Nang fell, and again the next. Sara told him about Josh's acceptance of the baby, and about every burp and coo. Each time she ended with, "Hurry home."

"As soon as the legals are settled," he answered.

Most of the time Bobby was alone in the house, packing up perishables, or alone in the barn wondering if he should pack and send all of Pewel's drawings and notes to the Old Russia Road cottage. Sometimes he walked through the orchard but he never made the circuit over the knoll, the spillway, up the west ridge to the sugarbush. Often he ventured to the cemetery. Linda came a few times. She'd arranged to work full-time for Simon Denham and his group.

On Thursday, April 3, he drove Grandpa's old Chevy to the reading of the will. "I don't think I understand," Bobby said to the lawyer after the first reading. Bobby, Brian, Joanne and Miriam were present.

"It's really quite simple," Michael Willings said. "You understand about the personal items, what's going to the church, what's going to each of you."

"Yes."

"What he's set up here is called a *tenancy for life*. And it's conditional. Essentially, Robert, he's giving you the farm, if you want it, but—"

Miriam made an odd hum, interrupted. "Don't be greedy, Rob. Don't be like your father."

"But, Mom—" Bobby smiled happily, "I am. Like you've always said. I'm just like my father."

"Just wait a minute," the attorney said. "You're not to make this decision for thirty days. With the weekend, I'll give you until May 5th, okay?"

"That's fine. I'm still not sure I understand . . ."

"The farm, Robert, is yours, for as long as you live. Upon your death the ownership will be divided equally among your heirs, Mr. Brian Wapinski, Ms. Joanne Wapinski, and Ms. Miriam Cadwalder Wapinski. Also, the conditions state that you must keep open books, that for ten years, fifteen percent of the net profits you derive from the farm, no matter how that profit is derived, shall go to those here—five percent each. Let me read you a note that he wrote to Robert but that is for all of you to hear.

Dear Bob,

I know you will not sit upon your talents, nor will you bury them for safe-keeping, but you will set them to work for your good and for the common good. Take care of your brother and sister and your mother. Make the most of what you are, of what you have in your head and your heart, and of what I bequeath to you. You can do it, Robert. I know you can. Think of the possibilities.

Love,
Grandpa

Phone conversation, 10 April, Old Russia Road: "Bobby."

"Yes. Tony?"

"Yeah. You gotta come back down, Man. Things are brewin. We're goin back. Be here Monday. They'll have details. And we gotta get Ty. We gotta get him out."

"Out?"

"Okay. Over and out."

On the sofa Sara was nursing nineteen-day-old Noah, praying through her exhaustion that Noah would fall asleep and for once stay asleep. He'd become colicky, had been awake most days nineteen hours. "Who was that?"

"Tony."

"Oh. How is he?"

"He didn't say."

"I wish we could do something for him. And Linda."

"Me too. Do you want me to take Noah for a while?"

"No. He's comfortable. If he starts again, you could put him in the Snugli and hike over to CondoWorld."

"Sure."

Then on Monday, on the roof, sixteen-strong, half-sitting against the alley-side parapet, half on cardboard sheets on the tar and gravel. "Listen to this, Man 'Rather than leave the necessary number of guards with the captured soldiers, the NVA shot them through the feet so they could not escape.'"

"What is that?"

"Classified State Department Telegram. Signed by the U.S. ambassador. This is only three days ago, Man. See. 'NVA/VC Treatment of People in Recently Captured Areas.' Goina be a fuckin bloodbath, Man."

"Can I see that?" Bobby asked.

"Sure, Captain," the man said. "Let me show you one more line. Here, '... recount the following massacre: the vanguard of the convoy stopped for the night short of Phu Tu hamlet, probably about the same time the massacre of the rear was ending at the floating bridge. About a thousand people near the front ... VC ambush ... The group was cut to pieces, despite its obviously being mostly civilians....'"

Bobby looked at the photostat pages. They'd been re-marked unclassified, but otherwise the roof rat was right. Bobby read on.

> Ban Me Thuot ... The hamlet's PF and PSDF, with no outside help, held out under constant attack until two days after Ban Me Thuot itself had fallen ... enemy tanks rolled in then and shelled the church to rubble. All but a few of the surviving population had taken refuge, and died there....
>
> Later in the day [14 April], in a clearing, they were surrounded by about fifteen Motolova trucks that began driving at high speed through the crowd, the drivers apparently trying to kill as many people as they could ... fifty or sixty were killed....

Bobby held his head. It was nearly impossible for him to grasp the extent of the collapse, the horror. "We still going back?" The words came pained. He felt torn. Noah, Nam, High Meadow, tenancy for life, San Martin, roof rats, Sara, Saigon—where did his allegiance lie? He looked at the man with the documents. The others were quiet, still, staring at different angles into the early evening sky.

"If we could get there ..." Bobby began, stopped. "It's late but maybe not too late. Did they really get a hundred thousand?"

"That's the word. There's like five thousand down in San Diego ready to go. But it's falling so fast. Man, ABC reported like a week ago, that the war was already lost."

"If they could hold," Bobby said, "we could counterattack."

"Yeah."

"We all agree. We're going back."

"You got it, Captain. There it is."

After the meeting broke up Bobby and Tony remained on the roof, spoke quietly inside Tony's box. "I just don't fuckin believe it, Man," Bobby said. "That it could happen just like that. Like that."

"Yeah. I guess it can, huh? But they'll stop em. We'll go. Launch the counterattack."

"Hm." Bobby fidgeted, dug his heels into the tar and gravel until Tony tapped his leg indicating that was a no-no. "Anything more on Ty?"

"They got him on fraud, tax evasion. I don't know what else."

"I can't bail him out."

"I know. We're hoping they'll release him on a PTA, a promise to appear."

"Good."

"I'm really sorry about Grandpa."

"Yeah. He . . . he was like my—" Bobby's voice broke, "my dad."

"Yeah," Tony said. "I could see that. I been flippin out ever since he had the stroke. Really weird dreams."

"Really?"

"Yeah."

"I thought I was the only one having those."

"Oh, Man," Tony said. "I'm like haunted. Between this shit . . . Man, I lay down and I see em issuing us 14s or 16s but we don't have any ammo. And we're moving up. We're waitin for the onslaught. If they kill me, it'll be the first time in five years that I'll be at rest."

"Geesh." Bobby was shocked by the depth and intensity of Tony's feelings.

"Hey, go home to your wife and kid. If anything happens, we'll call."

On April 17th Phnom Penh fell to the Khmer Rouge. At Xuan Loc, twenty-four miles northeast of Saigon, the ARVN 18th Division reinforced with a regiment of the 5th and a "brigade" of the Airborne, had been battling first two, then four NVA divisions. Four more NVA divisions were sweeping toward Saigon from the south, two from the north and three from the northwest. The government had all but run out of tactical air support and the allied troops at Xuan Luc were down to their last rounds. Above San Martin, in the Old Russia Road cottage, with Sara sleeping on the sofa, Noah in his crib, and Josh snoring under the dining table, Bobby flipped TV channels. He'd watched CBS's report on the NVA massacre of South Viet Namese officials, and NBC's coverage of Kissinger's speech. To him, things were getting more and more disgusting. On ABC Howard K. Smith said we *should* give aid to South Viet Nam—the one hundred and first day of the *ad absurdum* and now moot debate.

"Sara, you awake?"

"Um-hmm."

"I think we should go back."

"Hmm?"

"We could sell this place. If you don't like it—after a year, we'll come back."

Sara sat up. "Bobby, what are you talking about?"

"I'd like to call Willings, tell him we're going back."

"To your grandpa's farm?"

"Um-hmm."

"Oh. I didn't think you wanted . . . " She leaned toward him.

"What do you think, Sara? Would that be a better place for Noah . . . "

Four days later Nguyen Van Thieu resigned as president of the Republic of Viet Nam. Suddenly, it seemed to Bobby, everyone was saying we should never have stopped the bombing. Kissinger was still requesting U.S. aid! Congress was still holding hearings on aid! The political-electronic absurdity increased. The roof rats, on the other hand, dispersed.

Tony called. "It's over, Man. There's no place to land."

Within days the local papers and local TV were covering the arrival of the South Viet Namese refugees at Hamilton Air Force Base. There was gallantry amid pathos. There was every imaginable emotion from anger and disgust to pride, from humiliation to indifference.

On the 29th, Bobby's 29th birthday, rockets rained down on the airports and into the city and a massive helicopter evacuation began pulling the last one thousand Americans from Saigon.

Then, on the phone, Tony. "It's over, Man. Mothafuck! Peter Jennings just announced, 'Viet Nam is now Red.' Hey, you know what, Man?"

"What?"

"It does mean somethin, Man. It means one fuck of a lot."

"Come up, okay?"

"I don't know."

"We're goin back, Tony. We're going back to Mill Creek Falls. To High Meadow. I called Willings. Come home with us."

Part III

HIGH MEADOW

October 1984

Back.

It is cold. I am chilled to the bone. My right thigh is stiff. The sky above is blueblack. On the horizon is Draco, the dragon, with its tail by the pointers of the Big Dipper. Toward me is Polaris and the W of Cassiopeia, and there is Pegasus, the winged horse created from the blood of the Gorgon, Medusa; Pegasus who transported Bellerophon into battle against the monster Chimera. To the east Leo is barely visible. The sky there brings first light.

Slowly I limp from the sugarbush down through the high meadow to the edge of the pond. I do not have the sustenance for winter nights in these hills the way I once had when I brought Linda to World's End . . . eleven hundred million eons ago. I am moving, going back to the barn. There is so much more to tell.

We entered a time of rapid transformation, a time without motion, a time of expansion and contraction, of rest, retreat, revival, of relief tainted with humiliation. The year 1975 began a time of great turmoil for veterans of the Southeast Asia war. For many it began the expatriation many others had been enduring. For America, though thousands of people spoke of putting that "dirty little war" behind us, '75 marked an acceleration, albeit muted, muffled, glitzed over, trivialized or Tinseltownized, of the fragmentation and polarization of our society. The preceding decade had stimulated our internal conflicts. Thesis had been crashed head-on into antithesis, forced toward synthesis, only to have '75 release the bruised and wounded to scatter, to separate, to fester silently, to reentrench and prepare for the coming rounds. For Bobby and me '75 began repatriation, and for Bobby it marked his awakening to the needs of the roof rats and the rest.

Climbing. The big barn looms before me. This was the heart of High Meadow. Squirrels have built a nest in the eaves and they scamper as I approach. Below, there in the shadows of the mouth of the tractor garage, is the forge. That first winter I lived below the big barn in a cubicle at the very back of the garage. I worked every day—alone mostly, not wanting to talk to anyone—setting up the forge, building it right into the barn's foundation, into the earth, adding first an archaic hand bellows, then an old motor, then three—a fan, a vacuum cleaner reversed, finally through belts and wheels geared up and up, the powerful motor from a discarded clothes dryer whirling a five-tiered turbo-charger into tubes and hoses, like a mad scientist's kid's Erector set, but powerful enough to melt steel or stone. I worked bare-chested before the furnace, searing my belly, my back to the opening that faced the pond, the wind freezing my sweat—me heating and banging, shaping and cooling, forging the long ornate hinges for the gate across the drive, trying to burn the toxins and anger and dreams from my mind.

Bobby came back to High Meadow in November of '75. It took all that time to sell his Old Russia Road house, Sara's car, and the office-mobile. Without even entering the farmhouse Bobby climbed to the cemetery. He carried Noah on his shoulders, the little guy wrapped like an Eskimo and supported by both of Bobby's hands. With Josh scampering in accompaniment, Bobby brought Noah to meet Pewel, grandfather and great-grandfather and nothing more or less than a simple stone set next to Brigita's. "Granpa, this is Noah Pewel Wapinski. Granpa, here's the plan. . . . "

I called Linda that night. What night? I don't know. Sometime later, sometime before. Before I arrived—I don't know—in December? I told her I could make it. I said, "I'm comin back, Babe. I'm comin home. I'm gonna make it." She said something like, "Make it, then come back," or "Prove it," or "I'll believe it when I see it." And I said, "Okay."

Ty did not come back with me. In May, Ty was released on a PTA but he split. They picked him up in June. The public defender led him through various legal steps, plea bargaining, swapping charges here for admissions of guilt there. In August he was sentenced to seven-and-one-half years in prison with the possibility of parole after three and one-half years.

The roof rats of San Jose did not come either—not yet—and some of them never because some never made it home. "Wildman" David Coffee left the roof, got a job, died of head injuries sustained in a motorcycle accident. Fuzzy Golan was killed attempting to break up a convenience store hold up. I don't know what happened to Big Bro Boyson. I don't know what happened to any of the others except Ty and Frankie "The Kid" Denahee, who told me about Wildman and Fuzzy in 1980, when he arrived at High Meadow.

Look in here. This is the main floor, the one Pewel fell to nine hundred million eons ago. Through the late seventies it changed greatly. That's the Pittsburgh machine for making the female joint in sheet metal duct work, and next to it is the Flanger. There's the Slitter, a roller-cutter that grasps and pulls through entire sheets, and back there is the sheet metal break. We may have been small-town backwater hicks but through Bobby we attained a certain level of technical sophistication. This electronic system can measure and record the thermal collection efficiencies of twelve separate panels simultaneously. At one point Bobby was experimenting with not simply flat, domed and parabolic collector shapes, and water and air as collector mediums, but with argon, helium and neon, and with thermo-syphonation tanks and photovoltaic ribbons. Step-by-step experimentation, maybe you'd call it R & D, attempting to understand How Things Work—perhaps that's what this is all about.

The sun is up. The landform, the natural south-facing bowl of High Meadow, acts as an immense solar energy collector. I am now in the barn office—we always called it Grandpa's office. I've laid my bedroll on the floor, been poking around. The office is intact, the files undisturbed. Bobby kept files on each and every vet—their stories, their interests, their participation in his programs—but he carefully coded every vet, numbers, and I think he destroyed the master list.

To us, at that time, the essence of the time could be summed up in the questions, What does Viet Nam mean? and, How does that meaning work on us? Was it horror? Was it a leaderless bureaucracy running a death machine? Was it gallantry? Heroism? Was it calling for the best, for the most noble cause, and getting the best? It was intense struggle, intense hardship, met with intense valor, perseverance and pride. To Bobby, to many of us, Viet Nam—as an experience, as a natural topographic region, as a political-ideological entity, and as a human culture—represented the best, the most beautiful nascent possibilities, and warm humanness; represented all this as a backdrop for the worst, for the cowardly, the horrific, corrupt, disenfranchised, and finally for the abandoned. Together, the experience, the nation, the best, the worst, had been set adrift in ancient and leaky trawlers to sink or float, to die, to be forgotten. But that is description, that is not meaning. That dirty little war. That foolish misadventure. Just made us the laughing stock . . . 'round the block, 'round the world. We could not yet peg it, could not nail it down.

24

"Happy New Year, Man," Bobby said. They could hear the peal of the midnight bells from St. Ignatius, and the Episcopal and Methodist churches.

"Happy New Year, Tony." Sara leaned in, hugged him, a buddy hug.

"Yeah," Tony said. He was quiet, bitter, dejected. Happy fuckin new year, he thought. They were in the living room of the farmhouse. Noah was asleep upstairs. Earlier Linda had stopped by with Gina and Michelle, had stayed only long enough to exchange wishes. "I'm headin out," Tony said. Then low, bitter, he quipped, "Three's a crowd."

"It's goina be a good year, Man," Bobby said. "I can feel it in my bones. I can really feel it. Tomorrow," he paused, "today I guess, I'll show you the plan."

"Yeah," Tony said. It was warm in the house, freezing outside, cold in the barn. "Right on." There was no enthusiasm in his voice. He slinked toward the kitchen.

"Tony." Sara stood like a schoolgirl with her hands and feet together. "We love you."

Tony snorted. He hadn't meant for her to hear it but she had. "Don't give me any of that second-grade California empathy crap."

"I'm not," Sara said. She was not offended. Tony's head was down, his eyes turned up. "I mean it," Sara said.

Tony sneered, then said, "Maybe Josh can come out with me."

"Sure, Man," Bobby said. "You wanta call your folks?"

"Naw. Might wake the girls. I can't believe she went out with Denham."

"Tony!" Sara's voice was laden with sympathy. "She didn't. Really. It's their group's party. She said you could have gone."

"Yeah. The monster and Miss Priss! Beauty and the Beast!"

"That story has a happy ending . . . " Sara began.

"Not when Beauty's lookin to be with Mister Rich Doctor."

"Screw the self-pity shit!" Bobby snapped. "Tomorrow. I'm goina show it to Sara tonight. Tomorrow, Man, we get to work."

Earlier that evening, after Linda had left, and left Tony in a funk, Brian and Cheryl and their children, Anton and Lara, had popped in for hot cider and Christmas cookies.

"Give me a week and I'll explain to you what I'm thinking," Bobby had told them.

"It's okay," Brian had said. Then he'd laughed. "But make us some money, huh? Two kids and Cheryl's not back to work . . . "

"I think it's going to," Bobby said.

Cheryl tried to hide her disappointment. Aside to Sara she said, "Why would anyone want to live out here?"

"I like the hills," Sara countered. "And the pond. We went skating earlier and it was lovely."

"You better be careful with that ice," Cheryl said. "There was a boy who went through on the Loyalsock this week. He got trapped under and drowned."

"Oh! I didn't hear about—"

"The ice just isn't thick enough yet."

"That's the river," Sara had said. "The pond's pretty solid."

"But even this house!" Cheryl wrapped her arms about herself. "It's so cold."

"We're planning to rebuild it," Sara explained.

"Well—" Cheryl shook her head slowly, "I don't know why. If you and Rob had just sold the place, we'd have the cash to move out of Miriam's guest house. You could sell it for a subdivision like the new one over in Hobo Hollow. Then we'd all be rich."

Bobby overheard her. "That would be one shot and gone," he said. "Let me develop this plan, make this place pay you something every year. Besides, it's like money in the bank. If it doesn't work, we can always sell it later."

Weeks earlier, months earlier, back to before they left California, Bobby had begun planning—game planning, financial planning, personal and business planning. It had gone slowly. The decision to split from his recent past had been made, yet the decision to step into his future had to be remade daily. What if it didn't work? What if he took this opportunity and blew it—not only failing but causing hardship for others, digging a hole he would not be able to refill in a lifetime? What if he made something bad, something evil?

With patience, using all his design ability, Bobby had created a framework, a five-year, open-ended plan. Yet despite his efforts there were major gaps and unresolved problems. High Meadow would be the base for Environmental Energy Systems—EES—which at this moment wasn't much more than a concept, and boxes of books, product pamphlets, technical reports and drawings. It would be a working farm, even if Bobby was not a farmer. It would be home—he had his family, his son to raise, his wife to cherish, and the house to rebuild. And High Meadow would be a gathering, a cause, an evolution of thought about energy, about veterans, about the self.

That was the design challenge. Financial planning was easier than planning a personal agenda, and that was easier than planning a code, an ethic for the times, a criterion of what presently was morally valid. "Values," he'd told Sara, "can be ethereal. They change with the society, with the times." He found he could not plot value projections in the same manner he once plotted income projections. To earn $30,000 a year in real estate commissions—the calculations had been simple. But how does one plan morality? Is it possible to project value goals? This year I will have 30,000 integrity points!

"Grandpa used to talk about living by a plan and a code," he reminded Sara. "That's the framework." Yet as he'd tried to define it, refine it, it had become clouded and obscure. How do things work? How do children develop? What's happened to the soldiers who fought in Viet Nam? What is the right way to live? Without a code could any plan, no matter how successful financially, produce the right, sustainable results? And if it did, would one know? And what were those "right" results? What is the final goal?

Even on paper it had become muddled, so Bobby had settled, temporarily, for Master Plan, Phase 1, Zero to Five Years; had settled, for one clamorous circuit of the carousel, one round with the calliope whizzing and banging, blaring and tooting.

Tony stopped, stared into the black overhead. He did not carry a flashlight. Beside him Josh too stopped, leaned lightly against Tony's leg. The temperature had continued dropping. On the pond the ice expanded, fractured. Cracks shot out, split the ice for two, three, five hundred feet, the sounds long and fast like rifles firing. Tony remained motionless. More fractures, more eerie, cracking shrieks. Tony did not turn toward the pond. Overhead, north, just above the high meadow ridge, he saw Draco, the Dragon—a small-headed dragon, he thought—with its long tail curled about the Little Dipper. To the west, over the spillway, he identified Orion, the Hunter, seemingly aiming from his shoulder star, Betelgeuse, a double-barreled thumper at Draco. Yeah, Tony thought. Get some. Get some, Man. Happy New Year. Happy fuckin new year. Fuck Denham. Right now, Man, she's probably unbuttoning his shirt. Screw the self-pity shit. New Year's Eve and they don't even have a beer! Not one fuckin beer. How the hell ken ya get fucked up without even one beer. Hot spiced cider!

Tony plodded forward into the dark shadow of the barn. He did not need to see. With one hand on the wood siding he edged downhill, into the wind, toward the tractor garage. His ears stung from the cold, his fingertips burned. Josh stayed next to him, bumping him every few steps. Tony reached down, ruffled the thick fur on the dog's back. Somehow, Josh allowing him to do that was reassuring. "Fuckin women," Tony muttered. "Playin games with men's minds. Bitchin. Bitchin they've been kept down and cut out. But shit, so have we. So's the average joe. They compare themselves with some wealthy motherfucker and call us chauvinist pigs. 'We love you, Tony.' Get off my fuckin ass, bitch. 'Why don't you come with me?' Sure Linda. You woulda shit your pants if I'd said yes."

Inside the tractor garage Tony worked his way to the forge. He'd dampened the firebox all the way down. Coals still smouldered and the stone and brick were warm. Josh nudged him. He grabbed the dog's fur, ran his hands over Josh's coat. "We could fire it up, huh, Boy? But that'd make a racket. Sara'd go through the roof if I woke Noah and Bobby'd have to come out and tell us to stop." Tony crouched, pushed Josh's jowls back, caressed the dog's ears. "I bet right now," he whispered, "she's licking his nipples." He stood, rolled his shoulders, thought to head back to his cubicle, his bunker. An immense cracking exploded from the far edge of the pond, blasted like artillery at him. He jolted, froze. Then whispered, "Tomorrow, Josh. Tomorrow 'we get to work'! Like what the fuck have I been doing all my life?"

"Can you envision it, Sar?" They were cuddled together, in bed, excited, energized by ideas, by New Year's resolutions, by plans.

"I think so," Sara said.

"We've got the start-up capital from the sale of the house. We'll probably never be in this position again."

"I understand the part about the house," Sara said.

"I've just made preliminary sketches," Bobby said. "I want to change the roof line a little, and drop the collectors between the rafters. Then we'll put the glazing on top of the rafters. The problem with most solar collectors is they're ugly. But if the installation is beautiful . . . if we can do it with this house, we could show it to people. It's really going to look sharp. Really."

"I believe you," Sara said. "I know you can do it. But . . . we're not going to rip the roof off—"

"Oh! No. Not till summer. Or late spring."

"Phew! I could picture us in here without a roof. And Cheryl'd be saying, 'I don't know how you can stand it.' "

Bobby chuckled. "You'd have to snuggle against me all the time." He pulled her closer.

"I'd do that anyway," Sara said. "But you're getting so thin."

"Naw. I've been gaining some back ever since we got here."

"How much?"

"I'm one fifty-five, now. Anyway, I want to ask Tony to take over the farm."

"You think he's reliable?"

"I've been thinking and thinking and thinking about those guys. In San Jose. I've been asking myself, what happened to them? Good men. Most of em. Did you know Tony was a platoon sergeant?"

"Are you going to ask some of them to live here?"

"All I know right now is I've got to do something. Put em to work."

"Building solar collectors?"

"Um-hmm. The whole works. Collection, control, storage. Retrofits. New construction. Whatever we can sell. Someplace along the line they gave up. Remember Granpa used to say, 'Never give up.' These guys learned to give up. They learned to be helpless. They can learn to achieve. I've got to show you it on paper. I can't keep it all in my head."

"Bobby, where are they going to sleep?"

"Well . . . maybe . . . in the barn . . . "

"Could you convert that old pig house . . . "

"Hey, the little barn! That's an idea. We could look at it in the morning. If . . . um . . . you know . . . like if we changed the roofline . . . I'm sure the foundation . . . then separate the length into cubicles . . . it'd be like the hootches we had over there. Like a low barracks or a bunkhouse."

"I could go back to work. Linda says the school system's expanding. But I'll need my Pennsylvania certificate."

"Me too. If Nittany Mountain will accept those courses I took in California, I think I'm only a few credits shy of my degree. And I've got to get my contractor's license. General and plumbing."

Sara laughed. "You mean you're going to be a plumber!"

"Yeah." Bobby chuckled.

"My husband the skinny plumber." Sara tickled him.

Bobby wiggled away, grabbed her hands. "And a roofer," he said. "If we're going to embed the collector arrays we'll need to be roofers, too."

"I could be a farmer's wife, a plumber's wife, and a roofer's wife all at once." Sara worked a hand free.

"And you could run the school. You could teach them everything they didn't learn in grade school. And everything they forgot."

"Ooo! All these men." Again Sara laughed.

"Yeah." Bobby laughed with her. Then he asked, "Do you remember what Granpa said about the self needing minimum maintenance? About being able to expand beyond one's self?"

"Um-hmm. Opening oneself to teach, to create, to love."

"How can you teach someone to expand beyond his or her self?"

"I'm not sure."

"But you know," Bobby said. "That's why you're such a good teacher. That's what you were teaching those spoiled brats in San Martin. That's what I hope you'll teach here."

By eight thirty the next morning Tony had the forge roaring and the first iron bar glowing. His shirt was off. Outside the temperature was five degrees Fahrenheit. Wind gusts buffeted, bringing in the cold wall, then the pressure backed up and the hot air about the furnace surged out—oscillating, purging like freezing baths and hot saunas except better because his activity was also purging, requiring 100 percent concentration on the furnace, the metal and the turbocharger. Even the artillery bursts of ice fracturing on the pond didn't divert his attention; even Linda was gone from his mind.

"*Hè*," Bobby shouted. He was bundled up in hooded sweatshirt, jacket, a scarf over his mouth and nose. "*Hè*." He shouted the Lenape word for hello, one of the few local Native American words he'd learned, found in a file tagged *Monsee-Lenape* in Grandpa's office. No response. Between the turbocharger, the furnace roar, the wind and the ice Tony didn't hear him. "Hey Man! Tony!"

Tony snapped his eyes over, then immediately back to his work. "Yo!"

"When you can, take a blow. I'd like to go over the plan with you."

"Be a while," Tony shouted. He did not divert his eyes.

"That's okay."

"We should fit the hinges on the posts," Tony bellowed. "That set's done."

"Looks great."

For a while Bobby stood watching Tony heat the bar then withdraw it, lay it on the old anvil and whale on it with the peen hammer, methodically flattening and forming the end of the thick bar into a hawk's talon—the one strap alone a week's work. Then he left, inspected the old pig shed, returned, watched Tony in his concentration. Finally he shouted, "I gotta show it to you."

Tony sighed, leaned back, withdrew the bar and laid it in the ash bin, then hit the blower switch. Immediately the turbo wound down, the roar of the furnace sank to nothing more than the creaking of the firebrick. Again the pond fractures could be heard. "You make coffee?"

"Yeah. And Sara made fritters with syrup."

"I gotta get these last two finished and the gate hung before it's time to set out the taps."

"Yeah. And more."

In the kitchen Bobby laid out parts of the plan. "The structural design of the solar collector is flexible. The more we learn, the better we'll be able to make them. Interested?"

"Hey." Tony shrugged. "If that's what you want, Man."

"We build one, sell it." Bobby could see Tony was not excited. "Build two, four, eight, sixteen. Sell em cheap. Get the venture rolling."

"Fine."

"And the farm's got to produce, too."

"That's not a problem."

"No, I don't mean the way it's been. You know that stuff you were doing for Granpa?"

"Yeah."

"Double it. Triple it. Sugarbush. Strawberries. Feed corn. Apples and pears. Maybe vegetables. Maybe some chickens."

"And alfalfa?"

"Yeah."

Tony looked to the side. "Get serious, Man. That'd take ten people."

"A whole squad, huh?"

Tony shifted uncomfortably.

"Maybe grapes," Bobby said. "Run em up the hill at the north end of the pond. Like they grow em in Sonoma."

"What the fuck!" Tony pushed his chair back.

"You were really getting into it, for Granpa. Getting inta those journals."

"One crop, Man. I just thought we could make money with strawberries. There's no fuckin ..." Tony peered around, through the hallway to the living room, through the doorway to the dining room. He didn't want to offend Sara or anger her by cursing where Noah could hear. "There's no fuckin way." His voice was low, dispirited; his eyes cast to the back door.

"Figure a way." Bobby was intense, leaning toward him. "You be in charge."

"It's impossible."

"Do it slow. Let it evolve."

"Where you comin from, Man?"

"Could you do it if you had ten people?"

"Who the fuck's goina—"

"Roof rats."

That stopped Tony short. His face came up, eyes suspicious.

Bobby broke the silence. "Better 'n sleepin on roofs?"

"Maybe."

"Vets. Only vets. You be in charge. It's time we took care of our own."

"Wait a fuckin minute." Tony slid his chair back to the table, leaned in, picked up his coffee. "In charge a what?"

"Our farm. Your squad. Your platoon. You teach em how to farm. Set em to work. Any income above expenses is for you and them to split. But it's got to be done right."

"How you goina get these guys, Man?"

"I don't know," Bobby said. "One at a time. How are *we* goina do it?"

"Well—" Tony put his cup down, gestured with his hands, "I could put the word out. The bartender at the White Pines, Holtz, he might— Hey, wait a minute."

"You're on, Tony," Bobby said. "We're looking for homeless guys. Down-and-out guys. Guys we can help. We want to bring em here. Let em help us while we help them. You with me?"

Again Tony eyed Bobby. "What about the solar collectors?" he asked softly.

"Guy wants to farm," Bobby said, "he farms. Guy wants to build, he builds."

"What's all that other stuff you got there?"

"This?" Bobby ticked the fat file folder on the table with his fingernail. "That's the . . . ah . . . program. Just ideas. It's not finished."

"For farming and building?"

"Yeah. And for rehabilitating the crop."

In the afternoon Bobby sat in Grandpa's office, alone. The roar of the forge two stories down was his background music, Sara's enthusiasm his sustenance. How had she phrased it? "Give a man a fish and you'll feed him for a day," she'd quoted the old proverb. "Teach a man to fish and he'll be able to feed himself for a lifetime." Then she had added, "But give him a cause and he'll learn to fish and he'll teach others to fish, too. That's how one learns to expand beyond the self. Give him a cause." With that she had kissed him and taken Noah back to the house, leaving Bobby alone with his clutter of ideas, books and reports, papers and outlines, flow diagrams and fiscal projections.

In his mind he had kicked things off exactly as he'd wanted. Now he was lost. He needed to envision the next step. Bobby restacked his program papers, began relaying them out. Taken separately, each general category was easier to understand. For a while he worked on questions: What do we want to do? How do we transform attitudes, develop minds, attain and maintain defensible, sustainable life positions? At the foundation of every economic system there are people—what microsystem is best suited to the High Meadow community?

Bobby shifted to the more concrete sub-subcategory of jobs—job counseling, portable job skills, training and apprenticeships, practice. Then to detoxification. Then to leadership. ("Even if they'd only made corporal, or PFC," he'd told Sara earlier, "they've learned something about leadership; and leadership principles are the same whether in the military, in business, or even within a family.")

Bobby returned to the overall outline. He felt stuck. How could he integrate all the parts? For a moment he envisioned a circle, but that was cumbersome. Then he saw a vertical cylinder made up of vertically separate and removable leaves, or files. That, he thought, would work but the cross-referencing would be a bitch. A computer might be able to do it, but you had to be a major corporation or a university to afford a computer. Stuck. He was stuck. On a clean sheet of paper he wrote, "Overcoming Stuckness—A Program for Veterans." Two stories down the high whine of the turbocharger slowed, lowered, ceased.

At the forge Tony was having trouble with the claw. His concentration was off. His back was cold, his front hot. He donned a T-shirt and rustic leather vest, returned to the forge. He'd been steamrolled. He'd been steamrolled in the kitchen, had been steamrolled by the last half decade. Even if he hadn't seen it coming, hadn't seen the steamroller at all, ever, he'd been flattened. He wanted to resist. He had no desire to *run* the farm. He didn't even want to talk. "Your squad. Your platoon." What was this shit? "Take care of our own." Hey, he'd done that. In San Jose. Hadn't he been the Catcher? But he'd barely been able to take care of himself. His stomach felt tight, bloated. He shut down the forge, went back to his cubicle, climbed into his sleeping bag, pulled the pillow over his face to shut out all light. "Fuck it, Man," he mumbled. "Fuck it. Fuck it. Fuck it." Again and again like a mantra, trying to drive the thoughts away, wanting to toke up, to drink, to mellow out, to vegetate with the boob tube, to dose himself out of the confrontation with Wapinski's challenge. Better en the roof. What the fuck does he know? Nobody asks you nothin on the roof. Steamrolled, Man. Just fuckin flattened. "If it doesn't work, we can always sell it." Don't go fuckin settin me up.

Bobby rose. How could he unstick himself? He needed a break. For some time he simply stared out the window at the graying sky and the fading landscape. Then he poked into old files, files he'd packed away more than five years earlier.

There was the *Newsweek* magazine from June 9, 1969, the issue he'd found in the airport on his way home. He glanced at the cover, flipped open to the article and photo of Dong Ap Bia, Hamburger Hill, and was swept with feelings—disappointment, excitement, revulsion, nostalgia. He wondered about the men who'd served, about Tyrone Blackwell Dorsey with whom he'd lost contact.

> The Nixon Administration, rattled by Congressional criticism over the battle, sought last week to disclaim responsibility for stepping up the pace of the war. . . . White House aides insisted to reporters that there had been no escalation of military operations . . . since President Nixon took office. . . . As with many arguments about the Vietnamese war, the truth in this case seemed to be . . . elusive. . . .

Again Wapinski was revolted by the article. In retrospect of Saigon's fall, he found it even more abhorrent. As he looked at the photograph, he thought of the sacrifices of so many; thought of the men who'd become, in an instant, his men; thought of the cause for which the sacrifices had been made. He skimmed the article. In the back of his mind he was thinking about stuckness, about Sara's "Give them a cause. That's how people learn to expand beyond the self"; about criticism, responsibility and achievement; about John Kennedy and Ted Kennedy. In 1963 President Kennedy had talked about "America's stake in Vietnam." He had said South Viet Nam was "a proving ground for democracy in Asia. . . . If this democratic experience fails . . . then weakness, not strength, will characterize the meaning of democracy" to Asians. Senator Kennedy had countered in 1969, "even before the battle was over" (*Newsweek*), by characterizing Bobby Wapinski's sacrifice and the cause for which he had made that sacrifice as an "outrage," as "senseless and irresponsible," as "symptomatic of a mentality and a policy that requires immediate attention."

Wapinski clenched his teeth. The political, the controversial, was mixed and muddled with memories of the repeated assaults, of the WIAs who'd been left behind. What had become of them? Bobby squeezed his eyes shut. To sacrifice, he thought. To expand beyond one's self. To expose one's self. The country had committed us, had given us a cause greater than ourselves and we expanded to a higher level, to defend freedom and establish democracy in Southeast Asia. Then the country withdrew its commitment, denied the cause, devalued the sacrifice and said, at best, we were only fighting for ourselves. That in turn caused the collapse of our ability to expand beyond our selves, caused us to shy from exposure, to isolate ourselves in our fears.

In retrospect Alsop, in that same six-year-old issue, had been right.

> What the Communist side is proposing, of course, is a Popular Front government, precisely patterned on the popular fronts established under Soviet sponsorship after World War II, as a prelude to total communist control. Hugh Trevor-Roper, the distinguished historian [described] . . . the process as consisting of three stages: "Government by a genuine coalition of parties of the left and left-center, government by bogus coalition, and a final stage in which the bogus coalition was transformed into a monolithic block . . . "

For Bobby there was a flash of clarity and the fog of neopolitical, historical interpretation.

Bobby took a new sheet of paper. "To become unstuck," he wrote, "make a decision." Again he paused. Perhaps this was not the right approach, he thought, but he realized it did not matter. To be stuck on theory or form was like attempting to decide, in the heat of a firefight, which weapon to use—thumper or M-16. One indeed might be superior but debate could make the point moot. There were people to care for. Practicality would have to dominate theory while theory was being developed.

He smiled, felt satisfied. Make a decision. That would work. In the outline under Personal he wrote, "Pursue Elation." That's important, he thought. "Without the pursuit of elation, responsibility, decisiveness, and self-authorization atrophy. Elation from expansion is the real aim of self-fulfillment. That is what satisfies. Being filled with our causes. When a cause is accepted a person will do anything, sacrifice anything. A man will assault a fortified enemy hilltop eleven times. This is grunt psychology. Debase the cause and you deny the pursuit of elation. Total debasement produces irresponsibility, indecisiveness, helplessness, stuckness, and resentment. In the wake come the disempowered, the indefensible, the unsustainable, the self-pitying, the dregs."

Again Bobby paused. The potbellied stove had cooled, the sky had blackened. He rose, closed the thermal curtains on the bay window. Then he sat, pondered for a few more moments, grabbed another sheet of paper. In block letters he wrote: "WAS THE CAUSE JUSTIFIED? WHAT REALLY HAPPENED? DID SOMEONE, SOMEHOW, GET TO OUR MINDS?"

The January thaw arrived almost as if it were scheduled. Beneath the snow cover rivulets trickled, in depressions puddles formed. The warm temperatures continued for ten days—above freezing each day, seldom dropping below twenty degrees at night. On Groundhog Day it rained. In the house Sara threw a "party" for Josh, and Noah, clinging to him, "cruised" for the first time. By midnight in the hill country the rain turned to snow and the snow stuck. At dawn, under a clear sky, Sara beamed to Bobby that the entire glittering, fluff-coated world was a winter wonderland.

An hour later Bobby and Josh walked to the tractor garage. Tony was up, out. The day was magnificent. "You've done it again, Lord," Bobby muttered quietly. "Absolutely perfect." He walked to the little barn, wished that Noah were with him, that his son could walk in the snow, or cruise holding Josh's thick hair. Surrounded by this beauty, with Sara and Noah secure, inside, Bobby thought, Dear God, you've given me this day, this beautiful day. I don't need any more.

Bobby caught up to Tony at the half-erected driveway gate. Tony had already bolted the second hinge set to the post and to the left swing section of the gate. Other than a perfunctory greeting and "Ready," "Yup," "Up," neither spoke. Carefully they lifted the section, positioned it, aligned the holes. Then Tony pulled the thick carriage-bolt pins from his pocket, wiggled them through the first two holes on top, the first two on the bottom, then tapped them in with a piece of two by four.

"Geez, Man—" Bobby stepped back while Tony tested the swing, "they look great."

"They work," Tony said.

"They're great, Man," Bobby said. "Those are classic."

"Hmm." Tony backed to where Bobby stood, admired his work. The bottom hinge strap on each side ended as a hawk's talon. The top on each side was a hawk's head. Tony had first rough-formed each, had then, with chisel and hammer, detailed each, the beaks and eyes perfectly smooth, the neck and upper wing feathers each individually lined and detailed. The talons too were lifelike.

"Where'd you learn to do that?" Bobby asked.

"Right there," Tony said. "They do look pretty cool, huh?"

"Yeah."

Again the temperature dropped, the slush froze. All through February it remained cold and Bobby tinkered in the barn, built an expanded siting table, while Tony worked in the tractor garage rebuilding the old tractor engine, or in the barn readying the sugar taps, or in the sugarbush cleaning the crowns and collecting wood for the evaporator. In March the second thaw came, the snow melted, the surface soils softened. Inches below, the ground remained frozen, impermeable to the melt and runoff. Paths turned to slippery ribbons of mud. Bobby became irritable. In contrast, in the sugarbush the leaves of autumn had fermented and so sweet was the smell of organic decomposition, sucking in the warm air, Tony became almost intoxicated. He began to feel he could live at High Meadow forever.

The pond surface became mushy, slick. Bobby cautioned Sara and Tony about potential thin spots, yet he still walked Josh daily onto the hardest section in the shadow of the south knoll. Again it rained and an inch of water covered the ice. Again it turned cold. The water froze crystal clear over old opaque ice. It remained cold for a week but now the sun hit the ice from a higher angle. Leaves had sunk and frozen in the new ice and their deep color absorbed sunlight which passed through the clear glaze. Beneath the surface the ice melted in perfect leaf molds—yet the surface remained intact. Bobby studied these miniature collectors, thought how beautiful, how powerful.

The third weekend in March felt like mid-May. Linda came with the twins to visit with their father, but Gina and Michelle were only interested in playing with Noah.

"If you want to go find Tony, it's okay," Sara said to Linda.

"I can't leave these two with you. You've got enough work."

"Actually, when they're here, Noah's easier to handle."

"Well, maybe, for a little bit. He's so angry with me. . . . "

"He doesn't like Simon Denham very much, does—"

"That's not really it, Sar. He's just packed with anger."

"Well, lately he's seemed pretty happy."

"Syruping, huh?"

"Um-hmm."

"He's always happy when he's doing that. I've got no idea why. It's not just a matter of being outside because he's had lots of outside jobs."

Tony was at the Sugar Shack unloading logs and branches from the tractor cart. He was not happy. He was bored, antsy, impatient. The oscillation in temperature should have produced treble the sap he'd collected. Things were no longer falling into place. The gate was finished. There was no more forge work. Seed had been ordered but it was too early to plant. He'd laid out an area for vegetables—nothing commercial, just a house garden—but the ground wasn't ready for rototilling. The fields weren't ready for turning, either, and there were no materials to begin the little barn project. Bobby had been spending so many hours tinkering in the barn that Tony felt invaded. And Bobby was insisting that he read something every day, something beyond farm journals. He'd fallen into the habit of reading the daily paper and was now convinced the Kremlin or the White House would soon blow half the planet to smithereens. He wanted to get his Harley from Linda's—why it was still there he didn't know. He had the urge to go, to move, split, change scenes—anyplace, anything, as long as it wasn't High Meadow, as long as no one asked anything of him.

"Hi Babe."

Tony started. He hadn't seen her coming.

"How ya doing?" Linda's voice was light, simple.

"Fine." He straightened his back, looked down from the cart. Linda's face caught the sun, her eyes glistened. "Where're the girls?" He asked. She looked prettier today than she had since he'd come back, but immediately he focused on himself, told himself she found him horrible, deranged, repulsive. He looked away.

"They're inside," Linda said. "Playing with Noah." She had not seen Tony like this in years. He was shirtless. His arms and shoulders looked sinewy, his stomach was flat, hard. "How's syruping going?"

"Ugh."

Linda interpreted his grunt as anger. "I saw Mr. Morris last week. Did you know he's looking for syrup?"

"There's not going to be much." Still terse.

"Why?" Soft, concerned.

"I don't know. It's the trees."

"Are they okay?"

"Um."

"It's been wet enough, hasn't it?"

Tony jumped from the cart, kicked a branch into the pile. "Old Man Lutz cut in a foundation for a new barn. I think he hit the upper aquifer. It's been draining steadily for months. You can see it. It's like a giant ice floe."

"Well, can't they stop it?"

"I . . ." Now Tony again looked at Linda's face—those hazel eyes, that auburn hair, those beautiful lips. How incredibly attractive she was, and how repulsive he felt. "I didn't connect it until you said that," he said. For a while they talked about the maples, about telling Adolph Lutz about the problem, about what if it killed the entire sugarbush. "Want to ride up on the tractor?" Tony asked, smiled, suddenly wanting this person, this one person, to think him attractive, to like him again. He felt excited and happy when Linda climbed up with him and sat behind him on the sap tank, and he felt rending pangs because he knew he could not meet her expectations. Then he thought, she's probably being nice so she can bring up the divorce.

The tractor rocked as it crossed from the dirt road to the high meadow to the path for the sugarbush. Gently Linda touched Tony's shoulders. It had been so long since they'd touched, but he knew his shoulders were disgusting, crusty with that acne that never went away, that had turned to two strips where his pack straps had once rested, two dry, rough, cracking patches.

"Bobby's thinking of putting in grapes down there," Tony said as the tractor rumbled north of the pond. "Use a windmill to pump the water up to a big tank, then use a drip irrigation system on the vines."

"Oh. What kind of grapes would you plant?"

"I don't know. He wants me to go up to some winery in New York. Find out what they're doing."

"Can you grow them here? With the way the winters get?"

"They do in Europe. And New York. I got a book . . . "

Trees. Grapes. Alfalfa. Linda listened, was easy to talk to. Maybe things were falling into place, he thought, but you just needed to show it to someone for you to realize it. At the edge of the sugarbush Tony loaded more cut branches into the cart. Linda bent to help. "Don't do that, Babe," he said. "You'll get your clothes dirty."

"I can wash them." Linda smiled.

Deep in the sugarbush they inspected the trees, the taps, the crowns. Then Linda hugged him as if for the first time ever and Tony could barely control himself. She tucked her head into his chest, rubbed her cheek very lightly against his nipple, then looked up for a kiss. Then they were kissing and feeling like a midsummer's day in Boston and thoughts and remembrances and fears were overridden by desire, love and lust. Then she said, "Wait."

Coming down from the sugarbush Linda sat between Tony's legs as he taught her how to drive the tractor, and nibbled on her neck. " 'They call me baby driver . . . ' " Linda laughed.

" ' . . . And once upon a pair of wheels . . . ' " Tony too laughed. He was hot, expectant.

Together they sang, " 'Hit the road and I'm gone . . . What's my number? I wonder how your engine feels.' "

At the Sugar Shack the afternoon breeze turned cool. Tony unloaded the last of the branches, drained the scant few gallons of liquid from the sap tank. Linda kept him at bay. Again he felt her rejection, revulsion. Again he saw how deserving he was of that rejection.

"Babe," Linda said tentatively. How hard it was for her to speak the words. "Do you want to come home?"

Tony looked at her, his eyes locked on hers, not with intensity but in pain. How he wanted to say yes. "No," he said. "Not yet."

*   *   *

For Tony things became more complicated. Bobby had asked him to talk to Adolph Lutz about the aquifer and to tell him that Tony would plant the lower thirty-six acres this year. Tony had agreed, had talked to Old Man Lutz without satisfaction. To make things worse, Bobby had begun to push Tony on "our agricultural master plan." Linda had come each of the next two Saturdays, had come into his bunker-cubicle, which even Bobby never entered, had cleaned it the first week!, made out with him, necked, petted, fondled without going "too far" the second; then didn't show at all on the third.

More confusion: Tony, with Bobby's help and the brand new EES Ford Econoline van, brought Tony's Harley back to High Meadow—ostensibly to be used to visit the New York wineries. But the Harley meant, for the first time since he'd returned, that Tony had the means of splitting, of avoiding, evading the assault forces of civilization.

More yet: the bartender/owner of the White Pines Inn, Aaron Holtz, had come up to tell them a guy named Dale Ivanov, an ex-brown water navy man, needed a place to stay. "Can I tell im to check you guys out?" "That's why we're here," Bobby'd answered. "He sometimes calls himself Ivanushka," the bartender said. "Ivanushka Durachok. It's some kind of joke." "Guy down and out?" Bobby'd asked. Holtz had answered, "Seems to be. Drinks a lot."

After Holtz had left, Tony had asked, "Where are you going to billet him?"

"That's a good question. We haven't really started the little barn."

"Not in my bunker," Tony said firmly.

"Ah, right. Do you think on the main floor . . . "

Bobby turned the big three-oh. April passed. He paid the capital gains tax on Old Russia Road and suddenly found himself with much reduced funds. May came and went. Ivanov did not show. Still, in Bobby's mind, the venture had begun. Bobby tinkered with solar collector plate designs, built three, mounted them on the barn roof—asking everyone who came for their reaction, their first impression—searching for something aesthetically pleasing, efficient, lightweight, cheap. He subscribed to the National Technical Information Service and was swamped with documents and data; his research advanced in leaps and bounds. He made trips to Pittsburgh, Williamsport and Harrisburg. He found potential suppliers everywhere. In Scranton he found a shower-door company that would make aluminum extrusions to any specifications, in any color, with any finish he wanted. He continued to experiment with materials; he set up the first test stations, the first assembly table.

At the same time he busied himself fixing parts of the old farm house—attempting to keep the lid on the can of worms he was certain any major renovation would open. He felt guilty if he worked for twelve or ten or even seven hours in the barn without returning to the house to relieve Sara—even if only for a few minutes—from the frustration of caring for a one-year-old. He postponed the house roof work because he wasn't satisfied yet with the collector design. Then the well pump burned out and needed replacing, and a spring storm washed out the lower drive. Bobby and Tony spent two days cutting swales, installing drainage and a new culvert, and regrading the drive. Then the refrigerator went, then the clothes washer, then the upstairs bath drain pipe sprung a leak and the ceiling in the downstairs hall collapsed, and suddenly the after-tax capital from the sale of Old Russia Road, the start-up capital for the new venture, seemed inadequate, minuscule compared to the projected master plan. The barn became Bobby's refuge. The plan, the program, the Grunt Theory of Psychology, and The Code were all put on hold. There was one and only one concern—sell a cash crop.

"Please come this way," Bobby said.

"Into the barn?!" the woman said.

"My office is upstairs," Bobby said.

"You understand we're only looking," the man said. "We're exploring our options."

"It would be foolish if you weren't," Bobby said. He led Mr. Jasper Vertsborg and Ms. Ellen Louwery-Vertsborg, husband and wife, into the barn, across the main floor to the rustic elevator Tony had built for Pewel.

"You don't keep any animals?" the woman asked.

Bobby chuckled. "Only Josh and Tony."

Neither Jasper nor Ellen responded. He was less than five seven, and frail. She was his height, taller in heels, about his weight. They were exploring the possibility of purchasing an old home in the Lutzburgh section of town. Jasper had just signed a three-year contract with the Mill Creek Falls Board of Education to fill the newly created position of school psychologist. Ellen, who was a children's clothes designer, had just leased the small building on Third Street that had been Pete's Barbershop. "This is quite a contraption," Mr. Vertsborg said as the small wooden platform with the single handrail slowly rose. "Does your insurance company know you don't have it fully enclosed?" He didn't give Bobby a chance to answer (Bobby thinking, Thank you. What insurance company?) but continued, "Someone could fall off. If they fell from here, they'd be killed."

"Yes," Bobby said. "I guess. We use the lift mainly for materials. One of my men is building a set of regular stairs."

"That's good," Jasper said. Then, as they entered Grandpa's office, "Oh! This is very pleasant. What a nice view. I didn't realize your pond was so large."

"Please," Bobby said. "Sit down. Let me ask you a few questions."

For half an hour Bobby asked questions about the house they were considering. He knew the house. It had been the home of his fourth-grade friend, Bobby Conner. He asked about the old apple tree with the tree fort in the side yard and told Jasper and Ellen about the apple wars he and Bobby Conner used to have with Mickey Turley and Bobby's brother, Brian. "Yes. Well . . . " Jasper gave Ellen the high sign.

Bobby knew he was losing them. "Let me come out," he said. "Let me draw a plot of the property, take some pictures and measurements. I think with the proper insulation that house could be eighty percent self-sufficient. Particularly . . . you know the way the back of the house has those two inset porches . . . "

"They remind me of my aunt Millie's house in Scranton," Ellen said disdainfully. "All they need are clothes lines running out to the trees and a couple of old biddies yakking between floors."

"Picture that entire volume as a three-story greenhouse," Bobby said. "It would unite the floors."

"Hmm! That might be nice," Ellen said.

"Put in a terra-cotta floor. Or maybe slate," Bobby continued. With his hands he shaped the forms in the air. "Lay it in six inches of concrete over a foot of crushed stone to create a giant heat sink."

"Um." Ellen glanced at Jasper as if to go.

Bobby rushed on. "And even though it's practical," he said, "it's also elegant. Think of it at night. Two and a half stories of glass, a glass canopy, the night crystal clear, the stars twinkling. Because the glass is thermo-pane you can actually have . . . oh, an orange tree, some potted palms . . . "

Now Ellen was interested. Bobby talked on, explaining the workings of an advanced Trombe wall system, how it worked as a massive collector, how its heating and cooling function could be expanded by encasing pipes and pulling off and storing heat in a huge basement water tank. The more he spoke, the more excited he became. Finally Jasper said, "Well, go ahead. Go out there. Work up a plan for us. And a price. By components though. We might not be in the position to do everything at once."

After they left Bobby was riding on air. "Sar, guess what?! I think we've got our first job. And it's a big one. We'd need a crew of five, at least, to do it right." And to Tony, "We could make enough to buy a cement mixer and the sheet metal break I was telling you about. This could really get us started."

Bobby set to work. For the Vertsborgs Bobby built the most elaborate model of Bobby Conner's old house. Then he constructed the modular changes he would propose and he placed the model on the siting table. Carefully he tested the orbital track lighting to see not only how sunlight would hit the roof and walls, but even how furniture would cast shadows within a room or at what time on any day sunlight would enter the bedroom and hit the eyes of old sleepyhead. Bobby then priced out the materials, estimated the labor, and tacked on a minuscule profit margin.

This was to be EES' first renovation and in Bobby's mind it had to be a showplace.

> Roll me over, lay me down,
> And do it again.
> Oh this is number two,
> Roll me over, lay me down,
> And do it again.
>
> Roll me . . .

Softly Sara said, "What's that racket?"

"Um?" It hadn't awakened Bobby.

"Listen. Someone's singing. Is that . . . it doesn't sound like Tony."

"God." Bobby propped himself on an elbow. "What time is it?"

"Three thirty," Sara said.

From outside, at some distance, came, " . . . this is number four and I'm knocking on her door. Roll . . . Hey! Anybody home? Oh geesh. Oh geesh!" Then quiet.

Bobby did not want to get up. He'd worked till one on the model greenhouse, creating openable bottom windows and roof vents—important in the summer for cooling. Sara, exhausted from a sleepless night with Noah, who had had a bad reaction to his second DPT shot, didn't want to get up either.

Josh began barking. From outside, closer: "This is number seven and I'm at her little heaven. Roll me . . . Son of a bitch! Wapishkis! Is thish Wapishkises? Thish is Ivan . . . Oh Geesh! Ivanushka . . . Ha! Hahaha! Ivanushka Durrag . . . Durreg . . . Oh geesh! Ha! Durachok. I need . . . Ha! help."

In his bunker cubicle Tony sat on the edge of his cot. He was angry, frightened. He did not turn on a light, did not flick on his flashlight. For months, at night, since shortly after those weekends in March when Linda had come, he had been expanding and reinforcing his bunker. He was not sure why. It was as if he were being directed by an outer force. Perhaps, he thought, it was because of all the nuclear freeze material he'd been reading. A bunker would be necessary to protect first against the nuclear storms the war would unleash, then the initial fallout, then the roving bands of starving survivors.

Tony had first pushed the back wall of his cubicle back three feet. Then he'd erected shoring and a false wall. Nightly, behind the false wall, he bored away at his three-foot-by-two-foot tunnel—first level with the tractor garage floor, then angling downward and back, under the barn foundation, toward the east ridge. There he'd begun to carve a room. "Fuck," he'd muttered to himself in the throes of digging and shoring, "any asshole can see they're on a course to fuck it all up. For good. Motherfuckers don't give a flying leap. They got their bunkers. Kremlin's building an ABM system and their bunker's twenty stories deep. Plan, Tony had thought. I'll show him a master plan. Tony tried to make two feet each night, picking, shoveling, chipping, at times using the big Milwaukee drill with a three-quarter-inch masonry bit.

On his cot Tony heard the commotion, the singing. He heard Josh bark. He was unarmed. His thoughts were barely coherent. It would be easy to slip out, to ambush. He needed to continue the work on his bunker. He could go down the tunnel, bring out another bucket of chippings, load it into the tractor cart. It had been easy dumping the chippings each morning before anyone rose, turning some of it in with the high meadow, some in with the lower thirty-six, using some out along the drive to reinforce the sides where the danger of washout was greatest. And Wapinski didn't care, didn't notice. He was completely absorbed with his Vertsborg project. The only real problem was the tunnel had again set off Tony's dreams, nightmares. Nightly, after finally falling asleep, exhausted from farm chores during the day and chipping and shoring at night, Tony woke to the smell and feel of the rotted corpse breaking, being dragged over him. He did not wake in terror. His heart would not be pounding, preparing him to flee, but thumping, glubbing, pushing thick volumes, a slave, a resigned, depressed, manic indentured servant.

But this! This noise! This singing! In the dark Tony tied his boots, edged to the thick door he'd made, ostensibly to keep out winter cold. Quietly he unbarred the door, opened it on well-greased hinges, shut and locked it behind him. His cubicle had been stuffy, airless. The bunker room at the end of the tunnel would be worse. Once it was full size, he told himself, he'd begin work on ventilation. Maybe even a well. From the tractor garage he peered into the night.

" . . . Durreg . . . Oh geesh! Ha! Durachok. I need . . . Ha! . . . help. Geesh. Oh God, I'm drunk. Wapishkish? Oh God. Drunker en a fly in a vodka vat."

Dale Ivanov was rotund, chalk-white, flabby. He had pale blue eyes, long, wild blond hair, a brushlike mustache, perfect but unbrushed teeth. In the kitchen, before he said two sentences, with Josh sniffing his leg, and Bobby excitedly thinking he could help, Ivanov blew lunch onto the kitchen table and chairs, onto Bobby's legs, onto the floor, splattering walls and cabinets as high as Bobby's shoulders. Then Ivanov whirled. Bobby reached out to stablize him, hesitated, reached but missed, and Ivanov collapsed out cold amid the puke and stench.

"Bobby," Sara called, hushed. "Is everything okay?"

Muted. "Um-hmm."

"Did he—"

"Um-hmm. I'll clean it up. Go back to bed."

"I can help."

"Don't—" Bobby began. His diaphram lurched, he caught the motion, stifled it. "Don't come down, Sar. I got it."

It was dawn before Bobby finished. He'd swabbed and disinfected the entire room, he'd cleaned Dale Ivanov and had laid his pallid flaccid body on a blanket on the floor. Bobby'd bagged the towels he'd used for cleaning and put the bag out back. Then he'd gone up and showered and scrubbed himself raw, then returned and made the day's first pot of coffee.

"What died?" Tony looked at the body. "Oh."

"Dale Ivanov." Bobby looked at the blob of a man on the floor. "Our first new vet."

"Um," Tony uttered somberly.

Then he looked at Bobby and let out a tiny chuckle. Bobby stifled a laugh. Tony rocked back, laughs forcing themselves out in bursts between tight lips. Bobby hunched, hands on his thighs, laughing loudly. "You shoulda seen im"— now both were laughing uproariously—"he wobbled . . ." (God, it was so good to laugh) " . . . said something . . . then . . . gooooshh! And BAM!" Bobby flopped his arm over like a tree falling. "I haven't seen anything that disgusting since Granpa found me in a gutter downtown. . . . "

A week passed. Ivanov was set up in a corner of the main floor of the big barn. He, like Tony, came into the house for his meals. At first he was contrite, quiet. "Man, I'll never forget this," he said to Bobby over dinner. "You really got me out of a jam. Thanks, Man. Thanks."

Daily he became more talkative. In the house, before Sara, even before Bobby, he was polite, almost formal. But in the barn, in the tractor garage, he was brash. "Man," he spouted at Tony, "I don't know who done it. Man, I was down there at the White Pines. Behind it, you know?"

"Yeah." Tony was suspicious.

"There was this great big fat broad down there. A real idiot. Shee-it, I was already drunk. I didn't give a shit what she looked like. I just wanted to get my dick wet. That's the thing, right?"

"Yeah," Tony said. He didn't like Ivanov, didn't like and didn't understand Ivanov's self-important, self-assured manner.

"Man, I'm fuckin away on this fat bitch. Jessie somethin. I don't know if she even knows her name."

"Big strong girl?" Tony asked.

"Oh Man, was she strong. Man, it took all my strength to pin her. Oh, but, Man, she loved it. She's moanin'n groanin'n buckin like a racehorse. I'm fuckin my brains out. And somebody musta called the cops. Man, I grabbed my bottle and cut a chogie. There's like three bubble-tops zoomin in, Man. Lights. Sirens. Shee-it. I didn't do nothin illegal. I humped up through them nigger houses. Man, I walked right through that nigger section. I'm scared, Man, but I'm drunk. I got my bottle by the neck, ya know?"

"Um."

"I figure any nigger try en butt-fuck this dude, he's in for a world a hurt. Right?"

"Yeah. I guess."

"You ken fuckin bet on it, Man. Next thing I know, Man, I'm so fuckin far out in the boonies . . . I'm singing my fool head off. And I remember . . . Shit, I don't know. Ha! I don't remember. Somehow, next thing I know is I'm sleepin it off on the floor in there and I open my eyes and some gorgeous dollie's washin dishes at the sink and her tight little ass is packed in these jeans wigglin and twitchin . . . What's the matter, Man?"

No response.

"Tell me you wouldn't fuck her."

"I'm goin up the north end of the pond," Tony said. "Comin?"

"Uh . . . " Ivanov shrugged his shoulders. "Hey, I'm just kiddin, Man."

"Yeah," Tony said. Then, "I need to figure out a terracing plan. For grapes. See if we can bench it without retaining walls. Just cut it. You comin?"

"Ah . . . ah . . . Nah. Bobby said I could work in the barn."

"Um."

"Hey. You ever fuck anybody in your bunker?"

"I"— Tony stared at Ivanov —"fuck over anybody who tries to go in."

"Vertsborg. Jasper Vertsborg," Bobby said into the phone.

"There's no one in the school," the female voice said.

"Yes," Bobby said. "I know. He's the new school psychologist they've hired. Doesn't he have to come in during the summer? Set up his office, or something?"

"I don't know anything about a Doctor Vertsborg," the woman said. "Perhaps you should try the Board of Ed number."

Bobby was exasperated. He'd been trying for four days to reach the Vertsborgs. At first he'd thought nothing of the no-answer at their home phone. By the third day he'd become concerned. He had added a heat-loss analysis to his presentation and he wanted to explain all the facets and options he'd produced. He drove on to Old Pete's Barbershop. Work had begun on the store, but no one was about. To be so ready, with such a superior package to present, and to be in limbo was maddening. He'd been able to sell Aaron Holtz on a four-collector array for the roof of the White Pines Inn. That'd be something. It would preheat the well water for the dishwasher so the electric elements wouldn't have to bring the temperature up from its constant fifty-one degrees. But it was a tiny job compared to the Vertsborg project. Bobby wanted them both. And he wanted to put Dale Ivanov to work.

That night at dinner Ivanov said, "I'd be real happy to help. But I don't want to handle the glass."

"That's not a problem," Bobby said.

"I'm just afraid for my hands," Ivanov said.

Tony looked at Dale's pudgy hands, at the stubby fingers. "What's with your hands?" he asked.

Ivanov held his hands before his face, palms toward him, fingers wriggling. "These are my ticket to fame and fortune." He smiled broadly, resumed eating, waited, wanting someone to ask. Then, seeing Sara eyeing him approvingly, he went on. "I'm a musician. I'm probably the best bass guitarist in the East."

"Oh!" Sara was thrilled. "Can we hear you play?"

"See, that's the problem," Ivanov said. "When I got in some trouble last time I hocked me git-ar." He laughed. "I need six hundred bucks to get it out."

"Six hundred!" Tony straightened. "For a guitar?"

"Oh, it's probably worth five times that," Ivanov said. "I was with the group that opened for The Stones."

"Is that right!" Bobby was as enthralled as Sara.

"That's why I was drinkin that night," Ivanov said. He hung his head in repentance. "If I hadn't found a brother vet . . . Man, I'll never forget what you did for me."

"Aw geez, Dale," Bobby said. "Really. Don't think about it. You'd have done it if it'd been one of us."

Tony coughed. Slid his chair back, coughed into his fist. He stood, turned away, turned back, indicated something had gone down the wrong way, turned away again.

"Tony, you all right?" Dale sprung to his feet.

Tony waved him back. He slapped his chest. Took a short breath, cleared his throat. "Yeah," he rasped out. His eyes watered.

" . . . when I'm on my feet again . . . " Ivanov was saying.

Another week passed. Bobby convinced himself the Vertsborgs had gone on vacation, taking the long Fourth of July weekend. Ivanov shadowed him everywhere, chatted constantly, ostensibly assisted him with the four collectors for the White Pines. For Bobby, Ivanov's inane banter was an amusing break.

"Listen to the frogs," Ivanov said one warm evening as Sara (she'd cleaned the kitchen and put Noah down for the night) joined the men on the back steps. "It's like they're in complete command of the farm. Just listen to that croaking concert, that raucous reverberation."

"You could write a song about them, huh?" Sara said sweetly.

"Yeah," Dale said. "It really takes me back. When we were young, my brother and I would walk in the fields and search for frogs in the spring when it was wet and lizards in the summer when the fields were dry, when they were parched by the sun. This was in Ohio, almost down to Kentucky. That's where I grew up. My brother'd remember."

"Does your family still live there?" Sara asked.

"No. They've gone," Dale said. "I remember one time following an old creek bed, late one summer, following it up to the hills. Nick had a new bow and two new arrows. It may have been his birthday. We were after rabbits. Nick wounded one. That ol' rabbit gave out this terrible cry, like a baby bein hurt. And it tumbled into a thicket. We couldn't find it. We lost the arrow too. It was the last arrow we ever lost and the only rabbit. After that, Man, we only hunted lizards and frogs and those by hand."

"Where's your brother, now?" Bobby asked.

"Beats me," Dale said. "When I got back they didn't want nothin to do with me."

"I know what you mean," Bobby said.

"Yeah," Ivanov said. "This is really somethin here. I was listenin to the frogs last night. I was trying to recapture that feeling I had but I've been removed from it too long. I could only recall, not recapture. And that's different. The voices of the frogs are the only thing that seem not to have changed. Their voices and the moon, maybe."

"Oh Dale," Sara said, "that's beautiful. You really should write a song about it."

"Yeah," Dale said. "Maybe. I'd call it 'High Meadow.' "

The next day Bobby paid Tony and Dale Ivanov and Ivanov convinced Tony they should give Bobby and Sara a break and go to the White Pines for dinner and some beers. By eight Dale was tipsy, by nine loud and obnoxious, by ten in his first scuffle with a Jappo-biker that Tony dispatched with a single leg sweep. When the biker returned with two friends, Aaron Holtz threw them all out and the Catcher in the Alfalfa ended up pounding one guy's head into the pavement while the other two kicked his sides and Ivanov ripped the plug wires from the three Jap bikes and somehow started the Harley—when he'd taken the key Tony had no idea—then waited for Tony to temporarily maim the other two, gain enough time to break contact and retreat.

At breakfast the next morning Ivanov raved about Tony's strength, Tony's fighting ability. "You shoulda seen im! These three guys were giving us the evil eye, ya know? Tony just lit into em. Man, I'd follow that guy anywhere."

Later, alone, Bobby confronted Tony in the tractor garage. "What the hell's this fighting shit?"

"I didn't start it," Tony said.

"You can't go hitting somebody because they give you the evil eye." Bobby was angry, tired, acting like a tired father with a nine-year-old son.

"Forget it, Man." Tony clammed up.

"Damn it. I don't want to forget it," Bobby snapped.

"It'll never happen again." Tony was tense, defensive, angry.

"Fuckin better not!" Bobby stormed away.

Three days later, over dinner, Ivanov gave Sara a sheet of paper. "I'm going to dedicate it to you," he said.

"Wha . . . " Bobby looked at Sara reading.

" 'High Meadow,' " Ivanov said. "The song about a man trying to recapture feelings he had as a boy. I'm never going to forget you. And Sara. All you've done . . . "

"Bobby . . . " Sara nodded at him. Then to Dale she said, "This is very good." Again she looked at Bobby. Bobby shook his head. Sara handed him the lyrics. "I think you should say it now," Sara said.

Bobby cleared his throat. Glanced at Tony, at Sara, then looked at Dale. "Okay," he said. "Dale, we'll lend you the money to get your instrument out of hock. You can pay us back a little from each gig."

Ivanov's appreciation was excessive.

"I'm glad I finally caught you," Bobby said into the phone. "How was your vacation?"

"We haven't been on vacation," Jasper Vertsborg answered.

"Ah . . . Oh. I've finished the redesign of the Conner house. I think you'll be impressed. The greenhouse is truly elegant. By shifting the staircase, the dining room flows in—"

"We're not sure about a two-story greenhouse," Jasper said.

"Let me just show it to you," Bobby said quickly. "I've built a detailed model and it's on the siting table right now. You can see exactly . . . "

"Mr. Wapinski, we've changed our minds."

"You've changed . . . "

"Yes. You knew we were just exploring our options."

"Of course. So at least look at it. It's really beautiful."

"Well, you know they're developing a new country club—Whirl's End . . . I'm certain you already know—"

"Whirl's . . . No. No, I don't know."

"Oh, it's going to be fabulous. Ernest Hartley's one of the partners. It's just above the section they call South Hill, or New New Town . . . "

Bobby had to think fast. "Then you're going to build?" he asked.

"Yes. The streets should be in this fall. We're going to build in the spring."

"Then let me design it for you," Bobby said.

"Oh." Jasper Vertsborg laughed amiably. "We've already found a splendid architect. Barnett and Robins. You've probably heard of them. They're the best in the Northeast and . . . "

Bobby heard no more.

"How many gallons of syrup did you end up with?" Linda asked. She was in the tractor garage with Tony. Bobby was in the house, making phone calls. EES did not yet have a separate line to the big barn. Sara, the twins, and Noah were on a "nature hike" to the apple orchard.

"Less than forty," Tony said.

They were in the same state of gentle ambivalence that had generally characterized their relationship for the past seven months.

"Are the trees okay?"

"Seem to be."

"Then Mr. Lutz . . . where he broke . . . "

"I don't know. Maples need lots of water. Maybe that was a different seam. Or maybe just the top. Maybe the trees reached deeper but they needed the whole spring."

"Oh. I hope it comes back." Linda moved closer to where Tony was installing a new oil filter. His hands were black and shiny. "What about the strawberries?"

Tony looked at her. A dark feeling descended upon him. His tone changed. "I'm not making squat, you know."

"Huh?" Linda was taken aback. She had lost six pounds and she'd hoped Tony would notice.

"That's what this is about, isn't it?" Tony tightened the can filter, cleaned the oil smear from the can and the drippings from the frame below.

"What what's about?" Linda was hurt, defensive.

"This 'how much did we make' stuff."

"I just asked because I—"

"You know what Ivanushka says?" Tony didn't give Linda a chance to respond. "He said his wife says she lived it more than him."

"Lived what?" Linda assumed the crossed-arm stance she used to scold the twins.

"His craziness," Tony blurted. "His combat schizo shit."

Linda squinted, pursed her lips. "Where is this coming from?"

Tony turned to her. He was leaning forward, one hand out as if ready to jab. "Look. When this place starts making money, I'll give you my share. I don't give a shit about money. I owe you. I know. I know you pay everything. Or maybe Denham helps—"

"Denham!" Linda yelled.

Tony clammed up.

"Is that what you think? You think I've come here for *money*?! You think Denham gives me *money*?! You . . . you . . . " Linda held her tongue. Then she blurted, "Your daughters' daughters will live with your psychosis long after you and I are gone."

That night Aaron Holtz called the Wapinskis. "Bobby . . . "

"Speaking."

"Holtz here."

"How you doing, Aaron?"

"Good. Hey, this Ivanushka guy . . . You give him some money?"

"Yeah. To get his guitar out of hock."

"You can kiss it good-bye. He just left with some bimbo. They're headin for the Jersey shore."

"What?!"

"You might catch im. They were in a big brown Olds with a dented right front fender. Headlight's cocked out."

"Shit."

"You want me to call the cops?"

"Naw. Thanks Aaron. I'll . . . ah . . . call . . . "

25

S ummer passed, autumn came. The gloom at High Meadow was palpable. On the morning of Saturday, 30 October 1976, in the tractor garage, Bobby ordered Tony to pack.

"Fuck it, Man," Tony said. "Don't mean nothin. Give me a couple a days."

"No. That's not what I mean." Bobby's head ached. As things had deteriorated, disillusionment had turned into disappointment with himself. He was about as communicative as the cold forge.

"Fuck, Man," Tony grumbled. "It's goina take a few days. I got things here."

"Pack a ruck," Wapinski said. "Field pack. Knapsack. Whatever you fuckin Marines called em. There's one in the shop. We're movin out in an hour."

Bobby scowled, left, returned. "There's rations there too. Three-day resupply."

The day was crisp, clear. They barely spoke. It was a patrol of two. Tony was acquiescent, pliant. He'd seen Bobby's enthusiasm die and

Bobby's despair had in turn left him without hope, with nothing but his final-bunker mentality. He had harvested lackadaisically in the attitude of "What the fuck for? To give her money for new dresses to impress Denham?" But he had not given up completely. He'd achieved a state of minimal subsistence, with one and only one, cause. By the time Gina and Michelle entered first grade, Tony's bunker room was ten-by-ten-by-seven and was shored up with every scrap of pipe, beam and post he could scavenge from every corner of the farm.

They dropped to the pond, picked up the knoll trail through the orchard, up to the cliff edge where they paused to scan the pond. They descended to the spillway, crossed the dam, climbed the back trail, pushed on, scrambled over the old stone wall in the woods, crested the ridge into the sugarbush, into territory Tony knew intimately. Bobby did not stop, slowed only to allow a pair of squirrels the right of way in their trek across the wood. Tony looked out to the high meadow, to the tractor road he'd improved. At the far edge the sugarbush gave way to scrub pines, ash and deformed beech, which grew in the shallow soil above the rock ledge. This gave way to the barren crest rock that led to the gap.

Tony did not know of the Indian ladder, the hand and footholds in the rock face. Still he followed without question. The movement, with direction, with purpose even if he did not know the purpose, charged him. On the gap floor stagnant pools rimmed with ice looked lifeless. They crossed quickly as if crossing an exposed rice paddy, then ascended into the forest of virgin eastern hemlocks and picked up the narrow and ancient Lenape trail that meandered under the 150-foot trees.

"This is the cathedral." There was reverence in Bobby's voice. He led slowly, paused for full minutes. His concentration was returning. Occasional sun rays filtered in but the cathedral was dim. At the trail spur Bobby whispered, "Tonight we'll come back. NDP there." Quietly he moved on. Twenty minutes later at a small, once-cleared site Bobby de-rucked. "We'll set up here," he said quietly. "This is where the survivors of the Pennamite War hid. Recon the north and west. I'll check out the east."

An hour later Tony returned. Clouds had begun to form. Crispness gave way to rawness. "Sit rep, negative," Tony said quietly.

Bobby nodded. He had cleared a small sleeping area, had cut a few branches and made a tight, low lean-to.

"Want me to clear an area for a campfire?" Tony asked.

"No. No fire here. Relax. I'll be back in a bit ... "

Bobby disappeared like a spirit. At first Tony sat back, rested, but immediately felt antsy. He fiddled with the backpack he'd taken from the barn, dug inside, pulled out a can of soup, opened it, drank it cold. His anxiety rose. He turned at every crinkle of leaf, at every woodpecker's drumming, every creaking branch in the light breeze. Then he rose. He could not see more than a few yards into the woods. Quietly he cleared the low brush. Within paces he found stones, logs, chunks of sod. He raised the back of the lean-to, dragged in a thick log, clawed out a trench for it, rolled it in place. At the sides he placed stones and sod, more logs, more stone. From the brush he carefully chose the most natural pieces to camouflage the low berms and the lean-to. He cleared fields of fire in all directions—not clear-cutting but thinning so from outside the campsite appeared natural. Even in Bobby's quietness, Tony spied him on his return at fifty feet.

"What's this?" Bobby still quiet.

"You can never overimprove a defensive position," Tony said. He laid another rock onto the revetment he'd built off one side of the trail.

"You can build a Maginot Line," Bobby said.

Tony eyed him. He hadn't busted his ass to be challenged.

"False security," Bobby said. "Makes you less secure because you lose flexibility, agility, vigilance."

"This?" Tony gestured to the berm.

Bobby shook his head. "Me," he said. "The plan's not working. I gotta regroup. I've been a fuckin jerk."

Tony chortled. "Yep."

"A sucker, huh?"

"You bet your sweet ass, Man."

"You knew about Ivanov?"

"All he wanted to do, Man, was to fuck your wife," Tony said. They were now sitting side-by-side, looking out from the shelter. Bobby stared forward. "How come you let him in the house?"

"How else—" Bobby began, changed thoughts midsentence. "What about you?"

"I'd like to fuck her, too," Tony blurted, laughed, sputtered between laughs. "Naw. I'm kidding. I mean I would but I'd never do it. Never even hint . . . you know . . . "

"Why?"

"Why?!"

"Yeah. Why? How come you wouldn't think of fuckin me over but Ivanov couldn't think of anything but?"

"I don't know."

"I got to understand this, Tony. I've got to understand. Otherwise, it'll never work."

"Bringing in guys?"

"Yeah."

"Maybe we ought ta put a separate kitchen in the barn. And a bath."

"Um."

"You can't be havin guys goin upstairs when like maybe Sara's in the shower."

"It's a matter of showing trust."

"It's a matter of stupidity, Man. I been there. I been in RRVMC. You're talkin about bringing in psychos . . . "

"I was talking about bringin in guys who were down and out."

"Some of em are schitzo, Man. Fox in the henhouse. Maybe you want to help the fox, but you don't kill the hens."

"Umph." That was hard for Bobby to take.

"Better for us anyway," Tony said.

"How?"

"Bein separate. Responsible for ourselves."

"We'd need a new septic system. New well."

"Piece a cake."

"God damn it." Bobby balled his fist, hammered his knee. "I still gotta understand somethin. Why is it that a guy like you, who comes from such a caring family, drops off the deep end? And . . . "

"I . . . " Now Tony clamped his jaw. How much easier it was to advise than to be advised, to analyze another than to be asked to analyze oneself. "Maybe I was kinda the odd man out."

"Oh," Bobby said, not sympathetically, not to draw Tony out, but in simple acceptance.

"Naw. I wasn't really like outside it. I wasn't like the black sheep. I was just tee-tee to the side of the main current."

Again the simple, "Oh," followed by, "Then why . . . "

"Maybe . . . " Tony paused. "Maybe because I expected everybody to be like my family. You know, in Nam, the villagers were like that. Not if you were on a sweep going through a ville, but the villagers if you lived with them. My platoon was like that, too. We were family. Even the guys I was with in Philly. We were like brothers. But gettin out, Man. The World hasn't been like that. I thought people cared. Nobody gives a shit. Maybe I felt not like pushed out, but not looked at. You know, like when somebody keeps their eyes down when you walk into a room. Then like I reacted to it with, 'Well fuck you too.' "

"Um." Again the pause to understand, to assimilate. "Like, 'Fuck it. Don't mean nothin'?"

"Yeah. But not us. It's those motherfuckers don't give a shit. They're goina blow the whole place up anyway."

Bobby turned his head, his brow furrowed.

"Nuke it, Man. Bobby, they're goina blow everybody off the face a the map. Why should we give a fuck?"

"That's a cop-out."

"Like hell."

"Sure it is. If you didn't give a shit you'd be like Ivanov. Damn it. I can't figure . . . I tried but I fucked up."

Tony had no more to say. Bobby too was silent. He'd put himself back in the funk he'd been in for months. Overhead the clouds thickened and the air gusted in sporadic dips. The two men lay back, closed their eyes, slept.

At dusk Bobby nudged Tony. "C'mon. We're movin out."

Tony sat up. He did not speak. The order, the movement, felt natural.

"Lights," Bobby whispered. "Water and sleeping bags."

They moved south out of the Pennamite clearing back to the Lenape Indian trail. Without speech they meandered back under the hemlocks, deep into the darkening forest, to the spur. Bobby turned northwest. A hundred yards in was the fire circle—nothing lavish, a slight depression, a shallow circular pit perhaps sixteen or eighteen feet in diameter with a small circular ring of stones, maybe thirty inches across, at the center. Stacked to one side was a neat pile of kindling, to the other slightly larger branches, nothing more than two inches thick or two feet long. Overhead a narrow shaft through the hemlocks opened to the sky. There were no berms, no fields of fire, no camouflage. Bobby struck a match, lit the small wood teepee he'd erected earlier, alone. Immediately flames spread, licked up into the air. In the deep woods Bobby and Tony were completely open. Anyone could see them. Yet with the fire they could not see even a foot beyond the larger circle. Tony nearly shit. His response was to flee, to hide in the dark, to shun the exposure. But Bobby sat, his sleeping bag wrapped tightly over his shoulders, and Tony, trying hard, followed suit. Bobby lay larger sticks on the fire. The original teepee collapsed, curled, oxidized, disappeared. In the flickering of the flames, to Tony, Bobby's face deformed, furrows became crevices, wrinkles became chasms, features became craggy outcroppings. There was no color, no warmth, no life: only time—past, present, future—fused and frozen.

They sat silently watching the fire, mesmerized by the changing forms. After some time Bobby picked a stick from the wood pile; it was perhaps fifteen inches long, an inch and a quarter in diameter. From part of it the bark had fallen away. Bobby held it close to the flame but did not drop it. Instead he broke silence, said calmly, "This is a truth stick. When it is held no one else can speak. To the stick the holder owes an obligation—the obligation to speak the truth. When you begin, you say *hè*, which is the Lenape word of greeting. If you stop and recommence say *làpi* [luh-pee] which means 'again.' When you are finished say *wëli* [wah-lee] which means 'good'."

"What?!" Tony stared across at Bobby, at his stone face. Then he rocked back, looked up the long dark shaft toward the invisible sky.

Bobby repeated the Lenape words, the explanation.

"You're kiddin, Man," Tony said.

"No," Bobby said.

"Where the fuck did you dig up this shit?"

"It was in one of Granpa's files. This is the Lenape ceremony of truth. It may have been performed right here for five thousand years. And the truth is, I'm lost. I don't have the answers I thought I had."

"That's what the fuck we're doin out here?"

"That's what the fuck we're doin out here."

"This is fucked up." Tony was angry. Bobby shoved the stick at him. He snatched it. "You're fucked up," Tony stormed. His rage multiplied, built on itself, spiked. "You're some sort of fuckin . . . workaholic. . . . You act like nobody's good enough for you. Fuck you. Fuck your pious help-the-dregs crap. Fuck your goody-two-shoes I fucked up, crap. Truth ceremony! You're the biggest fucking hypocrite I ever met!" With that Tony whipped the stick back at Wapinski.

Bobby's arm shot from under the sleeping bag. The stick nicked his ring-finger knuckle, spun, hit his leg. He ground his teeth, grasped the truth stick, restrained his urge to bash Pisano with it knowing full well Tony expected to be bashed, was ready for him to lunge. Bobby's breath came hard. His hands trembled. "*yuho* [yooh-oh]. Okay." Slower, longer breaths. "I . . ." He paused. Bobby could see Tony was still ready to throw off his sleeping bag, ready to get into it. "I haven't been truthful. Not completely. I wanted you to do the farm but I didn't tell you about all the other parts." He could see Tony sink back. "I feel like we've been doing everything right but we're still losing."

"Yeah," Tony snapped. "Definition of a Nam vet. Do everything right, lose. That's me. That's my cousin Jimmy. Losers."

"Why?" Bobby pushed the stick out but did not release it. "I got an article says ten percent of the prison population is Nam vets. Says we lost the war. Says we were druggies during the day and praying to God at night we wouldn't be killed."

"Fuck em."

"Right on. But it doesn't answer the fuckin question, Why? Everything I've been reading, everything I've been thinking about, all the planning for a program of retransformation . . ."

"Of what?"

Bobby did not acknowledge. "It didn't do any good with Ivanov."

Tony snorted. "And it hasn't done squat for you."

"Leave me out of it."

Again Bobby pointed the stick at Tony. "Loser!"

Again Tony snatched it away. "That's fuckin right. I'm a loser. Even back in school. If one side picked me, that side lost. If I bet on a Super Bowl team, they'd lose. One hundred fuckin percent." Tony flipped the stick.

"You didn't lose at Dai Do." Bobby held the stick out.

Tony grabbed one end. Bobby didn't let go. Their hands and wrists were just off-center of the main heat rising from the fire. "What'd you know? We didn't win, either." Tony refused to flinch. His hand was very hot.

Bobby too refused to move. "Maybe you did. Just like we did at Hamburger. Even if they called it losing. But I've been reading. If they'd never been given the A Shau, they'd never of been able to win farther south."

"I don't give a fuckin flyin leap."

"We gotta learn more . . ."

"That's more of your shit. You can win every fuckin day, you still die, In the end everybody loses."

"Naw." Bobby pulled on the stick bringing Tony's hand into the fire. "That's two different games. When you came home, were you a loser?"

Tony pulled back. His fingers were baking. "No fuckin way," he snarled. "When I left we'd been makin progress."

"Me too," Bobby said quickly. He was having trouble holding on. "We'd virtually won. Who the hell lost it?"

"I don't know."

"It's not till Saigon fell that anybody called us losers. Even though we were out of the country, militarily, for two and a half years! Kick ass of anybody who tells you we lost the war. We didn't. The politicians did. The American people. Not grunts. We couldn't even of been called losers before April '75 because there wasn't any loss until then. Who lost it?!"

"Not me. Not my cousin."

"Me neither. So how come we're losers?"

"Cause maybe . . . cause maybe if you're a loser, it's not your fault. Nothin's your fault. Ow!" Tony released the stick, pulled his hand back.

For a long time neither spoke. Occasionally Bobby or Tony added new wood to the fire. The bed of coals thickened, glowed continuously. Sporadic flame tongues leaped. The faces of the two men dried, toughened like jerky; their backs chilled; their muscles tightened.

Now talk came more easily. Tony accepted the stick, passed it back, learned the Lenape words. His mood was less acquiescence, more exhaustion. He wanted to sleep. Bobby said there was no way back without flashlights. They'd brought none.

"You were a grunt," Bobby said. Tony nodded. "Grunts can do anything. Wëli." Bobby passed the stick.

"Hè. I might be fucked up. Neurotransmitters. All that stuff they talked about at Rock Ridge. But you're right. A grunt can cope. But he's got to have people around him who don't just listen, but understand. I . . . I could tell you some stories . . . "

"Tell me," Bobby injected.

Tony told Bobby about the corpse in the tunnel, about his nightmares, about once grabbing Linda. He moved on to Dai Do, the hand-to-hand fighting, the machetes, how he'd hacked and slashed like a madman in order to save himself and his platoon. Bobby shuddered, controlled his expression.

"You know what my biggest fear in Nam was?" Bobby said. "Getting stabbed. I didn't care about getting shot. I mean, I didn't want to get shot. But I never thought about it. But Man, I thought about bayonets."

"I got stabbed," Tony said. "Here." He touched his thigh.

Bobby winced. "I . . . I hate being stuck. With anything. Like at the dentist. The moment he touches me, even if I like him, I just think, I'm outta here. I can't stand . . . you know, needles even."

"No big thing."

Now their talk was every place. Tony told Bobby about Manny being shot in his arms, and about the village, the mother and the children. He did not tell Bobby about shooting them. He was still uncertain, and he sensed that Wapinski, with his theoretical perspectives, did not want to know about American atrocities. To Bobby it would add another blemish to a record he seemed intent on defending.

Bobby told Tony about Hamburger Hill, about the multiple assaults, about giving the order, about the mud, about losing Americans, not knowing if they'd been wounded, killed, or captured. "It's the difference between the officer's perspective and the enlisted man's," he said. "You guys would condemn a decision because you had to carry it out. Our condemnation came later. You had to tell this person to walk point, this person to walk his slack. You knew what you were doing. You knew where you were, knew the consequences. We got orders, we gave orders. Sometimes we were mortified by those decisions. We weren't sitting in some boardroom saying to our staff, 'I think we ought to buy AT&T. What do you guys think?' We made decisions that if they weren't right on, maybe three, four guys died. And you can't afford three or four guys when you only have thirty. And if you weren't right on, the guys are saying, 'That son of a bitch. Where was he? Why'd he lose my friend?' When I got back, my nightmares . . . Shit."

"*Yuho*," Tony said.

That released Bobby's tension and he chuckled. Now he was happy Tony was with him. "I had one that repeated for years," he said. "About triage. It finally stopped. Then it started again when my granpa was dying. But it stopped again."

They moved on. The mood ebbed, flowed. "I need your fuckin help." Bobby was nasty, demanding. "I can't do it alone. Either commit or go."

"Fine, fuckhead. I've been planning to go back to RRVMC anyway. Lick some nurse's ass."

"Yeah. Right!"

"Let em take care a me."

"Enable you to be a fuckhead like Ivanov?"

"Why the fuck not?!"

"What the fuck would turn you on? What would make you . . . make you pursue a dream? What would elate you?"

"Elate?!"

"Rev you up? Satisfy you? Be meaningful?"

"I don't . . . Maybe like at the forge."

"Why?"

"I don't know. I'm not there. I'm not paying attention to me. I'm focused. It's happening. Something's being created."

"Yeah," Bobby said. "That's my theory of pure elation. Get out of your self, into a cause."

"Fuck causes," Tony said. "They all got causes. Nuclear freeze movements. ERAs. BMWs. Ivanov had a cause—get the head of his dick wet. Fuck people with causes. Causes are fucked."

"We're using it differently," Bobby said.

"I've never been more elated than when I was stoned out of my fuckin gourd."

"Oh boy! You gotta help me. Cause and elation. That's what makes the world turn. That's the key to retransformation. It sounds stupid but the final piece of the puzzle is *fun*. Unselfish fun. That's why we've had all these false starts. It wasn't any fun."

From across the circle Tony glared at Bobby. For some time neither spoke. Finally Wapinski said, "We had a cause that was greater than our selves and we expanded to a higher level. We went to defend freedom and help establish democracy in Southeast Asia. That's different than just trying to get laid. Trying to get laid is concentrating on the self. Think about falling in love. When you really fall in love, where's your focus? Not on yourself but on the other. You go outside yourself. That's the difference between latching on to a cause with the focus on you, and adopting a cause with the focus on the cause. If the focus is on you it brings stress and kills joy. But if the focus is on the cause you enter a state of elation."

"Maybe—" Tony shifted, opened his bag.

"Why can't I grasp it?" Bobby asked. "So much of this self-indulgent self-fulfillment stuff is really shallow, but there *is* a core there. It's the key to becoming unstuck. It's the key to meaningfulness. *Pursue* is the wrong word. But *elation* isn't. Excitement. Fun. Playfulness. Without that, responsibility becomes drudgery. Without it decisiveness is unsustainable."

On and on, deeper and deeper into the night; deeper and deeper into each other's thoughts. "I missed Jimmy's death," Tony confessed. "We were putting up the gate. I'd just finished the hinges, remember? I didn't remember until later. That's been like a holy day of obligation to me and I didn't keep it holy. I didn't even remember it for a week. Even in San Jose I kept it holy."

"It was partly my fault," Bobby said. "I'm the one who ran off with his girl."

"Who? Red?"

"Yeah. I think maybe he wouldn't of gone back . . . "

"Naw. Naw, Man. He was goin back Red or not. She . . . you know, Man, she was like his pet. She was . . . You know, she wasn't a cause to him. I mean, he liked her. But he was never committed to her like he was to . . . geezo, like even to Li. I wonder if Linda's still got her drawings. You gotta see em, Bobby."

"He had a gal there?"

"An orphan, Man. A kid. That was his cause. Helpin them people. Me too when I was at the ville level."

At dawn they returned to the Pennamite camp, ate heartily, crawled into the lean-to. Before they went to sleep Bobby whispered, "Dear Lord, please bless us and watch over us; deliver us from evil, forgive us our trespasses . . . "

Tony, to Bobby's surprise, completed the beseechment. "And give us the strength and guts to try hard and never give up."

Bobby propped himself, craned over toward Tony.

Tony chortled. "Ah, he taught it to me, too."

He is not in the fire circle but to the side, in the dark, in the blackness of space. The images form, coalesce out of slow churning glowing blue gray black fog. It is a sphere, a skull viewed from the blackness, from the void, viewed from above, beside, before, a skull, a globe drifting in space, drifting away, the jaw opening, slowly, painfully, a silent anguished cry escaping. There is no sound. He is viewing the skull from miles above as it floats, spins slowly in the blackness, and there, there, falling from him a black dot, small, smaller, falling, being pulled into the anguished globe until it is imperceptible a second before it hits against the occipital crown. The jaw again and then the eye sockets—how can they, dead, inanimate—cry in silent pain. The bone cracks at impact, a black jagged hole in glowing blue, one, two, three, four seconds—it seems an eternity as he watches from miles above—then slowly, silently, a cone of gray brain matter explodes toward him, not high enough to touch him, but close enough for him to feel the earth's pain of millions of man-years of devastation, of death and dying drifting farther until he sees them all, sees the entire galaxy, sees Jimmy and Manny, sees hacked globes rolling, sees the mother, her children, the specks flying from him, they frozen, strong, Gina Michelle Linda . . .

"Tony?"

. . . blood gushes, erupts . . .

"Tony." Wap called him gently. "Tony. It's 1976. We're at High Meadow."

"UH!" Tony's eyes opened. He did not breathe. His eyeballs flicked. On the open side of the lean-to he could see their small camp, the low berm he'd built the day before, vegetation, open lanes. The sky had faded to deep blue. It was dusk.

"Almost time to go," Bobby said softly.

"Um." Tony sat up. His back was stiff. His right leg tight.

"Movin out in one five," Bobby said. "Best eat something."

An hour later they sat across from each other at the fire circle. Through the shaft between the hemlocks they could see the clear sky, yet with their vision so tunnelled Tony could make out only Cepheus.

"*Yuho*." Bobby was laconic. Then, "Damn it, Man. I've been marchin in place since I returned. That's what hit me in the lean-to. You too. Just marking time. Losing six fucking years. Yeah"—Bobby's voice rose, his hands began to shake —"some good stuff's happened. But *some* good stuff happens to a blob of shit on the sidewalk. There's no fuckin time to waste anymore. This is URGENT!"

"What is?"

"Getting off the fucking ground. Understanding why we haven't be-fore. Correcting it. Taking off."

"What does that mean?"

"It means you gotta transform. It means the next move is up to you."

"Maybe the next move is up to my chemical im-fucking-balances."

"You control it."

"You don't know what the fuck you're talking about. It's a neurotrans-mitter imbalance that causes mania and depression. That's what the *doctors* say."

"Fine. Did they tell you *why* you had a chemical imbalance?"

"Why?!" After last night's finale, Tony had not expected to be back in a pissing contest. "They don't know why! That's what ticks me off. Cause I killed people. It's . . . They don't have a clue. You got a broken leg, they give you a crutch. That's their approach."

"Exactly," Bobby said. "That's all they can do. Chemical imbalances are caused by something. Maybe something you saw. Or did. Or maybe it's diet. Who knows? But something caused the onset. Then the system went out of whack. That increased the depression, pushed the imbalance. Fuck the drugs. That only keeps you from getting to the original prob-lem. Makes you stick where you're at. Keeps you from taking off."

Spit flicked from Tony's lips. "I know the goddamned problem. Ev-erything's been fucked in my life, everything since Nam. And I'm not takin any drugs."

"No it hasn't," Bobby said. "Not since Nam."

"How the hell do you know?"

"In Philly? You were crazy then? When you met Linda? Go ahead, tell me you were nuts then."

Tony did not respond.

"In Nam? Were you crazy in Nam? I mean truly schitzo?"

Still no response.

"Once you had to pull your weight and you did."

"I do now."

"You work hard. You're a great worker. But you're not pulling your weight. You're hiding. And so the fuck am I. We did it once. We can do it again."

Tony was exasperated, exhausted. "What the fuck, Man. Over."

"No," Bobby said. "There's no 'what the fucks' to get you off the hook. It's decision time, Man. It's time to make the decision and never look back."

Tony reached out, grabbed a stick from the pile, ran a hand over it breaking off a few dry twigs. "*Hè.*" He held the stick vertically before his face, grasped it in a steel fist, glared at Wapinski, at the drawn wrin-kled features reflecting the sporadic bursts and ambient glow. "One con-dition," he said. "Consult me. Fill me in. Don't treat me like your fuckin pet. Like you keep no animals except Josh and Tony. And don't you ever give anybody any unconditional handouts. You want a platoon sergeant?! I'll fuckin out-sergeant anybody in the fuckin world. You develop the programs. You let me run em." He snapped the truth stick straight out, his hand just above the flame.

Bobby reached, grabbed, quickly, attentively, neither being burned. "This is the program," he began. He spoke at length, spoke like a military instructor first mentioning the main points, then backtracking to fill in. He spoke of his own family, moved on to EES, not simply the technical and production ends but the cause he called *attitude evolution*. From there he outlined his thoughts on farming and was surprised to have Tony adopt his phraseology of cause and attitude evolution as Tony took over to describe reduced-pesticide methods, water and soil conservation techniques that would allow for minimal chemical fertilizer usage without affecting yield. For the first time he listened to Tony's report on chardonnays, ". . . drinkable, marketable, in demand."

Then Bobby asked, "Can we produce wine here?"

"You mean actually be a winery instead of selling the grapes?"

"I mean if we're going to be detoxifying guys—"

Now they spoke of the dilemma of starting a winery with workers who might be alcoholics. "I've been through detox," Tony said. "Only about one in ten are actually physically dependent. It's genetic. The rest drink for other reasons. To be numb. To take the edge off. Sometimes for fun. Sometimes it becomes habit and after a while habit becomes something you depend on, physically."

"That begs the question," Wapinski countered. "If we're going to have alcoholics here we better be dry."

"Not true," Tony said seriously. "For a year you've been talking about responsibility. We're dry here. A guy's fine. He leaves here for the real world. You haven't taught him a fuckin thing. Sometimes I want a drink. Sometimes I want to get drunk, fall down, laugh, be stupid. So fuckin what?! We're developing a fanatical antialcohol attitude in this country when the real issue is drinking *and* driving. You talk about risks, you talk about decision making, about taking the plunge, about fun, about getting out of the self. If you're physically addicted, you've got to learn to stay away. Otherwise you just have to learn to drink responsibly. Control it."

Bobby burst out laughing. Tony was so serious.

"Fuck you," Tony snapped. He sat back, crossed his arms, jammed a heel into the rock ring.

"No. No. No." Bobby coughed out the words. "It's . . . it's just . . . " He rolled to his side laughing, making Tony even angrier. Then he grabbed the small pack he'd brought, opened it, pulled out a new fifth of Jack Daniel's. *"Hè."*

Tony stared. Then he too began to laugh. Bobby took a swig, passed the bottle. "The Yards in Nam," Bobby said, "wouldn't trust you unless you'd get drunk with them."

Again the bottle passed. Bobby moved on to the Community. He didn't know what to call it. Still he laid out the plans he'd made, fully including Tony for the first time. "... take care of our own ..." he repeated. "... a retreat. A center. Teach them to become unstuck. To take off. Grab a piece of life. An incremental program to teach them to make decisions. Stay as long or as short as you want. No government regulations. Work in the barn, the vineyard ..."

"Just don't give me all the shitheads," Tony said.

"What does that mean?" Bobby was perplexed.

"You talk about dregs, Man. About down-and-outs. Open it up, Man. Open it up to just guys in need. Or guys who want to be here. Want to help. Let some of em set examples for others. If you only take the worst, we're not goina move off square one."

"Well ... "

"Make entry formal. Like basic. A series of rites of passage. Each passed means greater responsibility, more freedom. Just like in the Corps. Call us NAM. Like we did in San Jose. That'll be our cause."

The night was crystal clear, cold. Both Bobby and Tony had their sleeping bags wrapped over their backs, pulled up over their necks to their ears. They were feeling mellow. Bobby talked of transformations, of attitudes, of building self-reliance and commitment, of tenacity and teamwork, of establishing habitual, efficient mechanics of everyday life, of his grunt theory of psychotherapy, which combined a teaching of basic life skills with a think-it-out, tough-it-out, no self-pity, one-foot-in-front-of-the-other philosophy. Very slowly it occurred to him, even if it had not occurred to Tony, that Tony had, in the past ten months, already transformed.

Bobby thought to say this to Tony but he did not. Instead he talked about the High Meadow Code, about his files, his attempts and false starts. "This is where it's all headed," he said. "This is what has to be done to get to an Ethic for Our Times." He moved a quarter way around the fire. On the ground he drew an arrow pointing away from the fire. Beside it, beginning at the arrow base, he marked the letters PFFEIPS. "I think it's kind of the time-lapse of the self," Bobby said. "Kind of time layers. Physical, financial, familial, emotional, intellectual, political, spiritual."

"I gotta pee," Tony said. He stood, swayed. They had eaten little. It had been nearly a year since he'd had a drink. The bottle was half-gone. Still, from the dark looking in, looking at the circle, at Bobby in the glow of the small fire, it struck him. He returned, sat, rehunched under the sleeping bag, said, "It doesn't work because it's not a circle."

"Yeah," Bobby said. "Yeah." He too was feeling the alcohol. "I like a circle," he said. "The Great Circle. The Fire Circle. Everything connected. A to Z. Alpha to omega."

In the wee hours they finished the bottle, laid it in the coals for a meltdown, talked on, ranted, chuckled, challenged each other. At one point Bobby said, "That's what we're goina turn around. Attitude ev-oh-lu-tion. Ev-oh-lu-tion!" At another, "Let's build a basketball court."

"Yeah, sure. Like the one you had in California."

"Something simpler."

"You ever play bladderball?" Tony asked.

"Huh?" Bobby focused on him, unsure he'd heard.

"It's a Viet Namese game played with a pig's bladder," Tony said. "Your grandfather had pigs, right?"

"Ye—"

"Jimmy once wrote about it. You take a pig's bladder and blow it up. The kids play soccer with it."

The night did not end. "Guy once said to me," Bobby said, " 'if you don't plan your life, someone will plan it for you. And he isn't interested in your best welfare.' Something like that. There's five billion people on earth, Man. A billion more than a dozen years ago. As the number goes up, as the species becomes more successful, the individuals lose value. Those that survive will be those that take charge of themselves."

As the sky lightened Tony Pisano and Bobby Wapinski were back to talking about layers in reference to the theory of expanding beyond the self. The idea fascinated Tony. "Maybe it's like stages. You have to go through the first to get to the second. But you've got to delaminate for the self to be stable enough to be the foundation for the expansion."

"Yeah," Bobby said. "That's the challenge. That delamination. That becoming unstuck. We're all affected by it. The whole country. We've got to decide right here and now. We've got to have the courage to decide, the discipline to try, the perseverance never to give up."

"Driven by elation." Tony chuckled.

"Yeah," Bobby said. "And it's urgent. Life is urgent. Me, you—we don't have the right to waste it. We're stuck because we don't know. We're stuck on unfinished business. Were we hoodwinked? Used? And if we were, does that negate the cause?"

"Um." Tony nodded but he wasn't certain he'd followed Bobby's line of thought.

"We went," Bobby said. "We fought. I saw it as an ethical obligation. But was it really right? Or was it wrong?"

"I don't know," Tony said. He rose. Shook out his bag.

"What could have been?" Bobby said.

"What should have been?" Tony countered. "Or should be now?"

"Yeah. Let's make a vow," Bobby said. He too rose. The fire was out. The bottle was a misshapen ugly gray form amid the ash.

"I vow," Bobby began, "to make the effort, to expend the energy, to discover the truth about—"

"No . . ." Tony interrupted. Bobby paused, frowned at him. "I . . . can't. Not just yet. There's . . . there's something I got to find out first."

October 1984

In another week or so it will be eight years since the first Fire
Circle, since the true beginning, for me at least, of community, of a
return to brotherhood, of the outset on the journey to the high
meadows of the mind.

By the end of 1976 Bobby had received dual degrees in civil and
design engineering, and by March 1977 he had his general
contractor's license and his plumbing I and II licenses. Sara had
obtained her Pennsylvania teaching certificate, and Linda was back
pursuing midwifery certification. I'd enrolled in a correspondence
course in sustainable farming and had received my first certificate. I
also began courses in veterinary medicine and economics. Farming
is much more than dirt and seed, plowing, soil erosion, planting
and reaping. It is more than irrigation and fertilization, pesticides,
fungicides, herbicides and cultivation. It is more than potassium,
phosphorus and nitrogen; more than chores and tractors, barns,
crop rotations and winter covers. Farming includes tax preparation,
crop per dollar per acre ratios, marketing, advertising, distribution,
labor laws, personnel management, EPA regulations and retirement
annuities. I'd just scratched the surface and Bobby was pushing me
to expand beyond the farm, pushing me to vow to discover . . . to
become unstuck . . . to grow beyond the self to the community.

He and I busted our butts preparing for the personnel expansion.
We installed a new septic system—tank, drywell, distribution box
and leaching fields—out beyond the little barn. (He'd wanted it
closer in but all I could think of was gallons of cold urine collecting
in my still-secret bunker, so I convinced him closer was ideal for the
basketball court he wanted.) He paid to have a new well pounded
and refracted. We cleaned the old pig barn, roughed in a kitchen, a
shower room and a two-holer bath. The guys, we figured, could
make finishing it their project.

It was during this time that the small array of solar collectors on
the roof of the White Pines Inn really began to pay dividends.
Aaron Holtz did for High Meadow and Environmental Energy
Systems what ten grand in advertising dollars could never have
accomplished. "C'mere." He'd grab lunchtime clients, dinner
patrons, evening drunks. "Feel this." He'd grab their wrists, turn on

the "cold" water tap before the dishwasher, and warm or scald their hands depending on that day's solar insolation. "Saving me a ton of money," Aaron would say.

From Aaron came the Bancroft job, our first solar collector implant retrofit. Others followed. Aaron had to wait in line for Bobby to schedule his home—a retrofit remodel with Trombe wall, greenhouse, rooftop array, and six-thousand-gallon basement heat-storage unit, EES's largest to date.

Suddenly there was money for tools—the break, the slitter, chop-saws, ladders. . . . Maybe it was the money, or luck, or fate, but in early January Jeremiah Gallagher of Williamsport and George Kamp of Towanda arrived; then ten days later came Tom Van Deusen from West Virginia. Each time one came Bobby treated him like he was a 'cruit entering basic training. He'd rant about urgency, about lost years and not becoming a lost generation. Then he'd give them to me and I'd tell them they could sleep for a week but then it was time to get-to, to work. With each of them I pretended to be unstuck. With each I judged the stage of the journey, the rest-stop at which they'd taken refuge.

High Meadow was becoming an institute. Grandpa's office bookshelves were moved down to the main floor of the big barn—into what had once been a workshop and toolroom. The place was sanitized. Additional shelves were built until, in the coming years, the walls would be completely lined. Farming books and journals occupied one section; another was devoted to solar technology and design; a third to light reading—novels, mysteries, westerns, even comic books; a fourth to Southeast Asia, to the war, the history, the people. In a subsection were Bobby's first books on veterans, their experiences, their adjustment problems. Here he had Robert Jay Lifton's *Home from the War*, and works by Charles R. Figley, Seymour Leventman, John Helmer, and Gloria Emerson. In each, in the margins, in his neat hand, were Bobby's comments and reactions, his agreements and often scathing criticisms. Bobby consumed these books, digested them, assimilated the nutrients and excreted the waste. And he encouraged every vet that came to High Meadow to do the same. Over the years the history section on the war in Viet Nam, Cambodia and Laos expanded to more than three hundred volumes; the fiction and memoir section to two hundred and sixty; the PTSD (psycho-socio analysis, help and self-help) to one hundred ninety. *Wounds of War* by Herbert Hendin and Ann Pollinger Haas became almost mandatory reading, as did (when it was published in '78) M. Scott Peck's *The Road Less Traveled*, which has nothing—and everything—to do with the combat veteran's experience. By the end, in 1983, this private library, including children's books and all the medical texts, had grown to nearly five thousand volumes. It became the legacy of one four-word question: How do things work?

An example: Do you recall Bobby and the different crystalline structures of ice? One cubic centimeter of water at one degree Celsius releases one calorie of energy when it drops to water at zero degrees Celsius. One cubic centimeter of zero-degree water releases eighty calories as it transforms into zero-degree ice. It is this quality of material state transformation Bobby and EES soon began to use in designing thermal storage systems for retrofits and new construction.

How things work. It came to pass that Bobby saw the release and absorption of energy at phase change, or state transformation, as analogy, as a property of humanness. "When one transforms," he would say, "from a state of egocentric indulgence or a state of being stuck on the self, to a state of expanding beyond the self to mate, to family, to community, energy is released. This energy can be absorbed by others. This is the essence of leadership. This is the essence of all healthy relationships."

With the energy tax credit passed by Congress during the Carter administration, EES was flying, overwhelmed with business, and making a fairly decent profit to boot. Only Cheryl, Joanne and Miriam were displeased. Miriam challenged Bobby on the expenses for the new well, the septic system, etc., saying they were neither business costs nor necessary capital improvements.

Perhaps they were not the only ones. In the theory of the self one comes to recognize that those who have not expanded beyond the self, those who have remained self-centered or who have returned to a state of seeking self-fulfillment, are energy-absorbers, energy consumers. Parasites. Exactly as I was for almost a decade. Focus on the self is self-defeating. The absorber/consumer ultimately becomes chronically depressed, is always stuck, often manifests a need for punishment or humiliation, at times coupled with a public vengefulness that can appear either sociopathic or altruistic.

I have not been here continually but have left to resupply, to meet with the principals.

26

High Meadow, Thursday, 3 February 1977—Tony's thoughts ran foul. Gallagher was being a pain in the ass. Kamp was so stuck he could barely drag his butt from his rack to the shitter, much less work. And Van Deusen, though he was energetic and enthusiastic, was so scattered he put all his energy into going nowhere. They were all in their late twenties, yet all acted like pubescent teens. Worse than FNGs. Worse than cherries. Rawer than the rawest 'cruit.

It was snowing. They were supposed to be keeping the drive clear for the delivery of the slitter—that machine that could take a ten-foot length of sheet metal and pull it through its rolling cutter in less than two seconds. They were supposed to have cleared the barn floor earlier, too, but Tony had done it, seething, grumbling, cursing under his breath.

That was only the tip of the foul iceberg. On Tuesday, the Pisanos and Pellegrinos had had Father Tom down at St. Ignat's say a memorial Mass for Jimmy, now seven years dead. It had not been like the one-year requiem. Only Aunt Isabella and Uncle James, and Jo, John Sr., Nonna, and Tony had come. When Tony called Linda, afterward, she told him she'd forgotten. But John Sr. hadn't forgotten. Nor had John Sr. forgotten that Tony had "chosen" to live in a barn instead of with his wife and daughters. It had been easier for his father to accept Tony's absence—his living homeless in California—than this nearby "nonexistence." "I'm sixty years old," he'd said to Tony after Mass. "Sixty. I never thought I'd live to so hate one of my sons. That's what you've done to me."

"Pop . . ." Tony had begun, but he'd been overwhelmed. Overwhelmed by his father's anger.

"He doesn't mean it," Jo had whispered to Tony. "He loves you just as much as I do. He just doesn't understand."

"I . . . Ma . . ."

"You don't have to tell me," Jo had said. "I don't understand either. Linda's so beautiful. But you gotta make your own way."

"Get the fuckin lead out!" Tony barked at Van Deusen.

"Sure. Sure. Sorry. I was just coming back for a shovel."

Tony slapped his head. "Geez! You guys got the tractor with the plow blade. He's gonna come in a big truck. He's not walkin."

"Oh. Sure. Of course. Sorry."

Tony sighed. "Look, Tom, forget the 'sorries.' Did you clean that section of wall . . . "

"Oh! I forgot. I'll do it in a minute. Let me tell Jer and I'll be right back."

Then: "Hey! Hey! I know you." It was the truck driver. He'd backed the semi with its forty-foot trailer all the way up the long drive, up through the gates, as if he'd delivered to High Meadow a hundred times.

"Huh?" Tom Van Deusen looked up to where the driver was standing in the trailer. Tony, Jeremiah Gallagher and George Kamp had just twisted and rocked the box with the cast-iron base onto a skid so they could use the tractor to pull it into the barn. All three were leaning on the crate.

"No. You." The driver pointed. "Yeah, it is . . . " He pointed at Tony, leaped down. "Ay! Ay Sarge! It is you. Sargeant Pizo."

Tony remained leaning on the crate, but turned his head up, sideways.

"Augh, you don't remember me."

Tony stared, searched the bearded face.

"Thorpe," the man said. "I was a newby. Fuck a duck, Man. You don't remember."

"Jim Thorpe . . . " Tony said tentatively.

"Yeah. Dennis. You called me Jim cause at Dai Do, Man, you remember that bad motherfucker, cause you said I ran like I was after the gold."

"Shee-it!" Tony laughed, straightened. "How the fuck you been?" He still didn't recognize this man.

"Ha! See, you do remember."

"Sure," Tony said. "You joined us . . . "

"Yeah, right there. Fer all a six days. Until I got hit."

"Yeah, that's right, huh? I remember . . . didn't you . . . "

"Just before you left I came back. Just before Loon. But shit. I'll never forget you and Dai Do. Man, you saved my ass. Hey—" Thorpe looked around, "your place?"

"Naw," Tony said.

"Nice place," Thorpe said. The slitter and cast-iron base were off. He was ready to go.

"You remember Dai Do, huh?" Tony now said. Then to the others, "You guys get this thing in there. You don't need me." And to Thorpe, "Wait a minute. I gotta talk to you."

It did not take long to get reacquainted. They had not known each other well. "Naw, Man," Thorpe was saying. "I'm just a temp. These guys are so busy they picked up a few of us. But they're cheap, Man. We got no bennies. And soon as they don't need us, they let us go."

"Maybe that's not so bad. No ties, no hassles."

"Yeah. I got no ties."

"Married?"

"Separated."

"Me too."

"Yeah. I got a kid," Thorpe said. "Down in Hagerstown. He was born crippled. Right hip was almost backwards. Left arm . . . ah fuck it. I couldn't handle it. Fuck em if they can't take a joke."

Tony chuckled. "I've got two girls. They're okay. But I couldn't . . . Hey do you remember the dink with the belt?"

"Dink with a belt?"

"At Dai Do. At that hamlet that afternoon. When that mama-san and her kids got wasted?"

"Oh. Oh shit, yeah. You mean the ones that dink fuckin stitched up the back?"

"Yeah. I . . . I been tryin to think, you know, about that time."

"Yeah," Thorpe said. "I remember. You were really pissed. That was the shits. Really a rat fuck."

"Yeah. I think maybe I shot em."

"You?!"

"Yeah."

"No way, Sarge. Don't you remember, you were down tryin to draw a bead on the dink with the belt but they were in the way."

"Yeah, but I fired. I must a hit em."

"You didn't fire, Man. Don't you remember?"

"No. I . . . I remember hearin my weapon . . . "

"Naw, that was me. I was across the trail from you. Like six feet away. I was behind that hump in the ground. I couldn't see the dinks but when that dink opened up I emptied a clip like straight up. I figured it'd maybe scare him."

"I thought I fired . . . "

"Naw, Man. Don't you remember Samuels teasin you cause you didn't return fire and that was like twice in one day and him sayin, 'Fuck the line of fire. Fuck the line of fire.' I was going to pound his head because he got so annoyin with that 'Fuck the line of fire.' You were really upset."

"Ha! Yeah, huh?" Tony laughed. "Yeah. 'Fuck the line of fire.' Ha! Ha! Hahaha . . . "

Now Thorpe began to laugh too. "And Maxwell kept yellin at you, 'What're you teachin the newby?' "

"Oh yeah." Tony was laughing almost uncontrollably. "I didn't fire. I didn't fire."

"Geez, Man," Thorpe said. "How could you forget that?!"

Friday night, 25 March 1977—Noah was asleep. Bobby was reading the local paper. Josh was on the floor by his feet. Rain was coming in sheets, hitting the windows on the south and west sides of the house masking the TV voices. Between gusts there was a constant tatter on the tarps where the roof was still open. "Idiots," Bobby blurted. He sniffed, swallowed. His nose was red, sore from blowing.

Sara was watching TV. They had barely spoken all day. "Who?"

Bobby dropped the edge of the paper. He was angry about Sara's low-level yet increasing bitchiness. He was sure it was because he'd said they didn't have the money to visit her folks and grandparents at Christmas but she denied it, passed it off to cabin fever. He didn't believe that. Her behavior fit the pattern of several case studies he'd been reading about enablers—cases where the attraction died when one partner, the enabled, began to expand, to become independent. With the Larson job completed, Sodchouski's underway, and Marrion's signed up; with the barn becoming a factory; with the vets cooking in their own bunkhouse; and with grumpy Tony, believe it or not, actually singing and smiling and doing the craziest little jigs, Bobby increasingly thought Sara *needed* to tear him down, to make them all dependent, again, on her.

"The town." Bobby did not want to confront her.

"What now?"

"They want to build an eighteen million dollar sewer plant on the crik below The White Pines."

"Doesn't that make sense?"

"That's more than six thousand dollars per house."

"Something needs to be done from what I've read."

"For that price you could buy everybody daily bus fare to Williamsport for ten years. Let em shit there."

Sara clicked her tongue. There was no talking to Bobby when he was in this mood. She sat up. "Listen to that rain. I'm going to check the roof in Noah's room. Oh! Damn it."

"What now?"

Again the tongue click. "Another flea bite," Sara said. "I can't take this anymore."

Bobby huffed. "I'll spray him again tomorrow."

On the stairs Sara covered her face. She was miserable, frightened. Every day she felt worse. Every day she tried so hard to be strong for him but he didn't care. It was impossible to do anything, to tell anyone, to seek help. They had been so broke all last year and now, even though there was money coming in, she didn't dare divert any for personal needs. Even for Noah's second birthday she'd skimped on the party. But Bobby hadn't noticed. He'd been off with the dog most of the day. Just a little bit of money, she'd wished, but now she just didn't dare. It wasn't, in her mind, hers. She wasn't working. She wasn't bringing home a check.

In the living room Bobby was brooding. The Soviets had arrested another member of the Helsinki Agreement group on "laws forbidding acts deemed to defame" the nation. In Uganda Idi Amin was waging a personal vendetta against half his people, and the bulk of American commentators were declaring him a nationalist, or at least asserting that we Americans had learned our lesson in Viet Nam and now knew better than to intervene.

The winter had been bitterly cold. In late February and March they'd been buried beneath nearly fifty inches of snow. Then a week ago it had warmed and the rain had come and hadn't stopped, had barely let up, and in the back of his mind was A Shau rain, Hamburger Hill rain. He didn't want to go out in it. He didn't want to walk Josh. He just wanted to wait it out, wanted his cold to go away, wanted the sun to return, wanted to forget about Sara's bitchiness. He fantasized about snuggling in a warm room in Rock Ridge with Stacy Carter. And too, Bobby had been doing almost all the labor on the Larson and Sodchouski jobs because Van Deusen couldn't decide to work with him or with Tony and each time he'd come, he'd left to farm (and each time he'd started with Tony he'd left for the EES job). Bobby, simply, was tired. Stacy had jilted him but she'd never been bitchy. Had he played it right, he'd be with her.

The back door creaked, a gust of wind rushed in, the door banged shut. "*Hè*," Tony called.

"*Hè*." Bobby rose.

"We got trouble."

"What . . ."

"Down by the spillway. It can't handle this," Tony said. He was soaking wet. "It's cutting around the side. The whole dam could go."

"Oh! Let's—"

"Kamp's refueling the tractor." Tony's words came quick. "Can the van make it up the back trail?"

"Ah, maybe . . ." Bobby's body was adjusting, pumping, his tiredness disappearing.

"We need the headlights. Ya can't see squat down there."

"Can we deepen the spillway?"

"I tried kicking out the bottom board but it's like . . . it's just rushing too hard. We need sandbags."

"We've got bags. Two crates for terracing the vineyards—"

"Then let's go."

Bobby tied on his boots. Josh was up, excited, whining by the back door, his toenails clicking on the floor. Sara appeared on the stairs, holding Noah. "There's a prob—" Bobby began.

"There sure is," Sara snapped. "The whole room up there is soaked."

Bobby gritted his teeth, shot a look of disgust at the ceiling. "Geez!" he cursed. "The dam's going. That's first. We'll lose the whole pond."

"It's raining in Noah's room," Sara shrieked.

"Damn it," Bobby yelled back. "This is more urgent. Do what you can."

He hurried. In the barn he found Van Deusen with three shovels and one crate of bags by the door. He was struggling with the second crate. "Hey—" he greeted Bobby, laughing, "life's a bitch and then you die."

"Good," Bobby said, focusing on the crates. Tony and George Kamp had already taken the tractor down the drive. Gallagher was in the tractor garage looking for a tow chain. "Let's get these into the van."

They worked quickly. The wind was gusting harder, driving the rain horizontally. They piled in, Bobby driving, testing to see if high beams or low gave better penetration. The driveway was soft, mud over still-frozen earth. Coming down toward the first culvert Bobby could see deep-cut gullies in the wheel tracks. He kept the driver's side wheels on the crown. They moved on, hooked around the mailbox post onto the back, stream-side trail.

This was tricky. This was not a road, not even much of a trail. Tony had gotten the tractor through, farther than Bobby could see. Bobby immediately got stuck. He turned. Without him asking, Tom and Jer were out pushing, rocking, timing their heaves, and Bobby timing the throttle with the swaying of the vehicle. The van spurted, stuck, made three feet, mired, caught for a hundred feet while Bobby attempted to maintain momentum and Tom and Jer ran, slogged, caught up, pushed to keep it moving, again mired, again spurted until they could see the tractor pushing up a dirt berm below the earthen dam.

They piled out, left the van running, the high beams cutting two long cones into the dark. The tractor could not climb the mud-slick wall. It could deliver dirt to the base but they would have to fill the bags—wet, sixty to ninety pounds—then hump them up to the top. Tony organized. One man held a bag, one shoveled, two carried.

At first they worked quickly, Bobby virtually running the bags up, placing them along the eroding edge beside the concrete spillway. After a dozen bags he was exhausted. Tony took over. Then Kamp, Gallagher, Van Deusen. Then Bobby again. Fifty bags were nothing. Waves, spray in the wind, lapped over the grass-covered dike. They were children at the beach attempting to save their sand castle from the tide. Now they worked more slowly, more methodically. The steps to the top became a slide. With a bag on each shoulder Bobby fell, slid to the bottom, cursed loudly. "You can do it, Captain," Gallagher yelled. Wapinski rose, slung one mud sack up, let it clump down, conform to his shoulder. With his right hand he grasped a second, swung it out, up, twisting it just enough to hold the loose end over his other shoulder.

From the top the scene was eerie. Below, the men worked back-lit in the mire and the wind-whipped, continuing deluge. But the top was dark, black. Pond waves could be heard, felt more than seen. For hours they dug, filled, humped. A single row across the dam top took three hundred bags, half their supply; took four hours, gained them three inches, two acre-feet of water. They were exhausted, becoming giddy, elated that they had thus far staved off the washout. The rain continued.

At one A.M. Tony grabbed Bobby's sleeve. "Let em take a blow." Bobby nodded. "We're not goina be high enough." Again Bobby nodded. He did not want to think it was useless. "I'm goina get the saw."

"What for?"

"We can take some trees. Stream side. Woods. Clean em." Tony chopped his hand down as if a chainsaw blade zipping branches from a trunk. "Then we can carry em over, lay em on top of the bags, put a few bags on top to hold em."

"Yeah."

"I'll have Kamp take the tractor."

"No," Bobby said. "I can go faster over the knoll. I could walk it with my eyes shut."

Tony did not let the others stop but he reorganized them to simply filling bags, stacking them in the mud pit by the berm for later use. With a flashlight he set off up the back trail into the woods, surveying trees to be taken.

"Man, I don't believe this shit," Van Deusen said. He was squatting, holding open a bag for Kamp.

"Yeah," Kamp said. "Sandbags. Fuckin sandbags. I haven't even seen one since I got back."

Gallagher piped in. "I didn't even know they existed back in the World."

"Man," Van Deusen said, "I can't believe it. I bet I filled a thousand a these over there."

"Two thousand," laughed Gallagher.

"Three," laughed Kamp.

"Four," said Van Deusen.

"You can't say four." Kamp flicked mud from his fingers at Van Deusen.

"Yes I can," Van Deusen countered. "Probably five." He hit Kamp in the leg with a mud ball.

"You said one," Kamp said. He emptied a shovelful of mud onto Van Deusen's legs.

"You fuck!" Van Deusen shouted, both hands filled with globs. The three of them were already soaked, mud splattered.

"Cool it," Gallagher said.

"Fuck you too." Van Deusen snickered. He flipped a handful at Gallagher, a second at Kamp, hitting each in the chin and chest.

"AH!" Kamp. "Take that." Now mud was flying, Van Deusen was backpedaling, Gallagher attacking, retreating after he threw, Kamp crouching, filling his hands with good sticky muck, letting it fly wildly, not seeing Gallagher sneaking up behind him, suddenly feeling his shirt collar grabbed, pulled out, feeling a handful of cold mud drop down to his belt. He shot up, let out a loud gasp, spun to see Van Deusen smack Gallagher in the face with a mushy wad. Then Kamp and Gallagher tackled Van Deusen, dropped him facedown, kicking, clawing to get loose, all three laughing hysterically, Gallagher picking Van Deusen up by the belt of his pants, Kamp stuffing huge gobs into the opening.

Bobby ascended the knoll. The darkness was total. He could not tell if he were on the trail, was afraid he might veer too far to the left, drop off the cliff. Slowly, trying to speed, he found the false crest, continued up. It was black. He was lost. In his mind he saw an image of himself falling, cracking his skull on the rocks on the way down, hitting the soft ice, going under, being missed. He saw the missing, the wounded. He heard the groans of pain in the water-rush from the spillway, in the wind and the creaking limbs of the trees. He reached the peak. There was not a single clue to give him direction. The wind, rain, stream-rush, masked the idling sounds of the tractor and van. One foot in front of the other, testing each step before weighting it. He shivered. He thought about Sara, about the town, the sewers. From the peak every way was down. Had he turned? Why hadn't he taken a flashlight? "Do it with my eyes closed," he'd thought. Guess not. Josh, soaked, shivering, had deserted him hours earlier. Fleas, he thought. Fuck the fleas. They've probably drowned. Bobby purposely edged to the right because if he was facing the right direction that would take him away from the cliff. But what if he wasn't facing the house? He visually swept the area around him hoping to spy a light from the kitchen window or from the barn. He saw nothing. Step. Step. Maybe he was going backward. Try to follow the fall line, he told himself. Step. "C'mon," he whispered, "one little light." One nice warm room, he thought. One nice warm Stacy. One roof that doesn't leak. One vet that pulls his weight.

Then, like a miracle, there was a light, a moving light, and he knew he'd moved too far to the right, come too far south, off the back edge toward the drive. He knew his exact location, moved, climbed left, watched as the light proceeded up the drive. He entered the orchard now seeing the faint kitchen light, the barn door light, then the car pull to the house.

He hurried, climbed. Sara was on the back steps. She had Noah bundled in a blanket. Linda was in the car. "What's happen . . . "

"God!" Sara exclaimed. "Are you all right?"

"Yeah. Fine. I came back for a saw. Where are you going?"

"To Linda's. The tarps must have blown off. Everything's wet. Are you really all right?" She touched his face.

"Yeah. Yeah."

"You're soaked. You're going to catch your death of cold. Is everybody . . . ?"

"Yeah. You should see them. They're really pulling together. If the damn rain would let up, I think we could save it. To Linda's?"

"I covered everything I could. All the blankets and stuff are in plastic bags and I put some stuff in the barn. There's two thermoses of coffee and buttered rolls in the bag on the counter. And apples and bananas. We'll be back when the rain stops. If you need me, call."

"Where's Josh?"

"In the barn."

"Give me a kiss." Sara came close, turned so Noah was on the hip away from him. She stretched but didn't want to touch him. He bent in for a peck. She planted a wowzer. "Love ya," Sara said. "Call when it's dry."

"Be careful," he called to her.

Bobby got the saw, fueled it, added bar oil, started it in the barn to warm it. He ran around getting a backpack for the coffee and food, a bag to cover the saw, twine to attach the bar oil jug and the gas can to the ruck. He found a flashlight. The batteries were weak and he decided that this was a sign. He was supposed to cross the knoll in the dark. He knew the thought was weird, maybe stupid, yet in his mind, in his jumbling thoughts, he believed it was the only way to bring back the missing.

Downhill to the pond was easy; up through the first part of the orchard was more difficult yet he did not lose his way. On the knoll, with the kitchen light blotted out by the rain, he was again clueless. But he did not think about the cliff, did not think about weighting his steps. He could see Sara and Noah in the kitchen light. He could feel the kiss, taste her mouth. He had fallen in love with her smile, her dark eyes. She'd lead him, or he'd lead her, progressing step-by-step, perhaps better than many, perhaps more aware—what we have is what we want—yet still, step-by-step as if it had been preordained and thus didn't need continual vigilance. He knew he could not think, ever again, about Stacy—not seriously, not in that way. He had made a conscious decision to love Sara. There could be no second-guessing. Bitchiness or not. She'd simply need to understand, to find out, that he had graduated from second grade.

By the first light of Saturday they had a solid tier of wood atop the first row of bags. Still the rain did not stop. By noon they had doubled the first tier and had added between a single-log second level, then, like beavers, they'd packed the spaces with branches and twigs, rocks and mud. The rain became a drizzle. Still Bobby worried: Had Sara, Noah and Linda made it to the apartment? Would the run-off continue to elevate the water level? Would the extended embankment hold? Tony, with the tractor, towed the van back to the road. He, Kamp and Van Deusen decided to break for a few hours while Bobby and Gallagher remained vigilant, reinforcing.

At six Tony's team returned. He was in a good mood. The rain intensified. "*Hè. Wëli.* Call Linda's. Call Sara."

"Did you talk to em?"

"Oh yeah. Hey, the drive held. And we refastened the roof tarps."

"Thanks. She say anything?"

"She said to give you a kiss. C'mere."

In the house with Jeremiah Gallagher standing close, eating cold cereal from a box, Bobby called his wife.

"I'm sorry the house is such a mess," he said.

"And I'm sorry I've been so bitchy," Sara giggled.

"Yeah. This house would do it to anyone."

"I've got something to tell you."

"What?"

"Not over the phone."

"Augh, c'mon Sar. I'm too tired for games."

In a lilting voice Sara said, "You're going to be a daddy again."

He was down in the hole. It was still his secret. Daily he'd added to it: a water blivet, a few cans of food, boxes of pasta, a radio, batteries, clothes, bedding—immediate survival needs. He included long-term, rebirth items—corn, wheat and vegetable seeds, tools. He'd brought down medical supplies, sanitation equipment, books on farming and machinery design—"because the loss of life will not be nearly as devastating as the loss of knowledge." Those had been Wapinski's words in one of their b.s. sessions. But Bobby still didn't know about the deep bunker. Tony included a reading text. He worried about Gina and Michelle. He wanted to impart to them, make available to them, all of humanity's cumulative knowledge.

This, to Tony, was urgent. He visited them more often now; took them, one at a time, for short Harley rides; hugged them, kissed them, sang crazy little songs to them. Linda didn't know what to expect. Was it too good to last? Tony took from the apartment the sketches drawn by Li, which Jimmy had sent. He framed them, put one in the barn, brought one down the hole. The worst thing, he felt, would be the loss of animals. But there was no room for species two-by-two. He'd further expanded the shelter, a second tunnel, short, only six feet, and a second tiny room. But it was becoming more difficult. By mid-May there were eight Nam vets at High Meadow. Dennis "Jim" Thorpe had come after being laid-off again; and Don Wagner and Carl Mariano. The place felt crowded—good crowded but difficult to covertly move tons of rock chips.

He secured a new shelf unit to a wall, then moved back to his cubicle, to his bunk. He lay down. A new death—the death of his grandmother—had triggered old dreams, nightmares. He understood this, understood the death of Maria Annabella, Nonna, was having this effect on him. But understanding made little difference. He had thought after Thorpe's first visit he'd dreamed his last dream, suffered his last depression. He'd told the dream to Wapinski. They'd talked Friday nights for hours, like at the fire circle, except now on the back steps of the farmhouse. It helped.

"Savor it," Wapinski had said.

"What do you mean?"

"Hold on to it. Try to be conscious of it. Don't stop it. Let the conscious observe the subconscious. Let the dream play out. And when you're back awake, try to immediately recall what happened."

Tony shut his eyes, drifted, exhausted, slept, turned. Then it came, came as it had sporadically for months, came with flashes of light on the dark screen of his shadowed retinas.

"Fast!" he screams. There is no sound. He wants to lift her, lift the old woman, lift the mother, the children. He wants them to dart, to vanish. He wants the men down, flat, hidden. Flash. Gina screams. He can see her. She has frozen. Flash. More screams. Flash. They are frozen by the noise, by the strobelike lightning, by each other's screams, shouts. There is no noise. The ground heaves. His belly—he is prone—jolts to his spine. His legs are splayed, flop in the tremors. There is no motion, no concussion. Flash. Blackness. Scream. He screams. They are prone watching him. He has frozen, erect, exposed, facing them, facing away, facing the noise, the flash. They want to advance, to save him. "Stay back!" He is vehement. "Get behind me." Flash. Stitched.

He bolted up.

"I want to run something by you guys," Bobby said. It was early morning. They were assembled in the big barn, ready for chores, for the day's work. Outside it was cool, crisp. Inside there was the smell of oil and paint and glass cleaner. "Twenty-one percent of World War Two veterans were discharged because of combat stress. Some could handle it. Some couldn't. That's what I've been reading. All along the line there are gradations of handling it. We're the same. Every army's the same. And whether somebody's got it really bad or just tee-tee, he's got to continually deal with his combat experience. Always. There are some things that made it worse for some, easier for others. Guy who was eighteen or nineteen had it tougher than a guy who was twenty-two. Guy who saw multiple heavy contact had it worse than a guy who was at the back of one firefight. Guy who trusted his own values, who wasn't ashamed of being scared shitless in scary situations, had cushions to protect him. See, I was kinda that guy. Maybe I saw a bunch a shit, but I was older. And I never thought being afraid did anything but made me properly cautious."

"I went at nineteen," Tom Van Deusen said.

"I was eighteen years eight months when I landed there in '69," Carl Mariano added.

"I was twenty-four," Don Wagner said.

"Yeah." Tony cut them off. "En daylight's burnin. We've got planting to do. I don't want the roots on those vines drying before they're in the ground."

"Aw, come on, Sarge." George Kamp laughed. Ever since the sandbag party, he'd buckled down, had taken an interest in the farm, in Bobby's fledgling program. "They'll wait a few minutes."

"I'm with Tony," Gallagher said. "Let's do this tonight. Bobby, we got concrete comin to Holtz's at one and the forms aren't finished."

"Whoa!" Bobby held up his hand. "Ah . . . thought for the week?"

"Learn something—" Thorpe began; the others chimed in, "every day to improve your self."

"*Yuho.* And DAARFE-vader?"

"Decide." They said in unison. "Act. Assess. React. Finish. Enjoy."

"You got it." Bobby turned, releasing them. "Let's go for it." The men rose, began scattering. "Carl, let me see you a minute, okay?"

"Don't you want me to go with Jer and Don?"

"We'll catch up to em. How long you been here?"

"Ten days."

"How's it going?"

"Okay." Mariano dropped his head, stretched out his neck, turned his face sideways and up—a suspicious glare—the same habitual posture Tony had had.

"Are you satisfied with your work here?"

"It's a job."

"I don't mean the job, I mean how you do it."

"Yeah. I guess."

"The hallmark of a High Meadow job is quality," Bobby said. "It's absolutely central to our cause."

"You goina fire me?"

"No, Carl. That's not the way we work. Besides, you're an independent contractor. That's the way the place is set up." Bobby led Carl up the new stairs to the loft and Grandpa's office. Mariano limped. His right leg and ankle had once been shattered by a concussion mine.

From below Tom Van Deusen yelled up, "Bobby, should I go with Jer or wait for you?"

"How many guys will it take to finish those forms?" Bobby countered.

"They can do it," Tom said. "But I can be working on the chaseway. You were right about his wife liking the way it looked."

"Okay," Bobby said.

In the office Bobby pulled out a file of forms, a box of labels, several ledgers. "One of our requirements here," he said, "is that each independent contractor keep his own records. The jobs you work. Hours. Equipment you supply. You've got to have your own checkbook, your own tax file. You can keep them up here or in the bunkhouse. Most guys carry their checkbooks but leave their files here. Periodically I'm going to go over them with you. It's completely confidential."

"I don't give a shit," Mariano said. "What do I need this shit for?"

"Keeps me honest," Bobby said. "Keeps you honest. Keeps Uncle Sam happy."

"Pay me cash. I'm not goina file no tax return."

"I told you day-one, that's one of our requirements. Remember— mainstream. Within the system. No hiding."

For forty minutes they filled out forms, applications for checking and savings accounts at The Bank of Mill Creek Falls, and, sketchily—Carl Mariano fighting it all the way—Bobby's DAARFE-vader form.

1. Decide: Pick a high-quality target.
2. Act: Advance on your target.
3. Assess: Assess your progress.
4. Re-Act: If not advancing, attack along a different route.
5. Finish: Persevere. Never give up.
6. Enjoy: Your actions, accomplishments, the results.

Bobby added a seven and the letter *P*. "Then," he said, "pick a new target."

"Ya know, Man—" Mariano said, his neck again extended, "this doesn't work for me."

"Is that the truth?"

"What da ya know, Man? You got it all. Farm. Business. Wife en kid."

"Yeah. You're right. Except the farm's not actually mine. I just have the right to use it. And that's what I'm letting you do."

"And I'm suppose to say thanks?"

"You don't have to. It might be the courteous thing to do, but I'm not dependent on thank-yous."

"You're really weird, Man."

Bobby nodded, pursed his lips, didn't answer. He packed up the forms, including a hundred dollar check to Mariano. "We'll stop at the bank on the way."

"Goina hold my hand?"

"Want me to?"

Mariano snorted.

"Give me a few minutes," Bobby said. "I gotta clear up some paperwork."

"I aint gonna become like these other guys," Mariano said. "They act like a bunch a brainless robots."

"Naw," Bobby said. "They're just on the program. They've picked certain quality targets and have committed to them. And they're enjoying the attack."

"That's not me."

"That's okay. Something I learned from Tony; I learned that self-esteem is more valuable when it's tempered with periodic self-doubt. Besides, you've got to earn it. No one can give it to you."

"I still ain't gonna be like them."

"You might be surprised. Quality's contagious."

Bobby knew it was working, but growth was again making money a problem. The vets were understanding, Bobby was open with them as to the overall financial situation. Still, to expand, to pay the vets' room, board and minimum wage, both the farm market and EES' clientele would need to increase. Nothing happens, he'd been thinking, nothing can be sustained without a salesman taking an order, without us selling our crop.

At this point, Bobby was High Meadow's only salesman. One of his targets was enough salespeople to create enough business to support forty vets—a five-fold increase. With that thought Bobby had scribbled a letter to Tyler Mohammed Wallace Dorsey Blackwell. It had taken Bobby an entire month to find Ty's location, a medium security prison between San Francisco and Los Angeles.

Dear Ty,

How's it going, man? Took me awhile to track you down. Guess they moved you a few times. I need your help, Ty. I'll explain in a minute. First I want to tell you I visited your folks and your brother Phillip. Carol's pregnant again. So is Sara! They're both due in September. Man, there's sure getting to be a lot of kids around here. Tony's living here with me, though he's been spending a lot of time with his wife and daughters. Anyway, Phillip and Carol are doing well. Little Tyrone's almost five. Cecilia's almost three. I didn't tell them I'd gotten your address—or your folks. But if you tell me to, I'll give it to them. Your mother sure worries about you. I saw Jessica, too. She's getting very pretty. I met Luwan for the first time. I've been over that way quite a bit on business. Life goes on, eh? Anyway, you should know they all wish you were back here.

Now, I need some help. Remember the community I talked about. It's becoming a reality, except it's nothing like I imagined. We've got eight Nam vets living here on the farm. We've turned the barn into a mill—producing solar heating systems. Business is taking off but I need a good salesman. You're the best I've ever seen. I want you to join us. Use us as a halfway house if you'd like. I'll submit whatever paperwork is necessary but you've got to take the first step—find out to whom I submit, and what I need to do to have you released in my recognizance.

Ty, you know my business and military background. Most people's lack of self-respect and their disrespect for others, for honesty, for truth, force us to seek out each other. Their attitudes don't work for grunts. You once looked for me, but I didn't understand. Now I'm looking for you.

Bob

P.S. If we could boost our sales, we could have a larger community.

" 'Oh the Thinks you can think, if only you try. . . . ' Dr. Seuss." Sara had handed him the book for the girls, had recited part of it to him just before he'd left for the apartment, and it kept repeating in his mind as he rode the Harley down Mill Creek Road, across town, over the new four-lane concrete bridge leading to the site of the future south-side Mill Creek Mall. He motored up 154 to Creek's Bend, thinking now of Blogs blowing by, or was it Rogs rolling round? Think, Think . . .

"Hi ya, Sweet Bumble-lee Beat."

"Papa." Gina ran up to him, hugged him. The late afternoon was warm, the sky still light.

"Where's Tumble-lee Treat?"

"She's up there." Gina turned, looked up the back stairs. Tony followed with his eyes. Michelle was on the top step. In her hand were two papers. Gina said, "Guess what? We wrote you letters in school today."

"You did?"

"Uh-huh. Read mine first."

"Should I read it before dinner?"

"Right now."

They climbed the steps together. Michelle was timidly waving the sheets. Tony bent, kissed the top of her head. "Tweedle-dee Deet," he said.

Gina jumped up and down. "Read mine. Read mine."

"Okay." Michelle handed him one sheet. Tony held it at arm's length, turned it, chuckled, "On the kwont of ε,🖑🖑." it read. "On the count of three . . ." He began to laugh. "One, two, three!" And he clapped his hands. Gina hugged him again. "Now let me see yours."

Shyly Michelle handed him the printed sheet. Before he was halfway through, his voice broke.

Memorial Day 1977

Dear Papa,
Thank you for fiting in the whor. It is graet you din't dy. I'm sorry some peepel you now dyed. Thank you aign.

Love,
Michelle

At the door, before she saw his eyes, Linda blurted, "Guess what?! Mark and Cindy eloped!" Then, "Oh Babe, you read Michelle's paper."

27

Mid-California, Monday, 11 July 1977—He read the 6 June issue of *Newsweek* with fascination yet without focus. He studied the photographs yet he barely saw them. He put his head back, closed his eyes. The room was warm, warmer than the unit in the prison. The bed was firm, yet softer than his cot. Still he wished he were there, not here, not for this. Again he looked at the magazine: "Battle over Gay Rights: Anita Bryant vs. The Homosexuals." He didn't care. How could he care? How could he care about anything anymore, with what they were going to do to him? At the back of the magazine were reviews of two books about Viet Nam, Larry Heinemann's *Close Quarters* and Philip Caputo's *A Rumor of War*. "Both carry the same message," the reviewer had written, "that the war was wrongheaded, an unspeakable waste of men . . . [a] war that reduced all combatants to a state of savage frenzy in which atrocities became not only possible but desirable."

He could barely concentrate. He was angry, angry at them all. "Caputo sent a patrol illegally into a village to seize two Viet Cong suspects. 'It was my secret and savage desire that the two men die,' he writes. The suspects were indeed killed, found innocent, and Caputo was court-martialed on charges of murder. The Marines, however, were embarrassed by the affair and dropped the case, allowing Caputo to float back into the real world, where he now wins prizes for his journalism."

Not angry, incensed! Fucka been black, Ty thought, they won't be no journalism prize. They'd hang his ass out on the firin range.

His thoughts tumbled. Billy Jo Trippan, his readjustment counselor, wanted him to admit to "the opportunities of incarceration." Ty thought, hang that Uncle Tom's ass out there too! "Opportunities!" Prison sucked. Worse than LBJ—Long Binh Jail. Not physically worse; this was a breeze. But here he had no links. The brothers weren't combat brothers. Maybe some were. But they didn't talk, except for Fats Knutsen, who wanted to organize a chapter of IVA, Incarcerated Veterans of America. A scam! That's how Ty saw it. Maybe had Knutsen been black . . . Ty had never had a visitor, never a letter. Except the one he'd just received from Wapinski.

"Take your frustrations," Trippan had said virtually every session, "and convert them. Make them work for you."

Every session, like a kowtowing Uncle Tom, Ty Mohammed bowed his head and agreed. Every session his thoughts blasted manically. You don't know nothin. You ain't ever goina know nothin. You no idea what I done. How it come back on me. Payback. Payback's a mothafucka. When I took an ear, He seen. When I snatched a ring, He watched. He a'ready punished me. You got no right. No right. I get out of here, it goin be payback time. You just write down how passive I am.

"There are a few others," a woman called in. She came into his room. Behind her were three young white men. "I don't think you can get a Negro's to transilluminate," she said to them. "None of the others' did."

"Do you mind?" one of the young men said politely to Ty.

The young men were all in loose white summer uniforms. The woman, the resident on duty, in a white lab coat and dark blue skirt.

Ty stared at them. He didn't answer. They didn't really look at him. Resignedly he sat up, swung his feet to the floor, grabbed the back of the hospital gown to keep it shut. Then he went into the closet and two of the interns and the resident entered with him and shut the door. God damn, how he hated this. He lifted the front of the gown, held his penis up and to one side. Two of them, he didn't look to see who, grabbed his scrotum. Immediately they had the skin pulled taut over a flashlight. "You can feel it right there," one said.

"Yeah, but you can't—"

"Oh yeah! I'm getting it to transilluminate."

"The light's got to come through the lump," the resident said. "Not through the sack."

"It is," said one intern.

"No it's not," said the other.

"Sure, look at it," said the first.

The resident bent down, tried to see what the first intern was seeing. "No," she said. "Even if the lump isn't so dense as to be opaque, I don't think—"

"But look . . ."

"Not with his skin pigment," the resident insisted. She stood up, turned on her flashlight, looked at Ty and said, "Sorry. I just don't think anyone can tell this way."

It had all begun a week earlier, on the Fourth. They'd been given the day off and Ty had lingered in the unit—a seventy-bed dormitory—a little longer than most of his unit-mates, had taken the time to fiddle with himself—not a lot, just a quick hand passed into his pants, a little friendly self-caress. With seventy of them on a floor designed for thirty— damn place was like living in an overcrowded fishbowl—there weren't many opportunities. He'd felt it immediately, an acorn cap, a half filbert, stuck to his left testicle. Right on the bottom. It was hard, maybe like half a marble, and securely attached. What the fuck, he'd thought. With one hand he'd maneuvered the ball so it was tight to the sack, with thumb and forefinger of the other he'd grabbed the lump, squeezed. It didn't hurt and immediately he'd thought that that was good. If he'd been sick, if the testicle had been swollen or sore, he'd reasoned, then it would be time to worry. Some sort of infection, he'd thought. But this was just a hard lump. He'd put himself away, caught up to the others. The thought had nagged at him but in the afternoon, playing basketball in the prison yard, he'd forgotten about it. At lights-out he rechecked. He wasn't certain he'd find it again but it was there—hard, secure— maybe, he thought, a little smaller.

On the fifth they were back to work, he in the woodshop making three-block ducks—a cube body, a thick dowel neck and a triangular head— for no one and no reason he could imagine. In the back of his mind it nagged him—something's not right, but he felt fine, healthy, clean. Indeed, he'd been clean, drug-free, since being rearrested. And he'd been warm, and fed, and clothed. He had not gotten his piece of the pie but he could bide his time, waste his time, waste these years, and still formulate his plan. Prison isn't forever. If he could stay clean on the outside, there'd be no holding him down.

On the sixth, in the showers, "Whatcha got there, Ty?" Laughs, other guys waiting, fuckin fishbowl, he'd checked himself again, breathed easier. It's a little smaller, he'd told himself. It's going away. But he knew he was lying. It was bigger. On the morning of the seventh he'd reported to the infirmary. "Just a cyst," he said to the doctor. "Huh?"

"I'm going to send you to a specialist," the man retorted.

"Just some pills, right Doc?"

The man was cool, efficient, no-nonsense. He didn't hide his disdain for inmates. He was not openly hostile. "I'll fill out the paperwork," he'd said curtly. "They'll tell you when and where."

"No big thing though," Ty insisted. "Right?"

"Maybe. Maybe not."

They had returned him to work and no more was said for two days. But Ty was afraid. Both nights he masturbated, making sure the equipment worked. Day and night, every time he went to the can, he checked. Every time he'd told himself, it's smaller. Every time he knew he was lying. He was appalled at how quickly it expanded. Six thirty Monday morning they took him from the unit to the holding cell, shackled him, then brought him from the prison to the county hospital.

He waited. Waited. The guard remained, happy to be outside, away. Ty would have been happy, too, except for the waiting, the fear.

A doctor examined him. As Ty dressed the doctor made a few notes in the new file. "Most guys get a little embarrassed," the man said when he closed the file. "They're reluctant to tell anyone. And seminoma is one of the fastest spreading of all cancers."

Cancer! "I got . . . ?" The word was like being hit with an AK round.

The doctor held up a hand. "I'm not saying that. It could be something else. I want you to understand a few things. We know a lot about testicular cancer, if that's what this is. For the most part they're ninety-five percent curable if they're caught in time. But a lot of men don't say anything until it's too la—"

"I jus found it on Monday," Ty blurted. "Really!"

The doctor smiled. He was in his fifties, gray, sympathetic. "Yes. That's good," he said. "If you hadn't done something about it, it could have spread into your lymphatic system and up into your abdomen. From there it can spread throughout your body. There's a number of different types of testicular cancer but seminoma . . . "

"Sem-a-no-ma," Ty repeated. He had his full attention on the doctor. His eyes were wide open. His entire mind was shifting—away from the prison, away from prison jargon, away too from roof-rat lingo, from junkie prattle.

"Yes. It's a cancer that strikes men between twenty-five and thirty-five. During World War Two there were an awful lot of GIs in that range. I forget the figure, one in a thousand men develop it. Something like that. You're not an isolated case. They used to handle all of this at Walter Reed. In Washington, D.C.?"

Ty nodded. The doctor continued. "One of the reasons why the survival rate is so high is they had almost an unlimited number of men to work on between, oh, I guess, 1941 and '45. Or '46. That's why we know it hits between twenty-five and thirty-five. Usually at twenty-eight or twenty-nine."

"I—I'm only twenty-six," Ty said.

"It's a matter of the maturity of your body," the doctor explained. "Perhaps you were exposed to something when you were small. We're not sure exactly. It may be caused by a very slow-acting virus that everyone's exposed to at some point."

"Herpes?" Ty asked quietly. He thought of Golden Gate Park, of the white girl, of his finger.

The doctor eyed him. "No," he said. "Something else. If you're susceptible, if you have the genetic tendency toward it, at a certain point in your maturation it manifests itself. The stimulus might be chemical instead of viral. We don't truly know."

Late that afternoon Ty had been admitted to the hospital. Then he had been examined by a urologist who straightforwardly announced, "It's either a benign tumor or cancer. It's not an infection and it's not likely to be a cyst. We'll operate tomorrow."

"Why, look here, Honey. Look what we got here." She is an old black woman, as old as his mother, older, bigger.

"What that there?" Another old black woman. This one has a mop in a rectangular bucket of dirty water. The bucket has four little wheels, casters, at the corners. The second woman is pushing the bucket toward him. He is in bed. The bed is small, low to the ground. Compared to the women he is tiny. They stare down at him. "Some big stud, huh, Sugar?" the second woman says.

"See what happen," the first says. "Your motha never tell you 'Don't touch yo'self'?"

The two women laugh. Ty is small. He is flat on his back, unable to rise. "You know what they gowina do ta this big stud?" The second woman cackles and the first joins her. "They got this big tool. Bigger en my mop here. They gon take that big ol Black 'n' Decker pecker wrecker, they gon make him sing soprano."

"Oh." The first woman titters. "Don't you go scarin this boy now. Don't you go eyein his privates." She can't hold back her gaffaws. She rocks up and down over him, her hands flailing like a gospel singer.

The second is laughing louder than the first, shrieking with glee. "He aint gowina *have* no privates."

"Fuck You!" he screamed. The anesthesia was wearing off. The morphine was inadequate. He was disoriented, paranoid. His arms were lashed, his legs restrained. There was an IV needle in his arm, and it *hurt*. His violent jouncing made the entire gurney tip. "I hate it," he shouted. "They made me. I never done nothin. AaaahhH! OW!" The pain was immense. His entire abdomen hurt. It was worse than the through-and-through of his ass when he'd been shot.

"You're going to be all right," the surgeon said. Ty had no idea who he was, where the voice was coming from. "We had to take it out," the surgeon said. "It was cancerous."

Ty's eyes flared. The pain was continuous. From the pain he knew they hadn't just split the scrotum, snipped out the nut and closed him back up. They'd gone in from above. It felt like they'd gone in from his lungs. "I already paid, Mothafucka. Here . . ." He tried to jerk his hand up, to show he'd paid a finger for a finger—but his arm was lashed flat. He twisted his head to show his ear, raised his lip to show his teeth.

"How long has he been like this?" Doctor Fenton turned to the postop nurses.

"Oh—" one checked her watch, "let's see, they rolled him in at nine thirty. He came around the first time twenty minutes later, then drifted back out."

Fenton turned back to Ty, put his hand on Ty's hand. "It's three hours," he said. "Most of the anesthesia should be out of your system."

Ty stared at him. He couldn't have been angrier, more afraid. Incarcerated. Restrained. Mutilated. He twisted his hand, grabbed Fenton's fingers. Snarled.

"Ow! Hey! I'm the doctor." He pulled his hand away.

Now Ty was in an even deeper funk. "What'd you do?"

"It's called a radical inguinal dissection," Fenton said. His voice was cold, that of an apathetic lecturer. "We took the testicle and all the lymph nodes on the left. To protect you from the spread of the malignancy. I'll call on you when we've got the pathology report."

Ty's postoperative recovery was quick. In a day the constant pain ceased, replaced by stabs anytime he coughed, sneezed, jarred his abdomen. In three days even that was tolerable. In a week he was back in prison, in two, back to his unit. He refused to talk about the operation. It was bad enough he had to shower—exposed, scars on his ass from Nam, now single hung—with seventy inmates, with a rotation of guards. His counselor, Billy Jo Trippan, Ph.D., wanted to know how it felt! What it meant! What changes Ty saw in himself! Fuck you, Billy Jo Bedpan. That was as far as Ty would go. Fuck you, all of you, he felt. I'm nothing. You control me totally. And I'm tired of this shit. They should of left me behind on Hamburger Hill.

The ordeal was not over. From the lymphangiogram they—the doctors, the warden, the state, they owned his body as much as they had owned his body when he'd been in the army—decided the proper course of follow-up treatment was 30,000 roentgens of radiation—15,000 from the navel down, 15,000 from navel to larynx, to be delivered 1,000 per day five days per week for six weeks, with a two-week break between the first and second sets. Or was it a 15,000 roentgen bolt each time? He wasn't certain and the doctors and technicians weren't into explanations. Again there was the fear, the leverage they used to prod him into acquiescence. "You've got a ninety percent chance of recovery," he was told, "if you complete the series."

"You mean," he'd countered, shy, concerned, revolted, all at once, "I'm either dead or alive."

"It might be higher. Probably ninety-five percent."

"That's same-same fifty-fifty." Ty hated them, hated this mealy mouthed probability shit. "Either you here or you aint."

The radiation treatment center was adjacent to the county hospital. On his first "visit" Ty was carefully, semipermanently, marked, diagramed, the graph pattern from the X-ray machine light traced onto his chest. Then he was zapped, ionized, irradiated, blasted, fried. No feeling. Little noise. Each time thereafter, it took only a minute to line him up, zap him, draw blood (to check his white-cell count), and send him back. The first zapping took place at eleven A.M., Monday, 1 August. By one o'clock he was ill. Not severely; he felt as if he'd eaten bad meat—something rotten from Fast-food Freddie's or something typical from the prison kitchen. By three he was nauseous but there was nothing in his stomach to vomit. Then it passed and he felt fine, felt like he was finally getting over on the entire system because they'd brought him back to the prison and put him in a private cell next to the infirmary. By comparison it was almost like being in a motel. No one bothered him. He was excused from details, work calls.

Tuesday was a repeat. And Wednesday. Leave early, get fried, return, get sick, do nothing, feel better, sleep. Except the "get sick" part got worse. By Thursday he was nearly broken. He had no idea how he could continue. He wandered about the cell, begged a guard to get him a book, some music, something to distract him. He lay down on the floor, piled blankets atop himself, focused on the ceiling for hours. Friday morning he felt better. Then they blasted his guts, took blood, returned him, and he was sick all night.

The next week was a repeat. *Bbzzzzzzzzzttt.* Blood. Sick. Radiation is cumulative. *Pzzzzaaa-oopp.* Blood. Sick. Sicker. Intestines, liver, bone marrow, the last of his reproductive equipment, and suddenly he was no longer bitter but only depressed and he wanted to see Jessica, his daughter, his baby, what had Wapinski written, he hadn't paid attention—the letter coming when it had, Wapinski referring to Luwan, Luwan dumb ignorant so desperate to have a baby she'd of had anyone's . . . Needs my mothafuckin help, huh? Oh God, just to see my baby once before I die. What I do with that letter?

The third week was worse. He could not think about Wapinski's letter. In the can he had seen the lining, like sausage casing, the lining of his intestines, his stomach. Take my other fuckin nut, he'd prayed. Just stop this. He couldn't even drink water without pain. Take my johnso—No! Not that. Just let me see my Jessica.

Then came the two-week break and he felt fine. The radiation was something he could weather. Hell, he'd been through half of it. It couldn't get worse.

But it did. Trippan visited him in the infirmary. It hurt to talk. Knutsen came. Other guys from the unit. "How ya doin, Man?"

"Whatda you care?"

"We care, Brother. We always cared. We didn't leave that on the outside."

Ty stared at them.

"Hey, I got this cool book, Man. Bippo said you was askin for a book. My old lady sent it to me. You take it."

"Yeah. Me too. I got a cassette player from my brother. En some bad tunes, Bro. You listen to em. Tell me what ya think."

Ty shook his head. A sheepish smile cracked his lips.

"Funny, huh, Bro?"

"Yeah," Ty said.

"What's funny?" a second inmate said.

"You," Ty answered. He gestured with his chin at each. "I must mean more to you than I do to me."

His unit-mates laughed. "Yeah," one said. "We all do."

"Eh." Ty looked away, looked back. "I was thinkin about friends I lost. In Nam. Things we went through. We were one body. Suffered together."

"You in that bad mothafucka?!"

"Yeah. I don't know why I made it back."

"Me too! One Seventy-Third."

"I got a little girl," Ty said.

The last week of the high zapping, of his lungs, heart, esophagus, brought a new level of pain and discomfort. It was Thursday, the twenty-second of September 1977. Today, he thought, today, tomorrow and Monday, and I'm home free. Just three more little blips. Just one foot in front of the other, Sir, Airborne, All the Way, Sir, Can Do! There's an end to this. There's an end to it.

"Hurts, huh, Man?"

Ty looked at Stiler. Stiler had killed his own father. Had shot him three times in the stomach. Stiler had been on shit, on dust, bad shit, stoned crazy. He hadn't even known he'd killed his father for three days. Ty did not speak, only nodded. His throat was so sore it hurt to breathe. His nose was running, he had a fever, the shakes.

"Ya know, in some countries, they do that to people, you know, political prisoners, as torture."

Ty nodded slightly. Burn the lining outta their throats, he thought.

"I never thought"— Stiler squirmed on the stool next to Ty's bed—" like nothin bout it when I read it. Now I see you bein fried. Microwaved from the inside out. Now I understand."

Ty nodded again, thought, Monday. That's it. And 95 percent chance . . . Shee-it. Jus so there an end to it.

But at the radiation center they did not zap him. His blood count was too low, or too high—how could he concentrate? Only three to go. "Come back tomorrow." Postponed. Not canceled. Postponed. There would be no end. He was a prisoner. A political prisoner. Incarcerated because he was black. Because . . . he'd . . . sure, he'd committed fraud.

But that was because he was black. Not being black caused it, but being black, way back in the army, even earlier, caused him to be stigmatized, caused the undesirable discharge, caused his drug problem. They done it to him because he was black. He'd given his left nut to their cause, to their bureaucratic disenfranchisement machine. It was the same as being politically prosecuted!

Friday, the twenty-third: "Ah, Mr. Mohammed, would you like me to put this lead shield over your Adam's apple?"

"No." His voice was thin, raspy. "I'm fine."

"Okay." *Bbzzzzzz-it.* "You know, you're doing very well. Usually by the eighth or ninth treatment we have to put that block on."

Ty stared. "You usually put—" He did not finish, but thought, Fuck it. Give me the whole thing. Two to go. I got this far. Don't you go ruinin my chances.

On Monday, the twenty-sixth, the machine broke down and there was a back up in the waiting room: a young white girl, maybe eight, in a wheelchair; four senior citizens, all white; plus an assortment of parents and spouses; and Ty and his guard. All the patients, victims, were weak, quiet. It was so obvious who was who. But except for Ty, the sufferers were all frail. Old or young. There was no one in their twenties or thirties; no one who'd been strong, healthy, in the prime of life. Drug addict or not, Ty had begun treatment much stronger than these people. And they were being zapped just like him. They were suffering just like him. And they weren't quitting. He glanced at the little girl. Her mother was reading a story to her. *Heidi.* His eyes shot to an old man with a curved spine and sunken chest. He seemed to be praying. His wife was doing a crossword puzzle. To Ty they all seemed alike, seemed weak, doomed. He was weak. The guard helped him to the changing cubicle, helped him remove his clothes, helped him to the deep-fry chamber. But he did not feel doomed. There was an end. Two more treatments.

"Get that little guy out of the way . . . "

Ty grabbed his privates. Most of the nurses and technicians had been nice, sympathetic, or cool and efficient. This one was bitchy. How many zapped people, people *you've* zapped into anguish, into pain, can one handle? He laughed. She gave him a dirty look. "Mr. Shrively," he hoarsed out.

Pzzzaaa-oopp. Needle. Blood. Ty rolled, pushed himself up, slid to the floor.

"Um." Not quite so bitchy. "You're the first person we haven't had to help up from the table today."

Ty forced a smile. "I . . . " The pain in his throat was intense but he wanted to joke with her. "Wife and I . . . " He looked at the nurse. What did he give a shit if his story was bullshit, was off the top of his head, just something to say. " . . . want to start a family . . . but Mr. Shriv—"

"Oh!" The technician was truly surprised. "Why don't you wait a little . . . "

"Mr. Shrively . . . " Ty smiled.

"You'll get it back," the technician said quickly. "But hold off on the family for about three years."

"Deformities?" Ty asked.

"Ah . . . " She turned cold again. "No. No sense saddling your wife with kids if you don't make it."

She was not there the next day, the last day, his last day of treatment! If he were not so sick he would have been overjoyed. His blood count was marginal. "Please . . . " He wanted to beg. He couldn't speak the words. Please. Just end it.

Pzzbzzz-aatt-ooppt. Never exactly the same noise twice.

"I'm impressed, Mr. Mohammed." This technician was one of the nice ones. Gentle. Empathetic. "We didn't think you'd make it this far."

"I . . . I had to. Didn't I?"

"Oh, not really. We take you to your limit but you could have stopped last week. We had a lottery going to see which day you'd quit. No one picked today."

Friday, October 7—Ty was back in the unit, back to his cot, back among the eyes and the ears. At lights-out they teased him about glowing in the dark. And the next day Knutsen told him to make sure the Classification Team had a full report because they would be more apt to transfer him to a minimum security facility because of his suffering. "Maybe even move up your parole date," Knutsen said.

"Yeah," Ty said. Yeah, he thought. But if I hadn't been in the house there'd a been no operation. I'd be dead. I'd be . . . Where's the Captain's letter? He said he needed my motherfuckin help. Didn't understand! Mill, huh? My chance. My piece a the pie. Golden Rule: He who got the gold, make the rule. Enough for a hundred operations.

October 1984

By the fall of 1977 High Meadow had reached its first critical mass point. Bobby could be away. I could be away. Things ran. George Kamp was a responsible worker/leader; so too Jim Thorpe. They got along well. Tom Van Deusen seemed to change overnight, a result of the great sandbag party. His intensity and focus changed. He became a savior of the pond. He wanted to run jobs, to help design projects, lay out schedules. And Bobby was only too happy to expose him to the resources and let Van Deusen take off.

Gallagher never developed that drive but he was now more self-assured. It was his idea to install an alarm system that could alert all High Meadow to crises. We installed an old air-raid siren that Bobby had scavenged from Johnnie Jackson's Salvage Yard, that had once stood atop the old elementary school in the Lutzburgh section of town. When activated that old siren could be heard over in Creek's Bend, Old New Town, and probably halfway to Rock Ridge. Along with the siren we ran army surplus ground-line telephone lines to links in all the buildings.

This was a time of building. Five more vets arrived. Howie Bechtel, Ron Hull, Steve Hacken, Mark Renneau, and our first non-European American, number fourteen, Art Brown—an African-American vet from Wilkes-Barre sent to us by Ty's brother Phillip.

Our labor was cheap. In the late fall we drew down the pond, widened and deepened the spillway—it took hours of jackhammering to bust up Pewel's work so we could rebuild it in a way that boards could be more easily removed in case of flooding. We reframed the roof of the farmhouse to change the angle, and the EES crew embedded the solar collectors between the rafters and installed the glazing—but before they finished the shingles Bobby pulled them from the job to work elsewhere. We added a "messhall" adjacent to the bunkhouse (some of the guys became outstanding cooks), redivided the bunkhouse into four single rooms and a two-bay dormitory. Across the pond in the woods, Bobby let Wagner and Mariano clean and repair Pewel and Brigita's first cabin. That was very emotional for him. Before he decided, if I recall correctly, he wandered half a dozen times—usually only with

Josh but maybe once or twice with Noah—up to the cemetery. I imagine he needed to ask permission, but we never talked about it.

We were going, always going, it seemed. I had to schedule meetings with Bobby. Grapes, that year, was our biggest farm topic. Through it all Bobby sniffled. His nose was always running and he was constantly popping over-the-counter antihistamines.

Nineteen seventy-seven was the year of the Great Energy Debate in Congress and in the Carter White House. Bobby followed it closely. EES made its first collector arrays to be sold wholesale, sold to a father-son plumbing outfit in Binghamton, New York. They liked our prices, the quality of the product, the design, the service. In '78 they purchased more than one hundred collectors. EES needed three more trucks to keep up with our crews. On the farming side we purchased a trailer/combine, a new tractor, and a used six-by farm truck.

Nineteen seventy-seven was the year Willie Joe Namath went to the LA Rams; the year of Son of Sam; the Ali-Shavers fifteen-round decision; the Nixon-Frost interviews. It was the year Elvis "the Pelvis" Presley killed himself because he was stuck and no one showed him the solvent to become unstuck. That left me all shook up, feelin like I was down at the end of Lonely Street.

By mid-'77 I was no longer stuck. I moved back in with Linda; told her about my dream the night Gina and Michelle were born; about so many of the things that had happened. Pop was talking to me again, too.

Linda received her midwifery certification. On September 23, 1977, she delivered her first baby. (She tells me *delivery* is not the right word. She says, "It's not like, 'Hey Lady, you the one who ordered an extra large with double cheese and pepperoni?' " How I laughed over that. "Maybe catcher is the right word," she'd continued. Catchers: catcher in the rye, in the alfalfa, in the birthing rooms—me and my Linda.)

On the twenty-third Linda caught Paul Anthony Wapinski, with Sara and Bobby and Dr. Simon Denham in the new birthing room at St. Luke's Hospital in Rock Ridge. The joy! I baby-sat for Noah at High Meadow. Most of the vets were at the house, waiting, expecting, playing with Noah—I wasn't the only one who'd missed these good years of his children's lives. When the call came we let loose with the air-raid siren and the cheers didn't stop until Ernest Hartley, Jr., the mayor's son, and three officers—Mill Creek Falls' finest—came screaming up in three squad cars demanding quiet and an explanation, and cited us for disturbing the peace. That triggered flashes of anger so deep I think had we not been so happy, we might have engaged those bozos in hand-to-hand. We blasted it the next day, too, Saturday, when we heard that Carol Simpson, Phillip's wife, Ty's sister-in-law, gave birth to Theodore

Jonathan Simpson—blasted the siren but only after we locked the driveway gate and when ol' fat-butt Hartley came screaming in we just hooted at him, unseen, from the orchard, the strawberry patch and down in the culverts. I don't think we could have had more fun.

Linda came up that night—Gina and Michelle were at Grandma's. It was the weekend of our eighth wedding anniversary. Bobby was inside with Noah. The guys were either on the basketball court or on our new soccer field, or in town. I took her to my old cubicle, then behind the false wall, into the tunnel, down to the deep bunker. I explained to her my fears about a coming nuclear war; my thoughts about joining Mill Creek's nuke freeze movement, my trepidations about that movement's "fringe" director, Joanne Wapinski, about not being able to tell Bobby because of Joanne. I was surprised, perhaps, jolted, that Linda didn't see what I'd done as paranoia. "Even Bobby doesn't know," I said. "Don't say anything."

George Kamp left at Christmas—our first graduate. He returned to Towanda and in January opened up a small auto-parts store. I might just as well finish him out. He returned periodically—sometimes just to visit but mostly with parts for our trucks or the old '53 Chevy—and of course each year he came back for the barn trial. By the Great Media Trial of 1981 George had two auto-parts stores. He had remarried, had his first child in 1982. In '83 he was elected to the township's board of aldermen.

By late '77 Bobby was looking for ways to speed up the High Meadow rehabilitation process. People were inquiring; we were receiving requests. "Could I come in June?" "Can you help me?" "I could get there by bus, I think." "Do you provide transportation?" On and on and on. Mouth-to-mouth word tends to become garbled. "Can I join your army? I'm a real good shot." "I'll pay whatever your fee is if you can help my husband (son) (brother)." Bobby wrote or called them all. "Can I come there to die?" To me it's unbelievable how many asked that question though when I rethink my own story, I should not be shocked. "No," Bobby'd answer. "We don't warehouse people. Come if you want to sleep for a while, or if you like apple fritters and maple syrup, and if you want to live." Constantly Bobby or I, Thorpe, Gallagher, Sara, and believe it or not, Carl Mariano, were explaining Bobby's approach, explaining High Meadow.

My brother, Dr. Joe, used to get on me when I'd bubble with enthusiasm about what *we* were doing, accomplishing, during this time. I'd say, "Viet Nam veterans can do anything." I'd say, "We're the best of the best—the heart of our generation." I'd say, "We're the vanguard, we are leading our generation and much of the world into the future, into the eighties." He'd say, "You're seeing a skewed sample. Most vets are bums with unresolved psychological problems." He'd try to be tactful, usually leaving out, "including you." I'd say, "Naw, look at us. Come up and visit us. See what we're doing." He'd say, "I know what you're doing. I think it's terrific. But who are you guys? Who do you attract? At least half of you are either Marines or Airborne, right?" "Maybe," I'd say. He'd say, "Don't you get it, Tony? Most of you up there chose to be something above average even before you entered the service. How can you compare the average vet with that helicopter pilot you've got? Or that ground radar technician? And everyone there is there of his own accord. It's not random selection but people who have elected to be something more than the mundane. I'm not putting that down. I think what you and Wapinski are doing is highly estimable. I just don't think you could do that with an average veteran population."

We'd argue on. I'd say, "Sure you could. We're not different." I'd think, but not say, "You're saying that because you're not a vet. You hid in school. You'd have to question your choice to agree with me." Instead I'd say, "You don't get it, Joe. We *are* average vets. For a lot of the guys this is a last resort. They've got no place else to go. They were all the way down with their backs to the wall." "Yes," Joe'd say, "but they chose not to remain there. Wapinski is an anomaly. You too. Not everyone is capable of pulling themselves up by their bootstraps. You watch TV. Most Nam vets are so psychologically scarred they either should be locked away for their own good, or for the protection of society . . . or maybe they're harmless but they're albatrosses on society . . . they're on welfare or sponging off relatives."

By this point I'd be livid but I'd be holding my tongue because on and off I'd sponged off Joe who'd helped to raise my daughters. Shit! Enough of that. I'd clam up, mutter something like, "What you see on TV isn't a random selection either."

At this time Bobby was telling us, "We've got to go beyond DAARFE-vader. It works when one is unstuck but it isn't a solvent for the glue of traumatic stress. That's going to require a new tool."

It was not by mistake or by chance that Wapinski was able to make such an impact. Bobby studied behavior. Not only screwed-up Viet Nam–vet behavior, not only successful vets—though this was one area of his focus—but behavior and behavior change in general. He interviewed the therapists at RRVMC (and came away enraged), talked to local psychologists and psychiatrists, went to Nittany Mountain College and purchased every psych text for every course they offered in the '77–'78 academic year. Bobby was driven as much to discover and implement a quick, workable program as he was to design solar homes and efficient, sustainable communities. He'd rant at "the idiots"—usually not to their faces but to himself, in the barn or the orchard, in the sugarbush or on a roof. He had no patience with people he believed "should know better"; people who he felt were ignoring available accepted knowledge; people who "strongly" supported this point of view or that WITHOUT having delved deeply in the subject matter; people who had taken the easy way out, accepted pulp.

"Hit em with the myth busters," he'd say. "People believe all sorts of inaccuracies. Yesterday, one guy said to me he sure was glad his father knew people at the draft board. Otherwise, he said, he would have been drafted, put in the infantry, and sent to Viet Nam, like everyone else. I said, 'Your chances would only have been about 3 per cent.' He couldn't believe that. I said, "Figure it out. Two point six million in-country vets out of ten million era vets. You had a 26 percent chance of going if you *were* drafted. And only 10 percent of those who went were assigned to infantry companies."

Ideas evolved. "For the guys who did go," Bobby'd say, "and who are now stuck, we need to develop a Quick Strike: Raid on the Brain solvent. Have them see they've got a gun to their heads—a major motivation to become unstuck. If a vet comes," Bobby'd say, "he's looking to change. He's already motivated. It's only a matter of pushing the right buttons, pulling the right triggers, transforming the meaning of the experience with the Raid. Look, right now much of the meaning, much of the interpretation of their experience is being foisted upon them from the outside. If we can bring it back to them, to the personal, if pride can replace shame, honor replace dishonor, camaraderie replace racism, and the military victory in which they were involved replace the political forfeiture to which they were not a part . . . "

Marvin Book arrived. Then Michael Treetop (a Native American). Then Knabe, Casper, Lorson, others. About this time too, Miriam, Joanne and Cheryl Wapinski (and Brian, though apologetically) enlisted the aid of Harold Rosenwald, Esq., to file charges against Bobby, claiming misuse of Pewel's estate.

Then came Gary Sherrick. "Bitta bing, bitta bang!"

28

The big barn, an evening in late May 1978—It was warm. Sherrick was hot. He sat on a box in the shadow of the Slitter, apart from the others. The day's chores and tasks were complete. The educational exercise—change the meaning by immersing into the truth, Bobby's first attempt at a Quick Strike program—was under way. Wapinski sat on layout table number 1. Pisano was on number 2. Gallagher, Van Deusen, Thorpe, Wagner, Hull, Mariano . . . sixteen vets in all, sat on crates, folding chairs, toolboxes, near the tables. Only Gary Sherrick was to the side, between the jerry-rigged elevator and the Slitter. Steve Hacken had been reading a David Ansen review of the film, *The Boys in Company C*, from a four-month-old *Newsweek*. " 'Vietnam,' " he'd read, " 'was not fought like any other war, and it can't be told the way old war movies were.' "

"What a bunch of crap," Sherrick muttered. He was just loud enough to distract the few closest to the elevator.

Bobby glanced over. He had not discerned the grumble but he'd seen the others turn.

" '...the film gives,' " Hacken went on, " 'a fresh and harrowing reading of a struggle so chaotic and irrational that it approaches the climate of hallucination.' "

"What," Sherrick yelled over, "approaches a climate of hallucination?" Heads snapped toward him. "What?" he barked loudly. He did not look at the group but talked toward the machine in front of him. "The film or the war?"

Hacken stopped. With his thumb on the column he squeezed the magazine. "The film," he said. "Did you see it?"

Sherrick could not control his voice. It was full of indignation and disgust. "That's not what it says. Reread it." Three or four guys groaned. Sherrick had been interrupting all night. Hacken reread the line. Sherrick snarled, " 'Climate of hallucination,' describes the word *struggle*. Not the film. *Struggle*. The war, damn it, seemed pretty fuckin real to me."

Gary Sherrick had been at High Meadow nine days. He was a genetic alcoholic and he knew it. He knew he was unlike most heavy drinkers and self-dosers. Once they learned why they drank, they learned to control their consumption. In Sherrick, one drink set off an immense craving for another immediate dose of alcohol.

Bobby had formally checked him in. He had made Sherrick fill out the new High Meadow Job Contract and Personal History form that Bobby, with Tom Van Deusen's help, had designed.

Sherrick had been an alcoholic since his first drink in his sophomore year in high school. For years he'd hid it, denied it, and except for the baseball scholarship incident, he'd held his life together until May of 1975. He'd more than held it together. He'd excelled.

Sherrick grew up in Indiana, attended Indiana University on an athletic scholarship until, in September '65, because of one drink that had led to one thousand, the school did not invite him back. He dried out. Swore off. He spent three years in the army, April '68 to April '69 in Viet Nam, a doorgunner on a Huey slick. By tour's end he'd been awarded a Silver Star, a Bronze Star, six Air Medals, a handful of commendations. After discharge he returned to Indiana University, graduated in '71 in the top quarter of his class, with a degree in history and government. For the next four years he worked as a policeman in Indianapolis. At night he took courses in law at the state extension. In 1974 Gary Sherrick was assigned to the Indianapolis PD Narcotics Investigation Division. In early '75 he took a drink, went on a bender, was released from duty. In the ensuing three years he was in and out of VA alcohol treatment programs eleven times.

"It helped at first," he'd told Wapinski during that first interview. "But I couldn't stay with it. I'd go back. Like iron filings to a magnet, it'd pull me. Then I'd check back in to the VA. Bitta bing, bitta bang. It'd be worse. If you're a repeater, the VA treats you like a parasite. They write things in your file like you're a manipulator or a malingerer. So you learn to manipulate the system because you get dependent on it same as being dependent on anything else. If you don't manipulate it, you've got nowhere to go. Then they make you feel guilty. You feel worse. Like what's the matter with me? It drives you to your next drink."

"Bad question," Wapinski had interrupted him. "Instead of, What's the matter with me? ask, How can I stay on the wagon and enjoy it?"

"Yeah," Sherrick had said. "They said that too. But that's not what they mean."

"Look—" Wapinski had tossed Sherrick's new folder on the desk, "here we don't keep records on malingering or manipulation. If you need help, we'll help. All you have to do is follow our rules."

"What rules, Man?"

"Simple stuff," Wapinski had said. "No drugs. No booze other than what's provided, which may not be much. We have a few blowouts now and then. Maybe some wine or beer—"

"I can't do that."

"Um."

"I can't control it . . . if I start."

"Then don't start." Wapinski had moved on. At this point he had never dealt with a genetic alcoholic; he assumed Sherrick was, like many others, a habitual self-doser.

"No individual firearms," Wapinski had said. "We have community weapons for hunting and target shooting but they're locked up. We target shoot most Saturdays twelve to three. It's not mandatory. Lots of guys find it therapeutic. You know the dangers, you've seen what a weapon can do. Some guys are afraid of em because of that, because of what they did with em. What we do is let you do it again, with supervision. Like the rifle range.

"Look," Bobby'd continued, "here it is in a nutshell. You don't hurt yourself, physically or mentally, and you don't hurt anybody else. Jessie Taynor, downtown, she's a big mentally retarded woman, she's off limits. You touch her, we kill you. No questions asked. You participate in work, PT—basketball or soccer, or, ah, Lorson and Knabe are setting up a weight room—choice is yours. And you participate in our discovery exercises. Thursday nights we meet in the barn, just vets, and talk about what we've discovered. As to work, you can work with Tony on the farm, with Van Deusen out on job sites, or with Howie Bechtel in the barn building collectors or assembling duct work."

"What if I don't want to?" Sherrick had asked.

Wapinski had eyed him. He did not want a repeat of the Ivanov affair. "You don't have to," he'd said. "Some guys start with a period where they just lay back. After a while everybody works. No work, no pay."

"How long do I have to stay?"

"Ten minutes," Wapinski had said. "It'll take you that long to drink your coffee. Look, this isn't a prison. This isn't a school. We don't give grades. We don't pay except food, board and minimum wage. We can help you out with clothes. If you stay and work, then maybe we pay a little more. Nobody, except you, is going to force you to do more."

"What if I fuck up?"

"Everybody fucks up sometime. Try not to. Don't fuck anyone over. These guys can be a mean bunch. At one time, you know, they were all trained killers." Bobby had grinned. Sherrick had laughed. "More coffee?" Bobby'd asked.

"Hey, let me get it."

"Sure. Few more things. Keep the swearing down around the kids. And there's no smoking in my house. My wife doesn't permit it."

"Okay. Where do I sign up?"

"You already have."

"That's it?"

"Yep."

"You're goina just let me come here? Nothing to pay! No obligations! You don't even want to see my DD214? Maybe I didn't get an honorable."

"You're a Nam vet?"

"Yeah."

"That's all I need. There's a desk with drawers and a file cabinet in the bunkhouse. There's paper and pens. And an address form for if something happens to you and you want us to notify somebody. You can keep it there or I'll keep it here."

"What about women?"

"We don't provide any."

"Ha! That's not what I mean."

They'd talked on. "Tuesday and Wednesday nights are reading and research nights. We tutor each other in everything from salesmanship to solar engineering to history. We've got remedial reading and math. Half the guys are taking correspondence courses. Look Gary, there's two common denominators why anybody's here. Every guy here is stuck. Caught. Snagged in a past experience. In the meaning they attach to it. If they weren't stuck they wouldn't be here. They wouldn't work for room and board. And they're all Nam vets. So when I talk about Tuesday and Wednesday being reading nights and Thursday being discovery night I'm talking about Southeast Asia, what it was to us, what it means to us, what really happened, what people think happened, how their thoughts impact upon us."

"Okay. I got a million stories. Bitta bing, bitta bang."

"Not stories," Wapinski had said. "You've got to take a vow. That's the one requirement."

"A vow?!" Sherrick had rocked back. "Are you guys some kind of cult?"

Wapinski had shaken his head. "Repeat after me. I vow to strive to discover the truth—" Sherrick had half-heartedly repeated the phrase, "to become unstuck . . ."

" . . . to become unstuck . . . " Sherrick's right hand had quivered. He hadn't been sure if he was supposed to raise it up like a witness in a courtroom.

" . . . to grow, to expand beyond my self . . . "

" . . . to grow, to expand beyond my self . . . "

" . . . to encompass community, intellectual development, and spiritual awareness."

Sherrick had laughed. It had seemed simplistic, silly.

In the barn, on his second discover night, Sherrick had been saying, barking, at the Slitter, " . . . seemed pretty fuckin real to me."

"Fuckin real to me, too," Mariano agreed.

"To me it was like a zoned-out nightmare," Mark Renneau countered.

Bobby put his hand to his forehead. There had been verbal snipes all night. Bad feelings were developing. Some vets were tongue-tied. Mariano looked like he wanted to punch Renneau's lights out. Norm Casper had turned his back to most of the group. There was an undercurrent of "fuck yous" and "fuck you, toos." Wapinski had originally imagined these sessions as thesis, antithesis, synthesis. Instead he saw anger, polarization. On no topic were the vets in total accord. Once opened up, every man had strong obstinate beliefs. "Let him finish reading," Wapinski said.

" ' . . . moral horrors of the battlefield,' " Hacken read. " 'Though [the director] suggests the distinctive anarchic quality of jungle warfare, he misses an essential factor . . . the paranoia that came from not knowing if the Vietnamese were friends or enemies . . . the moral lines were never so clearly—and smugly—drawn as they are here . . . ' "

"For God fuckin sakes." Sherrick exploded. "If we're going to debate the moral lines of Viet Nam . . . This is stupid. This is fuckin stupid. You guys are a bunch of fuckin idiots." With that Sherrick walked out from behind the elevator, out to the middle of the floor, sneered at Wapinski, at everyone, and stormed out.

The next week Sherrick did not work in the fields. He had no interest in strawberries, grape vines, grains or vegetables. He did not work in the orchard, nor would he clean the Sugar Shack. He even declined to drive or ride shotgun in a delivery truck. For a time he watched Gallagher, Book and Bechtel assemble collectors, but to him the job was dull, something "any cretin could do." And he did not like Book. Or Bechtel. To him all the vets were idiots, ants, slaves. He even asked Art Brown how he could slave for a white man after having slaved for white men in Viet Nam.

What Sherrick did was tail Wapinski. "Out to save the world, Bobby?" he chided Wap.

"Somebody better be," Wapinski answered.

"You're a throwback, Man. You belong to a different age. Bitta bing, bitta bang!"

"When I was in school," Bobby said, "in my strength of materials class, there used to be a poster by the blackboard: 'The only thing needed for the forces of evil to win in the world is for enough good people to do nothing.' "

"That's what got us into Viet Nam in the first place. Bitta bing, bitta bang."

It made the vets angry to watch Sherrick. They knew *they* were a team. His blatant defiance challenged them. To a man, since the arrival of the eighth or ninth vet, the peer pressure of everyone working, pulling his own weight, had made each fall in line. But not Sherrick. They saw him as an obnoxious slacker. They began to view him as the enemy.

Except Wapinski. "You satisfied with your life, Gary?"

Defensive, but hidden behind a smile. "Why not?"

"Where are you going, Gary? What's your direction? What's your target?"

"I'm not going anyplace. I'm fine right here. You said I didn't have to work."

"You don't. I'm just askin."

The next encounter. "Hey Gary, what are you afraid of?"

"Nothin."

"You seem like you're afraid to be a part of us. Man, you've been in the scariest situations in the world and you faced your fear. Face it now."

"You don't know diddly, Man."

"Then tell me."

"Someday. Maybe. Bitta bing, bitta bang."

Then, on a Tuesday, over coffee, Sherrick. "You were an officer there, huh?"

"Yeah."

"And in your twenties?"

"Yup," Bobby answered.

"I was too. In my twenties, not an officer. That's a different experience than these kids. We were old enough to know better."

"Yeah." Bobby laughed. "I guess so. You want to come up to the Poundridge job?"

Sherrick shook his head.

"It's an interesting job."

Sherrick stepped back a few paces.

"Gary, you got any idea where you're going?"

Sherrick didn't answer.

"What's keeping you back, Man? What's holding you down? What do you need to change to get rid of it?"

Sherrick chuckled. But all he would answer was, "Bitta bing, bitta bang."

The next day Bobby spent an hour with Sherrick in Grandpa's office. "Why do you want to change, Gary?"

"I didn't say I do."

"It's written all over you, Gary. You're almost thirty-four, huh?"

"You're seeing things that aren't there."

"You're perfectly happy, huh? Degree? Law school? Being an ant? A slave?"

Sherrick smiled. "Maybe," he said. He liked the tête-à-tête, the verbal head-to-head.

"Well, it's up to you," Bobby said. "But you know you can better manage your mind. You don't have to be stuck in neutral. You don't have to let others get to it."

Sherrick snickered, "DAARFE-vader, huh?"

"It works for most of us. But you have to learn how to decide. That's the first step."

"Like to play in those stupid soccer games?"

"Sure. To play it right you've got to make decisions. That's the beauty of it. And basketball. Everything is player-directed decision making. Yet it requires teamwork. Responsibility to the team."

"Don't tell me. When I was in school I had pro scouts after me."

"So what happened?"

"Maybe I got drafted."

"Maybe you didn't really want to be there?"

"What the fuck do you know?"

"You didn't try to go back. Since you've been here, you've never acted like you want anything. You don't even stand like you want anything."

"I don't stand . . . "

"That's right. Your posture says, 'Don't give me the time of day.' "

"Then why do you?"

"Forget it, Gary. Forget me. Right now look at yourself. What do you see?"

"Whaaa-dd?"

"C'mon, Gary. Play my game. Tell me."

"Tell you what? Like I hate my wife. Like I don't have a wife anymore. That I don't have any kids. Easy for you, Man. Your wife loves you. You got two kids."

"How do you know she loves me?"

"I can see it."

"If you wanted to feel loving towards your wife, if you wanted her to know it, how would you have to act? Make believe it's a new wife."

"I'd . . . I'd . . . Hmm. You know."

"No, I don't. It's different for every individual."

"Well, I'd . . . I'd look at her more."

"Okay." Bobby pulled out a sheet of paper, wrote down, "Look at her more." "What else?"

"I'd ah, assist her. You know, physically. Help her carry in the groceries."

"Good." Bobby wrote. "What else? This is your old wife. You want to change the way you feel from being angry at her to feeling loving."

"Um. I'd . . . I'd drop my facial expression. When I'm angry I get my face all knotted up."

"Jaw tight, teeth clenched?"

"Yeah. My hands, too. I ball them into fists."

"Show me."

Sherrick hesitated, then made a fist.

"No," Bobby said. "Stand up and show me the whole posture."

Sherrick rose. "This is stupid."

"Do it for me," Wapinski said. "Okay," he said as Sherrick rose, made fists, sneered. "Good. Now show me loose jaw and open hands."

"Like this?" Sherrick loosened totally, not just fist and jaw but arms, shoulders, his entire face. He stood a little straighter.

"Yeah," Bobby said. "Now, how do you feel?"

"I'm not angry," Sherrick said.

"Okay," Bobby said quickly. "Now angry again."

Sherrick transformed to angry.

"Now loving."

Sherrick transformed back.

"Angry," Bobby said. Immediately Sherrick tightened. "Loving." Quickly Bobby alternated. Then, "How did you feel each time?"

"Well," Sherrick said. "I could put myself into those states."

"You mean," Bobby said, "you control the way you feel?"

"Well, right here."

"But if you wanted to do it, you could?"

"Yeah. I guess."

"Then, if you want to feel more loving with your wife, what you have to do is decide to be that way. You'd have to figure out why you want to be more loving. What's good about it. What's bad about not achieving it. If you physically transform to the attitude you want to have, you'll have that attitude. Your mind will follow your body."

"That's too much, Man," Sherrick said. "I don't believe it."

Bobby smiled. "Bitta bing. Bitta bang."

The first of the barn trials were anything but. They were neither trial nor inquest; indeed, the first were not called trials but discovery exercises. As academic exercises they left much to be desired. As a "brain raid glue solvent," they were ineffective and disappointing. That spring and summer the vets rambled from topic to topic, touching only surface images, the interpretation of the war in popular culture—the first films and novels—and how closely the vets felt these vehicles represented their own experiences.

"I wanta go back to that review of last month," Mariano said. "I read it. I got some things to say about it."

They were in the big barn as usual. Sherrick was still in the shadow of the Slitter. George Kamp had come down from Towanda. Tom Van

Deusen and Steve Hacken were absent, trying to finish the Maxwell job, pushing hard to install the electronic control panel and make the final hookups before the building inspector arrived.

"It was in the February sixth issue," Mariano said. "There was that stuff about moral horror, remember? And chaotic or hallucinogenic warfare."

"Yeah," Mark Renneau said. "That's what it was like for me. One long cluster fuck of purple haze."

"Naw," Mariano said. "I got the two issues earlier than that one. Here. This one's on the New Indochina War. Between Cambodia and Viet Nam. And this one's all about Cambodia. 'Land of the Walking Dead.' It's like these prove that we were right."

"Bitta bing, bitta bang," came quietly from the Slitter.

A few vets glanced over. Mariano gritted his teeth. Because he now worked in the office he saw more of Sherrick than the others. And he disliked him more. He disliked Sherrick's attitude in the bunkhouse. The "house" was communal living. Of all the vets, only Sherrick was a slob. Thorpe had repeatedly told him to straighten up his rack, had helped him the first few times, had nearly lambasted him. "What are you going to do?" Sherrick had confronted Thorpe. He'd relished the antagonism. "Have Wapinski throw me out?" Thorpe had backed off. Most of the vets withdrew, distanced themselves from Sherrick. Even those who were less than neat, as if to heighten the contrast, had doubled their cleaning efforts.

"Commies against commies," Emil Lorson said. "I hope they all kill each other."

"Yeah," agreed Ron Hull. "Why should we give a shit?"

"Yeah," Mike Treetop concurred. "We all tried to save their silly asses. They want to kill each other, let em."

"Naw," Mariano said. "That's not what I was goina say. I mean, maybe we oughtta let em, but see, like here, like this picture of this baby." Carl held out the magazine. Wagner took it, looked, shook his head, passed it to Brown. "That baby was about as old as little Paulie. Man, that kid's no commie."

"That's Asian, Man," Renneau said. "That's how they treat life. Shee-it, there's like a billion people in China alone."

"Yeah," someone agreed. Most of the guys, however, were quiet, heads down, shaking, disagreeing but not overtly, saddened by the photograph of the bloody, dismembered, dead child.

"THAT—" the voice blasted from the Slitter, "is because of us. Because of America. Because we got involved. That war was a criminal enterprise foisted upon us and the Viets and Cambos, by a bunch of self-serving politicians and generals and by money-hungry defense contractors. What the fuck is the matter with you guys?! Why can't you admit you were just cannon fodder? If it was up to me, I'd put every one of you fuckers on the stand . . . make every one of us stand trial for our part in that carnage. The only people I have any respect for are the conscientious objectors. The rest of us . . . " Like all the weeks before, Sherrick emerged, sneered, turned, stormed out.

"Hey," Mariano yelled. "Bitta bing! Bitta bang!"

Gallagher, Wagner, Treetop, Lorson, others snickered, hooted.

"WHOA!" It was Wapinski's turn to shout. "He just may have something there."

"Ah, come on, Bobby!" Tony wanted the peer pressure to force Sherrick into line or from the fold.

"No," Wapinski said calmly. "He actually may have something. And, every one of us vowed to discover the truth."

"Do you want to bury this asshole?" They were in the barn office. Carl Mariano was to the side filing receipts and bills. Tom Van Deusen was at the drawing table sketching a detail for the bid for the Fyodor job. Steve Hacken had been popping in and out, asking Van Deusen questions about trim details on the Maxwell job. Josh was at Bobby's feet, asleep, twitching in his dog dreams, passing gas which could be cut with a knife. Sherrick was leaning over the desk, rereading the letter.

"I just want to do what's right," Bobby said.

"You want to get this asshole Rosenwald off your back though?"

"Yeah."

"You have a copy of your grandfather's will?"

"Gary, I just want to send him a letter explaining that I have, and will continue to, abide by the terms of the will."

"Hey!" Gary was brusque. "You have to hit them with quad-fifties. You have to gain fire superiority. Otherwise this guy's going to overrun your position."

"He's representing my mother, sister and brother," Bobby said. "Not Hanoi."

"You better wake up, Man. I know guys like this. I almost became one. He's going to push you so hard you either fight or sell out. You're not going to have a choice."

"He can't. I *am* abiding by the will."

"Not the way they see it."

"But I keep open books. They can go over them. You go over them. They're—"

"I'd rip you apart in five seconds. You're in my kill zone, Man. Stop thinking justice. Look at the landlines. Can you justify that cost? What about the bunkhouse? What about paying guys that don't work? You can't give away their money."

"We're turning a profit and I'm giving them their percentage. Actually, this year I paid them before I took out the capital expenses for the buildings."

"But after the trucks, huh?"

"That's stricktly part of the business."

"If you were their attorney, would you see it that way?"

"But that's the way it is!"

"Damn!" Sherrick smacked his palm onto the desk. "Stop thinking 'fair.' These guys don't care about fair. Think 'adversary.' Think 'enemy.' Fer God's sake, Man. You were a company commander! No wonder we lost. You didn't learn a damn thing about tactics."

Bobby responded angrily, defensively, "They're still my family." He leaned back in the swivel chair. "We'll try the open approach. If they come after us, we'll do it your way."

Sherrick snorted. "Suit yourself, Henry," he said. "Give em a decent interval, huh? Suit yourself Henry da Kay."

Despite the adversarial relationship between Gary Sherrick and most of the vets, Steve Hacken befriended him. On Saturday night half a dozen guys went to the White Pines Inn. The place was packed, the music loud, the air smoke-filled, smelling of stale beer and greasy steak sandwiches. Guys out-numbered gals five to one. Voices were loud, sharp. Drinks flowed like spring runoff.

Arguments, bickering, began in the van on the way down. "Don't give me that crap about pride," Sherrick accosted Mariano.

"I'm proud, too." Art Brown backed Carl's position.

"That's because you're stupid, Art," Sherrick said. "You soul brothers were used. How many times do I—"

Wagner cut in. "Bullshit. We were there together."

In numbers there is strength. Mariano, Wagner, Brown and Casper held to their position. Hacken felt divided. He had befriended Sherrick because Sherrick was bright, aloof. To Hacken, Gary held a personal power none of the others, except Wapinski, possessed.

Sherrick stood alone. "We raped, we pillaged, we murdered millions with indiscriminate bombings and H & I artillery and you're proud!"

Inside the bar, angry with each other, they still clumped. Half the patrons were young men in their early twenties. When the vets had been that age they'd felt healthy, strong, invincible, immortal. But every one of them had seen young, strong, mortal bodies shredded, traumatically amputated, blown to pieces. Now in their late twenties to mid-thirties, though some days they felt strong, some days they felt all too mortal, especially when confronted by a younger, larger, more boisterous drinking crowd.

They ordered beers, commandeered a booth, sat where they had the visual advantage of the aisle, the door, the outside, and direct lines of sight to the crossed legs of two nearly identical barflies in black miniskirts perched on vinyl-covered stools.

The first beers went down quickly. The vets began to feel their oats. Except Sherrick. He sat inner-most on the bench. He was quiet. He stared at the mug before him, at the condensation, the water drops growing, reaching critical mass, dripping, miniature rivulets gathering weight, running to the bottom of the mug, forming a circular puddle.

Brown and Casper were in the outer seats: Mariano and Wagner in the center: Hacken sat across from Sherrick. Mariano nudged Brown as one of the barflies shifted, flashed them a crotch. The girl smiled coyly, slithered from the stool, wriggled her skirt down, strutted toward the ladies' room. "Ooo! I'd like to poke that piece," Mariano said. Brown giggled. Casper leaned from the booth, his head ass-high, leering at the girl's back.

"Hey, Aaron!" Wagner called. "How about another pitcher and six cheese steaks with extra peppers."

"One without peppers," Sherrick called.

The girl who'd left rejoined her friend. The noise level was rising. They ordered another pitcher. Then another. Sherrick's beer was going flat.

"If we could get the mortars set up," Norm Casper said loudly, "the whole town'd be ours."

"Mortars?" Sherrick leaned over the table. "What mortars?"

Wagner elbowed him. "I got the crates in yesterday." His voice, too, was loud. "I didn't think they'd of let me in the depot but Wapinski knew the manager."

"What are you guys talking about?" Sherrick asked.

Again Wagner elbowed him. He sensed that one of the girls at the bar had heard. "Look guys," Mariano said matter-of-factly, yet strong, as if he needed to be heard over the jukebox and chatter, "somebody's got to stay sober enough to remember the password. I don't want to be shot by the sentries."

Sherrick still didn't get it. Hacken leaned over, whispered to him. His eyes turned to the barflies, then back.

Brown joined the other three with loud talk about their armed camp. "... armed to the teeth ..." "... booby traps ..." "... pigs mess with us again they'll be sorry ..." "... mechanical ambushes ..." "... more tunnels than Cu Chi ..." "... C-4 ..." "... phugas ..." "... Hartley's a pig ..."

Around the table they went bragging, boasting, b.s.ing, except for Sherrick, entertaining themselves and people close by. Then the barflies left with guys who'd talked with them. Around the table of vets the mood fell as flat as Sherrick's untouched beer.

Sherrick leaned back, snickered. "Idiots," he muttered. He reached out, grabbed his warm mug.

"Don't!" Mariano was curt.

Sherrick eyed him. "Who's going to stop me?"

The others didn't know what was going on, but Carl had been working in the barn office when Sherrick discussed his drinking problem with Wapinski. Even before they'd entered the White Pines, he decided, not altruistically, nor paternalistically, but out of resentment and brotherhood, that he would not let Gary drink. Mariano's head came down, his eyes squinted, his jaw jutted, tightened. "Me. Order a Coke."

Sherrick snorted. He still held the mug. "Watch this," he said. He began to lift the beer.

Mariano growled. "You touch it, I'll break your face."

"Hey," Casper said, "this is too much for me." He got up, went to the men's room. Wagner slid away from Sherrick.

"Me too," Art Brown said. He stood, went to the bar, ordered another pitcher.

"You touch me," Sherrick snickered, "you'll be in jail. I'll sue you, this place, Wapinski . . . "

"Don't drink it." Mariano had his hands and forearms on the table, had pulled his bad leg up onto the bench seat, was ready to pounce.

"Go ahead, Gimp! Hit me." Sherrick's posture showed nothing but disdain.

"Hey guys . . . " Hacken tried to interrupt.

"That touches your lip," Mariano sneered, "and I'm on you like a mad dog."

Sherrick winked at Hacken. Defiantly he raised the mug up to his mouth. Over it he said, "I'll visit you in your cell."

"You don't understand, Man." Mariano was higher. "I'd rather smash your ugly fuckin head and be in the clink than not smash your face and watch you drink."

Sherrick smiled. His eyes were locked on Mariano. He leaned back, pulled the drink up, tilted his head back, brought the mug to his mouth, began to tilt it.

"Hey!" Wagner's hand shot out, grabbed Sherrick's beer. "Hey! Hey Art! Aaron!" he yelled. "Make the last round Pepsis. And get us new glasses."

Sherrick was afraid. He knew most of the vets didn't like him. He'd been getting over on them, he'd been abusive, contemptuous. He'd stomped out of seven straight discovery exercises. "Discipline to act, my ass!" he'd glared at Wapinski. "This is a bunch of old ladies grumbling unfounded opinions. Idiots!"

But now Wapinski was gone. With Sara and the boys, he'd flown to California following the death of Sara's grandparents. In his absence, Mariano, the Gimp, had slide-tackled Sherrick during the last soccer game and nearly broken Sherrick's back. Bechtel and Thorpe had piled on. Gallagher, who was supposed to be refereeing, who'd called Sherrick for every minor shove, elbow, or high kick, had "missed" it. "Screw this crap about pride, eh!" Mariano had hissed the second time he'd taken Gary down.

Pisano was supposed to take charge in Wapinski's absence but there was no unity of command with regard to Sherrick. And Pisano had no intention of spending two weeks away from his wife and kids. Thorpe,

Gallagher and Van Deusen were next in line, and Mike Treetop below Thorpe on farm matters, and Wagner was moving into second spot on the fire circle–Pennamite Camp truth-stick sessions. Another half-dozen vets had come. Two in Wapinski's absence, checked in by Mariano. Only Hull, the strawberry man, had left. The bunkhouse was overcrowded. Sherrick was more than afraid.

By the discovery exercise of 6 July, Gary Sherrick was a nervous wreck. All week he'd been snapping his head, looking over his shoulder, sure he was being stalked. He'd tried to talk to Steve Hacken but Hacken had been busy, days, on installations of collector arrays, and evenings, beginning study for an electrician's license. Sherrick had approached some of the new guys: Wilson, Rooker, Cannello, Murray, Koch and Bixler. They'd all been warned off. He tried Brown but Brown had taken a Fourth of July leave. He tried Carl Mariano.

"Talk to the mirror," Carl said sternly.

"Yeah, right! Thanks."

"I'm not kidding."

Sherrick's head drooped. He felt he might just as well let them jump him, get it over with.

"I'm not kidding," Mariano repeated. "Wapinski taught me. Just like he tried to teach you."

"Teach me what?"

"Go ahead. Look in a mirror. Look at that sneer you've always got. See it. Feel it. Know how it feels?"

Sherrick didn't answer.

Mariano's voice lightened, he stood straighter, prouder. "Look at yourself, Gary. Take a look at the message your face is sending your brain. Take a look at the message you're sending others. Wapinski made me do it in a mirror. You try it."

The vets didn't let up. Under the silent treatment, Sherrick's paranoia spiked. On Friday the 7th, Wagner grabbed him. Sherrick nearly pissed his pants. "I'm taking three guys out to the fire circle," Wagner said. "Across the gap. Why don't you come? You haven't been."

Sherrick began to shake. He hadn't seen the Indian ladder but he'd heard, he knew. This was it. They'd push him. Say he'd slipped.

"One chance," Wagner said. "Decide. Go or no go."

"Naw. Naw, Man. I—I'm going to be reading. Wapinski had some documents he wanted me to read."

Sherrick did read. He skimmed Frank Snepp's book, *Decent Interval: An Insider's Account of Saigon's Indecent End Told by the CIA's Chief Strategy Analyst in Vietnam.* "It is not too much to say that in terms of squandered lives, blown secrets and the betrayal of agents, friends and collaborators, our handling of the evacuation was an institutional disgrace," Snepp had written.

The entire war was a disgrace, Sherrick thought. He heard something, lurched, settled back. His concentration was broken by every real or imagined footfall. Sherrick did pull from the reading some ideas, some conclusions. In the margin on one page Wapinski had written, "But Frank! ARVN intelligence correctly identified NVA's '75 attack points! You, CIA chief strategist, from your own writings, incorrectly interpreted NVA moves and overrode ARVN command, forced them to improper shifting of their forces! Your mistake led to immediate NVA successes which precipitated Saigon panic, led to loss of Central Highlands, led to final collapse!"

Sherrick added under Wapinski's note, "What led to Snepp being there in the first place? Would correct disposition of forces have made, ultimately, any difference?"

Ignored, alone, even at mealtime when everyone pitched in, a family, a brotherhood, Sherrick stayed aside, not spoken to, not acknowledged. By the time Wapinski returned in mid-July Sherrick was sullen, haggard, on the verge of a complete breakdown.

In contrast Bobby Wapinski looked great. He looked healthy, relaxed. His nose was dry. He'd gained ten pounds. Sara too looked great. Her dark eyes danced. Their normal somberness, the weight of responsibilities they'd elected to shoulder, had evaporated in the California sunshine. Although there was a sadness over the death of her grandparents and especially that they had never met Paul Anthony (who'd begun to walk the day of the wakes) there was a happy recognition of the fullness of their lives.

Two days passed. Bobby settled in. Sherrick kept his distance. Bobby didn't notice. Sherrick's twitching became worse. Everyone held back, waiting, feeling that Sherrick needed to make the first concession. It came on Sunday, July 23d.

"I quit." Sherrick cornered Bobby, alone, in the tractor garage.

Wapinski glanced up. He'd been cleaning and checking the forge. "Go ahead," Wap said. "Won't be your first time. Won't be your last."

"That's it then, huh?" Sherrick had expected resistance.

"Yeah, Gary. There's no locks. You know that. You really are a manipulator."

"I thought you didn't put that in the files."

"I don't." Wapinski turned back to the forge. "Doesn't mean I didn't see it, though."

"I'll pay you for what I took. What I used. I'll send it to you."

"No you won't, Gary."

Sherrick huffed.

Wapinski added, "You're a smart man. You're probably the smartest guy here. But you can't hack it. Forget us. Forget what we're building here. Take the easy way out."

"Easy way, my ass! Not one of these idiots here gives a rat's ass about me and I don't give a rat's ass about them. I'll show you. All of you."

Wapinski smiled. Didn't answer. Measured the depth of the firebox.

"I'll show you," Sherrick repeated.

"Naw, Gary." Wapinski was very slow, very calm. "You'd have to buck us to do that and no one's got the energy to buck the brotherhood. We can easily out-flank and outmaneuver you. And that's just what we're doing. We're manipulators, too. See, Gary, whether these guys give a damn about you or not, they give a damn about the brotherhood. You'll learn. You're part of it."

"Well goddamn it then—" Sherrick spun agitated, his arms flailed comically, "then take me. Take me to your goddamned fire circle. I'll—I'll—I'll tell you why ... but just you ... why I can't accept this shit."

Wapinski eyed him, bit his lip, attempted to gauge Sherrick's sincerity. "Why you choose not to accept this shit?"

"It's not my choice. They—I'm—they made me ... "

"Uh-huh." Wapinski shook his head, turned back to the forge. "When you hit bottom, come back. Things don't stop when you're on the bottom. Life goes on. When you get there, when you understand that, come on back. We'll start climbing back up together."

"Shit! What do I have to say?"

"Can you stay like you are?"

"NO!"

"Do you need to work hard to change?"

"Yes."

"Are you capable of changing?"

"Sure."

"Are you trying to change?"

"Ye ... No."

"Why not?"

"Cause I'm stuck here!"

"And?"

"And"—Sherrick was frantic—"and ... "

"And?"

"And I can't stay like this!"

"What?"

"I can't stay like this!"

"Um." Slowly, then terse, fast, "Okay. We move out in one five. You know the routine. Get the rucks. I gotta change."

It was the same scene, the fire circle, late late night. Only it was Sherrick, not Pisano. And the weather was warm.

"What really gets me, Man, is—is—I—I think I knew ... I think I suspected even while it was happening, I think maybe a second before I opened up ... Maybe long ... "

Bobby didn't say anything. Sherrick held the truth stick. Earlier, at the Pennamite Camp, Sherrick had reentrenched. He was a tough nut to crack. Once across the gap and through the cathedral his anxieties abated. No one had sent him to his death. Bobby talked to him about eating right, sleeping right, standing right. "Decide. Develop a cause, a reason to become intense. To be cool is uncool. To be uncool is cool. Get hot, Gary." Bobby pushed on. "Experiment with yourself. Learn your triggers. Use them. Practice switching to confident, to interested, to sensitive. Practice getting into the posture where you care about people, about things, where you care about quality work. Let your physical self lead your brain."

Sherrick took it as a challenge, not to meet, to surmount, but to resist. "Quality work?" Sherrick laughed. "To me that crap's got no value. I don't care about solar panels. And farming stinks."

"What's your mission, Gary?" Wapinski refused to let up. "Unless you desire excellence," he said, "you'll miss your target. Unless you are on a mission, driven by a cause, you will be outgunned, outmanned, overrun and left on the triage pile of humanity. You'll be left in the corner to cool."

Sherrick snickered. "Personal growth bullshit, huh? You Californians . . ."

Wapinski cut in. "You're not an inert object. People grow. You're right. A lot of that movement is pabulum for the masses, the ticket to fame and fortune for the high priests and practitioners. But there are core insights. No one, no matter how stuck, is completely static. Everyone changes. You get older, fatter, more reclusive, or maybe more widely read, more accepting, a better decision maker. The things to understand"—Wapinski held up a fist, extended a finger with each point—"there's constant change even if one is stuck in one compartment of his life, and to some extent one can direct that change. Change doesn't necessarily destroy the foundation you're built on. It might realign the blocks, reinforce one wing, change a facade, deepen a well, install a more sensitive perceptual system or rewire the rooms for better lighting."

"Man," Sherrick lay back in the lean-to. "You're a real piece of work. Change everybody. Change the past." He pointed at Wapinski. "That's why you believe the way you do. You're a revisionist. All you're trying to do is clone yourself. That's the problem with guys like you. You want to revise personal histories just like you want to revise the war. The thing happened, mister. Motherfuck, I can't believe I came out here!"

Through the afternoon, into the early evening, the tit-for-tat continued. "If you make a mistake on a collector plate," Wapinski said, "take it apart and redo it. Quality counts. If you make a mistake in your life, take it apart and reassemble it. Quality counts."

"Revisionism." Sherrick spat.

Wap continued. "If you won't do it for yourself because you need to be punished, do it for the brotherhood. They need you. I need you. You once pulled your weight . . ."

"Revision . . ." Sherrick twitched. "I don't need to be punished!"

"Change your focus, Gary."

"God bless you, Man."

"You can smell the fertilizer or you can smell the grapes, Gary. What you focus on is what you get."

"Fertilizer, huh?" Sherrick laughed.

"How you act, Gary, is determined by how you feel. And how you feel, Gary, is determined by what you think about and what you sense. What you sense is determined by what you're looking for. Fertilizer or grapes."

"What I think about! I think about booze. I think, 'Why can't I stay on the wagon when I'm away from a shithole like this?' Aren't you gonna say it? 'Gary,' "—Sherrick threw his voice into a screechy falsetto—" 'you've got so much going for you, why can't you stay sober?' " His voice reverted. "Because I don't fuckin want to. I don't give a shit."

"I never asked you that," Wapinski said.

"So what?" Sherrick shot back. "You wanted to. You all wanted to."

"How can you stay sober and enjoy it?" Wapinski asked. Sherrick stared at him. Wapinski repeated the question.

"All I gotta do is want to." Sherrick sighed. "I thought you weren't going to ask that."

"Ask what?"

"Why I can't stay sober?"

"I didn't. I asked, How can you stay sober and enjoy it? If you ask your question, you'll come up with an answer. If you ask mine, you will too." Wapinski sat up. It was almost dark. "I gotta git," he said. "Think about when you were most happy. I'll be back in a bit."

Sherrick started. "Whatda ya mean?"

Wapinski was already out of the lean-to.

"I aint stayin here by . . . " He poked out. Wapinski was gone.

At first Sherrick thought it was a joke, but night descended. The mosquitos came. And the chirpings, creakings, croakings, buzzings. Sherrick broke into a sweat. He hated being in the woods, alone, without a light, without a weapon, without a pilot, copilot, crew chief. He didn't want to stay. He didn't dare leave. He cursed. He damned Wapinski to hell for all eternity. He inched to the back of the small shelter, crouched, wrapped his arms about his legs, rocked quietly. His nares flared at every noise. His ears strained. The night could not have been darker. When was I happy? The thought simply leaped in. In school, his mind answered him. Maybe in the courtroom in law school classes. And in the courtroom when I cross-examined. The answers cascaded in on him. Except the judges were all jerks. Always siding with the junkies. I was a good student. I loved getting my grades. I loved making honors. I liked cleaning up neighborhoods. How can I stay sober and enjoy it?! How . . .

When Wapinski returned Sherrick was no longer sweating. Bobby led him slowly, quietly to the fire circle. He flicked a match, set the kindling ablaze, added larger sticks, explained the rules, the vocabulary. "Tonight," Bobby said, "I will call you Tëme [tah-may], Wolf."

Sherrick chuckled. That's cool, he thought.

"*Wëli* [wah-lee]," Bobby said. "Good."

"*Yuho*," Sherrick responded. Okay.

The talk evolved. The truth stick passed frequently.

"Maybe," Bobby said at one point, "the only people you respect are conscientious objectors of the antiwar movement, but I don't know why. You say the antiwar movement stopped the war, but the war did not stop. The war did not stop in '73 when we left or in '75 when Saigon fell. They had no effect on ending it. They only affected the outcome. So they're really not antiwar, are they?"

"Yes they—"

Wapinski held up the stick, continued. "They were simply anti-American–war effort, Tëme. Which I recognize as a valid position. But let's get the verbiage straight. I was antiwar. I was an antiwar soldier. I tried to stop the violence by winning. They did not try to stop the violence. They did not even see the other side. They only wanted to stop me. And you. We were their focus. And they did. But they didn't stop the violence and now they're trying to get to our minds, trying to convince us they did, or that if they didn't, it was our fault. They still want to control the focus. The people I most respect are the conscientious participants. Conscientious participants, Tëme. Of the COs . . . what's conscientious about ignoring people who are being tortured or murdered? What's conscientious about standing by while one nation overruns another—" Again Sherrick attempted to object but Bobby raised his voice, raised the stick, pushed on, "OR standing by when one faction within a nation enslaves or overruns the people of that nation?" Sherrick shifted anxiously. Bobby clutched the stick like a tomahawk. "And what's conscientious about abandoning an ally in the name of ending the war when in reality the war was not ended and our ally was uprooted, forced into third-class citizenship, starved, slaughtered? What's conscientious about denying the successes of the American effort? Right now everybody, most of the brotherhood, wants to make everybody else, those that didn't go, believe that the whole time they were over there the entire country was a free-fire zone and they were always in peril. That's bullshit. You know it. I know it. But it serves a lot of people's purpose, some of those that went and lots of those that didn't, to make it out like it was *constant* peril. Your chances of being killed in Viet Nam—if you were black and from New York City or Washington, D.C.—were less than being killed in your own neighborhood! *Tèpi* [teh-pee, 'Enough']." He passed the stick.

Sherrick exploded. "Revisionist bullshit! Bullshit! Bullshit!" He shook the stick as he spoke. "I'll prove it to you. I'll prove it to you with your own books. You want to run discovery exercises?! I'll show you discovery. I'll teach you discovery. You've got these guys on wishy-washy bullshit detail. If you seek shallow solutions to deep puzzles, you'll only solve the surface of the problem." Wapinski didn't speak but his eyes bore intently across the fire, into Sherrick. He had seen Sherrick turned on only once before, when he'd asked him for legal advice over Miriam's attorney's letter. Sherrick was leaning in close, into the heat. "You're such a fucking revisionist! What that did to me! What Nam did to me—"

Sherrick clammed up. Begrudgingly he passed the stick. Wapinski grasped one end, forced the other back into Sherrick's hand so they both held it. "When something's been misrecorded," Bobby said, "or only partially recorded, is it revisionism to correct or expand the record?"

"It is," Sherrick said, "if you change the meaning without justification."

"Then I think we're not revisionists."

"I'll prove you are."

"*Wëli.*"

Again longer exchanges, probes, attacks, withdrawals. "You're stuck, Tëme, on something that is past, something set, something static. Instead why not be concerned about something now, something ongoing like the circumstances of this veteran community, or of the peoples of Southeast Asia—today?"

Then late, late night, talking about Nam, about incidents, about punishment:

"I think I suspected it even while it was happening." Sherrick held the truth stick. His head was down, his voice low. "Maybe a second before I opened up ... maybe longer ... You know, Man. I mean all door gunners fear it. You train so it doesn't happen. You know it can. You're always aware of it so you don't let it happen. You know, you're right at treetop level. You're sliding past a hill. Guys down there are callin for help. They're gettin hit. You're the cavalry. You're comin to the rescue. Jungle's black as the inside of an unlit coal mine at midnight. Black as these woods. You see flashes. You're told our guys use red tracers, their guys use green. But you get there and both sides are using red and the RTO's yelling, 'The C.O.'s been hit. The F.O.'s been hit. Fire on em.' And you open up. You know how it is. Your adrenaline's pumpin. Your weapon's pumpin. Your 60's like a jackhammer. It's exploding. You've got it in your hands, jarring you, mount or no mount shakin like crazy. Then you're taking fire and you're jacked up so high you're squeezin trying to make the cyclic-rate zoom, wanting to turn the 60 into a hose of solid lead. Then the peter pilot's screaming, 'FRIENDLIES! Hold fire.' You're so jacked up, you're firing, hearing him in your ears but not in your head for what seems like a month but is probably half a fuckin second.

"And then you're back at base refueling, checking for damage, fuck all, and the dust-offs are coming back and there's six dead and sixteen wounded and you know you got some of em and they're your own fuckin troops!

"Man ... I knew it. I knew it. I knew it before I fired em up. I was the cavalry. I was ... " Sherrick paused for a long time. Bobby did not speak.

Slowly, quietly, Sherrick began again. "Man, no matter what you ever tell me, no matter what the reasons, what the cause, what happened afterwards, I'll never believe we had any fuckin business being there. We never had any right. For me to have done what I did, Man . . . no matter what the gooks were doing to each other . . . Man, no matter, there was never, never, *ever*, a justification for an American presence. You understand?"

Sherrick's voice trailed off. He passed the stick.

"Tell it to me again," Bobby said. He passed the stick back.

Sherrick was reluctant. Bobby nodded. Sherrick repeated the story adding times, dates, units, names of his crew members, the number off the rotor on his slick, details and more details. Again he handed the stick to Bobby. Again Bobby handed it back, saying, "Tell it to me again."

Sherrick sighed. He began a shortened version. As he got to the point where he was about to fire Bobby held up his hand. "I'm sorry. I gotta wiz, Man. Just hold it right there, okay?" Bobby returned. Sherrick finished the story. Again Bobby asked him to repeat it. Now as he got to the point where he'd just begun firing Bobby disrupted the story to build the fire back up. On the fourth go-through Bobby interrupted again, a few words further in, to get the old army blankets they'd brought, to wrap themselves against the predawn chill. The fifth time Bobby stretched his legs, kicked over the fire, caught the corner of his blanket on fire, had to scramble to beat it out. "Continue, please," he said.

"Continue what?" Sherrick asked.

"You were telling me about your premonition that you were firing up Americans even before you fired."

"Oh, yeah. I guess it was a premonition."

"Yeah. You worried about it all the time, huh?"

"Shit, yeah!"

"They bring charges against you, Tëme?"

"No! They knew . . . we weren't the only bird firing. There was no way to tell . . . "

"But you know it was you?"

"I think it was me. At least one. Had to be me."

"Probably was, Tëme."

"Shi—it happened again. Not—not in Nam. But when I was with narcotics investigation. We busted into this one house. And I knew it was going to happen. We blew away this old, unarmed black guy."

"You shoot im?"

"No. It wasn't me. But see, I knew before—"

"Yeah."

"Really."

"Yeah, Tëme. When you're trained to be aware of those possibilities, like you said before, like door gunners are always aware, then you always have those premonitions, huh?"

"Yeah."

"And if one comes true, you've got to punish yourself because you knew you were going to—"

"But I fired . . ."

Bobby's legs again shot onto the fire.

" . . . even when they yelled 'Friend—' What are you doing??!"

Wapinski jolted, rolled, yelled, "I'm on *fah-yar!*" The blanket smoldered, the burning wool smelled horrible.

Sherrick burst out laughing.

Wapinski regained his seat. "Tell me again, Tĕme, ah, from just as your bird was coming in."

Sherrick began the story but he couldn't stop laughing. "I was fah-yar-in . . ." He chuckled. "God, you stink."

"Quick Strike, Man," Bobby said.

"Huh?"

"I'll explain later. Hey, you know a lot about school. You were a good student. Why don't you set up the discovery exercises?"

"Those things?" Sherrick gasped. "Those guys are full of shit. They barely read anything. You oughtta set up mock trials. That'll force them to compete. They'll have to work as hard on getting facts as they do on their jobs or when playing soccer."

1 November 1984

Back again. In the big barn. On the main floor. On the table adjacent to the sheet metal break. The court has ordered that the equipment—tables, machines, tools, test apparatus, et cetera—"shall not be put up for auction or for sale or in any manner disposed" until the court has made its final ruling.

Seems like a lot of court stuff affects this place. In late '78 Gary Sherrick hit Miriam, Joanne and Cheryl with a slap-suit on the grounds of harassment and interference with business. Something like that! Sherrick understood the system, knew exactly how to manipulate it. He obtained, in Bobby's name, a temporary restraining order or a cease and desist order, something, while the court investigated (at Bobby's request) whether or not High Meadow, as operated, met the terms and intent of Pewel Wapinski's will.

We pressed on. Everything was getting better, falling into place. More of the High Meadow program jelled. The Quick Strike: Raid on the Brain Solvent—disrupting the meaning associated with the experience that causes one to be stuck and inserting a stairway or a ladder—became a formal, structured process, essential to the early phase of every vet's program. High Meadow was proving to be highly successful at transforming stuck and bitter men without hope into competent, productive and responsible citizens.

At this point I lost count of who came, who left. Between mid-'78 and mid-'79 we had better than a 100 percent increase in population including our first resident families. This taxed our water supply and sanitation facilities. We built a sewage composting plant, and all waste water was directed into a new, separate pond where by biological means—bacteria, algae and various marsh plants—the water was purified then used for irrigation. This worked so well Bobby attempted to get the town's Water Quality Authority interested in the concept as an alternative to the now $36 million proposal for a town sewage system and treatment facility. They wouldn't even look. Bobby attended public hearings, meetings, objecting to the town's plan as ultimately environmentally unsound and as nothing more than a town-wide tax to subsidize the development of South Hill, the New Mall, and Whirl's End Golf and Country Club.

By mid-'79 High Meadow had lost, via graduation, nine vets. Three didn't make it through the program: two by choice; one, Kenneth Moshler, was killed in town in a freak accident where a front tire on a panel truck blew out, the driver lost control and swerved into our newest EES van, pinning and crushing Kenny. For a time everyone was thrown into a retro-state—back to when close friends or hardly known unit-mates could be killed at seemingly any moment. Kenny was buried at High Meadow. That brought us all closer together.

Many of the new guys were hardcore dropouts. They had deeper feelings of self-disgust, longer-term drug habits, criminal records. They were victims of society and they played the role into which they'd been cast. "Not my fault, Man," "Shit happens." "You gotta roll with the punches." ("Roll," Bobby'd interrupt. "Not roll over.") They had little hope, little trust in anybody or anything. I don't remember a single one arriving without a bad attitude. They were more fucked up than I ever was. Stuck! They couldn't get off first base. Hell, half of them couldn't even get out of the dugout.

Because of the expertise long-term residents had acquired in either the solar business or the farm, there developed what was essentially a chain of command. The cherries, the newbies, the newfers, they came to us almost the way the rotation system worked in Viet Nam—new guy in, lowest of the low, in-country training and acclimatization, then into a work-team and the first mission, the newbies pulling the basest duties but always supported by, and always knowing in turn that they were supporting their team, their unit, the entire complex. Knowing too that via rotation there soon would be a new cherry, and eventually they would rise to the top, become short-timers and return to the World.

This was not basic training. High Meadow never stepped back that far. But there did develop more regimentation and requirements. For example, at work, everyone assigned to EES wore blue-and-white uniforms with name tags. This was no different than any other service company with men going into people's homes. Team leaders required their crews to be clean, tidy, to walk as if they were proud of their product, their team, their organization; as if they possessed total knowledge of the job, were skillful, confident, focused, learning.

Some of the work crews carried this to unexpected heights. Howie Bechtel's collector builders became The Energy Cell, and Steve Hacken's EES installers became The Power Pack. They demanded to stay together during PT. They purchased team uniforms—soccer shirts, shorts, socks—and challenged everyone and anyone, including regional league teams. Eventually they set off a scramble for new guys who looked to be promising wings or strikers or midfielders.

I was sure Bobby had discovered a program that could, if used on a massive scale, turn around not just the ailing vets but any ailing or stuck group. Farming and EES were vehicles. Any honest enterprise would have worked. I was sure it could be used in prisons, in inner cities, with junkies and juvenile dropouts. Linda could barely believe the High Meadow results. She and Sara established a vets'-wives group and used a modified program successfully.

Bobby had so many ideas some had to wait. To his collectors and storage equipment designs he did add a new branch—windmills. We built three to pump water from the ponds into holding tanks that fed our drip irrigation systems. These were towering edifices, one very traditional with large blades and its own house, the other two on poles looking like elevated plane props. Bobby wasn't finished. He began tinkering with mini-mills that could be mounted on roofs, that looked like weather vanes. These mills turned small generators producing electricity which in theory could be stored for later use, but he never developed a battery system.

Gary Sherrick never worked on the farm, never for EES. He became the director of the High Meadow Institute of Southeast Asia Studies. His countenance changed. No one acknowledged that it was a result of the fire circle. No one acknowledged that Wapinski's Quick Strike had changed the meaning of Sherrick's experience, of his premonition and role in the deaths by friendly fire.

As I review this I would not want one to think adding new associations to a vet's experience somehow changed or sugar-coated that experience. The opposite is true. We faced the subject squarely, immersed ourselves in our experience, and the overall American AND Asia experience, expanding our knowledge, our understanding. If anything our feelings became deeper, sometimes more caustic, yet every vet became more mobile with his emotions, became unstuck by the new associations and deeper meanings. One can call it developing proper coping mechanisms. We learned how to handle it, NOT to move on or put it behind us. For us there became nothing "post" about our personal traumas—they are with us here, now, forever, as they should be—but, because of our emotional agility, they are not debilitating. Indeed, they have become sources of personal strength, pride and motivation.

When Wapinski announced that Sherrick would head the institute, there at first arose low grumblings, then a cresting, raucous wave of protest. Sherrick's posture and expression may have altered but to the vets he had not shown any substantive change. He was still obnoxious, quick to judge, verbally abusive. Yet, within days for some, within weeks for most, the vets understood. This man's niche was not in physical or design labors but in the volumes and documents of the growing library, within the barn classroom, within the bunkhouse study halls. Quick Raid released in him a sense of urgency, of time wasted. Sherrick was on fire with How Things Work. When someone would ask, "Why are vets powerless?" or bitch, "Why are we voiceless?" Sherrick would respond, "Change the question. Ask, 'What can we do to have power? How can we have a voice in our own lives?'" If they asked, "Why are we still stuck in Viet Nam?" he'd reply, "How can we become unstuck from our Viet Nam experience of 1966, or '68, or '70, and enter into our own lives in 1979? How can we become unstuck from our limited American experience and know the Viet Namese experience? Viet Nam and the Soviet Union recently signed a binding Friendship Treaty. This has set off wave upon wave of refugees. Why? How? What's going on?"

By mid-'79 High Meadow had moved on to yet a new phase where Gallagher, Van Deusen, Sherrick, Wagner and I were permanent cadre, and both the farm and EES, beyond being part of the program, were businesses in their own rights. High levels of leadership led midlevels. Perhaps it was Gallagher. In his quiet beliefs, quiet management style, reinforcing Bobby while in turn drawing strength from Bobby; and like a conduit passing strength down, accepting and passing reinforcement up. Call it brotherhood. Call it family. Perhaps it was Van Deusen. Once unstuck, once turned on to learning, his enthusiasm was a beacon for others. Maybe even it was me. By 1979 I could answer farm problem questions with the same authority I once ran a platoon. Area farmers sought me out, studied our innovative techniques of water and soil conservation, pest and weed control. Down our informal chain of command everyone became a leader. Call it personal empowerment.

New causes. A dozen of us, at one time or another, had been "incarcerated" at RRVMC. We organized a formal protest. We went to hearings at the state capital. We objected to the warehousing and the drugging of our comrades. Everything was going well. We were having an impact.

I pushed for the development of a winery, drew up plans to carve out a subterranean cavern—cut right into the Pocono sandstone—and put the aging vats there because of the constant temperature. I explained to Bobby we could go through the back of the tractor garage, tunnel in just like Buena Vista Winery in Sonoma. I still had not told or shown him, or anyone other than Linda, the deep bunker.

George Kamp brought Jim Reitmeyer—not to enroll but to speak to us. Jim was the first in a long series of successful veterans of the Southeast Asia war to address a Thursday night meeting. He didn't know what to expect any more than we did. Jack had convinced him by saying, "Just let them see you. You're a role model. Don't hide from them. Tell them what you do, how you do it." Jim was the principal of a regional high school in the Towanda area. He'd served with Company F, 52d Infantry (Long-Range Patrol), the Ready Rifles, attached to the 1st Infantry Division.

Everything was going well. Rick MacIntyre arrived. He stayed only a month but he made a major contribution. Rick was Rick of 2/4, Rick of Philly, legless Rick who was so bitter in the hospital, who was determined to have the doctors cut his legs off at his neck. I don't know his journey but I know that when he came he brought the concept of *limiting beliefs*, that is, beliefs that limit the holder to actions consistent with those beliefs. As Rick put it, "I once believed I was a cripple. Then I found out I wasn't."

What an inspiration! He'd already become unstuck. In his first week he descended the Indian ladder, crossed the gap, scaled the far side, spent the night at the fire circle. After seeing him who could refuse to try? Thorpe and I were so proud, and I was relieved of some of my guilt for never having revisited him.

Everything was in place. Everything we did worked, was working. So why did it attract assault?

29

igh Meadow, Thursday, 21 August 1979, 6:40 A.M.—Wapinski's mind was scattered, attempting to solve a score of problems simultaneously. Nothing came out. His body too was bloated. He was in the upstairs bathroom, on the toilet, afraid to push again. Already the water was bright red. Damn, he thought. Damn it. I don't have time for this.

He clenched his teeth, rested his forehead on the heels of his hands, his elbows on his knees. His back hurt. Not horribly, just pressure-pain and constipation. His hemorrhoid had been bleeding since Tuesday, since it had blown like a high-pressure line letting go and his pushing had produced the first *ptsssssss* and the bowl full of blood. Ten months earlier it had happened for the first time and it had scared him. He'd gone to a general practitioner who'd chuckled about the cold "butt-hole scope," who'd laughed out loud, saying, "There it is. I can see the hole in the vein right there." Wapinski had felt violated, humiliated. Since that time he'd treated himself with creams and suppositories. It had popped again in the spring and he'd worried but he had not told anyone.

That flare-up had gradually subsided, had left him feeling embarrassed, vulnerable, angry, slightly anemic, slightly depressed.

Bobby rose, flushed, cleaned the red splatters from the porcelain and the seat, flushed again.

Noah was downstairs. Sara was in the boys' room. Paulie, in a diaper and T-shirt, was holding her leg. "Igooutsidetoo?" He said it as one word, one long singing sound without any syllable being emphasized. Sara cocked her head questioningly. "Igooutsidetoo?" Paulie repeated. He looked anguished. "Igooutsidetoo?" he said again.

Bobby looked in. He stood with his buttocks squeezed tight. Sara bent, grasped Paulie's hand. To Bobby Sara seemed bigger this pregnancy than she'd been with either Noah or Paul, and more tired. "Igooutsidetoo?" Paulie pleaded. Bobby chuckled at the babble. Sara kissed the boy. "Sure," she said. It amazed her how complete and grammatically correct, if slammed together, were his sentences. "After breakfast," she said. "Then you can go outside, too."

Sara turned, saw Bobby watching them. Slowly she straightened, sighed. For five years she had been either pregnant or nursing or both. Noah was four years four months; Paulie twenty-three months. Sara was exhausted. She was not simply taking care of the two boys. There was Bobby, Josh and the house; there was the women's group, the vets she tutored, and Tony with his new problem. She was six months along; her career was on hold; and she was feeling as if she hadn't just married Robert J. Wapinski but had married his causes, High Meadow, EES, and the constant chatter about Viet Nam.

"Talk to your son, will you?" Sara said.

"Noah?"

Sara nodded.

"What'd he do?"

"I caught him with two pieces of candy this morning and I found broccoli stuffed behind his booster seat. And Josh is still shedding! Can't he stay outside?"

Bobby lumbered to the kitchen doorway, spied Noah with half a dozen small cars and trucks lined up in a column on the kitchen table. He was pushing the last, tittering as the first crashed off the table edge. Bobby brightened. Then wailing like a police siren he barged in, twanged "Hold it! You're under arrest. Anything you say will be held against you."

Noah giggled. "Cut it out."

"This is the High Meadow vice squad," Bobby said. "No cutting it out allowed."

"Papa!"

"Ahha!" In a cartoon characterlike voice. "A code name. Write that down, Sergeant."

"Papa, what sergeant?" Noah was becoming unsure of his father's intention.

"Sergeant Sara informs me that you have been observed perpetrating a vicious vice," Bobby continued the charade. "That without provocation or permission you viciously attacked and ate two—not one but two—pieces of candy before breakfast!" Wapinski grabbed the boy about his chest, lifted him. Noah squirmed, half-heartedly attempted to escape. "And broccoli behind your booster seat?! Yeck!"

"Paulie did it." Noah wriggled to the floor.

Bobby had been up since five. There were so many things going on, so much to do. Yet his ass was dragging. He blamed it on the hemorrhoid. He blamed it on Sara's tiredness and his extra effort helping her with the boys. He blamed it on Paul Volker, chairman of the Federal Reserve. The discount rate had been rising steadily since its 1977 low of 4.75 percent. It was now at 11.75 percent. Construction loans, if available, were at 13 percent or more. Bobby blamed his tiredness on all the prominent economists who were predicting recession, and on the national financial columnists who, in spite of the recent Three Mile Island nuclear plant accident and OPEC's July jolt to oil prices, were declaring that "Energy from the sun may be free but the capital outlay for the collection apparatus is so high it is cheaper to heat, even today, with conventional fuels."

High Meadow sales were not bad. The columnists declared a solar water and space heating system would cost between $13,000 and $20,000. EES was installing equivalent systems for $6,600 to $8,000. The columnists claimed the solar equipment would not last long enough to reach a monetary break-even point. Bobby was confident that EES collector panels were of such quality and design they should be trouble-free for forty years. Every collector panel, every control box, every storage system now carried a small engraved brass plaque:

MADE IN AMERICA
by Veterans of The Viet Nam War

Bobby was absolutely committed to quality workmanship, to the belief that only quality workers produced quality work, and that anyone who strove to be a quality worker would be a quality worker. Further, he believed that with superior product design and superior craftsmanship any company would succeed, would ride the rough economic waves of recession, the changing tides of social attitudes.

High Meadow's problem was not product, not price, not even buyer resistance. It was simply that High Meadow and EES still had but one full-time salesman. Bobby had tried to induce Tom Van Deusen into a sales role but Tom had shied away. He'd tried Charlie Knabe and Gary Sherrick without success. Erik Schevard showed some interest, but he was still at the beginning of the program and simply wasn't ready; and Don Wagner, who may have been ideal, was running fire circle sessions full time. *Tëpi*!

Bobby was out of steam. Even on the farming side, Bobby was the prime seller. Tony could sell, did sell, but he didn't enjoy it and always settled for the initial offer. Mike Treetop and Mark Renneau helped, but . . . Bobby knew, selling is an art. None of them were sales artists.

Cash flow was again a problem. Attempting to support thirty-five vets plus three families on the two businesses was stretching High Meadow and Bobby to the limit. Vets were sympathetic—they hadn't come because of the wage structure—but Bobby insisted they be reasonably paid because that was essential to their understanding of their own worth and their learning successful money management attitudes. Bobby held stringent reins on his and Sara's expenditures. That too sapped him.

And, though he had not yet realized it, he was empty because High Meadow had grown so fast that it had outpaced its goals. Each facet of business and program individually was chugging along but collectively High Meadow was adrift, unsure of where it was going. Bobby was so busy selling, acting, re-acting, there was no time to plan, redecide, pick new targets, assess. Elation evaporated.

In the hour before Sara and the boys rose, Bobby had thought about these problems, about his own energy, about how, in California, he'd planned a running regimen, gotten into shape, finally run the Dipsea and felt strong, full of energy and endurance. And he thought he'd better get back into shape if he was going to keep up with his sons and the vets. Yet after fifteen push-ups and twenty sit-ups he'd been puffing, fatigued. He'd told himself, one higher each day. That'll do it.

He'd thought too about Father Tom Niederkou at St. Ignatius who had announced on Sunday that the parish was going to sponsor a family of Viet Namese refugees and would everyone volunteer a little time or clothing or . . .

And he thought about the newest vets, about his conversation last night with Sara. She'd said something about their dreams having been crushed. He'd answered, "That's a problem, Sar, but that's not the biggest problem. People have to have dreams for dreams to be crushed. Some of these guys have never had one. Their 'pipe dreams' were put down at one or two or three years old and that damaged the dream-making machinery. They have no dreams, no images, no visions. They can't see themselves being anything other than what and where they are." As the sun had risen, Bobby'd thought hard about this syndrome being worse than posttraumatic stress because there was virtually no foundation upon which to build.

Sara came down with Paulie. Now Bobby was at the table, reading a story in the newest issue of *Newsweek* entitled "The End of the Hmong." More crushed dreams, crushed dream machines, he'd been thinking. Noah had taken his cars into the living room where he was crashing them against Josh's legs. Without speaking Sara put Paulie in his high chair, shuffled to the stove where the teapot was whistling. We're like the 101st, Bobby thought. We've got a rendezvous with destiny. A rendezvous with those crushed dreams, with the Miriams, with the dream crushers.

It was not yet seven.

Gary Sherrick was in the barn library. He, too, had been up since five, reading, studying, making notes. The 1979 barn exercise, as he conceived it, would put both the American government concept of the war, and the prime American players in the war effort—from Dwight Eisenhower and John Foster Dulles to Richard Nixon and Henry Kissinger—on trial. Sherrick had had no difficulty persuading the vets to participate, nor any problem getting pro and con volunteers, but the vets had resisted his tight rules of evidence and procedure, issues of law and discovery phase exchanges. "Damn it." Sherrick had seethed at Wagner and Mariano. "There's a format here that's got to be followed."

Mariano had countered, "Gary, I thought you hated attorneys because of that shit."

"You dumb shit, no! It's because they don't follow it. They twist it, use it to harass the other side, use it to bury facts and evidence."

Sherrick wanted to charge the federal government with not being true to the founding principles of the nation. With that as the formal charge, he'd set out to prosecute while Steve Hacken and Jim Thorpe had taken the roles of defense attorneys. The trial was set to begin in October. Currently the vets were in investigation, abstract, and the first phase of discovery.

Gary continued with his notes. He was adapting a speech delivered in another time. He had been reading Joseph Buttinger's *The Smaller Dragon* and *The World's Famous Orations, America*, Volume III, edited by William Jennings Bryan. By changing the parties, Sherrick thought, the words could have been spoken in the late '40s or early '50s by Ho Chi Minh.

> Who among you, my countrymen, that is a father, would claim authority to make your child a slave because you had nourished him in infancy? 'Tis a strange species of generosity which requires a return infinitely more valuable than anything it could have bestowed. . . .
>
> Courage, then, my countrymen; our contest is not only whether we ourselves shall be free, but whether there shall be left to mankind an asylum on earth for civil and religious liberty. . . .
>
> If ye love wealth better than liberty, the tranquillity of servitude more than the animating contest of freedom—go from us in peace. We ask not your counsels or arms. Crouch down and lick the hands which feed you. May your chains sit lightly upon you, and may posterity forget that ye were our countrymen!

Sherrick was thinking, could Ho have said to the Viet Namese "colonists" what Samuel Adams had said to the Americans in 1776? The question was difficult. Hacken, Sherrick was sure, would first attack him on the phrase "shall be left to mankind as asylum on earth for civil and religious liberty." All year there had been a steady flow of news stories indicating that united Viet Nam was anything but an asylum for liberty. Sherrick thought to strike the phrase but he also thought if he could find a speech by Ho that stated the same idea, he'd be able to support the entire Adams' speech. What had happened post-1975, he reasoned, should not demean Ho's early intentions. Sherrick bracketed the phrase, picked up his photocopy of Uncle Ho's March 6, 1946, speech to the "multitudes" before the Municipal Theater in Hanoi, on the occasion of the government accepting French reoccupation. Underlined were Ho's words, "I would rather die than sell our country."

Sherrick stopped. Outside there was a rush of cars. Then banging.

"I'm gonna make it. Man, I'm gonna make it." Tony was muttering, talking to himself, trying to convince himself. He lay on the cot behind the barred door in his old cubicle. It had been a long time since he'd spent nights there and the past two nights had not been by choice. Linda was irate.

"How could you?!" she'd screamed.

"It was years ago." He'd twitched. He'd fidgeted. He hadn't thought she'd get so angry.

"Zookie! Zookie, that bitch with the neck tattoo?!"

"The kid could be anybody's," Tony had stammered.

Linda yelped. "That's not the point! Get out!"

He'd withdrawn, shaking, more upset at Linda's reaction to the paternity suit than to the suit itself, not understanding Linda's reaction was not to the suit at all but to his admission of liaison with someone she'd met, someone she loathed.

Tony put his hands to his head, massaged his temples. Things had been going so well for them. On August 11th Jo had taken Gina and Michelle, and Tony had taken Linda to Philadelphia for a beer at the EM Club where they'd met eleven years earlier, then to dinner and dancing and an evening at the Hilton Hotel. The girls were now nine years old. Linda's career was established. Tony had been in Mill Creek Falls for four years, back with Linda for two, more stable and secure with every passing month. They'd begun talking, tentatively, about another child. "I'm thirty," Linda had said. "If we're going to have another, it should be pretty soon." Tony, one of four brothers, had been dreaming about a son. Then the summons and papers and a demand for $12,000 in back support had arrived.

"I'm gonna . . . " Tony mumbled. He rolled on the cot. "Goddamn pig! If those motherfuckers . . . Kid's probably Gaylord's. Could be anybody's. If they tie it to me that's it. I'm gone. I'm on the Harley. I'm outta here. I'll be goddamned if I'm gonna work the rest of my life for some pig and her kid. Shit! When the hell was that. Five years ago? Six?" He hit his forehead with the palm of his hand.

Cut me a huss. All night his heart had been pounding, jarring him as he lay on the firm bunk. Finally he'd stammered to himself, "How would Bobby handle this? Could it actually be mine? I gotta maintain. I gotta main-fuckin-tain."

Through the heavy door the shouting above was muffled.

Tom Van Deusen had been up early that morning. He was sitting at the drawing table in Grandpa's office. Spread before him was the schematic for a domestic hot water and space heating system. The solar heat collection loop was in black; the space heating loop including five radiant floor zones was in red; domestic hot water was in green; and incoming cold was blue. Domestic hot water and space heating each had separate two-stage storage tanks and heat-exchanger coils; for all loops combined there were eight pumps. Bobby had taken one look at it the day before and had said, "More complicated is not more sophisticated. We're looking for simple, inexpensive, elegant solutions."

"Right," Tom had answered. Right, he now thought. Atop the schematic he laid a blank sheet. On the first line he wrote, "Bechtel's Energy Cell." Then he diagrammed a soccer field, sketched in positions, inserted player's names. On Sunday the 26th, The Energy Cell was scheduled to play Rock Ridge's Pulaski Club.

Van Deusen startled. "What the fuck's that?!"

The reaction at the dam was similar. They too were taken totally by surprise.

An hour earlier they had set out from the big barn; six of them in rucksacks with two-day resupplies; led by Don Wagner in his old red plaid shirt and bright orange pants (designed purposefully to interrupt old mental associations); with Rick MacIntyre at slack; followed by balding Kevin Rifkin, "Blue Dog" when he was with the 1st Cav; then Juan Varga, who'd served with the 4th Infantry Division; Joe "Doc Trash" Forbes, 1st of the 5th Mechanized; and Dave "Bro" Bailer, 3d Battalion, 5th Marine Regiment.

Their progress was slow. Legless Rick used his arms and thickly gloved hands to raise his torso, then swing his body forward, rhythmically banging out three-foot steps. The Corps had once fitted him with prosthetic devices but he'd found them slow, confining.

"We'll break on the dam," Wagner said. The morning was cool, crisp. It had rained violently the night before, then snapping gusts had blown the storm from the Endless Mountains almost as if the winds were blowing the hot, hazy summer away and bringing an October day. Wagner noticed the transformation on the trees of the woods they were about to enter. Overnight, scattered leaves had turned yellow, some had already dropped, here and there splotches of red had erupted. Don thought it was too early, felt it was an omen of a long, hard winter.

Juan Varga fidgeted. Water crashed through the spillway. Varga was a city dweller. The water rush unnerved him, the woods terrified him. "I can't sleep in the dark, Man," he whispered to Bailer.

"Me neither, Man," Bailer said. They were sitting on the dam leaning against their rucksacks. "This dumb. I . . . you know, Man, I thought we'd jus de-tox like at the VA. We goin in there." Bailer lifted his head toward the trailhead and the woods. He too was a city dweller. The gap, the Pennamite Camp, the fire circle meant nothing to him. And to him Wagner's *hè, tèpi, wĕli,* and *yuho* were Mickey Mouse Boy Scout bullshit.

Refkin broke out smokes, passed his pack. MacIntyre shook his head. "Can't, Blue Dog. I gotta keep my wind." Rick shifted. The trek over the knoll was hard on him and he could feel the pain in his legs that were not there. "If I do that, I can't keep my upper bod in shape and I can't do what I'm doing now."

The four newbies lit up. "Shee-it," Bailer whispered to Varga, "I aint done humped since '66. Fall a '66. Jus fore the monsoon hit. We moved . . . we was like near Da Nang . . . we moved up with the others and we run smack into an NVA regiment. One moh fuck-over, Man. Jus one moh."

Most of the vets who'd arrived in '79 believed being a veteran of the war in Southeast Asia was a terrible blot upon their character, a stigma that had destroyed their lives. Yet they identified with that period more strongly than with any other. They projected their "stigma" like a giant scarlet *A*.

"You been fucked, huh?" MacIntyre said flatly.

Bailer's eyes jerked to Rick. He glared. He hadn't meant for anyone but Varga to hear his comment. He looked away. "Yeah," he said. "Fucked royal."

"By Nam, huh?" MacIntyre said.

"Yeah." Bailer was defensive. He tried to act cool. "You too?"

"No," MacIntyre said. "Not me."

Bailer, Forbes, Varga, looked at him warily. Blue Dog didn't look at all. For them, in this early encounter, it was as if they could not show their recognition of Rick's condition.

"What?!" MacIntyre blurted. "My legs, Man?"

"You aint got no legs," Bailer said. His voice was icy, tentative.

"Huh!" MacIntyre lurched. "Hey, you're right. Hey, who took my legs?" He began to laugh. "Aw, who the fuck needs legs? Maybe it'd be nice. I'm going to tell ya something though. No matter what your experience, wounded or not, physical or mental, you've gained something by having been there. Seeing what you saw—what no one else in this country has seen—makes you a deeper person than those who never went. You just don't recognize it yet. The more you experienced that place, the more you saw the good and the evil, the corruption that was with our forces and all the other forces too. . . . Man, once you recognize it as a great teacher, then you'll understand what you have to offer.

"And to your Nam experience you've added the homecoming experience," Rick continued. "How you were treated. You know from that how to treat others, how not to treat others. And hey! Now you've got another experience. You're experiencing High Meadow and the Brotherhood. That's something deep, strong, more than most people in their station wagons and ranch houses and bank accounts ever know."

"Where you comin from, Man?" It was Blue Dog. His eyes flicked furtively to Rick, away.

Doc Trash added, "You sound like that g-g-guy, Wapinski."

"How come he don't come?" Bailer asked.

"He's in the office so much"—Wagner shifted in closer—"or in his car on sales, he's got no wind for the climb."

Blue Dog interrupted. "I asked this man"—he gestured toward Rick—"where he comin from."

"Way down," MacIntyre answered. "Down below the bottom. Man said to me, 'Why you here?' I said, 'Shit if I know.' " Rick chuckled as he spoke. "He says, 'What's your reason?' I say, 'Fuck off, hair breath.' He says, 'Everybody's got a reason for being here. Why are you here?' I begin to answer but he says, 'Don't tell me.' Then he split. Why you here, Blue Dog? Doc? Don't tell me. I'm not talking here at High Meadow. *Comprende?*"

"I don't g-get it," Doc Trash said.

Rick eyed him playfully. "You think you're the only one, don't cha? You're not," MacIntyre said. "I've been down that road. Maybe not exactly the same as you, maybe I hit different potholes, maybe I avoided some scattered clumps a dung from the dung wagon, maybe you stepped in more or less. But it was the same road."

"Da-da-don't go minimizing m-m-my feelings"—Doc sputtered bitterly—"ya wa-wa-weird little fucker."

Wagner's anger rose like a mortar round launched. He shot up but Rick guffawed so loudly and with such jubilance Wagner dropped back.

From the woods, from the knoll, from the downstream trail, men with rifles emerged. The newbies thought it was part of the exercise.

The first time Ty Mohammed went before the parole board he was turned down. This had little to do with his behavior during his first three and one-half years of incarceration. Indeed, his behavior and attitudes, after the operation and radiation therapy, swung back to the Tyrone Dorsey of San Francisco—back to the man studying his speech, expanding his vocabulary, walking, talking, being proud, reading, learning about the world's greatest salesman, examining the plight of minorities, their seemingly growing economic divergence from the wealth-path of the mainstream. He did not expound upon his views to the board. He acted the quiet, remorseful, contrite recalcitrant the board most favored. But boards are political. And parole boards are vindictive in the name of social responsibility.

After four years in prison, after his second hearing, Ty Mohammed was paroled on 1 August 1979. It took three additional weeks of complicated exchange and extradition procedures for him to be allowed to return to Pennsylvania. On the morning of 21 August Ty drove a leased gold Cadillac into Mill Creek Falls an hour after local, state and federal agents rendezvoused at the esses near the Old Mill on Mill Creek Road.

Suddenly there was commotion. Clumping on the front porch, then banging on the door. Bobby's head snapped up. Sara's instantaneous reaction was anger, interpreting the noise as vets playing grab ass. She was barefoot, not even dressed except for a loose-fitting muumuu her mother had sent her when she'd learned of Sara's new pregnancy. Commotion erupted in the yard. Sara's eyes riveted to Bobby, flicked to the back window, then to Paulie and Noah. Josh barked. The back door burst open. Bobby's heart froze, jolted, raced. Men rushed in. Bobby's eyes locked on their weapons, pistols, M-16 rifles. Instantly he searched for his own weapon, anything.

"Freeze!"

"Don't move!"

The voices were hard, harsh, threatening. The men wore black shirts, black pants, black hats.

Bobby exploded forward between Sara and the men. "What the hell are you—"

One man grabbed him. Outside there was shouting, screaming, cursing. Sara plucked Paulie from the high chair. A second man smashed Bobby behind the knees with a club, the first hammered him down with a pistol butt on his collar bone, then held the pistol, cocked, barrel on Bobby's temple. "Freeze!" Josh barked viciously, leaped, his old dog legs barely getting traction on the floor. Immediately he was clubbed across the nose, knocked to the floor.

"Don't move!"

"Don't move!"

Paulie shrieked.

Noah was frozen rigid in the living room, watching the men hit his father, hold a gun to his father's face, his father on his knees, his mother holding his shrieking brother, another man with a rifle leveled on them, his dog on the floor before him, between him and the others, bleeding from the nose, twitching. Men yelling things he didn't understand, three now on his father, pushing, frisking even though his father had on but a T-shirt and sweatpants. Then men grabbed his mother, grabbed his brother. More men came. Noah couldn't see them wrench his father's arms behind him, handcuff his father, handcuff too his mother. Armed men darted by him, rushed the stairs, leap-frogged forward, up, frightened someone upstairs would fire on them.

There was no break in the motion. Sara was now down, kneeling, trying to reach Paulie, frantic, trying to see Noah. They'd been caught so off guard, so unaware, then were so dumbstruck by the assault, there was no time for thought, no concept of what was happening, how to resist.

More men spread through the house, secured it room by room. In the kitchen Bobby's ankles were shackled.

"You've got the right to remain . . . "

A deafening blast erupted from the roof of the barn. In the kitchen, agents lurched, dropped to the floor, one smashed Bobby. One plowed Sara over, knelt on her. In the living room Noah peed. All over High Meadow noises, shouts, banging, could be heard amid the deafening shriek of the air-raid siren.

"Here's the search warrant!"

Bobby still did not know who the men were. He was furious. What was happening was just beginning to come together, to form a pattern in his mind.

" . . . probable cause . . . "

Sara was lifted, led to the other room. Bobby was turned to face the kitchen cabinet below the sink, unable to see where they had taken his wife and children, unable to see out of the room, out of the windows.

" . . . stipulates any and all terrorist documents, explosives, weapons, military equipment . . . may be seized . . . additionally any military plans, electronic schematics for detonation . . . axes, saws . . . bombs, gas masks . . . additionally all children . . . probable cause . . . "

Bobby pulled at the cuffs, seething, exploding, "Who the fuck are you?! What the fuck are you doing?!"

"Shut up. Where are the weapons?"

"What weapons?!"

"And the tunnels? Where are the tunnels? You better cooperate."

In the barn library Sherrick too was caught off guard. It wasn't unusual to have supply trucks coming and going all day, to have relatives visit, to have the farm or EES vehicles leaving this early. But the noises had been different. As he'd come onto the main barn floor he'd been greeted with, "Put your hands up! Don't move! Hands on your head! Take four steps forward."

Immediately Sherrick obeyed. "I'm DEA," he shouted. "Don't shoot. Let em surrender. Let everybody surrender. Don't shoot."

"You're . . . ?" Sherrick's confidence confused the officer. He hadn't been told that undercover agents had infiltrated the camp. Other men spread through the barn. A pair with rifles raced up the stairs to the loft while two covered them from the middle of the floor. A fifth man mounted the stairs.

"Let everybody surrender." Sherrick's voice was loud, firm, commanding. "They're not armed." Sherrick had been through it before— not as an American soldier in a foreign land but as an American drug-enforcement officer storming suspected drug dens in Indianapolis. He knew the fear of the agents, knew the "law and order" loathing of the perpetrators, knew the hair triggers. And he knew the best way to respond, the right things to say, the proper way to negotiate in order not to be accidently shot and killed. He remained still with his fingers laced behind his head. He glanced up as two men prepared to burst into Grandpa's office, a third scurrying to cover their advance. "We're not armed," Sherrick repeated. "Why don't you just take us all out front?" His voice was calm. In his mind he was already delineating the police harassment case—High Meadow vs. the State of Pennsylvania, the Town of Mill Creek Falls, and . . .

The siren sounded. Everyone jumped.

Tony was up, hunched behind the barred door. The alarm siren was shrieking and even in his old cubicle behind the tractor garage the noise was intense. His head was forward, flicking back and forth, searching for a weapon, some way to protect himself. He flashed on retreating into the old deep bunker. With the flash came the smell, the ooze, the rot as strong as the moment they'd pulled the body, dismembered it and pulled it over him, over him jammed in that tunnel . . . He grabbed the bar from the door hooks. It was a dry, rock-hard, rough-hewn oak two-by-four he'd taken from an old pallet years earlier. Let em come. He backed a step, set, not hinge side, not behind the door swing, but before it, to the open. Let em come. He was pumped. Eyes focused. The door burst open, two men stepped in. *SMACK*—Tony clobbered their arms, the M-16s clattered to the earthen floor. Immediately Tony shifted, attacked the pressure, the ambush, holding one end of the bar with his left hand, the middle with his right, hammering forward into the stunned officers, the now bleeding, downed men, Tony banging their heads with the wood bar . . . kill or be killed! escape! evade! never surrender! never be captured! Then . . . bam.bam.bam . . .

In Grandpa's office, Van Deusen, when he'd looked out the window and seen rifles, had grabbed up the papers from Bobby's desk, tossed them, not really knowing what they were or why he was doing it, into the fire-resistant safe, slammed the door, twisted the dial. Then he'd hit the air-raid siren. Then the door was kicked open.

Immediately he'd raised his hands. To two men shouting, "Don't move!" he'd nonchalantly shrugged, stammered, "Yeah . . . sure."

Another man came. Van Deusen was read his rights, cuffed.

"You want the siren off?" Van Deusen asked.

"Yeah." The reply was curt.

"That switch." Van Deusen pointed with his chin.

"Don't touch it!" one agent blurted.

"Geez." Van Deusen chuckled. "I'll do it with my forehead. It's not booby-trapped."

With the siren off the atmosphere became more relaxed. The agents

were in radio contact with their control unit. "Barn, Team Five, over."
One man said into his walkie-talkie.

The radio responded. "Go ahead, Andre."

"There's only one up here. Unarmed. There's a locked rack with four
rifles. You know, regular gun rack. This is just a real nice office up here.
Desk. Bookshelves. Over."

There was a pause, then, "Hold him there for questioning. Chief
Hartley wants to come up."

"Roger that."

Van Deusen stood quietly, looking more relaxed than he felt. One
agent held him at gunpoint, not aimed at Tom but at the floor before
him so should he move the officer could simply flick the rifle up. The
other two nosed around, one checking out the desk, the other, the one
with the radio handset, perusing the drawings on the drawing board.
None of them had heard the shots fired two stories below.

"Hey, what's this?"

Van Deusen glanced over. "What?"

"This is a soccer field, isn't it?"

"Yeah," Van Deusen said.

"What are you doin with a soccer field . . . "

"Lineups. We got a game Sunday morning."

"Yeah?"

"Yeah."

"Me too. Who do you play for?"

"Bechtel's Energy Cell."

"You guys the Energy Cell?!"

"Yeah. Who are you?"

"Andre Paulowski. I play for the Pulaski Club over in Rock Ridge."

"Yer shittin me?"

"No. I thought the Energy Cell . . . you know, was like sponsored by
a company . . . Bechtel's . . . "

"We are. That's who we are. We make solar heating panels and stuff.
Howie Bechtel's our team captain. He's a team leader, ah, you know,
like a production foreman, downstairs . . . where we make the solar panels."

"What about the bombs?" Paulowski asked.

"What bombs?" Van Deusen was truly surprised.

"They said you guys are building terrorist bombs up here."

One hundred twenty-nine federal, state, and local law-enforcement officials descended upon High Meadow on the morning of Thursday, 21
August 1979. It was a well-planned, well-executed assault. Agents from
the Bureau of Alcohol, Tobacco, and Firearms, state SWAT teams, local
police officers, town officials, state child-care workers, and command,
control and liaison personnel—all participated. Twelve men were as-

signed to the main house, six to each of the vet-family trailers, ten to each bunkhouse, twenty-two to the big barn, thirty-six to land search, and sixteen to tunnels and bunkers. At the dam, particularly after seeing Rick MacIntyre, the police officers were calm, almost gentle. They did not become edgy until they received the report, via radio, that one of the terrorists had badly beaten two officers before being shot and subdued. An ambulance had been on standby less than a mile down Mill Creek Road. It was advancing on the farm. A second ambulance was called for the terrorist.

Linda was on the verge of tears. On the car radio they were playing Elvis oldies—"Are You Lonesome Tonight?" then "I Can't Stop Loving You." She was half-singing along, half-talking to herself, half out of her mind, half talking to Tony. "Babe, I'm sorry I got so angry. I know it was a long time ago. I know we were separated then. Please come home. The girls are at your mom's. I can't stop loving you."

Linda did not drive fast. She wanted to practice what she would say to Tony. What kept coming out was, "Why? Why Zookie? Maybe I could understand it if it had been someone like that Stacy Carter. But Zookie? Sometimes you're such an ass . . . such a . . . bad little boy . . . No, that's no good." She passed the New Mill, the Dump Road turnoff, approached the esses by the Old Mill. From behind her came an ambulance with its siren whining. She pulled over, let it pass, continued on. Two police cars and another ambulance came from the opposite direction, whizzed by. "I'm—I'm sorry, Babe," she muttered. "I let the green-eyed monster control me. We can work it out."

Before Adolph Lutz's farm she was stopped by a police roadblock. With a tissue she dried her eyes, blew her nose. "Road's closed, Ma'am."

"Why?" Linda asked. "Was there an accident?" She leaned out slightly. Behind the barricade was a television van, men with cameras, a woman Linda recognized as a reporter from the 1st Witness News Team of Channel Five.

"No Ma'am. Just turn around please. The road will be closed for some time."

"Wait a minute." Linda got out of the car. "I saw two ambulances. One going, one coming. I'm a registered nurse. And my husband works—"

"Ma'am, there's an illegal, armed, paramilitary organization up here. We don't want anyone else hurt."

Linda immediately grasped at least the surface of the situation. She tried to stall, to learn more. The trooper stonewalled her but she overheard the reporter. " . . . allegedly a cover for a one-hundred-man paramilitary terrorist force . . . " The woman smiled into the camera. Her blond hair barely moved in the morning breeze. " . . . state and county officials are urging anyone who purchased or had installed any solar equipment, including electronic boards, from any of the following companies—EES, Environmental Energy Systems, The Energy Cell or The Power Pack—to immediately call local police. Do not touch the equipment! There may be explosive devices..."

Inside Linda's mind flares rose, alarms sounded, red flags waved. She knew immediately what to do.

Slowly, appearing from various structures about the farm, half-dressed men, their wrists cuffed behind their heads, the cuffs held by safety wire to each man's belt, were being marched like POWs to a cordoned area between the main house and the big barn. All minors were taken into protective custody by the state child-care authority. Suzanna Shallier, Tom and Joycelyn's eleven-year-old, kicked, scratched, and bit her handlers, but Erik and Lindsey Schevard, Erik and Emma's children, stunned or in shock, went "peacefully." High Meadow was officially subdued and secured in just under eight minutes.

In the cordon: "I wish I were in Nam again, Man. Back in the A Shau. Someplace safe."

"Yeah. We need heavy ordnance, Man. Call in some fuckin arty. Call in ARA."

"Pop smoke. Bring in the fast movers. Let em come in right on top a us. Blow these pigs away."

Individually the vets were read their rights. "You pressing charges?" It was Sherrick, loud, angry. They didn't answer him. "Are we charged with something or not?"

They separated Sherrick from the others, to the side, but not out of sight. Again he was read his rights. "I asked you a direct question, Sergeant. Are we being charged or not?"

"No." The man was terse, hard. "There are no charges right now. But, at any time they may be filed...."

"There's no charges because you don't have any goddamn charges. Why don't you fuckin admit it. You guys blew it."

"You may be arrested at any time." The sergeant stood square to Sherrick, stood looking like he'd like to club the cuffed man. "You can be charged with additional charges if you talk to anyone...."

"Bullshit!" Even with his hands behind his head Sherrick seemed threatening. "You asshole! You can't demand that unless you charge us. What the fuck are you going to trump up?"

From the tractor garage, from the main barn floor, from the Sugar Shack, black-clad troops came with knives, axes, saws, hammers, utility knives, toolboxes—all the equipment that any farm or small manufacturing company would normally have. The items were tagged, recorded, loaded into various police evidence vans. Then they came from the house, from the library, from Grandpa's office, with stacks and boxes of records, plans and ledgers. And from the main floor they took all the electronic control panels under assemblage and all the boxes of components.

Then from the tractor barn—Tony had been evacuated without anyone even knowing he'd been wounded—came word of the tunnel, the deep bunker, the survivalist supplies—mostly food, water, seeds, medicine and books, but also a shotgun (a cheap single-shot 12-gauge) and four boxes of shells.

In the house Bobby and Sara were still on their knees, still in separate rooms. Three times Bobby had been read his rights. Twice they'd showed him the warrant:

> There is probable cause to believe that property described herein may be found at the location set forth herein. This property is seizeable pursuant to Penel Code 1524, as indicated below by Xs. The seizeable property is evidence which tends to indicate that a felony has been committed, or a particular person or persons has/have committed a felony.

"Where's my wife?"

No answer.

"Where are my sons?"

No answer.

"Are they with my wife?"

No answer.

"You motherfuckin cocksuckers. We fought for freedom. Every man here fought for freedom! This is not freedom when for no god damned reason you motherfuckers can come in here and point a gun at my head!!"

"Sir," an officer behind Bobby said to a man who had just entered. "This is Robert J. Wapinski. We're sure of that. His sister identified him."

Wapinski snapped around. An officer twisted his head back forward.

"Humph!" The man who'd entered snorted. Then, loud enough so Bobby could hear him, he said, "His own mother tipped us off. She said she was worried sick about what he's been doing up here."

"Yes Sir. That's what Mayor Hartley said too. Did they find the mortars or those phu . . . What were they called?"

"Phu-gas."

"Those canisters?"

"Just a matter of time. We've got enough to lock these perverts away for life. Half these bastards have records long as your arm. There's so many drug addicts, convicts and psychos up here . . . Shit, they picked up another one coming in from California. Driving a big gold Cadillac. We've got to stop this before it spreads."

Bobby's knees ached. His back ached. His wrists and shoulders and feet ached. The longer they held him on his knees the more furious he grew, the more he felt disconnected from the present, the more he heard her voice, "Pig. You eat like a pig. You sound like a pig. If you can't eat properly . . . Get down on the floor. Get down there! Down!"

Killing me. The thought displaced Miriam's words. They're killing me. They want to kill me.

Sara too was still on her knees, alone, thinking the boys were with Bobby, terrified, miserable, afraid for her baby, her fetus, totally horrified at what the men were doing to her house. Every piece of furniture was inverted, every drape taken down, every rug rolled back. She could hear them upstairs going through drawers, closets. In the living room, before her, where the wallpaper had buckled from the water damage the weekend the dam nearly washed away—they had never repaired the wall—an officer split the bulge to check for drugs. Sara could hear them in the basement, too, and on the roof. They could not have been more thorough. After three hours she was allowed a drink of water; after four she was allowed to sit. Her legs were numb, her feet swollen. Slowly the feeling came back. After six hours, at one o'clock in the afternoon, she was uncuffed. The vets had disappeared from the yard. Bobby and the children were gone. Josh was nowhere to be seen. Still there were police in the house, in the yard. "This is an ongoing investigation," one man told her. "You're not allowed to say a word to anyone. Speaking to anyone will result in additional charges being filed against you."

Finally, at three o'clock, John Pisano, Sr., along with Linda, Isabella and James Pellegrino, Father Tom Niederkou, Johnnie Jackson, and Albert Morris of Morris' Grocery (now also head of the Mill Creak Falls Chamber of Commerce) were allowed through the barricade. John Sr. was livid. Sara did not know whom he was yelling at. "You tell Hartley he's gone too far this time. Too goddamned far. Sorry Father." Then, "Sara! Sara are you okay? Where's Tony?"

2 November 1984

Broken, twisted bodies, lifeless yet still seeping blood. Others wounded, in pain, in agony, in shock. Yet others dying, some so recently dead they don't yet realize it. Bodies. Piles of bodies. Drugged, seeping saliva, drugged, naked, dead, hidden, gasoline dripping, lights sirens bodies rotting buried disrupted. There is pain in my arm, my entire arm, my back, shoulder, legs. More images. A lifetime of images. I cannot tell you how beautiful the angel looks, her eyes—green, her hair—auburn, her teeth—glistening, and her bod—what a bod! She holds my hand, my good hand. Smiles sadly. Turns her head just so. Her mouth moves, emits soft sighs, songs.

Aftermath and change, withdrawal, rewithdrawal, rerage, renumbing. Are we so fragile, so vulnerable, they have gotten to our minds? They had gotten to my body. My wounds were serious.

Odd. The bells of St. Ignatius are ringing. It is noon but it's Friday and the bells are now only rung at noon on Saturday and Sunday. I miss many things being up here—burying myself in the past. I'm in the library. The bells were faint but I'm certain I heard them. Bobby used to pause when he heard them. More so after the raid. He'd nod, direct our attention away from ourselves, our business, to the community. How badly he wanted for us to be part of the larger community.

After shit hits the fan there are three options: one can either walk away, live with shit everywhere, or clean it up and move the fan so it doesn't happen again. Bobby, most of the vets, chose to clean it up. Me too, when I returned.

Not so Tom Shallier and his family. They left late the afternoon of the 21st, less than an hour after the kids were returned. No letters, no commo since. Six other vets abandoned the program within a week because of lack of security and new feelings of betrayal.

That first night many stayed up all night. Every sound made them uneasy. They posted guards, maintained constant if laconic communication between the bunkhouses, the barn, the trailers and the house. LPs, listening posts, situated themselves on the orchard knoll overlooking the drive and on the barn roof amid the various collector arrays and minimills. One group sat in subdued light on the main barn floor rehashing the events of the day, speculating on Bobby's release, on my condition, on if the high authorities had planted recording devices in the house, or barn, or bunkhouses, and if the occasional car or truck passing on Mill Creek Road was really surveillance, a vehicle with night scopes, listening devices, people sniffers. The vets whispered—hush . . . they'll hear.

Except Sherrick. "DAMN! You assholes! How does it feel?!"

"*Sssssshh.*"

"Jerks!" Gary exploded. He stood. He ranted. He paced amongst those on the floor. "It's exactly how we went into the hootches of the Viet Namese. Into their homes. Probable cause! Now you know how the Viet Namese felt! Now you know! Every time we went into a village: 'Don't move!' 'Stick em up.' 'We've reason to believe you're terrorists!' 'Freeze!' We did NOT have to rape; we did NOT have to pillage; we did NOT have to burn the village down or harm a single individual, for them to feel VIOLATED."

"*SSSSSSHH!*"

All night they talked, vented their angers, fears, frustrations. Linda returned, stayed with Sara. Bobby, only Bobby, was held overnight. He returned the next day at noon and sequestered himself with Sara and his sons and Josh—poor ol' Josh, the babysitter, his nose broken, his brain scrambled by concussion, barely able to walk a straight line—until dark. Then Bobby and Josh came to the barn. He vented his wrath and concerns and listened to the vets vent theirs and again every night for weeks, for months, every day at work, at rest, in class.

"We'll handle it. Grunts can handle anything."

"Yeah, anything."

"But not kids."

Noah became withdrawn, defensive. He tested his position by misbehaving, purposefully provoking punitive responses, confirming to himself, to his four-and-one-half-year-old mind, his badness, his need for punishment, for terror. Why else would they have taken him away? Why else would they have beat his father, restrained his mother, clubbed his closest friend until his nose ran blood and he could but twitch on the floor? At night, for months, Noah woke, screaming, unable to breathe, to catch his breath, unable to stop crying, becoming rigid when touched, then eyes like saucers, still, silent, numb.

The SWAT team did not use the same high-velocity rounds that were used in M-16s in Viet Nam. The rounds did not tumble, did not shatter. I was hit in the left hand an inch below my thumb, and in my left shoulder or back, near the base of my neck. Because I was leaning forward, and because of the angle of the shot, that bullet entered the upper trapezius muscle, passed through ten inches of meat and lodged in the lower dorsal region a finger's

width from my spine. Both wounds were mainly to muscle tissue—
to which the doctors, for days, kept saying, "Amazing! An inch this
way and you'd have lost the use of your hand. An inch there, you'd
have been paralyzed." And to which Linda said, "You must be here
for some reason, some higher cause. To have had all the close calls
you've had . . . God's got something planned for you." Linda. She is
so beautiful. I wanted to marry her again, that day, that night, then
and there, in postop. I wanted to live with her forever.

More shit hit the fan. Old shit. Old shit as if it had been shoveled
and flung and had hung in the air for years, hovering, slowly
floating in the air currents toward the blades. I still had to deal with
the paternity suit. And I was charged with resisting arrest,
assaulting law-enforcement officials, breach of the peace, concealing
a deadly weapon (the forty-four-inch oak two by four!), and half a
dozen other charges. Incredible!

For all the blustering about High Meadow the vets had done
down at the White Pines Inn, and elsewhere, the having mortars,
sentries, booby-traps and the tunnels of Cu Chi, the authorities
essentially found nothing. Are you surprised? Guys had been
vigilant but there never had been sentries. The gates had always
been open (except that one time when we hooted at Chief Hartley).
As to weapons, High Meadow had the few rifles, a few registered
pistols and my old single-shot shotgun. The way it was pictured on
the front page of the local paper the day following the raid, it
looked impressive. Yet considering the number of vets and what
could have been, or would have been had High Meadow been an
armed camp, we were highly underarmed.

Sherrick did the legwork but officially I was represented by Mark
Tashkor and Jesse Rasmuellen of Williamsport—both veterans,
though Jesse Rasmuellen was only an era vet. Charges, and never-
filed charges, against High Meadow, against Bobby, against me,
slowly disintegrated. Fuming rage mellowed, became fuel, became
drive. In the end, local, state and federal officials had made so
many errors—for example, the search warrants had been stamped
by a clerk, not signed by a judge, and the warrants' numbers were
blank (improperly recorded prior to authorization)—that Tashkor
was able to get the assault charges dropped. Then the concealed
weapons charge, and all the minor charges were withdrawn, and
the breach of peace charge was found unprosecutable.

We did not have the funds for a major legal countersuit, and
Sherrick, in spite of his law school years, really wasn't qualified. For
a time he attempted to get the Public Civil Liberties Union to take
our case but they were not interested in veterans who seemingly
were proud of their service. The PCLU saw our case as
contradictory to other cases it had supported over the past decade:

draft avoiders, resisters, and service members desiring early release from active duty.

Still Gary wanted restitution, revenge. He struck back. He wrote up the account of the raid, had it printed, names, addresses, every detail he could uncover. Then he mass-mailed a copy to every address in Mill Creek Falls and the surrounding area. He implicated Ernest Hartley, Senior and Junior, and dozens of their cronies in a politically motivated ploy that had illegally involved state and federal authorities. Gary got away with it by declaring his publication to be a biyearly investigative reporting magazine! Freedom of the press! Hartley, after sixteen years as mayor of Mill Creek Falls, did not run for reelection in 1980. Still, the new sewer plant and system was begun (is still under construction at a now estimated cost of $48 million), and the South Hill development of Whirl's End Golf and Country Club, the mall, the mall extension, and Hobo Hollow Estates never missed a beat.

We withdrew further, fought our withdrawal. Bobby had been devastated by the raid, had, like all of us, turned inward. Ty Mohammed was a godsend. If sales is an art, Ty was a true artist. For months Bobby was afraid to speak to new people, afraid they had seen him being taken into custody on Channel Five's 1st Witness newscast. He was afraid clients would fear their EES systems would explode. Ty was oblivious to the point of ruthlessness. He was the kind of salesman who could sell coal to Newcastle. Given an honest, well-priced product, given the cause of the vets and the environmental and financial justifications, Ty saturated half of Pennsylvania and southern New York with EES's message. While Bobby called every past client, every distributor, every supplier; while he explained how the misunderstanding had occurred, how EES and High Meadow had been totally exonerated; while he virtually begged everyone to remain with him, with us, and "rest assured nothing is going to explode"; Ty couldn't have cared less. Black, bearded, in a leased gold Cadillac and three-piece suit, nine-fingered, one-eared, one-testicled, golden-smiled Ty, within six months of his arrival, even with the recession of 1980 grasping the nation, tripled EES sales! He buried our withdrawal in work. EES was rolling again, business was good, the crop was being sold.

Work buried other emotions for Ty. He would not visit Luwan. He was cool to Randall, to Phillip and Carol, to his mother. He opened an account in Jessica's name, deposited half his earnings there, but he did not let her know, did not let her see him. He told no one. Nor did he tell anyone at High Meadow of his cancer.

Wonderment. *Am* [ahm] is the Viet Namese symbol for the female principle—much as is yin in the Chinese yin-yang dichotomy. They named her Brigita Am until my mother, Jo, pointed out that the baby's initials were BAW, which to Jo and then to Linda and Sara, too, were terrible initials with which to saddle any little girl. So they renamed her Am Brigita Wapinski—no one objected to ABW except Aunt Isabella who thought Am should be changed to Eva for Sara's grandmother. They named her on Thanksgiving night, eleven hours after she was born. Some of the vets liked the name Brigita but most called her Amy. Like all the other children—Noah and Paul Anthony, Erik and Lindsey Schevard, even Gina and Michelle when they were up—Am was virtually adopted by everyone at High Meadow. But being the last born—being born when the population was again rising, when we were so badly in need of a lift in the aftermath of the raid—Am became special. We marked her birth with the planting of an oak tree over her placenta, me acting the preacher, saying, "As this oak grows strong, so shall you and as it lives long so shall you." Thirty men said, "Amen." Am had more uncles than any girl in history, and that brought us closer, made us feel more like brothers. Through her, through all the kids, with Sara and Linda and Emma's help, we, and Bobby too, slowly re-began the expansion, the conscious turning out to embrace the community.

Another month passed. The trial of Eisenhower and Dulles, JFK, LBJ, Nixon and Kissinger, was a dud. Not that a lot wasn't learned but concentration had been disrupted, research time usurped. Had or had not the governments of the United States been true to the nation's founding principles? We never reached a verdict.

Five months from the day of the raid: There is a statute of limitation on paternity suits. Mark Tashkor wanted to invoke it. I wanted to know if Zookie's kid was mine. I tentatively agreed to help support, only to find that Zookie had dropped the case, refiled naming Gaylord as the father.

More changes. What changed more than anything was Bobby's re-realization that the world, that people, run on elation, spiritual elation. It is the fuel that makes things go well. It is what makes life good. Life is supposed to be happy. The pursuit of happiness is a basic human right. Ask Tom Jefferson! Ask Sam Adams!

> ... whenever any Form of Government becomes destructive of these Ends, it is the Right of the People to alter or to abolish it, and to institute new Government, laying its Foundation on such Principles, and organizing its Powers in such Form, as to them shall seem most likely to effect their Safety and *Happiness*.

And yet happiness seemed to have been legislated out of our lives. Happiness had been destroyed by governmental overcomplication; by reduction to triviality by academia; by a narrowing of perspective by the media's interpretation of our lives; by fear of risk and loss by insurance companies and school boards; by those who, wishing to provide equal opportunity to all, were seeking to level all by reaching for a common denominator and inadvertently finding that the only true common denominator is mere subsistence. We'd become competent men doing competent work—trudging on without joy like so much of America, without pleasure in our achievements, seeking passive "pleasures" like spectator America, boob-tube America, dumbed-down America seeking lowest common denominator sustainability, forgetting that true sustainability requires work; requires striving for quality, for substantive value, for elation that is an adjunct of hope, freedom and achievement.

Bobby reasoned it thusly. "We made ourselves vulnerable by becoming, as a microcosmic community, stuck. We did not reach out, expand ourselves, except in business and in an antagonistic political manner. For all our elegant, internal solutions, for all our simplifications, we have not gone public! We're building a tower of cards on a kayak when the structure requires a supertanker."

Wherever, whenever his ears told him, Bobby would raise his head, gesture toward town, "Hear that bell?" he'd ask. "That's St. Ignats. This town's got to know who we are, who we were. Not who they thought we were, not who they think we were because they saw *Apocalypse Now* or *The Deer Hunter* or *Rambo*, or 1st Witness News."

The expansion of unstuck vets, of the unstuck microcosmic community, grew into the larger community not simply as a business element like EES or Kinnard / Chassion or even the Mall, but as one-on-one volunteers helping the elderly, tutoring school children—especially "problem kids" of which and for which the vets both had a special understanding and an affinity, coaching in-town youth basketball, soccer and hockey, joining the PTA, the Rotary and Chamber of Commerce (after all, EES was now the sixth-largest company in town), helping the financially disabled—particularly with the reconstruction—plumbing and heating—of their homes, volunteering for church or temple functions which lead to assisting St. Ignatius with the sponsoring of the Huynh Thanh family, and finally to opening up High Meadow, the institute, the library, the mock trials.

Where we helped others, others helped us. Pop helped Linda and me buy a house in Old New Town. After ten years in the apartment in Creek's Bend, Gina and Michelle finally had rooms of their own, Linda had her study, we all had a rec room, and there was a yard where we planted trees and expected to watch them grow for fifty years.

Call it reaching out. Sara, Linda and Emma expanded their women's group, opening it to any abused woman. And as a Viet Nam vet group we began networking with other Viet Nam vet groups—first in Pennsylvania, then Texas, California, North Carolina, the entire country. We may have or may not have had the most comprehensive program but we were not a unique grouping. Viet Nam veteran groups were springing up all over America. By 1980 the movement was a snowball turned avalanche.

On July Fourth the bells of St. Ignatius rang while we marched as a unit in the town's parade. We had a strack color guard unit but behind we were loose, having fun, tossing candy into the crowd, handing out American flag decals, letting the children come out and pet our mascots—Bobby's Josh and the nucleus of my new agricultural venture, three Viet Namese potbellied pigs. (We'd dressed them in blue uniforms provoking hoggy snorts from the pigs and squeals of laughter from Jessie Taynor.)

On the 5th the bells rang again marking the arrival of the Huynh family and of Vu Van Hieu, a lone boat person, a CPA, a man who, after years of communist reeducation camps, repeated escape attempts, and a year in a Thai refugee camp, had finally reached the relocation center at Indian Town Gap only to lose his sponsor. Bobby hired him unseen.

This was a happy time—perhaps the happiest and most fulfilling in Bobby's life. Frankie "The Kid" Denahee, our 128th vet, came, brought with him the sad news of Fuzzy and Wildman. Still T-n-T and The Kid were together. I had to step back in time with them, as Bobby taught, becoming a ladder, giving them the ability to move on without taking from them the ability to return. All year I had been chided about the tunnel, the bomb shelter. Frankie joined right in.

Lea Balliet, Linda's youngest sister, came to visit, to sing and entertain. She was as pretty as Linda, maybe prettier. At twenty-two she drove the guys wild—so naive, so innocent, she'd been only eight or ten when most of us had been in Viet Nam. Marcus came, too. And Lem, the Tunesmyth. And Lee, Corky, Spider, Steve all the way from Idaho, Big Don, and Chuck in Jody's Cadillac—entertainers all of them, bringing their guitars, their music, their bands—veterans, all of them.

Later Bobby would look back and tag the year between the first raid and the next onset The Help Years, and he would snarl that the destruction of The Help Years had begun the week of Monday, 7 July 1980, with the letter he received from the IRS, and with the revolt of the excluders, and with the blood.

30

T he wind blew cold. The street was empty. He lifted the receiver,
dialed the number. Snowflakes fluttered in the lee of the open booth.
The sky was gray, not yet dark, late January, late afternoon.

"Internal Revenue Service. Criminal Investigations. Gilmore."

"Yes." He altered his voice. "I'm—I'm calling about one of your programs."

"Uh-huh."

"I'm calling about the program you've got for turning people in for
tax evasion."

"Yes."

"You give rewards, right?"

"There's a program . . . "

"Percentage, right?"

"That can be arranged. Who am I speaking with?"

"No. I—I can't tell you that. I'm talking the anonymous program. I
know you do that."

"In substantial cases . . . "

"That's what I'm talking here. Major fraud. Big time evasion. Maybe a hundred thousand. Maybe a million. None of the penny ante stuff."

"Can you hold, please?"

"What? No!"

"Excuse me?"

"I'm calling from a pay phone. Don't try to identify me."

"No." In the agent's voice there was irritation, boredom, apathy. "I'm just getting a file to issue you a number. When you call, identify yourself by the number."

"How do I get paid?"

"To bearer. Sent to a post office box."

"Yeah. Yes. That's what I want."

"Can you give me some information?"

"First give me a number."

"Okay. Your number is *R* as in Romeo, *T* as in Tango, *L* as in Lima, six, seven, six, four. Do you want to repeat it back to me?"

"R. T. L. Six. Seven. Six. Four."

"Now, tell me who we're talking about."

"First tell me who you are."

"I'm Special Agent Stan Gilmore."

"Mr. Gilmore?"

"Um-hmm."

"Keep this file open. This is going to be big. I'll call again."

Monday, 7 July 1980—

> Round and round the mulberry bush
> The monkey chased the weasel,
> The monkey thought it was a-all in fun,
> POP! goes the weasel.

The song was in his head, swirling, mixed with other immediate demands and concerns, new and old, swirling like flakes in a winter storm, Peppin, Zarichniak and Denahee, all, all morning, pulling at him, joy-terror-fear-questioning.

It was Noah's first day of summer camp, first time on a bus, alone, going off without Sara or Bobby, without Linda or one of the vets. It had taken three months for his night terrors to abate, six for the acting out to subside, nine for him to again appear the confident little boy he'd been before the raid. Bobby thought of him at breakfast. Sara and Am had been upstairs. "What did the monkey say?" Noah had asked.

"I don't think the monkey said anything," Bobby'd answered. "Only the weasel. He goes—" Bobby put his right index finger into his mouth, blew up his cheeks, "Pop!" Bobby smiled.

"But Papa, why didn't the monkey say anything?"

"I don't know, Noah," Bobby said. "That's not part of the song. Just, 'the monkey thought it was aaa-lll in fun. Pop! goes the weasel.' "

"What did the weasel think?"

"He was being chased by the monkey."

"But," Noah persisted, "what did he think?"

"I think he thought it was fun too. Don't you think it's a fun song?"

Noah hadn't answered. Paulie, too, had been quiet, but he was always quiet unless he had something to say. Bobby wasn't worried about him. Somehow, perhaps because of age or because he'd screamed through most of it and thusly had not seen much, the raid had seemingly not traumatized him.

"Noah?" Bobby said.

"I don't know," the boy answered quietly. "I just wanted to know what the weasel thought. That's all."

"Hmm." Bobby had been about to continue when Sara came down with Am dressed in a yellow sunsuit and a big yellow sunbonnet.

"He's going to miss the bus," Sara had said to him. Then to Noah, "You don't want to miss the bus on the first day, do you?"

The bus had come. Sara and Bobby, Paul, Am and Josh had all accompanied Noah on the long walk down the drive. Then quickly Noah, never before having even been in a school bus, scrambled up the stairs as if he'd commuted that way for years. In seconds the bus had gone. Then Paulie had burst into tears because he couldn't go too.

Bobby was not focused on the here and now. He was checking in Frankie "The Kid" Denahee, the 128th vet, the ex–roofrat, ex-gunbunny. Vu Van Hieu was at a small desk in one corner, bent over the master ledger, entering figures in his impeccable hand. It had taken him one day to learn Bobby's system. Carl Mariano was at a second desk that had displaced Van Deusen's drawing table. A third desk was empty. Bobby looked at Denahee, continued talking, not listening to his own words but blabbing on automatic. "We're brought up with the dual concept sane-insane. But, like in so many seeming logical tautologies it narrows the field and restricts our view of reality. So here we add *a-sane*, meaning without sanity, or beyond the bounds of reason, but not meaning weird or deranged or crazy. Asane, like baseball, the color green, dreams, intrusive day thoughts. Your reaction, your feelings, like most of us here, are normal and extraordinary. The circumstances, the events you're reacting to were extraordinary. . . . "

Bobby bent over the organization chart of High Meadow. There were now sixty-eight vets in residence—one of Asian heritage, one indigenous American, six Hispanics, ten of African ancestry, and fifty genetically European or Middle Eastern. The main office or headquarters consisted of Bobby, Tony, Carl, Don Wagner and now Vu Van Hieu. Tony also headed the column titled The Farm. Beneath him, with specific titles, were Thorpe, Treetop, Renneau, Cannello, and Rifkin, then eleven others. Van Deusen (design), Gallagher (construction/installations), Bechtel (assembly), and Mohammed (sales) headed the thirty-seven-man EES unit. Sherrick and Hacken plus five more ran The Institute; and in a new structure, Family Services, two vets assisted Sara, Emma, and occasionally Linda.

"Um . . . Where was I? Oh . . . ah, for now I'm going to list you under Tony's command, okay?"

"Sure."

"Did I mention to you about the grand jury indictments?"

"I didn't really get that."

"They're deciding who to indict. Last year's trial was of the five administrations starting with Eisenhower. The guys have been working on this year's candidates for some time. Maybe Ngo Dinh Diem, Ho Chi Minh, Sihanouk, or Jane Fonda. They get pretty lively. . . . "

Again his mind shifted to automatic, the conversation running now here, now there, routine chatter. "Your first ten dollars each week automatically goes into your education fund. After you're settled you'll start classes. . . . " Bobby's eyes shifted just an inch, just enough to look away from Frank Denahee to a stack of mail. A second stack held letters from veterans who wanted to come to High Meadow—or from relatives who wanted to send them. Where to put them? How to support them, have them support themselves? The place was bursting at the seams. The drive was lined with private cars, trucks—many old, rusted, mechanically defunct, making the farm look more like Johnnie Jackson's Auto Salvage than the pristine mountain meadow farm he'd known as a boy.

"You were talking about classes that are available downtown . . . "

"Oh yeah. There's things we can do up here but there are things we can't. Couple of guys who were medics are taking nursing courses—"

"Ha!" Denahee snickered. "To change bedpans!"

Bobby's face turned to stone. For a second he repressed an agitation that wanted to blow, then he released. "Don't be an idiot! Don't act like some stupid, spoiled school brat. If you're interested, we'll get up into a good course. Aim for RN. Specialize in emergency room care. Or ICU. Shit. I don't care what you study. Everyone here studies. Quality counts. You come to me, you come voluntarily. We'll take you in but you've got to follow the rules, you've got to strive. Look where you're at! No money. Never learned how to handle it. You told me that yourself. Trouble keeping a relationship. Right? We're going to confront that. It doesn't do any good teaching a guy a skill and having him get a job if all he's going to do is blow his pay. Fact is, you don't know how to live in this society."

Vu and Mariano popped their heads up from their work. Carl had never heard Bobby take this tone, this early. Bobby snapped. "You're number one twenty-eight. Not one guy who's stayed through a year has fucked up again on the outside. This is basic, modern life skills. You listen in class. You take notes. Part of our in-processing is reading evaluation. If you score low, it's mandatory you take Sara's reading class. Mandatory. The circuit includes nutrition. If you put enough shit into

your mouth, sooner or later all you can talk or think is shit. Your outcome depends on your attitude . . . but I guarantee . . . if you put in the
effort, it'll turn your life around." Bobby puffed, exhausted. He dismissed Denahee, sat slumped, slouched, in his chair, angry beyond reason.

All day waves of agitation rolled over him, receded. His thoughts
jumped from project to project, then back to the song, the conversation
with Noah, the boy getting on the bus. What effect will it have on him?
he thought as he sorted the mail, passed invoices and checks to Hieu,
inquiries to Carl. He hefted a letter from the Department of the Treasury,
Internal Revenue Service, split the envelope with a North Viet Namese
Army bayonet a new vet, Michael Yasinsky, had given him. The letter's
type was small, closely packed.

> Date of this notice: 7/1/80
> Social Security Number: 038-27-8907
> Form: 1040   Tax Year: 1978
>
> Proposed Changes to Income, Payments, Credits, or Deductions
>
> Employers, banks, and other payers furnish payment information
> on forms such as W-2, W-2p, 1098, 1099. . . . The proposed changes
> are listed on page 2 of this notice, and the reasons for making them
> on page 3. . . .

What the hell is this crap? Bobby thought. There were six more paragraphs of tightly compressed words. He skipped them, turned to
page 2.

Changed Item(s)	Shown on return	Allowable payments	Increase
Payments to Contractors	$105,750	$00.00	$105,750

Changes in Adjusted Gross Income

1. Total Increase	$ 105,750.00
2. Taxable Income per return	8,474.00
3. Corrected Taxable Income	114,224.00
4. Corrected Tax	28,525.00
5. Credits, as corrected or shown on return	11.00
6. Other Taxes, as corrected or shown on return	3,657.00
7. Total Corrected Tax	32,993.00
8. Tax as shown on return	1,271.00
9. Tax Increase	30,922.00
13. Interest from 4-15-78 to 15 days after the date of this notice	12,532.00
14. Presumptive Negligence Penalty	2.00
15. Send this amount to the IRS	43,447.00

Bobby smirked. The figures were ridiculous. If he had had an income of $114,000 in 1978 he'd be living like a king. And if he took everything he now owned—cars, trucks, machines, personal items—the value would not reach $43,000. Bureaucrats! he thought. Error after error. One more thing to straighten out. He handed the letter to Hieu.

On Thursday evening, the 10th of July, the vets met in the big barn amid the tables and machines, half-assembled duct work and plenums, control panels, windmill rotors, dust and debris. There were the usual announcements, old business and new. "We've completed the planting of a thousand seedlings on the south side of the knoll above the drive-way," Tony reported. "Four hundred Scotch pine, two hundred each white pine, Doug fir, and Austrian pine. There's room for another thousand next year; maybe five hundred in '82. By '85 we should be able to sell the first of the cut-yer-own Christmas trees. Final figures are in from this spring's strawberries and, actually, we made almost as much off the market-truck as we did selling to Morris', the IGA, and RRVMC. We might consider pick-yer-own, there, too, next year. And pumpkins in the entire lower-thirty-six amid the corn. Cannello's experimenting with them on two acres. . . . "

Bobby was still in a foul mood. Nothing, all week, seemed to break it. Just the opposite. It had been building, getting uglier. Wednesday after-noon Sara had gone into town for groceries, then to see Linda, then Louise Taunton, a member of her women's group who had missed the last three meetings. By dark Sara had not returned. At ten, with the children in bed, Bobby could no longer stand it. He'd paced, he'd read the newspaper, but he couldn't focus through a single full paragraph. At every sound he'd been up, down, looking out the windows to the drive. At ten thirty he'd called the Pisanos. Tony had answered. Sara had left three hours earlier. "Did she say she was going to the Taunton's?"

"Let me get Linda. I was watching a ball game."

Bobby had called the Tauntons. The line was busy. He'd sat. He'd sprung up. His ass hurt. One more thing. He'd worried about his hem-orrhoid—had it become infected? Daily his ass had been getting more sore but the five-hundred-dollar deductible on their medical insurance was enough of a deterrent to keep him from seeking help, from com-plaining. Except that he *had* been complaining. Not about his ass. About Larry Peckham and David Quinn. For all the work Bobby had done, for all the programs, the ladders, one foot in front of the other, one rung at a time, he, with Wagner and everyone else, had not been able to make the breakthrough. And Peckham and Quinn were not the only ones. Even Ty, in Bobby's opinion, was ghosting, getting over. Not on work— he was selling up a storm—but on self-development, on expansion be-yond the self.

It was the McDuffie thing, fallout from McDuffie. What had never been a problem before was now a situation to confront. High Meadow did not exist in a vacuum. Ty, Rodney Smith, Calvin Dee and Hector Jackson had set up an informal, exclusive Black Vets group. And they were actively recruiting the newest of the newbies, John Peppin. Bobby saw it as separatist at a time when all needed to come together, as a turning in when he believed they needed to turn out.

Wednesday night at eleven Bobby had called the police. Sara was not yet home. The police receptionist had seemed to shrug, to say, "So." Bobby had called Tony again. "Where could she be? Where the hell is she?" He'd called the Tauntons ten times. Then he'd called the bunkhouse. He was heading to Louise and Tom Taunton's as soon as Steve Hacken could get to the house to baby-sit.

Carl Mariano, Jeremiah Gallagher, Mike Treetop, Juan Varga, Ty and Rodney all had come to the house with Steve, all ready to pile into Ty's gold Cadillac to search for Sara. Van Deusen and Sherrick had shown up with walkie-talkies, a map of Mill Creek Falls, and plans for a house-to-house search. Another two dozen vets in a dozen vehicles were ready to set out when Sara had pulled in wondering what all the to-do was about.

Tony finished the farm report. Tom Van Deusen and Ty reported on EES: Tom on difficulties obtaining the proper anodized aluminum channels for the rafter embedded systems because the company that had been supplying them had gone out of business: Ty on the first drop in orders since he'd taken over sales. "Recession, Man," he said. "Credit crunch. Bankruptcies are getting pandemic." Carl Mariano reported an hour-per-man decrease in educational effort, and Gary Sherrick told the assembly the "grand jury" had been unable to decide who to indict.

Bobby clenched his jaw with every *can't-do* or *didn't-do* that followed Tony's *can-do*s and *did*s. Vu Van Hieu also had bad news. The IRS letter, according to his preliminary calls, was no mistake. There was "at least $105,000 of unreported income," Hieu said. "Everybody here say they file return, but IRS say not anybody file. Even you have not less than four hundred dollars income, if you independent contractor, you mus file Schedule C and Form 1040. Maybe you owe nothing. Maybe the IRS owe you. You still mus file."

"Fuck the IRS," someone called out.

A dozen vets agreed. There was resentment that the newby, the gook, the dink, had moved so quickly into the HQ, into a seeming position of power over them, telling them what papers to file, what they had or had not done. Chatter erupted. The group had been unruly from the moment they'd come together this evening. Some were talking about the Pirates, some about the Phillies, some about a pick-up soccer game Van Deusen and Andre Paulowski of Rock Ridge's Pulaski Club had set up for Saturday. There was talk about the hostages in Iran, and the political conventions. Reagan and Carter had secured nominations, and third-party candidate John Anderson was polling a strong 20 percent. They talked of the Midwest and the south, baking and turning to dust in the heat wave and drought.

In the corner by the Slitter, exactly as Gary Sherrick had once sat, was Sal Ianez who had lost his left arm at the shoulder to an RPG in 1969. Sal had settled in under Sherrick and Hacken as an institute researcher. The meeting, any crowd, overwhelmed him. He'd withdrawn between the elevator and the machine, slid into a fantasy where he was at a great formal party with beautiful women, powerful men, waiters in tuxedos carrying silver trays of crystal glasses filled with champagne.

At the opposite end of the room between the glass-cleaning and final assembly tables, Frankie "The Kid" Denahee was listening to Steve Travellers soft-voiced tale of the Highlands. Travellers was a two-tour Special Forces NCO, a year in Ban Me Thuot, a year at Duc Co near the tri-border. He was African-American. Earlier that day, in the High Meadow library, he'd read, for the first time in detail, of the People's Army of Viet Nam, i.e., the NVA's, policies and treatment of the mountaineers, the Montagnards, the Yards, "his people."

"My people are good people," Travellers whispered to Denahee. "I didn't know. I didn't know what happened."

Denahee didn't know either. Not in detail. Not what had happened since '75. And he felt too new to High Meadow yet to express himself.

"Good people," Travellers muttered. "Strong people." He'd said it to himself a thousand times since returning in '71, to himself because he hadn't known anyone who would listen, to himself to reassure himself that his people were still okay. "Good, strong people." His chin wrinkled, tensed, in restrained anguish. He'd inferred the details, yet he'd ignored them, denied them, for five years. For five years he'd blurred details through boozy bloodshot eyes.

"Yeah." Denahee nodded. "I knew some from when we—"

"Fuck America!" Travellers interrupted. "Fuck the land of opportunity. Fuck freedom. It's a sham. I'm sick of it. America's a take-it, grab-it, greedy, slovenly sham wrapped in highfalutin words. There's not a fucker gives a fuckin flyin leap—maybe there's some in this room— about my people. My people are being slaughtered. Exterminated."

A dozen vets were within earshot. Venom expressed, even if one is in agreement, is unsettling. Most guys glanced over, up, away. A few nodded. It was more comfortable to talk about the Pirates or the Phillies.

"This country stinks," Travellers said. His voice was louder, clear. "Stinks! Shovin Haagen Dazs in their fat faces, lettin my people die."

"Amen," said Calvin Dee. He, Hector, Ty, Rodney and John Peppin were at the center of the barn, before the sheet-metal break. Travellers sneered. His expression showed he didn't believe Calvin understood.

Jeremiah Gallagher moseyed over. "We're with you," he said to Travellers.

"Yeah," Tony said. "We're here together."

"Fuck it," Travellers snapped more angrily.

"Right on!" Ty stood, held up a power fist. Rodney, Hector, Calvin and John joined him. "They doin it to our people."

Michael Treetop stood. "They're doing it to all our people," he said calmly. "Let's not be doing it to ourselves. This isn't Liberty City."

Calvin cackled. "Burn, baby, burn!"

Wapinski watched. He hadn't been concentrating on the meeting any more than he'd been focused on anything all week. Ty and four black vets stood in the center, defiant, hostile, gesturing with fists. Three blacks remained seated. Dave Bailer stood alone, not gesturing, not hostile. Steve Travellers stood with Denahee, Gallagher and Pisano, angry, a different anger.

Two months earlier the tension had erupted into violence—not at High Meadow but in Florida. In December '79 a black man, an insurance salesman, a vet, ex-Marine Albert McDuffie, on a motorcycle had run a red light, had been chased by police, had freaked out, led the police on a one hundred-mile-per-hour chase through twenty-five blocks of the city until the police finally trapped him. Angrily the police had beat McDuffie, crushing his skull and killing him. The officers then re-staged the incident to look like an accident, and they falsified their reports. Within days some of the officers came forward, exposed the crime, and four policemen were charged with second-degree murder. The trial was moved to Tampa. In late May an all-white jury had deliberated for less than three hours before acquitting the officers of all charges. Miami's inner-city black ghetto, Liberty City, went up like an ambush zone surrounded by daisy-chained claymore mines. For three days the city had burned, the night sky glowed, the day sky smogged. Looters and rioters did a hundred million dollars in damages, killed sixteen, injured four hundred. Thirty-six hundred militiamen, essentially an army of occupation, had quelled the bloodied streets.

"You fuckers don't know . . . " Travellers began. He was staring at Ty.

Ty interrupted, parried the comment. "Our people, street people, people of color, people who are with us, they know. My people know this government won't do anything for them. This government givin handouts, givin businesses, givin houses to Viet Namese boat people. It gives breaks to Cubans. It gives nothin to African-Americans. People aren't going to sit back and starve. They're going to fight. Better to die fighting than be a slave in ghetto America."

"That's not what—" Travellers moved toward the center. Joe Alamont scrambled out. Black versus black. He wanted no part of it. Most of the white vets stayed seated, exactly like Wapinski. Robert Ortez stood with Ty. "—I'm talking about!" Travellers stopped. "I'm talking about Montagnards. The communists got an extermination campaign going against the Yards."

"That's cause they're dark-skinned." Ty barked his words. "I've been in white homes all over this state. You think I don't see racism?! Every day?! This is the most racist society—"

"Shut UP!" Steve Travellers's hands shot forward as if to grab, to strangle. "You bastard! You've completely turned what I'm saying. You're the racist. I'm talking my people."

"I seen it too." Erik Schevard stood. "I've been reading too. They pulled the rug from under em. I read where the dinks took over my area and carved up half the population. We had this village in our area—the people were Northerners from '55. They hated the communists. The communists hated them. Had em all listed for death as traitors. I seen a report said the dinks clear-cut the ville and plowed every man, woman and child under . . . along with the water bo."

"Cap it, Man." It was Joe Alamont. "They'd never kill the water buffalo. That'd be like holding a dude up, stiffin im, then throwin him and his wallet in a dumpster without stealin the money."

"They'd do that," Hacken injected, "to teach the others a lesson."

"That's it." Wapinski's voice was forceful yet low. The bickering ceased. "Steve, is there anything we can do?"

Eyes turned toward Hacken, back to Wapinski, then to Travellers.

"Fuck it," Travellers muttered. He backed toward Denahee. "I'm . . . I'll be all right."

"No." Wap stood, bent as if he had a stomach cramp, straightened slowly. "I mean is there anything we can do for your people? Something. Something short of stealing a SAC bomber and nuking Hanoi." Travellers didn't respond. "What about you, Ty? Can you do something positive for your people?"

The meeting continued, not simply that night but on into August and September. Bobby was frustrated, on the edge of control, fighting to hold himself, the vets, High Meadow, together. To Ty, Calvin, Hector, a mixed score of vets: "You want the government to take care of you?! Are you crazy? The government can't even take care of itself. How many of you guys have spent time at RRVMC? That's how the government takes care of people. That's what you want?! What do you think they do in Washington? Figure out how to make you rich? Make you happy? Make you successful? You are nuts. They applaud themselves if they can show— even by smoke and mirrors—a one percent increase in personal income. If you had one percent more, would that make a difference in your lives? One percent! You can have five thousand percent! That's what we're working on."

Then again, "Hey, who have you given control over your life? Promoter Don King, maybe? The baseball owners? Budweiser beer? Some fucking demagogue here or there? A rented gold Cadillac? Who's controlling you? You or them or it? Did they get to your mind? Madison Avenue ad men? You've got the choice. Political demagogues? Right now you've got the opportunity. You can use it or blow it. Your choice."

It was a tit-for-tat game. And Bobby was losing. Throughout this period, as the barn meetings continued, Vu Van Hieu handled the IRS and the retroactive accounting beautifully but he was not able to account for many of the vets who had graduated or who had quit. Perhaps Hieu would have handled it even more elegantly, more efficiently, had it not been for Bobby. Bobby refused to allow Hieu to force the vets to comply with the IRS demands for independent contractor status. At that time he did not realize or understand that to the IRS this demonstrated High Meadow's willful noncompliance with the law, and therefore justified the IRS's refiguring of the '77 through '79 returns as if all vets had been employees, and as if Bobby, as employer, had willfully not withheld from the employees, nor paid to the government, FICA, Federal Unemployment, and Social Security taxes.

Bobby brought Hieu with him to the first meetings with the case officers. They were open with the government men, explaining that they believed the problem was not theirs but the IRS's; they explained in detail what High Meadow was, how it worked, how and why he paid the vets, and how they in turn were liable for their taxes which, because High Meadow's pay scale was minimal, were not much. The case officers seemed amenable, happy to accept Bobby's explanation. Then the IRS re-sent notice of payment due for 1978, with additional interest charges.

In ensuing discussions, the auditors disallowed Bobby's claim that the vets were independent contractors responsible for paying their own taxes. In addition, they showed that at least fifteen vets had been receiving veterans disability payments. The IRS then stated that if Bobby attempted to claim High Meadow was a drug, alcohol and behavioral treatment facility, High Meadow would, because its "patients" were receiving federal funds, be subject to all federal laws and regulations— including building access and safety codes, procurement contract procedures and reporting, and reportage of racial composition of staff and patient populations.

In October the auditors went further, stating that because of the unpaid taxes of 1978, all years would be re-examined and present income and contracts might be attached. The fact that Bobby didn't "own" High Meadow but only held "tenancy for life" rights, set back the IRS attorney's plans to lien the farm. But Vu Van Hieu (and quickly Mark Tashkor and Jesse Rasmuellen, High Meadow's attorneys) didn't believe this obstacle would hold the IRS at bay for long. Vu, Tashkor and Rasmuellen, along with Lucas Hoeller, a Nam vet and corporate tax specialist, set to work, retroactively, reforming all High Meadow activities under a single conglomerate that would allow Bobby to write off "wages" and "care" (bed and board) of the "participants" as expenses.

The IRS agents in turn asked for details of local bed and board establishments, (the value of bed and board they later called barter and treated it as wages, subject to taxation, and soon part of the overall assessment). Hieu was horrified. "These men," he moaned to Bobby, "they act like your friend but they are not your friend. Many officials just like them now in Viet Nam. These men are your enemy. You must be more cautious. Must have Mr. Lucas Hoeller come every time. And Mr. Mark Tashkor.''

''Naw,'' Bobby objected. ''This is not Viet Nam. He's just doing his job.''

''He do his job with vengeance,'' Hieu retorted.

''No,'' Bobby said reassuringly. ''Really, Hieu. He's looking for a win-win situation, just like us.''

In late October the IRS sent yet another demand. This time they claimed Bobby was liable not just for the previously mentioned amounts, not just for the 7½ percent employer's contribution on all wages, but 15 percent, plus interest, plus various other penalties, plus—and this was the kicker, *''A 100 PERCENT PENALTY FIGURED ON ALL UNPAID TAXES, CONTRIBUTIONS, INTEREST AND PREVIOUS PENALTIES.''*

These tax-related events, the entire process, was more than Bobby (or Hieu) wished to grasp—more bewildering, more frightening. Bobby suspected his mother, possibly in conjunction with Ernest Hartley, of being the stimulus behind the IRS probe. For all his reaching out and expanding into the community, his relations with his mother and his family had gone from bad to worse. Only Brian remained cordial, but their talks were never intimate. Still Bobby never missed, never considered missing, paying them their yearly percentage as per Pewel's will.

What truly frightened Bobby, and Hieu, was one auditor's comment to Lucas Hoeller. ''We never would have caught him had it not been for that informer.''

Sometime between the meetings of October and December, maybe before Sherrick's cancellation proposal, maybe shortly thereafter, Bobby went to a doctor, again for his ass. And for his knee. ''Forget the knee. I want you over at St. Luke's immediately. You're all infected.''

''Can they do the arthroscopy at the same time?'' Bobby wanted the medical business finished once and for all.

''Just get your buns over there. Take care of them first.''

Time was a cloud. Bobby did not want Sara to know. He instead called Tony who took him to the ER. Bobby was examined, waited, was reexamined, again asked to wait. Finally, ''The procedure is called an anal fistula repair,'' the doctor explained. ''Here, let me show you.'' The doctor drew a diagram of the anal sphincter and surrounding tissue. ''A fistula,'' he said, ''is a channel caused by injury or infection. It connects an abscess to an open cavity. You've an infection up here. Pressure causes the seepage. You shouldn't have let it go so long. It's the infection that's probably been making you feel so weak. What we'll do is open up the channel, then suture it back up. But from the inside. See, we cut the sphincter here—''

''Oh,'' Bobby moaned. ''Oh. I gotta get out of here. I gotta get some air.''

Bobby emerged from the examining room. "*Hè.*" Tony chuckled. "How's the ass?" Bobby was ashen. He glanced at Tony. Then his eyes rolled back and he toppled silent as a tree in the woods.

Two days later, after the surgery, the doctor told Sara that Bobby would be fine but that his hematocrit level "was a bit low."

Still the meetings continued—beyond the outbreak of the Iran-Iraq War, past the election of Ronald Reagan, through falling inflation rates and Thanksgiving and Christmas and to the new year. As the pressure of the local recession and the pressure from the IRS increased, as the daily news brought new setbacks in the hostage negotiations, as the Soviet expansion into Afghanistan solidified, Bobby intensified his harshness, his demands, on the assembled vets.

"If there's anyone here who wants to remain stuck, get out. This isn't a fucking rest home. If you want to be warehoused, go to the VA. If the vow means nothing to you, leave."

To a man the vets sat quietly, heads hung. "You're expected to know the truth, the overall picture of what happened there. Why it happened. What America's role was. The positives. The negatives. What we were up against. What the enemy did. Goddamn it! Today's social problems are caused or exacerbated by misperceptions dating to Viet Nam. This new racism, this new polarization—skinheads, the Klan, Latin Kings, the Black Mafia, street gangs—their growth is a direct result of the media's narrow focus on racial tension and violence and its neglect of racial harmony. We're teetering on the brink of disaster. Individually and as a nation. Do you know that NVA terrorists assassinated a hundred South Viet Namese village leaders each month in 1960? A thousand a month in '62? People wonder why America has lost its will! Every terrorist incident, every hostage-taking to which America does nothing, destroys our will. Tony, you said this. We were America's will: the will to survive, to fight, to pull the trigger. And we were wasted by self-serving politicians, by the media, by big business, by the left and the right. And in using us they have killed America. Sherrick, is America over? Are the founding principles dead?

"You guys want to believe the worst about yourselves? Go ahead. Focus on every error, on every failure you've ever committed. But be aware, individually or as a nation, it makes us suckers for other people's propaganda. If it's you as an individual, go ahead, believe you're nothing, believe you're worthless, inept, because you don't have a tenth of the shit Madison Avenue tells you you gotta have to be anybody. If it's you, us, as a nation, go ahead, believe the worst because of the skewed perceptions propagated by ourselves, by Americans, about who we were in Southeast Asia.

"But every person here has taken a vow. Repeat it with me. I vow—" Bobby paused, waited for the chastized vets to lock in, "to seek to discover the truth, to become unstuck, to grow, to expand beyond myself, to encompass community, intellectual development and spiritual awareness."

Again Bobby paused. The vets were silent. "The vow . . . " Bobby said. "This is an irrefutable obligation. If you are not willing to take it, or if you are not willing to live by it, LEAVE!

"Gary, how did Sam Adams put it? If ye love the tranquillity of servitude better than freedom—and whoever or whatever you give your mind to is your master—go from us in peace. What did he say, Gary?"

Sherrick spoke up. " 'Crouch down and lick the hands which feed you. May your chains sit lightly upon you, and may posterity forget that ye were our countrymen.' "

"Um." Wapinski was motionless yet he seemed to be burning. "Leave. Call us not your brothers. Do you know why you were where you were when you were? Was there valid tactical, strategic or political reasons, or was it totally meaningless? Is it because you were never shown the overall reasons and you, to this day, believe there were none? Maybe you're right. Maybe not. That's what the vow is about!"

Gary Sherrick rose. "I propose," he began, stopped, straightened, cleared his throat. Formally he said, "I propose we place on trial, in this next year, the information, and the sources of that information, to which the American public had been exposed, regarding the entire American–Viet Nam era. In addition I propose that we incorporate the research for this year's trials of Jane Fonda and Robert Komer into a massive effort to discover the truth or nontruth of that previously mentioned information, and those sources of information, which allegedly have so poisoned our culture that America, as a concept, is endangered and on the brink of extinction."

"Seconds?" Bobby called.

"Aye." Forty hands rose.

On December eighth the temperature dropped below freezing, and for twenty-seven days it remained below zero, did not break above freezing until the hostages were released and yellow ribbons bedecked the land. It was as if that record cold winter was naught but one long meeting interrupted by daily events. Guys were hot with the topic, with their research. Arguments disrupted work. Bobby saw this as good. Vets switched basketball teams to be with like-minded players. New vets quickly became engrossed. Vets taking courses at Nittany Mountain involved nonvet students, and some nights the barn and library were packed with more than one hundred "investigators," "prosecutors," and "defense-team researchers." It was an exciting time, a striving time, generally a happy time.

Bobby was still sick, still irritable, still blaming it on allergies or the flu or burn-out or IRS-induced stress. Tony, Sherrick, Vu, Van Deusen, joked with him, chided him, told him just because he had a pain in the ass didn't mean he had to be a pain in the ass. He took it good-naturedly, but soon the frustration would spike and the ire of slow progress or no progress would grab him and he'd snap at one of the vets and the core staff would find itself buffering the most vulnerable vets from Wapinski's wrath.

In mid-January Mike Treetop and John Cannello left High Meadow to open their own restaurant in downtown Mill Creek Falls—the Shuke Ápeilìsh Pàkawenikana (Lenape for sugar apple dumpling, or the Apple Fritter). That sparked an immediate celebration but in Bobby it was followed by deeper stress. To Tony he said, "When I was in school, even in the army, I never thought I'd live to thirty. Even when I was first married, I figured thirty. When I married Sara I knew I'd be like Granpa, live past eighty. I'm going to be thirty-five. This IRS bullshit is killing me. I don't know if I'll make it another year."

"Cut the shit," Tony responded.

"No, Man. They really got me. They don't want to work it out. Hieu's right. They don't want me to be in business. The easiest thing for this agent to do is to shut me down. That makes his life easy. He's got nothing vested in working it out. The government gets nothing if I close down. And it has to pay these guys' unemployment. It gets whatever I can pay if I stay open. But these agents don't care."

"Yeah, but Man, your guys are going like gangbusters. They've been fixing frozen pipes around the clo—"

"Business is great. We're making money. We're paying taxes. But the more that comes in, the higher percentage they disallow. I don't know what I'm going to do."

At this time it was not so much to Tony that Bobby spoke. Nor to Sara. Nor Josh. Not even to Grandpa up in the cemetery. Instead Bobby spent hours talking to Hieu as if Hieu's trials and ordeals made him the most worthy confidant, as if Hieu was not Hieu at all but was Pewel Wapinski reincarnated.

3 November 1984

How can I tell you the story here of Vu Van Hieu? It is long, complex, a story of woe, a story of courage. Late at night Bobby used to visit him in his cubicle in the old bunkhouse. Hieu would be sitting on the edge of his cot, chain smoking, staring fixedly at the cover of a closed dictionary, concentrating, seemingly absorbing the content by the power of his focus. Bobby would sit, maybe smoke a cigarette with Hieu, maybe say nothing for a while. Then they would talk about Viet Nam. Hieu told Bobby about his war, thirteen years in the ARVN, '62 to '75, about his imprisonment. "They say, 'You come for three days. Three-day reeducation seminar camp.' They keep me for three years. They keep me much longer but my wife's father have some money to bribe the guards to let me escape. If I stay, if I not escape, I would not be alive. Sometime for two month they put me in a steel CONEX. You remember the steel CONEX box. My ankles in iron shackles. Eat only one bowl of rice each day. Two cups of water. You read report from the Aurora Foundation. That report has pictures of the CONEX they put me in. You know, they tie our elbows together. Lock us in under the sun for two month straight. Most men die. I can see all my bones because I have no muscle left. When the guard say, 'Okay, your wife pay. You can escape tonight,' I cannot go. I cannot stand up. I cannot crawl. I have no skin on the back of my leg, only scab. When I move they break. I cannot escape for three weeks until my wife's brother come and carry me.

"Then I hide. All Viet Namese people suffer food shortages. Some say America has blocked everybody from giving food to Viet Nam. But why does Viet Nam need anyone to give it food? My country grow food for many millions more people than it has but the communists won't let us grow food. No one want to work for the communists."

Hieu seldom talked about himself to other vets. But he talked to Bobby, shared with Bobby his deep sense of shame for having left Viet Nam, his profound desire to return. "It take me nine time to escape Viet Nam. Nine time I bribe this official, that official, this boat captain, that river watcher. Eight time they catch us. Once they send me back to the seminar camp where they work people who have no more money for bribes. They starve them and work them until they die, then they throw them like cherry pits into the jungle.

"The communist always know when someone trying to escape. They always know how many to let be successful, how many to intercept. Half of my people die at sea. These boats very small. Just coastal fishing trawlers. Maybe one hundred people on one boat. No one can move. Some baby born on boat next to some old woman crapping or some old man seasick. Many boats sink. Many attacked by pirates who kill the men and children and take the young women.

"We should have fought the war different. We try to fight on fronts while the communists terrorize our rear areas. We should have fought that way too but LBJ say, 'No Sir.' If he said, 'Okay,' in 1965, there would be no CONEX boxes, no seminar camps, no pirates, no refugees.

"In Thailand I take classes in English and in American accounting practices. My wife die. My children in Viet Nam with their grandfather. You help me write to Ambassador Jeanne Kirkpatrick at UN. You help me write to President Reagan. Because you are a citizen they must listen to you.

"Bobby, you help me go home. Someday—you hear my words— some motherfuck day, we go back and kick ass. Then I come back here with my children and my wife's family and my children get American education. They think I'm Eastern! Bullshit! I am fundamental American values."

31

The wind blew cold. The street was empty. RTL6764 waited. Gilmore had not been in but had been expected within a few minutes, yet the informer refused to wait on hold. Instead he'd walked upriver from the booth by the old two-lane steel truss bridge over Loyalsock Creek; had passed through the small mill area where many of the old brick buildings were now boarded up: had shied from the White Pines, worked his way through the tight, cramped streets of the millworker houses, uphill, past St. Ignatius, into the even more tightly packed homes of the minorities, to the phone booth at the edge of that neighborhood, beside the converted house that was The Church of the Golden Shepherd.

RTL6764 waited, stared back into the neighborhood at the dark angular forms with only an occasional light illuminating drab curtains hung in drab rooms. He stared at the dark rounded hulks of poorly maintained vehicles that lined the twisting darkened streets of the darkie neighborhood euphemistically labeled "minority homes" in a town much like his town. He turned to the booth, an open booth; they didn't install the kind with accordion doors anymore, at least not in a darkie neighborhood. The wind gusted. A chill caught him, ran up his back, out his shoulders. He didn't want to call. The excitement had gone out of it. But he was committed—for his people. For my people, he thought. He turned toward the neighborhood. The wind caught his face, made his eyes water, his lips sting. He eyed the houses, the vehicles, thought of the twisted path that had led his people, "only my people," into the minority neighborhoods of the north, the south, the east, the west. Led them there, kept them there, he thought. Killin em. That's what they doin. Nine black children in Atlanta, kidnapped, murdered. Half dozen still missin. Cuttin the hearts outta black men in Buffalo. Right down there in Johnstown, wastin black people. How that man put it? You pick up the paper, you read about blacks being killed here, being killed there. It does somethin to your brain. Tells you it's huntin season on blacks all over again.

He stared into the closest illuminated window. He could see the forms of people moving, but through the curtain, the dirt-coated glass, he couldn't tell if the forms were male or female. Yet he imagined an old woman, and children being scolded.

A dry, icy draft hit him, pushed him. He leaned into it. It pressed the cloth of his trousers tightly against his thighs and sucked the heat from his legs and his legs and feet were very cold. I done my part, he thought. I wasn't no rear eschelon mothafucka in Nam. I wasn't no clerk or jerk diving for a bunker every time a mortar landed half a mile away. I picked up pieces. Human pieces. Policin up bodies, strippin em, searchin em, lookin for documents. Shee-it! Intelligence! Never cut out their hearts. They cut out their hearts in Buffalo. God! I know! I know somethin they don't know. I know they feelin it. I know they felt it first time. First time you touched somebody you killed, you feel it, you feel it jumpin from them, feel it goin right inside you, right into your body. First time you feel it go in and spread throughout you like electricity, like heavy electric syrup. Then you don't feel it no more. Then they aint nothin but cold meat. Pieces a cold meat. But it's in you, takin you apart. Honkey racist murders in Buffalo goina die losin their hearts. And Bobby, dinky dau mothafucka, want "to interrupt *my* racism!"

"Internal Revenue. Criminal Investigations. Gilmore."

He altered his voice. "Stan."

"Yes."

"R.T.L. 6764."

"How ya doin, Good Buddy?"

"I'm freezing my ass off."

Gilmore chuckled, asked, "What d'ya got?"

"Nothing new. They are still taking federal dollars . . . ah, indirect recipients of federal funds. Two new guys this week. Both are on VA entitlements. That puts High Meadow in direct violation of the Civil Rights Restoration Act of 1972, doesn't it?"

"Same as before. He's not screening the participants?"

"He asks. But they're not going to give up their entitlements. They earned them."

"Do you have some names for me?"

"Yep. I even have their service numbers." He turned out from the booth, looked back to the illuminated window. "When do I get paid?"

"Not until the whole thing's settled."

For a moment he was quiet. His daughter lived in a house like that, a house with imitation-brick siding, maybe with an old woman like that, scolding. "His attorney says they're going to beat it," he said.

"Not a chance," Stan Gilmore answered.

As things got better, as they seemingly returned to normal, they went from bad to worse. The federal Occupational Safety and Health Administration cited High Meadow Corporation with twenty-two job safety violations, and proposed fines of $72,000. Among the "willful" infractions: not displaying an OSHA poster; not training workers how to handle hazardous chemicals (fertilizers); no guardrails on a section of the barn loft (Don Wagner figured they'd have doubled the fines had they ever seen Rick MacIntyre climbing down the Indian ladder at the gap); no safety gates and enclosed safety zone beneath the barn elevator; not using hard hats in the barn; debris on the barn floor; and improperly spliced electric extension cords.

"They might just as well fire me up," Wapinski said to Mark Tashkor.

"Easy," Mark told him. "Let me handle it. We've got two weeks to negotiate or file a written challenge. Just get something under the elevator, and paper the barn with their damn posters!"

"That's not it, Mark. They'll just keep coming back. They want to close us down. They're killing me."

"Let me handle it."

"You know, I had a dream last night. I dreamed I was in supply and that I had two units out by Dak To. One was U.S., one was ARVN. And they were under siege. Both of em. They were being hit. Rockets, mortars, heavy caliber machine guns hidden in caves in the surrounding hills. And I was in supply back in the rear and it was a beautiful day. But I can hear all this activity on the net and these guys are calling for fire support and for resupply. And I was the wagon train; I was the wagonmaster. 'Move it,' I'm screaming. 'Get this show on the road.' But there's a glitch. There's this bureaucratic snafu from higher-higher that's got us on hold. We can't move until we get their authorization. We're raring to go. Calls are coming in for medevacs. These guys are being picked apart and this is going on for days, weeks. And we can't go out and help. We know they're out of ammo. Out of food. We're sitting on tons of it. But we're not being allowed to go."

*   *   *

Some things really did improve.

John Sr. sat on the sofa in Tony and Linda's home. It was noontime, perhaps mid-August. Linda was at work. Gina and Michelle were at a friend's. Tony was in the kitchen filling two tall glasses with ice, water and wedges of lemon. In an hour and a half Tony would be addressing a growers meeting in Rock Ridge about the expiration of credit reprieves and the deflation of land values. He'd researched the topic in depth, had accepted organizational help from Sara, financial explanations from Vu, and delivery assistance from Gary Sherrick. The example that Tony was using was that of a Midwest farm valued, two years earlier, at half a million dollars. Banks held liens on the land for $260,000 and the owner had been extended $100,000 in credit for improvements and equipment. With 30 percent deflation caused by the recession the farmer was over-extended and the bank refused to extend or refinance the loans. Throughout the district others were in similar shape. Ramifications within the community included business closings and layoffs, and the closing of local banks because they had to charge higher rates to cover uncollectables, and new business was going elsewhere.

Tony's speech and appearance—he was in a suit and tie, had cut his long hair and shaved—to this point had been the topic of conversation with his father.

"Hey Tony, what are these?"

"What's what, Pop?" Tony reentered the room with the glasses.

"On the wall here?"

"Oh. My certificates."

"You got three Purple Hearts!"

"Um-hmm."

"And a Silver Star?! And a Viet Namese Cross for Gallantry?"

"Yeah. It seems like a long time ago."

"Did you do the frames? These are nice frames."

"Naw. Linda did em, Pop."

"This is why you asked me over . . . to show me this, huh?"

"Naw, Pop. I wish Mom came too, though. And I wish Linda were here. She's on call, and you know, if a call comes in . . . "

"You know . . . " John Sr. said these words slowly. He looked directly at his son but he did not keep his eyes on Tony's eyes. His throat was tight. "I'm very proud. Look at you. In a suit with a white shirt. Jo would be very proud of you, too. Tony, our Tony, off to deliver a speech. When I see you up there . . . When I see what you and Bobby and all you men have done . . . What you men are doing up there . . . Tony, Jo is proud of you. And I'm very proud of you."

"Aw . . . " Tony stammered. It was, for him, a lot easier to hear criticism from his father, from anyone, than it was to hear compliments. "You know, without you, without all your help . . . All the times you and Mom helped Linda when I wasn't here . . . And with the down payment and all . . . "

"Hey. What are families for, right?"

"Yeah."

"But you've done High Meadow on your own. You and Bobby. Since I retired, when I've been up there these last few months, for the meetings, I didn't know any of that stuff about Viet Nam."

"It seems nobody does."

"I know," John Sr. said. "I never said this before. I . . . Each time I heard or read about World War Two, where I was on the march north through Italy, my insides would grind. I still get angry. I think, like you say up there, I'm still coming to terms with it. When I hear what those boys describe, I see myself. I can see that progression, the assimilating and reassimilating the experience and each added fact or new story. I've heard so much crap . . . You boys talk about how good you were and everybody only talks about your atrocities. For me, for thirty-six years, it's been the opposite. I've seen people, civilians, they could have been our family, I've seen them butchered. I've seen them cut down. I've seen them blown up. How do you assimilate that?

"I keep wishing," John Sr. continued, "that I could do something more. I—I feel so limited. I tried to be the best person to you and your brothers and to your mother—"

"Pop, it showed. It always showed. Everyone always knew you *really* cared." Tony checked his watch. "I gotta go, Pop." He checked his watch again. He moved closer to his father. "Don't tell Mom, yet, okay? But I'm bursting to tell you."

"What? What?"

"Ah . . . " Tony whispered, "Linda's pregnant. Three months. We already know it's going to be a boy."

There was low murmuring, some coughing. Forty-five vets sat before the collector assembly tables. Bobby, as judge, sat on the edge of table 1. Before him at a small card table was Sal Ianez, the court recorder, then two long tables, one for the prosecution, one for the defense. Beside assembly table 2 there were twelve vets in folding chairs—the jury. Calvin Dee was chairman. In clusters behind the vets were "civilian observers," including Sara, Linda, Emma, John Pisano Sr., James and Isabella Pellegrino, and Professor Arnold Tilden of Nittany Mountain College with seven of his students. The proceedings had been going on for an hour.

In the jury box Howie Bechtel nudged Kevin Rifkin. "Hey, Blue Dog. How was your unit reunion?"

"Great, Man," Rifkin said. "We had this one speaker . . . an attorney. He said we should all get blood tests for this Agent Orange thing."

"Fuckin attorneys, Man!"

"I don't know, Man. But I told Wapinski. Half a dozen of us are going tomorrow morning. Over to RRVMC . . . "

Gary Sherrick cleared his throat, smiled, glanced back at Wapinski, returned to face the courtroom. "As per order of this court and per the findings of the grand jury of High Meadow"—his voice was loud, distinct—"this court has set the date of Thursday, October eighth, nineteen hundred and eighty-one as the commencement date for the trial of The People of the United States of AMERICA versus THE MEDIA."

At that moment he felt very down. For weeks he'd expected the final action, his final reward. He'd dreamed it, dreamed of reclaiming his daughter, of having the means to support her. Yet he'd dreamed too of the legal battle, of the judge saying, "There's no reason for this court, Mr. RTL6764, to award you custody. We do have your medical records, the record of your cancer. There is no reason for you to be the custodian of this child when you may not live long enough to see her grow up."

He felt very ill. But it was not the dream, not the delay of the award, reward, not even the cloak and dagger covert running about, spying, passing information on to Stan Gilmore of the Internal Revenue Service. It was something Bobby had said and he couldn't even remember the words. Something about Judas Iscariot. Something about Hamburger Hill. Something about interrupting his belief that his blackness in white-controlled America was the source of all his problems—"true or not, that's overcomable"—something about needing to interrupt his need for dismemberment because he wasn't a Judas goat leading lambs to slaughter.

"Gilmore here. Whatcha got, Good Buddy?"

"I—I—" He felt sick to the pit of his stomach. His breaths came shallow, quick. He glanced over his shoulder, up Third Street, past the new restaurant, past the 7-Eleven, past the intersection with Callar Drive to the T with Crooked Street and the big Victorian with the screened porch. "I—I think something big is coming down."

"Go on, Good Buddy."

"I—I need some money to get away from this. He's getting weird. Remember like Jonestown, like all those people killing themselves with that grape Kool-Aid?"

"Tell me more."

"I told you about the vow, right? And irrefutable obligations?"

"A regular demagogue, huh?"

"He's got an awful hold on em. And he's really—he's really sick. He looks terrible. He looks . . . He's almost crazy with frustration and anger."

Gilmore tittered. "He-he. That's what happens to people who try to screw Uncle Sam, Good Buddy. You're doing the whole country a service."

"I don't know what he might do next."

"Okay, thanks for the tip."

"Stan?"

"Yeah."

"You've got to get me some mon—Oh!" He hung up.

"Hey Man." It was Mike Treetop. "What's happenin, Bro? Come on in."

"I . . . Oh . . . I . . . I got . . . "

"Johnny and I saw you from the window. Come on. You've never been in, have you? Use our phone."

"I gotta go, Mike. I . . . ah . . . gotta split. I was just making an appointment."

"Yeah. Okay. Look, Ty, sometime, huh? We miss you guys."

"Sure Mike."

"We'll be up for the trial. You and Rodney going to do the race war thing?"

"I can't talk, Mike. I gotta go."

"Egalitarian inclusiveness," he wrote. He stopped. There were papers everywhere on the pine desk. It was Friday, 18 September 1981. Most of the vets had quit early. Vu, Mariano, Van Deusen and Wagner had taken Joe Alamont to RRVMC for a second screening. Earlier Joe had gone with Bobby and some others but he'd been denied Agent Orange screening because of a less than honorable discharge. Several dozen guys had gone to Mike and Johnny's The Apple Fritter—which was becoming their afterwork hangout. Others were at the White Pines; more were in the bunkhouse. Through the window High Meadow looked deserted. Even the grass and weeds seemed lonely, uncut, unkempt, abandoned.

Bobby glanced at the correspondence stack. The very size of it intimidated him. On top was a letter from Jinny Reed, Tim Reed's wife, a voice seemingly reaching across space and through time. "I remember," Jinny had written

> he told me when he hired you, you were someone who might shake the place up. Henry didn't like you at all (I think he felt threatened) but Tim insisted. When Henry fired you, Tim was devastated. After his first heart attack he talked about you incessantly, about your windmills and electrified road surfaces, about having an impact, and about how myopic Henry and all the planners were. At any rate, Bob, Tim wanted you to have the enclosed. Sometimes I think the only thing keeping him alive after the first attack was the thought of breaking into Harrison's cabinets and getting your drawings and proposals. The night after he got them and told me to send them to you was the night of the fatal heart attack . . . I wish you and Sara were still here. Your wedding was beautiful.
>
> Love,
> Jinny

Bobby tapped his fingers. It was hard to comprehend: Tim Reed, dead. He hadn't yet opened the package, hadn't yet told Sara. Beside the package was a design file containing Bobby's sketches for a quadracycle car:

twenty-one forward speeds, double derailleurs, very bicyclelike except with four wheels, a light, aerodynamic fiberglass and Plexiglas shell, supine seats for two pedalers, and a clutch-flywheel system for stability (gyroscopic effect) and assistance in hill climbing—all unproven, unprototyped. One more unfinished project, he thought.

There were other projects before him: an outline for a national Viet Nam Veterans Antidefamation League; a revised logo for EES reflecting the new phone number 626-6475—Call Nam-'64-'75; and a 200-year plan. Amid the projects, too, was the ever-expanding IRS file, and the new file on Agent Orange screening.

Bobby's exam, as cursory as it had seemed, had been distasteful. They'd drawn blood, checked his pulse, temperature, reflexes, and asked about skin rashes. He'd been treated like a 'cruit, like a prebasic trainee. Yet, he'd gone to set an example. On the floor beside Bobby, Josh thumped, twitched in his sleep, opened his eyes, looked up sleepily, sighed, went back to sleep. "How ya doin, ol' boy," Bobby whispered.

With the end of a pen Bobby flicked open the IRS file. The latest form, 668(Y) Notice of Federal Tax Lien Under Internal Revenue Laws, stated:

> ... notice is given that taxes (including interest and penalties) have been assessed against the following-named taxpayer. Demand for payment of this liability has been made, but it remains unpaid. Therefore, there is a lien in favor of the United States on all property and rights to property belonging to this taxpayer for the amount of these taxes, and additional penalties, interest, and costs that may accrue.
>
> This Notice of Federal Tax Lien has been filed as a matter of public record. . . . Penalty and interest accrue until the liability is paid.

On all property and *rights* to property . . . Bobby thought. Then he muttered, "There's no fucking way, Josh. There's no fucking way out. Hundred percent penalties! It's the damn *Empire Strikes Back*, is what it is. No wonder people are sick. We've been betrayed by our own government. How'd Granpa say it? 'First you have to sell your crop.' He didn't tell me what to do when the government doesn't want you to sell your crop. They're killin us, Josh. Aw, fuck em. We've been broke before and bounced back. We can do it again."

Bobby sighed, flicked the pen from the file, let the cover close. It was wearing him down. Last night, after everyone had left, Sara had donned a salmon-colored silk teddy, had caressed him, had looked so beautiful, so sexy, Bobby's silver Jumping Mary medalion hanging in her cleavage, and he had fallen asleep.

Bobby yawned. He looked at the sheet he'd begun. "Egalitarian inclusiveness," he'd written. His concentration had been broken. He could not remember where he'd planned to go with that idea. On a new sheet he wrote:

Just as if any sector of a defensive perimeter is breached the perimeter is breached; and if any sector of our economy is ailing, the economy is ailing; or if any cell in our body is sick, we are sick; if any human on earth is denied hope, freedom or opportunity, our hopes, freedoms and opportunities become tentative, precarious, subject to denial.

It is 205 years since the words "When in the Course of human Events . . . " gave birth to this nation; and 194 years from the penning of "We the People of the United States, in order to form a more perfect union, establish justice, insure domestic tranquillity. . . . " These founding documents projected their ideal, their plans, pangenerationally 200 years into the future. These documents, their spirit and their reach are models for us today. Dual citizenship of the state of residence and of the United States—though not formalized until the ratification of Article XIV in July 1868 (when the concept was a radical departure from existing systems of government)—has today, in 1981, become so accepted as to be virtually unnoticed, unrecognized as a concept, and in reality has become a system of triple citizenship—citizens voting for, and in turn being taxed by, local, state, and national governments.

The future must be one in which Human Beings will have triple (or quadruple) citizenship of (town), state, nation and world ("We the people of the United Nations, determined to save succeeding generations . . . "). The concept of world government is not original. It predates Caesar. But putting the power of that government into the hands of the people as citizens, world self-government, has never been attempted. A 200-year plan must be one of universal, egalitarian inclusiveness.

For years Bobby had mulled these concepts, let them foment. The urgency he felt in September 1981 motivated him to condense his notes. All citizens of the world were to be seen as created equal, with equal rights and equal opportunities under a unified system of global laws— which Bobby conceived of as equally restraining citizens *and* governments. Bobby was aware of the potential for great abuses, exactly as the founding fathers of America recognized the potential for the great abuse of a federal system of government and the needs for checks upon the powers of that government—not just internal checks and balances between the branches, but external checks by the states and by citizens. Bobby recognized how any government must first be a servant of the people, not first a controller of people. Therefore this new system of world government necessarily would have a federal form—a union or federation of independent governments, not a dominant world government that might deform into a dictatorship . . . perhaps evolving in stages, citizens of Europe, citizens of North America. A form that would be limited; that would deal only with abuses recognized internationally—either between states, by multinational commercial bodies, or within renegade states tyrannizing world citizens who were simultaneously citizens of that state.

Of course, having been subjected to out-of-control government—"The rights of the people to be secure in their persons, houses, papers, and effects, against unreasonable searches and seizures, shall not be violated"—being caught in the grasp of the IRS and the administrative authority of OSHA, Bobby saw the potential for tyranny, via taxes and bureaucratic regulations, in his strong global formation. Therefore, to give it teeth to deal with abuses yet to restrain it so that it itself would not become abusive, was the dilemma to be resolved. Bobby wrote, "How not to create a monster! The system must be able to expand for crises, then must have a built-in mechanism that automatically shrinks the system when crises pass."

Bobby stopped. This one concept, this multilevel citizenship concept, would be the basis for a global plan, an expansion of the Great Experiment that is America. "I, too, have a dream," Bobby wrote.

> I dream of a community, a nation, and a world not polarized into ethnic or racial factions, of a citizenry not fearful of stepping from their homes, not fearful of losing their homes . . . of a world citizenry that puts private interests and personal gains second, behind the glory of a worldism in which each separate nation, each separate state, each separate community lives and exists in a mutually profitable manner. . . . I want to see every man, woman and child living in their land in environmental harmony with the world ecosphere. . . .
>
> Become intoxicated with the myth, with the dream for your own good and the good of all your neighbors on earth. . . .
>
> . . . without abandoning the primacy of nationalism, for a hazy homogenized all-humanism;
>
> . . . without abandoning individualism and distinctiveness for robotic conformity;
>
> . . . without adopting the new dehumanizing aspirations of the mega-techno-capitalists with their economic primacy theories that seek to inherit personal and national sovereignty via the piece-by-piece transfer of power and influence to the officers of international corporations without the consent of the governed.

His juices were flowing yet he was exhausted. "The American dream," he wrote, "is a human dream. It is one an individual creates because he has the freedom and opportunity to create it. It is NOT something anyone is, or can be, given."

Bobby breathed deeply, closed his eyes. He could feel an expansion of human spirit, feel it through his back, from the back of his head, a four-dimensional image in time and space exploding from him, behind him, quick but not violent, expanding inclusively from past generations through him to the present, to the future, without him, happily, sensing himself nothing more than a temporary vehicle, weightless, a conduit . . .

"Bobby." Louder, "Bobby!"

"Huh?"

"Were you asleep?"

"Oh." He turned. His face was captured by a huge smile. "Sara! I didn't hear you."

"Are . . . Why are you smiling?"

"I was just having these ideas. It was almost like . . . like I could see the future. And it was beautiful."

"Do you know it's eight o'clock?"

"You're kidding?"

"Unt-uh. The doctor's been calling. He's called three times. They want you to come in for a retest. He said your blood values were so far out of line there must have been a lab error." She paused, cocked her head sideways. "What are you grinning at?"

"Just you," Bobby said.

November 5, 1981—Vu Van Hieu could not smile. An urge to return had seized him, an urge to continue the resistance, to resist the tyrants. Viet Nam had joined COMECON, the Soviet-dominated economic alliance in 1978. No longer was Viet Nam a mom-and-pop-type independent contractor communist government but now it was a branch-franchise outlet under strict control of the Moscow CEOs. Directed by the distant corporate headquarters, the franchise had, in December '78, invaded Cambodia, a hostile takeover of a competitor's franchise, had expanded the rape, pillage, and plunder for higher shareholder profits.

But that was not all. Had it been only Viet Nam, he would have quit High Meadow immediately—maybe joined the resistance. But it was bigger. It was global. His new country, the world symbol for freedom, on this day, at the very pinnacle of the Great Media Trial, had declared Robert J. Wapinski, d.b.a. the High Meadow Corporation and Environmental Energy Systems, Inc., to be insolvent due to unpaid and presumably unpayable back taxes. The "Service" had ordered all assets of the above to be seized and disposed of in order to make restitution.

Sunday, 4 November 1984

It is late. Late in the day. Or maybe not so late, just dark because of the rain, the clouds. I hear thunder approaching. It is late in the year for such a storm, the kind of storm that used to make so many of us anxious as if the thunderclaps were artillery bursts; the kind of storm that brought thoughts, images, of monsoons, of jungle valleys or hilltops, Hamburger Hill for Bobby, mudslides, hamburger hills for so many under monsoon rains and darkened skies late in their year.

I'm sitting on the loft floor, my legs dangling, like from the side of a Huey, over the main assembly area, over the flanger machine. In the dimness, before the tables, they emerge as if it were 8 October 1981. There are the vets, most anyway, some of the wives, families. In addition there are students from Nittany Mountain College, and Professor Tilden and his associate, James Alban, an instructor in history; and Montgomery McShane. From town there are dozens including Ernest Hartley, Jr. and Detective Don Fredrickson (to keep an eye on things?), and Uncle James and John Pisano, Sr., my Pop.

Gary Sherrick is beaming. He is prepared, has prepared the teams through general allegations, bills of particulars, discovery, detailed interrogations and requests for documents and records (research exchange). Sherrick is beaming with pride. This is his masterpiece. He has coached, lectured, cajoled and encouraged. "There is a politically correct way to think about the Viet Nam War," Sherrick has said. "There is an academically acceptable perspective from which to write about the war. There is a socially agreeable position; and there are media-tolerable projectibles. These manners, perspectives, positions and projections have fluctuated over the years but have swayed only slightly since 1968 when Lyndon Johnson declined to run for a second full term, and when Walter Cronkite converted and established an acceptable antiwar posture for nonradicals. That these ossified perspectives are narrow seems to have bothered few politicians, academics, John and Jane Does, reporters, editors or film makers. And after nearly a decade and a half most everyone is in agreement—and most everyone, because of the exact narrowness of the perspectives, is half wrong."

Sherrick, obnoxious Sherrick, sounded more like Wapinski all the time. "It is only through ever wider, patient research and deeper analytical knowledge that we can gain true understanding of any complex issue. And it is only through true understanding that we can plot reasoned courses of thought and action."

And there is Wapinski, as judge, sitting on the collector assembly table 1, now with his feet on the sheet metal break, which had been pulled over for a job I no longer remember, with the jury and the recorder, the bailiffs and opposing attorneys, the witnesses and researchers, observers and guests, and even ol' Josh, all before him, about him, above him sitting on the floor of the loft with their legs dangling. "I vow"—as a judge he would not put up with bullshit, with games; this was truth-seeking, not adversarial or even competitive judicature—"to become unstuck, to grow, to expand beyond my self . . ."

There is a lightning flash. Two. Three. Four. Now thunder, deeper darkness, heavier rain. Light, dark: a polarization accentuating differences. I can barely see the room now. The formal charges are about to be read.

32

Opening and Closing Arguments
and Highlights of
the Great Media Trial

S ession One—8 October 1981—"The Media," Bobby began, "is hereby
defined as the information promulgation branch of our society. This
branch's activities consist of collecting, compiling, analyzing, condensing and distributing information. The media includes, but is not
limited to the major news organizations of radio, TV and the press; the
entertainment adjuncts of film, TV, the visual and audio arts and literature; plus public historical, political and commercial presentations. We
name here as codefendants the Free World and United States television
networks; news magazines and newspapers; film studios; academia—in
particular history, political science, government and law, and sociology
departments; and the national political parties and their information
arms."

Bobby paused. Murmurs arose, crested. To the prosecutors—Mark
Renneau, Don Wagner and Tony Pisano—the definition had been too
restrictive. To the defense counsels—Gary Sherrick, Carl Mariano and
Frank Denahee—the construct and designation had been too broad.
From some vets came hoots of approval, from others jeers of derision.
Behind the audience Arnold Tilden glanced at James Alban and both

professors smirked. The atmosphere was light, happy, as if at the gala opening of a new play.

"Counsel for the prosecution," Bobby said, "are you ready?"

"Yes, Your Honor," Mark Renneau answered crisply.

"Defense?"

Sherrick stood, looked at Wapinski, turned to Renneau, then to the jury. "Yes Sir."

"Bailiff, read the charges."

"Sir." Kevin Rifkin acknowledged Wapinski. In a clear voice he said, "The Media is hereby charged with: collusion with the enemy resulting in Communist victories in Viet Nam, Laos, and Cambodia; with willful misrepresentations leading to the polarization of American society; with conspiracy to undermine the U.S. government and military; with the malicious skewing of information, which has damaged the democratic aspirations of peoples around the earth; and with incompetence."

"How do the defendants plea?" Wapinski asked.

"Not guilty on all counts," Sherrick answered.

"Let it be so noted," Wapinski said to the court, "that the defendants have entered pleas of not guilty."

"Naturally!" Don Wagner blurted. Before he could be silenced, he added, "The media's the only unaccountable element of our society. They always deny—"

"Order!" Wapinski rapped his hammer on the sheet metal break. "Order!"

"Put a cork in it," Mariano snapped at Wagner.

"Order!" Wapinski raised his voice.

"Sanctimonious jackasses," Wagner shot back.

Witnesses and observers began to laugh. In the jury box Calvin Dee nudged Felix Defabretti, was about to speak when Wapinski boomed, "SHUT UP!" That snapped faces forward. "Prosecutors, present your first opening argument." Wapinski started his stopwatch.

Mark Renneau rose. Slowly, emulating Gregory Peck in *To Kill a Mockingbird*, he sauntered to the jury box. He looked from juror to juror making eye contact with each. "Gentlemen," Renneau said. "You meet someone. He says, 'Who are you?' You answer with your name. But he says, 'You are not your name. Who are you?' Again you answer but this time you tell the story of yourself because that is who you truly are." Renneau paused. At the defense table Gary Sherrick scribbled a note.

"Gentlemen," Renneau backed away from the jury, "you have heard the charges and the defendants' pleas. The prosecution will break the Viet Nam War down into five phases and, in regard to each phase, will demonstrate the media's guilt on each and every charge. We will detail the media's collusion with Hanoi's propaganda ministry and how this led to the debasement of the allied cause and the collapse of will. We will show how the willful misrepresentation of story by the media has led to or exacerbated many of our nation's present political and social problems; how elements of the media conspired to undermine faith in and allegiance to this nation, its government and the armed forces legally raised, armed, and deployed by this government. We will present evidence of the malicious and purposeful skewing of information leading to the derailment of democratic aspirations. And finally, we will document the unquestionable incompetence of the media, particularly the broadcast medias, as a system for full, accurate, and unbiased information distribution to our society. And we will show that the ramifications of these acts have so poisoned our culture that our national myth, our story, America as a concept, as a noble experiment, is endangered and on the brink of extinction."

Again Renneau paused. He turned from the jury but did not return to the prosecutor's table. Casually he edged to where Sal Ianez was tape-recording the proceedings. "You gettin this, Sal?" Renneau asked quietly. Ianez raised his one arm, shook his fist in affirmation. "Good," Mark said. Then, to Wapinski, then turning to the audience and back to the jury, he said loudly, "Your Honor, we additionally will show that basic American actions and policies, and the causes and reasons behind those actions and policies, were justified and noble. And we will show that generally the policies were carried out efficiently, altruistically, and with competence. But first, the prosecution would like to establish the reach of the media into our lives and the importance to our culture of the story thereby told."

"That's your time, Mark," Bobby said. "Let's hear the first of the defense's opening arguments. Then we'll go back to the prosecution for . . . Who's going second for the pros . . . "

"I am," Tony Pisano said.

"Okay." Bobby nodded. "Let me remind all of you that comments are limited to four minutes but that we will return to any counsel or witness as many times as necessary to fully probe, detail, and quantify the topic. Gary, your first counsel."

"Thank you." Sherrick rose quickly, moved quickly to the center before Wapinski, moved as if emphasizing the difference between himself and Mark Renneau. "Your Honor," Sherrick commanded everyone's attention, "the defense moves for immediate dismissal of all charges."

"Excuse me?" Bobby was caught off guard. Again the ambient murmuring rose, filled the big barn with a cacophony of grunts, snickers, huhs? and ooooos.

"The defense," Sherrick repeated, "moves for the immediate dismissal of all charges on the grounds that the defendants have been falsely charged with crimes they could not possibly have committed."

"Wait a minute," Bobby began to chuckle. In the corner of his eye he caught Tilden and Alban gesturing positively to each other. "Sherrick, c'mere. What's going on?"

In full voice Sherrick stated, "This court has charged the media with collusion, conspiracy, and malicious skewing of information. You have further claimed that the effects of these alleged activities were the fall of Viet Nam and the polarization of American society. This is ridiculous! The defendants were not principals in this war, and could not have had the effects they are charged with. They were not in charge of policy. They directed no troop movements. They produced no weapons or ammunition. There are no provisions in law under which these charges, even if substantiated, could be considered crimes. The media, indeed, were not party to—"

"Gary!" Wapinski was baffled. He had not expected Sherrick to seriously pursue the request for dismissal. "You yourself proposed the charges."

"That was in a different role," Sherrick declared.

"Your Honor." Tony Pisano came to the bench. "I'd like to say something."

"The prosecution has already delivered its opening arguments," Sherrick said.

"I'll allow it," Wapinski countered. "Without charging it to anybody's time."

"Your Honor," Tony said, "the prosecution will show that the media were very much party to the war, to every stage of the war, to the final outcome and to the aftermath."

"Yeah, right!" Sherrick snapped. "One cannot be a party to—"

Wapinski overrode both. "Step back," he ordered. He shook his hammer at the two counsels. "Cut out the b.s. The charges will not be dropped. The trial will continue. The defense is directed to offer its opening arguments. Now, Gary, is this you, Carl, or Frank?"

Denahee stood. Despite Sherrick's unsettling maneuver the barn quieted. "There was no malice," Frank began. "No collusion, no conspiracy, no damage. The defendants did their jobs in a manner consistent with the highest journalistic standards the human race has ever known. That this nation experienced, and is experiencing, polarization over the war is due not to freedom of the press, nor to freedom of speech, but to the nature of that particular war, the manner in which it was conducted by five American administrations, and by the deceitfulness of U.S. government, military, and industrial officials.

"The prosecution will tell you that our clients mindlessly repeated erroneous facts and theories, or maliciously exposed information damaging to the government and the military. But the prosecution must *prove* that the facts and theories presented by the media were purposefully slanted to one ideological perspective; that broadcasts maintained a general thematic pattern so as to dupe the American people; and that the 'networks,' 'Hollywood,' the press and academia colluded with the intent to conspire. This they will not be able to do.

"It is the position of the defense that no collusion, no willful misrepresentations, no conspiracy, and no malicious antidemocratic skewing exists now or ever existed. As to incompetence, I would remind the court that errors in reportage are not the equivalent of deaths by friendly fire.

"Indeed," Denahee continued, "the defense will demonstrate not only the innocence of the media but will establish, beyond any reasonable doubt, that this unjust 'cause' for which fifty-eight thousand Americans were sacrificed was and is the stimulus for today's polarization and lack of will. We will show that despite the courage of many individuals, despite the camaraderie, despite the self-sacrifice to something larger than the self, the war was stupid, evil and immoral; that it was a criminal enterprise created by myopic politicians and greedy military industrialists; that it was unwinnable and at the same time a killing machine; that the battlefields had no immediate tactical or long-term strategic importance to the peace and freedom of this nation; and finally that the 'story' the prosecution so adamantly wishes to defend is the exclusionary story of wealthy, white European males, not the inclusionary story of all of America's people."

Bobby held up his hand. "Thanks Frank," he said. "Tony, you're up." Bobby reset his watch.

"Your Honor, we have chosen to present the data on the reach of the media and the importance of story in our opening arguments instead of through expert witness testimony because we believe this is crucial for the understanding of 'How Things Happened.' Supporting documents have been submitted for the court's records."

"Proceed." Bobby nodded.

"To deny that the media," Tony began, "is the teacher, the conveyor of information and story, and the shaper of opinions and the national myth would be to exonerate the media from any responsibility for the tragedies that have struck us at home and others abroad. Yet is it possible for this branch of our society to have had such impact? The prosecution has no intention of allowing this jury to remain in a state of ignorance with regard to the reach of the media, especially television. Nor will we allow the accused to sidestep wrongdoing.

"These are network figures," Tony said. "They come from an article in an advertising trade magazine on the *concerns* of television network executives. 'TV viewing hours are declining,' the report states, 'and this is costing the networks millions of dollars.' Listen to these figures. 'In 1973 the average American household watched six hours and fifteen minutes of TV each and every day. In 1974 that figure fell by one minute. In '75 it fell by an additional nine minutes.' This was a television disaster. This was the loss of at least fifty-three million viewer-hours.

"From another report, 'one hundred million Americans are mesmerized by TV every evening. They are soothed into states of heightened suggestibility.' Another report. 'TV is habit forming and addictive. Viewer self-esteem and enjoyment decrease as viewing time increases. Many people wish to cut back or quit but can't. They become as dependent upon viewing as any substance abuser becomes dependent upon his drug. Often an abuser expects to take one or two hits, one or two nips, one or two shows, but is seduced into more . . . into so many hours of watching that family and personal responsibilities are shunted. Withdrawal produces stress, tension and at times depression.' "

Tony shook his head sadly. "Another report," he said. " 'American children, before they enter first grade, view an average of 4000 hours of TV. Children who watch more,' this study suggests, 'do not become more sophisticated but lose or never develop the verbal proficiency and emotional security essential to learning.' Moreover, the study claims, 'these children also lack normal moral awareness. They come to view the world as a hostile and scary place.' "

Tony slapped his hands together. "Back to adults. Forty-nine point eight percent of all adult Americans obtain *one hundred percent* of their news from TV. During the Viet Nam War years, the Big Three networks pulled better than ninety-five percent of all prime-time viewers. To whom, I ask you, did we and are we giving our minds?"

Tony consulted his notes. "This," he said, "from a network insider's memo. 'News stories without dramatic footage are not lead stories. *Find something else.*' Implied here is that *importance* is a secondary criterion to the network executives who control the information to which most Americans are exposed, and upon which most Americans rely. Drama, controversy, theatrics and visual histrionics are paramount.

"And yet television news is not simply *the news*. It is not merely the communication of specific stories and data. *The news* is our national and cultural identity. Just as an individual's speech reflects who he or she is, his deepest thoughts, or perhaps no thought at all, so too do media projections, as our cultural speech, reflect who and what we are. TV is our past and present behaviors, our current self-image, our hopes, aspirations and optimism, or our debasement, fears and pessimism.

"The news is more than what is reported, much more than a recapping of events. Television defines us. Via its calculated projections it directs our focus, it tells us what to think about, and how to think. It tells us what we like and dislike; what to eat; what to wear; what to buy; what's cool, what's not. This cheap, ubiquitous medium tells us who we are, who we should be. It defines our sexual roles; it develops stereotypes of men and women, of vets and races. It tells us what is funny, what is fun, what is square. It defines what is politically correct and politically incorrect, what is socially acceptable. And it has defined our perceptions of the Viet Nam War.

"Above all else television is narrow, manipulative, not an information distribution system but a slick marketing tool designed to elevate material consumption to ultimate levels, a fabric of lies woven for private gain—a soulless, self-serving medium. We are in a battle for our national myth, a battle for history. A—"

"Whoa!" Bobby broke in. "Time's up, Tony. Way over." Bobby reset his watch.

Immediately Carl Mariano was up. "Television is not a monolith." He lambasted the prosecution even before he emerged from behind the defense table. "None of the media, including television, speak with one voice."

"They did about Nam," George Kamp shouted from the audience.

"Like hell . . . " Denahee shot back.

"Order." Wapinski rapped the table.

Mariano darted to the sheet metal break. "I request this exchange not be deducted from my time."

"Agreed. Go on."

"The media do not speak with one voice," Mariano repeated. "Nor do they reflect, in any aspect, a single opinion, perspective or theme. Television may articulate public concerns, but it does not, as the prosecution suggests, create single-minded public sentiment. Nor could it!

"Allow me to explain. What is the sum of plus one and minus one? What is the condition of a liquid mixing equal parts of equal strength acid and alkali? What is the net result of news stories from *The New York Times* and *The Wall Street Journal*? Please! Do not tell me nothing! Zero is not nothing, but is a neutral zone between plus and minus. Mixed acid and alkali do not create nothing but reach a balanced midpoint. And net results of the *Times* and the *Journal* are not canceled out but are deeper-and broader-based knowledge. *Time, Newsweek, U.S. News & World Report* often present identical topics but seldom present identical facts, identical opinions, or identical conclusions. The result is an ever-widening definition of *us*. Our range and scope as individuals and as a culture become more inclusive. We are set free by the freedom to choose from various news and entertainment sources. If the media define us, they define us in the broadest possible terms. If they tell us what to think about, and how to think, the menu they offer is so comprehensive one must see this not as limiting propaganda but as general education. Narrow? Manipulative? Lies? Come on, Tony. The media present such a vast potpourri of opinions and facts no one could possibly peruse, much less assimilate, all the data.

"TV stopped the war in Viet Nam and saved many of us here from death. It stopped the war not by being 'antiwar' but by exposing the harsh realities of that war. For nearly six months my own unit marched through dried-out rice paddies. We spread out, advanced on line in broad daylight. Our job was simple. We were flypaper. How many flies could we attract. The idea was to get them to fire at us so the technocrats could go to work, bring in the gunships, fast movers and arty. We could have handled the opposition toe-to-toe but that wasn't our mission. I remember for six months thinking, 'What bush can I get to? Where's the closest dike for when they open up? Where's there a hole?' But you had to stand up and walk. Sweeps! We lost a lot of men. Just wasted.

"A TV crew captured on film men in my unit being killed by snipers; it was TV that exposed this absurdity; it was TV that brought it into living rooms in suburban America.

"Viet Nam was a bad war. The defense will show that every American administration reached this conclusion: Eisenhower; Bobby Kennedy after his brother was killed; Robert McNamara; Lyndon Johnson declined to run because he knew; Nixon won election because he had a 'secret plan' to end the war. Viet Nam was the single dumbest endeavor America has ever undertaken. Today's heroes are the people who opposed the war, who brought about its conclusion. The media, instead of being tried for collusion, conspiracy and incompetence, should be applauded for their courage, convictions, and accomplishments."

"Good job, Carl," Bobby said. "Great job. We'll hear the last prosecutor, then take a ten-minute break. Don."

Don Wagner held a thick packet of file cards. "I'm, ah . . . I'm going to read some of mine, okay?"

"Fine."

"I can't do it like . . . I can't keep it all in my head."

"That's fine, Don," Bobby said.

Wagner fidgeted. "But first I gotta say—the war didn't stop! It's still going on. Carl's presumption that the media stopped the war is one of the absurd myths the media has promulgated and continues to reinforce. Ah . . . I can't get into that . . . But geez guys, fer godsake, ask Hieu. The war didn't stop in '75. Our witnesses will prove that."

Wagner stood so one leg was lightly touching the recorder's table. Though he'd rehearsed his presentation, he spoke nervously before the nearly one hundred people in the barn. "There was a time in America," Don read, "when we believed we were an altruistic people, a time when we believed we could help the oppressed, the needy, the cowering masses. There was a time when we vowed to go anywhere, to bear any burden, in the name of freedom. Now we exist in a time in America where we believe in looking out for number one, in the me generation, in getting our piece of the pie no matter whom we screw-over or abandon. Once duty was considered a virtue. Now it is equated with depravity. Our cultural story has changed. The ancient Greeks used to say, *Ethos anthropou daimon.* A person's story is his fate. And a nation's myth, the story it tells itself of itself, is a nation's fate. Our story is our self-image. Our self-image controls our behavior. We act in accordance with our beliefs and image; in a manner consistent with our story.

"Despite Carl's assurance that freedom of the press and of speech have given us a full menu, we will see that the media, time and time and time again, have oversimplified and misconstrued that story—specific stories about specific problems, from Viet Nam to racism, from the gender gap to energy production—and that this oversimplification has led to atmospheres of public sentiment in which specific solutions have been inadequate or inappropriate. It is not just Viet Nam, but it is Viet Nam again and again. The media, particularly the TV networks, have acted like vain, conceited peacocks always assessing their own image, operating in dread fear of self-embarrassment, sanctimoniously presenting themselves with false humility, with artificial neutrality, in serious and solemn tones as if the media are the new church, as if they are defenders of the victimized, as if they alone define good, represent good, and challenge evil.

"So overtly possessed of itself is TV that it dare not air anything that is not politically and socially correct, as the media itself defines and acquiesces to that 'correctness.' This is self-imposed censorship motivated by Nielsen ratings, by responsibility to shareholders, by greed. This creates, for the purveyors of information, dilemmas in which they are unable to present anything other than the inane reduced to the absurd. As to Viet Nam, the result was not a comprehensive picture but a lack of understanding; not an analytical approach but a nonhistoric, noninterpretive dramatic projection. Cultural forces, with the exceptions of simplistic nationalism and anticolonialism, were ignored. Viet Nam changed not just quantitatively but qualitatively from phase to phase, yet the media fixated on the theme of a quagmire of seemingly meaningless firefights. Perhaps this was good theater, but it was poor education.

"The story told, the story that is an inaccurate portrayal of *us*, is the source of personal and national disempowerment. Story is important. Story is effected by selective observations, selective remembrance, selective editing and selective retelling. What affects selection? Personal histories? Personal agendas? Political gains? For the media, the great storytellers, I go back to Nielsen ratings, market shares, greed.

"We are the story of ourselves but our story has been usurped by a medium without integrity. I would like to close with a quote from Alexander Hamilton.

> It is an unquestionable truth that the body of the people in every country desire sincerely its prosperity; but it is equally unquestionable that they do not possess the discernment and stability necessary for systematic government. To deny that they are frequently led into the grossest errors by misinformation and passion would be a flattery which their own good sense must despise.

"That was 1788. During Viet Nam, public misinformation incited passionate antigovernment movements. Incompetence in reportage led to administrations being overwhelmed and finally forced into an unnecessary, ill-advised, and—unfortunately for millions of Southeast Asian human beings—genocide-producing forfeitures of the allied military victories of 1968 and 1972. This lengthened, not shortened, the war. As someone said, 'They snatched defeat from the jaws of victory.' "

After the recess Gary Sherrick delivered the defense's final opening argument. His segment was disappointing. He reiterated numerous points covered by Denahee and Mariano, refuted little of Wagner's attack. Sherrick seemed antsy, anxious to delve into the meat of the exercise, the testimony of the expert witnesses. Tony and the prosecutors sensed he had something up his sleeve.

Session Two—15 October 1981—The air was charged. All week vets from each side concurred in private, speculated what their opponents would do. The prosecution's plan was to demonstrate that various beliefs or myths about American involvement in Viet Nam were widely held by the American public; that those beliefs—the elements of the story of American involvement—were established by biased information promulgation; that the stories, by commission, omission or reductionism, were skewed or untrue; and finally that these mistaken beliefs had serious social, political and martial consequences. Renneau tagged the prosecution's witnesses Myth Busters.

Jeremiah Gallagher took the stand. "The story changed drastically after publication of the Pentagon Papers," he explained. "These documents, or at least the fraction carried by the mass media, about ten percent, seemed to prove that America under Truman and Eisenhower supported French colonialism and opposed Viet Namese nationalism.

"Yet," Gallagher continued, "as a result of an agreement by the Big Three at Yalta, in the immediate post-World War Two period, France, prodded by the United States, set, if reluctantly, upon a course to grant independence to its colonies. By stages France did grant Cambodia and Laos independence, with full independence being given during the year preceding Dien Bien Phu. One can argue that 'granting' and 'giving' were not the just rights of the colonial powers—that colonies always had the right to independence. If you feel such, substitute the word *acquiesced*. The reality is the same.

"But in Viet Nam the independence process was thwarted because of a violent anticolonial movement. Ho Chi Minh and the communists needed the antagonism of the French to rise to, and to consolidate, power. Instead of supporting nationalist causes, Ho actually undermined all non-communist, anticolonial, proindependence organizations through various means including the assassination of their leaders. After the Geneva Accords divided Viet Nam into the communist North and the noncommunist South, Ho's party, between '54 and '56, consolidated internal control via Stalinesque tactics. In 1956 the peasants of Ho's home province, Nghe An, revolted. This uprising was crushed by the communists' 325th Division. At that time the Hungarian Revolution was also being crushed. Media attention was focused on Europe, and the tyranny in Southeast Asia was ignored. Nghe An was one of thousands of incidents of communist oppression that were virtually disregarded by the media. Today those barbarities are continuously left out of the retelling of what happened, and of how America became involved."

Gary Sherrick cross-examined. "Might not the rise of Ho Chi Minh and the communists be seen as a justifiable reaction, as a backlash, to colonialism?"

"Yeah. Maybe. But they didn't have to—"

"And might not it be said that Ho Chi Minh was driven by his abhorrence of imperialism?"

"That doesn't justify—"

"Maybe," Sherrick said. His expression changed. "There was a navy doctor, Tom Dooley, who wrote several books about this period." Sherrick smiled. "Did you read them?"

"Yes," Gallagher answered.

"And you've cited other sources for your claims."

"Yes. You have my bibliography."

"Um. It was extensive. You found quite a bit of information, huh?"

"Yeah."

"Then it wasn't ignored, was it?"

"It was by the mass—" Gallagher began.

Sherrick cut him off. "It's available to anyone who wishes to look, isn't it?"

"Come on, Gary. That's not what this is about. We're talking general public knowledge."

"Are we?" Sherrick asked. "You've accused my clients of fraud, cover-up, malicious skewings and misrepresentations, yet you have used sources produced by my clients to establish that my clients haven't produced those sources."

"The information's only there if you dig for it," Gallagher snapped.

"Then perhaps you should accuse the public of laziness, not the media of conspiracy."

Ed Fernandez testified about the early period in the South. "Despite having to deal with a deluge of refugees from the North—the equivalent of the U.S. attempting to resettle nearly eighteen million refugees within a two-year span—the Saigon regime was developing a modicum of political legitimacy, international acceptance and economic growth. In contrast to the severe regimentation in the North, the South, with American economic assistance, was blossoming. Ho Chi Minh's agents saw that Ngo Dinh Diem not only was not on the verge of collapse, as had been anticipated, but that the South held more promise and more hope than did the North. These observations were reported in May 1959 to the Hanoi politburo at the Fifteenth Plenum. In response, Ho Chi Minh ordered the establishment of a supply trail from the North to the South, and the resuscitation of the guerrilla war—this time against the Saigon government.

"The myths here," Fernandez said, "are first that the South, because of its chaotic pluralism and observable repression of various sects, was highly unstable; and that Ho Chi Minh was the legitimate leader of the North, while Ngo Dinh Diem, a Catholic in a Confucian and Buddhist country, was an illegitimate ruler in the South. Without denying any of the South's significant problems, these conclusions simply are not true. Had the North Viet Namese communists not launched their war against the South, including, by 1962, the assassination of approximately one thousand hamlet, village, district and province officials each month, South Viet Nam today might be the democratic and economic equal of South Korea."

"Objection," Sherrick blurted. "Conjecture."

"Sustained," Bobby agreed.

Sherrick's cross-examination again demonstrated that the "myths" the prosecution perceived were mirages the prosecution had created and then dispelled using information from public media reports.

Deeper into the session historical myths about the '60 to '67 period, and Tet of '68, were presented and parried by the defense. Every prosecution witness was followed by a defense witness who reestablished the foundation for the "myths," and who in turn was cross-examined by either Renneau, the Wagner or Pisano. Like the defense, the prosecution was able to discredit every testimony by showing how each was limited in depth and focus.

After the break the Myth Busters altered their tactics. "Americans were animals at My Lai but that incident was minor in the scope of the war. Yet of a total of 9,447 network evening news stories about the war that aired between 1963 and 1977," Al Palanzo testified, "473 dealt with the atrocity at My Lai. The media focused and fixated on this single incident which represented three of every one hundred thousand war deaths. The NVA assassinated six thousand Saigon government civilian personnel in 1970. That did not receive one minute of American television air time. Not one minute!

"The ramifications of this reportage are the labeling of allied soldiers as baby killers, and the dissolution of the moral rightness of the cause. By the way," Al added, "these media figures have never been made public, and are not now in the public record. They have been derived from an internal network report."

That seemed to catch Sherrick and the defense off balance. He questioned Palanzo at length about his source and how the information had been obtained. Then he requested that the evidence be declared inadmissible. Bobby ruled against him. Sherrick called Derrick Eaton and Steven Smith to the stand for the defense. They spoke of atrocities they'd seen, exclaimed that My Lai itself may have been a drop in the bucket but that it represented all American atrocities, reported and unreported, "which probably numbered in the millions." Renneau cross-examined Eaton; Pisano took on Smith. The point stalemated.

The role of the media with regard to the Easter Offensive of 1972 was examined next. Data was presented about the NVA's 200,000-man, 500-tank, three-pronged attack that included the communist four-division assault on Quang Tri and Thua Thien provinces, their successful capture of Dak To, and their siege of An Loc. Civilian casualty figures were presented along with a picture of the vast uprooting of millions of South Viet Namese. Then John Manfrieda explained how, without this massive, communist conventional-military assault, none of the casualties would have occurred. Manfrieda continued on about how the bombing of Hanoi and the mining of Haiphong were reactions to that NVA assault. "Yet," Manfrieda said, "the story was skewed away from communist assaults on civilians, away from communist atrocities, and away from Soviet and Chinese collaboration, *to* U.S. military reactions and antiwar demonstrations in the U.S. Even when South Viet Namese ground forces, assisted only by U.S. air power, blunted, countered, and defeated the attacking force—causing the infamous NVA general, Vo Nguyen Giap, victor of Dien Bien Phu, to be relieved of command—the media concentrated its attention on American bomb damage to civilian areas of Hanoi and Haiphong, and on antiwar speeches by members of Congress. Just as Tet '68 was reported," Manfrieda continued, "so too was the communist Nguyen Hue Offensive first labeled a communist victory, then, when the counteroffensive crushed the attacks, this real victory was ignored and *never* reported. That is collusion. That is misrepresentation. Four hundred seventy-three stories on the several hundred American-committed murders at My Lai; but only twenty-six stories on the upwards of 25,000 civilian deaths caused by that NVA offensive. That is malicious skewing of available information.

"It is only through military documents of the time, not through public press stories, that I was able to document these assertions," Manfrieda continued. "In light of communist documents released in 1978, what I have told you is irrefutable. These documents, too, were essentially ignored by all but the most esoteric journals."

Sherrick and the defense were not deterred. That perhaps the prosecution had established a beachhead to biased reportage was of no concern. The charge was malicious skewing, and the prosecution had yet to present any evidence of malice.

Session Three—22 October 1981—The prosecution directed its attacks away from historical phases myths to ambient myths: the "Viet Cong as a ragtag peasant army of 'minutemen' instantly abandoning their paddies when called to arms" myth *versus* the "highly structured proselytizing organization partially directed by Northern cadre, and composed—only one in ten was an armed combatant—primarily of unarmed, impressed peasants, of part-time bureaucrats, and of full-time autocrats" reality; the "unwinnable war" myth *versus* the "allied military victory and political forfeiture" reality; the "no safe place in Viet Nam because there were no 'front lines'" myth *versus* the "physical distribution of violence, which clearly showed, with the exception of the major offensives of '68, '72 and '75, that there were, albeit vague, 'front lines,' and that the populated areas were relatively peaceful" reality; the "war never changed and was a quagmire of meaningless firefights and death" myth *versus* the "phases coupled with their adjunct social, political, economic and martial evolution" reality; the "all GIs were druggies" myth *versus* the "actual figures for different periods, which showed early drug use was virtually unknown and that it did not become epidemic (ten percent users) until the withdrawal phase was well under way, and that overall heroin addiction was less than one percent" reality; and on and on.

After the break Hollywood and literature were examined. "Images are Tinseltown's business," Mike Hawley stated. " 'High concept,' " he quoted a trade journal, "that is, a story so simplified it can be reduced to one sentence, 'is what producers want today. How it is said is more important than what is said.' " Hawley reviewed images from *Apocalypse Now, The Deer Hunter, Heroes,* and *Coming Home.* He identified "prowar" and "antiwar" themes and gave detailed examples using well-known scenes. " 'The stories,' " he quoted from a *Newsweek* review, " 'tend to be relentlessly downbeat and the protagonists are invariably antiheroic—war-numbed GIs who lop off enemy soldiers' ears, or unhinged veterans like the character . . . in *Heroes.*' The problem," Hawley concluded, "is inherent to the nature of this medium—simplicity, drama, and temporocentricism. As one major publisher put it, 'There has been no counterwave of exculpatory literature to balance these bleak accounts.' "

"Temporocentricism?" Carl Mariano asked on cross-examination.

"The pattern or need of centering on only one's moment in time," Mike Hawley explained. "Ethnocentricism and temporocentricism narrow our perceptions and knowledge by ignoring other-culture activities and historical antecedents. For example, if the storytellers relay only what Americans did in a specific and limited circumstance, without relaying the antecedents that placed a faceless enemy in the sights of the home-boys, the viewer can only judge the American action in the snapshot of presented time. Meanings, motives, and reasons are lost. Gary himself talked about shallow conclusions being drawn from shallow presentations."

Rich Urbanowski followed Hawley and attacked literary produce. He quoted one best-selling novelist who'd written about the emotional baggage of his dope-smoking, cocaine-sniffing, baby-killing characters and then said in an interview at Nittany Mountain College, "They aren't me. I wasn't like that."

Sam Linderman presented his analysis of the syllabi from forty college courses being taught on the war. He took academia to task for "its politically driven curricula," for its lauding of the works of Noam Chomsky and D. Gareth Porter; and he demonstrated that thirty-six of the forty courses were highly slanted. As Linderman explained, "There seems to be a preponderance of sixties liberals who are now professors or assistant professors because they stayed in school to avoid the draft."

*   *   *

Session Four—29 October 1981—"A race war," Ty Mohammed said. "Racism pervaded every aspect of our lives there and it ran the war." In the audience, in the jury box, on the loft floor, even behind the prosecution's table, white vets and white students slightly bowed their heads or shifted their eyes. Of all the topics this was the most discomforting. Feelings of guilt, of being from the privileged class, of being one with the Oppressor, of a need to listen and acquiesce, ranged from subtle to strong, but they were universal. On the other hand, the black and Hispanic vets were vocal and virtually split down the middle on the issue of racism in Viet Nam.

"Black soldiers went and fought," Ty testified, "because we wanted to prove we were part of America. We wanted to show whites that we held the same ideals. We thought that going would gain us respect. We thought racism and stigmatization would end. Then we got there. Millions of us, some of us part of McNamara's Hundred Thousand that was really two hundred forty-six thousand, that took indigent young black men with dismal educations—See, they knew what they were lookin for. Get the dumb niggers to go be-boppin in the paddies like . . . who said it . . . flypaper. They were lookin for cannon fodder and scarfed up nearly a quarter million young bloods. Then they exploited us. It is well documented that there were more black soldiers killed in Nam than white soldiers. I know a lot of you are thinking, shee-it, I saw lots of whites killed too. And that is true. But mostly it was blacks, browns and reds because The System put us in infantry units while it put most whites in supply or transportation or even artillery. Whites, when they got killed, were helicopter pilots or doorgunners or truck drivers that hit mines. When a brother got greased he was humpin a 60 in the boonies or he was on the perimeter at a forward base like Khe Sanh. You understand me. I don't mean all. I mean in general. I mean the average white and the average black and that is the story the media told because they told about average guys.

"I know lots of guys here, white guys, humped too. I know whites bled just like blacks. But it was disproportionate. And we shouldn't have been there in the first place. Dr. Martin Luther King, Jr., said, 'We are taking young black men who have been crippled by our society and sending them 8,000 miles away to guarantee liberties in Southeast Asia which they have not found in Southwest Georgia or in East Harlem. So we have been repeatedly faced with the cruel irony of watching Negro and white boys on TV screens as they kill and die together for a nation that has been unable to seat them together at the same school.'

"See," Ty continued. "I'm not sayin anything against white vets. I'm sayin blacks gave more and got less. I'm sayin the true evils lay with The System. When I was charged with possession, Man, The System that prosecuted me, including my own defense counsel, was all white. That is not justice. I'm ashamed of things I did in Nam. But I shouldn't have been there. And even though I served, I have a racially instigated bad paper discharge that stigmatizes me. Rodney says the war was a ruse by white capitalists to eliminate a lot of young bloods because we were just beginning to come into our own. Racism is about power and the power hierarchy knew how to maintain. If lots of whites were wasted that was acceptable because whites outnumber blacks nine to one. This was a war within a war. It cost one hundred and twenty billion tax dollars. That don't include interest. The war was fought by sons of minorities and by sons of the poor."

"Amen," Rodney Smith shouted.

"No questions," Tony Pisano said.

"You may step down." Wapinski shook his head. "Who's next?"

"The prosecution calls Steve Travellers," Mark Renneau said. The buzzing within the barn remained subdued but the craning of necks and the rocking of bodies was pronounced.

"Uncle Tom," Rodney hooted. From the jury box Calvin Dee flashed Rodney a power fist. Then Rodney and Ty began an elaborate dap.

"Order," Wapinski called out.

"A lot of dying was done by black soldiers," Steve Travellers began. "And it is true that significantly more blacks than whites, in relationship to their respective percentages of U.S. population, started out being killed and wounded in Viet Nam. Quantifying that significance, however, illuminates the story. Especially since some in the old antiwar movement, and some historians today, regard the U.S. effort as racist, that is, 'a white man's war fought by the sons of blacks and other ethnic minorities.' Or if the effort wasn't racist, they describe it in economic or class terms; 'a rich man's war fought by the sons of the working-class poor.' But is this true? And if it is, or if it isn't, what ramifications has the story had?

"African-Americans constitute 12.9 per cent of the U.S. population. In the early years of the American build-up, there is no doubt that this minority was disproportionately deployed in infantry units. In '65 and '66, blacks accounted for 20 percent of all combat deaths. The armed forces recognized this, perhaps because of media exposition, and took corrective action. In '67 black combat deaths fell to 13 percent of all American KIAs. By 1972, and remember half of all U.S. casualties came after January '69, the percentage of KIAs who were black dropped to 7.6. From the beginning to the end, of 47,244 American combat deaths, 5,711, or 12.1 percent, were African-American. This is a statistically significant difference but not only is it not the 'half of all deaths' some politicians, commentators and 'historians' have claimed, it is actually significant in the opposite direction. Hey, Ty, maybe it was a race war, huh? But then you'd have to say it was to kill whitey. By the way, other racial minorities accounted for less than two percent of the KIAs.

"Damn it," Travellers continued, "that argument, that image, hurts black pride more than it enhances it. It pushes people who believe the racist-war theory into a victim-sucker self-image. Is that you, Ty? Calvin? Rodney? You *want* to live that stereotype? Maybe you *want* that to be your story because it excuses you from overcoming the very real racism we are up against.

"Black soldiers in Viet Nam, in general, like white soldiers, did an outstanding job of soldiering. It was the first war in which the armed forces were truly integrated, and the physical closeness and interdependency of blacks and whites created intense and meaningful friendships. This had *never* before happened in America on such a massive scale. That the media missed that story and instead chose to report racist fraggings says to me those reporters and editors were more interested in the sensational than the truth, no matter the consequences. Perhaps the vested interest in racism is not held by the capitalists but by the journalists.

"Consequences!" Travellers balled both his fists, placed them on his thighs, leaned forward in the witness chair. "The consequences of the race-war story are a new and deeper polarization between races in America. That was unnecessary. It is tragic.

"U.S. policy wasn't antiblack. There were other social and cultural phenomena working in America in the sixties that created the early bias and the lopsided results. For example, the percent of blacks in The Old South was higher than in the rest of the country, and The South was the most promilitary, or the most patriotic, region in the U.S. That led to higher enlistment rates. The percent of southerners killed is significantly higher than troops from other regions. But southern blacks and southern whites were killed at rates proportionate to their regional demographics.

"I examined serious incident reports, too. Fraggings, mostly. I don't know how pervasive fraggings were, but the black director of the army's Office of Equal Opportunity reported that in Viet Nam 1970 was the worst year. That year two hundred GIs were wounded or murdered by fellow troops in racial incidents; two hundred out of 500,000 in twelve months, including rotations. It is significant, but keep it in perspective. That's one in every twenty-five hundred. And it can be argued that the racial tension that led to many of those incidents was stirred up by inaccurate and misleading media reports. That's their vested interest again.

"I strongly believe that the separation of white and black America today, and the resurgence of hate groups, is directly tied to the misinformation aired by the mass media about blacks and whites in Viet Nam. I also believe that the decline, economically and socially, of the three-quarters of all African-Americans who did not advance under the Civil Rights laws, is a direct ramification of this misinformation, which robs black vets and the black community of their pride, and fills them with additional and unnecessary resentment at government and at whites in general.

"What would have happened had the media focused on interracial harmony, interracial cooperation, interracial camaraderie that existed in Nam? Let me project a different scenario. What if the media had told a different, and in reality a more accurate, story? What would have been the ramifications to the present?"

"Objection," Sherrick spoke up. "Conjecture."

"Overruled," Wapinski countered. "He's only asked the question, not answered it."

"It's still leading," Sherrick said.

"Screw it," Travellers snapped. "These guys don't want to hear this stuff. It interrupts their self-image."

The Last Session—5 November 1981—All week the vets had bickered, aided, cajoled or snubbed each other. The weather turned colder. High Meadow lay shrouded in a thick mist. Inside the barn Vu Van Hieu took the witness stand. He was neither prosecution nor defense witness.

"I will just say some things and you use how you like," Hieu began. He then related his experiences after the fall of Saigon, told of the imprisonments, tortures and killings he'd seen, of the extrapolation of thousands of refugee reports into the conclusion that a bloodbath— 70,000 killed in the first ninety days—had indeed occurred. "Maybe the media," Hieu said, "say little about this because we are not Americans. Or maybe because that would shame them because they say earlier no bloodbath will happen.

"Viet Namese people do the same. We too were blind. Before we lost our country many of my friends say we live under the yoke of American imperialism. My countrymen were free to say that. Even members of my family called for us to support this communist five-point plan or that communist ten-point plan.

"During the American time my countrymen stick their noses into every ministry and every prison in South Viet Nam and they raise hell about corruption and moral turpitude. They show the world tiger cages. They say their own families are cruel and inhuman. They expose this general for bribery, that one for having a fifteen-year-old mistress. They cheer when an American flag is burned, and when they see pictures of Americans ripping their draft cards, and when the pictures are of someone waving a communist flag on the steps of the U.S. Capitol.

"On 30 April we were liberated and we were no longer blind. Even for NLF leaders like Duong Quynh Hoa and Truong Nhu Tang, and opposition journalists like Ngo Cong Duc and Ly Chanh Trung, liberation too gives the miracle of sight. Now they see with their own eyes how all Viet Namese live happily, united in peace and freedom. We are so happy now that maybe two million enemies of the state are locked away in new economic zones, that maybe one million risk escape in tiny boats, maybe half happy to end up as fish food. Since liberation no tiger cages. Since liberation no opposition. Since liberation no prostitutes, no marijuana, no terrorists.

"Since liberation tiger camps! Since liberation opposition stamped into the earth by the PAVN which has more than five million soldiers to control the people. Since liberation twelve Buddhist monks protest Hanoi's repression by self-immolation. Why are there no pictures in the world press? Why are there no pictures, is because there are no photographers in Viet Nam except those approved by the state? Since liberation prostitutes can only work for party members, dope only sold by government cadre, terrorism only run by the state.

"Yes, now I see. There was much disinformation, and I was blind, but now I can see. If you still suffer disinformation, maybe it covers just how wrong so many were about the war. They say liberation and oppression just happen or are inevitable and not a communist long-term plan. Americans don't want to believe the communists had their plan and worked their plan and not just in the South but in Laos and Cambodia, too. Americans don't want to believe there was preconceived malice. The communists have a plan for America, too. To me this is very frightening. They hide from us their intent. Then Americans say communists have no plan. Communists do not enslave Viet Nam. If you gain your sight you too must see, must believe the communists have a plan—for your country, too."

After the break Tony Pisano delivered the prosecution's closing argument. He was at a loss as to where to begin, what to include. Wapinski had warned both sides they needed to reserve time for the jury to deliberate and report its verdict.

"Who are we?" Tony looked at the jurors, then the audience. "We are the stories of ourselves. We are the ethos and the mythos. We are our history and our interpretation and selective recollection of that history. This shapes us. This tells us who we are, what our beliefs and ideals are, what our behavior must be to be consistent with that self-image. Upon story one can forecast the future.

"The communists, too, have a story. They were and are determined to remake all Southeast Asia in their own antidemocratic image—no matter the cost, no matter the lives lost, no matter the misery produced. Their determination lured us, albeit as their opposition, into their story. We clashed militarily. We clashed culturally, not so much American versus Viet Namese but free democratic idealism versus rigid Asian communist tyranny. Today's true story is the story of the clash of these stories.

"We have examined both stories in regard to the war. We have seen how and by whom the combined story was told, where it was accurate, where skewed from reality. We have seen the impact of story on America. We've felt the impact. Hell, we are the impact!

"Because of this, we have indicted the media on the charges of collusion, misrepresentation, conspiracy, malicious skewing, and incompetence.

"Remember back to a time when we were young, when we were enthusiastic. Didn't we believe in our decency? We have always been decent men. In having gone, in having served, we affirmed our ideals, our belief in the value of every human life, in the value of freedom, democracy, self-rule and self-empowerment. Many of us made this choice in the face of 'anti-war-ism' and with the full knowledge that we may be wounded or killed. But we went, fought. We upheld an ethical obligation to human rights, and the ethical principles of freedom and democratic aspirations which we believed were the inalienable rights of all humans.

"For this we have been assaulted because the mistelling of our story is an assault upon us. For a decent person to be accused of deplorable acts is devastating. Yet the story told of our involvement has been the story of atrocities, of drug abuse, of racism, of disspirited and incompetent fighting, of cowering at night and bullying by day—all for an immoral cause.

"The media and the Left have usurped the moral high ground, and have held it tenaciously for thirteen years. Yet it is a lie. In the early sixties, some of America's most influential journalists, feeling betrayed by LBJ, lost sight of the cause of freedom. Their personal meaning was debased. They projected their own loss of meaning as if it were universal. That is the origin of many of the myths we've exposed. That is the reason for the denial of victories and valor. That is why victories, valor and altruism have been lost in the national myth-making process.

"Every one of you here knows of the problems of evil and the possibilities of virtue. The media set out to convince the world of the destiny, the inevitability, the fate of Viet Nam. Essentially they labeled the American effort evil, the communist effort virtuous. The universe is not the Great Machine of the Mechanistic Determinists of centuries past. Predetermination, fatalism, manifest destiny, the lack of free will, and the inability to impact situations for the good are lies that soothe the complicity of the liar.

"We have shown how, by omission, by biased selection, and by ethnocentric focus—AND because of greed as defined by Nielsen ratings—the media-created myth destroyed the American sense of duty that characterized the great bulk of our fighting men in Viet Nam. We have shown that the media's concentration on American shortcomings and failures was, beyond reasonable doubt, a conspiracy; that this conspiracy has altered the American myth and thusly the American character in negative ways. The tragedy here is that into the void has seeped skepticism, intolerance, and hatred. We tell ourselves we are no good. We are evil. We are sick. We kill infants and civilians. And we accept and assimilate those characteristics as part of our national character. We fret about what we've become, and the scapegoat for that fretting is the American veteran!

"Once idealized as a melting-pot of opportunity, American society has become a victim of altered self-perception, has been purposefully polarized by the media to its ultimate gain in both wealth and power.

"We have shown that 'antiwar' was not antiwar; that 'conscientious objection' was not conscientious; that 'idealists' without action or understanding hold no ideals; that the 'moral high ground' of the media is a veneer hiding a soulless and greed-motivated multibillion-dollar industry—a mind junkie that few can resist."

Bobby interrupted. "One minute left, Tony. Speed it up."

"Oooo. Ah . . . The results of the misinformation we've come to believe as our story is that we no longer believe in freedom—that will be the downfall of America. Our cause is dead. What is left is money. What is left is, 'What's in our national interest.' The liberty of others is not our concern. We no longer believe in sacrificing to maintain government of the people, by the people, for the people. Our only belief is in economic determinism, the power of money. This is penultimate. It will shatter and we will fall.

"This is not to say we did not make mistakes over there. Nor that some of the lessons we've learned aren't valid. It is to say that the one paramount thing America has grasped from our involvement—call it the Viet Nam Syndrome—is that we can't, won't and shouldn't fight for freedom, for others or for ourselves. I maintain, the abuse of power in the pursuit of freedom does not justify the abandonment of that pursuit. Nor does the abuse of freedom justify the elimination of freedom. Choosing to *not* defend freedom, integrity and human rights leads to abuses, atrocities and holocausts far worse than war. In war there remains an element of hope; under tyranny, hope is destroyed.

"The media's role and tactics have been to hold out to us images of suffering and need, then once action has been taken to depict pitfalls and failures, to criticize via negative dialectics that attack the solutions of the problem solvers without offering alternatives. In this way the critic becomes immune to criticism, the media's projection of its own moral mountain fortress is secure. For the nonmedia what is left is hopelessness. And the hopeless, the disempowered, are easy to control."

"Time," Bobby said.

"Just one more point," Tony pleaded.

"We're running late," Bobby answered.

"Knowing what really happened there," Tony plunged on, "what we did and didn't do, who we fought and what they did and didn't do; knowing who we are; knowing that we contributed to this country and the world; it insulates you from all those subtle attacks and all those insidious references and then no one can ever again make you into a second-class citizen. Thank you."

Tony shuffled to the prosecutor's table. His head was down. The barn was generally quiet. Tony felt terrible, felt as though he'd failed miserably.

Gary Sherrick rose. This was the moment many vets had anticipated, some with loathing as if they were in an NDP awaiting an enemy assault, some with glee as if payback time had arrived.

Sherrick paced his words. "Walter Cronkite is an evil man." Sherrick chuckled. He raised his eyes to the rafters. "Chet Huntley, David Brinkley, Harry Reasoner—evil, evil, evil." Sherrick crossed his arms, let his gaze descend to the men in the loft. "Who amongst you," his voice rose, his head came down, he spun, locked the jurors in his stare, "believes this?! Who here believes NBC, CBS, or ABC had men in Hanoi who met with the communist information minister and reported his propaganda as the sole truth? Or even the sole story?! Were there reports of communist programs? Of North Viet Namese policies? Of Hanoi's perspectives? Of NLF plans?" Sherrick paused. Then he barked out, "Certainly! The prosecution acts as if the U.S. media should be the propaganda ministry of the U.S. government. Is that what you want?! Is that who you want to control your story? Are you willing to give the government your mind?!"

Again Sherrick paused, stood still. Then he stepped toward the jury, and just above a whisper said, "Gentlemen, think what you are doing here. Collusion with the enemy. We have seen evidence that the media reported Hanoi's perspectives but we have seen no evidence, let me repeat that, *no evidence*, of collusion. Not once did the prosecution even suggest that network officials or film directors met behind closed doors with communist leaders to plot against America's role in Viet Nam. One American actress sitting on an antiaircraft gun is no more collusion than one actor coming down from his mount with his clay tablets and declaring our cause just.

"These incidents are but single grapes in entire bunches; but one sheet of glass amid an entire visible collector array. What of films; what of academia? The prosecution has equated academia with Noam Chomsky and D. Gareth Porter. These are but two men of an entire group. Whether they are right or wrong you cannot convict academia of conspiracy on the expressions of a few individuals who may hold views which oppose your own. Do these men not have every right to their opinions, every right to express those opinions?

"On misrepresentation leading to polarization, particularly racial polarization, the prosecution has acted as if Africans were not brought to America in chains to slave in fields for whites—as if the cause for polarization is not deeper than the prosecution's own temporocentric perspectives; as if, had the racially motivated fraggings not been reported, three hundred years of repression would have been forgiven and forgotten. Please, tell me . . . No, tell yourselves, who is misrepresenting The American Story.

"We have been told that there existed a media conspiracy against the government, that this conspiracy caused the debasement of the cause, the loss of hope and meaning, and the ascendance of brain-dead politicians and slick willies. The defense has consistently demonstrated that the media do not, did not, and have not ever spoken in one thematic voice—which would be necessary for conspiracy. We have also examined alternative explanations for the debasement of the cause, and these include the perspective that the cause was indeed debased from its inception. That the administrations may be the stimulus behind the loss of hope and meaning is more plausible to me than laying this charge at the doors of this information branch which is so vast not all the condos in Pittsburgh have enough doors . . . well, you get the picture.

"What of malicious skewing? We have seen evidence of misinformation, this is true. And we *have* seen evidence of skewing and of ethnocentric reportage. The defense does not deny this. But this is not the charge. The charge is malicious skewing resulting in damage to democratic aspirations." Sherrick snickered. "Perhaps we could rewrite the story and title it 'The Malice of Walter Cronkite.' Would that please the prosecution? Humph! Is there malice in attempting to stop bloodshed? Is there malice in bringing into our living rooms proof positive of the failures of our own government policies? NO! This is not malice. This is the identical idealism of which Tony spoke. And if the democratic aspirations of some Southeast Asians were damaged, well, as Hieu said, most of his countrymen were blind to democratic aspirations—"

Bobby interrupted. "That's not what he said, Gary. The jury will disregard that comment. Wrap it up now."

"Hmm. Okay. Lastly I want to address incompetence. Who here is infallible? Who here has never made a mistake? You can point to errors and call the media incompetent but that also is not the case. Indeed, the American public has never been so well informed. We are awash in a sea of data, of stories, of information which covers an entire three-dimensional spectrum. We are today the most informed people on earth.

"Think, Gentlemen, about what you want. Hieu described a world in which there are no independent photographers. Where only the state releases information. Is that what you want? That is what you will have if you convict the media."

"Have you reached a verdict?" Bobby asked.

"Yes, we have, Your Honor," Calvin Dee answered. The entire jury stood. They had deliberated and written the verdict together. "On the first four charges—collusion, misrepresentation, conspiracy, and malicious skewing of information—though we find that the evidence presented substantiates each point, and that many myths do exist, we find the charges to be too sweeping, and the prosecution's argument of media causation to be unsubstantiated. The media are therefore found to be not guilty. On the fifth charge—incompetence to fully and accurately inform our society—we find the media guilty as charged. Further, Your Honor, we, the jury of High Meadow, recommend that the media, because of their greed and foolishness, be sentenced to be the information branch of a polarized, overly yet poorly informed, disintegrating society which will continue to make mistakes in its decisions based on skewed information, will continue to act based on ethno- and temporocentrically limited stories, will continue to assess, re-act, and follow blind paths based on erroneous data the media feed this society."

5 November 1984

On Friday, November 6, 1981, one day after the IRS declaration of insolvency, the Treasury Department moved in without notice and seized all bank accounts that had Bobby or Sara Wapinski's name, including all corporate accounts, their personal checking, their small personal savings, and the three accounts Bobby had opened in his name "In Trust For" Noah, Paul, and Am. The seizure removed all monies from the accounts, left High Meadow, EES, The Institute, the farm, and the Wapinskis, unknowingly, absolutely penniless. On Monday, the ninth, Sara attempted to cash a twenty-dollar check at Mill Creek Falls Savings Bank but was turned away without explanation.

On that same day Bobby returned to RRVMC for an Agent Orange screening retest. Why he'd put it off I don't know, or maybe I do. Maybe I'd have done the same. The doctor had called him numerous times, had ceased trying to get him, instead had talked to Sara. Half an hour after Bobby'd left, federal marshals arrived with demands that all property and all rights to all property be surrendered to the federal government. They politely demanded that everyone exit the barn, empty handed (including not even being able to take the warm Styrofoam cups of coffee Van Deusen and Mariano had walked in with half an hour earlier), then they proceeded to padlock the barn doors. That some property belonged to individuals other than Bobby made no difference. Eviction notices were served on every person at High Meadow.

By midafternoon Bobby had still not returned. However, Mark Tashkor, Jesse Rasmuellen, and Lucas Hoeller all had come, had argued with the marshals, had set off in different directions to challenge the orders, to file appeals, to obtain a stay of the seizure proceedings. Anything to buy time.

Nothing worked. Nothing worked completely. As the weather turned cold, as Bobby returned to RRVMC again and again for more tests, more needles, blood samples, and rechecks, vets began to leave High Meadow. Some of the newbies checked into RRVMC's new PTSD program. (Postraumatic stress was now officially recognized by the psychiatric community, and thus by the veterans hospital system, as a distinct disorder.) The hospital enthusiastically accepted any vet claiming PTSD problems—because its new, expanded funding was directly proportional to the number of PTSD-vets it serviced. RRVMC encouraged all its Nam vet patients to lay the blame for *all* their problems on their Viet Nam experience—an outgrowth of the funding process and Binford's research.

EES closed.

Many of the High Meadow staff—Van Deusen, Mariano, Wagner, Gallagher, me—picked up part-time employment in town, then quickly pirated portions of EES's equipment, moved it to my yard and garage, and to other locales about Mill Creek Falls. That enabled the vets to regroup, reopen—not at High Meadow but soon in a vacant mill by the Loyalsock, and not as EES but as ETS (a pun on Estimated Termination of Service), the new letterhead reading Environmental Thermal Systems.

Stronger legal efforts ensued. Hoeller, Tashkor and Rasmuellen took it upon themselves to force a reversal of the IRS ruling. They first obtained limited relief; the farm being allowed to operate within limited parameters—specifically disallowing any capital expenditures. The IRS (via court alteration of the initial ruling) allowed Sara and the children to remain in the house. The judge further acquiesced: Although he closed High Meadow as a community and as a corporation, he allowed it temporarily to be run as a family farm with "no more than twelve nonfamily employees." That allowed needed latitude. Rifkin stayed on, as did Thorpe, Renneau, Denahee and others. Sherrick split, went back to Indiana or maybe to Illinois or Iowa. Said he had old business to straighten out. Erik Schevard took over farm sales. Vu Van Hieu still handled the books. Ty stayed, not in the bunkhouse with the others but in Pewel and Brigita's original cabin in the woods on the far side of the pond. I don't believe his depression could have been deeper but with all that was coming down, and all the scurrying to regroup, none of us noticed.

Bobby had no gumption left for legal battles. Instead he found himself battling for his life. "We don't want to make any conclusions from one test," he was told. "There's a chance something else caused these results." Then, "We won't know for sure until we take a biopsy and analyze it. We don't want to jump to conclusions until we can verify the findings."

In short order his symptoms spiked—fever, fatigue. He lost sight in his left eye. He moved, temporarily, bitterly, hoping they'd find it was bacterial or amoebic, maybe melioidosis or liver or lung flukes, not to the provincial RRVMC but to the Veterans Administration Hospital in West Haven, Connecticut, where the hematologists were among the top blood experts in the world.

On Wednesday, 16 December 1981, Robert Wapinski was diagnosed as suffering from aplastic anemia.

33

Saturday, 9 January 1982, Mill Creek Falls—How much time? he thought. How much time left? He didn't want to talk to anyone. His eyes were bloodshot, his arms ached, his stomach felt hollow, bloated yet empty, nauseated. Eating did not fill the void. Drinking did not take the pain away. How had they explained it? The low platelet count had caused a spontaneous bleed behind the left retina which caused the loss of sight in the center of the eye. A blind patch. He lifted the glass, sipped, swallowed. The beer was tepid. The last glass from a pitcher he'd killed alone.

"You think you're dying," she had said to him earlier. He hadn't answered, had shaken his head but he'd thought, I know I'm dying. It's just a matter of time. Again he sipped from the warm glass. He'd eaten, cleaned the plate, mopped up the last of the tomato sauce with a piece of buttered bread, eaten braciola, Grandma Pisano's old recipe which Linda had given to Aaron Holtz, which had become a favorite at the White Pines Inn.

There were few patrons. It was cold, Endless Mountains January icy, windy cold. And early, midafternoon, too early for the vets to come, to start the Saturday night shots and beer ritual which used to anger Bobby who did not understand their need for release but saw instead their drunken carcasses on his porch the next morning, saw too their flimsy bank accounts on review days, felt he wasn't paying them enough, sure they were blowing too much on eat-drink-and-be-merry, sure for so long that tomorrow you will not die.

"You're not dying," she had said.

He'd looked into those eyes, into those beautiful hazel eyes, and he'd thought about detaching retina, about blind spots, about personal, cultural, governmental blind spots. "I know, Babe," he'd said. "I . . . It's just . . . "

"You have a cold," Linda had said.

"I just feel for him," Tony had answered. "I feel . . . I feel ambushed. I feel . . . And I was in those same areas. This Agent Orange shit . . . "

"Babe, I have to go."

"I know. Good luck with the birth."

"We'll talk when I get home. There's chicken in the fridge. And noodles. Slice up some apples for the veggie."

Apples, he thought. That's where the other vets are. At Treetop and Cannello's Apple Fritter. Or at the new McDonald's at the mall. Working. Washing floors. Swabbing tables. The country was going to hell in a hand basket. Some government economists said the recession was ending. Blind spots! Or maybe just blind. They'd dropped the federal discount rate from 14 to 12 percent to stimulate the economy and it had stimulated only the service sector. American steel was dying. Forty-seven percent steelworker unemployment. The ripple effect from the Monongahela Valley rust belt led Kinnard/Chassion to close all but one of their toilet paper–making Yankee Rollers, to lay off two-thirds of their workers. Recession or not, don't people still shit?! Were they using leaves? It was times like this when the lure of the old Harley surged and Tony wanted to say, "Fuck it. Fuck it all! Don't mean nothin. Tomorrow it could be me."

Aaron Holtz had put a large sign over the bar, above the bottles. "Hungry? Out of work? Eat your Sony."

Maybe . . . Tony thought. Maybe if it were only Linda and the girls . . . they really might be better off without me . . .

Aaron brought a fresh pitcher. Tony shook his head. "On me," Aaron said. "I'll join ya for one in a minute."

. . . especially if . . . I got it on my knees. My shoulders. Chlor-fuckin-acne. We were in the same area, drank the same water, slept in the same mud. If I'd known I'd never of gotten her pregnant again. Teratogenic. Monster making!

"Hey, paesan!" Aaron returned, sat, filled Tony's glass, his own. "How ya doin?"

"Agh. *Mezza-mezz.* Just trying to get some space. Trying to close myself off to deal with it."

"He's goina be all right, isn't he?"

"This is serious shit, Man. You know, maybe if he hadn't been so ambitious . . . You know, not for himself. Altruistically ambitious?"

"Yeah, Tone. That's a good phrase. He was like that."

"Fuck!" Tony shot from limp gloom to anger. "Don't talk of him like he's dead."

"Naw. Naw, Tone. I didn't mean it like that."

"Damn it, Aaron." Tony slowly banged a fist on the table. "I want to scream. I just want to scream. I'm on overload. On tilt. We got ourselves overextended again. And . . . shit! I'm thirty-four, Man. I can start again but I'm feeling awful old to start again."

"What about your classes?"

"Augh . . . they're . . . you know, I'm doing pretty well. I . . . I keep wondering though, how much time? How much time do I got left? Am I next?"

"Maybe . . . you know what Bobby'd say? He'd say, 'What are you going to do with the time you've got left?' "

"Yeah. He would, huh?"

"Yeah."

"Yeah. And what have I done with the time God gave me that he didn't give Jimmy or Manny or all them Magnificent Bastards? Why did I get the extra years? I don't deserve—"

"Unt-uh." Aaron interrupted. "What am I going to do to deserve them?"

Monday, 11 January 1982—Sara climbed onto the bed with Noah and Paul. Am sat at the foot. The upstairs was cool. Bobby had never finished the roof work over the boys' room, had never fully insulated the attic. The boys, Noah almost seven now, and Paulie a preschooler, slept in one double bed beneath a country red-and-blue gingham quilt. Am, a month over two, had toddled in at first light and Sara had followed, singing softly. "Hello, everyone. Today, we're going to have some fun . . . " It was a song she used with the first- and second-grade classes she substitute-taught.

She sat, her back to the wall, her legs under the quilt, the boys snuggled close to her. At the foot of the bed, Am stood, her chubby, little legs wide, bounced, giggled. "We start the day with exercise . . . "

Paulie sat up, kicked his feet under the quilt attempting to topple his sister, then moved back in close but not touching. Noah was still, quiet. The moment Sara had come in he'd clung to her thigh, nuzzled his head on her lap. She stroked his hair. Cuddle time. A new ritual. Morning and night.

Without moving, barely audible, Noah said, "When's Daddy coming home?"

"Hmm?"

"Is Pop gonna come home today?"

"No," Sara said. "Not today. But on Friday we can go back up to West Haven."

"I don't want to," Noah said. His voice was still shallow.

"I thought you liked the motel . . . "

"That's cause it was Christmas," Noah said.

"Um," Sara acknowledged. She'd gone up with Bobby, without the children, on the 16th of December, had stayed three days. At that time they'd expected only a three- or four-day stay. Alone Sara had returned to High Meadow on the 19th, brought the kids to West Haven for Christmas, a motel Christmas, a tiny-hospital-room Christmas with little to do except peer out the window, over the town, down the leaf-less tree-lined roads to the sound, with no way to use the new sled, with too many candy canes and chocolate Santas attempting to compensate for childhood expectations. They'd returned to High Meadow on the 26th. On the 31st Sara had again driven back, again alone, forcefully separated from either her husband or her children, forced to make the choice.

"Why can't Pop come home?" Noah asked.

"Hmm?" Sara hadn't heard him.

"Why can't Pop come home?"

"Do you remember what we discussed?"

"How come they haven't fixed his blood?"

"Well . . . I guess it takes time. He has to grow some new cells."

"They could just give him some."

"Um-hmm. And they have. That's what the transfusions were."

"Then why can't he come home?"

"He will," Sara said. "But first they have to be sure he can make more blood on his own."

"Because it leaks out of him?"

"No." She kept her tone even.

"It leaks out of you sometimes. Sometimes you use a bandage in the bathroom. Why don't you have to get more?"

Sara was startled. "I . . . In a woman . . . Everyone is always making new blood. Just like you make new skin. Do you know what a cell is?"

"Like those pictures . . . "

"Um-hmm. But they're teeny-tiny teeny-tiny. And some, when they get old . . . They're like cars and trucks, really. Blood cells especially. Because they carry passengers and supplies to all the other cells, food and oxygen passengers. And like old cars they get used up and they have to be junked. But your body always builds new ones. Daddy's body isn't building new ones right now so it's not just a matter of giving him new ones but of fixing his factory where he's supposed to build them."

Noah, gloomily, "Oh."

"Come on now. Everybody up. You two've got school and I have to see if I can get our records back from Mr. Gilmore. And Mr. Mohammed needs to be checked on. And Mister Vu—"

"He let's us call him Hieu."

"And Hieu needs my signature to order—"

"Pop's supposed to sign, isn't he?"

"While he's not here, I sign for him."

Noah sat up. His countenance changed. He beamed, got to his knees. "Blue Dog said he'd take me skating after school."

Friday, 15 January, 1982—He sat on the table, cold, nervous, shivering, naked except for the green hospital gown which, sitting, split open in back, rode up in front exposing him if he did not constantly hold the cloth down. His arms, legs, were exposed, were chalk white, bony, ugly, ugly to him, especially his knees which looked like bulbous knobs and his ankles and feet which seemed oversized, cartoon feet dangling from skinny cartoon legs except there was no humor in the sight because he did not feel like a cartoon, did not want to see himself as a cartoon. He had now been a patient for thirty days, one month at the VA, one month of proddings and pokings, bone scans under a massive machine that was like being overrun by a T-54 tank, a month of needles, enemas, questionnaires—What insecticides and herbicides do you use on your farm? When was the last time the well water was tested? Do you smoke? And bone marrow biopsies. They'd be back in a minute to do his fourth bone marrow biopsy and his hands, arms, his skinny legs, up his back and his neck, everyplace, was shaking, quivering uncontrollably because of the cold, the anticipation of the needle, the damn syringe, aspirator, the size of a turkey baster, the needle itself as thick as a car's radio antenna. They were with him now, on him, controlling him, laying him down, restraining him, tying his right arm, painting his back and hip with Xylocaine, injecting the local anesthetic—for nothing, he thought, for no damn good. He hadn't slept the night before knowing it was coming, the needle, a car's antenna with a drill, no not a drill, more like the twist-punch on a Swiss Army knife, puncturing the hard outer layer of the ilium, right through the crest to get to the sponge cake inside, to suck out the marrow, then out and back in with a corer, just like a tree to find its age except he was sure he felt it more than the maples felt their taps. His body trembled from felt pain and anticipated pain, future pain even when it was no longer in him, when they would slice the coring, scope it out, count the cells. "It's not leukemia," they'd told him the first time. Or the second. "Oh, thank God." "It's primary refractory anemia or aplastic anemia." "Oh, thank you, Lord. Fantastic! *No problemo*. When can I get the hell out of here? What's aplastic—" "Bob, you've got no blood." "Huh?" "Well, it's atypical aplastic anemia. You've got some. Just not very much. You are in a disease process called aplastic anemia. Tell me about your farm chemicals? . . . "

Bobby shuddered. They were aspirating the marrow now. He tried to tune out, drop out, replay the conversations, escape the pain. "Is this because of Agent Orange? I was exposed. I . . . I just confirmed that." "We can't prove it, Bob, but too many young guys are in here . . . too young to be this ill. And the missing chromosome . . . " "Was I born with that? Was this inevitable? A rendezvous with medical destiny because . . . " "No. You could not have been born missing the seventh. You would have been spontaneously aborted. This is an acquired syndrome. The missing chromosome is highly significant. Agent Orange is a causitive factor."

Decreased hemoglobin, decreased white cell count, decreased hematocrit, decreased platelet count, decreased red cell count, decreased cellularity, deletion of the seventh chromosome—a complete reduction in all aspects of the blood-forming system—pancytopenia/aplastic anemia—all messed up. "We found leukemia, but it's such a low percentage we can't truly call it leukemia nor can we treat it as leukemia. It is, however, preleukemic."

Conversations: "Mark." On the phone to Mark Tashkor. "Mark, this is what they've told me. I'm preleukemic. Agent Orange is a causitive factor." "Bobby, I can deal with the IRS. But the VA and this medical stuff . . . Bobby, you need a medical lawyer." On the ward with other vets. "Hey, Man, you're lucky." "Lucky?" "Yeah, Man. You talk to the other guys around here. Wait till you've been here as long as I have. You're lucky, Man. It's just you, huh?" "Just me?" "Not your kids. Your kids are healthy, huh?" "Yeah." "You're lucky, Man. Two guys died in hemo last month. Two brothers, Man. Nam vets, like you. Not these old geezers from WW Two, Man. One succumbed to leukemia, one to complications of testicular cancer. They were lucky, too, Man. Not like Boyer or Doone or Soloman or Rozini." "Who are they, Man?" "Their kids, Man. Fahhcked up!! Boyer's daughter is six, Man. Six years old. Still don't weigh ten pounds. Doone's kid is so hyperactive she needs twenty-four–hour, in-sight care. His wife takes the day shift, he takes the night. The kid's never slept. Never. Not once. Climbs the walls. All kinds a birth defects, Man. You remember thalidomide. Same kinda shit."

Bam! He lies perfectly still, on his side, his legs, body beneath a gray-green shroud, his right hip protruding, white, like a flag, easy to see, seeable from the treelines of the sound, the sea, from the hills, from wherever the attack has come, has come like a wave rumbling unseen, slamming into his hip, the pain exploding upward. He feels, hears the bone being crunched, feels the shards, the chips, sees the syringe, the red swirl, the masked people hovering. He does not move, does not dare move. They are firing at him, he submerged beneath the gray-green shroud except for his blasted white flag hip and his head, trying to keep his head up. He coughs. Immediately pain grabs him, grabs his face, contorting, biting his eyes, his retinas, then falling, letting go, losing, the small room coming back into focus, the masked people pushing, shoving, moving away, leaving him empty, sucked dry of what he'd been, of the good he'd been, of what he'd done, of virtue, pride, courage, liberty, elation, sucking out the unself, leaving only self upon which to focus.

Escape! This is not me, not my disease, but a disease that has inhabited me and I must evict it. Evict!

"How's Josh?"

"He's fine. I think he misses you."

"I miss him too. Are you coming up Friday?"

"I think so. Tony said he'd stay with the kids. I don't want to leave them with Blue Dog. He took them out on the ice yesterday. I don't think it's safe. It just hasn't been that cold this year. I'm going in for Mrs. Ploffkin Friday morning so I won't leave here until after three."

"Be careful, huh?"

"I will. Ty said he wanted to come up. He said he has to come up. Has to tell you something. Anyway, he said he'd drive his Caddy."

"Good. Better than Granpa's Chevy."

"What was that stuff they're giving you again? I want to ask Linda."

"Deca-Durabolin. It's an anabolic steroid. It's supposed to promote tissue building. But, God, my ass is sore. It's all black and blue. Can you stay through Monday?"

"We don't have enough money . . . "

"There's a family here named Boyer. They've a little girl who's really ill. They rent out rooms to visitors. It's cheaper than the motel."

"What if I get called to sub?" Then anxiously, "What's Monday? Are they doing something . . . "

"A transfusion. That's all. I just want you here."

Saturday, 16 January 1982, 4:00 P.M.—"You finally got here."

"Hey. Yeah. How are you feeling, Captain? Sara didn't get away until five because some kid had some problem. Then this morning I had problems with the Caddy."

"Oh."

"Fuel pump. Nothing serious. Tony put in a new one. Just ate up the time. Sara's downstairs talking to Joan Boyer."

"Good. They seem really nice. I bet their place is nice . . . "

"Come on, Captain. How you really doing?"

"I—" Bobby snapped, "I'm pissed as fuckin hell." He jerked forward, peered at the door checking for Sara. Ty's head, too, snapped over, then back to Bobby who was settling back into the propped-up pillows. Quietly Bobby said, "Fuck it, Ty. This sucks. This just sucks. One of these perverted assholes came in here and said I should have my nuts chopped off. Asked if I wanted to see a shrink."

"Yeah. Stop the testosterone production which is facilitatin the growth of the cancer."

Again Bobby leaned forward. He furrowed his brow.

"I . . . ah . . . " Ty laughed. "Ha! I ever tell . . . Nah. I never told nobody." Ty's voice became conspiratorial, his eyes searched Bobby's eyes. He pulled up a chair. "They took one a mine when I was in prison."

"What!"

"Yeah. Sshhh. Testicular. I . . . ah, Man, I—I wanted to tell you—"

Bobby interrupted. "You're okay now?"

"Yeah. They . . . When they took the nut it hurt but nothing like the radiation treatments after. That was like being cooked. Like being slow fried. But . . . I . . . Look, I done some stupid things, Captain. I—"

"But you're okay?"

"Yeah. Yeah, I'm fine. I'm never going back. But wait a minute . . . "

"I want to hear more about that. You know about that? There was a guy here, before I got here . . . Sara!"

Sara and Ty stayed until eight. The three chatted, talked about Josh, about the IRS, Sara dismissing the topic with a quick, "I can handle it," about California. Surface talk as if they were simply old friends meeting by chance in a supermarket aisle, husband and wife restrained by the room opening to the busy corridor, the lack of privacy, and by Ty's presence. Ty, too, was restrained, needing to confess but unable to tell Bobby . . . awkward, ashamed, never believing it could have come to this, postponing his tale, his reasons, justifications, looking for the right moment.

The right moment did not come on Sunday. Sara and Ty had stayed with the Boyers', had seen their sparse quarters. Joan Boyer was renting rooms to raise money for medical expenses that no one could cover, was accepting experimental treatments for her daughter Tara, was letting Tara be a "research patient" because without money, without that arrangement, and the other—"We got divorced so I could qualify for welfare. You could do the same"—there would have been no treatment at all. That had shocked Ty, shaken him, he wanting so badly to make amends, yet knew, thought, what he'd done, where he'd taken Bobby, the vets, High Meadow, was not amendable any more than Tara Boyer was amendable. Ty felt ashamed because he could not just blurt it all out. Instead he blathered about sales, about clients, about home and homes—"I talked to your mother, Captain. She don't seem so angry anymore." Then he became taciturn, then rude, giving Sara and Bobby no time to be alone, resentful when Bobby suggested he check out the area, do a lone recon, Bobby thinking let me touch my wife without you present even if I don't have the strength to do more than hold her hand. That too went unsaid. So too did Sara keep to herself Noah's terrible nightmare of Thursday night, and the fact that on Friday it had not been "some kid" but Noah who was terrified to let his mother go, who clung to her all night and only parted because on Saturday Uncle Tony brought cousins Gina and Michelle, and Noah needed to be seen as strong in their presence. All three, Bobby, Sara and Ty, were sure there would be better opportunities on Monday to speak openly.

Then Monday: Bobby was hooked to an IV drip. Sara and Ty, not looking at each other, not talking to each other, in chairs on opposite sides of the bed, vied for his attention. A few vets, patients, had popped in, exchanged greetings, news—"Hey, Man, they say your crits all the way down to nineteen." "How'd you know?" "Aw, you know, Man. They hooking you up?" "Yeah. I'm supposed to get four units. Then if it maintains, they're going to let me go." "Go for it, Man."

A nurse came in with the tray and setup for the transfusion, Bobby's third. She was very pleasant. A second nurse came, checked the setup. He too was pleasant. "Wilcoxson will be up in a few minutes," he said. "He wants to talk to you before we plug you in."

Bobby nodded. "Okay."

"Will this take long?" Sara asked.

"Not too long," the nurse said.

"We've got a five-hour drive," Ty said. "Thought we might get on the road by noon. It's too cold to be on the road at night."

The nurses left. There was crying in the hallway. "Ty," Bobby said, "shut the door."

"What's—"

"Sshhh. I think he might have died. I didn't think he was going to make it."

"Who?" Ty asked.

"Old guy across the hall. World War Two vet. I don't know what's going on but I think they took him to surgery last night. They brought him back with oxygen. I'm not sure what his complications are."

"Poor man," Sara said.

Doctor Wilcoxson knocked, entered, along with the first nurse. Bobby introduced Sara and Ty. Wilcoxson asked them to step out for a few minutes while Bobby was hooked up on one side and while the nurse drew a few vials of blood from the other.

Very relaxed. Very confident. Very matter of fact.

In the hall the visitors watched the family of the old vet amble away. His room door was closed, sealed. The hallway was dim, the air stuffy, the floor gritty. At the end of the hall was a south-facing solarium waiting room. Even from six rooms back, Sara and Ty could see the brightness, the distant treetops, the water of Long Island Sound. Like a current it pulled them, they still barely acknowledging each other, resentful of each other yet in the same boat, shuffling, meandering, being cautious to keep their eyes out of other patients' rooms, moving toward the solarium.

Suddenly, behind them, there was noise, scurrying. People running to Bobby's room.

"Stay here," Sara ordered. She ran. Ty froze.

Inside Bobby was twitching, his temperature rising, his breathing hesitant. In seconds he began convulsing, his back arching, his entire body in spasms—"Shit. Transfusion reaction." "Temps one-oh-five eight"—

his lips, fingernails turned purple, blue. Sara, in the doorway, began trembling, her arms shaking violently. Ty now was behind her, watching too, seeing too as Bobby's face contorted, as they forced his head back, forced in an airway, then a nurse, seeing Sara and Ty, shut the door, sealed the room.

It may have been minutes, maybe hours, back and forth, the pendulum of the clock not marking time, the light in the solarium growing dim, a phone call to Linda, another to Tony, trying to remember what the doctor had said, trying to repeat it. And to Joan Boyer, "Can we stay one more night?"

"Oh God! Oh God! God damn it. What kind of God are you?! If you're so all powerful why are you letting this happen? Oh God! Please. Give him one more day. Please. Give him one more sunrise."

"One more first light." Quietly, not to each other, yet in each other's presence.

"Please God. Let him see his children one more time. I should have brought them. Let him see High Meadow one more time."

"You son of a bitch. You lettin all these dregs hang on. You lettin all these druggies live a hundred years drinkin their rotgut wine, shootin up, fuckin everybody over. You The Man. Take me. I'm worthless. Look what I done. Look what I done to the Captain. He saved lives. He saved my life. I set im up, Man. It was me."

Then it was dark. From the solarium they could not see the leafless trees, and Long Island Sound was but a darkness beyond the twinkling of streetlights, car lights, house lights, starlights.

Tuesday, 16 February 1982—What will I teach him? he thought. I don't even know his name. Low lights. Quiet. Linda sleeping now. I'll teach him that if he leaves a light on, everyone can see him but he cannot see anyone. Geez, no! Not yet. He's so terrific. Linda's really something. He's got to be named for Jimmy. Name him for Pop, too. Or Thorpe. Or MacIntyre. We could name him after Bobby, but . . .

"Babe, are you still here?"

"Right here. You can sleep if you want."

"Do you want to call him Tony?"

"No."

"Robert?"

"Maybe."

"Your father'll be hurt."

"We could call him Robert John."

"And James."

"Three names?"

"As many as you like."

"Then I'd call him John James Robert Rick Dennis Emanuel Pisano."

"Then that'll be his name. But let's call him Johnny."

* * *

Forward. Life. Time. Momentum. A steamroller. A freight train on new track rolling smoothly forward, downhill, the momentum of a million boxcars, a billion lifetimes, following the dips and rises, downward, pushed, unstoppable, the same track only different cars, different views sought, taken, through the narrow slits between the boards. Such limits! Such desire to see more, know more, take more in.

It was a warm winter. The pond froze, thawed, refroze. Warm for a winter in the Endless Mountains. Ty returned to the original cabin on the far side of the pond. Through the remainder of January he'd brooded. I done this. I brought this on him. On em all. Like I pulled the trigger. Like I . . .

In early February it had rained, cleared, become cold enough for Ty to cross the pond when he came in, but not cold enough for Sara to trust the ice, to allow Tony or Blue Dog to take the children skating. Then it had snowed, heavy, wet, sinking the ice. Then again it had cleared, cleared for Johnny's birth they all said, so, like old times, they blasted the air raid siren to shake the town and the mountains and the firmament and they partied but Ty did not stay to party but crossed the pond again, feeling the ice sag, aware of the muffled fracturing under the crust of snow, aware of his weight causing the fracturing, pausing, wishing he could stand lighter, looking back at the path he'd made, thinking he should retreat, take the trail around the pond, through the woods, hating that trail, hating himself for having made the cabin his hootch, his place, his lonely place, estranged, alienated, in a self-imposed exile in deep woods beneath a howling winter wind that scared him, frightened him the moment he'd moved in, had, at night at least, never ceased frightening him.

Again it warmed. Again it cooled. They said Bobby would soon be coming home. They said he was in remission—a decrease or subsidence of the manifestations of the illness. Decrease of manifestations! Not reversal, not cure, maybe not even getting better. They said he was 100 percent transfusion dependent. Remission was a plateau, a terrace on the hillside where the freight train rolled more smoothly, where it did not accelerate, where the multiple and varied androgen treatments worked temporarily.

Ty Mohammed sat in the cabin. It was Monday, 22 February 1982—sixty years to the day from Brigita Clewlow's marriage to Pewel Wapinski. It was evening, dark, cloudy, cool, raw. Ty Mohammed sat wrapped in a blanket, brooding, confused, angry. Why had Bobby done this to him? Why had he become ill, frail, unable to sustain the battle? Ty hadn't wanted to put him out of business. That had never been his intention. Nor had he wanted the vets to leave. They'd been a kick. They'd been suckers but he needed them. The cheaper they worked, the more he sold, the more he made. His piece of the pie. He deserved it. And hell, without him, Ty Mohammed, they'd have gone belly-up long ago.

Ty pulled the blanket tighter. He did not want to get up, to go to the back room, to the bed. It was colder there. He was already too cold. He didn't even want to use the bathroom, even though he had to pee and the pressure kept his thoughts fragmented. God damn Travellers! Him and his "research." Only twelve point one percent of the KIAs! Where'd he dig that up? And why'd he say it? Betrayer! Oreo! Judas! Makes no damn difference. The Man, The System, set against us. And Rodney, fuckin changin sides, sidin with them racist mothafuckas. Shee-it. Near three billion dollars a year on disposable diapers! Then lay-offs. They just automatin so they can keep the pie to themselves. Keep the minorities in minority housin. Won't let a man work! Cut off his nuts. That's what they do. Agent fuckin Orange. They all think they got it. How many have a nut lopped off?! How many got sores from some herpetic clit? Time I go. I know my way back to San Jose. Left some works in a flop house there. Left a psycho-bitch there. Black on white, Man. Don't go judgin a book by its color or a man by the shade a his skin for deep down we all brothers. There as much in black as in white, or white as in black. Dig it! We dealin on them suckers. On them suckers dealin on us. For real! Defoliants! They gettin their piece a the pie. That's all I was tryin ta do. That's all.

Confused, agitated, cold, babbling to himself for an entire week, some days emerging only to pee in the snow, some days dressing, crossing the pond, trying to work, feeling ill, feverish, achy, blurting words disconnected to his thoughts, thinking: rapacious—what the hell that mean? Thinking: Jessica, thirteen years old.

Saturday, 27 February 1982—Cold again, crisp, clear, bright sunshine melting exposed snow, shadowed roof run-off freezing into long icicles.

"You wouldn't believe that jerk," Sara said. She and Linda were at the kitchen table. Gina and Michelle were in the living room with Noah, Paul and Am. Johnny, eleven days old, nuzzled in a snuggle-pak strapped to Linda's chest.

"What's he say?" Linda asked.

"All of them," Sara said. "You wouldn't believe it around here this week. First Vertsborg calls me in about Noah. That was Monday. Or Tuesday. I know Noah's been having some trouble. I mean, it's understandable, isn't it?"

Linda nodded. "Vertsborg gets forty-five thousand a year, you know. He's got to justify his position."

"Maybe that's it. I thought he was going to ask like, what do you think we can do to draw Noah out? Instead he asks, 'Has he been withdrawn at home?' "

"What'd you say?"

"You know, Noah's right there. I didn't want to upset him any further. I said, 'He's been very good.' So Vertsborg looks at him, he's not even seven, and he says, 'Is it hard living in your house?' "

"And?"

"Noah just looks at him. You know how he is right now."

"Didn't you tell him about Bobby?"

"I'd sent in a note two months ago. You know, we didn't know what was going to happen. Right after the transfusion reaction. And you know Noah. He can read my face like a book. I thought it had to be addressed. I felt the best possible way to deal with it was through honesty. So I told Noah, 'I don't know what's going to happen today and I don't know what's going to happen tomorrow. But I do know the four of us are going to get through it.' And I told that to Vertsborg. And that son of a bitch turns to Noah and says, 'Would you like to live with another family for a while?' Linda, I almost died. I teach with these people. It's been one crisis after another, and this bastard's trying to put together a case for child abuse."

"And Brian and Cheryl? No. Finish the Vertsborg thing."

"Bobby and I talked about it. You know, after it first happened. And he said, and I agree with him, 'Your part in this thing is never to lie. If the kids ever come to you . . . you know, you never tell them more than they're ready to hear. You don't have to sit them down and say, "Listen, Pop says he's going to live but the truth is he's dying." But if they come and ask, "Is Pop going to die?" You don't know that. I don't know that. Someday, of course, but not too soon.' Anyway, I asked Noah to go back to class, then I told Vertsborg, I said, 'I'm ordering you to stay away from my child. I'm reporting this to Superintendent Carson.' "

"Good for you."

"Hm. I'm not home two hours and Cheryl calls. She and Brian want to come up. Sure. We haven't seen them in I don't know how long. I mean, Bobby's called and told Brian what was going on. And I've called Miriam. Once! She says, 'How is he?' I said, 'He's lost the sight in his left eye and he's preleukemic.' She says, 'Oh. Other than that, how is he?' "

"Really!" Linda snickered. "People! How dense." She began to nurse the baby.

"So Cheryl and Brian come up and she says, 'We're making out our wills.' And Brian says, 'If something happens to us, we want to leave the children with you and Robby.' I must have looked shocked. Here's Bobby in the hospital and all. Cheryl says, 'If you don't want them, we want you to do whatever you want with them.' See, Bobby being ill is making them deal with their own mortality."

"Sounds like it's making them make you deal with it."

"She says, 'If you don't want them, find a foster home or something.' Linda, I can't deal with this. I swear half the vets think they're dying, too."

"I know. Tony's been a real baby. But he's back and forth. Having a son . . . he's bought camping gear, balls and bats and hockey sticks. He even brought back a little Yale sweat suit on his last trip up."

There was a knock on the back door. Without waiting Ty burst in, dropped a load of packages, went back out, came in re-laden, closed the door with his foot, shook, shivered, smiled. "Whoo-ee!" he sang out. He was dressed to the nines. "Am I interrupting?"

Linda put her breast away, shifted Johnny across her lap to burp him. Sara chuckled. "No. Give us a second. Come on in."

"Ooo! I been downtown. I been uptown. I been to the mall. I been here. I been there. You gonna like this."

"What's all that?" Sara asked.

"Jus stuff." Ty beamed. He removed his coat, a new coat with a fur collar and fur cuffs. Beneath he had on a new suit. "Like it?" He spun. He pulled out his tie. "One hundred percent Chinese silk." He spun again, then came to the table, gave Sara a peck on the cheek, then Linda. "Can I hold him?"

"He's just nursed," Linda said. "You're apt to have curds and whey all down your back."

"That's fine." Ty could not have been more jovial. "I got somethin for this Johnny-boy."

Linda and Sara were baffled.

"And where's Noah? I got him his birthday present—a little early."

"Ty, that's so nice. You shouldn't—"

"Sure I should."

"Oh—" Linda said opening the gift Ty had handed her. "Look at this. Ty . . ."

"It's like a sleeping bag." Ty's gold teeth flashed. On his right hand he sported a new diamond pinky ring.

"But . . . " Linda objecting.

"No buts! I got somethin for the ladies, too. This is for you." He shifted Johnny, handed Sara a small box. "And this—ha! I knew you was goina be here—is for you. And where's them kids?" Ty spun, blustering, kissing Johnny, handing him back, grabbing boxes, heading into the hallway to the living room from which Gina and Paulie were peering, checking out the commotion.

"Oh!" Sara was shocked. "Ty Mohammed. You can't do this." She held up a gold chain. "Ty!"

And Linda too! "Ty! What's—"

"Not now!" He called back. "Not now!"

"This must have cost a small fortune. Ty, you get right back in here!"

From the other room, squeals, laughter. "A boomerang! And a glove!" "What a pretty blouse!" "I was goina get matching ones but I figure you two got enough matching clothes to last . . . " "A radio controlled car!"

Linda and Sara both in the doorway, "Ty! What's going on?"

"I jus sold my Caddy. Some sucka give me thirty-six hundred which is more than I paid not includin the lease."

Sara shook her head, befuddled. "Why . . . "

"Because I want to. Life's too short. Cause spring's almost here. Cause the sun come up. Cause there enough doom and gloom happenin around here. And ... cause ... ah ... I need to ask ... "

"Huh?"

"Jus a small"—he gestured back to the kitchen—"favor. I need a small ... "

They retreated to the table. Sara brought out coffee and biscuits. Ty's countenance changed. He became quiet, focused. Still he smiled, a subdued beaming. "I want you to do something for me cause I can't do it myself. I ... I jus can't. And I don't want to talk about it."

"About what?"

"Linda, you be the witness hear her say, 'Okay.' "

Linda nodded, not sure what was happening, not sure Ty was serious.

Ty reached into his inner jacket pocket, took out a sealed envelope. "You know my brother, Phillip?"

"Uh-huh."

"An his wife, Carol?"

"Umm."

"An my baby, Jessica?"

"Yes. Of course. What do you have ... "

"You jus give this to Phillip. It's my account for Jessie. I don't want Luwan gettin her hands on none—"

"But Ty. Why don't you—"

"No questions. You jus say, 'Okay.' "

"Oh ... really!" Ty fixed her with his eyes. Sara hesitated, nodded. "Okay."

"I'm goin. Howie en Blue Dog en Hacken all doin a bang-up job sellin jobs fo the new shop."

"Where are you going?" Sara asked. "And why?"

"Jus for a while. I'll be back. I got some business to attend to. Maybe in San Martin. Or San Jose."

"Did you get a job out there?" Linda asked.

"Um. Maybe." Ty winked. "Maybe jus my time to get a piece a the American pie."

"But you can give this ... "

Ty's eyes saddened. He hung his head. "For me, huh? Like I asked. Not till I go but I want to get things set. I got some stuff in Grandpa's cabin and some stuff I need to get the guys that'll take me a week or so. Bobby be back in a week ... "

"Maybe on Tuesday."

Monday, 1 March 1982, late night, Grandpa's cabin—Ty is again wrapped in the blanket, sitting in the chair in the small main room of the cabin. He is again feverish, talking to himself or thinking to himself, not able to tell the difference, sure it does not matter, he, alone, in the woods, the cold, the dark, knowing Bobby will be home tomorrow, afraid to confront him, afraid to look in the face of the man he has betrayed. I can, he thinks. I will. Straight down the arm so it can't be stopped. What will they think? What will they say about me? Bobby goina be like me. Nutless. He'll know. He'll understand. If they'd taken his ear and his teeth and his finger . . . any of em'd understand. They'd do the same. Any of em . . . If they done time, they'd know. If I'd known, I'd nevah called. Nevah. It was my turn to catch up. My turn for all the brothers The Man fucked over. Twelve point one percent! I swear I'd read thirty-seven. Maybe forty-seven. It was a race war. I know it was. I . . . I can do it. Won't hurt. Straight down. Then jus lie back. Won't hurt none. Jesus! If I had my works. Then it wouldn't hurt. Tie off, slap up, shoot . . . then jus nice and slow pull the blade across . . . Rodney sold his mind to The Man. Who's crying? Don't cry. Dead meat don't hurt. Dead meat don't feel nothin. Dead meat don't betray . . . All I gotta do is tell im. He'd forgive me. I could make it up to im. I could give im my piece a the pie. Taxes! God, it's freezin in here. My feet are freezin. I can do it.

Ty held the knife in his right hand. There was no light in the cabin, no light in the woods. Slowly he rolled his left hand over, exposed his wrist, rested it calmly on his left thigh. Dead meat don't hurt, Bobby. You'd be better off dead, too. Better than suffering them transfusions. Stop crying. You are worthless. You . . .

He moved the knife to his wrist. I could tell him. I could still tell him. The whole story. Write it in a letter. I could say . . . I could say Jessica need . . . Luwan needed . . . I could say . . . I'm not terrible. I'm not. I didn't mean to hurt . . . I didn't know. I . . . Do it. Do it.

The tears came hard now, fast now. His breath was short, choppy. He could not see, could not feel, wanted to . . . to . . .

Unweight. Float. Sure. He'll understand. I'm being stupid. Sit up straight. Put down that knife. Get blood on my suit! What a mess. At least get a towel. A towel. Where the hell I got a towel? Put down the knife. Ha! Who's laughing? I'll go. I'll go now. I'll go barefoot. I'll stand in the snow, all night, barefoot. I'll beg him to forgive me. He will. I know he will. And . . . and if he doesn't, then I'll do it. Sure. Sure. I'm not terrible. I'll take a nap. Be like that pope. Or that king. Barefoot. I'll go. Take a nap, then I'll go. Then I'll . . .

Ty woke with a start. It was still dark but no longer black, maybe five, maybe five thirty. He was still cold but he no longer shivered. The knife was on the floor, its edge barely visible. He checked his wrist, felt it, checked to be sure he was whole. He rose. Determined. Focused. He was colder than he could ever recall, but not shaking, not chattering. His muscles ached. His entire body hurt. Yet he felt relieved, felt strong. Aches were nothing. Soreness was nothing. Cold, numbness, all nothing. Ty opened the door. He removed his shoes, his socks, stepped out. It was dark but not lightless, wet, not raining but misty, a thick damp fog, a fine drizzle hanging, suspended, neither falling nor rising. The ground was cold. Snow remained in patches. Autumn's leaves curled, held ice crystals, minute frozen ponds, entire miniature winter landscapes. Ty peed. He aimed the flow onto a miniature world, melted it, shifted, melted the next. The cold of the ground stung his feet. He saw the pain as good, as cleansing. He stepped farther from the cabin. The pain was wonderful. The soles felt numb, dead, but stinging rose up through his heels, his ankles, to his calves, his knees.

Shee-it, he said, thought. That does hurt. Get my things. Take my things. Take Bobby's present. Come clean then clear out. Give em the whole story. What Sara goina think. She'll hate me. She'll . . . she'll grab up the children, pull em back like I'm dirt, like I . . . I . . .

Ty returned to the cabin. The soles of his feet felt dead, the tops stung. He sat, massaged them back to life. He replaced his socks, shoes. He pulled on rubber boots to protect his dress shoes, straightened his clothing, retied his tie, donned his new winter coat. Then he meandered through the small cabin grabbing his personal items, tossing them into his blanket, tossing in his gift for Bobby, his sales order forms, pens, a few knick-knacks he'd brought out, his small radio, nothing orderly, hit and miss, bouncing from wall to bed to the over-stuffed recliner to the table, here, there, without reason, until the blanket was heaped. Then he grabbed the four corners, twisted them together, threw the bundle across his back, left. His knife was still on the floor.

His mind was as scattered as his motion. In the cold, mist, just light, he stumbled, nudged trees, ricocheted like a steel ball in a pinball machine rolling to the bottom, bumpered here, there, always descending the narrow path to the pond.

In places the ice was still snow-covered. Elsewhere it was wet, smooth, impervious, holding broad, flat puddles. The water made it slippery and he trudged carefully, slowly, through the mist, unable to see his past footprints, which had melted, unable to see the far side, the rear edge too disappearing. Only the area immediately about him was visible. He paused. There was a brown leaf imbedded in the ice exactly how Bobby had once described the ice-leaf solar collector. He spied a second leaf, meandered to the right, spied a third, sloshed farther off course. For a few minutes he looked from leaf to leaf. He felt giddy. Then he could barely recall why he was on the ice, why he was dressed so early, carrying all his belongings in the mist. Under him the ice sagged. There was a low creaking—not the sharp cracking of frigid winter but a dull creak. He expected it. He took another step. The ice broke. That he did not expect. It broke in a very large piece, a slab, fracturing clean before him. He fell to his knees to distribute his weight but the ice continued dropping. At first it gave him a nauseous feeling. The cold wet of the surface soaked through his pants, felt cold on his knees. For a brief moment he felt silly, felt he'd overreacted to the sagging, felt glad the fog over the pond was thick and no one from the barn or the house could see him. But the ice continued down under his weight. The huge piece tilted like an immense trap door. He slid back toward the edge. His arms flailed. He released his bundle, the four corners opening, dumping his goods. Now he was prone on the ice though the slab had tilted almost to the vertical. He tried to climb, to dig his fingers in and hang on but he could not get a hold in the frozen surface. He grabbed for the blanket, for the box with the gift for Bobby. His legs sank in the water. Instantly the cold penetrated his pants, his skin, into his muscles. The water hit his scrotum, his penis, jolted him. When it reached his navel he began to panic. Then he purposely whipped his face into the water remembering it was the only way to close down the peripheral vascular system and retain body heat. He came up. The ice slab, like a bank vault door, dropped, slamming closed. His arms shot up to hold the ice off, his legs strove for support in the water, in the muck-bottom. Under the ice he searched for an opening. He looked up, it was lighter above and he knew that the ice was up. For a brief second he thought that they all would think he'd done it on purpose. He clenched his teeth as tightly as he could, closed his entire face down. His whole body stung. It was no longer cold. He tried slamming his fist into the ice but the only motion was his body sinking in the water. He was amazed at the hardness of the bottom of the ice. He searched for the slab edge. His body would not move, became numb. It no longer hurt.

He was frail yet he looked healthy, healthier than he'd looked in months. His face was different. Changed somehow. Altered from within as if they'd snatched his body, replaced his soul, or gotten to his mind.

Wednesday, 3 March 1982—Rifkin, Thorpe, Renneau, were there, celebrating more than Bobby's homecoming, celebrating the very first High Meadow wine—a barrel tapped long before its time. Smith, Stutzmeyer, Denahee and Erik Schevard and family were there. So too Vu, Van Deusen, Mariano—almost every veteran who still lived at High Meadow, plus a dozen from downtown and half a dozen from afar. And families came, the Pellegrinos and Pisanos, the Tashkors, Rasmuellens and Hoellers. Andre Paulowski popped in. And Father Tom Niederkou. All talking at once, in twos, in threes, in fours. Bobby was back.

"Man, this is bitchin."

"Sooo bitchin, Man . . . "

"Yeah. Bummer, that shit up there. Glad you're home."

"Yeah. Hey, they say anything up there about these rashes?"

"They talk about numbness in like hands and feet?"

"You hear about this guy, Reutershan, who died of liver cancer. Said it was caused by bioaccumulation of dioxin. We've been collecting lots of shit, Man. Establishing a whole new section in the library . . . "

"Hey. You hear that Ty cleared out?"

"Naw."

"Yeah."

"I can't believe he left. I can't believe he left without saying good-bye. He didn't even leave an address?!"

"We didn't expect him to go yet. We thought he was going to be here."

"He's a neat man, but Man, he had a heavy dose of the flakies. Sometimes he had his sh . . . stuff, rolled in a tight little ball. But then it would all spill out . . ."

"This wine sucks."

"Anybody see the kids?"

"I'm switchin back to cider, Man. This stuff's hurtin my head. Shee-it. I can't drink no more. One beer knocks me on my ass. Gives me a three-day headache. I used to be able to drink a case."

"You read those documents Mariano and Wagner got . . . on this Agent Orange shit and alcohol and headaches. Talkin about people not being able to metabolize alcohol and about abnormal EEGs. Right into people's brains . . ."

"Anybody seen Noah?"

" . . . into people's dicks."

"Keep it down, Man. Father Tom's right behind you."

"What! He doesn't have a dick?"

"Yeah. But I was reading where it cleaves the DNA chains in your cum so if you knock up your old lady, that's what causes these multiple birth defects."

"Yeah. I read that too. I read that the chemical companies knew it too. A long time ago . . ."

"Anybody seen Bobby?"

In the barn office, alone, just the three of them, Bobby, Noah and Josh. "Papa?"

"Um-hmm." Noah didn't ask his question. Bobby waited, then said, "What do you want for your birthday?"

Shyly Noah smiled. Then more broadly. Then he blurted, "A puppy."

Bobby pulled back, then nodded, managed a smile. Then he knit his brow, cocked his head, scratched Josh behind the ears, said, "What about ol' Josh, here?"

"He's—" Noah clammed up.

Gently Bobby asked, "He's what?" Noah, eyes to the floor, mumbled something. "Hmm?"

"I . . . said . . . I want a dog that's just for me. Josh is too old. And he stinks."

"Oh—" Bobby moaned sympathetically, "poor Josh."

"He's your dog," Noah said. "And I don't have anyone to talk to."

Monday, 8 March 1982—"You need a good lawyer. You need a lawyer who's like an alley cat. One nasty focused son of a bitch. The nastiest son of a bitch you can find."

"Mark, you handle it. Just submit the claim."

"You're a hell of a lot more forgiving than I am."

"I'm not forgiving. I . . . Look, it's open and shut. Here's the proof that I was exposed." Bobby flipped through the file on his lap. "Here's the letter from Wilcoxson—on VA letterhead. Nice, huh? Listen to this. 'In view of the history of exposure to AGENT ORANGE, we feel the probability of this exposure as an etiologic agent is a distinct and serious consideration.' "

Bobby produced more pages from his file. "Here's copies of the studies I told you about—'Impairment of the Blood-forming System by Exposure to 2,3,7,8-tetrachlorodibenzo-para-dioxin'; and, um, 'Chromosomal Aberrations Associated with Phenoxy Herbicides'; and 'Cytogenetic . . .' "

"Okay." Mark Tashkor held up his hand. "Look, I'll file the claim but a one hundred percent disability isn't just compensation for what you've gone through. And anything more is beyond my scope. If we don't—"

"Thanks, Mark. We'll get it. This one's from Dr. Lilly Dachik. 'Various courses of androgens have had short duration effects. Robert Wapinski is now totally transfusion dependent and with but a few exceptions requires four units of blood every two-to-four weeks to stay alive.' I . . . Mark, I can't pay . . . yet . . . When the IRS releases . . ."

"Don't worry about it, Bob. We're in this as one."

A month passed. Then another. To Bobby each sunrise seemed a blessing, each day brought new trials, new trepidations. Three times he returned to West Haven, three times nearly scared to death to accept the transfusion, the blood, fearful of another reaction, yet knowing his blood values had declined into the critical zone. One week they made it a family outing, driving up Tuesday, finding a motel with a pool where Noah and Paul could swim and Am could hang on to Sara and be swished through the water; then all taking Papa to the Wednesday "filler-up" clinic; Sara staying with the children, downstairs, praying, concealing her fears; then release, and up to Mystic to the whaling village before the long drive home.

During this time Bobby "went public" with his disease. He called his brother, tried to make peace, found Brian unaware of, or unwilling to confront, their schism. He talked to the vets, to attorneys, to doctors, to students. He was invited to address distant veterans groups and small classes of school children, and he responded to the degree his strength allowed. He talked to Father Tom and to Johnnie Jackson, to Aaron Holtz and Albert Morris. The latter responded by asking him to be Grand Marshal of the 1982 Memorial Day Parade.

It was a strange time. Bobby became almost proud of *his* illness; wore *his* illness like a badge of courage, like a Congressional Medal of Honor, like a shield or maybe like a mask.

"It's a reading from Paul to the Romans," he told Sara, told Tony, told Dennis and Mark, Juan and Joe.

Now that we have been justified by faith we are at peace with God through our Lord Jesus Christ. Through Him we have gained access by faith to the grace in which we now stand, and we boast of our hope for the glory of God. But not only that—we even boast of our afflictions—we know that afflictions make for endurance, and endurance for tested virtue, and tested virtue for hope. This hope will not leave us disappointed.

Juan listened rapt. Sara squeezed him. Others seemed embarrassed. Tony stared into his eyes, unconvinced, until Bobby said, "Just accept the part on affliction, endurance, virtue and hope."

On Memorial Day he stood on a makeshift stage before the 1883 obelisk in River Front Park. A throng of three thousand citizens had gathered, had cheered him earlier along the parade route, had actually frightened him with their mood, their attitude transformation from seemingly anti-American a decade earlier to seemingly militant patriotism now. Bobby stood, shy, frail, glancing up from the podium, seeing the crowd, attempting to concentrate on a short patch of cleaned and raked gravel between the crowd and the stage, attempting too, to concentrate on his speech, his breathing, hoping his words had meaning but not hearing his own voice, in midspeech not recalling if he'd delivered the beginning.

We recall the names, faces, shared laughs and hardships of our friends yet what we truly honor on Memorial Day is not just their deaths or their lives but it is their spirit. We honor their belief, their moral heroism. From the distant past to the future it is essential we understand "we can not hallow this ground. The brave men, living and dead, who struggled here, have consecrated it far above our poor power to add or detract . . . It is for us, the living, rather, to be dedicated here to the unfinished work which they who fought here thus far so nobly advanced." These words, of course, are from Abraham Lincoln's *Speech at Gettysburg* one hundred and nineteen years ago.

We remember, we honor, by continuing to advance that unfinished noble work. Theirs is a legacy and a promise. Ours must be a covenant. . . .

The covenant of Memorial Day includes the passing of the torch of the values—even if at times those values have been tarnished or corrupted—for which they made the sacrifice.

Ahhhhhoooooommmm. From faith and covenants Bobby moved on to meditation—bouncing like an ultradense polymer ball; place to place, house, barn, fields, going to pot, to seed; and topic to topic, always shifting, never finishing, never reaching ultimate satisfaction; straw to straw.

He lay on his back in the barn in Grandpa's office, alone, without even Josh there by his side, perfectly still, an old OD army jungle sweater folded and placed over his eyes. He saw High Meadow as it was when he was a boy. He saw his grandfather and grandmother. He saw Josh when he was a puppy running in the fields, loping effortlessly after butterflies on sunny spring days with soft breezes. He looked inside himself, saw his arterial system, saw his blood, each cell, saw it flowing, saw it fighting for life, battling the hill, the mud, friendly fire, searching for the enemy to find, fix, fight, finish. He saw the marrow chambers, the little factories squeezing out new cells, beautiful smooth, firm, healthy cells. He sent memos to the chambers. "Good job. Quality counts. I love what you do for me. Keep up the good work. I love you." He sent light beams, cobalt blue beams, high intensity beams, energy beams, reinforcements. "I'm behind you guys. I'm with you all the way. The supply convoy's ready, packed with all the beans, bullets, and batteries you'll ever need. And here's a new weapon, a new treatment, new chemical. Use it in good health. Use it against the bad guys. Get some, good guys. Waste that scourge. Grease em. Knock em out.

Ahhhhhoooooommmm. Ahhhhhoooooommmm. He saw Sara, saw her smiling, saw that spectacular smile which was iron bars reinforcing him, iron molecules in his erythrocytes. He saw Noah, Paul and Am, he saw them in school, on soccer fields, on stages, he saw them at birth, at present, at high school and college graduations, and he saw himself with them, proud, beaming inside if not outwardly, beaming subdued, purposefully, not wishing to steal from them their glow, their wonderment, whether they knew it, saw it, or not. He saw the next sunrise, the next and the next. Ahhhhhoooooommmmm.

With meditation he combined exercise. Walks. He was capable of little more. He walked with old Josh, often alone, often up to his grandfather's grave. He walked with Sara. Sometimes talking, sometimes in silence, thinking, pondering, observing.

I married the girl of my dreams, he'd think. And she is here with me. We have three beautiful healthy children. I've run the farm, the solar business. I think we've expanded awareness about environmental issues and veterans' issues, which overlap. Maybe I've helped someone along the way. Now all I want to do . . . All I want . . . All I ever wanted . . .

"Brian, he's getting worse. Did you talk to your mother? He needs a bone marrow transplant. He won't make it without one."

"Maybe Cheryl can talk to her. You know how Ma—"

"Brian! He's *your* brother! And she's *your* mother!"

"Sara, I've done everything I can."

Sara squeezed the phone striving to maintain control. "I know," she said. "And we really appreciate . . . "

"If I was a match I'd give him some."

"I know, Brian. It's just so frustrating that Miriam and Joanne refuse to be tested."

"You shouldn't have told her they'd poke the needle right into the bone."

"God!" Sara snapped. "Bobby's had it done six times."

"Well, you know Miriam. When Cheryl talked to her the first time
... She was, you know, 'NO WAY!' She said it was immoral to ask someone who's sixty-two ... "

"Oh God." Sara sighed, closed her eyes. "It could mean keeping her
son alive!"

"Well, like I said, if I could ... "

"Brian, what about your uncle? Were you able to find out anything
about him?"

"Only that, ah, his name is Fredrick. Fredrick Cadwalder. And he married a Jennifer Morton like thirty-five years ago. In St. Louis. You know,
I'd forgotten about him. I don't think I've seen him since I was maybe
eight."

"Hmm. Thanks. I'll ... " Sara scribbled the names on a pad, squeezed
her hand, tensed her arm in hope. "I'll follow that up. Ask Joanne again?
Please."

In late June, alone with Josh, Bobby smelled it. They had climbed
through the orchard, crested the knoll, descended to the dam, crossed
the spillway, entered the path to the far woods. Bobby took his time,
paused, observed, remembered a day with Red, remembered days fishing, remembered the nights and days when the dam almost washed
away. He walked slowly, carefully. Then, "Oooo! Smell that?"

Josh stood by him, looked up; his old body sagged between his shoulders.

"Geez. Ha! I ... I remember when we first walked back here, Ol' Boy.
Remember? And we smelled that but we couldn't find it. Maybe a dead
raccoon, huh?"

Josh's head dropped, swung indifferently to one side, the other. He
looked up again as if to say, "If you'll go on, I'll go on."

And Bobby answered, "Naw, Boy. We'll go back."

That night, returning from a lone trek across the gap to the fire circle,
Don Wagner, in his orange plaid pants, discovered the source.

"Why would it take so long for the body to come up?"

"This is the shits, Man. This is more fuckin problems."

"Poor fuckin Ty."

"Yeah. They goina let us bury im here?"

"What'd his brother say?"

"It was the boots and all. That's what weighted him down. And if he
didn't come up because of the gases, you know, the decomposition,
maybe because of the ice, then the gases worked their way out and the
body became waterlogged."

"We're lucky he had his boots on. That establishes it happened last
winter. Man, they've been all over the place, again. FBI. IRS. Staters.

Hartley's lackeys. That bitch from 1st Witness News . . . that's all they needed."

Two weeks later there was additional fallout. In the barn a score of vets huddled, close, almost like the old days, barn trial days, except closer now, beneath the loft where the Slitter used to be.

MARIANO: Did you hear that guy, Gilmore?

VU: He is the one from IRS.

MARIANO: Yeah. I heard him say, "He was my ears."

VAN DEUSEN: Like an informer?

MARIANO: Yeah. I think.

PISANO: What the hell did they need an informer for? You guys kept the books open. They coulda come up any—

VU: It make Bobby sick again.

PISANO: I don't believe it. I don't believe Ty would of done it. He wouldn't. He just wouldn't.

GALLAGHER: They didn't find anything. There were no signs of foul play. The autopsy said "by drowning."

THORPE: Didn't stop 1st Witness News . . .

VU: My cousins are in Connecticut. Tomorrow I will drive him. I have many connections, now. He has a fever . . . an infection . . .

PISANO: I'm sick of this shit, Man. I'm just sick of it.

WAGNER: I think I got a lead. We have to keep networking.

GALLAGHER: On what?

WAGNER: His father, Man. His old man. He'd be like sixty now. Maybe he had a family. Maybe Bobby's got a half-brother out there that'd be a match.

Sara felt guilty. She could not accompany Bobby, could not sit with him through another transfusion, through the new antibiotic infusion that would control whatever infection he had, allow his temperature to return to normal. Instead, along with the other newly hired teachers, she was inspecting her new classroom—a third grade in Thomas Jefferson Elementary in Rock Ridge. She felt torn. She liked the principal, a matronly woman in her late fifties. She liked the building, an old, two-story, red-brick edifice whose vacant halls echoed with the click of her heels, halls that seemingly held the smiles and laughs and smudges of thousands of former pupils. She liked that her career was restarting, full-time. But to be away from Bobby, from the boys, from Am who was only two and a half! She did not know if she could pull it off. It was tearing her apart.

When they returned it was not Bobby who seemed different but Vu Van Hieu. He seemed bigger, stronger. Perhaps it was because Bobby had not shaken the fever, had come back with six different prescriptions, had returned shivering, hunched over. Still, Hieu looked bigger to Tony, too, when he stood next to Carl and Bobby was not present.

"What's happenin, Hieu?"

Hieu put a finger to his lips, "Ssshh!" He leaned forward, indicated for Tony and Carl to come closer.

"What's goin on, Man?"

"Ssshh." Hieu looked about, checked the doors, windows. They were in the small mill building on River Front Drive.

"What is it, Man? You're smiling like the cat who ate the canary."

Hieu looked at him questioningly.

"House cat that ate the pet bird," Carl explained. "You know, ah . . . never mind. What's up?"

Again conspiratorially. "I told you of my cousins, eh?"

"Up in, uh . . . up in New Haven?"

Hieu nodded. "He say . . . you must keep this secret."

"Sure."

"Certainly."

"Okay. I tell you. I have not told Bobby. He is too sick to tell."

"What, Man?"

"Maybe two months, maybe three. They establish International Coalition of Free Viet Namese."

"What's that mean, Hieu?"

"Ssshh!" Vu Van Hieu squirmed restless as a small child over a secret dessert. "I am among first to join."

Tuesday, 10 August 1982—On VA letterhead—"There is no evidence that this veteran had the claimed condition in military service nor manifest to the required degree within one year. There is nothing at this time in the medical literature which relates any exposure to AGENT ORANGE to this veteran's condition. The letters submitted by the West Haven Chief of Oncology/Hematology provide nothing new or material. Notice of denial of disability is hereby . . . "

Son of a bitch! Son of a bitch! Son of a bitch!

Anger erupted, spewed massively. How much can one man be screwed? How far could they push him? Now he was over the edge. Now he believed the absolute worst about his government, his society. Now he thought greed controlled all, in retrospect controlled the media, in retrospect controlled the war, controlled why and how and by whom it was fought and perhaps Ty was right in his ambiguous "The Man" because now Bobby was being punished by The Man. Everything he'd worked for now seemed ruined, destroyed, ephemeral. The peace Sara had provided, the joy of his children, the elation he'd gotten from his own accomplishments, from those of the vets; the satisfaction of his tinkerings, his designs—at that moment were meaningless.

He had long avoided the natural anger of someone who discovers he has a terminal disease; had avoided the bitterness, the feeling of victimization. He had never felt like a victim, never seen himself as a victim, until now, until the denial of his claim, until the VA's personal rejection of him. The VA denial was so outrageous everything erupted, spewed from Bobby like the explosion from Mount St. Helens. He took it out on himself, on Sara, on Noah, Paul and Am, on Tony, on all the vets.

Cheaters, liars, betrayers, rejectors! Everyone. Everyone around him. Or suckers! Pawns, like he himself, lied to by presidents, by congresses, by governors and aldermen; cheated by politicians, by attorneys, by bureaucrats; betrayed by manufacturers, by shippers, by big business, by small striving to get their piece of the pie. SCREWED! Conspiracy, treason, deceit aimed directly at Robert Janos Wapinski, at his wife, his children, his dog.

"How dare they!" Bobby kicked a kitchen chair, sent it crashing. "Son of a bitch. How can they . . ." His voice tapered. He did not want the children to hear. Thoughts: Can't they see? I've given everything, to improve everything, every aspect of every life. . . . They've set me up. Screwed! Taking it all away! Taking it all. Everything. Even the dignity of acknowledgment. Screwed! Screwed! Then loud, angry, "SCREWED!!!"

On 8 September Sara returned to work, full-time. The situation fueled Bobby's rage. It was part of *their* machinations designed to divide and conquer, designed to debase his pride, his ability to provide for his family—not like his father but like his grandfather who had been a rock, a foundation upon which an entire nation could build, but no more, no longer would that be allowed.

Bobby did not object to Sara working. He took pride in her abilities, her quality as a teacher, her strong and principled positions. And he took pride in the accomplishments of his children, and in the independent attainments of the vets. Almost daily he received reminders.

> Dear Bobby,
> You made quite an impression on my husband. You have given him back his life and you've restored mine. People need heroes and leaders. There aren't many anymore. It pleases me that Joe's role model seems to have been such a kind, gentle and strong man.

But neither his acceptance and pride, nor the acknowledgments, insulated him from envy, anger, bitterness.

A different flood of letters also poured in, fanned the flames of his fury. "I'm dying from Hodgkin's disease . . ." "I'm in my third remission . . ." " . . . liver . . ." " . . . a soft tissue sarcoma . . ." "The cancer registry here shows a rate among Viet Nam vets 1,100 percent over expectations . . ." " . . . eleven birth defects and counting. My wife cries every night . . ." " . . . the rash is so bad—it now weeps constantly—I can no longer use my arms. My mother dresses me before she leaves for work in the morning. She's writing this for me now. (Hi! I'm glad to meet you, too.) . . . " " . . . his headaches are so bad now he never leaves the bedroom. The psychiatrist at the VA said it's from the emotional stress of combat but Danny thinks it was from that spray . . . " " . . . the doctor told me to take aspirin. He insisted Agent Orange never has and never will hurt anyone, and he showed me both a VA memo to its physicians and a VA pamphlet which specifically stated these facts. I think they're afraid if they admit it, it'll be the Pandora's box that'll bankrupt the entire system . . . " " . . . the VA pamphlet *AGENT ORANGE: Information for Veterans Who Served in Vietnam* says, 'there is no medical evidence that exposure to Agent Orange has caused birth defects in the children of Vietnam Veterans.' The lawyers for the class-action suit have at least 2,000 documented cases of polygenetic birth defects due to chemical mutation of chromosomal . . . " " . . . they denied my claim." " . . . they denied my claim." " . . . they denied my claim."

"God damned fuckers! Screwed royal!"

Tony sighed. "Yeah, I know."

"Screwed to the fuckin wall." Bobby's arms flailed.

"Yeah. They're treating it exactly as they treated PTSD when that first hit em. Deny, deny, delay, deny. Not our fault. Nothing we did. You brought it on yourself. You're a malingerer. They weren't particularly tight with a buck when Daddy Dow presented them with a bill for eleven million gallons of that shit but they're pretty tight now."

"I can't work . . . I . . . " They were alone in the barn, in Grandpa's office. Bobby couldn't finish the sentence. His face tightened, wrinkled, his eyes squeezed closed, his lips separated. At first without sound, then without control, he cried. He babbled. "I can't even . . . If I could just . . . I'm not finished . . . I'm sorry, Tone. I'm . . . " Tears seeped from his eyes, dripped from his jaw.

"Naw. Naw. It's okay." Tears came too to Tony's eyes but he forced them back. "I'd be doin the same. Shee-it. I have."

Bobby snorted. "It's okay to die," he said.

"Yeah. We all gotta go sometime."

"No. I mean . . . It's okay for me to die. I die, I die."

"Yeah, what happens, happens."

"What I mean is, I know it's okay . . . I don't want to extend it unnaturally . . . But god damn it, they owe me! They owe my family! I'm disabled and they deny it. They deny they're part of it. It takes away more than money, more than my being able to help support my family. It takes away more than life. It takes away hope. It allows chaos to reign. It allows those fuckers to get away with it. I've been physically assaulted, and they're getting away with it! And flaunting it! Their fucking diamond logo is on every fucking grocery store shelf in America. Screwed, Man! And the VA says in five years or so their study will be completed! In five years we'll all be dead! Epidemiological studies! Feasibility prestudies! Protocols for the prestudy! Study-design review! Prestudy study design reviews. And challenges to each step! And reviews of the challenges! Purposeful delays. They've developed the perfect legal tactic—bureaucratic stonewalling. When we're all dead, the suit is moot!

"Listen to this," Bobby continued. "This is from Fred Wilcox's *Waiting for an Army to Die.* '. . . if Dow Chemical knew in 1965 that 2,4,5–T was contaminated with dioxin, and the U.S. knew in 1962 that dioxin is toxic, then why were extensive scientific studies not conducted on the possible mutagenic, carcinogenic, and teratogenic effects of Agent Orange *before* it was used in Vietnam?' In '62 the chemical companies even sent letters to the government warning of health problems. This is a cover-up, Man. This makes Watergate look like a leaky faucet. We're talking conspiracy to commit murder! If they don't deny it, they've got to throw all these fuckers in jail!"

Bobby's treatment at the VA in West Haven continued, and it continued to be quality treatment. What a paradox, what a contradiction, to be treated by a monstrous, multitentacled organization that went beyond denying responsibility, which essentially denied that treatment was needed! Bobby was not angry with his doctors, or with the VA hospital staff. Many of these individuals shared his anger at the political process, the governmental hierarchy that controlled that process, the Washington leadership that controlled the hierarchy. "Whatever happened to taking care of our own?" they'd ask rhetorically. "Whatever happened 'to bind[ing] up the nation's wounds, to car[ing] for him who shall have borne the battle and for his widow and his orphan'?" That the average age of World War II vets was sixty-four years, that these older vets were entering VA facilities in record numbers for long-term care, that the cost to the government was astronomical and rising, that the nation was still in recession and tax cuts were politically popular, and that younger vets were still viewed as having lost their war (denying funding for Agent Orange claims was an additional boon to the myth that the military lost in Viet Nam), all impacted the decision to delay or deny Viet Nam veterans compensation for bioaccumulated poisoning.

Bobby hung his head. "How, Man, how did we miss this?"

"I don't know."

"Geez, Tony. I think back on my own health, I should have realized . . . "

"Yeah, but . . . you know, you weren't in a void. There was all the other shit comin down."

"But even here. We've been in touch with so many people. When I'd come across these health problem articles . . . isolated pockets all over the place, people organizing in small groups, being put down as crazies . . . I'd file em without reading em. It was like I wanted to deny it, too."

"You were handling other problems."

"WBBM-TV out of Chicago, in March of '78, aired 'Agent Orange: The Deadly Fog.' How'd we miss it?"

"Could you have done anything about it?"

"If I had had the tools . . . "

"But you didn't. If we couldn't handle it, maybe it's better we didn't try. We can't chelate dioxin from our systems, can we?"

"Maybe we can. Maybe we could learn how. Develop a program to wash it out before it manifests its damages. Instead we let the VA see that documentary, and react by secretly establishing their no-health-effects-from-Agent-Orange policy. We could have objected."

"That's what we're doing now, eh?"

Screwed!

A week passed. Maybe a month. Bitterness built on bitterness, anger on anger.

"What the fu—" He was on Route 154 coming back from the pharmacy at RRVMC. It was a pleasant day. He felt decent. In the rearview mirror flashing red interrupted his thoughts. "What now?" He slowed, pulled to the side, let the car idle as he watched the officer approach, watched red and blue blips sparkle from the officer's polished brass belt bullets, from his mirrored sunglasses, his badges and buttons. Bobby rolled down the window. He felt like a child about to be berated by his mother for something of which he was unaware.

The officer looked in. "We're making random stops to check to see if drivers are complying with the new seatbelt law."

"Oh." Bobby felt relieved. "Sure. I've got mine on."

"You really didn't have to in a car this age. What is it, a '54?"

" 'Fifty-three. My granpa added em a number of years back."

"Okay," the officer said. "Have a nice day. You can go."

The officer turned, headed into the flashes. Now Bobby watched him in the sideview mirror, watched him retreat, watched the smug strut. Bobby leaned out the window. "Hey! Wait a minute." The officer turned. "Wait one damn minute," Bobby shouted. He opened the door, got out.

"Yes."

"You stopped me just to check my seatbelt?!"

"That's right."

"How dare you! How DARE YOU pull me over for this!" Bobby was livid. "What kind of police state tactic are you running? You stop people at random? Pull them over? Don't you EVER do that again!"

"Take it easy, Buddy . . . "

"Fuck you, you son of a bitch! What's your name?"

"What did you say?"

"I said, 'Fuck you!' I'm reporting you." Bobby was like a madman. He walked right up to the officer. His skinny arms flew. "Get in my car. I'm taking you in. This is an outrage. This is criminal."

"Get back in your car and move along." There was no warmth in the officer's voice.

"I will not! You have criminally violated—"

"I said get in your car."

Again Bobby's arms flew. "You motherfu"—the heels of his palms hit the officer's chest—"cker."

"Bobby, settle down." It was Mark Tashkor.

"I'm sick of it. They treat men like criminals. We're citizens! We're being denied our rights."

"Tell me what happened."

"I'm sick of it, Mark." Bobby's manner was harsh, threatening. "That arrogant, incompetent fuck. Bureaucratic authorization to criminally destroy a man's credibility. We just keep being abused."

"Oh Boy. Look, I can get them to drop—"

"I'm not going to let em drop anything. Make em put me on trial. Make it a test case."

"Bobby, we're not going to do that." Tashkor was firm.

"Why the hell not?! We just let the state creep in here, chip away there, taking freedom after freedom. I wasn't doing a god damned thing. I'm just driving along—"

"Bobby! Bobby. Bobby. The guy's just doing his job."

"Mark! For God's sake. You're an attorney. Don't you see? It's not that lackey puke. It's the law. It's the law that allows them to enforce this seatbelt law by stopping—"

"Yes." Mark cut him off. "You're right. But . . . "

"Just like the goddamned VA." Bobby switched to a falsetto. " 'Oh! That oozing rash! That leukemia! That's just your irrational response to delayed combat trauma. Let me set you up with a shrink.' " Then in a deep, accented bass, " 'Why thank you, Commissar. Do you also condemn objectors to the gulag?' "

7 November 1984

I could not bear it any longer, the anger, the bitterness, the wasting away. I spent more time in the fields, or at the small mill, or in the market arranging for the sale of our crops. And I spent time at home, studying, or with my family. My eight-and-one-half-month-old son was crawling everywhere, gnawing or gumming everything in the house. Gina and Michelle were blossoming into young ladies. Linda had earned her own office in Denton's Ob-Gyn group. (To the chagrin and resentment of some of the physicians, Linda was more popular with the pregnant ladies than any of the docs.) And I spent time with my mother and father, too—feeling, being, becoming traditional American middle class. Even enjoying it.

At High Meadow the number of resident-vets dropped to nine with Denny Thorpe returning to Hagerstown armed with volumes of information on birth defects and VA compensation procedures; and Van Deusen, Mariano, Wagner, and Gallagher buying an old two-family house on the hill above the small mill. November came. Bobby's health seemed to stablize. My thirty-fifth birthday came and passed. In Washington, D.C.—after years of exile and expatriations—the nation finally welcomed its Viet Nam vets home. Or perhaps I should say we gave ourselves a welcome-home parade and a memorial, for it was Scruggs and Wheeler, two of our own, who were the prime movers behind the memorial. The dedication touched off a national reacceptance.

I missed the dedication ceremony. It is as important for a parent to spend his birthday with his children as it is for him to be there on their birthdays—it shows them they have something valuable to give, not just that they are valued and thus will receive. Bobby's thought. He missed the ceremony too. A group of fifty High Meadow and ex-High Meadow vets went. They returned on Sunday, the fourteenth, with story after story. I went down, rode the Harley, had to, didn't I? for Jimmy? went down alone in December, perhaps looking for greater distance, for escape from that rage, arrived late at night, in fog, mist, drizzle. A slight wind shifted the haze. The roar of jets from Dulles was the only distraction. I came around the corner. I will tell you it is not the same memorial today as it was in December 1982. At that time there were no lights, no stone walkways. There was mud. For the November dedication they had lain sod but hundreds of thousands of feet and poor drainage had destroyed it and the pit before the apex was—to me appropriately—thick, oozing muck. I had come in from Constitution Avenue, from the back where the top of the memorial is level with the ground, so from the back you see nothing at all—and in the low flowing mist and drizzle I was not even certain I was coming upon it. Then I made the corner, the west corner, the one closest to the Lincoln Memorial which in all its splendor and light was visible only as a glow, occasionally in thinner troughs of the moving mist, as an outline. Then the memorial, the first inch. A one-inch-high black polished stone. A pitiful, insignificant one inch. Inconsequential, much like the beginning of the involvement, a tiny wedge but one by forty inches. Then the first names, deaths. Step by step it grew. In the mist, in the dark, with the backglow from Lincoln not entering the pit, with the roar of unseen Dulles-bound jets unsettling. I could not see, focus upon, more than two or three panels, the one beside me, the one in front, the hazy one beyond, me not wishing to read the names, not yet, thinking this is all? This knee-high, waist-high wall, a memorial? More names. More names. Five per line, chest high, panel after panel, muck squishing from beneath my advancing feet, no longer able to see back, to see the beginning, to see the inconsequential thin wedge, unable to halt the descent, panel by forty-inch panel, the names, numbers, growing, slow steps, panels above my ears, over my head, blocking the sounds of the street, the city, capturing like a giant ear the overflight thunder, engulfing, enveloping, until the panels are more than ten feet, until I am submerged in the dark mist and the memorial itself, until I have descended through 29,000 names, 29,000 fallen with 29,000 fallen before me, reaching out, narrowing to the east, to the far inconsequential, insignificant wedge.

There is a man with a beard, ponytail, and headband, kneeling silently in the apex. I do not speak, do not acknowledge him, allow him the privacy of his prayer, his mourning. I am glad I am here, alone, here when there is no one except a kneeling figure. I advance. The east wall tapers. I slow. I do not yet know the order of names but have been told by others to look at 53 and 54 East, the panels that hold the dead from Dai Do. In the darkness, the mist, I cannot read, then can just barely read, but do not recognize any names, think to myself that I would not recognize them anyway because I do not remember the names anymore, maybe never knew some by other than a first name, or last, or moniker. Then I see, sense, Malnar, John Malnar, Big John, our sergeant major, then—it is strange, eerie, names emerge as if they want to be sensed, remembered, as if they come to me, as if they are branding irons, yet cold, dark, yet burning, searing my face, my mind, wanting me. I drop. My legs are liquid. My body has evaporated into the mist. I drop to knees I cannot feel, into mud I do not know is there. I am there with Manny, Emanuel, there with Harold, Richard, Robert, John, Carlos, William, Emmett, James . . .

James . . . I cannot move, do not move, cannot leave my brothers because they have reached out to me, hold me, touch me, and I them, them, eighty-one names from Dai Do, with me until I must find James, until I am sucked back down into the swirling vortex, amid tears, I am no longer, I am mist in the dark mist of flowing spirits clinging to the earth, come with me to find James, Jimmy, panel 14 West, I'd walked by him, by him without noticing, by him on the original descent without knowing.

34

B obby's anger abated, perhaps was assuaged by the season, the lights, the smiles and good cheer, perhaps by something Father Tom said to him, or said at mass on Christmas morning. Bobby's health seemed to improve. He regained some weight. The changes were like lifting a cross from the shoulders of all.

He was still transfusion dependent but his body was reacting positively to whatever new therapy they had him on and he returned to work, part-time, and to spending long hours reading and writing in Grandpa's office. With his improvement, with the new year, came an improvement in the local economy—or so it seemed. The solar business was slow, but general and construction plumbing and heating were steady. Bobby's mind remained sharp.

"I've tried." Don spoke softly. It was a Saturday in January 1983. Don Wagner and Carl Mariano were with Sara in the kitchen of the farmhouse. Noah, Paul and Am were in the living room. Bobby was in Grandpa's office working on his writings or his designs—he'd been vague in describing, to Sara and the others, his latest project.

"Nothing?" Sara asked. She pursed her lips.

"Dead ends," Don said. Immediately he felt self-conscious for having used the word *dead*. Quickly he talked on. "I've found every Wapinski in Texas, Oklahoma . . . I think from Missouri south. But no relatives. I've checked Wopinski, Rapimski, Wapin, a dozen variations. And if there ever was a Cadwalder . . . well, they're all unlisted."

"It's okay, Don."

Carl too spoke softly. "Have Bobby call his mother. He's *got* to ask her."

"I told him that," Sara said. "He said, 'No friggin way. I wouldn't have her marrow in me. Just no friggin way.' You know . . . he . . . "

"Sara"—this time Don used the word on purpose—"I'm at a dead end."

"I . . . " Sara put a hand to her forehead. "Don't . . . you don't have to try anymore. This last time up . . . don't say anything, okay? Doctor Dachik, Bobby's hematologist . . . she . . . "

"What?"

"She said Bobby only has a twenty percent chance of surviving a bone marrow transplant. It's too . . . it's gotten too risky."

Vu Van Hieu disappeared, or so it seemed, without a trace, without notice. Some vets searched the pond, recalling Ty. Most were afraid to call the police, afraid of repercussions, yet more afraid of an unknown, perhaps ill-fated demise. A few knew. They'd been asked to remain silent.

Early March 1983, in the vicinity of Mill Creek Falls: Hieu, Bobby, Tony, Carl, Don and Jeremiah Gallagher, a small room, curtains drawn.

"*Salute,*" Tony said. He wished he had a glass of High Meadow wine to raise to Hieu but they'd brought nothing with them.

"Thank you, my friend," Hieu said. "I will be commuter rebel," he joked. "I will be back."

Bobby clapped Hieu's shoulder. "You take care of yourself."

"Oh yes. You too. I . . . " Hieu paused. His discipline wavered. "I once tell you I am fundamental American principles, you remember?"

"I sure do," Bobby said.

"I am still," Hieu said. "But I am not fundamental American behavior. It upset me so much how they treat you. Your people, the VA, the IRS, the FBI. How they treat veterans! They see you as cause of the war. They see Viet Namese people as victims of *your* war. They treat you like piranhas . . . "

"Pariahs," Bobby whispered.

" . . . but to me, they condescend like I am a child victim. Like you say before, slavery by alms. Thank you for letting me work hard."

"Ah, Hieu. I never paid you what you could have earned on the outside."

"You pay okay. I save my money. Now I invest in the liberation effort."

"Are you sure?" Don Wagner asked.

Hieu smiled. "Yes. I am sure. You know, I see Viet Namese who came here, who fled maybe before Saigon fell. Maybe with very much gold. Now they make much more. They live in mansions, drive big cars. I have no respect for them. I detest them. I throw them out from helicopters in my mind. That money they arrived with, that was my country. That was Viet Nam's blood that they drained."

"Seems"—Tony turned from the group—"like a long time ago . . . but, you know, if . . . really, if I didn't have Johnny and the girls, I'd join you."

"No," Hieu said.

"I would," Tony said. He turned to Bobby. "Remember San Jose? We almost did—"

"No." Hieu interrupted. "You cannot. I know you would, but you cannot." Hieu tapped his chest. "This is for me, for Viet Namese men, to recapture our dignity, to atone for our shame."

"There's no shame . . . " Tony began.

"Tony, you are my friend. I know you very well. I know your battles. I know Dai Do. I feel such shame. I know the 2d ARVN Regiment at Dai Do. They were on your flank on the move to Dinh To. They the shits, eh? They run, huh? I know their commander a collaborator with the communists. Evil man. Evil agent. I didn't know then. He brings me great shame. I will forever feel shamed by him, and by others like him.

"That is why I return," Hieu said. "With my cousins we will regain Viet Nam. We do it ourselves. You pray for us. You hold us in your thoughts. We can never again ask you, ask for American bodies, ask your support like that."

Jeremiah Gallagher nodded. "He's right. This time you guys do it."

"Yes . . . " Hieu smiled.

"Get some for me," Carl cut in.

Don clenched his fist, shook it. "For all of us!"

"Right on!" Hieu beamed. "Now I go. You thank Sara. You thank Linda. You tell everyone I go on vacation. I go see my cousins but you don't know my cousins."

Only Bobby looked sad. "Cover yer ass, Man."

With spring came new growth, new life. The VA denied the appeal of Bobby's disability claim but the Social Security Administration approved his disability application, back-dated the effective date, paid him three months' retroactive benefits. To Bobby that acceptance, that acknowledgment, was of as much importance as the reimbursements. It gave him, returned to him, something intangible, something invaluable. And with a kick from Sara he became lighter, mentally more mobile within his physical limitations. The weeks, months, he had spent in fear, fear that his mind was going ended. Slowly assessment, action and assimilation replaced anger.

"Ever since I came back," he told Sara, "all I ever really wanted to do was to walk in these woods." They had climbed through the orchard, descended to the spillway, crossed the dam and entered the far woods. Josh had accompanied them as far as the orchard but had lain down and let them proceed alone. "I mean, that's almost fourteen years ago. When I first came back. I never thought of it as getting away from all that's out there. I didn't think of it as hiding. But I guess I did think of it as a safe haven from which to interact with the rest of the world, a base camp, you know, which would allow me to interact with them on my own terms. And I did. But then, coming back, I kinda withdrew and I guess I've been hiding out. I think the more I hide the more I separate myself from what the world is, what it's doing to itself, the more I feel totally exposed to it. We can't hide, can we?"

"No."

"For me it's been fourteen years. For America the war ended eight years ago. We've all been trying to get on with our lives but we haven't . . . It just keeps coming back."

"Um."

"Have I been carrying on like a complete ass?"

"No, Bob. Never." Her voice was soft, kind.

"But I have been hiding."

"Maybe. I don't know. You seem pretty well immersed in the whole thing."

"I don't feel like I've touched anything for a long time."

"There's not a person who's been here who isn't better for the experience."

"They did it themselves. I just opened the door. And if I hadn't, someone else would have. It's not even my door. It's my Granpa's. He touched them more than I. I haven't even been a gentle breeze. Geez, that's it, that's what I've been. A breeze. A slight touch on a few blades of grass. Bent them a little. But they'll straighten back up in a second. And at the same time there's ten tornadoes lined up about to rip through the fields. Great! Gentle breeze before the storms. Means nothing. Every single blade of grass is about to be uprooted, and I stood by and blew a gentle breeze and then stroked myself into believing I've had a positive effect."

"Bobby, you've had a wonderful effect." Sara was louder now. She didn't like it when he became maudlin.

"Sara, do you know, right now, if I could, if I could, I'd push the button that'd destroy Hanoi. And the Kremlin. I would. Where do they get off enslaving . . . not where, why? Why do they get away with enslaving millions of people? We went because of it. The enslavement came first. That's the origin of what's happened to me.

"Like so many of the guys . . . I felt most . . . effective . . . when I had a rifle in my hands and I was hunting communists in South Viet Nam. Damn it! That's where I should be right now. With Hieu. Not blowing blades of grass but blowing away evil shit. Not picking up the pieces of their aggression—not enabling that aggression by alleviating the side effects. Defense. We have a responsibility to help people hold their freedoms. Regain their freedoms. We have that responsibility because we have the ability. We're not some flat-broke emerging third-world nation. We're America! We can have an effect—a clean, positive effect. If it weren't for the simple-minded slime buckets that run this place, the greedy jackasses that'd rather make a nickel today and screw the future, the world could be beautiful. It could be safe."

Sara faced him squarely. "As long as you're in it, for me," her voice was clear, chastising, loving, "the world is beautiful. God's made us a beautiful universe. Maybe we've spoiled parts of it, but not all of it. Definitely not High Meadow. Because of you. High Meadow is a Garden of Eden."

They strolled on in silence. Then Bobby said, "God. If I could have a disease where they don't jab the bone marrow . . . God, that lumbar puncture was the worst . . . It would be a blessing. I'd be able to work more . . ."

"Bobby." Sara interrupted him. "Why do you feel you have to do more than you've done?"

"Because . . ."

"Because?" Bobby's brow furrowed. Her challenge tired him. She saw it as getting him out of himself. "Because?" she repeated. The day was clear, the scant new foliage delicate, deliciously light green, the sun penetrating easily to the earth. "Do you remember," Sara began, "when we got married?"

"Of course."

"Father Paul's words?" Sara asked. "When you truly love you love the other the way the earth loves the sun on the first warm morning of spring . . ."

Bobby stopped. "I remember that."

" . . . and you must have faith that spring will come again, and again re-light the land . . . in the light of this new light."

"New light," Bobby said. "That's what I think every night. Give me one more sunrise. One more first light."

Sara prodded, "Because . . . ?"

"Because I love you. And . . . because I think we're losing."

"Losing?"

"To the greedy."

"Then what are you going to do about it?"

"That's it. I'm at the end—"

"Damn it! No you're not."

"But really . . ."

"I'm not asking you to deny . . ."

" . . . my disease . . ."

"It's not *yours*. You don't own it any more than you own a mosquito bite . . ."

"I do have it . . ."

"You also have mosquito bites . . ."

"They're not the same."

"No, they're not. So you've got two things to struggle with. The greedy and this thing which has infected you."

"And how do I struggle?"

"You tell me," Sara said. "How do they work?"

Now Bobby's life, and Sara's, revolved around Agent Orange: research, the class-action suit, and Bobby's own health maintenance. Typically, Bobby concentrated on gathering and understanding every shred of information available, on turning his limited energy to designing a program to counter the ill effects.

The more he, Tony, and others learned, the more they rejoiced that their children were not born with major defects. And the more they empathized with Dennis Thorpe whose son had been born severely deformed, who, without the recent revelations, had blamed himself and his wife and she had done the same, until the strain dashed their marriage. Bobby, Tony, the others, felt for the families with malformed children. "Who, god damn it," they said to each other, "thinks—I mean you're twenty-fuckin-years old—that you've got your kids with you, genetically, ten years before they're conceived? Who anticipates that something you inhale at twenty, or something you eat or drink, is going to cleave the genes in your juice so that at thirty, thirty! it's going to make you father a monster! That your kid is going to be WIA from your war? That our grandchildren are going to be casualties, too. Or does this wipe out our genetic line?"

"Here's another set of questions," Tony said. "Does dioxin cross the blood brain barrier? Or any of the herbicide's or the dioxin's metabolites? Can it cause rages, violent behavior, insomnia, flashbacks, abnormal EEGs? PTSD caused by toxicity?!" Tony paused. He read aloud from a journal, " 'Some of the dioxin-biotoxin research indicates that a portion of combat stress reactions probably are *not* caused by delayed traumatic stress but are caused by defoliant poisoning of neural tissues which slows axonol impulse transmission as evidenced in abnormal EEGs and direct nerve tissue studies. The brain interprets and reacts to this lethargic activity—not as if one has suffered brain damage for which a brain will attempt to compensate via plastic recovery where other areas or structures take on the function of the damaged area—but by allowing the poisoned section to limp along and frustrate the rest of the brain. These studies hypothesized that biological frustration causes the stress reactions of many PTSD veterans.' "

"Geez, Man," Van Deusen said. "Then the entire scope of veteran maladaptive behavior needs to be reexamined."

"Yeah," Mariano said. "Except the VA's reacting identically to the Agent Orange studies as it did to the initial PTSD evidence. Listen to this. 'Like a poisoned brain in which one segment contradicts another,' " he read from an article, " 'The $24 billion per year Veteran's Administration officially denied all the evidence it was housing and treating—or mistreating.' "

" 'Men were treated like criminals,' " Bobby read from a legal magazine. " 'Their rights were denied. Victor Yannecone, the prime attorney for the veterans in the class-action suit against the chemical companies, asked if the VA attitude was changing, answered, "Yes. The attitude has hardened. The attitude had become patently vindictive. The attitude has become *militantly* anti-Vietnam veteran. . . . The trail of broken bodies and dying veterans is getting longer." ' "

"It is not a matter," Bobby continued, "of trying to hide from technology. Or of being an adversary of technology and going back to the soil like some reincarnated Thoreau at Walden Pond. We couldn't stop it if we wanted to. Short of a thermo-nuclear war, we couldn't get rid of all the polluting chemical companies, mining retorts, or manufacturing toilets. And we shouldn't want to. You know, we really do live better today than a hundred years ago. We live longer. Our bodies are stronger. It's difficult to dodge the carcinogens in our food, the teratogenic substances in our water, the embryotoxic waste in the air. But we can do something about it. We can band together. We can follow The Code. We can purchase only products manufactured by "clean" companies, or we can build our own chemical companies, run them cleanly—seeking new methods to guarantee that toxic by-products are not produced or that they are neutralized. Not stored. No storage is safe. If we pull together we can produce our chosen product lines more cheaply than the conglomerates. And slowly, through the best capitalistic device available to us—fair competition—we can put them out of business."

Knowledge did not slow his decline. Nor did it serve Sara well. Her constant thoughts were now of greater information, of "there's something out there on how to treat this that we haven't yet dug up. Some monoclonal antibody therapy, some oncogene . . . some magic dart . . . "

The trips to West Haven became more frequent. The dosage of antibiotics was increased, the potency elevated. Still the freight train chugged as if unstoppable.

Bobby paused. Suddenly, to him, there was no longer any sense in searching the literature, in looking for proof that TCDD had caused his aplastic anemia. It was beyond reasonable doubt. The class-action suit that had been filed in January of 1979 in the names of four hundred veterans had grown to represent 40,000 veterans. To him it made little difference. For him it was the wrong approach. If the veterans won, he asked himself, would it significantly change his life? Compensation? Money was not his ultimate concern, had never been. And vindication was not sweet, not bitter, not positive other than it nudged the scale toward zero balance, toward the center, toward neutral perceptions and policies that had gone askew. But vindication would not right the wrong, would not give him four-month erythrocytes. Vindication and money were not inherently negative but, to him, their tendency to break his focus, to refocus his concern, his disciplined concentration away from his work, away from his expanded self onto his central self, was ruinous.

For him to understand what was happening to him required an expansion beyond the search into toxicological effects, required of him first a fundamental understanding of his own biology, of the biophysical functioning of affected basic units, of his own cellular-molecular composition. At this point, though he did not yet realize it, the search for understanding, for How Things Work, the delving into human cellular mechanics, was but a new step to a deeper search, understanding, expansion.

Bobby read about, studied, made drawings of microtubules, lysosomes, Golgi, ribosomes. He meditated on cell membranes—walls that actively discriminated, selectively regulated the immigration and expulsion of living and dead materials; on mitochondria, the power companies of the cells; on the endoplasmic reticulum; and the headquarters, the tactical operations centers, the Pentagon complex, the nucleus itself with its double helix structure and its fifty to sixty thousand separate dioxyribonucleic acid (DNA) offices each with its own nucleotidal foreman, plans sets, and fax machines transmitting or capable of transmitting via intra- and intercellular chemical communication lines, pools, RNA messages—do this, don't do that, link these amino acids together like Lego blocks in this exact sequence, multiply and/or divide, or cease multiplying, dividing, or commence until this exact condition is encountered at which moment your present mission is complete, and get back to me, chemically, for debriefing so I too can rest. Genes! Construction drawings. Much more. Executives, decision makers. Still more. Stimulators, movers and shakers, motivators, prime movers, holders of the life force. Inside each gene a *desire* to be alive! An intimate and inseparable relationship of life forces, of strong, weak, love and . . .

Bobby could not yet grasp, conceive, conceptualize, the primary forces within atoms, the subparticles, quarks, muons, and their relationship to atomic structure, to molecular structure, to genetic desire, to cellular communication, to the production and reproduction of cells, to the reproduction of aberrant cells.

He studied, searched, analyzed, pondered.

Hemoglobin is constructed—actively and purposefully assembled—of four porphyrin molecules "glued" to a molecule of iron. Herbicide poisoning has a destructive, though indirect, effect upon this bonding that can be measured in urine samples by testing for coproporphyrins. Reaching backward: TCDD has been shown to be stored in the fatty tissues of those exposed to Agent Orange. Reaching forward: Is there a way to flush the toxins from human fatty tissues without endangering other, more active tissues such as blood-producing bone marrow, or egg/sperm-producing sex organs? Maybe an in-home purge? Fast and deluge the organism with endless quantities of pure Endless Mountain water, enough to cause diarrhea? Chelation: The process of chelating, or combining, with a metallic ion to form a chelate; or to form a ring with one or more hydrogen bonds . . . Hydrogen bombs! Vaporize me!

The attempt to formulate a workable design exhausted him yet he pressed on. Chelation therapy introduces a chemical agent—how he abhorred that tag—that will combine, chelate, with a specific toxic element producing a precipitate that *can* be flushed from the organism. . . . Backward: to a conceptualization of the 2,4,5–T molecule, of the 2,3,7,8–TCDD molecule, to an analyzation of their surface topographies, to the reverse, inverse topographies, to picturing and constructing molecules with those reverse topographies—nature does it all the time, antibodies to antigens—which can key into the toxin, lock on, together fall to the "bottom" like a child's suspension of backyard dirt in a water-filled beach bucket.

He attempted to enter the mind, to be the mind of an experimental pathologist, toxicologist. "TCDD induces malignant tumors"—he addressed a conference within his mind—"in exposures as low as five parts per trillion . . . causes carcinomas of the liver, lungs, palate . . . testicular cancer, lymphomas and leukemias . . . delayed effects . . . more toxic than the most lethal nerve gas in the military arsenal . . . causing failure of all elements of the blood-forming system, causing victims to hemorrhage, to be defenseless to infections, essentially to deteriorate, literally to fall to pieces . . .

"Yet . . . But . . . However . . . TCDD is eliminated from human tissue via bile fluid from which, by which, it is transported to the intestines to be defecated . . . Yet . . . However . . . here it is reabsorbed, the enterohepatic cycle, recirculated to liver, lungs, bone marrow, the body constantly discarding and inadvertently recycling unwanted trash like pissing into the wind . . . Yet . . . if it could be chelated, combined, as if the wind ceased, combined perhaps with cholestyramine used as a salt binder in patients with high cholesterol, used as a chelation agent in kepone toxicity . . . then not reabsorbed but indeed deposited, the mark being left, the throne room's excreta whisked away by the simple act of depressing the lever."

Again he reached back, reached forward. What causes cancer? No! What caused my cancer? No! No! When I was wounded, light shrapnel in the legs, I did not say, "Corpsman, take *my* shrapnel out." Nay! I said,

"Medic, get this fucking shrapnel outta me!" I said, "Take this out. It's not mine. It belongs to the NVA." So take this cancer. Take this aplastic anemia. I didn't ask for it. I don't want it. It's not mine. It's somebody else's. Give it back to Dow. Give it back to Daddy Dow. What has caused this cancer that has attacked me? Is it the Agent Orange? Sara is certain. She is leading the technical information search, the search for new treatments. She is the advocate. She is addressing civic groups in my name. She is the leading advocate for veterans, for humans. Certainly TCDD is a trigger. But what pulled that trigger?! Is it something in me? Something deeper in me than the strict biomechanical process, the reaction to a toxicant that has cleaved the genetic lines of chromosome Δ allowing for translocation of gene x on arm q of the heavy chain to relocate to chromosome A where it lodged next to gene y which enables it, chromosome Δ, to evade the mechanism that controls its expression? Why was it set off in me, in this manner, and not in others who were equally exposed? Why in my bone marrow? Why my blood? Why, in affected others, did it trigger brain tumors, or liver . . . or testicular . . . ? And what, if it is something inate in me, beyond the biomechanical, is it? What is the triggering and the site selection determinant? And if it is beyond the physical, is it something I can reverse? Is this something, if I can determine the trigger, I can psychologically or spiritually untrigger? And if untriggerable, if chelated and flushed, what happens to the chromosomal damage previously done?

Bobby searched into himself for hours on end, day after day, week after week. He sent messages, explored hidden regions, sought information, gave orders. "Headquarters, free the infiltrators, expel the double agents, arrest the saboteurs." Can the damage be repaired? Can the war be won though major battles have been lost and the nation is on its knees? Will a win at Xuan Loc keep Saigon from falling?

Daily Bobby studied, contemplated, ruminated. Daily he unfocused, disciplined nonfocused meditation. He lay still, on his back, on the floor of Grandpa's office, alone, wrapped in a blanket, a bedroll, warm yet not aware of the warmth, secure though without cognition of that security. Over his eyes he laid the old OD jungle sweater that reduced the dimmed room to utter darkness, to the void in which the search could be continued. He looked in. He traveled to sites of unrestrained growth, of mutant self-destructive platelets. He attempted to spy on the man-made environmental toxins triggering the aberrant cellular mutations. He tried to infiltrate the mutants' base camp to discover their need for suicide. Why have you allowed these substances to enter the walled city of the cell? Why have you not expelled them? Why have you let them come to headquarters? Or have they simply gained control of the commo center, altered the messages and production orders, to their choosing? And why have you not recognized the abnormalities of the new structures? Why have you allowed them to replicate endlessly their chimeric clones? Or do they, themselves, or do you . . . ? Surely there is not and never has been a TCDD alien for each and every cell. Then why are all new cells aberrant? Surely the answer to this, like a change in the cultural norms of a society, explains the delayed onset of the disease, and like a society the aberration began with a tiny pocket of radical . . .

So what?!

Re-unfocus and flow. He is a microscopic entity, not matter, not energy, but thought represented within his unformation by a blue glow flowing within his own arteries, veins, capillaries, a pinball ball ricocheting from concave disks but 0.0003 inch in diameter, inspecting each; a blinking cursor in the three-dimensional holographic computer screen of his body, leaping through tissues, randomly interviewing a sample of the one hundred trillion cells of his being, checking that each contains an identical headquarters with identical blueprints—though with different assignments, tasks to perform, different rooms to construct, different systems to maintain—checking randomly, then comparing blueprints, finding that hair cells and skin cells and toe cells all know the proper way to make blood cells so how come the bone marrow that makes those blood cells is fucking up?!!! Fire the CEO! Chastize the nucleotidal foreman! Send in a . . . a what? A messenger with proper prints! "Ah, hey look, Buddy. You spilled coffee on yours and you're building the wrong stuff, Man. See? Here's a good set. I borrowed it from your patella."

"I'll make what the hell I want. Leave me alone."

"What? Man, you keep makin that shit, you'll kill us all."

"Says who? You follow your prints, I'll follow mine."

"Man . . . see, you spilled that TCDD coffee right there and the cell lysosome isn't complete and it's leaking its enzymes into the cytoplasm and causing quick self-destruction."

"Says who?! Where do you get off telling me my job?"

"Naw. Naw, Man. You don't understand. You keep doing that they goina poison your food. Hide somethin in the food that'll cause *your* lysosome-stomach to cramp until you're a goner, Man. Then they'll replace you. You know, Man, transfer in a bunch a scabs. Chemo followed by bone marrow transplant, Man."

"They wouldn't dare!"

. . . now feeling the warmth of the cocoon about him, then again not feeling it at all but sensing on some level that he is warm, protected, cared for as Sara cares for him, linked eternally, secure in this care, this warmth, this cocoon, liberated to deepen the search, millimeter by millimeter, nanometer by nanometer, searching for the commo line between triggered cells and healthy cells, searching through April, May and June.

The trigger must yet be something more, something else, something different. If the trigger is in me, or of me, what am I? I am more than the sum of my cells, more than a heap of organelles, just as a book is more than the linkage of words, more than a pile of letters. The relationship of the parts, the format, is essential. And the force that organizes the format is essential, is perhaps the life force, the soul, is the essential me. How has that force, how have I, gone awry? How can I right the bias? Trying to understand, trying to construct the parallel universes of mind and body, of corporeal and spiritual, attempting to unite them within a code, to explain them in The Code, in a search for the universal tie.

"Aren't you getting into the car?" Sara's words were quick, light. The early morning was delightfully cool.

"Hmm." Bobby turned, looked out across the pond, let his gaze fall on a pair of mallards by the near bank.

"I told Linda we'd meet them at River Front Park ten minutes ago," Sara said. "We're late." She slid in behind the wheel, turned, checked the children, insured they'd buckled their seatbelts. Bobby remained motionless, leaning against the car. It was to be their first real family vacation. With the Pisanos they'd rented a cottage on the Jersey Shore. "Bobby?"

"Um."

"Bobby, are you okay?"

"Yeah. It's—" his words came slowly, "that I'm just looking . . . at the ducks."

"Come on. Get in. Bobby . . . are you feeling okay?"

"I'm a little cold." He settled into the seat beside her. "And my head's pounding."

"Your crit's low?!"

"I just got a refill. . . . It's . . . I think it's because of my eye. It's like there's a blob of water over everything."

"Do you want the patch while we're moving?"

"No. Maybe. I'm going to just close my eyes awhile."

He rested his head on the seatback, zippered his jacket. In back Noah and Paul were drawing pictures, Am was munching a bagel, all being "good," being quiet, not irritating their father. The car rolled. Bobby sat up, took in the drive, the old gate, the orchard and Christmas trees. Then he closed his eyes again. He thought of Josh in Rodney Smith's care, felt like he was abandoning him. The thought didn't last. Almost immediately it was replaced by slight vertigo, by nausea, by pains in his joints, arms, butt. Pain, the inner experience, the thought, the word alone can induce it, enable it, allow it to spread. Pain, the process, exactly the opposite of DAARFE-vader, capable of being controlled by DAARFE, capable of destroying DAARFE. And cancer! What caused the . . . No. He would not think of it, would not meditate on it. This was vacation time. Time with his kids. And none in diapers! What JOY! Let Tony change little Johnny; Bobby was through that stage. Better to build sand castles . . . splash each other, maybe a sand dragon . . . maybe an entire sand city at the edge of the rising tide.

"Man, you all right?"

"I'm just kinda hot, Tone."

"Open your jacket, Bobby. You're all flushed."

"Shit! I can barely move my arm."

Tony pushed his hand through the open passenger window, laid the back of his fingers against Bobby's forehead. "Man! You're burning up!"

"No. I can't be. It'll be . . ."

"Sara?" Tony kept the alarm from his voice. Sara and he were changing places so he could drive with Bobby, Sara with Linda, the girls, and Johnny. "Sara?"

"It's nothin, Tone." Bobby leaned forward, smiled weakly. "I musta been leaning on it, put it to sleep." He raised his arm, began to unzip, leaned forward gasping. Tears welled to his eyes. Beneath his breath he muttered, "This is *our* vacation!" Then he leaned back, tightened his abdominal wall. More loudly to Tony he said, "Get in. We're goina have this time."

Bobby held out for three days. He built sand castles with Am, waded in the surf with Paul, let Noah bury his legs, winked at some bikinied beauties with Tony, and spent hours watching Sara. Then he could hold out no longer. His legs swelled, he could barely walk, had to ask Noah to help him, Noah so serious, only eight years old, had to ask him to be strong for his father.

On Wednesday 27 July 1983 Bobby returned not to the cottage at the Jersey Shore, not to High Meadow, but to the VA hospital in West Haven. His temperature had risen to 104. They started him on IV antibiotics and IM steroids. Doctors Dachik and Rosenwald prodded, poked, identified a grossly infected hematoma in his right arm. They stuck him, slit him open, sucked pus from his arm—not once, not twice, but over five days seven times. The direct pain and the throbbing pain were tremendous, yet were askew of the deep hematoma site and the first time they'd found only a small pocket, and the second too, and nothing the third and fourth until the ultrasound technician suggested Bobby tell the surgeon to do the next cut down right there in the lab so that the technician could show him the exact location. The fifth and sixth times the surgeons ignored the offer until so frustrated they did the seventh under ultrasound, stuck in the needle, dead center, and withdrew 70 ccs of blood.

"Did you hit it on something?"

"No," Bobby answered. "I don't think so."

"Maybe?" the doctor asked.

"So what if I did?"

"If you didn't," Dachik said, "it's possible that it was spontaneous. Spontaneous bleeds are significant."

"My condition's deteriorating, isn't it?"

"Not necessarily. It may be the low platelet count. We've some responses to that."

More tests. New fever spikes. More blood drawn. Another bone marrow biopsy, another Wednesday at the transfusion clinic. "You're platelet count is low. And . . ."

"And?"

"The tests show an increase in leukemic—"

"Leukemia!"

"There are a number—"

"Leukemia."

"...chemotherapy..."

Bobby was barely hearing.

"...treatment has come a long way in the last several years..." the voice empathetic, matter-of-fact, professional, personal.

"I'm a goner. Holy shit!"

"...you're very early in the leukemic process...a six-week course of cytotoxic...and cytosine arabinoside..."

Then, later, on the phone with Tony, afraid to tell Sara over the phone, "Leukemia."

"Bummer, Man."

"Yeah. Ambushed again."

Meditation: Mid-August—See them, he tells himself. Feel them. The august stem cells of the marrow produce immature or precursor clones that differentiate into specialized cells as they mature. Differentiation and maturation are controlled by specific inducer proteins produced by the stem cells or by other cells in the surrounding support tissues. Immature myeloid (marrow) stem cell clones become macrophages or granulocytes, erythrocytes, megakaryocytes, eosinophils or mast cells, depending on the inducer that binds to the immature cells' DNA. Picture this, he urges. See this. See the pool, the mixed-inducer ocean, with millions of immature floating rings. When these cells differentiate and mature, growth inhibitors, produced by the mature cells, block these cells from further multiplication. But leukemic cells—immature, undifferentiated—produce their own growth inducer independently of the stem or support tissue and this allows them to steadily, though nondifferentially, multiply immature clones. These immature clones do not produce differentiation inducers that would cause them to mature and stop reproducing. Picture it. See them. How can I turn on the differentiation-factor producers that might stop the uncontrolled growth of leukemic cells? How can I keep the leukemic cells from asynchronously producing their own differentiation factors?

Swimming in meditation, floundering: If all myeloid leukemic clones have abnormal chromosome arrays—that is, the deletion or malarrangement of a chromosome segment—how can that segment be restored or replaced? See it. See it happening. Expect it. What value knowledge if not...See it being fulfilled.

Bobby remained in the hospital through July and the first twenty-six days of August. On the twentieth he was interviewed by reporters from the *New Haven Register*, the *Hartford Courant*; on the twenty-first by a man from UPI. In them, in the media, Bobby found a strange bedfellow—truly interested, sympathetic investigative reporters delving into Agent Orange illnesses and death, exposing personal tragedies in America, Australia, Southeast Asia. They seemed delighted with the new mace, the new battleax with which to bash both the government and corporate America. Yet Bobby found in their seemingly sensational revelations, little ungrounded sensationalism.

"It's working?" the reporter asked. There was surprise in his voice.

"Seems to be," Bobby answered. For six days he had not spiked a temp. His platelet count and hematocrit were up. Other elements of his blood seemed to be responding. The fact that he had not had a fever all week indicated the new antibiotic regime was controlling his infections. He was up, out of bed, the July swelling in his legs gone. He walked the halls morning, noon, night, cautiously, afraid of bumping or being bumped, afraid of causing a new hematoma, yet anxious to be in motion.

The reporter sat in Bobby's room, making notes in a small cardboard-bound pad. Additionally he recorded the interview on a Panasonic microcassette. "Hmm. I thought you were much ... "

" ... closer to dying?" Bobby finished the question.

"More seriously ill," the reporter countered.

"It's serious." Bobby smiled. He liked the man, liked his direct yet relatively sensitive approach. "You want me to be dying, huh?"

"No Bobby, I don—"

"But it's a better story if I am."

"Unfortunately. Newspapers do want you to be dramatic."

"Well, I am." For half an hour Bobby explained his leukemia to the man, made certain the reporter understood the process, the short-of-a-miracle irreversibility, the temporary positive signs, responses to the chemo.

"You don't seem bitter," the reporter said.

"That comes and goes."

"If you had it to do all over again, would you go to Canada?"

"You mean ... Hell, no! I'd go again right now if I could."

"You would?!"

"I certainly would. I'd go back to Viet Nam in a minute. Shit ... I don't think I'd like the person I'd be if I hadn't gone. And if living with this pain ... is the price, then I'll take it. I've seen the best. And the worst. But seeing the best, the very best, seeing it just once inspires one forever. That makes it worth it."

"Worth dying for?"

"Yes. It was worth it then. The cause. It sucks now ... being sick ... having these constant reminders that your body's self-destructing. But that doesn't change the value of the cause. Still, I won't let a Dow product in my house."

"What about your sons? You have boys, don't you?"

"I ... " Bobby paused, his mind raced, his face reflected anguish.

"If they were to be drafted . . ." the reporter began.

"They won't be." Bobby turned hard, surface hard, voice hard, but inside, flashing on Noah, on Paul, juxtaposing them to Hamburger Hill, to the A Shau, to the mud and violence in a way he had never imagined, inside he turned sour, clammy. "No way," Bobby said. "The government's gotten enough Wapinskis."

Saturday, 27 August 1983, High Meadow—"Bobby's home."

"He's been waiting for ya, Man," Rodney said. "Every day. Every mornin, ya know? I let him out an he disappears. Then I find him by the road. Just sittin. Waitin for ya. He makes me call im a hun'red times. I don't think he hears anymore. He's gettin awful old."

Bobby slid his hands over Josh's head, kneaded the base of the dog's ears. "Aw, good ol' Josh. Good boy." Josh groaned, stood, leaned in, then shook his head. Bobby rocked back. "Don't bump me, Boy. There." Josh stopped, looked up. Bobby sighed. "Ah . . . let me just scratch your ears."

"Hey Man. Good you're back. You made the front page of the paper."

"I did?"

"Yeah. Look at this

DYING VET BACKS
CHEMICAL COMPANIES

Says He'd Go Again

"Says I backed who?"

"Hey, you're a celeb. UPI. That's carried all over the country. Calls you a 'self-made man.' Talks about you as a 'manufacturer of environmental products.' Let's see, 'entrepreneurial spirit upon which America was founded . . .' I liked this part. 'Wapinski claims that the causes over which America went to war were noble and just and that Agent Orange was a legitimate weapon in the fight against communism.' "

"That's not what I said."

"It says here you hope your corporation will become as large and as powerful as Dow Chemical. That you hope someday to be in the same manufacturing association."

"No, that's not what I said at all."

Later that afternoon Bobby took Josh into the barn. They climbed aboard the creaky old homemade elevator constructed for Pewel a decade earlier. Slowly it raised the old dog and the frail man up to the loft. They entered Grandpa's office, opened the thermal curtains letting the room flood with light. For nearly an hour Bobby sat, scratching Josh's ears, both just sitting, Bobby covering one eye, looking out at the farm, the pond, the woods, thinking of the gap, wondering if he could ever again attempt that hike or walk through the cathedral of eastern hemlock or sit at the fire circle.

After a time Bobby removed the file of ideas and notes, of half-written thoughts and collected articles, that he had labled "The High Meadow Code." The file was thick. Indeed it was not a single file but three files: one with articles on environmental policies and plans; one with the best thoughts and plans for housing, energy, and a sustainable future; and one, the main file, containing Bobby's own writings. Slowly, purposefully, he spread the sheets, sorted them into beginning and end, into myriad central elements. By the time the work was spread and organized it was eight o'clock, dark. Josh had slept through Bobby's labor. Now, happily, he rose, nuzzled Bobby's legs, descended with him to the main floor, returned to the house.

Sara was hurt. Angry. Bobby apologetic. Sara, her back to Bobby as she washed the dinner dishes, "Can't you spend some time with us?"

"I'm sorry. I lost track of the time."

"Noah's really upset about that 'Dying Vet' story. He spent all evening decoding it."

"I'll talk to him. I . . . You remember Granpa's code?"

"Uh-huh."

"I want to finish that. That story, you know, 'the self-made man' stuff. It set me thinking about all . . . like Granpa used to say, 'Civilization is a gift.' We think we're so independent yet really everyone of us is heir to this incredible complex structure that passes on language and light, everything from when to cut your toenails to advanced chemical treatments which can reverse aging and disease processes. It passes to us an education system which bathes us in inducer factors which cause us to differentiate into functionally different individuals which civilization requires to remain healthy."

"Bobby—" Sara turned from the sink, "what are you talking about?"

"About the inducers of greed and the inducers of altruism."

"Maybe you should talk to Noah."

Then, with Noah, halfway up the stairs, seated like two buddies plotting a caper, "You get more publicity," Bobby said softly, "if the newspapers . . . They want you to be dying."

Noah's eyes opened wide. "Can they do that?"

"No. They have no effect on my health. What I mean is, in their story, if I sound like I'm dying, it makes for a more dramatic story."

"Oh."

"It gets more sympathy and they sell more papers that way," Bobby said.

"And the chemical company," Noah asked, "do you really back it?"

"No. He misquoted me. I was explaining to him that we had a small company. That all companies aren't bad. That lately it seemed to me the media, you know . . . "

"Uh-huh."

" . . . has tried to paint them all, ah . . . to describe them all as if they were all poisoning the environment. I said to him, What does that do to our civilization? To our children? If we eliminate the production-inducer from the bathing solutions of our culture . . . " Bobby paused, simplified his explanation. "What attitudes will children have, when they're grown, toward producing, toward working with materials, with their hands? Will they know how to work? Will they understand the benefits of manufacturing?"

"I know how to work."

"I know you do. You're an excellent worker. I'm very proud of you when you tinker out in the shop. But the papers, and especially TV, give us the impression all manufacturing is bad for—"

Noah broke in, "If you went back to Viet Nam, you'd leave us."

"I . . . but . . . "

"It says you said you'd go back."

"Hmm. That's . . . Noah, I can't explain that to you. That's the nature of guys who were airborne. Why we agreed to go in the first place. But I wouldn't leave you to go there. I love you guys too much, and Mama, to go now."

On Sunday morning Bobby and Sara took the children to Mass at St. Ignatius. Then, back home, Bobby again retreated with Josh to Grandpa's office.

PREAMBLE—DRAFT
Before I am a living being I am an element of the earth . . .

All afternoon Bobby wrote, rewrote, conceptualized, diagrammed the Ascending Line of Life, and the Great Flowing Circle of Nourishment. When it was again near dark he returned to the house.

On the twenty-ninth of August he spiked a temp of 101.

All the way up Bobby was nauseated, freezing. He lay, in the stifling car, the windows opened but a slit, wrapped in a blanket, one end over his head, covering his eyes. His head hurt. He lay rigid, seemingly holding on for dear life even though Tony drove more smoothly than he'd ever driven in his life.

The pain was different than all other pains Bobby had experienced. Other pains—mental, emotional, physical—had always, after the initial onset, given him strength, given him insight, stirred him to action. But this pain robbed him of focus, of his disciplined nonfocus, forced him to concentrate vaguely on himself. His body seemed to react to its self-destruction with a physical terror he could not control.

"This is not me . . . " Tony heard him mumbling under the blanket. "Grant me the strength and courage to try hard . . . " Fragmented thoughts or fragments escaping, seeping outward, reaching Tony's ears, making Tony want to accelerate, to get there faster, yet afraid of bumps, of jars, of causing a bruise that might start an uncontrollable bleed. "I could run the Dipsea . . . I've climbed the Indian ladder carrying Josh . . . I could play full-court for hours . . . "

"Hey Bobby, you hear the one about the bulimic party?"

Bobby only groaned.

"You know the difference between a rubber tire and three hundred and sixty-five used condoms?"

"What?"

Tony sighed inwardly. He'd broken through, gotten Bobby off himself. "One's a Goodyear. One's a *really* good year."

A laugh, a groan. Silence. Tony's mind scanning for new jokes. He heard more mutterings.

" . . . and to never give up."

Labor Day, 1983, was September 5th—Sara was required to be in her classroom on Friday the 2d and again Tuesday the 6th. Students returned on the 7th. Sara did not come to West Haven on the 30th but came instead, for two days, on Saturday the 3d, her 36th birthday.

At this time, Josephine Pisano moved into the farmhouse at High Meadow, nearly full-time. Through September John Pisano Sr. went up daily. He brought up Johnny, who was now eighteen months, and who liked being with Am and Paul. Noah, assumed the roles of teacher, baby-sitter, supervisor, director. Jo cooked, cleaned, did the laundry. Linda helped. Annalisa assisted. John Sr. puttered in the gardens, fixed the wobbly front porch railing. Sara taught full-time, worked when she came home, still hosted rap-group meetings—the women's group, the couples' group—in the living room on Tuesday and Wednesday nights, and let the old staff run, covertly, new barn sessions. Sara was responsible, too, for the farm—planning, with Tony, ordering, overseeing, with Tony, paying bills, alone, paying percentages to Miriam, Joanne and Brian, and, alone, by arrangement, virtually everything else to the IRS. Every night she called; every Friday she packed up the kids, headed to West Haven. Every Sunday night she returned. Everything she did, work, chores, time with the children, with the groups, was scheduled around Bobby—getting to see him, talk to him, help him. And every week, almost every day, there was something new: a new infection, new fever, new bleed. Every day throughout September Bobby was scheduled for a possible surgery the next day. Every day, at High Meadow or in West Haven, Sara attempted to find, to convince, matching platelet donors. The fear of another transfusion reaction was constant. The fear of bleeds was continuous, of infections, of not having the money to make the trip, of paying everyday bills, the old Chevy giving out . . . The list was endless.

And every day, something new.

"That's how paranoid I am," Bobby told Tony. "It's the steroids. The doc thinks they're responsible for my rib. I'm afraid . . . I could stand up and my ankle might crumble. Or I could blow my nose and bleed to death."

To Tony it wasn't real, wasn't fully tangible. Bobby looked frail but not so frail. Back on IV antibiotics and transfused he sounded healthy. Whatever unacknowledged fatalism his body held, his conscious actions did not betray. Then his crit would fall. Then a new infection or an unfound infection would erupt, re-erupt. Then Bobby's mind would sag, cave in upon itself, and he would have to fight to rise to zero, to overlook positive; and his doctors would grasp at new treatments, attempting to find the specific yet elusive magic bullet for his changing condition.

—Another bone marrow. "To see how fast the leukemia is spreading, growing," Doctor Dachik told him. "If it's the slow-growing kind, a very slow-growing leukemia . . . well, the chances of you surviving a slow-growing leukemia are greater than of you surviving chemotherapy."

"Huh!"

"If it's the fast-growing variety . . . chemo will be . . . "

"A last ditch effort?"

—"Ahhh! No change from the last biopsy. No chemo."

—"Sorry. Low-level chemo. A continuation of the August treatment but changing the mixture . . . "

—"Sorry. Another bleed. We need a chest X-ray. Need a gallium scan. Need a CAT scan."

—"You're still popping fevers."

"I know. One oh one, eight. That's the highest . . . "

—"Seems to be a hairline fracture. . . . Can't find it. . . . Could be a pleural effusion. . . . Could be . . . "

—"The multiple transfusions and the ensuing bilirubin have caused gall stones which may be the source of the infection . . . gall bladder . . . removal . . . "

"Forget it! It took you guys seven times to do my arm. We're talking periphery there. You're talking deep inside . . . "

—Tony: 20 September: "What the hell you doin here, Man? Are you ready to die? What are you stayin in the VA system for? You got leukemia. That's curable, Man. You don't have to die from leukemia. Hey! Look! What the fuck do you think the VA's goina do for ya? The VA wants you to die! It cost them money to have you in here. You're not payin. They're not makin a profit on you. You cost them money! It is in their best interest if you die quickly. They're not trying to cure you. Get your fuckin act together, Man. Get the fuck out of this hospital. Get your . . . Aah, stop feelin sorry for yourself and get your ass up to Boston General or to that Jewish hospital out on Long Island that specializes in leukemia. Man, they'll have you in remission in five, six weeks."

Bobby chuckled. "And who's going to pay . . . "

"I will. I'll sell my house."

"No you won't."

"I'm serious, Bobby. It's not you. It's not part of you. Why do you need it? You don't need to be sick for me. We're all sick of you being sick."

"Me too."

"Man," angrily, "you're letting it do to you whatever it wants. And you're saying, 'Look what it's doing to me.' "

Joking. "Makes a good media show."

"Fuck it! Fuck them hangers-on. Those bastards hooked on tragedy. Don't mean nothin, Bobby. What means somethin is what you're going to do about it. Your words."

"My words?"

"Uh-huh."

—On Friday the 23d Sara and the children arrived to celebrate Paulie's sixth birthday with Bobby. Aside, while Bobby blew on a noisemaker, Noah explained to Tony, "I'm eight and a half. Pop's going to buy me a bicycle when I'm nine." And a little later Am said, "Pawpee, know what? For my birthday I want you to get big and strong again."

—On the 26th: "Don't tell Sara."

"What?"

"Do you remember Stacy Carter?"

"Oh yeah! Great—"

"She sent me a card."

"Yeah?"

"Yeah. You know, nothin much. Just a blank card. An Ansel Adams photo of Half Dome in Yosemite. And a 'Get Well Soon' written inside."

"Who's the cute doctor down there with the nice legs?"

"Her? I don't like cute doctors. She makes me nervous. She always wants to see my butt. I hate that. Leave me alone. I'm sweaty. I stink . . ."

—Tuesday the 27th—Tony on the phone to Linda. "They just aspirated 300 cc of blood from a pleural effusion which was causing his lung to collapse. They want to reenter the cavity with a larger needle but they're afraid that might create even more bleeding. They want to try but his bleeding time, you know, in you or me it's maybe two minutes, they can't do surgery if it's over nine minutes, and even after infusing ten units of platelets and rushing him to the OR his bleeding time was twenty-five and a half minutes!!! It's driving him crazy. Sara too. It seems, you know, because of potential liability . . . Good God! Like how much more liable and how much greater remuneration . . . Shit . . . Seems every night they ask him to sign a permission and liability release agreement okaying the next day's procedure. And he knows full well that he's approving a procedure that could cause him to bleed to death. . . . "

—On the 28th of September they suspended the chemotherapy, explaining to Bobby that it might be the chemo, not the leukemia, which was causing the bleeds; explaining further his options: full guns chemo, change the chemo, no chemo. Over the next few days he agreed to a two-month ceasefire to give his body a chance to regroup, rest, rearm enough to sustain him through the next chemo battle.

—"Bob, the problem is we can't seem to stop the bleeds."

—"Bob, the problem is you keep spiking these temps."

—"Bob, I've got to be straight with you. There's only a ten percent chance you'll survive a full course of traditional chemo."

—Sunday, October 9th: "Don't tell him."

"I know. But he should be told."

"It'll kill him. You know how attached . . . "

"What if one of the children says . . . It would be better if he were told."

"No. Shit! Poor Josh."

"You know he couldn't hear anymore. I'm sure he never heard the car. You know how he was always down there at the road."

"Yeah. Rodney's really broken up over it. He blames himself."

—Monday, 15 October: "Full guns chemo, Bob. Your choice. It's designed to force the cells to differentiate and mature but it will make you very ill. Nauseous, vomiting, hair loss, and there's only a ten percent chance . . . "

To chemo or not to chemo?

Bobby explained it to Sara, detached, as if he were saying, "One b.l.t. coming up. Mayo or no mayo?"

She couldn't answer. She let him talk on. "It's like attacking a hill," he said. "You attack it because if you don't, it means eventual defeat and loss of the entire country. But by attacking we risk immediate defeat, yet there is hope for eventual victory. Even if it's only one percent, you go for it."

Sara touched her chin, ran her hand down onto her neck. She despised the green walls of his room, the buffed aluminum frame of his bed, the uncomfortable chair for visitors in which she'd spent so many days. If it means . . . she thought but she could not say that. She tilted her head, gazed at Bobby. "When?" she asked softly.

"Not till after Thanksgiving," Bobby said. "When my strength's up."

Bobby reached out his arm. Sara grasped his hand. Bobby winked. "You better go," he said. "It'll be dark before you hit New York."

"Um. Guess I'd better."

"Give me a call when you get in so I know you're safe."

"I might wake you."

"I'll feel better if I know. Give the kids a hug for me, too."

Through October, into November, Sara came every weekend. Every weekend she brought the children. They visited twice each day but spent most of their weekend time at the Boyers'. Tony had stayed Monday through Friday in September, but less time as the fall progressed. Don Wagner filled some of the gaps: and Jeremiah Gallagher, and Carl Mariano, Tom Van Deusen, Kevin Rifkin, Rodney Smith, Renneau, Denahee, Fernandez, Bechtel and Hacken. Each pulled his stint at guard, at watch, never leaving Bobby without someone close by.

Through October and into November Bobby's condition worsened. Some days he read. Some days he wrote letters. Some days he talked with other patients or with official visitors—a local Catholic priest, a national reporter—or with whichever vet was up from High Meadow.

But visitors were discouraged. Bobby was technically, if not practically, in reverse isolation. Visitors were required to wear masks, gowns and gloves so as not to expose his frail immune system to worldly viruses. The rules were not enforced and Bobby seldom mentioned it to anyone. Instead he closed his door. A week before Halloween, he began recording the tapes.

Hi Noah. This is your pop. I'm talking to you on a tape recorder at the West Haven VA. Today is Wednesday, October 26th. I'd rather be with you but right now I can't be and I want to say some things to you I may never have the chance to say.

You are my eldest son and I love you very much. The day you were born was the happiest day of my life. If I close my eyes I can see you and hear you on the day you spoke your first word, the day you first learned to walk holding on to Josh, the first time you went to camp, your first day of school. How proud you were to walk up the steps of the bus that first time. Most recently I think of you at the beach, burying me in the sand, then running for the surf and turning back to me and saying, "Let's go!" You're already a great person, a great brother to Paul and Am. Always believe in yourself. Listen to your heart. Noah, you've a good heart and a good mind. When someone's yelling at you for something, judge yourself. Trust yourself. Trust your feelings, Noah. Even if it is Mama yelling at you. You've a good soul, a good mind, and a good heart. Look inside yourself for answers.

That's the essence. Here come the particulars. The drug that I'm about to take might kill me. And if it does, then you'll have this tape to remember me by. If it doesn't, you'll simply never have this tape. There's so much I want to say to you, because I love you so much. I don't want my death to be something that ruins your life. I don't want it to be an excuse for you to not achieve all you're capable of. Rather it should be a reason for you to succeed. To be the best person you can be. And the happiest. I guess I worry more about you than I do Paul or Am because, well, you are the oldest.

And I guess the biggest problem right now is, I don't feel I'm going to die. I think this drug is going to work. And I'm going to get better. And you and I, Paulie and Am and Mama, we'll have a great life together.

One of the most important things I want to say, Noah, is I don't want to see you in a war. I don't want you killing anybody. And I don't want anybody hurting you. That may sound selfish, and people are going to give you arguments about loyalty to country and duty to humanity. You remember this. You remember how sick your Pop was. And you see what loyalty and duty did for him. See how loyal the country was to him when he needed them most. Noah, you don't have to go into the service to prove to anyone you are a man. You are going to be a fine young man. There is no doubt about it. Should you *need* to fight, pick your causes and your battles carefully. And be equally careful picking your allies. No matter your strength, no matter your fire power, a weak pointman can lead you into a kill zone.

I hope you stay active in sports all through school. It shows respect for your physical body. And please study. Do your best. It shows respect for your mind.

I don't have to tell you to love your mother. You do. And you always will. I know that. But don't forget that you have your own life, too. And don't be afraid to explore that. I hope that you and Paul and Am will always be friends, and that all of you and Mama will always be a family that helps each other. And if you get married and have children, you can go to Mama's house and the grandchildren will be there, and that you're all happy. That's what I want for you, Noah. I want you to experience the elation of learning and doing, loving and growing, living and expanding.

I want you to remember that you have responsibilities, too. When you get old enough to drive, don't you do any of that drinking and driving business. And when you're dating, remember, treat the girls with respect. You have responsibilities. I certainly hope you don't get any young girl pregnant. That's one of your responsibilities. There's nothing wrong with being a virgin when you graduate high school. I was, and you still were born.

I wish I could hold you right now. You're always the one that comes back for a special hug. You were such a beautiful baby, and are such a handsome boy. And strong! I love you, Noah. I loved you from the moment you were born. I was so proud and so worried that day. You had respiratory distress and had to be suctioned a number of times and I stood by you every time watching over you. Someday you'll be on your own, standing on your own two feet. And you're going to do just fine. You're very fortunate. You have a mother who really cares, who loves you and takes care of you. And you have a brother and a sister who put up with you when you become "the Director." You're good at that. As you get older you'll learn how to do that with a lot more class. It's called selling. And it's called leadership. Lead by principles. By a code.

I think about all the things that could have been between you and me. All those little milestones in your life when I'd like to be there. When you turn sixteen. When you graduate from high school and college. When you get married. When your children are born. I'd like to be there to see the smile on your wonderful face. To pat you on the back and say, "Way to go, Kiddo."

I feel so frustrated. I never knew my father. And I want to be a Pop for you as long as I can. I hate this disease, Noah. It's taking me away from you. It's stopping me from being a Pop. I made it without a mother, too, so you're light-years ahead of me. Your mother and I love you so much. We're rooting for you all the way. I want to be there with you just to see the look in your eye.

This is an important point, Noah. You are worth all the good things that can happen to you. You are worth having a good life. You are worth all the blessings of God. One thing I don't want you to worry about, you're not going to get what I have. It is not something that is passed down from father to son. You're healthy. Agent Orange has not affected you. Don't worry about it. Just go out there and live your life.

I don't want to say good-bye. There's so much I want to say, I could ramble on for hours. I want to hang on, Kiddo. I don't want to leave you. Don't blame yourself for what's happened to me. You had nothing to do with this. Don't blame God, either. All the good things in the world came from God. You and Paul and Am came into Mama's and my lives from God. And Mama came into my life, not by some fluke, but she was a gift. When you were little babies people used to say, "What do you do with little babies?" And we'd say, "You cherish them. Ya hug em and you hold em close." I cherish you, now, Noah. Still. Always. I'd love to see you become a man. I can imagine what you're going to be like when you're a teenager. Oooo-weee! It makes me happy right now thinking about you having a great time.

It's hard to talk right now. There's a lot of noise in the hall. I feel good today. I think I'm getting better. I want to get better. I don't ever want to give you this tape. I'd be happy just watching you get up in the morning, making you breakfast, seeing you go off to school. Maybe that sounds boring but to me it sounds like a great life. You know, Mama brought your picture, and Paulie's and Am's. It's on my bedside table. I look at you, at all of you and I say to myself, "There it is! Because of them, I'm going to get out of here." That's what you do for me. Because of you and because of Mama, I'm fighting real hard to get better.

You've brought so much joy into my life, Noah. I want to thank you from the bottom of my heart. Thank you for being you. I'm not going to say good-bye. I don't want to say good-bye.

Take care, Noah. Love yourself. Think good things about yourself. I love you.

On Thursday the 27th Bobby made a similar tape for Paul, with specifics just for his second son. In this tape Bobby's voice was weaker. And he did not mention recovering. On Friday the 28th he made a tape for Am.

. . . God blessed me with being able to be there when you were born. And it was scary and it was beautiful all at the same time. We counted your fingers and your toes. I counted them for Mama. And I told her you were definitely a girl. And all your fingers and toes were there.

And the tears that your Mama cried, the tears of joy. She was so happy. You were so beautiful. And all your fingers and toes were there. You were perfect. You were the prettiest baby born that day. When other parents would come to see their babies they'd see you in the little bassinet in the nursery, they'd point to you and they'd say, "Isn't that a beautiful baby." And it's true. I was in love with you—well, I was in love with you the moment I knew Mama was pregnant. And I fell in love with you again the day you were born. And again the first night I changed your diaper. And the first night you slept in the crib that Granpa made. As a matter of fact, I slept under the crib that night because I was afraid you'd be lonely. Now you're getting older and I love you even more. I guess that's why this is so hard. I want to get big and strong for you again. You're going to be a beautiful young lady and by the looks of it, I won't be there.

That's not really true.

I will always be there—my spirit will be with you—never to look over your shoulder but there for you, to give you strength. That is what comes to us and is available to us always from our ancestors and especially from father to daughter. I'll always be there with you, I'll always enjoy your pleasures, your joy at having your first child, at winning games, at every achievement—when you have your own company, when you are chairperson of the board, when you are president. Know that when things are tough, when things look bleakest, that I am in you to help you and to give you strength. You are a precious person. You are my daughter.

When I die, my spirit will pass on to you. You will have all my strengths plus all of your own. And because there is Noah and Paul, the strength is multiplied. When I spoke to Noah, on his tape, I said I will miss most of all not watching you three grow up. But I know now that I will not miss that. No, I will always be watching. I will smile with your smiles and cry with your tears as I now know my granpa and granma have watched over me. My wonderful children, if ever you feel sad or weak or down, if ever all things seem to be set against you, dig down, dig deep into yourselves, and you will find strength. There is strength in you that you don't even know. Some of it comes from me, through me, from the beginning of time. My love for you grows every day and in the next life it will know no bounds.

Mill Creek Falls, 31 October, 6:00 P.M.—They looked like the descending bars of a xylophone. Michelle was dressed as a skeleton, Gina as a ghoul; then Adam, Nate (John and Molly's boys) and Noah as Ninja warriors; then Paul as He-Man; Am as She-Ra; Johnny as a pumpkin; and finally Mark Jr., the newest Pisano, as either a mummy or a bowl of spaghetti. Mark and Cindy had agreed to take them all trick-or-treating. John and Molly went to get the pizzas. Linda and Tony were alone, setting the table for the return of the masked marauders, ooooing and ahhhing at the costumes of the children who rang their bell. Tony was in no mood for the party, felt guilty not leaving for West Haven, not being with Bobby on this Monday.

"Don't pour the soda yet," Linda said.

"Why not?"

"It'll go flat before they get back."

"Oh." Dull. He sounded and felt numb.

"Babe, please don't pour it."

"Oh! Geez. I didn't even realize . . . " Tony stopped, stood still, blurted, "What do you think of macrobiotic diets?"

"You're thinking of Bobby, huh?"

"Yeah."

"I've seen some articles that suggest they can be effective. I've seen others which say they lack basic nutrients."

"You know what he said to me? He said he wanted a pine coffin."

"Oh." A pause, then, "How's he looking?"

"He . . . he's wasting away. He's just wasting away. He's getting these sores on his arms and in his mouth. There's nothing left to him." Tony's voice dropped off. He began filling the plastic cups with soda again.

"It's terrible," Linda said. "It's a terrible thing."

"I don't know. . . . " Tony stopped again, realized again he was pouring the soda. "He said he wanted it lined with burlap. And he said it should be pegged not nailed together and the handles should be pine also. He wants me to make it."

"His coffin?!"

"Uh-huh."

"Why would he want—"

"So it'll rot. He wants to be buried near his grandfather and grandmother. Without any concrete vault. So his body might return to the earth and nourish—that's what he said—nourish future plants and animals."

"Are you going to do it, Babe?"

"I . . . I hate thinking about it. I hate playing his nurse. I hate playing his good buddy. Do you remember, he used to have blond hair. He used to be really hard. Sinewy. I don't know what's keeping him alive."

"You are, Babe. All of you."

Sara too was depressed, exhausted. Though she had spent the weekend in West Haven it had almost been as if she'd never left Pennsylvania. The exhaustion was numbing. And frightening. Sunday night, on the way home, with the children in the car, coming up the last stretch of dark road from Eagles Mere, she'd nodded at the wheel, been jarred awake by the tires bouncing in the grass and by the slapping of small branches against the windows.

She sat in the bedroom. The children were with Tony and Linda. She sat, numb, slowly gazing from one object to the next, not actually seeing them, thinking though she did not want to think it, What will it be like after he dies? Will I meet someone else? Someone who doesn't have all these problems? Oh, what a horrible thought. What a horrible person I've become. How could I . . . I didn't even call . . . Thank God Jo's helping. I couldn't . . . Oh God, this cancer has taken over my life too! I can't breathe. I can't think. I can't sleep. How can I teach? How can I bear this cross?

For three weeks all was status quo—the trips, the worry, the prayers, the exhaustion. Except for Bobby. He'd gained a few pounds. His voice was strong, and the sores in his mouth and on his arms were healing. On Wednesday morning, the 23d of November, the day after Am's fourth birthday, Bobby called his mother.

"Three-one-five-four."

"Hi. Happy Thanksgiving."

"Who is this?"

"It's your son, Rob."

"Oh, Rob. Thanksgiving isn't until tomorrow."

"I thought I'd call early. How are you?"

"My condition's worse. My ankles are swollen. My knees ache. And you know how my stomach is. I went to the doctor's, three different doctors in the past three weeks. But they can't find anything. I think they say that so they can do more tests. Did you know that most of the labs are owned by doctors?"

"Really?"

"Yes. And . . . " Miriam rambled on, "this one said . . . Then that one gave me . . . Then I took . . . I already had that test but I couldn't tell Doctor Denham because I didn't tell him I was seeing . . . " Finally, "Why did you call?"

"Just to say Happy Thanksgiving."

"Did you catch something from one of those girls you go with?"

"What?!"

"Those floozies. That redhead! I don't think our family will ever live that down."

"What red . . . You mean . . . "

"And that Carter girl! She's been married five times."

"I don't think s . . . "

"But you're all right?"

"Huh? I've got . . . "

"From that floozie. Is she part Negro?"

"Sara?!"

"Oh, if Mrs. Meredith ever saw her . . . You know, you could move back here. You could leave that floozie and come home."

"Back off. That's not what I called for."

"Well, if that's not what you called for, why did you call?"

"Do you know that I'm very ill? From Agent Orange."

"Oh, come, Rob! Agent Orange is a crock of poo. I saw that on TV. Now if you'd been a decent young man . . . "

"I don't believe I'm listening to this."

"Just as long as you remember the check. Why didn't you sign it last time? How come *she* signed it? It wasn't even—"

Bobby hung up. His arms were shaking. His breathing was shallow.

By the time Sara and the children arrived, along with Tony, Linda, and their children, and Don Wagner and Tom Van Deusen, Bobby had calmed. But tiredness lingered.

Sara acted as gatekeeper. She would not allow the visitors to enter en masse. She parceled his time, granted them brief audiences, even Noah, Paul and Am.

"I've got something for you."

"What, Pawpee?"

"It's your birthday, isn't it?"

Am wiggled. "Uh-huh."

"Give me your hand." The little girl reached up, grasped Bobby's hand. He squeezed. "How's that?"

"What?" She giggled.

"Pretty strong, huh?"

"Uh-huh."

"You told me you wanted me to get strong for your birthday. So I did."

"Can you give me a piggyback ride?"

"I don't have any clothes on."

"Ye-ees youz do!"

"Just pajamas. Maybe next time. I . . . I gave Uncle Tony your present. Did he give it to you?"

"Uh-huh. I got a crown."

"A tiara, huh? That's because you're a princess. It's a magic tiara."

Paul came in. Shy, quiet. "I love you, Paulie. Hold my hand a minute."

"I love you too, Papa."

"Trust your own heart in all things. Do you know what that means?"

"No."

"Trust yourself."

"Don't go, Papa."

"I won't. I'm so glad you're my son."

Then came Tony. "How ya doin, Man?"

"Ah, the kids . . . you know, I really want em here but it's a real struggle."

"Hey—" Tony's face brightened. "You know the definition of a real good buddy?"

Bobby began to chuckle. "No."

"He's a guy," Tony said, "who goes to town and gets two blow jobs, then comes back and gives you one." They both laughed. "Maybe," Tony continued, "you heard the one . . . "

Noah entered, remained, came out, came to the solarium waiting room, sat on Tony's lap. "Pop says, on my birthday, he's going to teach me to ride a bike. He's going to tell me tomorrow. I'm going to come back tomorrow and he's going to tell me. Just Pop and me."

On Thanksgiving morning Noah had the sniffles and Sara decided neither the children nor the adults, except Tony, should enter Bobby's room, should expose him, immunologically spent, to a potentially lethal virus. Instead they talked, gestured, waved from the hallway. By evening Sara would not let the children be exposed to the sight of their father.

He was frail. His hair was gray. A large patch had fallen out from one side making it look as if there was a hole there. From morning to evening his entire countenance changed. The sores that had been healing cracked and oozed and Linda helped the nurse re-bandage Bobby's arms and legs with white gauze, and his back with large patches. His eyes teared. He drooled, coughed up bloody mucus.

"Where am I?"

"You're at the West Haven VA." Sara's voice was firm, controlled.

"Is this our house?"

"Yes."

"We live here?"

"Yes. We live here."

Bobby's words began to slur. "You and me?"

"Yes. You and I."

"Just you and I?"

"Yes."

"What about Josh? Where's Josh?"

"He's . . . upstairs."

"Good."

In the hallway, Sara, "Tony, take the children home."

"Okay. I'll drive em, then come back. Or Linda could drive . . . "

Word spreads quickly in a small town. By Friday it seemed everyone knew Bobby was dying. And everyone was upset.

She banged on the door.

Miriam answered. "Yes."

"Mrs. Wapinski?"

"Cadwalder-Wapinski. Who are you?"

"Josephine Pisano. I've been taking care of your grandchildren for three months."

"Oh. Which ones?"

"How could you?! Your son is dying!"

Now defensive, her voice sharp, piercing, "How could I what?!"

"If I had only one kidney, or one lung, or my heart, and one of my children needed it . . . "

"Well, I'm not you!"

"You didn't even go for the blood test. Three hundred of his friends went. They're his true family. You wouldn't lose anything. You—"

Miriam slammed the door.

The road, the dirt mud road with the stone wall running to the mountain, the paddy. Why am I in white? In white! Snipers! In white. Next. Cover me, Man. One more assault, Sir. We almost had em last time. We lost three bodies . . . Ty? Ty! Ty, go over . . . up Man, cover me, we'll have a beer when this is over. Then we'll talk. Next. Not that one. Put him in the . . . One more sunrise. One more first light. Are you my dad? Dad! Dad, I'm just like you. Am I just like you? Death is unlife. Death is not being part of life. Death is an inducer of false exile, false estrangement, false expatriation. One more first light, Josh, ol' Buddy. Good buddy . . . two blow jobs . . . mallards on the pond. You don't have to scare em. Look at those hinges. They'll last a hundred years. Who'll cut the Christmas trees? Put this one in the corner . . .

For a week Bobby's hallucinations, flashbacks, periods of confusion and delirium flip-flopped with periods of total lucidity. His physical deterioration was erratic. At times, though bedridden, he seemed strong. Emotionally, when lucid, he was confident. Twice he received whole blood transfusions. Twice he received platelets. Three times his antibiotic mixture was adjusted. On Wednesday, 7 December, the hematologists began a new chemotherapy, a totally new treatment that had never before been used on leukemics. Dachik was hopeful. Wilcoxson had reservations. Before deciding, he had outlined the procedure, the theoretical response, the actual response in culture and animal studies. Bobby, totally lucid, had asked a multitude of questions, had read the new permission-to-treat form, signed it, signed too a form titled Permission to Perform Autopsy. "Don't withdraw on me now, Doc," Bobby had said to Lily Dachik.

"As long as you understand the risks," she'd countered.

Bobby'd smiled. "Let's give it a shot. No pussy-footin around. We're not politicians. We don't have to do just enough to appease . . . "

"Bob—" Wilcoxson had laid a hand on Wapinski's bed but had not touched him. "We're at a very critical point. But I don't want you to think last shot and give up."

"No, Doc. Really. I understand. We're going to get through this."

"We're going to get through this," Bobby repeated to Tony that evening. He was nauseated. The new chemo was kicking in.

"Yeah." Tony wanted to believe, wanted to sound up, sound positive. "Hey, I ever tell ya—"

"About the good buddy?" Bobby chuckled.

Tony laughed too. "Naw, I was doing the farm books. This last spring, we got a hundred and fifty gallons of medium amber syrup from two hundred taps. At fifteen bucks a gallon that's over twenty-two hundred bucks. Not bad, huh?"

"Is that right?"

"Yeah."

The conversation lapsed. Bobby became more nauseated. He coughed. Tony cleaned his chin.

"How old am I?" Bobby asked.

"Thirty . . . Yer about a year and a half older than me. Thirty-seven, huh?"

"Um. I thought I'd die at twenty-five."

"Across the pond?"

"No. I mean even before Nam. When I was a kid. I thought I'd die by twenty-five. Even after Viet Nam—" again the cough, the cleaning, "I thought, you know . . . "

"Yeah. I think I . . . When I was bumming around. I figured . . . "

Bobby wasn't listening. He wanted to talk. He cut in. His words began to slur again. "God gave me twelve more years. I did a lot in twelve years, didn't I?"

"Come on, Man. What kind of talk is this?"

"I married Sara. Then Noah—" coughing more frequently now, "Paul, ha! you should have seen your face when we named him Paul Anthony. Am . . . "

"Paulie's starting swim classes in January. I remember last summer, in the pond, he's going to be a hell of a strong swimmer."

"Um. Twelve years. The farm. The . . . "

"Cut the shit, Bobby."

"Really . . . "

"Shit, Man! You're bleeding. You've got blood in your mucus. I'm getting the nurse."

Alone, in the solarium—Bobby in his room asleep, being watched by the floor nurses—they took special care of him—Tony sank into a cheap chrome-framed armchair. He too wanted to sleep but he couldn't. He wasn't sure if he should call Sara. He'd talked to her earlier. Talked to Linda, too. Had angrily told Linda about them asking Bobby to sign the autopsy permission form, but she'd answered that it was pretty much standard. He told his wife about Bobby, fully lucid, saying, "If it ever comes to where I'm on a respirator, I don't want anybody but you or Sara deciding on the quality of my life. If I want the plug pulled, I'll pull it myself."

"Don't," Tony mumbled, "go unassing this AO, Man. Just don't." He slid farther down in the chair. His head rested on the hard seatback, his butt hung two-thirds over the edge, his knees were bent at ninety degrees supporting him uncomfortably, almost lying down. Tony's eyes closed. His face sagged. He was in the room with Bobby but the room was dark, dank, small. They could not stand, could not sit, had to lie prone. Bobby was coughing, spitting up. He needed to pull him up, pull him through. Above, far above, outside the tunnel, they pulled, pulled the rope he'd looped over Bobby in the deep. Tony coughed. In sleep, dream, he raised his hand to clear his mouth but his hand was filthy with others' sputum. His stomach tightened, churned . . .

Tony sat up. He was stiff. His neck was sore, his legs below the knees were asleep. He could go to the Boyers'. Could find an all-night diner. Could sleep on the floor except the floor was dirty. He rose. It was after two. He checked on Bobby. The night-duty nurse was sitting in the chair beside his bed. The table lamp was on. In its light she'd been writing her shift notes. She looked up, put a finger to her lips. Bobby was not asleep but seemed to be resting. Occasionally his chest trembled in a feeble cough.

On Friday night Sara and the kids arrived. Bobby's condition had remained stable. He had not eaten in two days, was being fed intravenously. His cough persisted. The blood content of the mucus had increased though not substantially. His eyes were bloodshot, the surrounding skin was black and blue as if he'd let his guard down and been pummeled. His skin was chalky. He was semilucid, semidelirious.

"Bob." She went to him, kissed his forehead.

The children remained in the hallway with Tony. Bobby turned his head, looked at her, didn't answer.

Sara kissed him again. "I'll be right back." She exited. In the hall she whispered to Tony. Tony nodded. To the children she said, "Pappee is very sick right now. And very tired. We're going to let him rest. Uncle Tony will take you to the Boyers'. I'm going to stay here. Right now he needs me more than you need me. Tomorrow we'll try to have you come in."

Bobby coughed again, and again. He hadn't slept since the onset of the coughing. "I talked to Mark Tashkor, today," Sara said. "He heard from Victor Yannecone. The number of claims against the chemical companies has risen to two hundred and thirty-three thousand. Eighty thousand are for serious ailments. Something beyond chloracne."

Bobby looked at her. His eyes showed no comprehension of her words. Sara gritted her teeth. She talked calmly of the children, of school, of the call from Vertsborg and of Jo having gone to see Miriam. Then she simply sat with him, held his hand.

Tony returned. He stood in the hall. He did not want to interrupt. He watched as Sara spoke, as Bobby watched her, as she repeatedly cleaned his face, as she silently cried, and as Bobby responded by crying too.

Then his coughing became much worse. There was much more blood. He gagged. Tony ran for the nurse. Sara stood. Her arms shook. She tried to clean him, his face. Her gentle hands bruised his chin. His platelet count had dropped to nothing. The nurse found no blood pressure.

No pulse. Another nurse came. A technician, a medic. Immediately they began CPR, injected him, through the IV tube, with digitalis and/or other drugs.

"Call Dachik. Call Wilcoxson." "Start a unit of platelets." "Call the unit. He should be down there." "Where?" "ICU." "No time." "I've got a pulse." "Start another IV." "Tony, call the Boyers." "He's bleeding everywhere." "Dachik's on her way." "Is he still on that new chemo?" "What should I do next . . . "

Next. Bobby tried to sit up. There are wires everywhere. Trip wires crossing jungle trails. His face is covered with blood. There is blood everywhere. Its stench permeates the room. He can smell it, taste it, see it. They've left him behind. Boyers. Bowers. Bowers and Eton. There is mud everywhere. The hillside is slick as blood mucus, sliding down, sliding down. "Cover me." Bobby's voice in the commotion. "I'm going back up."

"Stop the antibiotics. Just saline. And platelets."

They did not move him but worked on him, over him, worked him over, all night right there in his room with Sara right there, Tony there, Bobby totally docile, flaccid, then springing up wide-eyed, shouting, being restrained, shouting, "Bowers! Eton! L-T . . . " Then mumbling, "L-T . . . L-T . . . I can't remember his name." Then docile again. Coughing, being suctioned. Resting. Then lucid, semilucid, "Tony. Tony, are they on the wall?"

"He's hallucinating," a nurse said. "Spiders on the wall. It's common."

Tony eyed her. Shook his head. Said to Bobby, "Yeah, Man. Their names are on The Wall. Right there in Lincoln's thousand-yard stare."

"Good. I think of them . . . "

On Saturday, they had moved him to the ICU, with the chemo and antibiotics suspended, with additional platelets, Bobby regained a sense of the present. His breathing came easier. His coughing subsided. His pulse was steady, his blood pressure palpable. He rested. Occasionally he woke, looked to see Sara, now in a surgical mask, beside him, holding his hand. "They stopped all the drugs," she told him. "Lily said they'll reintroduce them one at a time to make sure they're safe."

"Um," he answered.

To her it was the sweetest thing he'd ever said.

"They said I could stay in your room," Sara said. She yawned. "Bobby, I'm going up to the room. It's all cleaned up. Tony's here. Bobby, I've got to rest."

"Um," he hummed again. Then he said to her, "We're going to get through this."

By Sunday Bobby had improved enough to sit up, to be propped up, for short periods. He was lucid, yet confused. When Tony came in Bobby thought he was the doctor. When Sara sat with him he thought she was his Aunt Krystyna. The children came but Tony told Sara he thought it best if they did not see him. "Not yet. Not until he's a little better."

Sara acquiesced. She was exhausted. To Lily Dachik she said, "How much longer do you think?"

"I don't know," the doctor answered.

"He's going to kill me," Sara said. "I can't stand this. I'm going to be dead and he's going to be lying in his bed. I hate this. I hate chemicals. I hate veterans. I hate what this has done to us. Why do we have to use up our energy for this?"

Doctor Dachik tried to soothe her.

"You don't understand." Sara burst into tears. "I've watched him lose. . . . He's lost the business. Lost the institute. Noah keeps collecting books for him so he can have more god damn books when he comes home. I've tried to be here for him. I have to work. I have to be in my classroom. It hurts. I've tried to be his wife. To take care of him. And . . . I can't watch him die."

"Go home, then," Dachik said. "He's responding well. It could be two or three more months."

Sara was too tired to drive home the night of the eleventh. She called her school principal, asked for Monday off. She spent the night at the Boyers'.

On Monday, the twelfth, Bobby was returned to his old seventh-floor room. The crisis had passed. He ate an entire breakfast, his first food in four days. Mentally, too, he was back.

"Oh, my God," Sara beamed. "I thought we were going to lose you."

"Naw. I'm okay. Are the kids at the Boyers'?"

"Yes. They're packed up. We were going to drive back."

"How's Tara?"

"You know."

"I don't know how they handle that." Bobby grinned. "Maybe I do."

"Um." Sara smiled.

"I saw him last night."

"Who?"

"It was very beautiful. Like coming out of dark water. Like our wedding."

"What was?"

"The Holy Spirit. I could feel his hand on me. I can't describe it. He was speaking in a tongue I didn't know yet I could understand. He told me to believe."

"Bobby!"

"Really."

"This is amazing."

"It was like a bright light but not glaring. Not like looking into a headlight but very bright. Very white. It came from the cathedral of the eastern hemlocks. I could see the hemlocks around us. It was very bright. And it was the light telling me . . . telling me about the healing side of believing. About the baptism in water and the baptism in fire."

"Bobby—" Sara said. He had never spoken this way before, spoken about a supernatural faith. They were Catholic but this went far beyond their religious learnings. If she were not so thrilled to have him back she would have been embarrassed. Still she did not know how to respond. "This is phenomenal!"

"We have this power," he said. "We've been given it by the Holy Spirit. I'm . . . I'm trying to believe. I'm struggling . . . I'm trying to get in touch with it each time. This isn't the first time but I didn't understand.

"Tell the kids," Bobby continued. "Tell them there is a God. That he loves them tremendously. That he loves me, too. Just as much."

"You tell them. Let me go back and get them."

When Sara returned Bobby was not in his room. "Where . . . "

"They've taken him back to the ICU. They shouldn't have brought him up so soon. His friend's with him."

"Tony?"

"I think."

Then, downstairs, Tony, pacing, to Sara, the children in chairs in the corridor, "Damn it. The shit's hit the fan."

Sara, "What? How? He was just . . . "

"His blood pressure fell through the floor. His white blood count's back to nothing."

"This isn't supposed to happen!"

"He's bleeding again. Coughing up . . . He thinks he's on Hamburger . . . "

"Is Lily . . . "

"She's in with him. Damn."

"I . . . I've got to take the children back to the Boyers'."

Later that night Lily Dachik said to Sara and Tony, "The quality of his life has reached a point that we have to know if anything should happen, which is possible at any moment, ah, how would you like us to handle that? We really feel that resuscitating him at this point would be of no value. It would be bringing him back ah, ah . . . only to die again."

Now Tony couldn't handle it. He kicked the wall. Stamped his feet. "Goddamn it! My best goddamned friend is dying. Best goddamned human being who ever lived . . . Goddamn Agent Orange . . . "

Sara sat with Bobby, alone, holding his hand. His eyes were shut. He was semicomatose. She was afraid to speak, to open her mouth, afraid she'd wail. She took a deep breath. "I'm back," she finally said. "I'm with you now. Do you understand that?"

Bobby squeezed her hand.

"Noah sends his love. Paul and Am, too."

"Um." Bobby's hum was very quiet, very weak.

Again she sat quietly, feeling helpless. Then she rose, left.

Tony entered, hugged Bobby.

" . . . omm." Very weak.

Tony put his ear to Bobby's mouth. "What?"

" . . . omm."

For a time he tried to understand but he couldn't decipher the word. Sara returned. " . . . m . . . omm," Bobby said.

"Are you saying 'home'?" Sara asked.

"hi . . . " Bobby said.

"High Meadow?" Tony asked. "Is that what you're saying?"

Bobby opened his eyes. " . . . m. take care of Noah," he said. "And Paul Anthony. And Am."

Tears flood Sara's eyes.

" . . . tony . . . take me home. I want to die at home. carry me home."

11 November 1984

Veteran's Day—It is cool, clear. The sky is not crying. It is dawn. It is nearly a year. I have four small flags with me, maybe six-by-ten inches, on small wooden dowels. Would it in some way have defiled them, those who served, had I brought up eight, one for each grave?

There's a sugarbush over the west ridge there. Can you imagine that spirit, that hope and trust which is optimism. I am the spirit, the will. I can control the will, see, read, taste the wind. From up here with the sun rising at your back you can see most of the place—the pond, so peaceful; the big barn and the small, the house, still unfinished; the vineyard, the high meadow, the knoll and orchard and cliff and dam. Out that way is the drive with the gate and the hinges I forged that first winter when I didn't want to speak to anyone. Over the hills, down there, is the town. You can see the breaks in the trees though without their leaves the breaks are less distinct. The first one is the Old Mill, then the New Mill, then the warehouse area down by the river. And you can see the steeples, the square one of St. Ignatius. Across the river, in what used to be Hobo Hollow, is the mall, then South Hill, New New Town, Old New Town, Creek's Bend, and way up to the left the Kinnard/Chassion plant. Out to the right is the old steel truss bridge. The White Pines Inn with its small array of solar collectors is just downriver.

The town sure has changed in the years since I first came to High Meadow, has changed greatly since the years of my boyhood. Still, perhaps it has not changed as much as the country. The entire perspective, the ideals, the hopes and projections . . . Perhaps that is why I'm here. To carry it forward . . . for you, Bobby, back here behind me. Next to Grandpa. And your grandmother. And with ol' Josh here with you, too.

Robert Janos Wapinski died 14 December 1983 at 5:57 A.M., less than an hour before first light, less than a year ago. I accompanied his body back, stayed with him through the wake, the funeral, the burial. We put him in the ground on Sunday the 18th, lowered him with his grandpa and grandma on one side and his aunt on the other. The two workers and Ty and Kenneth Moshler, who'd been

crushed by that panel truck, and Josh, too, are in the row behind
them. The sky didn't cry that day, either, but Noah did. Noah
sobbed for days. He was angry, hurt. He took it out on Sara. "He
needed you. Why didn't he need me?"

Paulie reacted differently. He didn't cry at all. He barely spoke
except I heard him say to Noah, "Please don't cry." Maybe he said
it to me. "It scares me when you cry."

Am cried. Not like Noah. She clung to Sara. It really was too
much to expect of her, to be there, to understand. We too. Isn't that
the origin, the nest, of rites and rituals?

Bobby's funeral was really something. I did not let happen to me
what happened when Jimmy died. I've grown, I guess. The will that
died with Jimmy survived him to die with Bobby yet it survives
him and lives on in you and me. There must have been four
hundred people there. Six of us, the core group, Van Deusen,
Gallagher, Mariano, Wagner, Denahee and I, carried the flag-draped
pine coffin up the hill, with Father Tom Niederkau, and the
deacons, the altar boys, family, extended families, vets, friends, even
a TV crew from Channel Five all trailing.

Father Tom was eloquent.

> In death there is life. In dying we are reborn. Evidence of
> the resurrection is less in the stories of the Bible than in
> every blade of grass that browns, every leaf that falls, then
> returns in the spring.
>
> We recall his face, his struggles, our shared laughter. We
> celebrate, we commemorate, not this man's life, not his
> death, but his spirit which has been reborn. We honor his
> altruism, his willingness to risk himself to help others. Bobby
> sent me a note, a quote from Lincoln. It was during the
> period when he was very ill. "It is for us, the living, rather,
> to be dedicated here to the unfinished work which they who
> fought here thus far so nobly advanced."
>
> He wished for us to continue advancing that unfinished
> noble work. He wanted us to remember the whys, the
> causes, the principles. He had accepted the torch, the light,
> had carried it gallantly. Now he has passed the torch to us,
> the work of spiritual love, of freedom, justice, equality,
> integrity, friendship, godliness.

Godliness! There was only one thing that to me that day, those
days, was ungodly—Miriam Cadwalder-Wapinski. The evening
before, she had come to the wake, thrown herself on the casket,
sobbed, wailed, "My baby, my son. My dearly beloved." I went to
assist her, comfort her. I thought . . . She rose, turned, vengeful,
pushed me aside, confronted Sara. "You bitch," she snapped.
"Why didn't you tell me he was so sick?"

The entire room was stunned, silent. Miriam yelled like a drill instructor. "You did it. You did this to him. You . . ." Thorpe, Rodney Smith, Rifkin, surrounded her. "You'll regret this," Miriam boomed. "You'll regret—" Rodney turned her. Sara was on her feet. Noah had frozen in his chair. Rifkin and Thorpe grabbed Miriam's arms, escorted her, she screaming, cursing all the way, out.

At the funeral Miriam seemed contrite. She stood just before Stacy Carter. Stacy had sent a large flower arrangement with a ribbon with the words " . . . imagine me and you . . . " She could not have looked more beautiful, more tormented. Sometime that day she said to me, "We were supposed to wait for each other. My . . . I hope he forgave me. I hope I can be Sara's friend." I told her, "I'm sure he did. And I'm sure you will be. After that."

Father Tom had finished. Lea, Linda's sister, was about to lead the gathering in song when Miriam huffed loudly, "Godliness! He was filthy. He and his floozies . . . " And Stacy Carter swung a roundhouse right and caught Miriam upside the head and knocked her down, and right there on Channel Five's camera Rodney and I and Ty's brother Phillip stepped in, grabbed Miriam, and Rodney said, loud, to the camera, "Tha's not his mother. Who is she? Get this lady outa here." And Bobby's brother—his sister, Joanne, had not come—but Brian, to the far side, covered his face and shuddered and shuddered again as Rodney and Al Palanzo escorted Miriam down the hill, she screaming all the way. "Sell it. Sell it. Give me my money."

Peace, godliness, returned with song. They had chosen it because he'd been a Screaming Eagle of the 101st Airborne. And I couldn't believe it, me a Marine, getting blubbery over the song. I couldn't control my tears but I controlled my voice. The refrain:

> And He will raise you up on eagle's wings,
> Bear you on the breath of dawn,
> Make you shine like the sun,
> And hold you in the palm of his hand.

I flashed back to Manny, to Ty, to Moshler, to Wildman, to Fuzzy, to so many guys. And to Jimmy. The third and fourth verses.

> You need not fear the terror of the night,
> Nor the arrow that flies by day;
> Though thousands fall about you,
> Near you it shall not come.
>
> For to His angels He's given a command
> To guard you in all of your ways;
> Upon their hands they will bear you up,
> Lest you dash your foot against a stone.

After the others had retreated to the house—the vets, led by Mike Treetop and John Cannello, had prepared an elaborate meal complete with apple fritters and maple syrup—I lingered here, at the family cemetery. I wanted to tell Bobby a few things—word from Hieu, word from Sherrick. Cards, letters. Every day for months they'd been piling up. Success stories. Guys who'd become what you would call "solid citizens." "Man, you got to be proud," I said. I did a little dance, a little jig. "Remember Ortez? Remember Peckham and Quinn? They've opened a small vet center in Chicago. Okay, they're not financiers or physicians but they're making it. Helping others to make it, too. Remember Ianez? Hawley? Bailer?" I sang a little tune, changed some words, an Elvis tune, "We can't stop lovin you . . . "

Life continued. Hardships. The farm was given to Bobby under a tenancy-for-life agreement, which meant upon his death Miriam, Joanne and Brian owned a controlling interest, and they forced it to be put up for sale. Sara was exhausted, at the point of a nervous breakdown. She wanted to run away. She packed up the most personal items, and she and the children moved to Sonoma, California. For a long time she didn't answer calls, didn't write. When I did hear from her she told me she had been praying, that on the day she felt the lowest she heard a song on the radio that went—

> Got a dollar in my pocket,
> got your letter in my shoe.
> Fresh out of the Infantry,
> I'm tryin to find you.
> Old '43 is slowing down
> to roll around the bend.
> I'm ON MY WAY TO SEE YOU AGAIN.

And she wrote that Noah had taught himself how to ride a bike.

14 December 1984

It seemed like the final betrayal.

I was going to tell you much more about the trial, the veterans' class-action suit against the companies that manufactured Agent Orange. I was going to detail the cover-up—what and when Dow and Monsanto knew about the contaminants, and why they kept the information to themselves. I was going to explain the $180 million settlement but there is no time, no time at all. I will tell you it is not over. There has been a settlement but not a final determination. Of the millions, Sara, it appears, will receive $3,600 as compensation from the chemical companies for Bobby's death. There is no compensation from the VA or the government.

I feel like the Mad Hatter, or the White Rabbit. Which one? Ah well . . . I'm late. I'm late. For a very important . . . You see, I can no longer attend to the past. I can no longer let them have my mind. Linda and I sold our house.

We're moving. Maybe that's what we're here about, to answer the questions on how it has all changed, to look at the future, at our hopes, to wonder why things have gone so awry, so out of whack, and to hope through our actions and our thoughts and through changing perspectives, beliefs and attitudes, perhaps we can regain control, re-right the ship of state and the ship of culture, plot and follow a course where all people can hope for life, liberty, and the pursuit of happiness.

So I've come here now, Bobby, to tell you this. Linda and I are going to attempt to resurrect the high meadows of your spirit. We're back in business. With my father's help we have purchased High Meadow. The core staff is returning. Gary Sherrick, too.